December 30, ¿

Bob and Tris...,

Thank you for being so
great friends. We always enjoy
the times we share together, whether
a wine-blessed dinner at the
fabulous Trattorias, or bluffing my
best at a game of Texas Hold-em.
We look forward to hanging with
you guys next year!! both up North
and "Down the Shore."

All the best,
Scott

Bob & Trish,

December 2006

Hope you enjoy reading my novel.

All the best,

Sue Hyun

A REASON TO DIE

A Novel by

Sal DeStefano

Llumina Press

Requests for permission to make copies of any part of this work should be mailed to Permissions Department, Llumina Press, PO Box 772246, Coral Springs, FL 33077-2246

ISBN: 1-59526-064-1
        1-59526-072-2

Printed in the United States of America by Llumina Press

Library of Congress Cataloging-in-Publication Data

Destefano, Sal, 1956-
  A reason to die : a novel / by Sal DeStefano.
     p. cm.
  ISBN 1-59526-072-2 (alk. paper) -- ISBN 1-59526-064-1 (pbk. : alk. paper)
  I. Title.
PS3554.E846R43 2005
813'.54--dc22   2005000578

Acknowledgements

Several carefully chosen readers—selected in part for their brutal honesty—endured the earliest versions of my manuscript. Their pain is my novel's gain. These polite, but truthful critics include Karin Fey, David Hyde, Charles "Chick" Krug, James M. McKenna, Joseph Muresco, Angela Saparata, Kay Sontz, and my son, Anthony DeStefano.

I am deeply indebted to Dr. Debbie Papa-O'Donnell for sharing her professional expertise in gynecology and obstetrics so that my novel's heroine might tend properly to her patients. I am thankful, too, for the indispensable insights of my sister, Elisa DeStefano, whose first-hand knowledge of Islamic customs and culture have leant authenticity to my story's characters and setting.

During the revision process, I struck up an e-mail correspondence with Asif Hameed Khan, a native of Srinagar, and medical school student in Pakistan. Asif's vivid descriptions of everyday life in the Kashmir Valley, as well as his keen ability to gauge and express the pulse of the Kashmiri people, particularly their yearning for peace through freedom, proved invaluable in lending credibility to my characters' motives and actions.

Two professional editors with major league experience have left an indelible mark on my tale and its telling—Katharine Turok, a freelance editor affiliated with Words into Print, and Lou Aronica, a former executive with Avon Books who now helps aspiring writers achieve their dreams through his editorial service, The Fiction Studio. Because of them, you are about to read a more compelling book.

Finally, I am thankful for the patience and understanding of the four most important people in my world—my wife and soul mate, Doreen, to whom this story is dedicated, and my children, Anthony, Rachel, and Sarah. They define all that is good in my life.

To Doreen

*whose unwavering love and steadfast support
gave this story heart.*

In Memory of
Joseph Muresco

Who confronted death as he savored life—
with courage, dignity and honor.

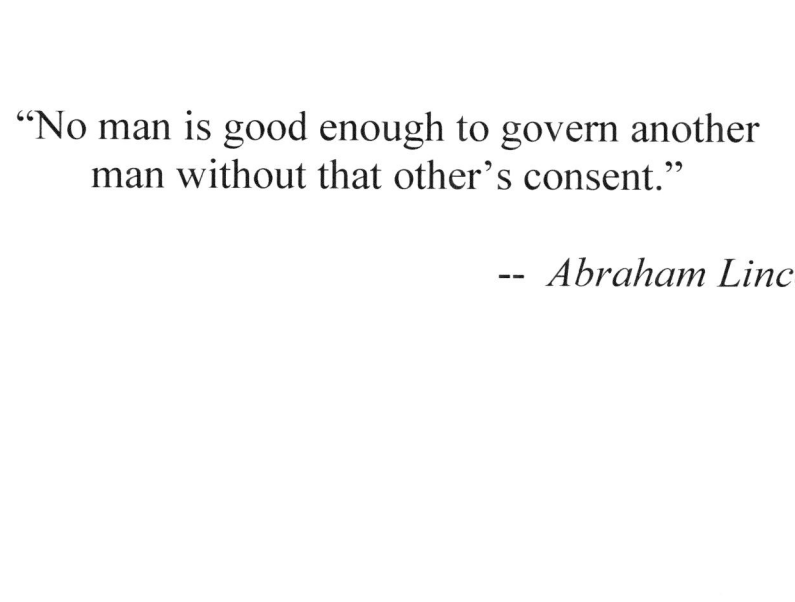

"No man is good enough to govern another
man without that other's consent."

-- *Abraham Lincoln*

"Political power grows out of the barrel of a gun."

-- *Mao Tse-Tung*

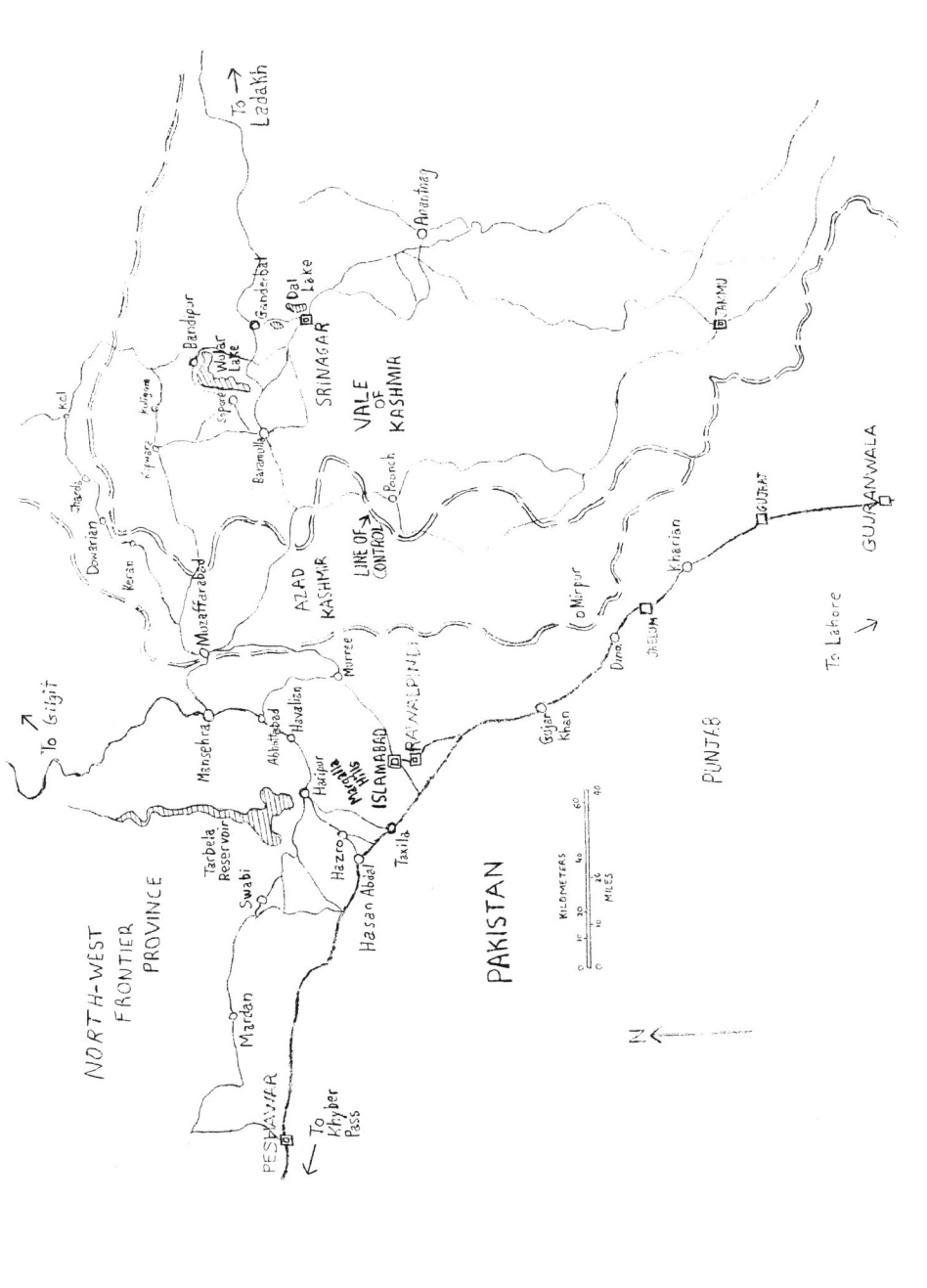

PART I

"I can think of no more honorable cause than preservation and protection of family to induce a man to sacrifice his life."

—*Edward J. Lloyd, President of the United States of America*

Perched at 4,300 meters in the lower Himalayas overlooking the Vale of Kashmir, Major Asan Rasheed poked his head through an opening in the concrete bunker and spotted Lieutenant Malik's squad pinned in an apple orchard on the outskirts of Baramulla. From atop a low ridge bordering two sides of the orchard, approximately 60 troops from India's Special Frontier Force were picking off Malik's men one at a time.

Ninety minutes earlier, Malik and a dozen commandos had blown up the primary fuel depot used by India's XV Corps out of Srinagar. They had moved to within 65 meters of their next target, an armory west of Baramulla, and were about to penetrate the armory's perimeter, when Major Rasheed received an unusual order from Khan's Citadel. Terminate Malik's mission immediately, and return his squad to the mountain outpost by 1300 hours.

Rasheed never questioned orders from central command, and quickly radioed the directive to Malik, who, as Rasheed expected, balked at the prospect of cutting short his mission. But Malik was a good Pakistani soldier, and requested instructions on the safest route back to the mountaintop bunker.

They could not return the way they had come because enemy soldiers from the Parachute Regiment of India's 9th Battalion had taken up positions around the fuel depot Malik and his men had demolished. Their best chance was to continue three kilometers north through maize fields and fruit farms until they reached the pine forest blanketing the west slope of PK-2761.

Malik and his commandos proceeded north, and had entered an apple orchard along a secondary road to Handwara when, at the bottom of a low ridge near the smoldering remains of a farmhouse, they were ambushed.

Rasheed pulled his head in through the bunker's square opening, glanced at his watch, and saw he had 12 minutes to meet General Khan's deadline. He grabbed a radio from his sergeant's hand. "Leopard 4, Leopard 4, do you read me?"

Static hissed through the speaker.

"Leopard 4, Leopard 4, come in."

"Mountain Den … read you … breaking up. Moun—"

"Leopard 4. What is your status?"

More static, loud static.

"I repeat. What is your situation?"

Through the radio's speaker, Rasheed heard four successive explosions followed by a staccato burst of machine gun fire. Twenty seconds passed before Malik's voice returned. "Four confirmed … five wounded. We need … rescue us? Are you—"

"Leopard 4, come in."

No answer.

Rasheed did not understand why Islamabad had abruptly pulled the plug on an operation that had been proceeding smoothly. Dangerous orders had been coming from Khan's Citadel in recent weeks, but this one was costing the lives of his men.

Rasheed turned to his sergeant. "How fast can we fly three Hueys to Malik's position?"

"Sir, there is not enough time."

"Answer my question."

"Fifteen minutes."

No one would know if he missed the deadline. "Get them up now."

"But sir, the order came directly from General Khan."

"Is it the Pathan who is stranded out there? Is it the Pathan who dies if we fail to act?"

The sergeant's narrow mustache twitched, and he stared down at the bunker's dirt floor.

Rasheed understood his officer's fear. "Very well, I shall give the order myself."

Within two minutes, three Huey Cobra gunships lifted off the helipad on PK-2761 and screamed northeast toward Malik's position.

Rasheed poked his head through the square portal and watched the choppers fly in V-formation, quickly putting altitude between themselves and the mountain's steep eastern face.

Pakistani officers were trained to make important decisions, but in General Khan's army, a wrong decision meant a career cut short at the end of a noose. Rasheed was especially nervous because he should not have been in charge of the outpost today. Late last night, his superior officer had flown to Islamabad for an emergency meeting at Khan's Citadel. Rasheed was not told the meeting's purpose, only that Pakistan's destiny hung in the balance.

Rasheed pulled his head into the bunker and checked the time. Four minutes left until central command expected Malik and his men back in the bunker. He glanced at his sergeant, who lowered his eyes. "Do not worry. For your troubles, I will recommend to General—"

The earth beneath Rasheed's feet started to shake, and he heard a low rumbling outside.

His sergeant looked at the ceiling. "What is that sound?"

The noise grew louder, like an approaching train, until the rumbling turned into a continuous, thundering roar. Rasheed ran outside through a narrow door at the rear of the bunker, looked up, and could not believe his eyes. A blue missile trailing white vapor soared west to east across the cloudless sky, passing so low over the mountain Rasheed could read the Arabic script painted along its side.

Gazing skyward, Rasheed stumbled to the front of the bunker overlooking the Vale, and leaned back against its cool concrete surface. Though brazen, Ali Khan was no fool. He must know Pakistan's army was not yet ready to carry out the boastful threats he had made against India.

Rasheed lifted his binoculars and peered up at the missile streaking toward Baramulla. He then focused on the orchard where the Indian Army had cornered Malik and his men. The three Huey's were hovering over the smoldering farmhouse. Too late to call them back, he whispered, "Allah have mercy on Ali Khan, Allah have mercy on us all."

His sergeant, beside him, raised his arms high. "Allahu-Akbar!"

Before Rasheed could reply, a brilliant flash of scorching light consumed the Vale. Rasheed fell to the ground, opened his eyes, but could not see. The heat of a furnace enveloped his arms and legs, and the stench of seared flesh, his own, scorched his nostrils. A deafening roar filled his ears, and then he heard no more.

The holiest of jihads had begun.

CHAPTER ONE

John Covello gripped the arms of the black vinyl chair across from Dr. Chandler's desk, and sat flush against the backrest. The sharp pains shooting through his belly left him little tolerance for bullshit. "Don't mince words, doc, life's too short."

Chandler picked up a manila folder on his desk and pulled out a single white page. "Pancreatic cancer, Stage IVB. The GI series, CT scan, ERCP, and angiography—all point to the same diagnosis. The PTC's not in, but that won't change anything."

John had grown accustomed to bad news, so why should today be any different? "What are my options?"

Chandler's long pause did little to boost John's confidence. "The cancer has spread. Your stomach, spleen, colon, probably your liver and lungs are involved. Removing your pancreas may reduce the pain, at least for awhile, and supplementing surgery with chemotherapy might slow the cancer's growth. With Stage IV, there's also a good chance you're eligible for experimental gene therapies."

John's composure surprised even himself. "Are you saying you can't cure me?"

"No one can. Stage IVB cancer of the exocrine pancreas is untreatable." He pulled a dark transparency from the file, an X-ray of John's abdomen, and slid the sheet across his desk.

John held the plastic sheet to the light and observed translucent gray smudges covering half his organs.

"Your only choice is undergoing palliative therapies to manage the frequency and intensity of the pain you'll experience over the next few months. They'll all improve your quality of life, but they won't change how long you live."

John closed his eyes. Chandler had handed him a death sentence and he felt nothing. Maybe because the pains had bothered him more frequently in recent weeks, he had expected this result. Or maybe he was content justice would finally be done. He had taken a life, and would now give his own.

He'd have accepted the news willingly, almost appreciatively, but in dying he'd leave Maureen and his daughters no better off. In fact, a protracted illness was likely to saddle them with more debt. There had to be a quicker way to die.

"You know my situation."

"What about your accounts receivable?"

John smirked. "Haven't heard those words in two years."

"Have you considered bankruptcy?"

"Certain debts can't be discharged, like federal tax liens and debts from fraud. I've got both."

"You may be eligible for financial aide through the indigent assistance program we offer at Jersey Shore Medical Center. It's decent, not great, since you still own a home."

"Guess it's my lucky day. If I don't raise a million bucks by the end of the month, I lose that, too."

"Any cash value in your life policies?"

"Tapped out."

Looking genuinely remorseful, Chandler sighed. "Why'd you let things fall apart?"

"He was five years old."

"You weren't responsible."

"Let's not rehash it, and yes, I was." The botched implosion was yesterday's news, and nothing could change the result. "What do I do now?"

Chandler placed the diagnostic results back in the manila file. He stood and faced the window behind his chair. With his back to John, he peeked through the blinds. "Palliative treatments will run hundreds of thousands of dollars, and in the end won't extend your life beyond three or four months."

"Forget the surgery, forget the chemo. I told you, I'm not dragging this out. Give me pain killers, and I'll deal with the rest."

Chandler descended into his black leather chair. He folded his hands on his fine wood desk, leaned forward, and studied John's face. "I know someone who might help Maureen after you're gone. Someone who can help her pay off your creditors, pay off your house, and pay your kids' college tuitions. Give her anything and everything you'd want for her, and more."

"I'm not even dead, and you've got her remarried."

"I don't mean another husband. This person works for the government."

"You don't understand. Between judgments I can't pay, three mortgages in default, and four overextended VISA cards, I owe more than $2,000,000. No government handout's covering that."

"It's not a handout."

"What is it?"

"If you qualify—and I know you do—in exchange for services you provide, Maureen will receive twice as much money as she needs to satisfy your current financial obligations."

John's company had once contracted with the FBI to implode an abandoned crack house in Dallas. He'd also consulted for the ATF, but no job he'd ever performed for the government paid that kind of money. "What sort of services?"

"The federal government needs a skilled demolitions expert."

"No way they'll cough up the kind of dough I need."

"In this case, they will."

John shook his head. "After Chicago, what makes you think they'll give me the time of day, let alone a contract?"

Chandler opened his desk drawer and pulled out a white index card. He scribbled down a phone number, and handed the card to John. "Call these people. I don't have a name, but they'll know why you're calling."

"Who are they?"

"A federal agency that'll guarantee your family never needs welfare or food stamps to survive."

"You know what they say when something sounds too good."

"Believe me, it's for real. Of course they'll want to meet you."

"I don't know."

"Look at it this way. Your death is inevitable, and right now, there's nothing you can do to stop Maureen from falling into a very deep hole. Wouldn't you like to leave this world knowing no creditor will ever hound her again?"

"What I'd really like is to stay in this world and pay my bills."

Chandler rose. "One important condition, and it's not easy."

"What's that?"

"You can tell no one, not even Maureen, about your cancer. If they find out you've told anyone about your illness, they won't help."

"Why?"

"Meet them and you'll understand."

"What kind of demolition?"

"Look, John, I'm only a messenger. They'll explain everything. But if you want to take advantage of this opportunity, call soon."

"How long can I think about it?"

"Tonight, tomorrow the latest. Someone's there 24/7."

Three months after the Chicago accident, before he'd cashed out his life insurance policies, he sat in his Mercedes with the garage door down and the engine running. Maureen had gone to the mall, and the girls had left for school. Only when he imagined Maureen's anguish when she discovered his body did he turn off the ignition.

John stood and stared at Chandler. "I'd like to discuss this with my wife."

"You won't if you're serious about helping her."

"Of course I wanna help her."

Chandler walked around his desk and placed his hand on John's shoulder. "Tell you what. I'm expecting your PTC images first thing in the morning. Stop back tomorrow at ten, and we'll discuss what they show. Then if you're still having doubts about making the call, we can kick it around some more." Looking mournfully into John's eyes, Chandler added, "I know it's difficult, but wait until after you've called these folks to break the bad news to Maureen."

Yesterday, while Christie was home alone, a vulgar bill hound had called four times in an hour. The jerk spared no profanity and had frightened his daughter to tears. "I guess I can hold off."

"Trust me, you won't be sorry." Chandler walked John to the door. "We've missed you at the Rotary meetings. People still ask about you."

"I've had other things on my mind."

"Have you ridden your Harley lately?"

The Friday before Memorial Day John was forced to choose between his Harley Heritage Softail Classic, equipped with an 80 cubic inch, 45 degree, V-twin engine, and his Buick LaSabre, reliable basic transportation. "Haven't been much in the mood for riding."

"Sold it?"

"Yeah, but now I don't worry about dying on a motorcycle."

Chandler smirked. "You haven't lost your sense of humor."

"And I've still got my Boston Whaler."

"I'm surprised you didn't sell your boat before your Harley."

"Been trying for two months. No takers."

When they entered the empty waiting room Chandler picked up *The Star-Ledger*, still folded in its rubber band, and glanced at the headline. "Terrible what happened in Kashmir."

John hadn't paid much attention to the story. "I don't care, so long as we don't get dragged in."

"Like it or not, what happens there affects us here."

"Right now, I'm not worried about people's problems on the other side of the planet. I've got enough of my own."

Chandler smiled. "Make that call soon. A conversation can't hurt, and trust me, you're doing the right thing for Maureen."

"I'll sleep on it, and see you tomorrow."

"By the way, use a land line, not your cell phone. Another of their silly rules."

John paused with his hand on the doorknob, and looked back at Chandler. "Why me? The government has hundreds of highly trained demolitions experts to choose from. What makes me so different?"

Chandler's smile faded. "What makes you different, John, is no matter what, you won't see your next birthday."

CHAPTER TWO

The pile of white confetti littering the top of the conference table told Denise Farrell all she needed to know about her boss's day. She had never seen Colonel Daley lose his temper. Instead, he always released his frustration on the nearest sheet of scrap paper, tearing the page into ever smaller strips until he transformed a single page into hundreds of wisps no larger than a dime. The higher the pile, the worse his day, and today his pile was two inches tall.

Colonel Daley had risen from his seat and stood to the left of a 60-inch flat plasma monitor mounted to the conference room wall of CRUSO's Active Mission Oversight Center. Deep under the Pentagon, this was the largest of AMOC's three conference rooms, which she and Daley now occupied alone. Twenty feet wide by 50 feet long, and paneled in dark-stained walnut, the room gave Farrell the feel of sitting in a tunnel, not a state-of-the art command center linked to the most advanced communications equipment on earth.

Looking at the giant screen showing a color map of the Indian subcontinent, Daley finished his assessment of their dilemma. "Not only must the president convince the prime minister we've recruited a qualified candidate, but unless Behari believes our operative has infiltrated Khan's Citadel by Saturday at 1500 hours, he has the support of his Council of Ministers and both Houses of Parliament to launch a nuclear counter-strike."

Denise Farrell had earned the rank of major in less time than it took most men to make first lieutenant. Several officers engrained in the army establishment, Colonel Daley included, resented her rocket ride up the ladder, but most did a passable job of hiding what Farrell considered their envy.

Farrell was proud of her accomplishment, not only because she was a woman, but because she was black. In her spare time she spoke at high schools and colleges inside the Beltway about military career paths for women. She planned on making colonel herself by the time she reached 40, and if CRUSO pulled this mission off, President Lloyd had promised her another promotion.

At the moment, a not-so-simple obstacle stood in her way. She picked up two stapled pages from the top of the pile on the table in front of her. "None of these candidates have the right skills, and this operation's not something you can train for in two days."

Daley returned to his seat at the conference table across from Farrell. "Take another look at Santiago. She had hands-on EOD experience."

"Sir, she's back in the hospital and not expected to live two weeks."

Daley folded his hands on his lap and began rocking in his chair, another nervous habit Farrell had gotten used to. After a moment, he stopped. "Have you tried our Category C agents?"

"I've reached out to everyone in the network. These are the only names that come close to a match."

"So basically, we're screwed."

Farrell looked up at the three rows of digital clocks mounted to the wall behind the colonel and honed in on the one labeled 'Eastern Time.' "If we find a qualified candidate within 24 hours, we can meet the prime minister's deadline."

"And if we don't, we drive the last nail into CRUSO's coffin."

Farrell said nothing, since she harbored her own doubts about CRUSO's ability to further US interests at home and abroad.

President Lloyd had assumed office a year and a half ago, inheriting CRUSO from his predecessor, who had launched the program in response to America's inability to impose its will on other nations without raising cries of "evil empire." The invasion of Afghanistan, the occupation of Iraq, and the defeat of Syria hadn't diminished the need for America to root out terrorism and influence world events, but mounting resentment toward Washington's monopoly on world power had made that task harder than ever. Even its staunchest ally, Britain, had begun shying away from joint military exercises with the US.

America had maintained a firm grip on the title of world's only superpower. Its nearest competitor, China, didn't come close. But America paid a price for military and economic superiority. Major military incursions in Asia, Africa, and the Middle East to smoke out terrorists had evoked charges of hegemony and imperialism. CRUSO—Civilians Recruited for Unrecoverable Special Operations—was established to give America another choice, an alternative tool for manipulating world events without giving the appearance of having caused those changes.

Ironically, the previous administration had never called upon CRUSO to act, yet President Lloyd, skeptical of the agency's methods from the start, had tapped the program twice. Both missions under the president's watch had failed, and he had made clear to Colonel Daley three strikes and CRUSO was out.

Responding to the first mission's failure, President Lloyd yanked Farrell from her post as Staff Advisor to the Secretary of the Army, and placed her under Daley's command as CRUSO's Deputy Director. Her appointment probably reinforced Daley's perception of himself as an outsider, a holdover from the prior administration—and he was right. Lance Parker, the current Secretary of State, and George Farrell, Denise's older brother, had been fraternity chums at Columbia University. At George's request, Secretary Parker had floated Farrell's name past the president.

Farrell and Daley both knew what her appointment was really about. As Deputy Director, she kept tabs on CRUSO, serving as the president's eyes and ears inside the agency, and during her first few months on the job, Daley made little effort to hide his animosity. Only after the failure of CRUSO's second mission had Daley warmed up to her. Following the fiasco in Argentina, she could have easily run to the president to say she had objected to Daley's candidate from the start. Instead, she kept quiet, and after that, her boss started showing her serious respect.

As much as Farrell hoped to make colonel by 40, Daley never made a secret of his own goal—promotion to brigadier general by 60. For Daley, 60 was coming next May, and if CRUSO failed to identify a qualified candidate within 24 hours, chances were good neither would achieve their ambition.

Colonel Daley, tearing more scrap paper, added another half inch to his pile. "Should we start looking at Level D candidates?"

"I'm as desperate as you, sir, but I wonder if that's prudent."

"For the hell of it, who do we have?"

Farrell extracted a folder from the middle of her stack. "Closest Level D match is a 32-year-old male from Texas, ex-Navy. He actually went through the Explosive Ordnance School at Elgin and spent 18 months with the 305th Civil Engineering Squadron."

"Why's he on death row?"

Farrell skimmed the candidate's profile. "Murdered two police officers in Abilene ... says here 'subject exhibits sporadic episodes of aggressive outbursts characterized by uncontrollable anger resulting in destruction of property and/or physical assaults on others, which episodes are typically triggered in response to' ... forget him."

"What's the rest say?"

"... 'in response to instruction from anyone subject perceives as holding a position of authority.'" Farrell closed the folder. "I'll keep hunting."

CHAPTER THREE

Turning onto a quiet street lined with mature oaks and spacious colonials, John debated heeding Chandler's advice, and waiting before breaking the news of his cancer to Maureen. He pulled into his driveway, entered the gate at the side of his house, and climbed the three steps onto his backyard deck.

Before going inside, John paused and looked behind him. A wooden bulkhead along the Manasquan River's north bank formed his yard's rear property line. On the wide river two speeding V-hulls chased one another toward the Manasquan Inlet. The male captain of the leading screamer, whose dark hair fluttered in the wind, looked about 40 years old. Two boys, probably the man's sons, sat glued to bucket seats in the stern. John watched them disappear downriver, remembering a time when that dad could have been him.

John entered his house through the kitchen door, dropped his keys on the table, and found Christie in the large den off the kitchen. She knelt backward on a club chair, and was looking out a French window with a panoramic view of the river.

"Hey kid, didn't you see me come in?"

Christie's head snapped in his direction. "Dad, how'd you do at the doctor?"

He wasn't very good at lying, especially to his children. "Fine, what're you up to?"

"Did you take along your lucky Hog?"

For his last birthday, Christie had given him a miniature cast-iron replica of a Harley Davidson ElectraGlide. She said the toy was his good luck charm, and she made him carry it wherever he went. He pulled the tiny motorcycle from his pocket. "Right here, as always."

"Don't lose it."

"I promised you I'd never lose it, and—"

"I know. You never break a promise."

"So what's up?"

"Just thinking about what a mistake I made going to summer school."

John smiled. "Especially on a day like today."

"And especially social studies."

His younger daughter had been recommended by her seventh grade teacher to participate in the middle school's summer enrichment program. History was Christie's favorite subject, except on hot sunny afternoons in July. "What's your assignment?"

Christie sprang backward off the chair and picked up an open text-book lying on a lamp table. She walked to a globe mounted on a chrome stand, and spun the sphere. "We're studying foreign capitals, and I'm looking for Bishkek."

"Fishcake?"

"Ha ha, Dad. Seriously, we're not allowed to use the Internet, and I don't know where to start looking."

"I can tell you this much, not the United States."

"No kidding."

What little fight John had left he'd dug for deep out of his love for Maureen and the girls. In fact, if he were sure they'd all meet in heaven, he wouldn't have minded Chandler's diagnosis. "Let's take a look."

Christie handed the textbook to John, who thumbed through the index, then flipped to a page in the middle. "Got it." He turned the globe slowly, and spread his palm over Central Asia. "Look around here."

Christie stared at the globe. "Kyrgyzstan."

"Good job."

"I wish we didn't have to learn about all these little countries. The only one that matters anyway is America … and Ireland."

"Don't forget Italy."

"Where Nana's from."

"The world's become smaller and scarier than ever. That's why they teach you about all the countries, even the little ones."

Christie took the book from her father and set it on the table. "So what'd the doctor say?"

"Did you get any more of those nasty calls today?"

"Don't worry about it."

"Tell me."

Christie cast her eyes down. "A man from AmeriCredit called, not the same one who called yesterday. This guy was a bigger jerk."

"What did he say?"

"Don't worry, Dad. What did Dr. Chandler say about the pains?"

She wasn't about to drop the issue. "Stomach virus. Some rare strain from South America."

Christie's light blue eyes pierced him. She had recently cut her blond mane into a bob, and by parting it down the middle, had turned herself into a miniature Maureen.

"You don't believe me?"

"Technically I'm a kid, but I know a stomach virus doesn't last four months."

"Really, it's a virus. He gave me muscle relaxants to ease the pain."

"Let's see the pills."

"I haven't gone over to Eckerds yet."

Christie stared at him, as if probing his thoughts. Slowly, almost imperceptibly, her expression turned from skeptical to somber, and tears welled in her eyes.

John held her close. He couldn't tell the truth, not yet.

She buried her face in his chest, and when she looked up, her cheeks were moist. "It's Billy, I know it is. I wish he were never born."

"Please don't say that."

"If he never lived, he couldn't have died, and if he didn't die, maybe you wouldn't be sick."

"One has nothing to do with the other."

"Yes it does. After the accident, everything changed. You used to like having fun. But after he died, it's like you went away." She wiped her eyes. "I miss you Dad, I want you back."

John gently pried his daughter's arms away and clasped her shoulders. "Listen. What happened to Billy was my fault, and I'm the one who's gotta deal with it."

"That's the point, Dad. It's been two years, and you still haven't."

"I'm trying, kid. I'm really trying."

"If you're trying so hard, why don't you go back to work? I miss the countdowns."

John remembered the last implosion Christie had tagged along on—the Spencer-Davis factory in downtown Charlotte. As she'd done a dozen times before, Christie pressed the red "fire" button triggering the detonator that ignited the charges that forced the six-story concrete structure to collapse in on itself. John loved when Christie's eyes lit up as she watched thousands of tons of cement, bricks, and mortar tumble to the ground in a synchronized display of destruction that always ended with a giant billowing cloud of dust.

That was before Chicago, before the lawsuits, before the bill collectors. One way or the other, time was running out. With three, maybe four months to live, he wondered if his family's last hope— and a slim one at that—had boiled down to the phone number Chandler had given him.

He couldn't look Christie in the eye. "I promise you, everything will be fine. You, Karen, and Mom, you're all gonna be fine." He pulled the toy Harley from his pocket. "And don't forget, I still have my lucky charm."

"I thought the charm would make you happy, but you're always sad. I can't remember the last time I heard you laugh." A tear rolled down her cheek. "It's a silly toy. You might as well throw it away."

"I promise, I'm gonna make things right again. No more nasty phone calls, no more worrying someone might take our house away."

"You don't understand. I don't care if we're rich or poor. I want my old dad back."

"Everything will be fine."

Through her tears, Christie glared at him. "Not if you don't come back to us."

"But—"

"Maybe you don't wanna come back. Maybe you're sick of us."

"That's not fair. I—"

"Leave forever, if that's what you want." Christie choked back a sob. "Anyway, it doesn't matter. It's like you're already gone." She swallowed hard, then turned and ran from the room.

Listening to his daughter's angry footsteps bounding up the stairs, John stared out the French window. Under the afternoon sun, the surface of the Manasquan River danced with sparkling light. He reached into his pocket and pulled out the telephone number Chandler had given him. Staring at the 12 numbers until they dissolved into a gray blur, he prayed they held an answer for the three people who mattered most in his world.

CHAPTER FOUR

Kneeling on the cool tiles in Ali Khan's penthouse suite, Dr. Salena Zamal rubbed the bloodied corner of her mouth, struggling to hold back tears. Her cheek throbbed where Khan had struck her. She slowly began to rise, then stopped when he lifted his hand.

"Do not get up."

Salena loathed how her tears brought him pleasure, but if today's beating were to end, she must weep openly, giving him the signal he had vanquished her. She let the tears flow. "Forgive me Ali Khan." She clutched the strings of her silk dupatta and cowered before the hem of his swirling white robe. Staring at the white floor tiles, she waited for him to speak.

"You may rise."

She dried her cheeks and addressed Khan in the way he had taught her. "Kind master, please allow me to speak."

"There is nothing to say. You shall not go to Srinagar."

"My mother has little time."

"She is no longer your family. You belong to me, and to me alone."

Too many nights Salena had fallen asleep pondering how to kill herself before September's end, when Ramadan was over and Khan planned to make her marry him. If the Americans did not contact her soon, she would be forced to spend the rest of her days as his wife. He had even forbidden her from visiting her mother, lying gravely ill in a hospital bed in Srinagar. "Suppose Captain Qadeer accompanies me? He can assure my safe passage to Kashmir."

"Even if I could spare him—and I cannot—I have told you before, the journey is too dangerous."

Salena had one tactic left, an appeal to the only love he placed above his lust for her. "Please allow me to do what the Qur'an expects of a good daughter—honor my mother."

Khan's blue eyes got big, and he laughed so hard the black turban on his head trembled. "My precious flower, do not insult me. You of all women cannot invoke the precepts of my faith."

"My faith as well."

"In name, not practice."

"The Qur'an is clear. 'You shall worship nothing but Him, and show kindness to your parents. Paradise awaits those who cherish and respect their mothers.' My only wish is to honor the words of the Prophet."

"Then why do you so often neglect the Prophet's most important words: 'the best woman is she who, when you direct her, obeys.'"

She did not wish to be hit again, so she stared at a Persian carpet adorning the wall behind him, and spoke softly. "I am trying to learn. Each day, I am learning."

Khan brushed her cheek, staining his fingers with her caking blood. "You have forgotten the tenets of Islam. Those infidel whores in Peshawar poisoned your mind. I promise after I vanquish Pakistan's enemies, I shall devote my life to restoring your faith."

Until Khan had abducted her, nothing Salena did even came close to what he expected of a Muslim woman. She had earned a Bachelor of Science at the University of Peshawar, then moved to New York City to pursue an M.D. at Mount Sinai School of Medicine. She remained in the States to complete her residency in Obstetrics and Gynecology at Saint Barnabas Medical Center, specializing in maternal fetal medicine.

But it was not her education that had aroused Khan's ire. In fact, he once let slip it pleased him having chosen an educated woman. What angered him most was after she had returned to South Asia and moved to Peshawar, she had joined the Revolutionary Association of Women of Afghanistan, an activist organization espousing equal opportunity for women.

In the city of Peshawar, 16 kilometers east of the Khyber Pass, where many Taliban sought refuge after their rout from Kabul, supporting such a cause came at a high price. Ali Khan despised RAWA and all it stood for. Declaring its goals contrary to the laws of Islam, he banned the group in Pakistan, and punished membership by public flogging and 20 years imprisonment.

Ali Khan's government and the humbled mullahs of the Taliban banished to northwest Pakistan had much in common. Both took Mohammed's words and twisted them to subjugate half of Pakistan's population. The better half, in Salena's view.

Salena loved her religion, and in her heart believed Allah's words bestowed spiritual and intellectual equality to women. Even her religious champion, the renowned Islamic mystic, Rabi'a al-Adawiyya, was a woman. Adherence to the Five Pillars of Islam—belief, prayer, fasting, alms to the poor, and pilgrimage—applied to all Muslims, and Allah made no distinction between the sexes as to what rewards obedience to His word would yield.

Salena doubted Ali Khan would ever view the Qur'an as a beacon for leading men and women down a common path to the realm of eternal peace. Instead, for him and his kind the Qur'an provided a sword with which to conquer the bodies and souls of women. On rare occasions when Salena suggested that freedom for women and Islamic doctrine were not mutually exclusive, he ridiculed, and sometimes, as now, hit her.

Still, she must convince Khan to allow her a last visit to comfort her dying mother. She spoke softly, submissively, "I am not a bad Muslim, I have learned much from you."

His response was gentle. "I must admit, with my guidance your behavior has improved."

"My mother misses me. I am her only child. She asks merely for my presence at the time of her death."

"Within two weeks, Kashmir shall take her rightful place among the provinces of Pakistan. Perhaps then I shall allow you to visit her with an escort."

"My mother will surely die before then."

"How do you know this? You are forbidden contact with Srinagar."

"The nurses. They speak softly, but I still hear."

Khan's tone hardened. "It is the Punjabi."

"What do you mean?"

Khan grabbed her chin and forced her to look at him. His dark blue eyes and bronze face, all angles, had earned him a reputation as the most handsome ruler in Pakistan's history. Salena agreed, but his contempt for women evoked such hatred in her, his perfect Pathan features had become invisible.

"You know perfectly well who I mean."

A warm tear slipped down her cheek. "Dr. Raja?"

"Why does he persist in feeding you news from Srinagar?" He released his grip. "Captain Qadeer has warned him once."

"He tells me only what his colleagues in Srinagar tell him."

"What good does that do you?"

"If I know her condition, I can suffer her pain."

"I shall have the captain pay Dr. Raja another call."

"Please, he is an old man. He cannot endure another night of the captain's abuse."

"The way that old man looks at you is reason enough I should kill him—and you as well."

The Pathan code of honor imposed death on any man or woman suspected of sex outside marriage. In the case of an accused woman, her executioner was the man most shamed by her conduct, usually her husband, father, or brother.

Pakistan's former president, Labib Razzak, had banned such brutal means of restoring tribal honor, but when Khan stole power in Pakistan, he reversed Razzak's prohibitions. He authorized the use of Islamabad's largest sports arena for public executions, and every week, men and women declared by their jirgas as karo and kari for violating tribal honor were handed over to Khan's security forces and, in front of thousands, stoned to death.

Salena had learned to keep her distance from men who made her heart flutter, afraid they might one day disappear, and in fact, several had. "Dr. Raja does not desire me. He sees me as a daughter, nothing more."

"Then he is guilty of incest."

"Please do not hurt him."

"He is already dead."

She heard herself breathing harder. "If you hurt him, I will kill myself. Then you will never have me."

Khan came at her and grabbed her hair. "If you harm yourself, I swear, I will personally go to Gilgit, cut off the heads of your little cousins, and hang their bodies in the middle of Garhi Bagh."

Salena's trembling lip yielded to muffled sobs, and she struggled to speak through her tears. "Dr. Raja ... he knows I love my mother ... he wants to help me ... I swear, he asks nothing more."

Her long hair tight in his fist, Khan pulled her close.

She shuddered under the force of his arms.

"Your beauty is all that saves you. But make no mistake, I will have you." He pressed his manhood against her. "For now I shall let the lecherous doctor live, but I swear, if you leave the Citadel you guarantee his death and the death of all your clan." He pushed her away with such force she lost her balance and fell to the floor.

From inside his robe, Khan pulled out a silver pistol, walked to her side, and pressed the muzzle to her head. "If you dare travel to Srinagar against my will, when I catch you I shall not kill you." He aimed the gun at her leg. "I shall shoot out your kneecaps and cripple you. Then you shall never leave me."

Salena grit her teeth to stop the tears.

Khan stuffed the gun in his robe. "My flower, you will learn to love me." He turned and walked away, leaving her sprawled on the floor. When he reached the stone arch leading from his suite, he paused to look at her. "I have an important meeting tonight. Go to your room and tend to your bruises. Tomorrow we shall fix a date for our wedding and discuss the many sons you shall bear me."

Khan's footsteps faded to silence, and Salena cried some more.

CHAPTER FIVE

J ohn Covello drove alone to pick up his older daughter, Karen, who held a summer job as a counselor for the Ocean County Childhood Care Center. Come September, Karen was starting her sophomore year at Manasquan High School. She had already chosen teaching as her life's work and, so far, shepherding a dozen six-year-olds from one craft station to the next hadn't dimmed her ambition.

He pulled into the circular driveway and got in line behind the cars of other parents, mostly moms, waiting for their own wannabe teachers. In his idling Buick, chilled by strong air conditioning, sharp pains pierced his belly, a reminder his death would not be easy.

John spied a pay telephone outside the administration building's front entrance. He wasn't sure what to make of Chandler's government friend who insisted he call on a land line, but he did know this: if this friend could deliver the big numbers Chandler had hinted at, John was gonna listen.

He turned off the ignition and walked to the phone. Pulling out the white slip of paper Chandler had given him, John tapped out his PIN and eight of the 12 numbers on the paper, then stopped.

What if this were a hoax? Why would any government agency give him the time of day let alone a lucrative contract after the botched Chicago job?

Still, he had nothing to lose. If Uncle Sam was willing to overlook the biggest mistake of his life, and pay him big bucks for what he once did as well as anyone in the industry, Maureen might dig herself out of the mess he'd made for her.

As he keyed in the last digit, Karen walked out the front door of the administration building. John hastily placed the handset on the cradle and stepped back from the phone. He'd try again later.

Karen looked parched and weary, and was mostly quiet during the drive home. She described how she had separated two boys on the soccer field who'd fought over the right to play goalie. Thankfully, she didn't bring up his appointment with Dr. Chandler.

As John approached their beige, vinyl-sided colonial, he saw Maureen's Dodge Caravan parked in the driveway. She must have left work early.

Last spring Maureen had taken a job as an accountant for a financial services firm in Toms River. John had asked her to postpone working full-time until Christie's freshman year. Neither wanted their girls coming home to an empty house. But when Verizon turned off their phones for the fourth time, and Silver Bay Bank served a default notice for the third, they had no choice.

In the two years since Billy Dwyer's death, John hadn't mustered the strength to solicit new business for his firm. He'd drive to his office in Long Branch, then spend the day strolling the boardwalk recalling his toughest jobs. His walks always ended with the same recollection—the botched implosion in Chicago.

Maureen had passed all four parts of the CPA exam after they married, and worked two years at Peat Marwick before Karen was born. With her strong credentials, and his lack of resolve, their only chance to avoid foreclosure was Maureen's going back to work.

John followed Karen in through the back door and found Maureen setting the kitchen table. He walked over and gave her a peck on the cheek. "Where's Christie?"

"Up in her room."

"I guess she's still mad at me."

Maureen grabbed a potholder, opened the oven, and pulled out a tray of meatloaf. She set it on the stovetop to cool. "What did Dr. Chandler say?"

"I should've been a plumber."

"Do I have to call him myself?"

Chandler had stressed his government friend couldn't help John if he discussed his illness with anyone, including his wife. "Don't bother, the results were delayed."

"Which ones?"

"The ERCP and the GI series."

"What about the angiography and the CT scan?"

Maureen was tough. That was the first reason he'd married her. "Yeah, I think those came in."

"Did the angiography detect any intestinal bleeding?"

John didn't know that's what an angiography did. Her smarts was the second reason. "Inconclusive. He's waiting for more results."

"When will he have them?"

Maureen's button-down blouse puffed softly over her ample breasts, and the slit in her blue skirt bared just enough leg below the knee to make him yearn for the delights above. Her subtle sex-appeal was the third. "Tomorrow. He made another appointment to see me at ten."

"Good, I'll go with you."

John knew he had to see Chandler alone. "What about work?"

"I took the day. I'm taking mom to see Aunt Liz tomorrow, but that's not until one. I'm free all morning."

"Great."

"You don't want me to go, do you?"

John took his place at the rectangular oak table. "Of course I do."

Maureen's eyes lingered on John before she turned and began slicing the meatloaf.

Karen walked in from the den and sat beside her father. "Where's Christie?"

Maureen spooned a sliver of meat onto Karen's plate. "Ask your dad." Before Karen could speak, she said to John, "Why don't you go talk to her?"

"I tried before, and she ran away."

"Try again."

John heard footsteps from behind, and turned to see Christie traipse into the kitchen with her head down.

"Don't bother. I'm not mad, just a little sad."

John needed to set things right, and fast. "Let's discuss it."

Karen dropped her fork on her dish. "That's a change. You never talk about anything."

Christie sat beside her mother and passed a small bowl of peas across the table to her older sister. "Karen's right, you never talk about how you feel."

John didn't answer, and instead, poked at the slab of chopped meat sitting forlornly on his plate. He looked at each member of his family, then put down his fork. "I've made a decision."

All three women stopped eating and looked at him.

"From now on, I'm sharing my feelings. I'm telling you everything that's going on inside, and I want you to do the same. Your hopes, your dreams, your sorrows—everything."

Christie's eyes got wide and misty. "I knew it, I knew you were sick."

This wasn't the time or place he had in mind to inform his family he was dying of cancer. He turned to Christie. "Today you said I ran away, and you were right. I never talk about the accident because it hurts. I've kept everything inside, and I understand that made you feel shut out. Believe me, I love you guys more than anything. If I didn't have my family, I would've died a long time ago."

Christie swallowed hard. Maureen and Karen stared at him.

"I'm not saying the change will be easy. It won't. But I'll make the effort."

Karen was first to speak. "Does this mean I can get that used Mustang at Downs Ford?"

John rolled his eyes. "Not quite, but don't give up. Along with an effort to express my feelings, I'm exploring new ways to get us out of this hole I've dug."

Maureen reached over and clasped his hand. "I'd just be happy to see a glimpse of the old John. I know the kids would too." She looked at Karen. "Once we pull together as a team, then we can solve our money problems."

For the first time in as long as John remembered, they talked about things he'd kept bottled up for years—the time he disappeared for two days after being acquitted of manslaughter but convicted of fraud, the time he almost rode his Harley into a tree after reading a letter filled with hate from Billy Dwyer's father, and the time he stole three jars of Nutella from Shop-Rite because it was Christie's favorite Graham Cracker topping. They laughed and cried and giggled and grinned as they hadn't done in years. Everything was perfect, until they returned to the subject of money.

Karen brought it up. "Allison and Kim from the Care Center are going to Seaside tomorrow night. Can I go with them?"

Maureen glared at her. "We've discussed it before. You can't go spending your savings on silly rides."

"Come on Mom, I've saved my entire paycheck for three straight weeks."

"If you plan on going to college, that's the way it'll stay."

"This sucks."

"Don't you dare talk to me like that."

"I wasn't talking to you."

"Now you're lying."

John couldn't take anymore. He threw down his fork, making a loud clatter as it hit his plate. "Stop it, both of you." He scraped back his chair and stood. "I told you, I'm working on a plan to get us back on our feet. I can't discuss it now, but trust me, I'm trying."

Karen frowned. "What's your big plan? Rob a bank, or maybe put us on the street to sell our bodies?"

Maureen shot up, leaned over, and slapped her daughter hard across the face.

Karen stared at her mother in disbelief. It was the first time John had ever seen Maureen strike one of their children. Karen shoved her dish across the table and ran from the room.

Maureen's expression turned instantly from anger to regret, and she looked about to cry. Christie timidly excused herself, and slunk from the room.

If not for the troubles he'd caused his family, Maureen wouldn't have snapped. He got up and held her. "She's frustrated and I can't blame her. She wants to live life like a normal teenager."

"She doesn't understand how bad things are."

"It's not her problem, or yours."

Maureen pushed him away. "There you go again, shouldering the burden alone."

"I'm sorry, you're right, but it's true what I said. I'm working on a plan to get us out of debt."

"A job?"

"Maybe."

"What kind?"

"I don't know, maybe a demo job."

"That's exactly what you need to get your confidence back."

"We'll see."

Together they cleared the table, then Maureen went upstairs to make peace with her daughter.

John walked out the back door, stood on the deck, and watched the dying sun descend over the Manasquan River. The wake of a passing boat gently thumped his Whaler against the rubber bumpers hanging off the bulkhead. That old boat gave him the last enjoyment he hadn't yet sold.

He'd try Chandler's friend again in the morning, maybe take a drive to Point Pleasant Beach where no one would interrupt him.

Through the open den window he heard a TV announcer cut away from a game show to the sullen voice of a newscaster. "We interrupt this program to bring you a special report, 'Crises in Asia.' Tonight in the Bay of Bengal, US surveillance satellites detected …"

John blocked out the rest. With any luck, Chandler had given him a way to fix his money problems. Why even think about problems he couldn't control?

CHAPTER SIX

Less than 48 hours remained until Prime Minister Behari's deadline, and CRUSO had yet to find a suitable candidate. Major Farrell glanced at the pile of shredded scrap paper on the table in front of Colonel Daley and did a double-take when she saw his confetti mound had swollen to the size of a softball.

CRUSO's strongest lead had been a telephone call one hour earlier from a Dr. Robert Chandler, who assured Farrell he had identified a qualified individual who would call CRUSO within 18 hours. Chandler's candidate had better call soon.

Side-by-side on the table in front of Farrell lay two preliminary Career, Character, and Cash Reports—one on Dr. Robert Chandler, the other on his candidate. Neither profile came close to a full-blown 3-C's Report, but from what Farrell had read so far, Chandler's man looked promising.

Daley got up and walked to the 60-inch plasma monitor. "Isn't Chandler Category C?"

"He is, but you said so yourself, we're in a jam."

"How long's Chandler been treating this gentleman?"

Farrell glanced at the report. "Since April 5th."

"Any connection beside doctor and patient?"

"Both belong to the Brick Township chapter of the Rotary Club."

"What else do we know about his referral?"

Farrell put down Chandler's preliminary 3-C's Report and picked up an even thinner profile with the name "John A. Covello" printed on top. "I covered his demolitions experience. His most impressive credential was the Carter Building in Dallas. Contract job for the FBI. It wasn't until after the Chicago incident that he stopped working."

"One screw-up doesn't make a career."

"His blunder in Chicago isn't my main concern."

Daley sauntered back to the conference table, and stood behind his burgundy leather chair looking down at her. "What is, then?"

Farrell had become familiar with her boss's power tricks. One was to stand while addressing a seated subordinate. Farrell rolled back her chair, got up, and locked eyes with Daley across the table. "I have several. No prior military service for one, and considering we have less than 24 hours to train, that's a serious drawback."

"I disagree. The most important quality is demolitions experience— building implosions to be precise—and that's exactly what he does."

"What if he's forced to defend himself?"

Daley pointed to the 3-C's Report in Farrell's hand. "Didn't you say he was star midfielder for his high school lacrosse team?"

"I did."

"Went on to lead Rutgers to three state championships?"

"Yes, but how is that relevant?"

"Fact is, no one shines at midfield without speed, stamina, and good hands."

Farrell held back a frown. "College sports hardly substitutes for military training."

"Apparently, you've never played lacrosse."

"What about his emotional instability? He's suffered a series of legal and financial setbacks over the past two years."

"Hogwash. That's why these people come to us in the first place. What are his other downsides?"

"He was informed of his condition three hours ago. He's still assimilating the news of an incurable illness."

"That's something they all have to deal with. Give me something better."

"How about a wife and two children?"

Daley plopped down into his leather chair, and began rocking.

"His younger daughter is 13, his older, 16, and he's been married to the same woman 18 years."

Daley stilled his chair and looked up at her. "Sit, you're making me nervous."

Having achieved her objective, Farrell obliged. "Sir, you know the rules."

"These are exigent circumstances. The consequence of failure is nuclear war."

CRUSO candidate selection guidelines disqualified men or women with minor children, except when no other suitable candidate was available. Even then, achievement of the mission's objective must be necessary to prevent imminent and irreparable harm to a vital national interest.

Farrell had to concede the present situation fit the exception. "I would've preferred someone with no children."

"Don't think I savor the thought, but we're in a bind."

"We still need a complete 3-C's Report on Mr. Covello, and for that matter, Dr. Chandler."

"We can run full 3-C's during the next two days."

"After the mission is underway?"

"Can they be finished before then?"

"You know that's impossible."

"My point. Now do you have a photograph of Mr. Covello?"

"I believe so." Farrell angled her chair to the conference table facing a keyboard and 17-inch monitor. She punched in a series of numbers and letters, and on the giant screen at the front of the room appeared a head and shoulders shot of a man with groggy brown eyes. Farrell keyed in more numbers and beside the first image appeared a younger version of the same man. She kept typing, and a third photo appeared beside the others. "His New Jersey Driver's License, his ID card for the FBI implosion ... looks like we have his prints on file ... and a yearbook photo from Red Bank High School. That's the best I can do in 30 seconds."

Daley rose and walked to the 60-inch wall-mounted monitor. "Not bad. Brown hair, brown eyes, olive complexion. He'll blend."

"He won't be confused for a WASP."

"What are his short-term symptoms?"

"Tim Sheehan examined the medical file Dr. Chandler e-mailed us two hours ago. Mr. Covello suffers severe abdominal pain due to metastases of the cancer to his stomach, liver, and abdominal wall. He hasn't jaundiced yet, and his urine shows normal, so the cancer probably hasn't spread to his bile duct. According to Drs. Chandler and Sheehan, without treatment, he'll be mobile four, maybe five more weeks."

"I only need five days."

Farrell wondered what Covello's wife and daughters looked like. Neither of CRUSO's prior mission candidates had left behind children, let alone young children.

Daley continued, "So basically we're weighing lack of military experience and no training time against a man who's an expert in his field and—"

A three-tone chime rang from the monitor in front of Farrell. Daley kept quiet as Farrell typed in the required six-digit password. Instantly, a laser printer beside the monitor spit out two pages. Farrell lifted them from the output tray. "Look's like Khan's army is on the move again."

"Where to now?"

"At 1748 hours DST the Anstat-4 picked up 15 PUMA's and eight T-80UD's on the ground at Skardu."

"He's making his play sooner than we thought."

US military strategists and Ivy League academicians had for years theorized scenarios culminating in a nuclear exchange between India and Pakistan. Such reports offered fascinating reads, but no one, not even Farrell, really thought it would happen.

Yesterday, the day after General Khan detonated a 15 kiloton tactical nuclear warhead 3,500 feet over Baramulla, incinerating 2,500 Indian soldiers and 7,000 civilians, and condemning an additional 5,000 to slow deaths from radiation sickness, President Lloyd sent Secretary Parker to Beijing to enlist Premier Jintao's help dissuading Khan from pursuing his policy of aggression toward India.

This morning the president had been informed Premier Jintao was willing to entertain America's request that China engage General Khan in meaningful dialogue over his expansionist policies. But nothing came for nothing in international politics. In exchange for Jintao's help, the president must publicly support the fulfillment of China's destiny—reunification under the flag of China's one legitimate government, the People's Republic.

The door behind Farrell burst open. She turned to see Mission Specialist Stacy Miller rush into the conference room.

"Sorry, but you'll want to hear this." She held up a blue file. "At 1702 DST, the Command Hub received a hang-up call."

Daley smirked. "With or without heavy breathing?"

"The caller used a number matching Dr. Chandler's referral tag, and we identified the source."

"By any chance, 356 River Road, Brielle, New Jersey?"

"No, a pay phone at the Ocean County Childhood Care Center in Point Pleasant."

Farrell tapped numbers into the computer on her left, waited for a reply, then looked up at Daley. "Exactly 4.3 miles from John Covello's house."

Daley smiled. "Looks like our man is interested."

Farrell wasn't so sure. "A hang-up might mean he changed his mind."

"Not a problem." Daley strode past Stacy to the conference room door, stopped, and looked back at Farrell. "What are you waiting for? If he won't ask us to dance, we'll ask him."

CHAPTER SEVEN

Crossing the lobby of the Citadel, Dr. Salena Zamal trailed two steps behind Ali Khan. His violent outburst the night before had marred her cheek with a dark patch of bruised skin. Salena hoped the thin layer of makeup she had applied that morning would be enough to conceal the blatant proof of her keeper's wrath.

Her throat tightened as Captain Qadeer approached from the opposite direction dangling one of those acrid Red Lamp cigarettes from his lips. He stopped and snuffed out his cigarette in a marble ash tray, then walked up to Khan with his arms spread wide, and firmly embraced his mentor. He ignored Salena, which was fine with her, since Azam Qadeer was the only man alive she despised more than Ali Khan.

"Come now, Azam, you must acknowledge the presence of Dr. Zamal. In two months she shall serve as your nation's first lady."

Qadeer bowed his head. "As you command."

"You two must learn to get along, if not for me, then for Pakistan."

Without looking at Salena, Qadeer gave a shallow nod in her direction. "As-salaam alaikum."

Salena thought of spitting at him, but instead replied, "Wa-alaikum salam."

Qadeer lit up another cigarette, took a deep drag, and blew his smoke at a slight angle from Salena's face.

Choking on the stench of burning tobacco, she turned away from Khan and Qadeer, but listened carefully to what they said.

She heard Qadeer speak first. "Lieutenant Siddique is bringing your car to the west entrance."

"Good. Have you set up my meeting with General Afzal?"

Salena recognized the name of the chief of Pakistan's Inter-Services Intelligence Agency. His wife, Nusrat, was her patient.

"Ten-thirty at Chaklala, then back to the Citadel for a one o'clock meeting with Admiral Mahmoud."

"Ach'ha. Has everyone confirmed their arrival times?"

"Yes, the last to get here will be General Abbasi. Frahat's forces have kept him occupied at Karambar Pass. He cannot leave until Wednesday morning."

"Assure his presence before we start."

"As you command, habib." Salena heard Captain Qadeer address her back. "Dr. Zamal, I will send two officers to your room in 30 minutes to escort you to the hospital."

Pulling her dupatta across her face, she turned. "I shall be waiting."

Qadeer bowed to Khan and walked toward the Citadel's main elevator bank. Salena spoke loudly enough for Qadeer to hear, "I wish he would not smoke in front of me."

Qadeer kept walking and disappeared into an open car.

"He is a man, it is his right."

"Smoking breaches Allah's law."

"His loyalty has earned him my leniency."

"But he smokes in the hospital. It is bad for the patients."

"Why do you argue with me?"

"Many of my patients are pregnant, some are nursing. And the babies. His smoke fouls the lungs of your generals' newborn sons."

Khan sighed. "Very well, I shall mention your concerns."

Time was running short, but Salena held out hope the Americans would contact her before next Wednesday. If and when the call came, she must be ready with specific information about Khan's location and movements over the next few days. She must also learn which generals and politicians he had chosen to attend Glorious Dawn. Despite her desire to stay far away from Khan, she knew the most effective means of gathering information about the man's plans and actions was to feign interest in the man himself. "Before you leave, please allow me to apologize for last night's insolence. I have come to understand that after we marry, my mother is no longer my family. I shall endeavor to drive her from my mind."

"My heart is not as cold as you think. I shall keep my word. After Kashmir is liberated, I shall allow you to go to her."

"Thank you, kind master."

He regarded her warily. "Why the sudden change of attitude?"

Khan was not a stupid man; she must proceed with caution. "The truth is, I have no choice. Either I fight you and be beaten, or accept my fate as your wife."

"Your intelligence serves you well."

"My only desire is relief from your blows."

His steely blue eyes scoured her. "Have no doubt, other desires shall follow."

The thought of intimacy with Ali Khan turned her stomach, but if she were to end his abuse, she must help the Americans, and find an excuse to spend time with him. "This evening I wish to prepare your supper—an expression of my gratitude for your mercy."

"Perhaps you crave me more than you know."

If Islam did not prohibit public displays of affection between men and women, she was sure he would have grabbed her right there in the lobby.

"Indeed you are handsome."

"I have dinner scheduled for seven o'clock with Lieutenant General Frahat."

She could ill afford to lose this opportunity. "Please, can the meeting wait? I am preparing jhinga karhai and chapli kabab."

"My two favorite dishes."

"Mine as well."

"But the lieutenant general and I have yet to determine which squadrons to move from Sargodha to Masroor."

"The war comes first, but if the truth be told, I am disappointed."

Khan rubbed his chin, as if mulling his options. Finally, he said, "I do not wish to discourage your efforts to win my favor. I shall meet with Frahat at four-thirty. He can make other dinner arrangements."

She smiled. "Thank you kind master."

"Now return to your room, and wait there until the captain's men escort you to your patients." Khan paused, grinning at her with two rows of perfect white teeth. "I was a fool to believe you would choose an old man over me."

"I say now as I said then, Dr. Raja is my colleague, nothing more."

"Any man who looks at you drives me to madness."

"I am yours alone."

"Tonight you shall have the chance to prove your words."

"Restraint is difficult for me as well, but do not forget the words of the Prophet, 'the woman and the man guilty of fornication, flog each of them with a hundred lashes.'"

Lust raged in Khan's hungry eyes. "Then may Allah forgive me if I take you tonight."

"In two months your masculine urges shall have legitimate outlet."

"Do not hide behind the dictates of Islam to preserve your virginity."

Salena was sure if Khan knew the truth, he would slit her throat.

CHAPTER EIGHT

John squinted at the lit numbers on the clock-radio beside his bed: 4:38 a.m. Haunted by his decision to hide his illness from Maureen, he had tossed and turned all night. He hadn't actually lied to his wife, but in his book, withholding an important truth was just as sleazy.

What plagued him most, though, were thoughts of his own mortality. The worst part of knowing death was imminent was mourning the loss of his family. He was supposed to grow old with Maureen. Together they'd watch their daughters mature into fine young women, pursue careers of their own, marry good, honest men, and make beautiful children.

The accident in Chicago, and now cancer's death sentence, had obliterated such fond notions. His only chance to give Maureen and his daughters a bountiful future lay in the phone number of Chandler's friend.

If that road led nowhere, he'd return home and confess the truth about his illness.

John slipped out of bed, put on jeans and a T-shirt, and kissed his sleeping wife.

Her eyelids parted into thin blue slivers. "Where are you going so early?"

"The Inlet Grill for coffee and *The Press*. Maybe watch the morning charters."

"On your way home, pick me up a large decaf."

He kissed her lips. "Sure thing, gorgeous."

Maureen smiled, closed her eyes, and rolled over.

John crossed the Route 35 drawbridge and entered the resort community of Point Pleasant Beach. He made a left onto Ocean Avenue and drove parallel to the Atlantic Ocean until he reached the northern tip of the barrier island. There the road veered sharply left and ran along the Manasquan Inlet. Two bait and tackle shops, three coffee shops, and a half dozen beach bungalows lined the left side of the road across from the water.

Approaching the Inlet Grill, John slowed to a crawl. Inside the coffee shop, where he knew he'd find a pay phone, he saw a dozen fishermen standing in line eager to get a jump on the morning fluke. During the last two years, John had begun many days here, not to fish, but to observe. He'd pick up a large coffee and *The Asbury Park Press*, grab an empty bench, and watch the bowriders, cruisers, and party boats heading for the ocean ply the inlet's tricky currents.

John angled into a parking spot beside a maroon minivan, and shimmied through the narrow space between his car and the van.

At the trunk of his Buick, he paused to look both ways before crossing the street. A dark green Ford Explorer approaching from the left stopped directly in front of him and a tall black man wearing a white collared shirt and blue tie jumped out from the passenger side. His voice was deep. "John Covello?"

John recognized neither the black man nor the balding man at the wheel of the SUV who kept looking around. John wondered if one of his creditors had decided to play rough. "Who sent you guys?"

"I'm told it's you who tried calling us."

Of course, Chandler's government friend. "This must be one hell of a demo job."

"Come with us, and you'll find out."

John climbed into the back seat of the Explorer, suppressing the urge to cry out in pain. The cramps cutting across his belly hurt worse than ever. Instead of dwelling on the cancer eating up his insides, he focused on where the two tight-lipped men were taking him.

He caught a glimpse of Riverwood Plaza on Route 70 west. Ten minutes later they turned right at the recently refurbished McDonalds, which put them on Route 547 north. So when the truck veered left into the main gate at the Naval Air Systems Command Station in Lakehurst, John wasn't entirely surprised.

They pulled up to a loading dock behind a three-story office building, where John's escorts led him up a cargo ramp through a pair of metal doors. Inside, the two men guided him through a labyrinth of well-lit hallways to an unmarked wooden door. One of the men opened the door, let John in, then both disappeared without saying good-bye.

John found himself in a small windowless office filled by a round conference table too wide for the room's dimensions. A tall white male, about 60 or so, stood to the left of the table. He wore a freshly pressed, dark blue uniform with a narrow bar patch stitched across the chest and a small silver eagle embroidered on each shoulder. What little white hair he had left was combed to one side. John looked at him, but the man's steely gray eyes gave nothing away.

On the opposite side of the table stood a petite black woman wearing a dark green jumpsuit. Her hair was cut in a pixie and she had a manila file tucked under her arm. John put her at about 30.

The woman spoke first.

"I'm Major Denise Farrell—United States Army. This is Colonel William Daley. I apologize for the abrupt circumstances of your delivery." She motioned John to the chair between herself and Daley. "Why don't we sit?"

John wasn't saying no to anything, at least not yet. They all sat and she continued. "By now, you've probably concluded Colonel Daley and I are affiliated with the government agency Dr. Chandler spoke to you about yesterday."

John nodded.

"I assume you're also aware earlier this week General Ghalib Ali Khan detonated a low-yield nuclear weapon over a town in the Kashmir Valley."

John cleared his throat. "Yeah, seems to be what everyone's talking about."

"Excuse me if I repeat facts you already know, but your familiarity with the region is essential for your understanding of why you're here."

"I'm all ears."

"The territory that makes up modern day India and Pakistan was once part of a single British colony called India. After World War II England could no longer afford to hold onto India, and in 1947 granted the colony independence.

"The great divider of the Indian people was, and still is, religion. Most are either Muslim or Hindu. During England's rule the two groups tolerated each other, though age-old resentments occasionally flared into communal violence. In the years leading up to independence, a man named Muhammad Ali Jinnah, the leader of the Muslim League, argued for a separate Muslim nation to be carved out of India. Mohandas Gandhi, leader of the Hindu-dominated National Congress, wanted India to remain united. By 1947 hatred between Muslims and Hindus boiled to the point where London realized they had no choice. They divided the colony into two sovereign nations based on religious affiliation.

"Partition of the subcontinent uprooted millions. Muslims left or were forced out of lands that make up modern-day India, and migrated to lands that became Pakistan. Hindus living in present-day Pakistan moved or were driven from their homes onto lands that became India. In the process of switching land and people, more than a million men, women, and children of both faiths were slaughtered. Needless to say, bitter hatred persists between Hindus and Muslims." Farrell paused and studied John as if gauging his reaction. "Are you with me?"

"High school was a long time ago, but yeah, I'm with you."

"So you had two new nations starting out as uneasy neighbors—their very existences based on a mutual desire to destroy each other. Three wars and numerous skirmishes later, they still haven't learned to co-exist. Toss in a Muslim fundamentalist acquiring control of Pakistan's nuclear arsenal, and what happened last Tuesday was no surprise."

"You saw it coming?"

"Three weeks ago the Defense Intelligence Agency observed a sharp escalation of military activity along the Indo-Pakistan border. In many places, General Khan's combined forces effectively pushed Pakistan's border two miles east into India. Khan's greatest gains came along the southern sector of the Line of Control, where—"

"Hold up. What's the Line of Control?"

"India and Pakistan fought their first war over the disputed state of Jammu & Kashmir. The Line of Control is essentially where the shooting stopped. Pakistan and India agreed, albeit reluctantly, to recognize the cease-fire line as their common border through Kashmir. That line more or less held until three weeks ago, when Khan's army rolled over India's forces from Mirpur to Potha."

"Didn't India fight back?"

Farrell nodded vigorously. "Last Friday the city of Poonch was about to fall into Khan's hands, when Prime Minister Behari ordered a major counter-offensive designed to achieve two objectives—prevent the capture of Poonch, and take Pakistan territory in the Jhelum Valley. By dedicating 80 percent of its resources to one region, India's army made swift gains. Tuesday's detonation over Baramulla was Khan's response to India's counter-attack.

"When Khan started making moves on India last month, we weren't sure of his end game. Since then, we've learned from an inside source he plans nothing less than the complete conquest of India's seven northwest provinces. He intends to annex half a million square miles of sovereign Indian territory to Pakistan, and he's prepared to use every means at his disposal. Our goal is to stop him before he starts.

"That's the broad overview. The historical circumstances that stirred and continue to feed the animosity between India and Pakistan are much more complex than I've outlined, but I'd prefer not to confuse you."

John shook his head. "Confuse me? I go out for a cup of coffee, and before I get a chance to call, you haul me off to a military base, give me a history lesson on a part of the world I'd rather forget, and expect me to understand what the hell's going on. No, Major Farrell, I'm still really confused."

"Our agency is aware of the implosion accident in Chicago you and your company were blamed for. We're also aware of the financial and legal impact that accident had on your family."

"I get it. You're holding me prisoner until I pay my taxes."

"We also know about your Stage IV pancreatic cancer. We're truly sorry."

"Why do I have trouble believing you?"

"In exchange for your help, our agency can lift the financial and legal burdens your family will be left with after you die. Dr. Chandler should have explained that."

"He did, but he wasn't clear on what's in it for me." From the sides of his eyes, John caught Daley frowning in Farrell's direction.

Either Farrell didn't notice, or ignored him. "Our agency is one of seven new implementation arms of the National Security Agency created after the 2001 attack on America. We draw on resources from all four branches of the US armed forces, as well as Homeland Security, and the CIA, FBI, and DIA."

"DIA?"

"Defense Intelligence Agency. A support arm of the Department of Defense that gathers foreign intelligence needed for planning and executing military operations."

"I hate asking the obvious, but with all those resources, why do you need my help?"

"The world has changed Mr. Covello. For one thing, combating terrorism at home and abroad costs US taxpayers billions of dollars every year. We simply can't afford to keep sending our armies into every country bent on destroying itself or its neighbors. More importantly, whenever we intervene in a dispute in some dark corner of the world, we breed resentment, not only among our enemies, but our allies too. The world is growing weary, and wary, of a planet dominated by one superpower. Let's be honest. Some countries have been around hundreds, even thousands of years. We've been around less than 300—yet we're the strongest nation on earth. That raises a lot of backs."

"So what? Whenever crazy men like bin Laden or Ali Khan hurt innocent people, we have every right to take them out."

"It's not so simple."

"Sounds simple to me. One Tomahawk missile through Khan's bedroom window, and we all sleep a little safer."

"You're right on the objective, wrong on the method."

"I don't get it. When we took out bin Laden, the world cheered."

"And where was the cheering loudest? You didn't see dancing in the streets of Cairo, Damascus, or Baghdad. Al-Jazeera labeled us the Big Bully of the West and the name stuck. You'd be surprised how many of Pakistan's Muslims are proud of Khan's gains against India.

They don't perceive him as a cruel dictator trampling their rights. They see him as a great leader willing to stand up to the big bully."

"Are you saying we created that monster?"

"Not created, nurtured."

"I still don't understand."

"Pakistan is an Islamic republic. Its laws and religion are integrally related. Don't get me wrong, Pakistan's Muslims have their differences. The two major sects, Sunni and Shiite, have very different takes on who gets to follow in the shoes of Mohammad. But whenever we flex our muscles in that part of the world, their differences evaporate. Many Muslims, regardless of ideology, resent America. Khan plays on that resentment to keep the support of his people, not as a dictator, but as a defender of Islam."

"So what? It's not like if we knock out Khan we'll feel the wrath of Pakistan."

"We fully intend to neutralize Khan, but without brewing more hostility in the Muslim world."

John remembered a radio report he'd heard on his drive to the inlet. "Why do we have to get involved anyway? Doesn't India have nukes of its own?"

"They do, and the last thing we want is for India to use them."

"I say they have every right to defend themselves."

"As does India's prime minister. Half an hour after Khan exploded his bomb over Baramulla, our satellites observed road and rail deployment of nuclear-armed missiles bound for northwest India. Within two hours, India was poised to launch a massive retaliatory strike."

"What stopped them?"

"We did, but only because President Lloyd begged Prime Minister Behari to give America first shot at ousting Khan."

"What happened to not breeding resentment?"

"The operation is covert. If it's done right, no one will know America was behind Khan's demise."

"I thought killing a foreign leader was illegal."

"Not after Executive Order 11905 was repealed."

John didn't recall hearing that hunting season had re-opened on crazed despots, then again, for the past two years he hadn't paid much attention to anything outside his self-spun cocoon. "So if America promises to assassinate Khan, that'll be enough to keep India from launching its nukes."

"Not indefinitely. Prime Minister Behari is chomping at the bit to strike back at Pakistan. If we don't prove to his satisfaction we've undertaken a mission to remove Ali Khan from power, he'll authorize a nuclear response. He gave President Lloyd until Saturday 6:00 a.m. to provide clear evidence we've commenced a covert operation."

"That's only eight days away."

Farrell looked grimly at Colonel Daley, who nodded back at her.

"I don't mean next Saturday—I mean tomorrow."

"What?"

"I mean by 6:00 a.m., Eastern Daylight Saving Time tomorrow, President Lloyd must prove to Prime Minister Behari we've infiltrated a US operative inside Khan's command and control center, otherwise, at 6:01 a.m., an Agni-III missile delivers a 20 kiloton payload to Islamabad set to detonate 5,000 feet over Rawal Lake."

"What's your plan?"

Major Farrell opened her manila file, removed two photographs, and slid them across the table to John. She pointed to a small octagon centered on an aerial black-and-white photograph. "Khan's Citadel." She pointed to the second photo. "Same structure, northeast elevation."

John examined the side view first. Floors one through five consisted of mirrored windows, and above that, solid concrete walls, except for the top floor, which was ringed by a balcony. Turning to the aerial photo, John picked out a cluster of buildings encircled by a wall directly across the street from Khan's Citadel. "What's that?"

"The Diplomatic Enclave."

"Enclave?"

"A 30-acre complex housing diplomats and their families. The large white building inside the wall closest to the Citadel houses the Enclave's elementary and secondary schools."

"One misguided Tomahawk, and then talk about Big Bully of the West."

"Absolutely right. Khan intentionally built his Citadel in close proximity to the Enclave's school."

"Well at least it's July, no kids around."

Farrell bit her lip. "The academic year runs differently in the Enclave. The third week of July marks the middle of their summer session."

"You're crazy. The school's too damn close."

"We have a 180 foot margin of error."

"You need a thousand." On the aerial shot, John pointed to a rectangular building abutting the Citadel. "What's this?"

"Pakistan National Hospital. It's linked to the Citadel by an elevated walkway crossing a 20 foot alley. Another reason a missile strike is out of the question."

John mulled the elevation shot of Khan's Citadel. He had a feeling where Farrell was going with this, and he wasn't happy. "Impossible. Even if you sneak some fool inside, he'll have to wrap the columns in wire mesh."

"No need to wrap columns."

"Bullshit. That's standard safety procedure."

"We have RDX."

John had previously worked with RDX, a copper-encased explosive capable of slicing steel beams at a rate of 27,000 feet per second. "Big deal, you'll still get flyrock."

"It's not like any RDX you've seen. Direction and explosive strength are digitally adjustable. We call it RDX-7S."

"Never heard of it."

For the first time, Farrell smiled. "We have lots of things you've never heard of."

"Including invisible dye so I can penetrate Khan's Citadel without being seen?"

"If you accept our offer, we've invented a legitimate cover for you as a hospital and health care systems consultant. You'd be going to Pakistan at the invitation of a highly respected physician employed at Pakistan National Hospital."

"Don't tell me you have someone planted inside."

"Not planted, but willing to help."

"Assuming you meet Behari's deadline, how long would I have to position the charges?"

"According to our informant, next Wednesday at 1:00 p.m. Pakistan time Khan plans to meet in secret with the leading members of his command structure to hammer out final details of his thrust into northwest India. The meeting is code-named Glorious Dawn, and as far as we know it's only the second time he's assembled all his top generals and politicos in the Citadel at one time. He's usually careful about dispersing his key people, but to insure flawless execution of Glorious Dawn's objectives, he's made an exception. That mistake has created a unique opportunity."

"Say something goes wrong—maybe you don't meet Behari's deadline, or your operative gets caught before next Wednesday—do you really think Khan would set off more nukes?"

"We know for a fact the Baramulla bomb wasn't the last in his plans. Our informant has advised us the initial prong of Khan's attack consists of low-yield nuclear detonations over the five largest cities in northwest India—Delhi, Mumbai, Ahmadabad, Kanpur, and Jaipur. We're looking at 30 million potential casualties—20 million in India, 10 million in Pakistan."

"That's insane."

"That's the start of World War III. With nukes exploding on their back doors, China and Russia are likely to jump in, then we have no choice but to jump in too."

"Just what America needs."

"Just what America doesn't want."

"OK, let's say everything goes as planned—next Wednesday Khan and his lackeys get buried under a hundred tons of rubble. Won't he be replaced by some other screwed up dictator?"

"Pakistan's former president, Labib Razzak, and a dozen of his loyal generals live exiled in London. The moment we confirm the Citadel is down and Khan is dead we'll fly Razzak and his generals back to Pakistan. He's assured President Lloyd he'll resume the policy of reconciliation he began with India before Khan ousted him."

John clasped his hands behind his head and sat back in his chair. "There must be a thousand demolitions experts to choose from who didn't kill a kid by mistake. Why pick me?"

Farrell looked down at the table and didn't answer.

Colonel Daley's eyes locked on John, and for the first time, he spoke. "Mr. Covello, I'm not sure you understand. We call our agency CRUSO—Civilians Recruited for Unrecoverable Special Operations. The key word is unrecoverable. The candidate we send to Islamabad is not coming home. We picked you because you're as good as dead anyway."

Everything fell into place at once. He whispered, "This is a suicide mission."

"I thought you knew."

He'd have to die to give Maureen and his daughters a chance for a normal life. "When would I go?"

"If you accept, we set up your disappearance, and in six hours, you're gone forever."

The pain slicing through his gut must have shown on his face. Farrell leaned forward and touched his hand. "Are you all right?"

"No, I'm not all right." John doubted they could ever pay him enough money to throw away what little time he had left with his wife and children. "Before I listen to another word, I'd like to know what's in it for my family."

Daley's impassive eyes grew big and he grinned. "As well you should, and I think you'll like the answer."

CHAPTER NINE

Alone in the bedroom of the lavishly appointed suite Khan had chosen for her on the 11th floor of his Citadel, Salena waited for her escorts to arrive so she could begin her rounds at the hospital. She looked into the mirror beside her bed and examined herself in the loose-fitting dress Khan had approved for her wardrobe. The baggy, light blue garment reached down to her ankles and left little hint of her gender. Tucking her hair beneath a matching dupatta, she thought how her life would be different had she married by 16, like many of her friends, and not gone to college. For one thing, Khan would never have known she existed.

Salena had met Ghalib Ali Khan during the spring semester of her third year at the University of Peshawar in a class called "Women and Islam." The army had granted Lieutenant Khan a six month leave to pursue courses in Islamic Law and Shariah. He boasted to the professor he had taken the class to better understand the mind of the fallible gender.

Khan pursued her relentlessly that semester, not in the crude way of the West, but subtly, in the way his bold blue eyes fixed on her when he thought she wasn't looking. He was 15 years her senior, and a magnificent Pathan specimen. If not for his opinion every good Muslim woman must hide behind the walls of her home or beneath the shroud of a burqa, she might have found him attractive.

After each session he badgered her with quotes from Hadith and the Qur'an, twisting the words of the Prophet to support his belief in the intrinsic inferiority of women. She countered with quotes of her own from the Qur'an, and whenever the debate was going her way—which was nearly every time—he flew into a diatribe, rejecting any rational argument that promoted secular and spiritual equality of the sexes.

To her great relief Khan left the university after the spring semester to resume his military career. She soon discovered he was not gone for good. He continued his obnoxious discourse through e-mails and telephone calls, and though she changed her e-mail address and telephone number several times during her senior year, he always found a way to contact her.

After graduating Peshawar University with high Honors and gaining acceptance to Mount Sinai School of Medicine in Manhattan, she left Pakistan and Ghalib Ali Khan behind, and moved to America. Even in the States Khan continued plaguing her with letters, cards, and e-mails. Over the years the frequency of his correspondence diminished, not because he lost interest in her, but because he became preoccupied with the one objective he sought above all—control of Pakistan.

Four and a half years after Salena returned to the subcontinent, Khan achieved his goal. Backed by eight regiments of Pakistan's Frontier Corps, in less than 48 hours Khan staged a successful coup against President Labib Razzak. In two bloody days, 45,000 Pakistani soldiers and civilians lost their lives.

Razzak had been ripe for the fall, perceived by the majority of his constituents as too quick to bend to the whims of the West, and too lenient on the question of Kashmir. Salena herself disagreed with Razzak's conciliatory overtures to New Delhi on Kashmir, but at least Razzak was a tolerant man, which explained why those saddened most by his departure were Pakistan's women.

The deposed president got lucky. With the help of America's CIA he escaped over the Iranian border with minutes to spare, but many of his loyal followers met far worse fates than exile. Razzak's Minister of Agriculture, Zaheer Uddin, and the minister's pregnant wife, Lateefa, were dragged from their home in Rawalpindi and beheaded on the National Cricket Grounds as their six year old daughter was forced to watch. The girl, Kalila, was one of many children Salena had removed from Rawalpindi's lawless streets and taken into Pakistan National Hospital.

Within a month of toppling Razaak's government, it became clear Khan intended to rule Pakistan according to his maniacal interpretation of Islamic law. He banned most television and radio programs, closed cinemas and nightclubs, and forbade public play of many games including cards and chess, and popular sports such as tennis and cricket. Last April he outlawed Basanth, a happy holiday when boys celebrated spring's arrival with kite-flying duels, and in May closed Kinnaird College in Lahore, the only women's college in Pakistan he had not shut down on the day he assumed the presidency.

Shortly after Khan's army gunned down the last of Khan's opponents—1,200 Punjabis assembled in Jallo Park near Lahore demanding Razzak's reinstatement—Khan authorized construction of the Pakistan Joint Forces Command and Control Center, a 12-story office building equipped with the most expensive telecommunications and surveillance equipment the country's treasury could withstand. Inside Pakistan, the structure was known as The Citadel, and around the world, as Khan's Citadel.

Had Salena not been forced to flee Srinagar only one year after returning to her homeland, Khan might have forgotten all about her.

Instead, when Khan discovered she was living under an assumed name, and working as Assistant Director of Women's Health Services at Lady Reading Hospital in Peshawar, he ordered the ISI to spy on her around the clock. After solidifying his power base in Islamabad, Khan made his move.

On the fourth Sunday of last March, while Salena was washing her hands in the operating room after delivering a baby girl for a Pathan villager, Captain Qadeer and three burly goons from the ISI burst into Lady Reading Hospital to carry out Khan's will. After Qadeer put her in the back of his jeep, he said nothing of their destination, but when they turned east on the Grand Trunk Road, she knew exactly where they were headed.

A knock on the door rattled Salena to the present. Tucking an errant strand of her dark hair beneath her veil, she lowered her head and left her suite.

Accompanied by two of Qadeer's lackeys, she walked through the elevated skywalk connecting the 4th floor of Khan's Citadel with the 4th Floor of Pakistan National Hospital. The air conditioned walkway, with windows for sides, spanned a narrow driveway linking the Citadel's front and rear parking lots.

Salena took the elevator to the hospital's 5th floor and entered her office, while her two army escorts positioned themselves outside her door. On a desk stacked with patient files, Salena booted up her computer and checked the toolbar on the bottom of her screen to see if the message she was waiting for had arrived. It hadn't.

She picked up five files and left her office with Qadeer's soldiers in tow. When they reached the automatic doors leading to the hospital's maternity patients, the two soldiers stopped abruptly. No men, including Qadeer's enforcers, were permitted to enter any part of the hospital housing women. As always, Salena suggested the soldiers fetch an early lunch in the cafeteria downstairs, and return in three or four hours. As always, they eagerly obliged.

All patients in Pakistan National Hospital, except the orphaned children Khan tacitly allowed Salena to house there, enjoyed private rooms. Unlike the hospitals in which she had trained during her residency in America, most hospitals in Pakistan, in all South Asia for that matter, squeezed up to 10 patients in communal rooms. She recalled an incident during her residency in the States when a spoiled American women complained bitterly of being forced to share a room with just one other patient.

The first patient on Salena's list, the wife of Khan's Minister of Justice, suffered from diabetes. Her illness had caused an excess buildup of amniotic fluid in the sac surrounding her fetus. Over the past four months Salena had monitored her condition carefully to make sure the fluid pressing her uterus and diaphragm did not trigger premature labor or cause her difficulty breathing. Now seven months along, she would spend the remainder of her pregnancy in bed.

Salena's next patient was a quarrelsome woman. Her name was Nusrat Afzal, and Salena found her sitting up in bed, moaning like a dying cow. Salena had difficulty feeling sorry for the wife of the director of Khan's Inter-Services Intelligence Agency, now seven months into her ninth pregnancy and suffering from placenta previa. Her placenta covered her cervix, and caused vaginal bleeding. Standard treatment included bed rest and delivery by cesarean section.

"You are 20 minutes late," she said. "Where were you? You should be coming to me first. Do you not care? Are you not listening?"

Salena sighed. She could tolerate Nusrat for five more days. "Reema needed an ultrasound, yes I do care, and no, I will not listen if you keep whining."

"Do you want me to lose my baby?"

The world would be a nicer place without people like Nusrat, but she could never say so. "Of course not, but you are not my only patient."

"My husband is an important man."

"The husbands of all my patients are important men."

Salena pulled a chart from a slot on Nusrat's footboard and checked her morning lab results. Satisfied with the woman's blood count, Salena left the Maternity Ward and took the elevator one floor down to the Pediatric Unit.

Pakistan National Hospital was Khan's creation, and he had spared no expense on staff and equipment. He built the hospital to serve the elite of his government, and nobody gained admission without his blessing—no one, that is, except the children Salena had sheltered there despite Khan's objections.

Khan's violent coup left 150,000 new orphans. Most survived the streets of Lahore, Karachi, and Peshawar by begging for bits of chapatti to nourish their scrawny bodies, and by scrounging together scraps of cardboard to shield themselves from the summer monsoons. In Islamabad, Pakistan's pristine capital, Khan did not allow orphans to live on the streets, so last autumn, at Khan's direction, Qadeer rounded up all the city's homeless children.

Boys older than eight were ordered to the rugged mountains of Azad Kashmir or the barren Thal Desert to train as soldiers. Girls older than 10 Qadeer gifted to Khan's generals, ministers, and cabinet members to serve as handmaids for their wives and daughters.

Shortly after Khan forced Salena into servitude at Pakistan National Hospital, Dr. Raja, the hospital's Assistant Chief of Pediatric Medicine, confided in her that Qadeer had kept for himself one particularly attractive child. Her name was Hana, and she was only 11 when Qadeer handed her over, half dead, to Raja for treatment of a lacerated vagina and torn cervix. Ten hours of emergency surgery failed to save the child. After burying the girl in an unmarked grave in the paupers cemetery, Qadeer paid Raja another visit, this time bearing threats of death if he dared tell anyone of the girl's horrific end.

Salena swore to herself, and Raja too, she would do everything in her power to prevent another child from suffering the same fate as Hana.

Before reaching the entrance to the Pediatric Unit, she stopped at a solid beige door and entered a large rectangular room without windows. Formerly a storage room, this was where she had set up 24 cots topped with lean mattresses for the unwanted children. Arranged in two rows of twelve against opposite walls, every bed was occupied—many by more than one child.

Salena lowered her dupatta, for here amongst the broken children in the midst of Khan's domain was where she felt closest to freedom.

Jamaal and Jameel, seven year old twins, ran to her offering grins and tight hugs. The others smiled or waved, except those truly sick, like Fawaz, whose liver had been severely damaged by Hepatitus B, and Taahir, who suffered the debilitating effects of an enlarged heart at the tender age of eight.

Umar, a sinewy boy of six whose wide umber eyes bared his soul, handed her a crayon drawing of two stick figures holding hands. "This is me and mommy. She always holds my hand. When she gets well, she will come for me."

"That is a beautiful picture, Umar." She got down on one knee and kissed the boy's forehead. "Someday you will have a family."

Salena rose and walked to the last cot on the left. A young girl with shiny black hair rippling along her side lay curled up on a flimsy mattress with her eyes closed. This was Kalila. Since the day of her parents' execution, the only adult she had spoken to was Salena.

Kalila opened her eyes. "Miss Salena, I wish to nap, but I cannot fall asleep."

"Would it help if I lie with you?"

"Could you, Miss Salena?"

"I would be honored to do so."

She slipped off her shoes, and lay on the cot beside Kalila. Wrapping her arm around the child's waist, she felt a tiny hand grip hers. Despite the tragedies visited upon her at such an early age, Kalila's thirst for learning was unquenchable. She had acquired the English language with ease, and had confided in Salena that one day, like Salena, she hoped to go to America and become a doctor.

Salena longed for the chance to help the Americans rid Pakistan of Ali Khan—if not for herself, then for the young girls of this land doomed to become women in a world dictated by husbands, fathers, and brothers too quick to maim, burn, or kill them if they dared chase their dreams.

Kalila fell quickly into a deep sleep. Salena rose carefully and covered the child with a cotton blanket crumpled at the foot of the thinly padded cot.

In what she referred to as the Freedom Ward—at least to good friends like Dr. Raja—she chatted with the boys and girls for over an hour. At 2:45 p.m. the time had come to leave. She said her farewells and left behind the only patients she derived joy from serving.

She entered the reception area of the Pediatric Unit, and saw no sign of her two escorts. They were likely loafing in the cafeteria. She turned and walked past the nurses station to Room 412 where, as she had hoped, she found the only person in Pakistan who knew of her plan to help the Americans.

Chapter Ten

F or John to even consider the mission Farrell and Daley had described, that shit-eating grin Daley was flashing at him had better mean good news for Maureen and his girls.

Sitting at the conference table, out of reach of John's fist, Daley leaned forward and said, "How does $10,000,000 sound?"

John nearly gagged. He had dropped his family into a hole $2,000,000 deep. Given ten million bucks, they'd not only climb out, but live on top for the rest of their lives. "All I have to do is say yes?"

Daley's gray eyes hardened and he sat straight in his chair. "Not quite. If for any reason the mission's objective is not met—you get caught, or Khan survives the implosion—your wife receives $1,000,000."

"What good is a million when Maureen needs twice that to pay off my debts?"

"Then don't fail."

John sprang from his chair and slammed his hand on the table. "You jackass, you'd rob me of the last three months I could have with my family, and if something goes wrong—something completely out of my control—you'd leave my wife and kids strapped. You know what you can do with your half-baked plan, Colonel Daley."

Farrell was shaking her head, glaring at Daley. She turned to John. "Please, John—"

"It's Mr. Covello. You don't know me well enough to call me John."

"Try to understand, Mr. Covello. Nothing less than world peace hangs in the balance."

"So by paying my family less if I fail, you think I'll do a better job?"

"Absolutely not. The payout contingency applies to all CRUSO candidates. We have complete confidence in your skills and abilities." She laced her hands, and folded them on the table. "Please sit down."

John did as she asked, but avoided looking at Daley. Farrell, though blunt, at least feigned compassion, not like that arrogant son-of-a-bitch sitting across from her. "I just assumed you dropped the value of my life because of what happened to Billy Dwyer."

Farrell regarded John at length before answering. "You know ... I know ... anyone who takes time to learn the facts knows, you didn't kill that boy."

During the two months after his father died a painful death from lung cancer at the age of 62, John dragged himself to work at Planned

Demolitions, Inc., the company his father had founded fresh out of graduate school. With Maureen's encouragement, John eventually came around and decided the finest tribute he could pay his dad was to move the business forward. In just two years he expanded Planned Demolitions into the third largest demo company in the US.

Riding high after the company's most profitable second quarter ever, John won a bid to implode the abandoned 18-story Demarest housing projects on Chicago's south side. The city council had approved the site for subsidized, two-story townhouses as an alternative to the high-rise projects that had for years accelerated urban decay.

It was Mayor Ronald Madden's idea to turn the Demarest implosion into Chicago's entertainment event of the year. Under pressure to start construction of the townhouses before the November elections, he set an impossible deadline of five weeks to prepare and destroy the twin buildings. The implosion, publicized weeks in advance, became the hottest ticket in town.

John had already spread himself too thin. At the time, he was managing projects simultaneously in San Francisco, Austin, Mexico City, and Quebec, and was relying heavily on subcontractors.

His sub for the Chicago implosion, Joe Vreeland of Allied Deconstruction, used the wrong type of charge. Instead of using a linear shaped charge made for cutting steel, he used a plastic explosive called Riogel, far less expensive, and designed to shatter rock. Vreeland overcompensated for his use of the wrong explosive by using too much, doubling the number of charges needed to bring the buildings down.

The City of Chicago exacerbated the problem by violating its contract with John. He had specified a 1,500 foot primary safety zone around the apartment buildings slated for destruction. Mayor Madden, in a misguided attempt to give his constituents the best possible view, set up police barriers that allowed the public to within 800 feet of the doomed structures.

John had planned to arrive in Chicago two days before the Demarest implosion, but problems in Mexico City and San Francisco delayed his arrival until the morning of the detonation. He managed a quick inspection of the sight, and when he saw Riogel instead of linear shape charges attached to the I-beams, he went nuts, screaming at the mayor to postpone the implosion. Over John's objections, Vreeland defended his use of Riogel, and the mayor, reluctant to disappoint 50,000 anxious spectators, gave the green light.

A young woman who had won a contest sponsored by a local radio station pushed the "fire" button that set off the explosives four blocks away. Standing beside her, John immediately sensed something had gone wrong. Pieces of wood, steel, and flyrock shot out of the apartment buildings in all directions. Instinctively, John ducked as debris flew toward the roof where they stood.

What he heard next was the sickening wail of an ambulance. Minutes later he learned five-year-old Billy Dwyer had been decapitated by a rectangular sheet of steel the size of a food tray. Not a day had passed when the boy's autopsy photos presented in evidence at John's civil and criminal trials didn't come back to haunt him.

Major Farrell, though compassionate, was wrong. He did kill Billy Dwyer. "The truth is Ms. Farrell, you do have doubts about my skills and abilities. You picked me because you had to. I'm the only candidate you've got."

Colonel Daley said, "You're right about that."

John ignored him and asked Farrell, "If I say yes, what happens next?"

"We take you back to your car in Point Pleasant Beach. You'll get home by eight o'clock. What time does Maureen leave for work?"

"She's off today."

"All the better. Dr. Chandler will call your house at eight-seventeen. Let Maureen pick up. He'll say emergency surgery forced postponement of your ten o'clock appointment to three-thirty. An hour and a half later, at 9:45 a.m., you'll take your boat for a spin in the Atlantic Ocean."

"This morning I heard a weather report. A storm's moving in."

"Yes, that works in our favor. At 10:05 a.m., you'll enter the ocean through the Manasquan Inlet. At the bell buoy, set a course for 135 degrees and head due southeast four miles. You'll be met at your destination by the Coast Guard cutter *Munro*. From there, you'll be flown by helicopter to McGuire Air Force Base, where—"

John raised his arms, making a 'T' with his hands. "Two hours? That's all I get to say good-bye to my wife and kids?"

Daley answered. "Better make every minute count."

John sucked in a deep breath and said to Farrell, "I'm really starting to dislike that man."

Farrell shot Daley a stern look that made John wonder who was really in charge. "Colonel Daley is concerned about our stringent time parameters. Remember, India's prime minister has given us only until tomorrow morning to confirm our operative has infiltrated the Citadel and made contact with Crescent Moon."

"Who?"

"Crescent Moon. The code name of our informant."

"How do I contact this Crescent Moon?"

"Everything will be explained before you leave for Islamabad."

"What if for some reason I make it to Islamabad but can't get into Khan's Citadel? Will I have time to get the hell out of Pakistan before Behari sets off his nukes?"

"Unfortunately, no."

John shook his head. "I'm lovin' this job more and more."

"After you land at McGuire, you'll leave immediately for Andrews Air Force Base. You'll be accompanied by a grief counselor."

"I don't need a damn shrink."

"You're mind is struggling to digest volumes of information in virtually no time. Sooner or later, your emotions will catch up. He's there if you need him."

"Another waste of taxpayer money."

"After you arrive at Andrews Air Force Base, about noon, Colonel Daley and I will show you blueprints of Khan's Citadel, teach you to prep the RDX-7S, and discuss how we'll deliver the charges to you once you're inside."

Nothing Farrell had explained so far addressed John's biggest question. "What about the payout? Maureen's no dummy. She might get a little curious when she opens her mail one morning and finds a check for $10,000,000."

"Your Boston Whaler Montauk is powered by a 150-horsepower outboard engine, a SeaStar Nautique, three years old."

"Damn, you people probably know what color crap I took this morning?"

"It's our job, Mr. Covello."

"You can call me John." He glowered at Daley. "But not you."

A flicker of a smile rose at the edges of Farrell's mouth. "I trust you haven't told Maureen about your diagnosis."

"Chandler made that crystal clear."

"Good. So once you're on the ocean in rough seas your motor will catch fire, explode, and your boat will be torn apart. A body won't be recovered, but they'll find debris, including your Whaler's transom with pieces of the motor still attached. Upon careful inspection of the burned out engine, the explosion will be determined to have occurred as a result of improper installation of the fuel line by the manufacturer—gross negligence at the factory. Maureen won't have time to call a lawyer, because one week after your funeral, SeaStar's lawyers will contact her. Hoping to sidestep devastating publicity, and because liability is open-and-shut, they'll negotiate a $10,000,000 settlement."

Farrell seemed like a nice enough lady, but with the stakes so high, he wanted more than her word. "Not for nothing, but when that goes down, I'm already dead. How do I know if I play your game, Maureen gets the prize?"

"At Andrews Air Force Base, President Lloyd will join us by videolink from the White House to verify terms of payment. You do trust the president?"

"Don't push it."

"If you insist he'll make a personal visit."

"No thanks."

"The money is no consolation for a premature death, but do you have any idea what pancreatic cancer does to your body?"

"If what I'm feeling now is any hint, I'd rather not know."

"You won't, and neither will your family. After the search for your body is called off, Dr. Chandler will phone Maureen and reveal your diagnosis. She'll feel terrible, but maybe a little relieved knowing she was spared the ordeal of watching you waste away."

John thought what $10,000,000 would mean for his family— Maureen never again bothered by debt collectors, Karen never denied a night out with friends for lack of a few dollars, and Christie never afraid to pick up the phone. "If anyone deserves a break, it's my wife and kids."

"They'll get that break, if your mission succeeds."

"Of course it'll succeed. With you people planning every detail, how can it fail?"

Farrell looked down at the table. Daley reached for a sliver of yellow paper on the table and tore it in half.

"I mean, you've done this kind of thing before, right?"

More awkward silence.

"Hellooo?"

Farrell and Daley exchanged tight glances, then Farrell spoke. "CRUSO has conducted two prior operations. Both failed to achieve their objectives."

"You guys are the brains behind the smartest, toughest military machine in the world. How could something go wrong?"

"The details of the prior missions aren't important. Besides, they're classified."

"Then count me out, because if you guys don't know what the hell you're doing, I might as well go home and enjoy what little time I have with my family."

Farrell and Daley stared at one another, as if locked in telepathic debate, until finally, Daley nodded.

Farrell leaned forward and said, "CRUSO's first operation, thirteen months ago, targeted a Russian crime boss, Yegor Kotenov. The NSA learned Kotenov planned to overthrow the leaders of Krasnodor, Stavropol, and Adygea, and break off from the Russian Federation. An unstable Russia is not in America's best interests, and CRUSO was asked to help. One of our referral agents—someone like Dr. Chandler—referred a gentleman suffering from an incurable liver disease. He spoke fluent Russian, served five years in the Marine Corps, and was a former employee of the State Department. He could also cook up a storm. CRUSO set him up as a chef on Kotenov's yacht. In the act of attaching an underwater mine to the hull, he was caught by Kotenov's security. Before he was interrogated, he did as instructed and bit the cyanide caplet."

"Guess I'll be packing one of those in my travel kit."

"You won't be given the caplets until you arrive at Andrews. There you'll get full instructions on their use."

"Goody, I can't wait."

"CRUSO's only other operation occurred last November. The target was a Columbian drug lord with a nasty habit of raping nuns and shooting priests. He also put half a billion dollars worth of genetically engineered marijuana on the streets of LA. Strong stuff, and highly addictive. CRUSO found a former Navy pilot in the last stages of lung cancer. His mission—fly an unmarked Lear jet into the target's private plane. In retrospect, well, we blundered. Waited too long. By takeoff time, our candidate was so weak he could barely pull the throttle. We tried pumping him with pain killers, but that only made matters worse. The target's pilot spotted our man coming, dove into the Andes, and a chase ensued. Our operative hedged on the throttle and slammed into the side of a mountain."

"You're not instilling confidence. Those men had military experience."

"For this mission a military background is helpful, but not essential."

"Did their families get paid the consolation prize?"

"Yes, however neither candidate had children. The pilot wasn't even married."

"So why'd they do it?"

"They figured they were dying anyway. Why not die for their country?"

"I appreciate what my country's done for me, but make no mistake, my family comes first. If I blow myself to bits inside Khan's castle, I'm doing it for my wife and kids—no one else."

Farrell checked her watch. "If you're going to accept our offer, we need your answer."

"Say I take down the Citadel without me in it. Can I come home?"

Daley's cheek muscles tightened into chiseled features. "You come back, your family gets nothing. That's the deal."

The sharp pains wracking John's stomach made it hard to think. He put himself in Maureen's shoes. Three months with a dying husband, half that time in a hospital bed, or $10,000,000 and set for life. But he had so much more to tell his wife and daughters than two hours could possibly allow.

John rose and locked eyes with Daley. "I guess you're right. I'll make every minute count."

CHAPTER ELEVEN

D r. Raja spun to face Salena. From behind thick lenses set in wire rim glasses his umber eyes grew wide. "What are you doing here?"

"I have come for news of my mother."

His voice was soft, but urgent. "You should not be seen alone in the Pediatric Unit, especially with me."

"My guards have gone off, probably to the cafeteria."

Room 412 held no patients, only two hospital beds, a few chairs, and two small tables. Raja was convinced Captain Qadeer had wired his office with electronic listening devices, and despised the thought Khan's security chief could monitor his conversations. To escape the scrutiny of Qadeer's bugs and wiretaps, Raja often came here to update his patient files rather than complete the task in his office. "You are still not intending to carry out your treachery?"

"If the Americans contact me, most definitely."

"Your scheme is too dangerous, for you—and for the children."

"If I succeed, the children need never again fear for their lives."

"Qadeer is suspicious. His cattle prod will loosen tongues."

"If I do not help the Americans kill Ali Khan, millions will pay the price for my cowardice."

Raja sighed. His tone turned melancholy. "If by chance you succeed, where will you go?"

Khan had many friends in Pakistan who would eagerly avenge his murder. If they discovered she had conspired with America to assassinate Khan, she was as good as dead. "I will leave immediately for Srinagar."

Raja shook his head slowly. "Srinagar is just as dangerous."

"I shall stay only long enough to visit my mother."

"Do you forget the Border Security Force? If they find you, you will end up just like your father."

Like her father, and proud to be. The last time Salena had seen her father they were standing on a runway in Srinagar. She was ending a two week visit home before starting her residency in the States. Her father's Pathan blood had not stifled his tears when he told her how much he would miss her, and how much her achievements had meant to him. She promised him next summer she would stay in Srinagar for a month.

Three days later neighbors reported seeing her father in the company of five Border Security Force guards. The BSF had been harassing him for years, claiming the articles and editorials he wrote for *The Kashmir Monitor* encouraged the militant separatists to bomb buses and police stations. In fact, her father abhorred the violence of the extremists, and wrote as much at the risk of assassination by one of 20 Muslim terrorist groups operating in and around the Vale.

All he wanted for Kashmir was peace through freedom, but in Kashmir a journalist could get hurt, and if he wrote the truth, he could die. Her father had been a victim of the truth.

Now she must assure Raja she would not share her father's fate. "Trust me, I will not venture beyond Lal Ded Hospital, or my home."

"You fool only yourself. You are Ali Khan's woman, and the police will use that in every imaginable way."

Salena swallowed hard at the memory of ten groping hands tearing off her clothes and veil. "As soon as I say good-bye to my mother, I will leave Srinagar, perhaps for China or America, but only until Kashmir is free. Then I shall return home again."

Raja gently clasped her arm. "Please do not take such a risk. You mean too much to me … as a friend."

He had never crossed the line with her, and she had never given him the chance. "Then as my friend, please understand why I must go."

Raja looked down at the floor. His emerald green turban contrasted sharply with his somber gaze. "This morning I received an e-mail from Dr. Qureshi."

"You *do* have news of my mother."

"Curse me for telling the truth." He lifted his eyes. "This morning she lapsed into a coma. Dr. Qureshi performed a CSF and she tested positive for bacterial meningitis."

Last November her mother had begun an uphill battle against pneumonia with empyema, and since then had been admitted on and off to Lal Ded Hospital in Srinagar. Dr. Raja and the hospital's Assistant Director had been close friends in medical school, and had corresponded over the years. During the past three months, Raja's friend had e-mailed him every few days with updates of her mother's condition.

Meningitis on top of pneumonia meant her mother would not last more than two weeks. "You have confirmed my decision. I must help the Americans."

"As I feared."

"Do not worry. By this time next week, I will have seen my mother and left Srinagar."

"The road to Kashmir poses perils to hardened thieves, no less a woman traveling alone."

"I can handle myself."

"Your Pathan pride robs you of good judgment."

Beside her mother, there was only one other whose welfare meant everything to her. "Have you any word of Naji?"

"He grows stronger every day, but he misses you."

"When I go to Srinagar, I shall visit him too."

"I would not have thought otherwise."

Salena had one more favor to ask. "Promise me, whatever happens during the next week, you will not allow my children to be expelled from the Freedom Ward."

"You have my word."

"I fear especially for Kalila. Tell her I will send for her. Tell her a Pathan's word is her honor."

"Of course, but you had better leave."

They must have caught whiff of the acrid odor at the same time. Both turned their heads toward the door.

Salena's stomach plunged when into the room strutted two soldiers led by Captain Azam Qadeer puffing on a Red Lamp.

Khan's enforcer strode up to Raja, his eyes narrow and seething. "What are you doing alone with General Khan's woman?"

"Raja's hands began to tremble.

Qadeer inhaled deeply on his cigarette and blew a stream of smoke into Raja's face. "Answer my question."

Raja gagged, struggling to answer. "I was … we were discussing … Dr. Zamal …"

The fiendish grin forming on Qadeer's face made Salena want to run, but she forced herself to stay.

Qadeer's tone was casual, as if what he said next he said often. "Perhaps an hour alone with me in the Citadel will restore your voice."

Salena knew of only one way to save her friend—and herself.

She swallowed hard and steeled her voice. "You have no right to barge in here and interrupt my consultation with Dr. Raja."

Qadeer's blood red turban shifted slightly as he snapped his head toward Salena. "Exactly what sort of consultation?"

Salena fixed her eyes on Qadeer. "I will not answer until you put out that cigarette."

"Do you forget who I am?"

Salena clenched her fists at her sides and stepped so close to Qadeer she could make out the faint lines beneath his chin where human nails had left their mark. "I have spoken with Ali Khan about your filthy habit. I have told him how the smoke harms the wives of his generals."

Qadeer's eyes narrowed to glistening brown slivers. He pinched the Red Lamp between two fingers, sucked a long drag, and blew the smoke directly over her head. When he had no more smoke to exhale, he smirked and flicked the lit cigarette to the floor.

Salena thought better of making him stamp it out. "For your information, I am here to ask Dr. Raja if he would telephone his colleague at Al-Shifa Hospital regarding a treatment option I intend for one of my patients—Captain Tareen's wife."

Qadeer squinted at her skeptically. "Exactly what sort of treatment does Captain Tareen's wife require?"

"Physician-patient privilege binds me to silence."

"In this hospital you have no privilege but to serve Ali Khan."

Salena slouched her shoulders in feigned resignation. "Madame Tareen has been unable to conceive. I have considered treating her with *bromocriptine mesylate*, a dopamine agonist agent which inhibits the secretion of prolactin, a hormone that triggers milk production. High prolactin levels interfere with the release of a woman's eggs, which causes faulty ovulation and irregular menstrual cycles. I'm hoping to use this drug to help Madame Tareen bear her husband a child."

Qadeer stared at her in dumb silence, as if struggling to register the meaning of her words. Finally he said, "Why must Dr. Raja make the call? Why not contact his colleague yourself?"

Salena replied in a tone of exaggerated sarcasm, "Certainly, Captain, you do not expect General Khan would appreciate me calling a man with whom I have never before spoken."

The bushy black brow above Qadeer's left eye quivered. "I can easily verify what you say about Captain Tareen's wife." He grabbed a sheet of paper from the patient file on the table beside him and yanked a ball point pen off the pocket of Raja's white lab coat. He scribbled down some words, then glared at Raja. "You queer little mole, if I catch you near Khan's woman again, I will teach you a lesson you shall not forget. Now return to your office and wait for me. You and I are not yet through."

The taller of Qadeer's two lackeys grabbed Raja by his collar and shoved him toward the door.

Raja spun and scurried from the room without looking back.

After Raja disappeared, Qadeer addressed Salena. "The diagnosis you claim for Captain Tareen's wife had better be true."

Salena frowned. "When you discover I am telling the truth, I expect your apology."

He barked at his soldiers, "Take her back to her office, and then to the Citadel. It is nearly five o'clock, and I am told she is preparing dinner for General Khan."

CHAPTER TWELVE

T he phone at John's house rang at precisely 8:17 a.m., exactly when Major Farrell said it would. John let Maureen answer, exactly as Major Farrell had instructed him to. When Maureen walked into the den and informed John his appointment with Dr. Chandler had been postponed from 10:15 a.m. to 3:30 p.m., he remarked that Chandler had some nerve ruining an afternoon he might have otherwise spent with Maureen and her mom at Aunt Liz's house.

For the next hour and ten minutes John groped for words of wisdom by which his wife and daughters would remember him, but torn apart inside he managed nothing more profound than useless small talk. Now, with 20 minutes until he was scheduled to leave his family forever, John struggled to concentrate on what Karen was saying.

"Dad, did you hear me?"

"I'm sorry, hon, what was that?"

"I was thinking, if I can't go to the boardwalk with my friends, could I at least invite Carrie to sleep over?"

"Sounds great."

"Thanks." She whirled and headed for the front door.

"Where you going?"

She stopped short and turned. "Dad, are you all right?"

"Yeah, fine."

"Paul's here."

"Where's he taking you so early?"

Karen approached him slowly, scrutinizing him as if he'd mutated into a two-headed gnome. "Where I go every day in July. My job at the Childhood Care Center."

Damn, he was losing it. He'd better think quick. "You didn't give me a hug."

"Since when do I hug you before I leave for work?"

"Well … hugs are nice. They're something we should do more often."

Karen smiled. "You really are trying." She wrapped her arms around his back and rested her head on his chest.

He whispered, "I love you, Karen, and I'm proud of you." He squeezed her tighter. "Please understand where Mom's coming from. She's worried about your future … about all our futures."

"I'm not mad at her anymore."

John pulled away and stared at his older daughter, etching her face in his mind.

"Have you been crying, Dad?"

"No …well, maybe a little. I promise you Karen, everything's gonna be fine. You, and Christie, and Mom, you're all gonna do real well."

"Great, Dad, let's talk about it later. Paul's waiting."

"I love you Karen."

"Love you too." She left in a blur for the last time in his life.

The phone rang twice and Maureen answered in the kitchen. Her words grew louder and harsher as her conversation progressed, and just as John walked in, she slammed down the handset.

Maureen confirmed his suspicions. "Another bill collector looking for money we don't have. CreditQuick this time. I guess they … John, you look upset."

He wasn't allowed to tell her much, but what he could say he'd make damn sure he meant. "I know I've bottled up my feelings for way too long. I'm sorry."

"Yesterday at dinner was a step in the right direction, at least for you. I'm afraid my little outburst took me in the wrong direction."

"Don't beat yourself up over Karen."

"That wasn't like me."

"I know that, and she does too. Don't let one mistake guilt you for the rest of your life."

Maureen chuckled. "You should talk."

He grinned, but the smile didn't reach his heart.

"You're worried about your test results."

"Yeah, sort of."

She slipped her arms around his neck. "We'll get through whatever Chandler throws at us, as long as we're together."

God, he was going to miss her. He planted his hands on her waist and guided her toward him. "I want you to know something."

"What's that?"

"You're the finest thing to come into my life. As tough as it's been these past two years, I'm grateful you stayed the course."

She caressed him with those soft blue eyes he'd been unable to resist since the day they'd met. "We help each other. That's what makes us a team."

They lost themselves in each other's gaze. Bending his head, she met his lips halfway and, embracing her, moved his tongue into her mouth with impassioned urgency. He longed to hold her forever, but the half-hour chime from the living room clock meant the time had come to prepare for his journey.

He pulled away, and brushed his lips against her ear. "You're the best."

"You are too, and don't sound so discouraged. It'll all work out."

"I'm counting on it." John released his hold on Maureen's hips. "Where's Christie?"

"Out on the dock."

"I'd like to take a ride in the Whaler, maybe cruise the bay."

"I don't think that's a good idea. It's supposed to start raining by noon."

"The river hasn't turned choppy, and the clouds will keep me cool. I'll only be a couple of hours."

"OK, but don't you dare go near the ocean."

"I won't." He had nothing to say except, "I love you."

"I love you too."

Giving his wife a long, final look, he branded his mind with an image of her silky blond hair, and penetrating blue eyes.

John opened the kitchen door, stood on his deck, and looked up at the shroud of gray covering the sky. The breeze was nippy for mid-July, but he figured for Major Farrell's purposes the weather was cooperating just fine.

Christie sat on the bulkhead with her back to him. Her legs dangled over the edge and she was staring across the Manasquan River at the backyards of stores and houses not far from where CRUSO's agents had picked him up shortly after dawn.

"Hi kid, what ya doin'?"

"Nothing much, just thinking."

He plopped beside her on the bulkhead, hanging his feet next to hers inches above the water. "About what?"

"All that mean stuff I said yesterday."

"About me being sick of my family?"

"No, when I told you to leave forever." Christie slipped her hand in the crook of his arm and squeezed him close. "I never want you to leave. Never."

John swore to himself he'd keep it together. "All kids say they want their parents to leave. That's part of growing up. But don't worry, the last thing I want is to leave any of you."

Christie looked up at him, her eyes betraying concern. "Do you think Dr. Chandler will say you're OK?"

John stared at the river's swollen whitecaps, staving off tears. "I hope so."

"You don't eat anymore. When someone stops eating, they're usually sick."

John ensconced her shoulders in his arm and pulled her close. "I love you, Christie, and whatever Dr. Chandler says won't change that. You and Karen and Mom, you're my life. Even if I'm sick—I mean really sick—with my girls beside me, I'll get through."

She pressed her head against his chest.

John wasn't sure what felt worse, the pain gouging his stomach or the doubt rending his heart. "No man could be luckier than me to have a family like mine."

"No girl could be luckier than me to have a dad like you."

"Then don't look so sad."

"I'm worried."

"I'll be OK." Breathing in the saltwater air, John held his daughter and listened to the waves lapping against the bulkhead. When a seagull overhead cawed a long, lonely cry, he released her shoulders and stood. "I'm going for a ride in the bay."

"You'll be late for your appointment."

"Dr. Chandler put it off until this afternoon."

When Christie started to rise, John helped her up. "Can I go with you?"

"Any other day I'd say yes, but this morning I need some time alone—time to think." He craned his neck toward the darkening sky. "Anyway, if I take you out, and it starts raining, Mom will have my head. Next nice day, you're my first mate."

"You mean that?"

"Kid, you know I never break a promise."

John climbed into his Boston Whaler and coaxed its SeaStar motor to life. He cast the ropes to his daughter, who tied them to a wood piling. As the boat drifted away from the bulkhead Christie yelled, "Did you remember your lucky Hog?"

John patted the front and back pockets of his blue jeans. Feeling nothing but flat denim, he grabbed the breast pocket of his polo shirt. There it was. He extracted the miniature Harley and held it high in his fingertips. "I'd never forget!"

"Don't lose it."

Burying her gift deep in his pants pocket, he shouted, "I won't," then blew his daughter a kiss. "I love you."

She smiled and blew a kiss back.

John flipped on the electronic compass and nudged the throttle forward. For the last time he looked at his home. Through the kitchen window he saw Maureen's face, and though he might have been mistaken, he could swear she was crying. He waved, but instead of waving back, she turned and walked away.

He wondered if the secret language of long-time lovers had revealed more than he had intended.

CHAPTER THIRTEEN

The rooms of Ali Khan's suite, large and luxurious, devoured the entire 12th floor of his Citadel, and provided an ideal ambiance in which to plot wars and seduce women. Salena had invited herself to Khan's penthouse palace, even cooked dinner for him, hoping to learn more about Glorious Dawn. Instead, when their meal had ended, he had not spoken once of his imminent war with India. His only interest had been in fulfilling his promise to her that morning—to have his way with her that night.

Salena pushed herself off the plush leather sofa and stood beside the nearest chair tucked under the rosewood table at which Khan entertained heads of state. Long enough to seat 20, the tabletop was adorned with two place settings, one at the head, the other to its right. No trace of the prawns and almonds remained in the bone china plate from which Khan had eaten, and every morsel of the jhinga karhai Salena had prepared with her own hands filled the other.

Biting her lip, she looked at Khan, who sat relaxed on the leather sofa, one arm draped across the top of its back. His flowing white robe and jet black turban lent him an air of elegance.

"Why do you run from me? Come sit beside me. You have served me well and deserve a rest."

She loathed his hypocrisy. How dare he seduce her before marriage when he had condemned to death scores of young men and women whose only transgression was their love for one another? "I have sat for an hour and am tired of sitting."

"We need not sit for long."

"What do you mean?" she said, knowing perfectly well the intent of his words.

"My flower, I grow weary of your false modesty."

"Please let us wait. By August's end Ramadan will be over. After that, I am yours to command."

"My decision is final. I shall enjoy your favors tonight." His lips curled into a menacing smile.

"What must I say to convince you we should wait?"

"You can say nothing. My passion has lost its patience." Khan rose and walked to her, grabbed her hand and dragged her back to the sofa. He pushed her backward into the soft black leather, then pinned her arms against her sides and pressed his firm, muscular torso onto hers. Squashing her breasts with his chest, he rammed his lips against hers.

Salena wriggled her hands free, dug her nails into his shoulders, and pushed on him with all her strength. Their mouths parted. "No, please. Not yet."

Khan pulled off her veil and grabbed her hair at the nape. Resigned to repeat the disgrace she had endured six years earlier, she heard from behind a loud pounding.

The general lifted his head and roared, "Go away." Not waiting for an answer, he pressed his mouth to hers and probed for an opening.

She grit her teeth to fend off his lust-driven tongue, and just as the wet snake bore through her lips, a loud knocking echoed again in Khan's chamber.

He released his hold and shot off the sofa. "This had better be important or you shall pay with a hundred lashes." He turned and glared at her. "Get behind the couch while I see who dares disturb our privacy."

Khan stormed across the marble floor to answer the door. Salena got up and knelt on all fours behind the leather sofa. She heard the voice of Lieutenant Siddique, but could not make out his words. After a brief exchange, the door slammed shut and she heard the sound of approaching footsteps.

"Get up," Khan said.

Rising slowly from the floor, Salena read in his eyes fury and frustration.

"You must go to the hospital immediately. Nusrat Afzal is bleeding."

Salena imagined the spoilt woman moaning and whining, screaming at the nurses, inflicting misery on everyone around her. On any other night, dropping everything to help Nusrat was the last thing she would have desired.

Khan gripped her shoulders and squeezed so hard, she winced. "If General Afzal were not so important, I would let his wretched wife bleed to death. How long shall you need?"

"That depends on the cause and severity of her bleeding."

"Curse that woman. Take what time you must, but I swear, if I do not have you tonight, I shall have you tomorrow."

"As you wish."

"I shall send a guard to meet you at the doors of the Maternity Unit. He shall return you to the Citadel."

Checking her urge to flee Khan's parlor, Salena walked toward the dining room door. At the threshold she paused and turned. Though she wanted nothing more than to spit in Khan's face, she smiled demurely. "Thank you, kind master, for your gracious company."

She boarded the elevator to the 4th floor, and crossed the skywalk into Pakistan National Hospital. As she had expected, she found Nusrat wreaking havoc in the Maternity Unit. In fact, her uterine contractions had caused more bleeding than usual. Salena ordered blood transfusions, and since the bleeding placed her fetus at risk for insufficient oxygenation, she ordered supplemental oxygen until her blood levels tested normal. To suppress her contractions, Salena prescribed four doses of Terbutaline.

Satisfied she had controlled Nusrat's bleeding, but in no hurry to return to the Citadel, she thought of ways to extend her time in the hospital. She walked toward the Maternity Unit's exit doors with the intention of going to her office. There she would document Nusrat's file, a legitimate chore, but writing even a lengthy report would require no more than an hour.

When Salena reached the double doors, the soldier Khan had promised to send was nowhere in sight. Taking advantage of the man's tardiness, she decided to check on her children before heading to her office.

To avoid a chance encounter with Khan's guards, Salena took the service stairs. Nearly ten at night, the 4th floor hall leading to the Pediatric Unit was deserted. She passed several darkened offices, three supply rooms, and a pantry before entering her makeshift orphanage.

By the glow of the Freedom Ward's nightlights, she saw her boys and girls fast asleep on their cots. The only sound was the rhythmic breathing of slumber. She tiptoed to the last cot on the left. Kalila rolled over, and her eyes, big and brown, opened wide.

Salena knelt by her side and whispered, "Trouble falling asleep again?"

"I had a bad dream."

"Move over, and I will lie with you a few moments."

"Thank you, Miss Salena."

Salena climbed onto the cot facing Kalila, whose eyes appeared moist and puffy. "What have you been thinking about?"

"Mummy and Poppy. I pray they will come for me soon."

"You know in your heart that can never happen."

Kalila's eyes clung to hers. "That is why Allah has sent me an angel."

"And who is your angel?"

"That angel is you."

Though Salena could easily take her own life, such a callous act of self-interest would bring misery to these boys and girls. Left to fend for themselves on the city streets, many would die, or worse, be forced into slavery. At least here she had given them a chance.

After Kalila fell asleep, Salena left the Pediatric Unit and climbed the service stairs one flight up. Rounding the corner, she came into view of her office, and saw Captain Qadeer standing outside her door puffing on one of his Red Lamps. As she approached, his eyes undressed her.

Qadeer's presence was somewhat unusual. On those rare occasions when Khan allowed her to enter the hospital without a chaperone—usually when responding to an emergency such as tonight—Khan dispatched one of Qadeer's subordinates to escort her back to the Citadel.

Ignoring the captain, Salena walked straight to her desk.

Qadeer followed her in. "General Khan demands you return with me now."

"First I must document Madame Nusrat's file."

"Make it quick."

"I need five minutes." She wondered how badly the captain had hurt Raja. "What took you so long to get here?"

"I had business with your friend."

"Dr. Nawaz?"

"Dr. Raja. He won't be coming to work tomorrow."

"Is he ill?"

"Let us say my visit shocked him."

Imagining the satisfaction she would derive gouging this fiend's eyes out, Salena did everything in her power to check her rage. "What did he say?"

"That is for your master to reveal."

If Qadeer had forced Raja to disclose her plan to assist the Americans, she would face torments many times harsher than those she imagined Qadeer had inflicted on her friend. Sitting in the chair behind her desk, Salena opened Nusrat's file. Pretending to read a chart inside, she wondered how much pain she could endure at the hands of Azam Qadeer before his torments stopped her heart.

CHAPTER FOURTEEN

C hoppy seas, cloudy skies, and a brisk wind made for a rough ride on the Atlantic Ocean, but John relished every moment. As Farrell had promised, four miles due southeast from the bell buoy outside the Manasquan Inlet, he found the Coast Guard cutter *Munro* waiting for him, along with a helicopter topside ready to whisk him away from his home and family forever.

The flight to the Naval Air Systems Command Station in Lakehurst took less than seven minutes. The instant he touched down, two junior officers in Navy whites hustled him to a jeep and drove 100 yards to a military jet idling on an adjoining runway. In two minutes, he was back in the sky, above the clouds, streaking toward Washington, DC.

The passenger cabin consisted of two rows of 10 seats lining both sides of a wide aisle. The plush leather cushioning John's back and buttocks made him wonder how much of the country's military budget was actually spent on the military. Surrounded by 39 empty seats, he guessed this was one expensive shuttle flight.

Ten minutes after takeoff, a young brunette in a dark green jumpsuit emerged from the flight cabin wearing what looked to John like a sympathetic smile. She offered him a bottled water, but the throbbing pain in his belly forced him to decline. She walked back up the aisle, stopped short of the crew compartment, and sat in the front row.

John closed his eyes and thought about how sad Maureen looked staring at him through their kitchen window as he pulled away from the dock. He tried recalling a happier time, the gift he'd gotten her for her 35th birthday, a pair of third row tickets to *The Producers* and room reservations at the Marriott Marquis, when a rasping cough from behind jarred his pleasant reminiscence.

"Hi, I'm Lieutenant Michael Hawley. Call me Mike."

John snapped his head toward the back of the cabin, baffled by where this 50-something gentleman sporting a trim gray beard had come from. He saw only two doors, and had assumed they housed the jet's lavatories.

"Great little plane, isn't it?" Mike, a portly man, squeezed himself into the seat beside John. "Mind if I join you?"

"I think you already did."

He wore a white wool turtleneck, which John thought odd for July, topped by a navy blue blazer. The large man flashed a wide smile so warm and fuzzy John wanted to vomit. "This your first time?"

"First time for what?"

"Flying."

Oh brother. This must be the army shrink Farrell had warned him about. "Well if you don't count the fifteen vacations and three hundred business trips I took while I was still working, I guess it is."

"That's nice."

John got the impression Hawley hadn't heard a word he said.

"So why *did* you stop working?"

Or maybe he had. "Slicing off a little kid's head didn't do much for my confidence."

"How did the Chicago accident make you feel?"

He'd better lose this bozo, and fast. John turned toward Hawley and leaned in close. "It's like this doc. I had no choice, I had to stop working cold turkey, you know—the way some smokers break their habit. I had this nagging urge to kill another kid, and rather than play out my fantasy, I ended my career."

Hawley's eyes popped open, and his cheeks lost their color.

"Only kidding."

His horrified expression softened into a look of pensive curiosity, and the pink returned to his bearded face. He smiled. "Denial is a common defense mechanism for dealing with loss. Humor works, too."

"Who's laughing."

"Let's talk about death."

"Let's not."

"What about death frightens you most?"

"The part when you stop breathing."

"It's perfectly normal to confront death with profound trepidation."

"No shit."

"Do you feel nervous about dying?"

"No, just mildly terrified."

"That's why we're taking this time to discuss the death process and your beliefs about the hereafter. Wouldn't you prefer to confront death properly?"

"Why? If I get it wrong, I get to do it over?"

"What I'm asking is this: Do you believe you're going to a better place?"

"You mean better than where I've been?"

"Yes."

"Well, to be perfectly honest, I kinda' liked New Jersey."

"That's not what I mean."

"What *do* you mean?"

"You know what I mean, John."

"Mr. Covello to you." This stranger had no right forcing him to talk about death, especially his own.

Hawley's tone lost its congeniality. "Between now and next Wednesday, Mr. Covello, you'll be conducting a series of complex, integrally related tasks which if you fail to perform properly could result in the deaths of 30 million people. That you should take seriously. If not for the people of South Asia, and if not for your country, then for the wife and daughters you're leaving behind."

"Then let's drop the death thing, OK?"

"Have it your way. But there are other issues we need to discuss."

"Like what?"

"Your familiarity with the socioeconomic standing of India and Pakistan. You may not be aware, but both countries have profoundly influenced our own nation's culture and economy."

"Yeah, I know. We'd fall in a heartbeat without gas stations and 7-11's."

Hawley shook his head and sighed. "On the flight to Bahrain, you'll be given two CIA brochures describing Pakistani customs and etiquette. I'd suggest you look them over."

"I'd sooner read *Knitting Digest*."

"We also need to discuss the chronic gastro-intestinal pain caused by your cancer. The activities expected of you require tremendous physical and mental exertion. There's a concern among some at CRUSO your chronic pain might interfere with your ability to focus, and hence, your ability to perform."

"What can you give me?"

"Unfortunately, not much. Most methods of managing pain in pancreatic cancer patients require more time than we have, and quick fixes cause unacceptable side effects."

"Can't you give me a shot of morphine?"

"Side effects from morphine are usually transient, and mental clouding is minimal after the initial doses, but opiate-induced response inhibition caused CRUSO's last failure. Palliative medication impeding mental clarity to any degree is unacceptable."

John recalled Farrell's story about the pilot who slammed into the side of a mountain. "What about radiation?"

"Radiation might shrink the tumor and relieve the pain, but don't forget, you get one hour at Andrews, and every minute will be spent briefing you on your mission."

"Do you have anything else that works fast?"

"Neurolytic blocking agents injected through the abdominal wall have proven effective, but often come with unpleasant side effects."

"What could be worse than what I feel now?"

"Bowl and bladder incontinence."

"Forget it."

"There's also gemcitabine, if you don't mind diarrhea, constipation, nausea, and vomiting."

"No thanks, I'll live with my pain for the next four days. Who knows, maybe the agony of a thousand knives twisting my guts will keep me focused."

Hawley stroked his beard, and regarded John thoughtfully. "I really wish you'd share your feelings about death."

"It's not my favorite subject."

"Dealing with death is never easy. Psychological reactions run the gamut from anger to despair, even guilt. It's a good idea to explore those feelings."

John had dealt with death before, first his father's, then Billy Dwyer's. He knew the drill and could handle his own. "I have a better idea. Let me die my miserable death alone, apart from everyone I love, and don't make me think about it so much."

CHAPTER FIFTEEN

C aptain Qadeer moved a chair from the nurses station into Salena's office just inside the door, lit up a Red Lamp, and began reading the *Pakistan Observer*.

Concentrating on Nusrat's file, Salena held her nose, but the stench from Qadeer's cigarette grew worse, and she started to cough. She looked up and saw only a crimson turban sticking up from behind a newspaper. "If you insist on babysitting me, get rid of that cigarette."

Qadeer lowered the paper, exposing cruel brown eyes. He got up, ambled toward her, then flicked the lit cigarette into the waste basket beside her desk.

Salena dropped Nusrat's file and stood. "Are you crazy? You will start a fire."

He shrugged and walked back to his chair.

Kneeling at the side of her desk, Salena dug furiously through the rubbish, found the cigarette, and crushed its glowing tip along the basket's metal sides. She gave Qadeer a long, dirty look, got up, and sat in her chair.

Holding open Nusrat's file, she reached for her computer's mouse. Her screen saver, a repeating series of Kashmir Valley vistas, was instantly replaced by a dozen icons lined up in two columns of six along the left edge of her screen. When a tiny blinking crescent moon popped up on the right side of her lower toolbar she let out a startled gasp.

Qadeer lowered his newspaper. "What are you doing?"

Salena tried hard not to gawk at the screen. "Oh, nothing. I yawned."

"Finish your business. The general demands I return you to the Citadel by eleven o'clock."

She peeked at the circular clock above her file cabinet, and saw she had four minutes.

Salena guided the mouse over the crescent moon, double-clicked, and opened an innocuous green screen requesting a password. She typed in 10 digits, hit the return key, and brought up a blue screen with a white box in the center. This time she keyed in a combination of six numbers and six letters. A third screen appeared demanding more numbers and letters. Twice more she repeated this ritual until after the fifth return there appeared a black screen with a blinking white cursor in the upper-left corner.

She glanced at Qadeer, making sure he was buried in his newspaper, then typed: cm live.

Nearly a minute passed with no reply. Maybe the Americans had given up. She was beginning to lose hope when two words appeared below and to the right of hers.

Home here

For the last five months she had mentally rehearsed the questions she'd been instructed to ask.

Being watched, have 1 minute

go with KGA, wolf en route

time of kill

7/21, glorious dawn

kill method

demo Citadel; help wolf enter den

wolf condition

male, pancreatic cancer, stage 4

Salena heard the rustling of a newspaper, looked up, and saw Qadeer walking toward her desk. She typed faster.

cover

computer systems consultant; Advanced Medical Systems, Newark, New Jersey

date/time of arrival

From the corner of her eye, she saw her last inquiry had been answered, but with Qadeer standing directly in front of her desk, she couldn't risk reading the reply. She minimized the screen and clicked on the Web2Net icon, calling up the home page of her Internet provider. When the home page appeared, she clicked randomly.

"I thought you were making notes to Madame Nusrat's file."

She looked up. "I am entering data from the nurse's chart. I do this for all my patients."

Qadeer leaned forward and cocked his head to get a better look at her monitor. "I see."

Salena glanced at the screen, did a double take, and her stomach plunged.

"And why does that data include the weather and traffic for Muzaffarabad?"

"No, I … her chart … I …"

"Are you arranging to take Madame Nusrat on a holiday? Not a good idea, since she is confined to her bed. Your own orders."

Angry at herself for having panicked, her mind raced. "I was accessing Nusrat's file. When you walked over, I accidentally clicked the wrong shortcut."

Qadeer's lips curled into a skeptical sneer. "It is time to return you to the Citadel."

"My work is not done."

"But you are already late."

"Late for what?"

"The general has a surprise waiting."

She assumed the surprise was Khan himself. "I need half an hour more."

"He wants you back by eleven o'clock. There will be no further discussion."

Salena was in trouble. Her virtual network link would take 15 minutes to self-disconnect. Anyone who maximized the crescent moon icon before then would discover her exchange with the Americans. She had to distract Qadeer and enter the 10-digit termination code manually.

"I shall go if you insist, but I must take my work with me." She turned and faced the stack of files on her desk. With her back to Qadeer, she discreetly knocked the entire pile to the floor. "Oh, no!"

"What happened?"

"You made me nervous."

Qadeer didn't budge.

"Won't you pick them up? You are the reason I dropped them."

For several seconds their eyes froze in a silent duel, until finally Qadeer grunted, walked to the front of her desk, and bent over to pick up the files scattered across the floor.

Salena closed her Internet home page, rolled her mouse to the crescent moon icon, clicked, and missed. She steadied her hand for another try.

"What are you doing?" Qadeer was standing, clutching the files.

"Closing my home page." She stared at the wall clock, hoping to draw his attention away from the monitor. "May I have my patient files?"

"I will keep these tonight."

"For what reason?"

"Never before have I seen you so diligent about updating your records. Perhaps there is more written here than diagnoses and prescriptions."

"Suit yourself, but I need them back by tomorrow morning."

"You have wasted enough time. Let us leave."

Avoiding eye contact with her computer screen, Salena followed Qadeer to her office door. As she entered the hall, she turned around, pushed in the handle lock, and silently implored Allah to allow no one near her desk.

CHAPTER SIXTEEN

Half an hour had passed since CRUSO's last transmission without a reply from Dr. Zamal. The entire time, Daley sat tearing up scrap paper, and in the last five minutes alone, the height of his confetti mound had doubled.

Farrell worried too, having not given Crescent Moon enough information about John Covello or his mission to adequately prepare her for John's arrival tomorrow morning. That Zamal had abruptly ceased messaging before they had completed their exchange only deepened Farrell's concern.

Daley began rocking his chair. "A nurse, maybe a doctor, walked in on her."

"At nine at night?"

"Who else?"

"One of Khan's watchdogs. She's been a virtual prisoner in his Citadel since the day he abducted her."

Daley stilled his chair and leaned forward. "You mean like that lunatic captain?"

"That's exactly who I mean." Farrell picked up a file labeled "classified," thumbed through its contents, and pulled out a sheet near the bottom. "Her transmission of 11 May at 1005 hours stated in part 'My greatest fear is Captain Azam Qadeer. He is insane and does not trust me. He wants me dead.' And we already know the story on Qadeer."

Immediately after Crescent Moon's May 11th transmission, the CIA interviewed tribal chieftains in Kabul and paid handsome sums to mid-level politicians in Pakistan to learn all they could about Captain Qadeer. Reading the captain's profile had given Farrell goose bumps.

A native of Kandahar, Azam Qadeer, upon turning 12, emigrated to Akora Khattak in Pakistan's North-West Frontier Province. Akora Khattak's claim to fame was as home of Darul-uloom Haqqania, a well-known madaris, or religious school that churned out Islamic holy warriors by the hundreds. Qadeer attended Darul-uloom Haqqania, as did Ghalib Ali Khan, and Khan, two years older than Qadeer, took the lower classman as his protégé.

Having earned his spurs as a full-fledged mujahideen, Qadeer returned to Afghanistan, where Mullah Mohammed Omar, then the Taliban's supreme leader, appointed Qadeer as a high-level officer with the Ministry of Vice and Virtue. Granted free reign as a member of the Taliban's dreaded religious police, young Qadeer handed out death sentences by the hundreds for crimes ranging from suspicion of adultery to photographing women.

After Ali Khan was promoted to lieutenant colonel with the Pakistan Frontier Corps, he recruited his old madaris chum as his personal assistant and primary enforcer. Striking terror into the hearts of 180 million Pakistanis required someone with the stomach to kill women and children—someone who lacked a soul. Qadeer was the perfect candidate.

Daley resumed rocking. "It could've been Qadeer, or any of Khan's goons watching her."

Farrell's heart fluttered the same way it had hours before CRUSO's last terminally ill candidate embarked on his mission. "With Khan's security people breathing down her neck, how can she be much help to John?"

"If she wants her freedom, she'll find a way."

"If she doesn't know who John is when he arrives, she'll lose a lot more than her freedom."

By 3:00 p.m. Pakistan time tomorrow Prime Minister Behari required conclusive evidence America had infiltrated an assassin into Khan's Citadel. So certain was President Lloyd of nuclear war between Pakistan and India if CRUSO failed, he had disclosed to Behari CRUSO's existence. To further gain Behari's trust, the president had suggested the prime minister send an envoy to Washington to personally observe the mission's progress from inside the Pentagon.

Behari had accepted the president's offer, and had chosen Ajay Agarwal, India's Deputy Foreign Minister and Behari's childhood friend as his special envoy to monitor the progress of CRUSO's mission. Agarwal was expected to join them in Washington later tonight with a front row ticket to CRUSO's big game.

The prime minister's concession to wait until tomorrow—6:00 a.m. Washington time, 3:00 p.m. Pakistan time—before launching his Agni missile had not stopped him from preparing for war in the event CRUSO failed. On its last pass over northwest India, the NRO's AmStar-50 spy satellite had photographed open missile silos near Jalwali, Gharaunda, and Kullu, any of which could reach Islamabad within seven minutes.

Colonel Daley stood, and began pacing behind the burgundy leather chairs along his side of the conference table. On his third lap past Farrell he gripped the back of his chair and looked down at her. "Say you're right, and Zamal was being watched. She'll wait until the pressure's off, then contact us. Maybe she'll transmit tomorrow morning."

"Tomorrow morning cuts it awfully close. Right now she knows only that our operative is a male systems consultant who works for an American company. She has no idea what he looks like, when he's arriving, or for that matter, his name."

"How many male systems consultants from America do you think will show up at Pakistan National Hospital in the next four days?"

Farrell didn't appreciate Daley's condescending tone. She rolled back her chair, stood, and faced Daley across the table. "Assume she does figure it out. So will whoever was watching her tonight if they happened to read our exchange. I can see it now, John lands, gets driven to the soccer stadium, and it's his-and-hers baskets for their heads."

"John leaves at 1420 hours. We're not waiting for another transmission."

"You're pushing too hard."

"We have no choice."

Farrell knew Daley was right. Between the runaround Premier Jintao was giving Lance Parker in Beijing, and the mounting pressure on Sanjay Behari in New Delhi to give Khan a dose of his own medicine, they had little choice but to proceed.

All she could do was pray John wasn't walking into a trap.

Farrell lowered herself into her chair and stared down at the conference table. She spoke as much to herself as to Daley standing across from her. "Just remember. After this mission is over, successful or not, we still have ourselves to live with."

Even if John wasn't arrested the moment he stepped off the plane in Pakistan, he had only six hours and five minutes after landing to clear customs, check into the Rawal Regency Inn, contact Crescent Moon, and transmit to CRUSO verification of their meeting.

Farrell wished they'd had more time to compile the character component of John's 3-C's Report. Something in his dossier might have convinced her he wouldn't crack under pressure. But so far, everything about this mission, including compilation of the 3-C's on Covello and Chandler, had been performed under extreme pressure.

CHAPTER SEVENTEEN

When they reached the 11th floor of Khan's Citadel, Salena followed Qadeer off the elevator into a maze of bland white hallways lit up by fluorescent lights. Salena's quarters occupied three rooms on the southeast side of the octagon structure, directly below Khan's master bedroom.

Qadeer kept two paces ahead of Salena. In one hand he gripped the handle of his holstered pistol, in the other a smoldering Red Lamp. Rounding a bend in the hall, Qadeer spoke without looking back. "Why did you need information about Muzaffarabad?"

Salena tugged the tips of her veil closer to her bosom. "I told you, it was a mistake. You made me nervous."

"Nothing makes you nervous."

When they reached the door to her room, Qadeer smiled grimly. "Enjoy your surprise. Against my best advice, Ali Khan insists on loving you."

She opened her door, unimpeded by a lock, for as Khan's chattel, she had no need of locks or keys to hinder his access. Pulling off her veil, she inhaled a sweet fragrance, and saw on top of a table between her parlor and her bedroom a red ceramic vase overflowing with a magnificent bouquet of white jasmine.

The delicate white petals of Pakistan's national flower reminded her of her homeland. The Moghul emperors, especially fond of jasmine, planted vast groves of the hardy shrub on the grounds of their summer palaces in the Kashmir Valley. When she was a little girl, at least once every spring her father drove her and her mother around the Vale to visit its splendid gardens.

Salena walked to the table, closed her eyes, and inhaled deeply the inebriating aroma. As a child, she dared dream of marrying a man she loved, unheard of in a world where love mattered less than the consent and dowry of a bride's parents. Her marriage would be different—the result of two free-thinking individuals choosing to share their lives, not the outcome of a contract between two families. At her wedding, her parents would sit beside the parents of the groom, not separate and apart, but as equals, amidst a nuptial garden overflowing with jasmine.

A small white envelope rested against the vase. She read the handwritten note inside:

Dearest Salena,

I love you more than life itself and am deeply sorry. The flames of my passion are difficult to control, but after all, those flames are ignited by you. I have reconsidered your plea we wait until after our wedding before I satisfy my passion. For that reason, I have decided we shall marry before Ramadan, two weeks from tomorrow. Sleep well my dearest Salena, and do not worry. As you have learned to serve me, you shall learn to love me.

Your kind master,

Ghalib

Salena tossed the card on the floor. Two weeks left until her final surrender.

She again considered taking her life, perhaps by swallowing a jarful of the medicine with which she intended to treat Captain Tareen's wife. Then she thought of her friend Raja, howling in pain under torture, and of her mother in a hospital bed, dying alone in a dying city. She imagined Ali Khan's eager hands groping her, and she shuddered at the thought of again submitting to a man she hated. She thought of Kalila, who spurned everyone but a single angel sent by Allah, and of Naji, waiting patiently for her in Srinagar.

Reasons to live, reasons to die.

Salena recalled her abbreviated transmission with Major Farrell. Farrell was telling her she had found the right person, perhaps someone who might give her another reason to live.

Until tonight, Farrell had offered only vague promises of freedom, both for herself and her beloved Kashmir. She had offered money too, but it was freedom Salena craved more than anything.

The Americans had first approached Salena during the last year of her residency at Saint Barnabas Medical Center. Zipping along the Empire Corridor on Amtrak's high-speed express to Albany, Salena looked forward to a weekend visit with a girlfriend in Schenectady. Admiring the green hills across the Hudson River, a blonde woman with a pasty complexion sporting a blue designer suit sat beside her and began talking.

During the next hour Salena learned the Americans had for years been watching Ali Khan ascend the ranks of the Pakistan Army. The general possessed charm, charisma, and a strong fundamentalist following. They suspected one day he might gain power, and if so, would pose a significant threat to the stability of South Asia. As a vociferous critic of President Razzak, General Khan made no secret of his ambition to bring Kashmir under the flag of Pakistan.

Salena also learned that for two years the Americans had monitored her e-mails from General Khan. Based on Salena's terse, sometimes nonexistent replies to Khan's declarations of love, the Americans concluded she had no interest in becoming his life partner.

In her rare responses she made clear she rejected his militaristic solution to resolving the Kashmir problem, as well as his twisted application of Islamic law to subjugate Pakistan's women. America's intelligence analysts viewed her as ripe for accepting an invitation to spy for the US in Pakistan. Rather than spurn Khan's love, they hoped she would fuel it, all the while feeding America information about his political and military ambitions.

But Salena had already made up her mind. After her residency, she planned to return home to Srinagar and offer her services to the overworked, often harassed medical staff at Lal Ded Hospital. She wanted nothing to do with Ali Khan. That is what she told the American agent, and that is what she did.

Thanks to the brutality of five officers from India's Border Security Force allegedly weeding out Islamic militants from law abiding Muslims, her return to Srinagar was short-lived. Exactly one year, two months, and five days after she had gone home, she was forced to flee the Vale. She moved to Peshawar, Pakistan, where a former undergraduate professor helped her secure a position at Lady Reading Hospital.

Last February while attending the World Conference of Obstetricians and Gynecologists in New York City, the US government again approached her. This time America's point person was a black woman who introduced herself as Major Denise Farrell. The politely confident Ms. Farrell claimed affiliation with a newly formed government agency seeking to oust General Khan from power.

By then Khan had solidified Pakistan's economic and military ties with China and had begun rattling his sabers at India. To western nations, a fundamentalist warmonger wreaking havoc in the midst of the world's fastest growing market for American and European products was intolerable. Khan had to go, and they hoped Salena would help.

Salena gave Farrell the same answer she had given the blonde American woman five years earlier. She had no intention of going anywhere near Ghalib Ali Khan. Farrell asked her to memorize a 10-digit code. If she ever changed her mind she should open the home page for Shenandoah National Park, append the 10 digits to the site's URL, and hit enter. Instructions would follow to put Salena in direct contact with Farrell's agency.

Back in Peshawar three days after the World Conference ended she was abducted by Captain Qadeer and delivered to Khan's Citadel. When she arrived, Khan divulged he had been watching her for a year, and had decided to act now before she left the country for good. He informed her she was to work at his newly built hospital for Pakistan's elite, and at the same time, make preparations to become his bride.

By early May, after too many beatings and shattered dreams, Salena contacted Farrell and began feeding the Americans information about Khan's activities. At best, Salena was tepid toward America, with its pampered ladies, bloated men, and loose morals. She helped the US out of desperation. She wanted Khan dead.

This past Tuesday after her kind master exploded a nuclear bomb over Baramulla she relayed to Farrell all she knew about Glorious Dawn. Within five hours, Farrell messaged her back. The US had devised a plan to destroy Khan and his military monster by severing its head. They needed Salena's assistance, which if given, guaranteed her a cash reward of $2,500,000 and freedom from Ali Khan. Farrell also pledged to reinstate Pakistan's tolerant former president, Labib Razzak.

Inhaling the sweet scent of jasmine, Salena wondered who this American was who would commit suicide for his country. He must be brave, someone noble with high ideals, an exception to the shallow, narrow-minded men she had met time and again during her years in the States.

If she helped the gallant American kill Ali Khan, freedom was hers, and she would yet have a chance to meet her perfect lover and celebrate with him her perfect marriage amidst an elegant pageantry of jasmine.

The risks were many, yes, but she had little left to lose.

CHAPTER EIGHTEEN

The jet carrying John to Washington, DC rolled to a stop at the end of the tarmac. The brunette in the dark green jumpsuit who had offered John water during the flight escorted him through the exit door and down a rolling stairway. Two Air Force officers young enough to be his sons stood stiffly at the bottom of the steps. They greeted John politely and hustled him to a jeep idling alongside the jet.

As the jeep drove around the nose of the jet that had flown him far from his family, John saw Lieutenant Hawley, the army psychologist, emerge from the cabin at the top of the stairs. By now Maureen must be worried sick he hadn't returned from his jaunt on the Manasquan River. He had the sudden urge to jump off the bus and beg the pilot to fly him back to New Jersey. Still not believing he had abandoned the three most important people in his world, an intense cramp shot through his belly reminding him why he was here.

The airmen drove John to a one-story brick building with a fenced side yard containing a plastic pre-fab playground. A sign at the foot of the walk leading up to the building read "Family Support Center."

A young woman in a green jumpsuit sprinted from the building and escorted John inside. She led him down a short hall to a bright, spacious room with a high sloped ceiling and recessed skylights. Bulletin boards pinned to capacity dotted the room's pastel yellow walls, and John guessed on any other day this room was used for playing ping-pong and checkers.

On metal chairs along both sides of three fold-up tables laid end-to-end sat six people. John recognized two: Major Denise Farrell and Colonel William Daley, who sat opposite each other at the middle table. John's attention was drawn to an elderly woman who sat at the first table. Her hair pinned in a bun, she wore a pale green blouse covered by a matching lightweight jacket, and she appeared unusually thin. A blonde female officer sat beside her.

Both Daley and Farrell stood as John approached. Farrell, the closer of the two, met John halfway and shook his hand. "How was your flight?"

"OK, I guess."

John sat on the same side of the center table as Farrell, leaving one empty chair between them. He noticed a TV monitor, turned off, set up on the far end of the first table.

After Daley sat, he nodded hello and promptly informed John the mission had run into its first glitch. He described CRUSO's abbreviated transmission with Crescent Moon, but assured John they expected to reach their informant again by tomorrow at 9:00 a.m., Pakistan time.

Daley's guarantee failed to boost John's confidence. "How can you send me into a hellhole like Pakistan when my contact doesn't even know who to look for?"

"We expect to reestablish our link with her before you arrive."

John didn't remember hearing CRUSO's informer was a she. "And if you don't?"

"In that unlikely event, you'll have to initiate contact on your own."

"What do you suggest? Walk up to her and say, 'Hi Crescent Moon, I'm here to destroy Khan's Citadel. Will you help?' I'll be shot on the spot."

"I told you, we'll get in touch with her, but if not, you'll have to try your best."

"You're right. I'm a penniless, dead man, anyway—why not waste me like yesterday's garbage."

Daley scraped back his chair, stood, and looked down at him. "Yes, Mr. Covello, you are a little fish with big problems. But we're giving you a chance to resolve those problems, if not for yourself, for your family. We explained the risks and rewards at the outset, so you shouldn't be acting all indignant now because of one minor hiccup."

John realized the colonel was right. He had accepted this job for Maureen and his daughters and, bottom line, nothing came for nothing. "I have one more favor."

"We've given you enough."

"It's not a big deal."

"We agreed on the terms. No changes."

Farrell glared at Daley. "No harm hearing him out."

Daley sat and gave John a begrudging nod.

"After I'm dead, make sure my children don't fall apart. Especially Christie. For them, this is coming out of nowhere. And Maureen, too. I don't care how many millions she gets, this is gonna hurt. Just look in on them to make sure they're handling things."

"That won't be a problem," Farrell said. "I have family too. We'll make sure yours pulls through."

John read voices well, and Farrell's came from the heart. "Thanks."

The major rose, and covering her mouth with her hand, cleared her throat. "OK John, let's get you ready. The more information we give you now, the easier time you'll have later." She motioned to the last table, where John saw two men sitting across from each other wearing business suits. One had black hair, brown eyes, and an olive complexion—maybe Italian or Spanish—and wore a gold-buttoned, navy blue blazer. The other man, with blue eyes, a full crop of sandy hair, and freckles on his neck, bore a slight resemblance to Maureen's younger brother. His muscular physique filled a charcoal pin-striped suit.

"First let me introduce you to Lieutenant Jeffrey Hall, US Marines, Special Forces." The big, blonde guy in gray flashed John an ear-to-ear grin so wholesome it could've come off a Wheaties Box. "Don't let that baby-face fool you. Ten years of training and experience in espionage, counter-intelligence, and reconnaissance has made him one of the Corps' best."

She turned toward the dark man in navy blue. "That's Sergeant Richard Banta. Also Marine Corps Special Forces. For the last three years he's worked closely with Lieutenant Hall. His specialty is unconventional warfare, and he's well versed in South Asian politics and Islamic studies."

Banta flashed John a polite smile.

"Those guys look like they belong in a Van Damme movie."

Farrell chuckled. "The movies glamorize what's actually a tedious vocation."

"Somehow I don't see unconventional warfare as tedious."

"These men will accompany you on both legs of your journey, first, from Andrews to Manama in Bahrain, and then from Bahrain to Islamabad. From Andrews to Bahrain, you'll fly the Air Force prototype ST-131, America's first super-sonic military transport. If it tests successfully, Boeing's slated to produce five for the Army and Air Force over the next three years."

"It's still in testing?"

"Don't worry, with over 250,000 miles logged, we've discovered only three minor design flaws."

"Let's not go there."

"The ST-131 is being refueled on a runway two miles from where we're sitting. It'll be ready in 30 minutes. At an average cruising speed of Mach 2, you'll land in Bahrain at the US Administrative Support Unit, Southwest Asia Installation, in about five hours. A helicopter will shuttle you eight miles to Bahrain International Airport, where you'll board Pakistan International Airlines Flight 486 to Islamabad.

"Timing is critical. You're leaving Andrews at 2:10 p.m. and arriving in Manama at 7:15 p.m. Eastern Daylight Saving Time. You'll have to adjust to the time differences. When you land in Manama, the local time will be 2:15 a.m., Saturday. That gives you 30 minutes to get onto PIA Flight 486 departing Bahrain at 2:45 a.m. Miss it, and the next flight to Islamabad doesn't leave for 12 hours."

John recalled his earlier conversation with Farrell in New Jersey. "But if I don't contact Crescent Moon by 3:00 p.m., Pakistan time, India wastes Islamabad."

"Exactly right. Miss your connection in Bahrain, this mission's over."

"I love pressure, I really do."

"The moment you enter the passenger terminal at Bahrain International, you lose your identity as John Covello and turn into John Cattano. Your passports, visa, airline tickets, driver's license, every document you carry will prove you're John Cattano from Brielle, New Jersey. We'll discuss your fictitious identity in more detail, but first let's finish the timing."

"Let's, because I'd rather die instantly under a thousand tons of concrete and steel than feel my flesh burn off its bones."

"Flight 486 arrives in Islamabad at 8:55 a.m., Pakistan time. You're only in the air four hours and ten minutes, but Islamabad is two hours ahead of Bahrain. The most important thing to remember, as soon as you enter the passenger terminal at Bahrain International, you may no longer speak with Lieutenant Hall and Sergeant Banta. They'll also be on Flight 486 under assumed names, but you cannot communicate with them in any way. If you approach them, they'll deny knowing you."

"Why's that?"

Farrell sat and raised her dark eyes to the ceiling, as if searching the skylights for an answer. Finally, she said, "Truth is, if you get caught—blow your cover, in layman's parlance—you cannot compromise the lives of anyone else involved with this mission."

John looked at Hall and Banta sitting at the next table. They probably had families of their own. "I understand."

"In Islamabad, after you clear customs, hail a cab to the Rawal Regency Inn. Of course, you'll check in under your assumed name. Lieutenant Hall and Sergeant Banta are lodging at the same hotel, but again, if you see them, steer clear."

"I don't mean to sound rude, but if I can't talk to them, what good are they?"

"Their primary purpose is to take custody of the RDX-7S charges from CRUSO's overland courier. They'll also reconnoiter Pakistan National Hospital, assess security, and determine the safest means to deliver the charges once you're inside. Believe it or not, they can help you in other ways too, but they'll be more effective if Khan's people don't suspect they're American agents. Wait for them to come to you."

John carefully studied the two men's faces. "If you guys come knocking, I better remember what you look like."

Farrell said, "Don't worry. On the flight to Bahrain, you'll have five hours to get friendly." She reached into a large briefcase and pulled out a wallet, visa, passport, and glossy blue folder, and set them on the table between herself and John. "These establish your fictitious identity. John Cattano doesn't demolish buildings, he works for Advanced Medical Systems, a consulting firm based in Newark, New Jersey that designs information systems for hospitals, health clinics, and physicians. In case the ISI, Pakistan's Inter-Services Intelligence Agency, checks you out, AMS actually exists."

"No one's that stupid. All they have to do is call and ask for my extension."

"That's why at this very hour FBI agents are meeting with Ted Dunne, the company's CEO, to inform him AMS has a superb systems analyst on staff named John Cattano who's worked there for six years. Mr. Dunne knows little else about Mr. Cattano, and he's receiving a substantial sum not to ask." Farrell pointed to the blue folder with the letters 'AMS' printed on the cover. "The phone number on the brochure connects to an existing line at the company's Newark office. The same folks meeting with Mr. Dunne are re-wiring that line to forward all calls to CRUSO's command center."

Colonel Daley leaned forward. "Anyone calling for Ted Dunne gets me instead."

John grunted. "I hope you're nicer to them than—"

"As I was about to say," Farrell interrupted, "this past February at the annual World Conference of Obstetricians and Gynecologists in Manhattan, you set up an exhibit showcasing your company's software. The conference ran four days, from February 22nd through 25th. On the last day, a respected doctor from Pakistan noticed your booth and expressed an interest in your company's comprehensive Linux-based hospital management software system, a product called Med-Link. This doctor was particularly interested in Med-Link's integrated modules allowing hospitals to add applications at their own pace, including components for patient registration, a master patient index, appointment scheduling, surgical suite management, physician scheduling, clinical data captured from bedside medical devices, patient billing, electronic remittance, and numerous other hospital application software modules."

"What the hell are you talking about? I get there and they start asking me questions, I'm screwed."

"We don't expect anyone to question your knowledge of computer-based hospital systems."

"And if someone does?"

"Read the materials in the brochure. They'll give you an overview. If you do get stuck, we're hoping Crescent Moon bails you out."

"Seems like a lot's riding on this Crescent Moon."

Farrell again reached into her briefcase, this time pulling out a white folder. She placed the folder on the table, face down. "The doctor you met in New York City is actually Crescent Moon. Her real name is Dr. Salena Zamal, and I'm the one who recruited her."

"Here in America?"

"She received her medical training in the US, and during the last year of her residency at Saint Barnabas—"

"In New Jersey?"

"Yes."

"You're kidding. Maureen delivered both our girls at the Community Medical Center in Toms River. It's affiliated with Saint Barnabas."

"Good, then you'll have something to chat about. Dr. Zamal agreed with us that Khan posed a grave danger. But in the end, she was less interested in the money we offered her than in returning to Srinagar."

"Srinagar?"

"Where she was born, the summer capital of Kashmir."

"I thought she was from Pakistan. Isn't Kashmir part of India? Or is it part of Pakistan?"

Farrell slumped back in her chair, sighed, and turned to Daley looking for an assist. Daley looked back and shrugged.

"What did I say?"

"If we have a few minutes before you leave, I'll discuss the Kashmir problem."

"What Kashmir problem?"

"It's not germane to your mission objective."

"If you say so."

"When I met Dr. Zamal in February, she had moved to Pakistan and was working in Peshawar. She never said why she left Srinagar, but I asked her to memorize a cipher for contacting me if she ever changed her mind. Within a week of returning to Peshawar, General Khan abducted her and essentially imprisoned her in his Citadel. He plans to marry her in September."

"Let me guess. That's when she came calling."

Farrell nodded.

"Nothing like enslavement to crush apathy."

Farrell continued, "At the New York convention, Dr. Zamal was so impressed with Med-Link she invited you to Pakistan to bid on installing the patient management module at Lady Reading Hospital in Peshawar. You agreed, but told her you were committed to a prior installation. Last month, you learned she relocated to Islamabad and was working at Pakistan National Hospital. You e-mailed her, asking if she was still interested in Med-Link, and she said yes."

"What about Mr. Wonderful? Won't he have something to say when an American businessman shows up in Pakistan rubbing elbows with his reluctant bride?"

"Dr. Zamal believes a systems consultant would arouse the least suspicion and give a foreigner widest access to the hospital."

"But I need access to the Citadel."

"If she gets you inside the hospital, she'll get you into the Citadel. That's what she's assured us."

"Like I said before, if she doesn't know my name, how—"

"Colonel Daley, we're ready."

John looked past Farrell to the first table where a young woman's voice had come through the TV's speakers. The monitor was aglow with an image of an impressive wood desk and an empty chair. The desk was flanked by two flags—the American flag, and a flag bearing the seal of the president of the United States.

Colonel Daley rose and spoke in the direction of the monitor. "We're ready here, too, Stacy."

Seconds later President Lloyd, not the man John had voted for, came into view and sat in the chair behind the desk. "Good afternoon Colonel Daley. Hello Denise."

Daley and Farrell replied in unison, "Good afternoon Mr. President."

"Good afternoon Mr. Covello."

Unsure whether the president could see him, John stared straight at the screen. "Hello sir."

"Good afternoon Mrs. Krause."

The gray-haired lady sitting at the first table nodded. "Good afternoon Mr. President."

"First, allow me to express my deepest sympathies regarding your unfortunate and untimely catastrophic illnesses. I am told you both believe in God. When our lives are visited by tragic events of cataclysmic proportion, we endeavor to take comfort in our belief that God has a greater purpose. At the very least, such events test our faith and courage.

"These past two days, Ms. Krause—only hours for you, Mr. Covello—have presented a unique opportunity to salvage from your profound personal losses a modicum of comfort. Ms. Krause, your philanthropic intentions are magnificently noble, and rest assured, shall be realized exactly as you have instructed.

"Mr. Covello. Devotion to Maureen, Karen, and Christie motivates your participation in this mission. I can think of no more honorable cause than preservation and protection of family to induce a man to sacrifice his life. Quite frankly, I understand you have expressed skepticism regarding the intention of the American government to honor its commitments under our agreement. Be comforted. I will personally direct the transfer of funds to your wife upon verification of your death and settlement of the fictitious litigation that comprises the circumstances under which she will receive your compensation.

"Finally, I say to both of you, though you have named specific beneficiaries to receive the bounties of your efforts, an entire nation, perhaps the entire world, shall benefit from the success of your endeavors. General Ali Khan is armed with weapons of mass destruction and has proven his inclination to use them. Diplomatic overtures to avert all-out war have made little progress. As such, the successful completion of your mission is quickly becoming the most effective means by which Ali Khan can be stopped. I am grateful to you, as is your country, for undertaking this difficult endeavor and for making the ultimate sacrifice. Good luck, and Godspeed to you both."

The monitor went to static, then to black.

John closed his eyes. This mission was becoming more real by the minute, as were his second thoughts.

CHAPTER NINETEEN

Everyone on both sides of the three tables stared silently at the darkened screen. A minute passed before John heard anything, and when it came, it was the sound of tearing paper—Colonel Daley ripping the top page off the yellow pad in front of him.

Major Farrell ballooned her cheeks, exhaled slowly, and said almost reverently, "I guess we should continue." She turned over the white folder she had extracted from her briefcase, pulled out an 8" x 10" photograph, and slid it in front of John. "This is Dr. Zamal."

John gasped at the waist-up photo of a woman in her late-twenties, maybe early thirties, wearing a taupe, form-fitting business suit over a white button-down blouse. Her thick chestnut hair cascaded past her shoulders. The shot captured a sideways glance, and in her large brown eyes and full pink lips John read a warning, "Look, but don't touch."

If this were Khan's reluctant bride, John could understand why he kept her near. "Interesting," he muttered.

"In what way?"

Colonel Daley grinned. "I think he means for a doctor, she's hot."

Farrell answered with a frown. "John's not that shallow."

"To be perfectly honest," John said, "that's exactly what I was thinking."

The major rolled her eyes and grabbed the photo. "Bring this along on the flight to Bahrain and memorize her face." Tucking the picture back in the white folder, she added, "though I think you already have."

John took the folder from Farrell. "Better safe than sorry."

"Leave that photo on the jet. The last thing you need is getting caught in an Islamic republic carrying a photo of a woman, especially when the woman belongs to General Khan."

"What's wrong with a picture?"

"Strict Muslims frown upon photographing women who aren't close relatives. In Khan's Pakistan, snapping pictures of the ladies has gotten more than one hapless tourist thrown in jail."

"I'll leave it on the plane."

Farrell got up, walked behind the TV monitor, and returned carrying two rolled-up, rubber-banded blueprints. She slid off the bands and lay the large sheets side by side on the table. John rose, as did Daley, and all three stood looking down at the plans.

Farrell pointed to the plan on the left, depicting seven floors of a rectangular building. "Pakistan National Hospital. Until four years ago, the CIA had 25 highly paid Pakistani agents operating in and around Islamabad. Since General Khan took over, we're down to two, and of those, only one's gotten a peek inside. Between that agent's reports and information supplied by Dr. Zamal, we've calculated an 80 percent confidence ratio in the accuracy of our hospital blueprint. On the way to Bahrain get to know the hospital's layout. As Dr. Zamal's software consultant, you'll likely spend lots of time there." Farrell nodded toward Lieutenant Hall and Sergeant Banta. "The hospital is where those gentlemen expect to deliver the RDX-7S charges to you."

John eyed the second print and counted six floors of an octagon building. "What's that?"

Daley answered. "The second, fourth, and sixth through ninth floors of Khan's Citadel."

"Where's the rest of it?"

"Those were all Dr. Zamal could get us, but that shouldn't matter. Implosion engineers don't rely on mechanicals."

For half the demolition jobs John had performed the building plans had long vanished, or over the years, disintegrated. When prints were available, he might examine them, but he never relied on them exclusively, since on-site inspections invariably disclosed major differences between as-built and as-drawn.

"I'll need the mechanicals to figure out how to get around once I'm inside." In the center of each octagon floor, John noticed a small rectangle labeled 'Main Elevator Bank.' He put his finger on one. "For example, how do I get in there?"

Farrell ran her finger across two parallel lines connecting the elevator bank to a small square inside one wall of the octagon. "An air vent runs from the passenger elevator shaft to a service elevator on the periphery. It's your best bet. I'm sorry I couldn't do better on the schematics, but Khan runs his command center like a fortress."

John scanned the other five floors depicted on the blueprint. "For my own edification, what's your confidence ratio on the Citadel drawing?"

"Roughly 20 percent."

"Wonderful."

"The Citadel is the most secure building in Pakistan. Thanks to Dr. Zamal we're lucky to have what we have."

"What about structural support?"

"Concrete columns and steel I-beams."

Concrete columns were relatively easy to destroy and usually required a small quantity of conventional dynamite packed into strategically drilled holes. Often 200 pounds was enough to fell a 10-story building. High tensile steel beams, on the other hand, required a high-velocity explosive to literally cut through the metal. Copper-encased RDX, physically attached to the beam, generally performed the task well. "How far did you say the Citadel is from the hospital?"

"Twenty feet."

"And from the Diplomatic Enclave?"

"Approximately 180 feet to the school."

Regardless of how technologically advanced Farrell's souped-up RDX was, this job would be no easy task. A demolition usually involved pulling a structure away from an adjacent building, street, or other exposure toward an area large enough to contain the debris. Strictly speaking, that sort of demolition was not an implosion. A true implosion occurred when adjacent buildings completely surrounded the building to be demolished, forcing the contractor to collapse the building onto itself. Of all explosive demolitions, implosions were the trickiest. "You're asking a lot."

"I know John, but if you can access the building's core through the main elevators, it's possible."

With any demolition the quantity of explosives was less important than the placement of the charges and timing of their detonation. Charges had to be placed where a structure would naturally fail if it were overloaded, or in the language of the trade, forced into its natural failure mode. For an implosion, that was usually the center.

To enhance a building's natural failure mode, the center was weakened and collapsed by timed charges, creating an open area into which the remainder of the falling structure could drop. Other charges were then fired in precisely timed succession toward the building's outer walls. The detonation pattern acted like a wedge to collapse the outside walls inward, similar to felling a tree. Gravity and leverage physics then used the weight of the structure to pull itself downward, toward the center, in a controlled process.

But that sort of precision required weeks of preparation—cutting away stairwells, studying the structures of neighboring buildings, attaching steel cables at specific points to guide the falling building inward, using a blow torch to weaken support beams, and drilling holes in carefully selected concrete columns. For this job he had days, not weeks, to prepare, and he must do so in total secrecy inside the most secure building in Pakistan.

Staring down at the Citadel blueprint, John shook his head. "You guys are dreaming."

Farrell and Daley eyed each other across the table. It was Daley who broke the silence. "We anticipated cold feet once you understood the complexities of the mission. The president has authorized me to increase your failure compensation from one to $2,000,000, but only if you detonate an explosion."

"I don't understand."

"Get caught or killed before you detonate, your wife gets a million. Destroy the Citadel, she'll get two million, even if Khan survives. Of course if he dies she receives the full ten million."

Two million dollars would put Maureen at break even—far better than getting stuck with a million dollar debt. "Let's see this high-powered RDX I'm pinning my family's hopes on."

Colonel Daley called Sergeant Banta over. Looking dapper in his navy blue blazer, the young olive-skinned officer was the last person John would have figured for an expert in unconventional warfare. Banta carried a small red package the size and shape of a cigar box. He set the box on the table in front of John, flipped open its lid, and pulled out a gray bow-shaped tube the width of a cigarette, and two inches longer.

Daley addressed Banta, "Show Mr. Covello why he shouldn't worry."

The sergeant proceeded to explain the bent tube was a prototype linear shaped charge developed exclusively for the military capable of cutting through titanium, dolomite, Kevlar, graphite-epoxy, and just about any other known material. With a maximum explosive force of 125,000 feet per second, its power was three times stronger than any charge John had worked with. Only three ounces each, the charges were compact and lightweight. Their unique features included a self-contained charging and ignition system, a digitally-controlled timer adjustable to .0005 second increments, a blast containment setting to focus the direction of explosive force, and a velocity regulator allowing calibration of the explosion's force from 2,000 feet per second up to 125,000 feet per second.

John was amazed. If the versatility and cutting capability of these charges were half as incredible as Banta described, they'd be more than sufficient to implode the Citadel—assuming John could position them where they'd do the right damage.

After the sergeant instructed John on the use of the RDX-7S, Daley cautioned, "Once you take custody of the charges, don't let them out of your sight. The charge you're holding and 41 others like it are the only prototypes available. Half the country's inventory is inside that box."

Impressed by the unique attributes of RDX-7S, John had only one question. "Where and how do I get them?"

Daley deferred to Major Farrell, who explained, "This mission will be CRUSO's first deploying two candidates." She turned and faced the gray-haired lady who'd been sitting quietly beside the female officer at the first table.

A flicker of a smile rose at the edges of the older woman's mouth.

"Allow me to introduce Ms. Patty Krause. She suffers from an incurable liver disease."

John nodded at her, and now understood why she looked so thin.

"She'll fly with you on the first leg of your journey. After you reach Manama, you'll part company. She and the 21 charges will be flown to Sharqpur, where a friendly Pakistani agent will meet and drive her into downtown Lahore. She too has been given a fictitious identity—a retired Asian Studies professor from UCLA with a desire to visit all the places she's described to her students for 35 years."

John wondered what Patty Krause had really done for a living.

"In Lahore she'll rent a Subaru. Followed by our Pakistani agent, she'll drive 460 miles northwest on the M-2 Motorway into Islamabad. The M-2 is a three-lane expressway, so the ride should take between eight and nine hours and put her at the Rawal Regency Inn by seven tomorrow night."

John noticed Ms. Krause inspecting her hands clasped on her lap, and asked Farrell, "Maybe its none of my business, but why do you need a second CRUSO agent to deliver the charges?"

"The RDX-7S is highly classified and can't get into enemy hands. If Khan's security forces intercept Mrs. Krause, she's been instructed to detonate the entire box from a wireless trigger attached to her cameo."

"I don't get it. You obviously expect her to reach Islamabad alive. I thought by definition CRUSO agents ended their missions dying."

"Ms. Krause has agreed to a regulated disappearance under the supervision of the US government."

John imagined this woman had family somewhere. Maybe hers was buried in debt too.

Farrell went on discussing his agenda. "Your first scheduled meeting with Lieutenant Hall and Sergeant Banta is set for 4:00 p.m. tomorrow at the Rawal Regency."

It occurred to John he wasn't the only person in the room with everything to lose if he missed the three o'clock deadline.

"During the day, while you're connecting with Dr. Zamal, Lieutenant Hall and Sergeant Banta will determine the safest means of transferring the charges to you at the hospital. When you meet with them, they'll advise you what they've decided. After you've taken possession of the charges, the lieutenant and sergeant will remain in Islamabad until after you implode the Citadel. As I said, under no circumstances can you go to them, even if you're in trouble. They'll come to you."

"Sort of like guardian angels."

"In a way, but when you're in the hospital or Khan's Citadel, you're basically on your own."

John again studied the incomplete blueprint of the Citadel and shook his head. "I don't know how I'm gonna take that building down without hurting innocent bystanders."

Daley leaned across the table and spoke in a tone devoid of emotion. "Your immediate objective is establishing contact with Dr. Zamal by 3:00 p.m. tomorrow. Your primary objective is imploding Khan's Citadel by 1:00 p.m. next Wednesday. Minimization of collateral damage is a secondary objective."

"So if I kill a kid or two across the street, no big deal, right?"

"Minimization of collateral damage is a secondary objective."

John balled his fists. "Mister, my handiwork already killed an innocent kid, and I'll be damned if I'll let that happen again."

Farrell cut in, "I don't believe the colonel intends you disregard the issue of harming innocent civilians. We have complete confidence in your ability to execute a clean implosion. That's why we chose you."

"Don't you bullshit me either, major. You chose me because I'm the only deadbeat demo man dying of cancer who happened to be available this week."

Farrell paused, as if hesitant to express her next thought, then spoke with soft conviction. "John, if you want out, now's the time."

He had made his decision, and he'd made it for his family. "Let's get going."

Daley handed John a wallet with $5,000 in Pakistan rupees—for greasing palms if he ran into trouble—and a black gym bag with enough clothes and toiletries for four nights. He told John to change out of his blue jeans and polo shirt on the flight to Manama, then passed him a garment bag he said held a dress suit, white shirt, black shoes, and a tie.

Farrell's expression turned somber as she handed John a tiny medicine bottle. "The label says Bayer aspirin. Each caplet contains 750 mg of potassium cyanide. If you find yourself in a situation where hostile forces discover your true identity, and you have no chance of escape, bite down on three caplets. You'll lose consciousness within a minute and die from respiratory arrest within ten."

"What if I don't do it?"

Daley answered almost gleefully. "Your family gets nothing."

"That's real sweet."

"Look at it this way Covello. Whatever happens, you're dead. Get caught, and you might as well help your family erase half your debt."

"I'm not sure who I like less, you or the guy I'm supposed to kill."

Farrell pursed her lips at Daley. "John understands the gravity of the situation, and he'll do the right thing." She guided John away from the table. "Remember, the only person you can trust is Dr. Zamal. Stick with her and listen to what she says. Her reasons aren't ours, but she wants Khan dead as much as we do."

With Patty Krause leading the procession, all seven people sitting or standing around the table walked toward the door. John held the gym bag in one hand, and with the other, slung the garment bag over his shoulder. Noticing the red box tucked under Sergeant Banta's arm, he whispered to Farrell, "I suppose it's too late to negotiate a regulated disappearance."

"That was never an option for you John. In fact, before you detonate, you should probably put yourself in the middle of the Citadel as close to the basement as possible. That'll increase your chances of a quick death."

John became quiet and followed the others out, grasping the certainty of his fate.

CHAPTER TWENTY

Eighty-eight minutes had passed since Farrell and Daley had returned to the long, narrow conference room under the Pentagon. Stage 2-C of CRUSO Mission No. 003 had commenced.

An hour earlier, Captain Robert Walters from the Coast Guard Station at Manasquan Inlet had driven to 146 River Road in Brielle to inform Maureen Covello stormy seas and high winds had forced his cutters and choppers to suspend their search for her husband. They would redouble their efforts with additional ships and aircraft as soon as the torrential rain and 50 knot winds subsided.

Farrell placed the phone back in its cradle. "As John expected, she's taking it hard."

Daley rocked in his plush leather chair. "I'm not surprised."

"Maureen's in shock. Her older daughter, too. The poor child was called home from her summer job, and when she heard why two police cars were parked in her driveway, she went hysterical. The younger girl, Christie, still doesn't believe he's gone. She's convinced herself he's coming home."

"Denial's a common response in children."

"I kept my promise to him."

"Which one?"

"Doing my best to make sure his wife and kids don't fall apart. Lieutenant Hawley agreed to put on a Coast Guard uniform and keep vigil with Maureen for as long as she needs his support."

"Covello's family will get through this. When Dr. Chandler tells Maureen about John's cancer, she may even realize his death at sea was better than what was about to come."

As much as the colonel's candor irritated her, he was right.

Daley rubbed his eyes. "Any word from Crescent Moon?"

"It's one in the morning there. I doubt we'll hear anything for at least six hours."

"Not unless she sneaks out of the Citadel."

"Won't happen, not with Khan's watchdogs around." Farrell picked up a one-page printout Stacy Miller had handed her when they returned to the Pentagon. "Looks like Chandler's eager to get paid."

"What's that you've got?"

"A Priority 4 update. Chandler called in at 1230 hours to give us his bank's wire instructions."

"Guess no one trusts us, referral agent or candidate."

"Stacy read in Chandler's tone a strong effort not to sound greedy."

"Two million's a substantial sum."

"Should I have Stacy call him, remind him of CRUSO's compensation guidelines?"

"I'd prefer you make the call yourself. He might breathe easier if one of CRUSO's top people called him directly."

"Very well, sir."

"While you're at it, thank him for coming through with a viable candidate on such short notice."

Since its inception, CRUSO had developed candidate referral relationships with 322 physicians in 42 states—mostly oncologists and cardiologists, and a smattering of GP's. After President Lloyd had moved Farrell into her job as Daley's assistant, she hop-scotched the country, personally meeting half of CRUSO's referral agents.

CRUSO sorted its referral agents into Categories A, B, and C. Two factors determined category—the duration of the physician's relationship with CRUSO, and the size of the doctor's practice. Physicians affiliated with CRUSO longest, and those offering the greatest number of potential mission candidates, earned Category A status. They were contacted first when CRUSO needed a mission operative.

The specifics of a mission's objective were never revealed to CRUSO's referral agents, nor were referral agents informed of the full scope of CRUSO's affiliation with the NSA. They did know the candidate chosen by CRUSO would train to participate in a high-risk military operation likely to result in the candidate's death.

Payments to referral agents came with the same strings attached as payments to candidates. If a candidate completed his or her mission objective, the referral agent received the full compensation agreed upon. If the candidate failed, the agent received a lesser amount, usually half.

Last September, Dr. Robert Chandler, a general practitioner, had been added to CRUSO's Category C list. Farrell hadn't had a chance to meet with him personally, and now wished she had made the time.

Daley stopped rocking. "By the way, when you do call Chandler, remind him he still owes us a copy of his Villanova transcript."

"Will do. That reminds me, I put in a call to Agent Marshall at the FBI. She promised they'd work all night to deliver complete 3-C's Reports on John and Chandler sometime tomorrow."

"Good work, Major."

CRUSO did not pay its referral agents or the families of mission candidates until comprehensive Career, Character, and Cash Reports had been compiled on both the referral agent and the mission operative. A nearly non-existent preparation period for Mission 003 had prevented CRUSO from bringing Chandler's 3-C's Report current and assembling a full report on John. However, completed 3-C's Reports on Patty Krause and her referral agent had been received and reviewed late yesterday.

Farrell recalled the barbed exchange between John and Daley two hours earlier. In his heart, the colonel was a gentleman, and she wished he and John had parted on friendlier terms.

Daley must have been reading her mind. He said, "John's an OK guy, but he's too damn blunt."

"Remind you of anyone?"

The colonel chuckled.

"You could have gone easier on him. He's under incredible stress."

"If he doesn't curb his tongue, he could find himself dead long before Wednesday."

"Put yourself in his shoes. Less than 24 hours ago he finds out, on top of all his money woes, he has pancreatic cancer and four months to live. This morning he's whisked off the street, hustled to a military base, and given the opportunity to earn a fortune for his wife and kids, but only if he leaves everything behind, that day, and travels to a foreign land where he's expected to blow himself up along with a crazed dictator. That's a lot to handle."

Daley snatched a blank sheet of paper off the table. "I'm not stupid, Denise, and I'm not cruel. This mission isn't like the others. Failure here assures nuclear war and thirty million dead. That's for starters. If China, Russia, and America get involved, no one honestly knows where a war like that will lead."

Her boss was right about the implications of failure. A lot more was riding on this mission than genetically altered marijuana or Russian underworld profits. If Khan weren't killed and President Razzak and his moderate policies restored, America was certain to butt heads with another major power somewhere in South Asia.

So much could undermine Mission 003 beside John shooting off his mouth, but maybe Daley was mistaken about him. True, he had a brazen streak a mile wide, but Farrell had a hunch he knew when to stop. Watching the colonel tear another white sheet down the middle, she said, "Don't worry, he'll handle himself better than you think."

"So long as he doesn't do something stupid."

"Like what?"

"Like hit on Dr. Zamal."

CHAPTER TWENTY-ONE

John's right ear popped as the ST-131 lifted to a cruising altitude of 42,000 feet. A few minutes off the ground, when his inner ear adjusted to the jet's elevation, a series of long sharp cramps roped his belly before settling into a dull throbbing.

The jet's passenger compartment was small, as the prototype transport flying John to Bahrain was designed to carry guns and bombs, not the men and women who might die using them. He had opted for a sixth row window seat, four rows from the back.

John figured he should do something useful, like read Advanced Medical System's glossy brochure to learn more about what a hospital systems consultant did for a living, or one of the CIA reports on Pakistan Sergeant Banta had handed him after they boarded. But right now he felt like closing his eyes, so that was what he did.

He had been impressed by the president's words of encouragement, though he found it ironic how the same government—a mere 12 hours earlier so eager to levy on his house for back taxes—was now prepared to pay his family $10,000,000 for destroying a single building. The difficult circumstances of no time, little information, and uncertain assistance made success nearly impossible, but hearing the president express support for the mission had actually gotten him pumped.

One point the president had made clear. The consequences of failure extended well beyond keeping Maureen, Karen, and Christie saddled with debt. Left to live, the target of John's mission would propel the subcontinent into a nuclear war killing millions. Sacrificing his life, already abbreviated by cancer, to secure his family's future was motivation enough to accept CRUSO's offer. That he might save entire countries from blowing themselves into nuclear wastelands offered another incentive to do the job right.

John recalled the blueprint of Khan's Citadel. The close proximity of nearby buildings—the school across the street and the hospital next door—gave John one more reason to do his best work. On the morning he died, Billy Dwyer was watching the implosion from 850 feet away, and as poorly as Joe Vreeland had prepped the Demarest projects, the negligent sub had taken rudimentary precautions. Even then an innocent bystander had died.

If he could demolish Khan's Citadel, killing only the warmongers America was paying him to kill, somehow Billy Dwyer might forgive him. Only a few government bureaucrats would know of his personal sacrifice, but he would know and God would know, and in the end they were all who mattered.

Noticing his thoughts getting grimmer by the minute, he opened his eyes and picked up a spiral-bound CIA booklet entitled "Pakistan: Customs and Etiquette." The report's introduction contained a litany of factoids about Pakistan's geography, government, and economy. He was relieved to learn that while Urdu was Pakistan's official language, English was widely spoken within the government, as well as in most medical and educational institutions.

He paid particular attention to the section on "Women of Pakistan." He was amazed that even in the 21st Century a typical Pakistani woman could expect to marry by the time she turned 14—a year older than his younger daughter—and carry nine pregnancies to full term.

Major Farrell was right. According to the CIA pamphlet, taking photographs of women you didn't know well was more than impolite. Snap a photo of a Pakistani girl, and you could find yourself in a duel with your subject's male relatives, and men in Pakistan packed guns as routinely as New York lawyers carried PDA's. Foreign men especially were warned to steer clear of Pakistani women.

The more John read about Pakistan, the more he likened it to America's Wild West. Visitors to the countryside risked getting caught in armed clashes between feuding tribal factions and warring bands of smugglers. Carjackings and abductions were constant threats in Pakistan's tribal areas, which generally meant any place not in the downtown district of a major city. Americans were particularly attractive targets, and excursions to the country's rural sections, especially the rugged North-West Frontier Province, required a travel permit from the Home and Tribal Affairs Department. A condition of issuance often included hiring an armed escort.

Fortunately his mission did not require he leave Islamabad, which the brochure described as a modern city even by Western standards. Good thing, too. He'd never survive the hazards of Pakistan's countryside, whether dodging gun-toting thieves starved for US dollars, or evading Islamic terrorists out to kill Uncle Sam's home boys.

He grew tired of reading. Glancing behind him, he saw Patty Krause sitting across the aisle three rows back gazing out the window. In the cabin's front row, her escort was flirting with Lieutenant Hall and Sergeant Banta.

John shut his eyes and fell into a deep sleep. He didn't stir again until he was awakened by a sharp stinging in his right ear. They had begun their decent to Bahrain.

Earlier in the flight Lieutenant Hall had explained the nation of Bahrain was an island in the Persian Gulf 10 miles wide by 30 miles long. From a 22-acre base leased by the US government, the United States Central Command orchestrated battle carrier group components of the Navy's Fifth Fleet.

John peered through the porthole. The city's street lights formed a crisscrossing pattern not unlike those on approach to Newark. Back in Washington, Major Farrell had said they'd land in Bahrain at 2:15 a.m. A quick check of John's watch proved she'd hit the mark.

The ST-131 bumped the runway twice and rolled to an abrupt stop. John rose, stretched, and looked back at Patty. The gray-haired lady had been rejoined by her female escort. Both got up and walked toward the cockpit. Passing John, Ms. Krause smiled and whispered, "Good luck."

John nodded and watched the frail woman shimmy up the aisle. Staring at her back as she stepped out the door, he shoved the white folder and glossy AMS brochure into his gym bag.

A voice barked from behind. "Let's move."

John turned to see Sergeant Banta approach. For someone who'd spent five hours wedged in a plane seat, he looked sharp in his navy blue blazer. "I'm ready to rock."

The Sergeant snapped, "What's your name?"

No mental lapses for John, not when his life depended on it. "John Cattano, hospital systems consultant for Advanced Medical Systems."

The sergeant grinned his approval.

John extracted his garment bag from an overhead storage compartment, grabbed his gym bag and followed the sergeant out the door.

Seconds after John's foot touched the tarmac, the sleek supersonic jet rolled toward a brightly-lit hanger on the opposite side of the runway.

The lieutenant, the sergeant, and John climbed into an open jeep driven by a grim-faced soldier wearing desert fatigues. The jeep peeled off the tarmac between two large concrete buildings and swerved onto a wide asphalt avenue lined with one and two-story shops.

They raced past the base's commissary, careened down a long, dark alley, and emerged onto another asphalt plane that stretched far into the night. Directly ahead, John spotted a helicopter, rotors spinning, ready for takeoff.

John glanced at his watch: 2:20 a.m. Twenty-five minutes to reach the overseas departures terminal at Bahrain International Airport and board PIA Flight 486.

They all boarded the helicopter, Lieutenant Hall last. As he slid the door closed, the chopper lifted off and banked sharply right.

Once in the air, no one said a word. Five minutes later, a parallel line of twinkling white lights converging at the horizon came into view. The chopper swerved away from the runway, flew over what looked at night like a passenger terminal, and landed at the deserted end of a vast unlit parking lot.

They jumped from the helicopter, which immediately flew off. Lieutenant Hall and Sergeant Banta walked briskly toward two yellow taxi cabs parked end-to-end at the fenced edge of the immense lot. Lugging his gym bag, John had to trot, at times run, just to keep pace with the soldiers in suits.

He gulped in the hot, arid air. "Why didn't we land closer to the terminal?"

Lieutenant Hall replied, "Seventy-five people know CRUSO exists. Until this mission, when India's prime minister was informed, none included a foreign head of state. The government of Bahrain has no idea what we're doing tonight, which means we pull up to the departure gate the same way as any tourist—in a taxi."

"What about the drivers?"

"For delivering three Americans to the terminal—us in one cab, you in the other—no questions asked, they get a thousand bucks each."

"Is there anybody you guys can't buy?"

"Not to my knowledge."

"America's tax dollars hard at work."

"Don't forget, tensions are high in South Asia and the Persian Gulf. Once you're inside the terminal, stay cool, show respect, and when you reach the boarding gate, do whatever security asks. You'll have no problem catching your flight."

Three minutes later John's cabbie dropped him off at the Departures Level of a spacious lobby adorned with abstract paintings, modern sculptures, and a dozen soldiers in desert fatigues clutching big, black semi-automatic rifles.

John got onto one of three lines queuing up to check-in counters, all equipped with walk-through metal detectors. He noticed Hall and Banta waiting on the line to his right, about five spots ahead. At the front of their line, a security officer was hassling a lanky black man about his carry-on luggage. John's line moved quickly, and he reached the transfer counter at the same time Hall and Banta walked through the gray portal on their line.

John glanced at his watch: 2:37 p.m. As if on cue, a man's voice echoed over the loudspeaker, first in Arabic, then in English, "Final call for PIA Flight 486 to Islamabad. Boarding at Gate 17."

He handed his passport, visa, plane ticket, and phony driver's license to a dark-skinned man wearing a blue jacket with a badge pinned to the pocket. The man scrutinized John, stamped his papers, and handed them back. John dropped his gym bag and garment bag onto an X-ray machine conveyor belt, then handed his watch to the transfer agent. Patting his pockets to make sure they held nothing metal, John walked through the metal detector.

Harsh buzzing pierced his ears, and instantly, two armed soldiers blocked his path. Beyond the portals, in the transfer lounge, he noticed Lieutenant Hall and Sergeant Banta stop and turn.

Two clearance officers sprinted over and, along with the soldiers, ushered John to a table in the corridor leading to the departure gate.

The taller of the two officers was a middle-aged man with short black hair. He addressed John through a light Middle Eastern accent. "What is your business in Pakistan?"

"I work for Advanced Medical Systems, a consulting company in America. I'm meeting with a doctor in Islamabad to market my company's software."

"What kind of software?"

"The kind that helps with patient indexing and clinical billing."

The officer squinted warily. "What is clinical billing?"

That wasn't what he'd meant to say. "Billing by clinicians for patient treatment."

"Empty your pockets. Everything on the table."

John pulled from his pants pocket the wallet holding John Cattano's business cards, drivers license, VISA card, and $5,000 in Pakistan rupees. He dug into his other pocket and fished out the aspirin container and Christie's toy Harley—the one made of metal.

The second officer, who wore a white turban and a thick black beard, picked up the plastic aspirin bottle, popped the cap, and shook out a single caplet. He rolled the clear casing filled with light blue powder between his fingertips, studying it like a diamond. "What are these used for?"

"Curing whatever ails you."

The turbaned officer gave John a dirty look. The taller officer continued, "Where in Islamabad do you intend to sell your software?"

Hoping Farrell had reestablished contact with Crescent Moon, John went for broke. "Perhaps you've heard of Dr. Salena Zamal."

The eyes of both officers opened wide.

"Apparently you have, so you probably know she works at Pakistan National Hospital—General Khan's hospital. I was introduced to her at a conference in New York City. She invited me to bid on a hospital administration software package. In fact, I'm scheduled to meet with her this morning at eleven-thirty."

The two officers stepped back and spoke to each other in Arabic. John glanced down the corridor to the boarding gate and saw Hall and Banta had disappeared. He checked his watch. In four minutes Flight 486 would depart without him.

The taller officer stepped forward. "Show me proof of your meeting."

The AMS brochure wouldn't link him directly to Dr. Zamal, but it did provide evidence of his job as a hospital management software consultant. John reached for his gym bag. "No problem, I've got something in here."

The bearded officer slapped John's hand away. "I will open it."

"Suit yourself."

The officer extracted two polo shirts, a pair of trousers, and the glossy AMS folder. The other officer grabbed the brochure from his colleague, opened it, and pulled a single page from the left sleeve.

"If you're interested in learning more about hospital administration software, I'd be happy to come back another day, but if I don't board that plane in the next three minutes, I'll need to take down your names and badge numbers."

Studying the paper he'd pulled from the blue folder, the tall man grunted and said, "This doesn't prove any—"

"What is this?" The bearded officer was holding the plain white folder.

John remembered the white folder held Dr. Zamal's photograph, but he was sure he had left it on the plane. He had to answer with something, anything, and spat out the first words that came to mind. "My wife. Isn't she pretty?"

"You are a liar. This is General Khan's woman."

"Oh yeah, you're right. I left my wife's picture at home."

The bearded officer grabbed John's collar. "You infidel, why you take picture of Ali Khan's lady?"

John shoved the turbaned man away. "Back off, buddy." He stepped toward the officer ready to push him again, but the cocking of rifles stopped him cold.

Damn. Farrell had warned him about pictures of Muslim women. He had to think fast. "I snapped her photograph in New York to remember what she looked like. Call her yourself, she gave me permission."

"I give no shit for her permission. Did General Khan approve?"

What was it with these people? A woman couldn't wipe her own ass without a man's OK. "Dr. Zamal said the general allowed photos, but for business purposes only."

"With no dupatta?"

"No what?

"Veil, her veil."

"What can I say? That's what she wore at the conference."

The taller officer pulled the white-turbaned man aside and they began whispering in Arabic. The two soldiers in desert fatigues held their rifles pointed at John's chest.

John checked his watch. Two minutes more and his mission was over. The taller officer came forward and handed John the blue AMS folder. "If the hour were not so late, I would call Islamabad myself."

John hastily crammed the brochure and his clothes back into the gym bag, and stuffed in his pockets all the items he'd been told to remove. "My photograph please."

"That I am keeping."

"What for?"

"To show the Director of Clearance when he arrives. He has friends in the Citadel."

"I'd really like the picture."

"For what purpose?"

"To remember what the doctor looks like?"

The officer leaned down and whispered in John's ear, "If you forget a face like hers, you are no man at all."

True enough. "But Dr. Zamal will ask for it back."

"If your story checks out, we shall mail it ourselves."

This round he wasn't about to win. "You guys sure have some strict rules."

For the first time, the tall officer grinned. "If you think we are difficult here, wait until you get to Pakistan."

Lugging his bags, John ran all the way from the transfer counter to Gate 17, struggling to ignore the intense pain ripping through his belly.

Chapter Twenty-Two

M ajor Farrell had slept less than two hours in the last 48, and her eyes had begun to sting. From her backpack under the conference table in AMOC-CRUSO, she dug out a small bottle of wetting drops, squirted her eyes with the soothing liquid, and lightly closed her lids.

She heard Colonel Daley say good-bye to President Lloyd and hang up the phone.

When Farrell opened her eyes she saw her boss scraping his hand across the conference table, shoveling his latest pile of shredded paper into a waste basket he'd lifted to the table's edge. His housekeeping chores complete, Daley looked across at her. "The president suggested if we can't reestablish contact with Crescent Moon by 1:00 p.m., Pakistan time, we assign Lieutenant Hall and Sergeant Banta the task of bringing her and John together."

"That's cutting it awfully close to Behari's deadline."

"It also increases the chances Lieutenant Hall and Sergeant Banta compromise their cover."

"I suppose if by then the doctor and John haven't met, there's little to lose by letting Hall and Banta try."

"Exactly the president's reasoning." Colonel Daley stood and rubbed his eyes. "What's our assessment of Ajay Agarwal?"

Thirty minutes earlier, the State Department had briefed Farrell on Prime Minister Behari's special envoy. "Mr. Agarwal was born and raised in Calcutta. He's Behari's principal confidante, and unfortunately, a member of Shiv Sena."

"Shiv Sena?"

"A fundamentalist Hindu party."

"I gather temperance isn't his strongest suit."

"No, and worse than that, Behari won't take a breath unless Agarwal gives him the nod. The State Department believes Agarwal views his trip to Washington as a waste of India's time and money. If the decision were his, Islamabad would already be toast. He said straight out to Ambassador Carlin he believes the American operation simply gives Khan more time to organize his regiments along the Line of Control."

"How soon before this bozo arrives?"

Farrell had a gut feeling Daley and Agarwal weren't likely to make fast friends. "Mr. Agarwal lands at Andrews in six hours and ten minutes. He'll be here by four-thirty tomorrow morning."

The colonel sighed. "That's 90 minutes before Behari's deadline. We'd better get in touch with Zamal long before then. What's the latest from the Diagnostics Lab?"

"Same as before. They've exhausted all seven IRC protocols, and tunneled each of 16 secondary backbones. Every gate's closed. Signal and satellite, no difference. They've tried coaxial, fiber, and cable. It's as if her computer disappeared."

"What about the tech-heads at ARPA?"

"Stan Mueller's looked at everything from WAN signal distortion to a TCP/IP tunnel encryption error, and keeps coming up empty."

"So what's the problem?"

"He says there's a good chance her station's dead. Someone could've kicked the cable connector loose from her terminal, or maybe ..."

"Maybe what?"

"Someone pulled it."

To secure communications with Crescent Moon, CRUSO had connected her to the NSA's virtual private network employing a combination of tunneling, encryption, authentication, and access control. Five levels of passwords permitted entry to verified tunnel users, and CRUSO's VPN used an encapsulated security payload whereby the entire Internet Protocol packet was encrypted.

The government was constantly testing new measures for reducing security risks to data and e-mail transmissions, including physical protection, firewalls, hardened operating systems, access control, authentication, and encryption. Still it seemed to Farrell every time she was briefed on a new method for limiting access to CRUSO's private network, some 15 year old hacker found access through a back door.

This time, Stan Mueller was sure all indications pointed to a problem other than illegal entry. CRUSO's network intrusion detection system for monitoring network traffic had detected nothing, meaning the problem could only have occurred on Dr. Zamal's end.

Deep in thought, Daley paced to the head of the long conference room, then back to his chair. "There must be some way to reach Zamal without relying on the VPN."

Farrell mulled the options. With the government's wealth of expertise, figuring out a way to inform Dr. Zamal of John's impending arrival shouldn't be so difficult. The more she dwelled on that last thought, the more she realized getting a message to Crescent Moon needn't be difficult at all. "I have an idea, and I'm sure it'll work."

"Great, I'll have Stacy ring up the Diagnostics Lab."

"That won't be necessary."

"You're good, Denise, but you're no IT expert."

"Sir, for this solution, I won't need Stan. But I will need a Yellow Pages."

CHAPTER TWENTY-THREE

Salena clutched her silk veil beneath her chin, and slowly opened the door to her room. Leaving behind the scent of jasmine lingering from the night before, she stepped quietly into the carpeted hall of the Citadel, and rode the elevator down to the 4th floor. At the checkpoint near the skywalk entrance, a guard standing at the counter asked her a few routine questions, then allowed her to cross into the hospital.

Her first priority this morning was to contact Major Farrell to find out when the American suicide agent was arriving. She did not wish to appear overly eager to get to her office, so she bypassed the main elevators that would take her to the Maternity Unit, and headed straight to the children in the Freedom Ward.

Taahir's enlarged heart did not stop him from running to greet Salena with a warm hug. Relieved to see Fawaz, her hepatitis patient, sitting up in his cot smiling, she thought about changing his medication to Valaxin, a new drug from SciClone recently approved in India to treat Hepatits B.

Mulling her options, she heard a child scream. She snapped her head toward a small, crayon-scored table between two cots and ran over to find Jamaal arguing with his twin brother Jameel about who had drawn the scarier soldier. She settled their squabble by heaping praise on both, and admonished them to love, not fight one another. Her mediation a success, she walked to the far corner of the storage room, where she found Kalila lying on the edge of her cot, crying.

Kalila's shoulders shuddered as she sobbed, and she kept staring at the white linoleum floor even though Salena stood directly beside her.

"What, no hug today?"

The child shook her head without looking up.

"But I miss your hug."

Kalila silently rose, wrapped her arms around Salena, and buried her face in Salena's long dress.

"What is troubling my pretty young lady?"

"Mummy will like you."

It broke her heart whenever Kalila spoke of her parents as though they might return. "I would have liked her, too."

"And Poppy will think you are nice."

"To bring a sweet girl like you into the world, they must have been wonderful people."

"Do you think they will come for me soon?"

Salena always reminded Kalila in the gentlest possible way. "They are with Allah now, and yes, you will see them again, but not for a very long time. You must first live many years, and then, after you are called home to the One True God, you will see them again."

"Why must I wait so long?"

Salena peeled Kalila's arms off her waist and dropped to one knee. She stroked the girl's long black hair. "Mummy and poppy watch over you from heaven. They wish only that you live a happy life."

"But if they are gone, how can I be happy?"

Salena thought of Naji, alone in Srinagar. "I will find another family to raise you, not to take the place of mummy and poppy, but to give you a happy life until you grow into a woman."

"Where will you find these people?"

"I do not know yet, but I promise with all my heart I will find you a good home."

Salena had never broken a promise, especially to a child, and she would not start now. After helping the American martyr rid Pakistan of its tyrant, she would find a loving family to adopt Kalila. She might even adopt Kalila herself.

She bid reluctant good-byes to her children and left. Hoping to avoid another confrontation with Khan's favorite goon, she decided she would take the stairs instead of the elevator up to the 5th floor.

Walking toward the stairwell at the end of the Pediatric Unit's main corridor, she passed Room 412, where Raja went to escape Qadeer's bugs and wiretaps. The door was closed and lights out. That wasn't like Raja, always an early riser. Qadeer's thugs must have hurt him badly. All the more reason to help America destroy Ali Khan and the puppets who kept him in power.

She climbed one flight and headed down a long hall, its tiled floor glistening from an early morning polish. In Washington, DC the time was 12:30 a.m., but the courteous black lady from the US government had told Salena she could contact her any time, day or night.

Salena's heart skipped a beat as she said good morning to three nurses hovering over patient charts at the nurses station in the Maternity Unit. They greeted her politely, but she had the odd feeling they were watching her back as she continued down the hall.

She came to her office and walked inside.

Her computer was gone.

Scanning under and behind her desk, she saw nothing but limp cables coiled on the floor. Her files were gone, too. One at a time, she yanked open her desk drawers to find out what else was missing.

"Looking for these?"

Her head shot up to find Captain Qadeer in his bright red turban watching her from the doorway. He held three manila folders.

"Why did you take my computer?"

He answered with a smug grin. "I think you know."

He couldn't know or she'd already be dead. "My computer is not broken and does not require an upgrade."

Qadeer sauntered closer and dropped the folders on the desk. "You can have these back."

"I need my computer."

"I will return it soon."

"I need it now."

"Why so anxious?"

"I have drug dosages and timetables stored on my hard drive."

"No paper backup?"

"Perhaps I can save you time. What are you looking for?"

Qadeer stroked his stubbled chin. "Your behavior last night was unusual. I intend to find the real reason you were checking the weather in Muzaffarabad. Perhaps you are planning a trip to Srinagar."

Her only chance was to invoke the name of Khan. "Do not forget, after I wed your general, you will answer to me."

"Stop your fretting. The more you whine, the more reason you give me to doubt your intentions." Qadeer pulled a Red Lamp cigarette from his baggy trousers and pointed it at the files on Salena's desk. "Anyway, if your computer proves as clean as those, you have nothing to fear."

He was probably right, complaining only made her appear guilty. "When will it be returned?"

"A complete inspection requires two or three days."

"That is too long."

"Make do with paper files." Qadeer struck a match and held its flame to the tip of the cigarette, igniting the shredded brown tobacco into hot orange light. He clutched the burning matchstick between his fingers, and looked down at the waste basket.

Salena clenched her teeth, and when their eyes met, the captain paused. Smirking, he raised the match to his lips and blew out the flame, then tossed the smoking stick into the pail. "If I discover you were planning an escape, your kind master will beat you senseless, then turn you over to me."

The thought of Qadeer let loose upon her sent shivers down her spine. Major Farrell had assured her the encrypted communications program linking their computers was so deeply embedded in Salena's

Excel data files, an army of analysts would need weeks to unravel the code. She glared at Qadeer. "And when you find nothing, you shall pay for your disrespect."

The captain's grin broadened into a wide smile revealing twin tracks of yellow teeth. "I doubt you will break as easily as Dr. Raja."

"Is that why he is not in his office?"

"Let me say it this way … he needs the day to recuperate."

She checked her Pathan urge to claw the flesh from his grubby face. "Get out."

In front of her desk Qadeer stood his ground and glared at her. She stared back defiantly, refusing to blink, until finally he curled his lips into a sneer, turned, and left her office.

Qadeer was gone, but not his stench. That was all he had left her, and nothing more. No relief from his scrutiny, no hope for her friend Raja, and no way to contact Major Farrell. She had no idea what the American assassin looked like or when he might arrive. For all she knew, he was on his way this very moment.

CHAPTER TWENTY-FOUR

Braced for a grueling interrogation and full body search, John Covello was surprised when clearing customs at Islamabad International Airport entailed nothing more than having his passport and visa stamped. The customs clerk ignored his carry-on bags, and didn't even ask why he had come to Pakistan. John speculated the security officers in Bahrain had decided not to contact the Pakistan authorities to verify his story about Dr. Zamal's photo.

Even the taxi ride from the airport to downtown Islamabad was uneventful. If anything, John found the trip fascinating. On the ST-131, he had perused the CIA's fact sheet on Rawalpindi and Islamabad, and had been lectured at length about both by Sergeant Banta, who had been to Pakistan twice before.

Referred to in most travel guides as twin cities, Rawalpindi and Islamabad had little in common, either in age or appearance. Islamabad, Pakistan's federal capital built in the 1960's, had no bustling downtown district. Instead, the city was laid out in an expansive and carefully planned grid apportioned into distinct sectors for administrative, educational, commercial, residential, recreational, and industrial use.

Located against the backdrop of the Margalla Hills at the northern edge of the Potohar Plateau, Islamabad's design included lush open spaces and wide tree-lined streets uncluttered by traffic jams or harried pedestrians. Neat rows of jacaranda and hibiscus trees shaded wide pedestrian promenades lined with colorful splashes of red roses, white jasmine, and purple bougainvillea.

By contrast, Rawalpindi, known to the locals as Pindi, exemplified the classic South Asian city—sprawling, congested, and chaotic—with 400-year-old bazaars, streets bustling with shoppers, and taxis competing with auto-rickshaws and horse-drawn tongas for road space and fares. Crumbling concrete storefronts leaned precariously over narrow streets filled with streaming masses of humanity, and the pungent aroma of spiced karahis, kebabs, and tikkas fried and grilled in open-air restaurants clashed with the stench of rotting garbage piled high in 10 foot heaps at the ends of slim shadowed alleys.

The cab driver, a dark-faced man in his mid-30's with large brown eyes, spoke fluent English through a mild Indian accent. He asked John a myriad of questions about his life in America—where he lived, what school he attended, how many children he had fathered, and what sort of job he held. He also probed John about his ancestry and asked why his great-grandparents had left Italy to start a new life in a foreign land.

He also spoke about Pakistan. He talked earnestly, and at times, eloquently, about his nation's push for economic self-sufficiency, and how Islamabad's symmetry and precision exemplified that impetus. He explained to John that Pakistan's founders had decided the new federal capital should be located far from the politically powerful business interests in Karachi. Yet to remain accessible from the south and west, the site could not be far from existing road and rail links to Pakistan's major cities. The northern reaches of the Punjab, close to the North-West Frontier Province, proved ideal.

Perhaps the deciding factor in choosing where to build the new capital was the area's proximity to Pakistan's Islamic neighbors in Central Asia and the Middle East, countries such as Iran, Afghanistan, Saudi Arabia, and Turkey. "That is why," the driver added, "they named the city Islamabad."

When the impassioned young man broached the subject of international politics and his country's relationship with America, he sounded genuinely hurt, as if America had turned its back on Pakistan in favor of India—even after Pakistan had cooperated with the American government during its war on terrorism. Preferring to avoid an argument, John responded with nods and one-word answers.

The taxi driver told John they were headed northeast on Murree Road, the main thoroughfare linking Rawalpindi to Islamabad, and had reached the halfway point to the Rawal Regency Inn. He pointed to a concrete structure coming up on the left, a wall three stories high surrounded by an asphalt parking lot. "The cricket games, they will return in September."

John did not instantly recognize the structure ahead as a sports stadium. What threw him were the two 20-foot high parallel rows of chain link fencing topped with razor wire coils encircling the arena. He'd never seen such harsh security, even at Giants Stadium when last season his beloved Big Blue had squared off against the Jets in the Super Bowl. "What's it used for now?"

"Some Pakistanis have resisted the changes of General Khan. Here is where they pay the price."

"You mean they get thrown to the lions?"

"Not exactly."

"Seriously, is this where he keeps them prisoner?"

"Only for a week or two, until they name other traitors."

"Then he frees them?"

"Then he executes them."

"And this is a good thing?"

The driver's eyes darted left and right, then up at the rear view mirror. "Myself, I hate the killing. Most Pakistanis wish Ali Khan would not kill so much."

"Why do your people tolerate him?"

"Why does any country teeming with poor tolerate a strong leader with an iron fist?"

"Yeah, and look what happened to Hitler, Mussolini, and Saddam Hussein."

The young man did not answer, and instead turned on the radio. Spying a digital clock on the dashboard, John adjusted his watch to Pakistan time: 10:23 a.m.

The music blaring from the cab's dashboard reminded John of a movie he had once chanced upon while surfing his TV's highest channels, a show where voluptuous, brown-eyed women wearing long silk veils, whose wrists dripped bangles and bracelets, danced and smiled, laughed and cried, and always sang in high-pitched wails.

They came to a major intersection crammed with cars, buses, and taxis, and for the first time since he'd landed, John spotted military vehicles—a procession of gun-mounted jeeps and green armored vehicles weaving through the traffic.

As the taxi squeezed through the intersection, John counted half a dozen near collisions. The driver informed him the intersection was called Faisabad, and marked the end of Rawalpindi and the start of Islamabad. As he finished his sentence, the young man calmly swerved left at the last second to avoid the bumper of a double-decker bus painted fire engine red.

John's heart leapt to his mouth, but the driver hardly seemed fazed.

He pointed out the window. "Those are the Margalla Hills."

That the driver referred to the peaks looming in the distance as mere hills struck John funny. The green carpeted mountains rising from the edge of the city must have reached over 4,000 feet. Sharp gullies and deep ravines lacerated their steep slopes, and by Adirondack standards, their summits appeared jagged and new.

On the left they passed a golf course, on the right, a large lake glistening blue. What impressed John most about Islamabad was the abundance of green. The white concrete buildings—streamlined, symmetrical, and spaced far apart—rarely exceeded three stories, and nearly all were surrounded by meticulously manicured trees, shrubs, and lawns.

They pulled into a circular driveway leading up to the front entrance of the tallest building John had seen so far, the 15-story Rawal Regency Inn.

John got out and handed 3,000 rupees to the young taxi driver. "Thanks for the ride."

The driver counted the bills and smiled. "Have a pleasant stay, and may what you learn in Pakistan surprise you."

John couldn't imagine learning anything in a country where people were thrown in prison and murdered for backing the wrong candidate.

Lieutenant Hall had described The Rawal Regency as a four-star hotel, and when John walked into an elegant lobby with high ceilings, walnut paneled walls, and marble floors, he understood why. Scanning the lobby's brown leather sofas and rattan chairs, he saw no trace of Hall or Banta. He checked in and rode the elevator to the 7th floor.

His room was spacious, and included a separate bedroom and a small parlor, both furnished in white wicker. The bedroom faced south, and offered a panoramic view of Rawal Lake, and beyond the lake, wooded plains extending far into the distance. Closer to the hotel along the lake's shoreline, John beheld a network of red, white, and yellow gardens connected by broad concrete sidewalks and high-spouting fountains.

All things considered, not an unpleasant place to die.

John had no more time to waste. He splashed his face with water and changed into tan pants and a white golf shirt. In his garment bag CRUSO had packed a brown leather briefcase. John pulled it out and slid the glossy blue AMS folder into the center pocket. Armed with the briefcase and a Nelles tourist map, John rode the elevator down to the lobby.

Outside, under the hotel's canopy, the temperature felt like a hundred. He walked down the driveway, through the main gate, and stopped on the sidewalk to watch the passing pedestrians. Nine out of 10 were men, and nearly all wore baggy white pants with long white tops that resembled nightshirts split up the side. If the temperature didn't feel like August in Miami, John would have thought the garments comfortable. Studying the long sleeved shirts, it dawned on him he was the only person in sight whose arms weren't covered.

Though he could probably walk to Pakistan National Hospital in ten minutes, he felt awkward with bare arms, and decided to flag a taxi.

Scanning the busy street for the next available cab, he noticed a man standing on the sidewalk some 50 yards away wearing the same baggy outfit as everyone else, but this man's face was familiar. It took a few seconds, but John realized he was looking at Sergeant Banta. The instant they made eye contact, Banta turned away.

A yellow taxi came into view and John stepped to the curb. He raised his arm to hail the cab when a green van screeched to a halt directly in front of him.

Before John could move, the van's side door slid open and two brown-faced men in desert fatigues jumped out, grabbed his arms, and dragged him toward the van. The van's front door burst open, and another soldier leapt out, ran behind John, and lifted his legs. The three soldiers carried John head-first to the van's side door.

John dropped his map on the pavement, and clung to his briefcase. From the corner of his eye, in the instant before he lost sight of the sidewalk, John glimpsed Sergeant Banta, wide-eyed and gaping.

The soldiers threw John face-down onto the van's metal floor. One of the men yanked his arms behind his back and pried the briefcase from his fingers. A door slammed shut and metal clicked at his back. His wrists had been cuffed.

John screamed, "What the hell is this! Who are you!"

The van lurched forward, made a sharp, squealing U-turn, and sped off in a straight line.

One of the soldiers rolled John to his side.

He found himself looking at a pudgy man with a thin mustache staring straight ahead.

The first time John had yelled. Now he would reason. "Excuse me, could you tell me who you are and where you're taking me?" He checked his impulse to add something like, *because if I don't get where I have to go in the next four hours, you, me, and all your children will burn to a crisp in a mile-high fireball.*

The man stared straight ahead, as if John hadn't spoken.

"Do you understand English?"

No answer.

"Please, it's important, I'm an American businessman, and I'm here to—"

Without looking down, the soldier rammed the tip of his black boot into the middle of John's gut.

John screamed. The pain was like nothing he'd felt before, as if his stomach had been ripped alive from his belly. After the initial shock passed, throbbing cramps strafed his abdomen.

These men were obviously in no talking mood. Fearing they'd burst his intestines if he tried again, he stayed quiet and prayed for the pain to stop.

CHAPTER TWENTY-FIVE

Salena had come to Khan's penthouse suite determined to find out why Captain Qadeer had confiscated her computer and detained Dr. Raja. Instead she found herself standing at the far end of Khan's dining room table evading Khan's innuendos and subtle accusations. Approaching him had been a mistake, but now she had no choice. "Dr. Raja knows nothing, as I'm sure your precious captain has informed you."

His chin raised high, as if sampling the air, Ghalib Ali Khan stood beside the carved teakwood chair at the head of his splendid rosewood table. "And your precious Dr. Raja—how can you be sure what he knows?"

"He keeps to himself and has nothing to tell."

"I understand he had much to say last night. In fact, the good doctor has cooperated fully with Captain Qadeer."

She wondered if Qadeer had really broken Raja's vow of silence. "If he has told you everything, why have you not punished me?"

"Then you admit your intent."

Khan's obsession with her may have blinded him to the truth. She would test what he knew. "Yes, he continues to give me information about my mother despite the captain's warnings."

Khan's eyes narrowed contemptuously. She took a cautious step backward.

He stormed toward her, stopping inches from her face. In a single, swift motion, he jerked off her veil and grabbed her hair at the nape. "If you persist in lying to me, I shall confine you to your quarters."

"What ... what do you want me to say?"

"The truth. I want the truth."

His breath reeked of a morning meal spiced with garlic and curry. She struggled to turn her head, but he held her fast. Stifling an impulse to cry, she answered, "You ... you already know the truth."

Ali Khan released her hair and frowned. "Yes, I know. I know because 200 volts for 30 seconds forced Dr. Raja to scream the truth. He said you would stop at nothing to return to Srinagar—do anything to visit your mother. He said you planned to leave this very morning. You even checked the bus schedule to Muzaffarabad. How dare you consider traveling to Kashmir after I explicitly forbade such a journey."

Salena bowed her head and inhaled a long, deep breath, praying Khan did not sense her relief. "Yes, kind master, I admit my folly. I did intend to leave against your wishes."

"Had you no thought of the consequences for the little haramzadas you hide at the hospital, or for Dr. Raja, or your cousins in Gilgit?"

"I prayed Allah's mercy would protect them."

"I grow weary of your thirst for Srinagar. After I have conquered Kashmir, my first business shall be the elimination of all that drives you to defy me."

"My mother is already near death. By the time Kashmir falls, she will be gone."

Staring down at the white ceramic tiles, Salena was not prepared for what Khan did next. He grabbed her forearm and drew her close, then planted his hand firmly against her back. Through his flowing white robe she felt his stiff member press against her.

"If Dr. Raja ever again feeds you news from Srinagar, I shall cut out his tongue with my own hand."

"Please, I must inform his staff. When will you allow Dr. Raja to resume his duties?"

He grunted and released her. "Like the doctor's will, his glasses were frail and broke. You shall be pleased to hear I am fitting him for a new pair at my own expense. He shall return to work tomorrow."

"Thank you, kind master."

His gaze lingered on her. "I have 20 minutes more until I meet with General Zeba."

"Then I will leave now, as you require time to prepare."

"I need no further preparation." The look in his eyes torn between passion and reason, Ali Khan grabbed her arm again. "Our wedding cannot happen soon enough. I must have you now."

Bracing for his vulgar caress, she was startled when he shoved her away. "Leave my sight, or I shall sin before Allah."

Happy to obey, she turned and walked slowly toward the stone arch leading from the cavernous dining room. When she reached the arch, she remembered her other reason for coming. She stopped and turned. "May I beg a favor?"

"That depends on your wish."

"I have admitted my transgression. May I now have my computer returned?"

"My precious flower, I intend to indulge the captain's request and allow him to keep it awhile longer."

"What is left to inspect?"

"He recommends a thorough examination of every program on your hard drive, right down to the source code. Mind you, he merely wishes to verify security has not been breached through the Internet."

A lump rose in Salena's throat. She nodded demurely. "As you wish."

Chapter Twenty-Six

J ohn estimated two minutes had elapsed since the three men in desert fatigues had tossed him into the back of the van and sped off. Lying on his side, hands shackled behind his back, John's belly throbbed with pain.

The van made a sharp turn, and an instant later, John's body bounced off the floor. The sunlight shining through the rear window disappeared, and the cargo compartment dimmed. Screeching tires echoed off walls, as if they'd driven into a large chamber—an underground parking garage was John's guess.

The vehicle stopped short and his vision went black as someone behind him pulled a cloth hood over his head, leaving him scant room to breathe. A door unbolted and clicked open. Large hands seized his arms and slid him head-first across the van's floor. His legs dropped to the ground and men on both sides gripped his arms and shoved him along.

After being led a short distance, John was ordered to stop. He heard a mechanical whir—the sound of an approaching elevator. The doors rolled opened and he was yanked aboard. The elevator rose quickly to its destination, where the soldiers pulled him out and tugged him along. They stopped again, and John heard a door swing open. Without a word, he was half lifted and half dragged up a stairway.

They climbed two, maybe three, flights before he heard a second door open. He was walked a considerable distance that included four turns before being shoved through a third door. There they stopped, and all hands released their grips.

John inhaled a strong odor, cleaning solvent, that clashed with a putrid, vaguely familiar odor—the stench of urine.

An arm slid between his upper back and cuffed hands, and held him firmly in place, while another set of hands grabbed and held his knees. He heard the snap of metal, and when he tried to move his feet, they didn't budge. His legs had been cuffed.

A hand rummaged through his left pocket and emptied its contents, then moved to his right for the same purpose. Other hands grasped his forearms and dragged him backward until the backs of his ankles bumped into solid metal. He heard another click, and his hands were free.

Someone shoved him hard against his chest. Falling backward, he braced for a cracked skull, but instead, found himself sitting on a chair with metal armrests. Though his hands were free, he dared not remove the hood.

He didn't have to. Someone grasped the cloth at the top of his head and yanked up hard, stinging his nostrils.

Harsh fluorescent light blinded him. Squinting through the glare, he detected about 10 feet ahead a dark-faced soldier in a tan uniform sitting behind a small table. The man's head was capped by a bright red turban.

Arranged in a neat row across the table's front edge were John's wristwatch, aspirin bottle, toy motorcycle, and soft leather briefcase. Behind his neatly arranged belongings he saw a pack of cigarettes bearing a label he didn't recognize.

John did not recall seeing the red-turbaned soldier during his abduction, but he was clearly in charge of whatever was about to happen. As John's eyes adjusted to the light, he realized the wall behind the seated officer was covered by thick black floor-to-ceiling drapes. He wondered if the drapes hid an exterior window, because from what he could see, the room had no outside view.

To his left John noticed a stainless steel table. On it lay a number of objects he didn't recognize, at least not immediately. One was a thin white tube, about two feet long, with a red handle on one end and a U-shaped prong on the other. John nearly choked on his saliva when he realized the object was an electric cattle prod.

Staring impassively at John, the soldier behind the table reached for his cigarettes. When he lit up, the burning tobacco emitted a foul stench like no cigarette John had smelled.

Grasping the pack, the turbaned officer stood, stepped slowly around the table, and to John's amazement, offered him a cigarette.

He'd been snatched off the street, had his guts kicked in, been blindfolded and dragged up a stairway, and now this guy wanted to be his pal. "No thanks, they might give me cancer."

The dark-faced soldier flashed a yellow-toothed grin. "When your time is up, your time is up."

John glanced at the soldiers to his left and right. "Yeah, and I hope mine's not up today."

The officer took a long drag on his cigarette, and walked closer to John. "My name is Captain Azam Qadeer." His tone was cordial. "What is your business in Pakistan?"

"I heard you have lovely weather and amazing cricket games." John couldn't help but add, "And I thought I might catch a hanging or two."

Qadeer bent over and faced John at eye-level. "We don't hang spies, we chop off their heads."

"All the better, hanging's way too boring."

"Perhaps we have much in common."

John was sure they had nothing in common.

Qadeer flicked his ashes on the floor. "Now why are you here?"

"Because you brought me?"

"I mean why did you come to Islamabad?"

"The bombs. My travel agent said if I came to Pakistan I might get to see nuclear bombs go off. I thought that'd be really neat."

Qadeer looked down at him, shook his head, then turned away. He sauntered to the stainless steel table, picked up the cattle prod, and turned around.

John figured this guy was about to get serious. "You obviously went through everything in my briefcase. Why I'm here should be perfectly clear."

Clutching the two-foot long tube, Qadeer walked back to John. "What is the real reason for your visit?"

John nodded at the small table on which his personal items were neatly laid out. "Do you think I invented that sales brochure and price list? That I'm some sort of secret agent? What's my mission? To stop nuclear war between Pakistan and India?" John chuckled. "I may be lots of things, but I'm no underworld spy."

His face barely a foot from John's, Qadeer drew deeply on his cigarette and brandished the smoldering butt close to John's cheek.

John gripped the seat's metal armrests and fixed his gaze straight ahead. From the corner of his left eye, he saw Qadeer bring the cigarette so close to his ear he heard the sound of sizzling tobacco.

Qadeer moved the cigarette down along John's shoulder and over his bare arm, stopping an inch above the back of his hand gripping the armrest. Qadeer lowered the glowing tobacco toward John's skin.

John screwed his eyes shut and braced for pain.

Nothing happened.

When he opened his eyes he saw Qadeer had snuffed out the butt on the metal armrest less than an inch from his wrist. If John's legs weren't shackled, he'd have kicked this asshole in the balls.

Qadeer backed up, stood erect, and began tapping the U-shaped prong against the palm of his hand. "Why did you choose now to sell your company's software in Pakistan? Unless you are deaf and dumb, you know my country is at war with India."

"Like I had a choice."

"Explain."

"I get paid salary plus commission. My boss tells me to fly to Mars, I fly. He tells me to swim to Atlantis, I swim. He tells me to go to Pakistan, I go. Simple as that. If I sound annoyed, it's because I am. I've got a wife and two kids at home, and right now, this dump's the last place I wanna be."

Qadeer turned and strode to the small square table. He picked up John's briefcase and brandished it like a gun. "Why were you carrying Dr. Zamal's photograph?"

Damn, the security man in Bahrain did follow through on his threat. John had no way of knowing whether CRUSO had reestablished contact with Crescent Moon, but the photo clearly linked him to the young doctor. "I was introduced to Dr. Zamal last February at a medical convention in New York City. You obviously know her, so you also know she's a big shot at Pakistan National Hospital."

"She serves in the hospital at General Khan's will."

"You mean she waits tables in the cafeteria?"

"She is a doctor."

"That's what I thought. Well, I was headed to the hospital to find her …" John nodded at the soldiers standing on either side of him, "… when Tom and Jerry here decided to take me on an unplanned tour of your city."

"Are you saying Dr. Zamal requested your presence in Islamabad?"

"No, I always make cold calls 7,000 miles from home, especially in cities where the State Department warns Americans not to travel. Of course she invited me. I'm here to evaluate the hospital's patient satisfaction gauges, physician endurance, and ventricular reticular systems for data capture and retrieval, then sell her the software that'll do the job best."

"With relations as tense as they are between Pakistan and India, I am surprised you are not frightened."

"I never mix politics and business, and this trip's strictly business."

Qadeer grinned. "You will learn quickly, Mr. Cattano, in Pakistan there is no difference between politics and business." All of Qadeer's facial muscles hardened at once. "Dr. Zamal did not say she was expecting a computer consultant from America."

"Are you her boss?"

"She does nothing without my approval."

John put two-and-two together. "I get it. You work for General Khan, he's marrying Dr. Zamal, and you make sure she doesn't run out on him."

"What does this mean, 'run out on him?'"

John saw nothing to gain by provoking this bully for no reason. "It's an American expression. It means she doesn't run out of love for General Khan and remains eager to obey his every command."

"Yes, in a way that is what I do, but it does not explain why Dr. Zamal failed to inform me of your visit."

"Maybe she's wrapped up in her wedding plans. After all, buying a new computer system is probably the last thing on her mind when she's about to marry a powerful world leader."

"General Khan is indeed powerful."

"Brave, too. In the flip of a switch turning thousands of men, women, and children into charcoal treats." Damn, he'd better learn to control himself.

Too late. Wielding his cattle prod, Qadeer stomped forward and screamed in John's face. "Like all Americans, you are ignorant. You know nothing of the plight of Pakistan and its people. Like fat cows you sit on the other side of the world and pass judgment with no idea of what you speak. You people deserve every misery the jihad has inflicted on America and its interests."

An image of flames licking the top floors of the Twin Towers, and innocent men and women leaping to their deaths came into John's mind. How dare this imbecile imply those people deserved their terrible end. If John made sure of nothing else these next four days, he'd make sure Qadeer was standing right next to Khan when the Citadel collapsed around their heads. For now he must play their game. "Sorry. Just so happens I don't like guns and bombs, especially the kind that wipe out whole cities."

"India would love for us to disappear. They realized half their dream when we lost East Pakistan. General Khan shall avenge our past disgraces."

"Look, Mr. Qadeer—"

"Captain Qadeer."

"Look, sir, I'm only interested in earning a commission so I can afford my monthly mortgage payments. If you wanna turn India into a big bowl of curry, go ahead. Just let me meet the person who's supposed to buy my software."

"I warn you, Mr. Cattano, I shall be watching you closely. You breathe, I know it, you sleep, I know it, you—"

"Yeah, yeah—I fart, and you know that, too."

Qadeer backed up to the small table. It was then John noticed on the floor a pair of wire glasses, their frames crumpled and lenses shattered.

Lifting John's hotel card key from the table, Qadeer said, "I suppose you shall need this." He set the card down and lifted the tiny motorcycle. "What is this?"

"A gift from my daughter ... a good luck charm."

Qadeer studied the miniature Harley up close. "Good luck charm? I think I shall keep it."

"You have no right to—"

"Shut up." Qadeer lifted the cattle prod and twisted a dial on its handle. "You speak only when spoken to." He picked up the small aspirin bottle, scrutinized the label, and pried off the cap. With two fingers he fished inside and pulled out a light blue caplet. "What are these?"

"My cyanide tablets, in case I'm captured and interrogated."

Qadeer's eyes popped open.

"You guys can't take a joke, can you? They're exactly what the bottle says. Aspirin."

"Why do you need aspirin?"

"For the headaches I get when big brown men wearing red turbans chain up my feet and threaten to electrocute me with cattle prods."

Qadeer scowled and held up the bottle. "I think I shall keep them too."

"Suit yourself."

He stuffed the bottle inside his uniform and set the electric prod on the table. Rummaging through John's briefcase, he extracted the blue AMS folder. "I will take this as well."

"I need that brochure for my presentation. Besides, you wouldn't understand what it says."

"Are you calling me stupid?"

"Not really."

Qadeer put down the folder. The big man's eyes spit daggers as he sauntered forward. "You arrogant piece of American shit." He nodded to the mustached thug on John's left. The soldiers flanking him grabbed his arms, pulled him to his feet, and with no warning, Qadeer smashed his fist into John's belly.

John screamed, blinded by exquisite pain. He instinctively tried pulling in his arms to protect his abdomen, but the soldiers held them tight.

Qadeer bellowed with glee. "I hardly hit you." He turned to one of the soldiers. "Do you see what I mean, without their GPS guided bombs, American men are soft. But this one seems softer than most." Qadeer got quiet and his eyes narrowed into a pair of thin slivers scrutinizing John's face. "You are not a faggot, are you? Do you know what we do to faggots in Pakistan? We no longer whip them in public. We tie them up and push stone walls on their heads. If they do not die instantly, we watch them writhe in the rubble until they bleed to death."

John struggled to catch his breath.

Qadeer continued, "Maybe you are not a man? Maybe you are girl."

A wave of nausea rolled up from John's belly and got stuck in his throat. He dropped his head, moaned, and heaved, but nothing came out. When the feeling passed, he lifted his head and groaned, until finally his voice returned. "You're quite a man yourself, hitting me with my hands out of reach of your ugly face. My 13-year-old daughter has more guts than you."

Qadeer grabbed John's chin and screamed, "You shall learn respect." He stepped back, aimed his fist at John's middle, and thrust it into John's stomach with the force of a jackhammer.

John shrieked but was abruptly silenced when his insides reeled and warm liquid dribbled down his chin. He stared at the floor and watched drops of blood trickle to the white tiles, smattering the floor's shiny surface with bright red splotches. The room spun and his head wobbled. Everything got fuzzy and gray. He opened his mouth to speak, but before his tongue could move, his world went black.

CHAPTER TWENTY-SEVEN

The monitor mounted to the front wall of AMOC-CRUSO magnified every pore on President Lloyd's skin, turning his face into a human relief map. The effect was particularly pronounced on his forehead, which now resembled a pair of rolling hills.

Since the day Farrell had met Edward J. Lloyd—two weeks after he'd lost an election for congressman in upstate New York—she noticed how his forehead wrinkled, especially when delivering bad news.

"I'm sorry, colonel, but the prime minister refuses to alter his position."

Standing beside the giant monitor facing the president's image, Daley said, "I don't mean to sound disrespectful, but the prime minister is being unreasonable. Two hours isn't a lot to ask."

"Behari's waited four days, and as far as he's concerned, that's four days too many. Now you're asking him to wait until five o'clock."

"Lieutenant Hall and Sergeant Banta are ready and waiting for Patty Krause. The Pakistani agent shadowing Ms. Krause checked in 20 minutes ago. She's an hour ahead of schedule, already 20 miles past Gujranwala. At her current pace, she'll arrive in Islamabad by 5:30 p.m. Pakistan time."

"The fact remains, as far as we know, Mr. Covello has not established contact with Crescent Moon."

"He will, but three o'clock doesn't give him much leeway."

Farrell was watching the exchange between Daley and the president sitting in her chair at the long mahogany conference table. On this point, she agreed with the colonel. Two hours more to verify John had made contact with Dr. Zamal wasn't much to ask.

"The prime minister believes it's an ominous sign her computer is dead."

Daley turned away from the monitor so the screen's built-in lens couldn't pick up his face. He rolled his eyes, signaling to Farrell for help.

The idea had been hers to begin with. She rose and walked toward the plasma monitor. "Mr. President, what about my telegram?"

"That was four hours ago Denise."

"Give it more time. Eventually it'll work its way to Dr. Zamal."

"Eventually may not be soon enough."

She knew the president trusted her, not because her brother and Lance Parker had been frat brothers, but because she had never given the president bad advice. Now was no time to squander her credibility.

Farrell looked straight at the camera. "Intelligence provided by the CIA, along with Dr. Zamal's own communications, indicates any written correspondence with her name on it, even junk mail, gets filtered through Khan's security. Global One confirmed delivery to the hospital's main reception desk at 0838 hours Pakistan time. If the telegram hasn't reached her yet, it will in the next few hours."

"Ajay Agarwal arrives at the Pentagon in 45 minutes—an hour and a half before the three o'clock deadline. Your telegram had better do it's job by then."

Farrell's eyes burned, and her patience was wearing thin. "The prime minister's obstinacy is beyond my comprehension. Our last report from Lieutenant Hall confirmed John checked into the Rawal Regency at 1105 hours. I'm willing to bet, as we speak, he's on his way to the hospital."

"I respect your instincts, Denise, but this time the decision isn't mine."

"It's crazy. The prime minister is willing to give our operative three days to plant the explosives, but not two extra hours to contact Dr. Zamal."

"His people want revenge, and they want it now. The only way he can justify holding off a counter-attack is if he knows our man is inside."

Farrell heard a door click open. She glanced back and saw Mission Specialist Stacy Miller enter the room holding a printout.

The president continued, "I'd love to give John those two hours. Frankly, if it were up to me, I'd give him two days."

"Has Secretary Parker had any luck in Beijing?"

"Lance believes the Chinese government won't discourage Khan's invasion. I'm keeping him there for one reason—to buy Mr. Covello four more days. As long as Lance is pleading hat-in-hand with the premier to check Khan's invasion of India, they're not likely to suspect we're simultaneously conducting a covert operation to assassinate him. Of course, Lance's shoe shuffle becomes meaningless if John doesn't contact Dr. Zamal before Behari's deadline."

Farrell heard the colonel curse beneath his breath. She turned and saw him standing beside Stacy, reading the printout and shaking his head.

"Denise, are you paying attention?"

Farrell turned back to the president. "I'm sorry, sir. Yes, and I still haven't given up hope John will reach Crescent Moon by three o'clock."

"I hope you're right. I'll call back in 20 minutes for an update." The president's face disappeared from the giant screen.

Farrell walked over to Stacy and Daley standing beside the conference table.

The colonel, who'd gone pale, looked at her as she approached. "We've got a problem—a big problem."

"What's wrong?"

"Twenty minutes ago Sergeant Banta witnessed three Pakistani soldiers kidnap John off the sidewalk in front of the Rawal Regency Inn."

"What are you talking about?"

"They drove southwest in an unmarked van to Murree Road and turned right. We have no other information."

Farrell put the pieces together, and the result wasn't pretty. Khan must have discovered Dr. Zamal was cooperating with the US government. The telegram Farrell had sent four hours earlier to Pakistan National Hospital, the one Farrell had counted on Khan intercepting, clearly linked John to Dr. Zamal. After John checked into the Rawal Regency Inn, Khan must have ordered John picked up as Dr. Zamal's accomplice.

Farrell's heart thumped against her rib cage. She could do nothing now but pray she was wrong.

Chapter Twenty-Eight

John opened his eyes to a field of vision filled with radiant white light. Squinting, he rolled to his side, away from the light, unsure if he were asleep or awake.

A female voice, a dulcet song wafting in his ear, uttered soft, soothing words. Maureen.

He must tell her of his terrible dream, of falling gravely ill and traveling to a distant land, of doing dangerous work for her sake.

John noticed another bed next to his, a bed with crisp white sheets and chrome railings along both sides. He raised his chin and looked around for his alarm clock. The old Panasonic with bright blue numerals was nowhere in sight.

The gentle voice again filled his ear, but this time it sounded nothing like Maureen's.

John slowly turned his head toward the light. His retina screamed and he squeezed his eyes shut. "Please turn it off."

The harsh light beyond his shuttered eyelids dimmed. He opened them again and gasped.

The woman he beheld was not Maureen. Unlike Maureen, this woman had long brown hair pressed against both sides of an olive-skinned face partially concealed by a baby blue veil. Her eyes were large and brown and shone with defiance.

Struggling to remember where he'd seen this pretty face, a fist of recognition jolted his memory. "You're even more beautiful in person."

Her rich dark skin flushed, and she glanced over her shoulder. She turned back to John with one finger pressed to her full, pink lips. "Shhh. Be quiet and listen." Her tone was urgent, not frantic, but firm and assured. "Captain Qadeer does not know the true purpose of your visit."

John figured as much, otherwise he probably wouldn't be breathing.

"He is unaware you suffer from pancreatic cancer and does not know blows to your stomach will cause you more pain than normal. You have convinced him you are a soft American businessman who has forgotten how to act like a man."

"Wonderful, just the image I was hoping to project."

Dr. Salena Zamal smiled, slightly parting her plush lips to reveal perfectly aligned white teeth. For some odd reason, John was glad not all women from third world countries were cursed with yellow teeth, or worse yet, none at all. "I did not intend to insult you. It is a good thing he believes you are weak. He will not suspect you are capable of deeds requiring great courage."

John caught her drift, but wasn't sure he liked the idea that in the days ahead prudence dictated he act like a pussy. He lifted himself to a sitting position and dangled his legs off the side of the bed. The room he'd been brought to was obviously an examination room in a doctors office or hospital. He saw no one else present.

The white lab coat Dr. Zamal wore, despite its loose fit and ankle length, failed dismally to conceal her femininity. "Am I in Pakistan National Hospital?"

"Yes, adjacent to Khan's Citadel, where you were taken by Qadeer's thugs."

Sharp pains sliced through John's abdomen and he rubbed his stomach. "Do you have any pain killers? Maybe a Percodan or two."

"That would not be wise. You will need all your wits these next four days."

"Gee, glad I'm in the hands of such a compassionate lady." John noticed a tiny black mole above Salena's upper lip, a punctuation mark that enhanced her smile. He detected no makeup coating her skin, except for a carefully blended smudge along her left cheekbone, as if to camouflage a blemish, maybe a bruise.

Salena lifted a blood pressure cuff off the table beside the bed, rolled up John's shirt sleeve, and wrapped the flat, limp band around his forearm. When her fingers touched his skin his arm tingled. God how he missed Maureen.

She stuck the tips of the stethoscope into her ears and began pumping the black bulb. "From now until Wednesday my job is to keep Ali Khan occupied while you place your explosives in the Citadel. As for Captain Qadeer, he is in big trouble with Khan. Pakistan welcomes all guests with warmth and hospitality. Qadeer grossly mistreated a health care professional who came to this country at my invitation."

The inflated bladder compressing John's brachial artery numbed his arm. "So you must have connected with Major Farrell while I was en route."

"No, Qadeer confiscated my computer last night."

"Then how did you know who I was?"

"The telegram." Air hissed out of the inflated cuff.

"What telegram?"

"Late this morning Qadeer intercepted a telegram addressed to me from your company, a reminder of your business trip to Pakistan. That telegram probably saved your life."

"Qadeer said nothing about a telegram when he was toying with me in his dollhouse."

"Did he ask if you had come to Pakistan as my guest?"

"I don't remember, I think so."

"He must have, to confirm the contents of the telegram. If you had lied and told him anything else, he would have killed you on the spot." Salena removed the cuff and wrapped it around his other arm.

"What are you doing?"

"Your blood pressure reading is 170 over 95. Much too high."

"You see, doc, I've been under a little stress lately."

"Dangerously high."

"That's the advantage of knowing I'll be dead in four days. No need to worry about eating fatty foods or getting enough exercise."

She paused a few seconds, studying him, and with no change of expression said, "As your physician, I'd recommend a long vacation to a deserted island in the South Pacific."

John managed a laugh. Collaborating with someone who shared his sense of humor might actually make his last few days on earth a bit more tolerable.

She smiled coyly and pumped the bulb. "After Qadeer finished with you, he summoned me to his office. He did not tell me about the telegram right away. He asked many questions. Was I expecting a visitor? I told him yes. Who was this person? A hospital systems consultant."

"Did he ask my name?"

"Yes, but I did not know it."

"My real name is John Covello, but in the time I've got left, it's John Cattano."

"Fortunately, Major Farrell told me the name of your company before I was forced to end our transmission. I told Qadeer you worked for Advanced Medical Systems, a software company in New Jersey, that I found you dreadfully dull and boring, and that I had lost your business card and forgotten your name."

"Great. Where's the captain now?"

"I am certain giving Ali Khan his own version of why he was rude to my American guest." Salena looked down at the blood pressure guage. "Slightly better. 140 over 90." She pulled the stethoscope tips from her ears and unwound the deflated cuff.

John noticed her fingers, long, lean, and dark, crowned with neatly trimmed nails naturally pink. Goose bumps pricked his arm when she removed the band. "You know, doc, Khan's gonna ask why you didn't say something sooner about a visitor from America."

"True, and I do not know what I will say, but an answer will come before dinner."

Dinner. Dinner? "Shit, what time is it?"

Salena frowned and craned her neck around the corner of a clothes closet beside the door. "About 40 minutes past two. Why?"

"How long was I out?"

"Two hours"

"Oh my God."

"What is wrong?"

"I have to contact Major Farrell."

"Why?"

"To tell her we've met and you're prepared to help me."

"She knows I will help you."

"No, she has to be told we've made contact."

"What is the hurry?"

"Trust me, if I don't reach Farrell in the next 20 minutes, bad things will happen."

"What bad things?"

John remembered she hadn't been told about the deadline. "A nuclear bomb."

Her eyes narrowed skeptically. "What are you talking about?"

John explained Prime Minister Behari's plan to retaliate against Khan, and his condition for postponing the launch.

"It is almost three o'clock now," Salena said.

"I have to get to a computer in the next few minutes."

"But my computer is gone."

John heard a commotion in the hall. "There's got to be some way—"

"Shhh, don't say a word." Salena lifted a clipboard and pen off the table, stepped back from the bed, and shoved the tips of the stethoscope into her ears.

Sitting up with his bare feet hanging off the bed, John watched the door closely. A tall man in a white robe and a black turban strutted into the room.

"Ahh, there you are my precious flower."

Salena dipped her head slightly in what John interpreted as a gesture of respect, possibly fear.

The man's light brown skin contrasted starkly with his piercing blue eyes. His jaw was set square, and those eyes, they could penetrate steel. Christie and Karen, even Maureen, would have branded him a hunk.

The man tipped his head once at Salena as he strode past her, then went directly to John. "You must be Mr. Cattano."

As John nodded, he saw a soldier clutching an automatic rifle enter the room and stand at attention inside the doorway.

The white-robed man smiled, and when he did, his features melted from stolid and distant to warm and friendly. The transformation was remarkable. The man extended a massive hand. "My name is Ghalib Ali Khan. Welcome to my country and its crown jewel, Islamabad."

John's only thought: if he didn't get to a computer in the next 15 minutes, Khan's crown jewel, and everyone in it, would shatter into a trillion pieces.

CHAPTER TWENTY-NINE

Denise Farrell had little patience for stubborn men, and Ajay Agarwal was no exception.

India's special envoy had landed at Andrews Air Force Base 45 minutes earlier. His first request upon waltzing into AMOC-CRUSO hadn't been a briefing on the current status of Mission 003. Instead he had asked Farrell to fetch him an avocado and muenster cheese submarine sandwich garnished with a nest of alfalfa sprouts.

Agarwal was now seated comfortably in a burgundy leather chair at the long, mahogany conference table two seats from Farrell, his half-eaten hero sprawled out on deli paper littered with green sprout droppings. He picked up the uneaten half of his overstuffed sandwich, took a large bite out of the rounded end, and swallowed the entire piece in one gulp. "Incredible."

Colonel Daley, sitting across from Agarwal, three seats down, was in no mood for the special envoy's culinary critique. "Dammit, we're asking for two more hours."

Without taking his eyes off the sub Agarwal lifted the bread to his mouth and paused. "This is the finest muenster cheese I am tasting in a very long time."

Daley got up and walked to the empty chair directly across from Agarwal, gripped its top from behind, and leaned forward. "President Lloyd has compromised the secrecy of a classified government agency for the sole purpose of allowing you to witness an operation in progress, and all you can talk about is the damn muenster cheese?"

"The avocado is delicious, too."

"What the hell is wrong with you? In 15 minutes your prime minister intends to launch an attack that could destroy a million men, women, and children. If any of Khan's warheads survive, he'll fire them at Delhi, and then we're talking tens of millions. Draw China, Russia, and America into the fray, and the only country left standing is England. Whatever crispy souls are still alive on the subcontinent had better get used to living under the rule of the second British Empire." Daley's fingernails pressed deep into the chair's plush leather. "Our man is on the ground and I know he'll contact us. Give him a little more time."

Agarwal gently placed the sub on the deli paper and looked up at Daley. "Your man, he has been captured by the ISI and he is dead."

"We don't know that."

Agarwal gazed wistfully at his sandwich, rolled his chair backward, and glared up at Daley. "India has waited too long in answering Khan's aggression. If not us, who will be teaching him he cannot get away with killing our people. Who will be avenging 10,000 dead at Baramulla?"

"If it makes you feel better, think of our mission as exacting that revenge."

"Now that Khan has discovered your plan to assassinate him, I am seeing no advantage of waiting one minute more."

Daley rolled out the chair he was standing behind, sat, and leaned over the conference table to within grabbing distance of Agarwal's throat.

Farrell's heart pumped a few beats faster.

The colonel locked eyes with Agarwal. "Our two support agents in Islamabad have not positively identified John's abductors."

Agarwal smacked his lips, and sent a lone sprout squirting from between his teeth, halfway across the table. "You insult me, yes?"

Daley sat back in his chair and began rocking. "Why did you bother coming?"

"The news that your operative fell into the hands of the ISI did not reach me until after I landed. Had I known in New Delhi, do you think I would have made this trip?"

Daley shook his head and didn't reply.

Farrell had skimmed the special envoy's NSA dossier moments before his limousine had pulled up to the Pentagon. She learned Agarwal had earned a doctorate in zoology from India's prestigious Allahabad University, where he met upper classman Sanjay Behari. Agarwal's credentials included service as consul general in Sao Paulo, a stint as India's foreign secretary and high commissioner to the United Kingdom, and ten years as vice-chancellor of the University of Mumbai. Three years ago, Prime Minister Behari tapped Agarwal to serve as his foreign minister. A poultry-eating vegetarian who drove a hard bargain, Ajay Agarwal was no dummy.

Daley had apparently given up on India's special envoy, but the stakes were too high to let Agarwal off the hook without a fight. In seven minutes, at 2:55 p.m. DST, President Lloyd and Prime Minister Behari planned to join them in the Active Mission Oversight Center via video-conference. If by then CRUSO couldn't prove John had contacted Crescent Moon, Behari would issue the launch order.

Farrell swiveled her chair to face Agarwal. "Why won't you consider what we know, and what we don't know?"

Agarwal regarded her over his shoulder.

"Mr. Covello's abduction obviously points to a problem, but we don't know for sure he's exposed his cover."

"I am begging to differ, major. The abduction of Mr. Covello and the failure of Dr. Zamal to contact CRUSO point to but one conclusion. They have been caught."

"How can you sit there and—"

The phone intercom buzzed and all eyes turned to the blinking red light above the keypad. Farrell hit the speaker button. "Yes Stacy."

The young woman's strong voice filled the paneled room. "Prime Minister Behari is set for AV feed into AMOC-CRUSO. Shall I make the transfer?"

Farrell glanced at the row of clocks on the wall behind Daley. "Advise the prime minister we're waiting for President Lloyd. When the president calls, make the transfers simultaneously." From the corner of her eye, she caught Daley nodding his approval.

CHAPTER THIRTY

Transfixed by Ali Khan's steely blue eyes, John couldn't help but shake the extended hand of the man he was sent here to kill. "How did you know my name?"

"This is my city. I know everyone who enters and everyone who leaves."

The pitch of Khan's voice reminded John of the low notes from the alto sax he played in high school. Enunciating his words perfectly, Khan spoke flawless English, which John found disconcerting from a man who wore a jet black turban around his head.

John glanced at Salena, who stood behind and to the side of Khan. "So I guess you read the telegram my company sent to Dr. Zamal." The doctor's lips tightened and her eyes got wide, as if signaling John to proceed with caution.

Khan released John's hand and smiled. "Yes, and I do accept Mr. Dunne's apology."

John sifted his memory for recognition of the name. He thought back to his last meeting with Farrell and Daley, and what he'd read in the AMS brochure. John hoped his vague response did not belie his ignorance. "I shall pass your sentiments along."

"Your supervisor would have been prudent to give me advance notice of your arrival."

Then he remembered—Ted Dunne was the owner of Advanced Medical Systems. "I'm sorry too. We've been so busy lately, we've hardly had time to breathe."

Khan's lips traced a subtle grin. "I might have mistaken you for a spy."

John's view of the clock above the door was obstructed by the closet. He guessed two minutes had passed since Khan had entered the room, leaving him only 10 to contact CRUSO. "Truth is, I am a spy."

Khan's face hardened, and he clenched his fists at his hips.

"I'm interested in learning everything there is to know about your hospital's physician coordination computer management modules. I'd like to get started as soon as possible, but first I'd like to call my boss and let him know I'm here."

Khan scrutinized John for a full minute, then slowly opened his fists and slackened his arms. "Actually, Mr. Dunne requested you, or Dr. Zamal, contact him as soon as possible after your arrival."

"Guess my boss and I are on the same wavelength."

"I was quite impressed by Mr. Dunne's gratitude. His deference was, how shall I say, uniquely un-American. He sincerely appreciates my allowing you to visit Pakistan on such short notice, and he apologizes for any inconvenience your visit causes."

"I thought Ted sent the telegram to Dr. Zamal."

Salena gave John a subtle shake of her head.

"Unfortunately, I have enemies eager to hurt those close to me." Khan burrowed his right hand under his robe, rustled around, and exhumed a short, yellow sheet of paper.

He thrust the paper at Salena. "Take it."

She put the telegram in the pocket of her lab coat.

Khan explained, "All of Dr. Zamal's letters and packages are previewed by Captain Qadeer, solely to assure her safety."

"Oh yes, the good captain. I've already had the pleasure of meeting him."

Khan clasped John's shoulder on what must have been a bruise inflicted by his abductors. He clenched his teeth to stop from wincing.

"It is my turn to apologize," Khan said. "When airport security in Bahrain advised Captain Qadeer you carried a photograph of Dr. Zamal, he was understandably curious. But the captain can sometimes act hastily, particularly when he perceives a threat to me or my betrothed. I hope you understand."

"Apology accepted."

"Once you get to know the captain, you may actually take a liking to him."

Maybe in his next life, John thought, when he came back as Attila the Hun. "I suppose everyone deserves a second chance."

"Nevertheless, I have chastised Captain Qadeer for treating you roughly."

John again glanced at Salena, but spoke to Khan. "Before I forget, congratulations. Ted mentioned you and Dr. Zamal are engaged." John leaned forward, and winked at Khan. "Damn good catch."

Khan squeezed John's shoulder in his iron grip, and John instantly realized his mistake. Farrell had warned him about Islamic taboos on discussing a woman's appearance. He groaned out his words, "I mean, she's extremely hard-working and intelligent."

"Thank you, but next time please remember in our culture men do not speak of another man's woman in such terms."

"Sorry, I'll try to do better."

Khan removed his hand from John's shoulder. "Technically, in Islam, the concept of engagement does not exist. The only way a man and woman can enjoy intimacy is through Nikah, the contract of marriage. The Qur'an refers to marriage as mithaqun Ghalithun—a strong agreement."

With the city around them about to explode, the last thing John needed was a lecture on Islamic marriage. He fought back the urge to jump off the bed and run.

"The sanctity of mithaqun Ghalitun becomes evident when one understands the term also describes the agreement between Allah and the Prophet Mohammad. It is interesting to note the Qur'an uses the word Hisn, Arabic for fortress, when describing a marriage. Marriage is considered the fortress of chastity."

Though John avoided looking directly at Salena, he couldn't help but notice a scowl marring her pretty face. He wondered if Khan practiced what he preached.

Khan folded his arms across his chest. "During the period leading up to the marriage ceremony, Islamic law prohibits a man from seeing his future bride except for the purpose of making preparations. Even then they may see one another only in the presence of the woman's mahram."

John had explained to Salena the consequence of failing to contact Farrell by 3:00 p.m., and he couldn't understand why she just stood there in silence.

"A mahram is any man who a woman cannot marry—a father, an uncle, a brother. To an American it may sound strange that a man and woman under contract to marry cannot be alone together, but to a Muslim it is haram, prohibited."

Angling his head toward Salena, John rubbed his cranium above his temple, pretending to soothe a headache, then opened his hand to shield his face and shot Salena a wide-eyed look of 'get moving.'

Salena shrugged her shoulders and looked down at the floor.

He had to try something different, something drastic.

Kahn went on, "A man may look at a woman when she is without her headscarf, so long as she covers her aworah—her body from her chest to below her knees. He may look at her hair, eyes, and face, but he must gaze upon her with the purest intentions."

"Excuse me, General Khan, sir."

"No need for 'sir.' General Khan will do."

"What you're saying fascinates the heck out of me, and I've got a question or two, but I'm still learning the ropes here and I don't want to say anything in front of Dr. Zamal that might get you upset."

"You wish us to speak alone as men?"

"That's right, if it's OK with you."

"Indeed, I have questions of you as well." Khan pivoted to Salena. "You have finished your work here. Go now and make your rounds. Mr. Cattano and I wish to discuss zar, zan, and zamin." Khan turned to John. "Gold, women, and land—three things any Pathan is willing to fight and die for."

Salena bowed slightly to Khan. "Thank you kind master."

Kind master? Was this guy nuts? Or was she?

Salena picked up John's patient chart and started scribbling notes.

John said to Khan, "General, if you don't mind, do you think Dr. Zamal could call Mr. Dunne to let him know I'm here and ready to sell my wares?"

Khan's tone became stern. "Dr. Zamal has already dallied too long. When I am through, you may call him yourself."

By the time Khan was through they'd all be dead. "But with a war on and what not, Ted's probably worried sick."

"A few minutes more will make no difference." Khan turned and glowered at Salena. "Leave us now."

Salena put down the chart, gave John a timid glance, and scurried past the soldier guarding the door.

John wondered if the war about to break out would impact Maureen and his daughters. Brielle was far removed from this strange part of the world, but still, nuclear war anywhere was bound to stir up fear and uncertainty in America.

Then again, maybe nuclear war wasn't such a bad idea. Preoccupied with survival, John's creditors might stop hassling his family. John knew that wasn't the answer. The answer rested with him, and for the second time in as many years he was about to let his family down.

John could do nothing now but hope in the next five minutes Salena somehow made contact with CRUSO, but if her spineless silence in Khan's presence had followed her out the door, that wasn't likely to happen.

CHAPTER THIRTY-ONE

Left in the hands of John Cattano, America's mission to assassinate Ali Khan was sure to fail, or so was the conclusion of Salena Zamal as she hurried toward the hospital's 3rd floor elevator bank. Not that Mr. Cattano was incompetent, and not that he didn't seem courageous. She would even call him likable—for an American. The problem was his tongue. Wag it too much to the wrong people and both of them would end up dead.

Waiting for the elevator, Salena recalled how most men she had met while attending medical school in America believed they had all the answers. They knew everything, and only backward dolts inhabited the rest of the world. Apparently, that was also the attitude of Mr. Cattano.

The handsome American had better not delude himself into believing Khan a fool, not if he planned to survive until Wednesday. Of course, if what Mr. Cattano had told her in the examination room were true, she had better contact Major Farrell within the next seven minutes, or few in Islamabad would survive the day.

The elevator arrived, Salena hopped on, and she rode to the 5th floor. With her computer in the custody of the ISI, she must find another means of communicating with the Americans.

Other computers were available—every nurses station was equipped with two—but they were useless to her since she had no e-mail address for Major Farrell. Her only contact with the major since her abduction from Peshawar had been their messages over the US government's virtual private network, and the initiation code to access that was embedded in Excel files loaded on the computer Qadeer had confiscated.

She considered placing a telephone call. After all, people still used telephones to communicate. She could call the Pentagon and ask to speak with Major Farrell.

Salena emerged from the elevator and hustled down the hall. Flashing obligatory smiles to familiar faces, Salena mulled two problems. First, Qadeer's intelligence personnel monitored all overseas calls, and second, even if she got lucky and hers slipped through unnoticed, it might take many minutes for an American operator to connect her to the Pentagon. If the layers of bureaucracy in Washington, DC were as thick as they were in Pakistan, by the time Farrell came to the phone, Islamabad would lay in ruins.

She remembered the telegram. Brushing past a mustached father cuddling his newborn son, Salena pulled the yellow sheet from her lab coat and spotted exactly what she was looking for—a telephone number.

Major Farrell must have realized the private network link to Pakistan National Hospital had been disabled, compelling her to find another means of establishing contact. Why couldn't the major have accomplished two objectives with one communiqué? The same telegram she had used to inform Salena of Mr. Cattano's imminent arrival, she might also have used to provide a phone number at which she could be reached. If Salena's hunch were right, the phone number for Advanced Medical Systems printed on the telegram would connect her directly to Major Farrell.

Salena glanced up at a clock behind the nurse's station in Labor and Delivery. According to Mr. Cattano, she had four minutes to stop India from atomizing him, her, and everyone around them.

Her office door in sight, she began running.

Salena entered her office and sprinted to her desk. Near her phone lay two drumsticks languishing in a plastic dish—the grilled tandoori chicken she had brought up for lunch from the cafeteria. Worried about the fate of her friend Raja, she had barely touched her meal.

She glanced at the clock above her file cabinet. Three minutes to three. Salena lifted the handset, and when a hospital operator answered, Salena requested an overseas line.

"What country code please?"

"001."

"Please hold."

Salena examined the telegram. The signer was a Mr. Ted Dunne, but her instincts insisted Major Farrell would answer. Because the ISI was likely to eavesdrop on her conversation, she must measure her every word.

Nearly a minute passed before the operator returned. "Dr. Zamal, you have a clear line to the US."

"Thank you." Salena punched in the 13 digits and waited. A few seconds later the phone rang once, stopped abruptly, then changed to a fast-busy signal. She pressed star-one to bring back the operator. "I was cut off. Please try again."

A half-minute passed before she heard another dial tone. She punched in the numbers, whispered a prayer, and the line began to ring. "Allah be praised." The third ring hadn't quite finished when someone picked up.

CHAPTER THIRTY-TWO

J ohn shimmied off the edge of the mattress, and with Ali Khan walking beside him, limped toward the foot of the bed. Vaguely aware of the cool tiles touching the soles of his feet, John's purpose was to get a clear view of the clock above the door. That way, the nuclear explosion's blinding flash wouldn't catch him entirely off guard.

On the floor near the footboard John found the black Nikes and gray sweat socks Lieutenant Hall had given him on the jet to Bahrain. Prior to his money troubles, John wore only designer sneakers, but these past two years, he'd made do with clearance bin specials. Because John's mission might require he climb elevator shafts and descend support girders, CRUSO had insisted he wear sneakers not likely to disintegrate under his feet.

Struggling to ignore the dull pain throbbing in his belly, John sat on the edge of the hospital bed, picked up his socks, and silently prayed Salena was headed for a computer wired to the Internet.

Standing nearby, Khan said, "First ask me your questions, then I shall ask mine."

Other than the soldier stiff at attention inside the doorway, John and the general were alone. John was now in position to see the clock above the soldier's head—seven minutes to Behari's deadline.

What could John say to a man with whom he had nothing in common? Best if he kept it bland. "Seems your country goes through a lot of trouble keeping its women covered. What gives?"

"You raise a difficult issue, a source of boisterous contention among heathen elements in all nations whose laws are guided by Islamic principals."

So much for bland. "Let's talk about something else."

"Be not timid, Mr. Cattano. You requested this time, now speak your mind."

What the hell. In a few minutes they'd both be dead. "OK, how would you like living life under a sheet? Isn't that degrading to a woman?"

Ali Khan smiled. "Quite the contrary. Islam views a woman as the most precious creature in human life. To protect her from harm and the lechery of vulgar men, Islam dictates Hijab, or the veil. When a woman leaves the family home, she must cover all of her body, except for her face and hands."

John shoveled his right foot into his Nike. "And that doesn't steal her dignity?"

"Not at all. Islam focuses entirely on a woman's dignity, not her superficial qualities such as her hair and her breasts. When a woman's attractions are covered, men concentrate on her more honorable qualities as a person, and do not view her solely as an object of lust."

"So what you're saying is when a man meets a woman, he can't be trusted to control his base instincts."

"Can you deny it?"

John recalled one summer night about a year ago, his last family outing to the Point Pleasant boardwalk. Holding Maureen's hand, with Karen and Christie in tow, they strolled past a game booth where players shot squirt guns into the mouths of plastic clowns. The water blew up balloons attached to each clown's head, and the first player to pop their balloon won the prize.

His daughters paused to watch five men, none less than 30, test their sharp-shooting skills. The winner, a man about John's age, claimed his plush toy, and with his buddies in tow, turned to leave. Apparently unaware her parents stood five yards away, the middle-aged winner stopped and stared at Karen. She averted his gaze, but that wasn't enough to discourage the jerk from flirting. He told Karen she looked hot and offered his stuffed toy if she'd let him get into her pants.

Furious a man old enough to be her father would hit on his daughter, John ran over and nearly pounded the pervert. John also remembered how utterly helpless Karen felt afterward. He longed to assure her not all men judged women first on their looks, but he couldn't. Truth was, that was the nature of men.

Bent over, sitting on the edge of the hospital bed, John knotted his laces thinking Khan's words might hold a grain of truth. When he finished, he rose and faced the white-robed general. "I suppose men do focus on a woman's appearance first."

"When it comes to women, Islam puts modesty, purity, and chastity first. Can that be wrong?"

John wondered how a women's freedom of choice fit into Islamic law. Maybe it didn't. "You make it hard to disagree."

"Then don't." Khan folded his arms across his chest. "Now I have some questions for you."

"Ask away."

"Tell me, Mr. Cattano, how would your company's software benefit Pakistan National Hospital? Many consulting firms would seize the opportunity for a lucrative contract with Pakistan. What sets Advanced Medical Systems apart?"

John's jaw dropped. The world around them was about to explode and Khan expected him to spit back all the AMS marketing crap Farrell had given him to read. Since there was still a chance Salena would contact CRUSO in the next three minutes, he'd better give it a try.

"You should know, first off, except for small clinics or group practices, there are no all-encompassing, off-the-shelf solutions capable of satisfying the existing needs of major health care institutions. Management information solutions must be developed to meet the specific needs imposed by the structure and function of each organization." John paused, having impressed even himself.

The general came back with an equally impressive question. "What factors, then, enter into a consideration of information systems options for individual health care institutions?"

Before John could answer, he heard a deep voice resonate behind Khan. "Forgive me, general, the matter is urgent." An army officer wearing a tan uniform and red cap stepped into the room.

Khan turned. "What is it?"

"At 1440 hours, General Abbasi reported from Karambar Pass. A fresh Indian regiment has been deployed to reinforce General Frahat's offensive. General Abbasi expresses grave reservations about leaving his post to return to Islamabad in the midst of intensifying hostilities."

Khan rubbed his chin. "Abbasi simply does not understand the magnitude of what is about to occur. I shall speak with the general directly. Give me a moment and I shall be along."

"Thank you, sir." The officer spun and marched out the door.

Khan turned to John. "We shall finish our conversation later." He leaned closer. "Let me be blunt. I believe we can do business. I am aware many world leaders question the strong measures I have taken to safeguard Pakistan's eastern border. I have read the accusations and slanderous labels—warmonger, zealot, lunatic. You will note, except for India, all my detractors come from the West. Engaging in business with AMS offers a small, yet important opportunity to prove I am willing to deal with America. I have no argument with the US. If my government can transact legitimate business with private enterprise in the West, perhaps I shall muffle those critics who accuse me of blind desire to impose Islamic fundamentalism throughout Asia."

"I get it. Use me to put on a happy face to the rest of the world."

"Use each other, Mr. Cattano. The value of our relationship shall benefit you in ways you cannot imagine."

Khan's proposition sounded great, but even if it were real, the time on the clock meant the fuse was lit on India's 20 kiloton nuclear missile pointed at Islamabad. "Thank you, and I look forward to working with you."

"You shall begin assessing my hospital's software systems this very night. I seek a program that smoothly links the data bases at major hospitals in Karachi, Quetta, Lahore, and Peshawar with those at Pakistan National Hospital. Since Dr. Zamal has worked both here and in Peshawar, and is already familiar with your software's capabilities, she shall serve as your guide."

"Great."

"Of course, you shall require an escort."

"I wouldn't have thought otherwise."

"Captain Qadeer shall make himself available."

There were loan sharks John would rather have follow him around. "That won't be necessary."

"I insist."

"Then Qadeer it is." It wouldn't matter anyway, John thought, if Salena failed to contact CRUSO within the next 60 seconds.

"Since you have come to Pakistan at the invitation of its future first lady, I also insist you lodge as my guest at the Citadel. The suggestion was the captain's."

John was sure hospitality had little to do with Qadeer's offer. "Marvelous. While he's feeling so generous, do you think he could return my good luck charm—a toy motorcycle my daughter gave me for my birthday. It's my only reminder of home."

"Consider it done. A car shall pick you up at your hotel at eight o'clock. When you return, you will have your photograph and fingerprints taken. Routine security measures. After that, Captain Qadeer will escort you to the hospital."

"I can't wait."

"To atone for the captain's excesses, I have arranged to supplement your western attire with clothing better suited for Pakistan's summers. They will be waiting for you in the Shah Rukin Suite on the 9th floor."

"Thank you." John wondered if he'd have two seconds after seeing the white flash to leap into the closet behind Khan. Probably not, since Farrell had told him ground zero was over Rawal Lake, a mere five blocks away.

Khan firmly grasped John's hand. "My schedule is tight, and I must take leave."

John shook Khan's hand, and the general left the room accompanied by the soldier standing inside the doorway. Surrounded by silence, John bowed his head, murmured The Lord's Prayer, and prayed for a swift death.

CHAPTER THIRTY-THREE

With Prime Minister Behari on hold in New Delhi waiting for President Lloyd to patch in from the White House, Denise Farrell scrutinized India's special envoy. "What will it take to convince you our mission hasn't been compromised?"

Ajay Agarwal lifted his submarine sandwich to his mouth, and like a jeweler admiring a well-cut diamond, paused to examine the sliced avocado and muenster cheese tucked inside. Without looking at Farrell, he replied, "I am needing reliable proof your operative has contacted Dr. Zamal, and that has not happened." For only an instant he took his eyes off the sandwich and glanced across the table at Daley. "I demand you put the prime minister through immediately."

Daley looked at Farrell for help, but Farrell had run out of ideas. All she could do was watch helplessly as the stubborn diplomat rammed the butt-end of his sub down his throat.

The colonel checked Eastern Time on the wall clock behind him, got up, and ambled to his chair directly across from Farrell. He sat and pressed the intercom. "Stacy, has President Lloyd called in?"

Stacy's crisp tone sounded through the speakers. "Four seconds ago. I was about to buzz you."

"Patch in the president and prime minister, and set up a—"

"Hold on, colonel."

"What is it Stacy?"

A full 10 seconds passed before Stacy replied. "I have an overseas call on the AMS line. A woman asking to speak with Ted Dunne. She says she's from Pakistan National Hospital, and her name is Dr. Zamal."

The colonel shouted into the intercom. "Tell the president and prime minister we're on the phone with Crescent Moon. Ask them both to hold." Daley paused. "Better yet, connect them to each other while I speak with Dr. Zamal."

"Very well, sir."

Swiping the tip of his tongue over his lips, the colonel glared at Agarwal. "I'm putting this call on speaker so you can hear every word."

Agarwal nodded.

Daley turned to Farrell. "I'm ready."

Farrell tapped out a series of numbers and letters on the keyboard in front of her, then nodded back to Daley.

The colonel's tone was all business. "Ted Dunne here. Good to speak with you Dr. Zamal."

"Thank you for sending the telegram."

The doctor's voice was exactly as Farrell remembered.

Daley's eyes focused on the intercom. "A telegram was the least we could do in light of Mr. Cattano's last minute change of plans. If Saint Joseph's Hospital hadn't postponed its installation until the end of the month, John couldn't have come any sooner than September."

"Then Pakistan National Hospital must consider itself fortunate."

Daley passed his hand across his mouth. "Tell me, how was John's flight?"

"A minor misunderstanding as to the nature of his visit delayed our initial meeting, but those misunderstandings have all been resolved. He was quite anxious for me to tell you he arrived safely."

"With tensions so high in the region, I understand his concern."

"To spare the expense of a call, he asked me to send you an e-mail, but my computer is not functioning."

"Maybe Mr. Cattano can sell you some hardware."

"A timely idea, as my PC is out for repair."

Speaking into the microphone, Daley looked askance at Agarwal. "John's tops in his field. He can hook you up with a reliable hardware vendor. Do you expect he'll get an opportunity to deliver his Med-Link presentation to your purchasing manager any time soon?"

"Do not worry. Mr. Cattano has already met the most influential administrator in Pakistan."

"And who might that be?"

"General Khan himself."

Farrell heard in Daley's voice a desperate effort to unravel his tongue. "They've met ... actually met?"

"Oh yes, and to my surprise, they seem to have hit it off famously."

"That can't be bad ... can it?"

"Let me say this. If Mr. Cattano can persuade General Khan of Med-Link's advantages, he will have no problem making a sale. The only obstacle thus far is his propensity for candor. In Pakistan, too much honesty is offensive."

Daley rolled his eyes. "Mr. Cattano is our number one salesman, but he does tend to speak his mind."

"If he can restrain his impulse to speak bluntly, his chances of selling Med-Link here will improve dramatically."

"Do me a favor? Next time you see him, tell him to call me. His last client has a few questions about our billing. It'll also give me an opportunity to remind him to respect your culture's high regard for discretion."

"A fine idea."

"While I'm on the phone, do you have any specific questions about Mr. Cattano or Med-Link?"

"Yes, does Mr. Cattano have all the materials he needs to make a persuasive presentation to the hospital's Board of Trustees?"

"He flew light. There's a knockout PowerPoint presentation loaded on his laptop, which should catch up with him at the Rawal Regency sometime this evening."

"I assume, then, after he spends a day or two analyzing our hospital's current software configuration he will be ready to tender a formal proposal."

"We're counting on it."

"It has been a pleasure speaking with you, Mr. Dunne."

"The pleasure's mine."

After an audible click, all three in the room exchanged glances. Farrell spoke first. "Based on that conversation, I believe we must conclude John has infiltrated Pakistan National Hospital, and with Dr. Zamal's assistance, is likely to gain access to the Citadel."

Daley nodded. "I'm in total agreement."

They both turned to Agarwal.

The ornery Indian was scowling. "Because the fox has entered the roost, does not mean he will be stealing the egg."

Daley shot up from his chair. "Is every government man in India as pessimistic as you? No wonder the country with the fastest growing economy in Asia can't pull itself out of poverty." He slammed his hand on the intercom. "Stacy, tell the president and prime minister we're ready. Tell them they're getting the best news imaginable."

Studying the envoy's cynical countenance, Farrell wondered if between now and Wednesday she might go for Agarwal's throat herself.

Their 20-minute video-conference with President Lloyd and Prime Minister Behari went better than Farrell could have hoped. Despite questions raised by Agarwal as to whether John's identity had been compromised, after twice listening to the taped conversation between Colonel Daley and Dr. Zamal, Behari agreed to postpone launching his 20 kiloton warhead. He did reserve the right to attack Islamabad if Mr. Covello were caught before the start of Glorious Dawn, however, he expressed "considerable confidence" the US operation promised a reasonable probability of success.

After the call, even Agarwal began to lighten up. Within 15 minutes he and Daley were actually conversing in a civil tone. Farrell suspected the special envoy's second avocado and muenster cheese sub in as many hours had something to do with his upbeat mood.

"I am believing these avocados taste better than those I ate in Brazil. You will ship me a crate to India, no?"

Daley replied, "I'd be happy to, but the secret's in the dressing, and nobody mixes a tastier dressing than Carney's Deli. I'll talk to Hal, the owner. Maybe he'll share his recipe."

"And if he does not, you will be ordering the CIA to steal it." Agarwal guffawed at his own joke.

Daley smiled, but Farrell wasn't sure he did so to be polite. "I suppose I could obtain a warrant to install a microphone in his kitchen."

Agarwal bellowed so loudly, Farrell almost didn't hear the intercom buzz and Stacy's voice come over the speaker. "Colonel Daley, I have Lieutenant Hall on the line with a Priority 1 message."

The colonel's expression turned dead serious. He picked up the phone. "Yes lieutenant."

Agarwal's laughter dissolved into an irritating simper. He turned to Farrell and pointed at Daley. "Your boss has a good sense of humor."

Keeping her eyes on the colonel, she answered, "He has his moments."

"Do you really think he will get the recipe?"

"If the colonel says he'll try, he'll try."

Daley's face turned ashen. He shook his head and his eyes glazed over, as if he'd just been sentenced to the gallows. Farrell heard him say, "Any identity trace?" and then a moment later, "I'll inform the president."

The colonel dropped the phone on its cradle and stared across the table at her. He was struggling to maintain his composure. "I have tragic news."

Afraid to ask, Farrell did anyway. "How bad?"

"This mission is over."

CHAPTER THIRTY-FOUR

At 14 minutes past three John had run out of prayers, but he began speculating the ones he'd said had done their job since Pakistan National Hospital, and apparently, the entire city of Islamabad had not been destroyed by a nuclear inferno.

Alone in the examination room, he remembered an image of Maureen, Karen, and Christie sitting and giggling on a bench along the boardwalk at Seaside Heights. Karen and Christie clutched to their hearts stuffed Minnie Mouse dolls John had won on a wheel of chance.

Carefree and content. That was his life two weeks before the Chicago implosion, when Billy Dwyer still lived. He chuckled to himself, stricken by the contrast between his outlook then—on top of the world, no end in sight—and now, cowering beside a closet in a strange land counting the seconds before an atomic blast turned him to dust.

Salena must have gotten through. A piece of him wished she hadn't, because now he must deal with the reality of why he was here—to implode a building for the sole purpose of destroying the lives inside. Evil or not, dangerous or not, they were human beings. Yet he had agreed to commit murder for the sake of preventing war. He had done so not for his country, nor for the world, but for his family. At times like this John wished his life's portrait hadn't been painted with so many shades of gray.

A dark-skinned nurse in a pale green veil entered the room with her head bowed. She spoke to John without looking up. "Are you the American guest of General Khan?"

John wondered if all women in Khan's Pakistan had been trained to avert the eyes of men. "I suppose I am."

"Will you need help finding the lobby?"

"I'll figure it out."

Staring at the floor, the sullen nurse nodded and left.

Not sure what to do next, John remembered his four o'clock meeting at the Rawal Regency Inn with Lieutenant Hall and Sergeant Banta.

John walked into the hall, spotted a bank of elevators, and rode the first car down to the main lobby. Inside the spacious lobby painted flat gold and adorned with contemporary leather furniture, he observed a pair of soldiers standing beside the hospital's automatic glass doors. The soldiers scrutinized everyone entering and leaving, and John had the feeling they were looking for someone specific.

John sucked in a deep breath and walked toward the exit, certain the guards would stop him. Making an all-out effort to stroll as casually as if walking through his own living room, John stepped onto the black rubber, and activated the pneumatic rollers to part the double doors. He heard the expected hiss, then the gruff voice of the soldier on his left.

"Stop!"

John grit his teeth and turned to the man who had barked the order. "Yes sir, what can I do for you?"

"The question is, Mr. Cattano, what can I do for you?"

"Huh?"

"We were told you might need directions to the Rawal Regency Hotel."

John speculated everyone from floor mopper to chief of surgery had been informed of his visit. "According to the street map I looked at this morning, I'm only a few blocks away."

"Please allow me to show you." The red-capped soldier walked through the open glass doors waving for John to follow. Standing on the sidewalk in the dizzying heat, he pointed down Constitution Avenue, a broad six-lane boulevard, and gave directions.

John smiled. "Thank you. Thank you very much."

"No problem sir, enjoy your stay in Islamabad."

If three hours earlier Azam Qadeer had not pummeled his belly, John might have thought all Khan's security men friendly, even accommodating.

John checked his watch. With 35 minutes before his meeting with Hall and Banta, he'd use the extra time to inspect the exterior elevation of Khan's Citadel.

The sidewalk fronting Pakistan National Hospital was bustling, but not crowded like Manhattan at rush hour. As he'd noticed earlier, most pedestrians were men, and nearly all paused to look at him. The few women he spotted, some in veils and long dresses, others shrouded in one-man tents, did not acknowledge his existence. How could they with their eyes focused on the cement.

He came to an iron rail fence about 15 feet high running along the sidewalk. Through black metal bars spaced eight inches apart he viewed Khan's Citadel. John assumed security cameras were monitoring all activity around the Citadel, so he did not stop, but slowed to a shuffle.

The octagon structure, set back some 100 feet from the street, appeared more imposing than he'd remembered from the photograph Farrell had shown him during their second meeting. He saw the same mirrored windows encircling the Citadel's 1st through 5th floors as he'd seen in the picture. The exterior walls of the 6th through 11th floors consisted of sheer white concrete, with air vents protruding at intervals demarking each floor. As in the photo, the 12th floor was encircled by a balcony.

John recalled Farrell telling him the building's structural support consisted of concrete columns and steel I-beams, but he could not confirm that until he entered the building's core. Once inside, he would determine where to place the charges and how high to set their explosive force. From the outside at least, this 21st Century castle appeared impenetrable.

From the Citadel's roof along Constitution Avenue, six soldiers looked down at the street. John guessed his movements were being watched. He glanced back at the hospital and saw three soldiers pacing along the north side of its roof facing the Citadel.

Inside the iron fence an asphalt service road wound to the left of the Citadel and disappeared through a narrow gap between the Citadel's south wall and Pakistan National Hospital. From his vantage, John could make out the enclosed skywalk spanning the service road connecting the 4th floors of both buildings. During his briefing Farrell had said the skywalk was 20 feet long.

He turned his attention across the street to the Diplomatic Enclave. A six-foot high cement wall separated the sidewalk from the grounds beyond. John surmised the Enclave covered an expansive area, since the concrete wall ran four blocks south toward Rawal Lake and five blocks north toward the Margalla Hills. The wall's entire length along Constitution Avenue was broken in five places by sturdy iron gates. The nearest was across the street in the direction he had to walk.

He crossed the avenue, strolled up to the gate, and peered between the metal bars. Inside on the left he saw a bland two-story building sheathed with white vinyl siding. Along the walk leading up to its entrance was a sign written in four languages. John read the English version: International Community Education Center.

He swallowed hard and wiped the sweat off his brow as he caught sight of something familiar—a playground equipped with swings, spring-mounted animals, and a wooden jungle gym. It reminded John of the park in Brick Township where he took Karen and Christie as toddlers.

John turned and looked back across the street. Farrell's estimate was probably accurate. A mere 180 feet separated the school from Khan's Citadel.

Despite the strong sun, cold needles pricked his flesh. The school was too damn close. No matter how precisely the RDX-7S allowed him to focus the blast, without proper weakening of the Citadel's support structure, no way could he prevent debris from flying across the street. Considering summer school was in session, and the time and day of detonation—1:00 p.m. on a Wednesday—children were bound to be sitting in their classrooms, or worse yet, running around the playground.

They were all crazy. Farrell, Daley, even the president of the United States. They were all nuts. How could they expect him to implode the Citadel without taking adequate safety measures?

He'd allow no more Billy Dwyers. He didn't care if the kids in this school were American or not, or whether CRUSO viewed them as—how did Daley put it—collateral damage. People were people, and that was the end of it. He'd sooner forego the money, even at the expense of his family's financial security.

John could no longer dally on the sidewalk. Anyway, he'd seen enough. He'd play CRUSO's game until instinct and experience told him someone other than Khan and his warmongers might perish in the blast. When that happened, he'd walk away.

Following the soldier's instructions, John started out for the Rawal Regency Inn. He was impressed by the city's cleanliness. Streets straight, wide, and free of litter leant a futuristic air to Pakistan's national capital. The graceful co-existence of man-made symmetry and natural beauty almost took his mind off the dull ache gnawing at his belly.

Upon entering the Rawal Regency's elegant lobby, John inhaled an invigorating breath of cool air pumped in from condensers and fans churning to capacity. He got on the elevator, checked his watch, and saw he had 10 more minutes until his meeting with Lieutenant Hall and Sergeant Banta. John recalled the lieutenant's instructions on the jet to Bahrain. Wait in his room. They would come to him.

In the hall outside his door, John inserted his card key. Glad he'd given himself a few extra minutes to shower and change before his guests arrived, he opened the door. That morning, before leaving his room, he had drawn the drapes in the parlor. In the dark, he groped for the light switch and flipped it on.

"John."

John leaped backward, smashing his shoulder into the edge of the door as it closed behind him.

"It's us. Jeffrey Hall and Richard Banta."

John recognized the voice of Lieutenant Hall. "You scared the hell outta me."

John turned on more lights and saw the CRUSO operatives had changed into polo shirts and casual slacks. John shook the lieutenant's hand, then reached for Banta's. The sergeant's grip was firm, but he cast his eyes to the floor. Come to think of it, the lieutenant wasn't smiling either.

"Gentlemen, why the long faces?"

The young men shot each other tight, somber glances. Lieutenant Hall walked into the room's parlor and motioned for John to follow.

John complied, noticing the room was too cool for the beads of sweat glistening on the lieutenant's forehead.

The lieutenant took a deep breath. "First off, great work getting Crescent Moon to call Ted Dunne."

The telegram intended for Salena, intercepted by Qadeer, must have included the AMS phone number that connected directly to CRUSO. "That wasn't my idea. It must have been Dr. Zamal's."

"It worked. Prime Minister Behari has agreed to give the mission a chance. That's the good news."

"And the bad?"

"Please sit."

John got the feeling it wasn't a request. He sat in one of the parlor's white wicker chairs, while the CRUSO operatives sat in two chairs facing him.

"Patty Krause is dead." John heard the words, but they didn't register. "She was intercepted at a security checkpoint on the M-2 Motorway four miles north of Dina. Khan's security must have set up a traffic stop sometime during the past four hours. That was the last time our satellite scanned the highway for trouble spots."

"How could she be dead?"

"Our agent was on line eight cars behind hers. Every driver was stopped and questioned—destination, purpose of visit, that sort of thing. The guards must have seen the charges, or come close. Ms. Krause had been instructed to detonate if their discovery was actual or inevitable."

"She wasn't supposed to die."

"All we know is she jumped out of her car and started running, clutching her cameo. She headed for an embankment along the shoulder. The guards ordered her to stop, and she did. A second later she disappeared into a ball of flame."

"I don't believe it."

"We hadn't instructed her to run, but we assume she did to avoid killing anyone nearby."

John's heart couldn't help but wilt a little for the frail, brave woman. He slumped back in the wicker chair and sighed. "What now?"

"We'll have to use a different explosive. Something readily available through a Pakistani agent in Murree."

During his career John had worked with many types of explosive compounds, and was sure he could handle whatever they came up with. "Flex-X, Composition-B, C-8? Which is it?"

"Dynamite."

"Dynamite?"

"Gelatin dynamite, 12 inch sticks, two lbs each, detonation velocity 15,000 feet per second."

"We're talking steel I-beams, not granite boulders. I'll need a damn truckload."

"Within the next 24 hours we can take delivery of 160 lbs."

"Only 80 sticks of dynamite. That's like trying to blow up a house with a firecracker."

"We'll have access to an additional 50 sticks of ammonia dynamite by Monday afternoon."

"Dynamite isn't right for this job."

"It is, if you know where to position it."

"Don't teach me my business. You can't destroy a steel-frame, 12-story building—no testing, no weakening, and limited access—with 130 sticks of dynamite.

"Sure you can. The hardest part will be delivery."

"You're not listening."

"I am and we have no choice."

"I need linear shaped charges. Dynamite won't cut it, literally or figuratively."

"All of us—Colonel Daley, Major Farrell, and President Lloyd—are well aware your mission has become 10 times harder."

"What about the other 21 charges? Farrell said there were 42 RDX-7S prototypes, and Ms. Krause was carrying half of them."

"CRUSO's weighing that option. The problem is finding another courier willing to blow himself up on a day's notice."

"You found me."

"That was part luck."

The lieutenant had a point. "Even if I say yes, how the hell do you sneak 80 sticks of dynamite into Khan's Citadel."

"By delivering it to the hospital."

"Right, I can see it now. You walk up to the main reception desk and say, 'Excuse me ma'am, I have a shipment of dynamite for Dr. Zamal. Sign for it please.' You're off your rocker."

"Clandestine delivery can be made, we just haven't figured out how."

"Maybe Colonel Daley will drop it off himself."

"Our job is delivering the dynamite, yours is setting it. We'll do ours if you do yours?"

"Do I have a choice?"

Hall stared at him and said nothing.

John was beginning to wish he hadn't awoken yesterday morning with a craving for fresh brewed coffee from the Inlet Grill. "How do I find out where and when the first load's coming?"

"We'll meet here again tonight."

John remembered Khan's invitation. "We can't. I'm moving into the Citadel."

The lieutenant's jaw dropped.

"That's right, the general personally invited me to stay as his guest at the Citadel while I'm analyzing his hospital's software systems."

Hall broke into a smile. "I can't wait to hear the colonel's reaction."

"Tell him I must've made a good first impression."

The lieutenant and Banta rose. "We'll figure out a way to contact you."

John got up. "I'll keep my eyes and ears wide open."

Hall reached out and shook John's hand. "Good luck."

The three men exchanged good-byes and John went into the bedroom. He closed the curtains overlooking Rawal Lake and lay down, hoping a three hour nap might rejuvenate him.

Eyes closed, he put the situation in perspective. Why not do the best he could with the resources available, even if they were essentially useless? He didn't care if Khan survived the blast. His family was guaranteed $2,000,000 so long as he set off an explosion.

John turned onto his side. Something still nagged at him— something about doing the job right—and at the edge of sleep, the elusive memory came to him. A black and white photo he'd seen on the third page of *USA Today*—a kindergarten snapshot of a smiling five-year-old boy, the photo of little Billy Dwyer.

PART II

"Kashmir is paradise on earth, and I swear, someday it will be free."

—Dr. Salena Zamal, Physician, Pakistan National Hospital

CHAPTER THIRTY-FIVE

A drumbeat pounding on the hotel room door startled John awake. He glanced at the clock-radio on the table beside his bed: 8:08 p.m. He'd slept eight minutes past the time Khan had said someone was coming to pick him up.

He stumbled to the door and found standing in the hall two soldiers wearing tan uniforms and cross expressions. The taller of the pair was the same goon who had kicked in his stomach on the floor of the van, and later held his arms while Qadeer used his belly as a punching bag.

"General Khan said be ready at eight o'clock, no?"

"I overslept. Give me five minutes to shower and change." When John released the door, the taller soldier thrust out his arm to stop it from shutting.

"Ok, come in if you want."

"We do not need your invitation."

"Sorry, I forgot I'm not in the land-of-the-free and home-of-the-brave anymore."

The two soldiers exchanged thin-eyed glances, then turned and glowered at John.

"No, what I meant is, I'm sure you're both brave, this just isn't a free country."

The tall soldier came into the room first. "You think freedom is so good. Look what too much freedom has done to you're precious America. Turned its men into faggots and women into whores."

"Are all Khan's followers misogynists and homophobes?"

"What do those words mean?"

He wasn't about to start again, not with one of Qadeer's enforcers who already had it in for him. "I meant, are all his followers as observant and wise as you?"

The soldier smiled. "Now you are learning."

John took a quick shower, shaved, and put on the blue pinstripe suit he'd received compliments of CRUSO. He hastily packed his bags, and the two soldiers ushered him downstairs to a limousine waiting at the hotel entrance. In less than five minutes they arrived at the Citadel, where the limousine driver made a left turn through the command and control center's iron gates and pulled up to a cement walk under a concrete awning.

As John followed the soldiers through the Citadel's lobby, he soaked up any detail of the building's structure which might prove useful.

The main elevator bank, located in the lobby's center, gave John his first good news. Though all implosions were difficult, symmetric buildings with hollow top-to-bottom cores offered a ready-made shaft into which debris could fall freely. More importantly, such a design negated the need to detonate explosives on every floor.

The number of floors detonated was determined by the building's age, height, condition, surrounding exposures, and the direction of fall. A tall building with a large hollow center often required the weakening of fewer floors relative to the structure's height to ensure the building inclined toward the middle. Depending on what John discovered upon closer inspection of the Citadel, he might get away with setting and detonating charges on only one or two floors and still do heavy damage.

John's two chaperones led him to a small office on the 4th floor, where another soldier took his photograph and fingerprints. In an adjoining office, a different soldier sat him down at a small table and, reading from a clipboard, asked him a series of questions about his health and personal history.

This time no cattle prods lay in sight. In fact, while John was questioned, a mustached man in civilian clothes served him a cup of tea that looked a lot like warm milk. The sweet-smelling beverage, the man told him, was black tea mixed with milk and sugar, and spiced with cardamom, cloves, cinnamon, ginger, and pepper. Reluctant at first, John found each sip tastier than the last.

After the questions were over, a single soldier took John through a series of corridors to a small lobby at the 4th floor entrance to the skywalk crossing into Pakistan National Hospital. John observed two soldiers with machine guns slung over their shoulders standing behind a high, narrow counter. Beside the counter stood Captain Qadeer.

Approaching the counter, John observed a young man wearing green scrubs emerge from the skywalk into the Citadel. The man stopped at the checkpoint and handed the guards a slip of paper. The guards scrutinized the document, asked him a few questions, then let him pass.

A different man, wearing blue overalls, walking a few steps ahead of John and his escort, passed the checkpoint and entered the enclosed walk without pausing. John made a mental note: no problem leaving, third-degree coming.

When John reached the counter, Qadeer instructed him to proceed through the skywalk. With the captain following a few steps behind,

John crossed the enclosed walkway and entered the hospital. The corridors were dim, which made sense since, according to a sign posted in the hall, visiting hours had ended an hour ago. He and Qadeer rode the elevator one flight up, where an overhead sign indicated they were about to enter the Labor and Delivery Unit. They walked toward a U-shaped counter, which John recognized as a nurses station.

Two women chatted outside the counter. One was a nurse whose head was covered by a dark green veil, and the other, looking away, wore a long burgundy dress and matching veil. When the lady in burgundy turned around, John recognized the face of Dr. Zamal, and even with a veil shrouding her hair, she was stunning.

Salena greeted John with a polite hello and ignored Qadeer.

John looked down, not so much out of respect for Muslim culture, but to hide his shame that when their eyes met, his heart had skipped a beat or two. "Thanks for making yourself available on such short notice to help me evaluate your hospital's software requirements."

"I welcome the opportunity to assist you. Your stay in Pakistan is short, and the sooner we start, the more help I can give you."

Some women, beautiful women, stayed with abusive men by choice. Others stayed out of fear. John couldn't figure out why Salena stayed, when with a carefully executed plan, she could have escaped. He forced himself to look into her exotic eyes. "General Khan has invited me to lodge at the Citadel."

"Yes, he seems to have taken a liking to you."

Unsure whether to interpret that as a compliment, John followed Qadeer and Salena inside the nurses station to a computer on one end of the counter. With Qadeer peering over her shoulder, Salena clicked through a series of menus. Some screens required data entry, while others displayed patient records. At each screen, Salena stopped and launched into a tedious explanation of its purpose, relating to John her understanding of how it was designed. John didn't understand half her techno-babble, but at judiciously spaced intervals, he nodded knowingly and interjected grunts of interest.

If Salena's strategy was to bore Qadeer senseless, it worked. Clutching a urine sample, the green-veiled nurse who had been chatting with Salena emerged from one of the patient's rooms. Qadeer backed off from John and Salena, caught up with the nurse near the elevators, and engaged her in conversation.

Feigning interest in Salena's discourse, John shot a furtive glance in Qadeer's direction. The captain lit up a cigarette and effectively cornered the nurse by planting his hand against the wall behind her head.

Speaking softly, he interrupted Salena. "Is Qadeer related to that woman?"

Staring at the screen, she responded without turning. "Why does that matter?"

"I thought Muslim men weren't supposed to flirt."

"Qadeer does not obey the rules he enforces."

"Why am I not surprised."

"Muslim men should not smoke or drink either. He does both."

"Lucky me. Four days to live, and I get to spend them with a hypocrite who likes playing with cattle prods."

Shifting her head slightly in John's direction, Salena looked at him from the corners of her eyes. The white light of the computer screen revealed plusher lips and smoother cheeks than he'd noticed during their first meeting at the hospital.

In hushed tones, John explained to Salena what had happened to Patty Krause and the 21 high-tech charges she was to have delivered to Islamabad. He also told her that two American operatives who had accompanied him to Pakistan hoped to sneak 160 lbs of dynamite into the hospital sometime in the next 24 hours. He needed access to the Citadel to determine how and where to plant the dynamite, assuming it was delivered as promised.

John shifted his eyes toward the elevator lobby where Qadeer had trapped the nurse. "I need to shake that guy for at least three hours."

"Impossible. Qadeer will never let you roam the Citadel alone."

"Without a close-up look, I have no way of knowing where to position the dynamite. I'd even take those half-baked blueprints Major Farrell showed me in Washington."

"Blueprints?"

"They'd be better than nothing. Why?"

"Blueprints are easy. Watch what I do, and play along."

Salena called out to Qadeer, who frowned, obviously annoyed at the interruption. She told him she wished to examine the computer files in the Pediatric Unit. The captain flashed the nurse a lecherous grin and returned to the station. As he approached, Salena whispered to John, "First we must make a quick stop."

"Where?"

"You will see."

Qadeer grumbled all the way as they returned to the elevators and rode one floor down.

Several feet before a sign signaling entry into the Pediatric Unit, Salena stopped at a beige metal door.

Qadeer grabbed the doorknob. "There are no computers in here."

"Get out of my way."

Salena stood eyeball-to-eyeball with Qadeer, and for 20 seconds, neither blinked. John balled his fists, ready to sock Qadeer if he so much as touched Salena.

Qadeer finally backed off, smirking. "There is nothing of value in there, anyway. You have 10 minutes."

As John followed Salena through the door, he was surprised Qadeer remained in the hall, but when he glimpsed the captain pulling a cigarette from his pocket, he figured wherever Salena was about to take him, smokers weren't welcome.

Entering a large room where the only light came from nightlights plugged into wall outlets, John made out two rows of beds, not the robust beds he'd seen in the examination room, but flimsy mattresses perched on sticks.

Every bed held a body, some held two. As his eyes adjusted to the dark, John realized these people were children, half of whom lay curled up snoring. Those who weren't sleeping lay on their sides, eyes open, or sat up in bed playing with dolls, cars, or tiny trucks.

As Salena entered the room, a rail of a boy looked up and ran over to her. The brown-faced child hugged Salena. "I draw another picture for you."

"Thank you, Umar, but it is time for bed."

Clutching Salena, Umar regarded John. "Is that man bad?"

Salena knelt in front of Umar. "No, he is from America, and he is my friend."

"Then I will not shoot him."

"No, this man must stay alive."

The young boy skipped back to his cot and leaped the last three feet onto the mattress, bouncing so hard John was sure the frame would buckle.

John followed Salena to the last cot on the left. On a frayed mat beside the bed sat a young girl whose long hair hid her face. She stroked a shriveled monkey that had once been full and fluffy. When the child turned and saw Salena, she sprang up and wrapped her arms around Salena's waist.

"Aren't you sleepy?" Salena asked.

The dark-skinned girl shook her head.

"It is past your bedtime."

The child buried her face deep into Salena's lab coat.

"Did you try falling asleep by yourself?"

The girl pulled away and nodded.

"At least you tried. Give me a minute, Kalila, I will be right back."

Kalila sat down on the mat and resumed playing with her monkey.

John was overcome with curiosity. "Who are these children?"

Salena led John away from Kalila's cot. In a soft voice, she explained the children were orphans she had rescued from the streets of Islamabad and Rawalpindi, sheltering them in what she called the Freedom Ward. She described her pact with Ali Khan. He tolerated their presence in his hospital as long as she remained in the Citadel. If she fled, not only would Khan expel the children, it is possible they might never be seen again.

John now understood why she stayed.

Salena described the psychological scars Kalila bore having been forced to witness the execution of her parents. "Since that terrible day, she has spoken to no adult but the angel who protects her."

"I assume that angel is you."

Salena nodded. "Please give me a moment." She walked back to Kalila's cot, lay on the mattress beside the girl, and gently clasped her shoulder.

John recalled Christie had gone through a difficult phase when she turned five. Fearing the monsters who lurked in her closet, she made Maureen or him lie with her until she fell asleep. Staring down at Kalila, John realized how fortunate for Christie her monsters weren't real.

When Kalila was asleep, Salena rose and tucked a thin white sheet around the girl's neck. She whispered to John, "You cannot imagine how much suffering she has endured."

"I only hope the bastard who murdered her parents is inside the Citadel with me next Wednesday."

She smiled. "You are brave indeed."

John surveyed the frail cots lined up along the walls. "Trust me, you're a lot braver than I'll ever be."

As they walked together toward the exit, the door opened. Qadeer stood at the threshold, dragging on a cigarette.

Salena strode up to him. "Put that out. Children are sleeping here."

"Children? What children? All I see here is vermin."

John sneered at the captain. "Then you should feel right at home."

Salena warned John off with a stern look.

"You're right, he's not worth the trouble."

As Salena led John to the Pediatric Unit's nurses station, John occasionally glanced over his shoulder making sure Qadeer kept well behind.

Salena said softly, "Never embarrass a man in front of a woman."

"He deserved it."

"Maybe so, but push him too far, and he will kill you before you kill him."

She was probably right. Imploding the Citadel would be payback enough. He changed the subject. "Did you always speak good English, or did you learn when you lived in New York?"

"How did you know I lived in New York?"

"Major Farrell told me everything she knows about you, which I'm beginning to think isn't much."

"What else did she tell you?"

"That you completed your residency at the same hospital where my wife gave birth to our daughters."

"Saint Barnabas in Livingston, New Jersey?"

"The Community Medical Center in Toms River."

"An affiliate. I spent two weeks there."

"Small world."

They came to a nurses station identical in shape and size to the station in Labor and Delivery. Salena greeted a white-veiled nurse sitting behind the low, front portion of the U-shaped counter.

When Qadeer caught up, he said to the nurse. "Get me tea."

The nurse looked at Salena, who nodded her approval. The nurse rose, walked from behind the counter, and disappeared down a hall.

Salena addressed Qadeer, "I must demonstrate for Mr. Cattano how physicians in the Pediatric Unit access patient history files and update treatment protocols. You are welcome to join us."

"I am already bored." He scowled at John. "Anyway, the smell of American chicken offends me."

John swallowed hard and looked away.

Qadeer turned and walked into a visitors lounge directly off the nurses station. The lounge's half-glass walls allowed John to see inside. The room, empty before Qadeer entered, was furnished with two plaid sofas, three chairs, and several tables stacked with magazines and children's toys. A color TV mounted to the wall blared a program in a foreign language.

Qadeer picked up a remote from one of the tables and started clicking.

Salena led John around the back of the nurses station and stopped in front of a computer on one of the high counters. Standing at the keyboard, she brought up a menu unlike any she'd shown him in Labor and Delivery. Instead of choices like 'Master Patient Index' and 'Patient Transport Schedule,' John read headings like 'Security Attachment 45-BMA' and 'Preliminary Plat: 4th Floor.'

John glanced at the lounge. Slumped on a sofa, heels propped on a table, Qadeer appeared mesmerized by the agitated ramblings of a black-turbaned cleric preaching at him from the television.

Salena said, "Since the day Khan brought me here, I tried breaking into his data files. I had no luck in Labor and Delivery, or the pharmacy, but a month ago Dr. Raja found a back door. He showed—"

"You told someone what you're doing?"

"Dr. Raja is a good friend."

"He knows you're helping me implode the Citadel?"

"No, I have told him only that the Americans plan to send a suicide agent, but not that you have arrived."

"How well do you know this Raja?"

"Raja is like a father to me, but Ali Khan hates him."

"I'll take a wild guess. Khan's jealous."

"Yes, he believes Raja is in love with me."

"Is he?"

"I told you, Raja is a friend."

John wasn't sure any man could stay mere friends with Salena. "What did he find?"

Four mouse clicks later Salena came to a screen entitled 'Command and Control Center: Revision 2,' followed by a list of links numbered 1 through 12. "Raja failed to find evidence of Glorious Dawn. Even after the detonation at Baramulla, he refuses to believe Khan would plunge the subcontinent into all-out nuclear war. But while he was searching, he did find something else."

Salena nudged the keyboard toward John, who clicked on the '1.' A menu popped up with choices including 'Electrical,' 'Heating/Cooling,' and 'Plumbing.' He clicked on 'Electrical,' and instantly the screen flashed a schematic of the Citadel's 1st floor wiring plan complete with switches, receptacles, and branch circuits. He closed the file and clicked on 'Plumbing.' "Have you examined the plans for every floor?"

"Qadeer and his goons are constantly over me. I have seen only a few."

Now and then glimpsing into the lounge, making sure Qadeer hadn't budged from the sofa, John scrutinized the mechanicals for each floor of the Citadel, starting on the 12th and working his way down. By the time he reached the 7th floor, he realized Farrell's 20 percent confidence ratio in the accuracy of her diagrams was way too high.

The white-veiled nurse returned to the station holding a capped Styrofoam cup. John suspended his fingers over the 'control-alt-delete' buttons, ready to reboot if she entered the nurses station. Instead, the nurse paused in front of the counter and asked, "Where is he?"

Salena nodded toward the lounge.

The nurse's lip twitched. With her free hand, she pulled her veil tight to her cheeks. John watched closely as she walked into the lounge, handed the cup to Qadeer, and turned to leave. John couldn't hear what Qadeer said next, but it was clear he had called her back. When she stopped and faced Qadeer, John read fear in her eyes, and as if sensing her dread, perhaps delighting in it, Qadeer forced her to converse with him.

When John opened the mechanicals for the 3rd floor, he paused. The 3rd floor plan showed no interior walls, only open space supported by vertical steel beams at regular intervals. "What's on this floor?"

"The passenger elevators do not stop there. I believe it is empty."

John closed the file and clicked on a different diagram of the 3rd floor labeled 'Completion.' This one showed the 3rd floor divided into office clusters, each one labeled with strange names. John whispered the names to Salena. "'Reserved for J & K,' 'Reserved for Rajasthan,' 'Reserved for—'"

Salena shuddered.

"What's wrong?"

"I think I understand." She pointed to the screen. "'J & K' refers to Jammu & Kashmir. I also see Rajasthan, Gugarat, Haryana, Punjab, Himachel Pradesh, and Delhi—India's seven provinces nearest Pakistan."

"The same provinces Khan plans to capture."

"Yes, and I am willing to wager the 3rd floor is where he intends to house their federal administrative offices."

"Perfect."

"Insane."

"No, I mean the 3rd floor. It's ideal for imploding the Citadel. Close enough to ground level so if it collapses, all the floors above will follow. Nine floors, four through 12, will pancake onto the 3rd floor, crush the first and second floors, and in a perfect world, continue straight down to the 2nd sub-level."

"Where Khan is convening Glorious Dawn."

"Exactly."

"Why in a perfect world?"

"Because I have serious doubts 160 lbs of gelatin dynamite can generate enough force to topple the support beams. I won't know for sure until I get a closer look."

"But the 3rd floor is closed."

John scanned the plan, found what he was after, and pointed at the screen. "What about the service elevator?"

"Guards are posted at the service elevators on every floor."

John continued examining the schematic. "I'll use the fire stairs—two sets on every floor."

"I have seen the fire stair doors on the 4th and 11th floors, but have never tried opening them."

"Were they guarded?"

"Not when I have passed them."

John cut a look from the screen to the lounge to make sure Qadeer was still harassing the nurse. Satisfied he was, John examined different diagrams of the 3rd floor's electrical, plumbing, and ventilation systems.

Studying the diagrams, he whiffed a pleasant scent—the fragrance of a rose, or was it jasmine? He turned his head slightly toward Salena. Wisps of silky brown hair had escaped the sides of her veil, and when their eyes met, she acknowledged his look with a subtle smile.

"Can you print the diagrams for the 3rd floor and 2nd sub-level?"

"That will not be a problem." Salena pointed to the raised counter on the opposite end of the U directly behind them. "Wait at the printer."

As John walked to the printer, Salena tapped out commands on the keyboard. Standing in front of the printer, waiting for the diagrams, John heard a stern voice from behind.

"What are you doing?"

John spun to see Qadeer craning his neck over the counter and around the side of the terminal at which Salena stood. Unable to get a clear view of the screen, he gave up and started circling to the rear of the nurses station.

By the time Qadeer entered the U and walked to Salena's computer, she had clicked back to the Pediatric Unit's main menu. "Why do you bother me? I am simply doing as General Khan instructed—showing Mr. Cattano physician treatment files."

The printer next to John began to whir. Salena's eyes opened wide.

Qadeer turned and glared at John. "And what are *you* doing?"

Too late to stop the printer from spitting out the floor plans, there was only one thing to do. He scanned the printer's control panel, found the button he was after, and popped open the cover. "Fixing a paper jam."

With the printer's internal machinery exposed, he looked at the letter-size sheet which had begun feeding from the paper tray. The page was still blank. He turned to Salena. "I think the rollers are worn. You should call maintenance in the morning."

"I will definitely do so."

"Additional use will only cause more damage." John reached down and pulled out the plug. "Better no one touches it until the rollers are replaced."

"Yes, I will tape a note to the printer."

Qadeer scowled. "Enough. I should have returned both of you to the Citadel 10 minutes ago."

Salena smiled sweetly. "Mr. Cattano and I have covered much ground for one evening. I will attach a note to the printer and then we can leave." Salena wrote a note and taped it to the printer's feeder tray.

John left the Pediatric Unit feeling a lot more nervous than he was acting. As soon as someone plugged in the power cord, there was a good chance the two Citadel floor diagrams would print out.

In total silence the threesome walked briskly through the deserted halls of the hospital, and crossed the elevated skywalk into the Citadel. With a nod from Qadeer, the guard on the Citadel side let them pass.

John wasn't sure how to communicate what he'd learned about the Citadel to Lieutenant Hall and Sergeant Banta. He hoped the two CRUSO agents would find a way to contact him.

At the 9th floor, Qadeer escorted John off the elevator. Before the doors closed, he turned to Salena, "Thanks for your help."

Salena nodded. "We will continue our tour tomorrow."

Qadeer directed John through a labyrinth of halls until they came to a door with a gold plaque labeled 'Shah Rukin Suite.' The captain informed him breakfast would be delivered at 8:30 a.m. He must be dressed and ready to return to the hospital by nine o'clock sharp.

John managed a half-hearted thanks and entered the room alone. He flipped on a light and found himself looking at a king size bed and a typical hotel dresser—nothing as large or elegant as the word "suite" implied.

He undressed and climbed into bed. Cooled by strong air conditioning, the sheets felt good against his skin, but sharp pains pierced his stomach. He thought about what might happen if Salena didn't return to the printer before Qadeer or one of his lackeys. The answer was easy. Tonight—not Tuesday night—would be his last on earth.

CHAPTER THIRTY-SIX

An hour earlier, at 1:00 p.m., Major Farrell had surpassed her record for consecutive hours with no sleep. That record she had set last November during CRUSO Mission 002. After 10 rigorous weeks of 16-hour days planning and practicing, she'd become like a sister to Kevin Blanchard, the pilot who had agreed to fly a Lear jet into the Cessna Citation transporting Carlos Guzman and 500 lbs of his genetically altered marijuana. Only since May had Farrell begun emerging from the cauldron of guilt into which she'd cast herself for Kevin's failure.

By contrast, she had met John Covello twice, once to convince him he should accept CRUSO's offer, and later, that same day, to cram more data into his head in 60 minutes than anyone could expect to absorb in 60 days. Still, Farrell had a hunch John Covello would succeed. His determination to see Maureen and their daughters flourish despite his hard luck was strong. Not only had he survived his trip to Pakistan, but he had gained quick access to Dr. Zamal and Khan's Citadel. Both accomplishments gave Farrell good reason for optimism.

Now the ball was in CRUSO's court.

She looked across the table at a bleary-eyed Colonel Daley. "Actually, the idea was Sergeant Banta's."

Farrell had not addressed Ajay Agarwal, but the special envoy answered anyway. "If you had not sent an old lady to do a young man's job, this crazy plan of yours would not be necessary."

Daley swore out loud, then turned to Agarwal. "Stay out of this, you're only an observer. When I want your opinion, I'll ask."

Agarwal stood, leaned low across the table, and waved his finger at Daley. "You are wrong colonel. My job is to assure India is not wasting precious time entertaining your president's folly while Khan is counting the days and hours before he murders 20 million of my countrymen. I am not caring if my opinion means nothing to you. It means everything to Prime Minister Behari, and he, not President Lloyd, is gripping the trigger of India's nuclear arsenal."

Daley shot up so fast his chair on wheels smashed against the wall behind him. "If your prime minister and his long line of predecessors hadn't been so stubborn on the Kashmir question, we wouldn't be sitting here wondering how the hell to sneak 80 sticks of dynamite into Khan's fortress before he starts World War III."

"There is no question on Kashmir. It belongs to India. Plain and simple."

"Damn you, Agarwal. It's not plain and simple. An overwhelming majority of Kashmiri Muslims firmly believe India stole the province out from under Pakistan's nose. And the half million soldiers you've stationed in Kashmir haven't exactly endeared themselves to the local population. Maybe if your Border Security Force resisted the urge to rape Kashmiri women and murder Kashmiri boys, we wouldn't have to contemplate this so-called crazy plan of ours."

"You ... you double-faced Americans. Always quick pointing the fingers. How easily you forget My Lai and Abu Ghraib."

"Those were acknowledged criminal acts. American soldiers were tried, convicted, and sent to prison for My Lai and Abu Ghraib. I don't recall so much as an inquiry coming out of New Delhi for what your army did in Gaw Kadal."

"Gaw Kadal was different. Those men were terrorists."

"They were praying."

Farrell stood. "Please gentlemen. Leave politics to the politicians. We have a man inside the Citadel waiting for CRUSO to deliver 160 lbs of dynamite. That should be our sole focus." She turned to Agarwal. "We're doing our best under difficult circumstances. True, Ms. Krause's death was a setback, but we now have good reason to believe John is in a position to carry out the implosion—if we can get him some explosives. All I ask is you let us do our job."

Agarwal frowned, but held his tongue. Daley retrieved his chair, and they all sat.

Farrell addressed her boss. "Lieutenant Hall is waiting for the green light. What should I tell him? "

"In your estimate, what's our greatest risk?"

"Khan's old madaris buddy."

"Captain Qadeer."

"He was ruthless in Kabul, and he's brutal in Islamabad. Our own intelligence and Dr. Zamal's statements suggest he's suspicious of eveyone. We have to hope she finds a way to keep him off John's back."

She's been resourceful up to now, I see no reason why she won't continue. Give the lieutenant authorization."

"Very well, sir."

Daley swiped a day-old mission status sheet off the table and ripped it in half. "By the way, what's the word on John's 3-C's Report?"

"The FBI, IRS, and local police components have all been analyzed. So far, no surprises."

"What about his medicals?"

"Stacy called Dr. Chandler at eleven o'clock. He was finishing up and expects his lab to deliver John's original ERCP and PTC by five. He prefers sending us a complete report rather than transmitting the results piecemeal."

"Do me a favor. Have Stacy call back and tell him to send us what he has."

"Yes, sir."

"No reason to add tardy paperwork to our list of worries."

Agarwal cleared his throat. "If I were you, I would be worrying more about smuggling that dynamite into the Citadel than finishing your paperwork. Reports will not be mattering if Mr. Covello is not getting the explosives."

Daley glared at Agarwal. "First of all, thank God you're *not* me. Second, CRUSO's internal operating procedures are none of your business. And third, I assure you, John will get that dynamite. One more thing. If you open your mouth again about something that doesn't concern you, those damn avocado and sprout sandwiches you gulped down this morning will be your last."

"Are you threatening me?"

"Interpret it any—"

"Gentlemen, the more we argue, the less we work. Let's put our differences aside and concentrate on what's important. Please."

Daley and Agarwal exchanged scowls, then turned in different directions. The special envoy opened his briefcase, removed a file, and began thumbing through its contents. Daley picked up a stale mission status sheet, and tore it in quarters and eighths.

Farrell pressed the intercom and directed Stacy to ring up Lieutenant Hall. While she waited for the connection, it occurred to Farrell she hadn't asked Stacy about the status of the 3-C's Report on Dr. Chandler. The paperwork never seemed to end.

CHAPTER THIRTY-SEVEN

Having awoken an hour early to avoid her morning escort, Salena dressed quickly, left the Citadel, and hurried to the nurses station in the Pediatric Unit. Any doctor or nurse who happened to retrieve the Citadel floor diagrams before she did would likely show them to a colleague. An investigation would ensue, and Qadeer, who had seen her at the computer last night, would instantly accuse her.

She arrived at the Pediatric Unit by seven and found Nurse Laldin sitting inside the nurses station scribbling notes on a chart. The petite woman looked up, said good-morning, and returned to her business.

Salena entered the station from the rear, walked to the printer, and saw the output tray empty. She bent over to plug in the power cord and froze when she saw it fastened snugly in the wall. Glancing behind her, she saw only Nurse Laldin hunched over her chart.

In frantic silence she rose, scoured the nurses station, and spotted a trash bin beneath the counter. She walked over and saw two sheets of paper, face down, inside the circular can. She turned them over and found a copy of yesterday's hospital menu, and the note she had taped to the printer last night.

"Looking for these?"

Salena bumped her head on the bottom of the counter as she spun to confront her questioner.

Dr. Raja.

Her friend's face bore no scars, but his eye sockets, dark hollows filled with sadness, confirmed her worst fears about the pain he had suffered at the hands of Qadeer. "Please forgive me."

"For what?"

"If I had not come looking for you ..."

"Eventually Qadeer would have found a reason. Your presence gave him an excuse."

Salena clenched her teeth at the sight of the dark telltale bags under Raja's eyes.

Nurse Laldin lifted her head and glanced over her shoulder. Salena flashed a phony smile, and the nurse turned back to her chart.

Raja held two sheets of paper, both folded in half. He opened the top sheet, revealing the schematic of the Citadel's 3rd Floor. "What is this?"

Salena had caused Raja enough trouble and was not about to involve him in more. "It looks like a floor plan."

"Of course it's a floor plan."

"How did you get it?"

"I arrived early to run a nosocomial infections update in the Pediatric ICU. When I saw the note on the printer, I looked under the counter and found the cord unplugged. When I plugged it in, these came out."

"Interesting."

"Neither Nurse Laldin, nor anyone else I asked, said they saw you here."

"You showed them the printouts?"

"No, but when I visited the Freedom Ward, Umar was up, and he told me you were there last night with a man you introduced as a friend from America."

"He is a software consultant."

Raja stroked his left temple where his green turban met the wire frames of his glasses. "You make a fool of me, Salena. No software consultant needs a blueprint of Ali Khan's Command and Control Center."

"I have never seen those diagrams."

"Then you will not object if I show them to Dr. Mehdi."

The hospital's chief administrator, hand-picked by Ali Khan, would undoubtedly deliver the printouts to Qadeer. "Trust me, Raja, better you do not know the truth."

"Let me decide what I should know."

When Raja became stubborn, he never relented, especially where her safety was concerned. "Please give me the floor plans and walk away."

"That will not happen, not until you tell me everything."

Raja was a mild soul, incapable of taking the same risks as she to rid Pakistan of its menace and her of her keeper. If she disclosed that John was the American agent sent to topple Khan's regime, Raja might expose him, if only to protect her. Unfortunately, her friend had left her no choice. "He goes by the name John Cattano, but his real name is John Covello."

"Is this the spy America has sent to kill Ali Khan?"

"We must speak in private."

They walked down a long corridor lined with offices and laboratories until they came to Room 412, the empty patient room where Raja found refuge from Qadeer's wiretaps and listening devices. Salena glanced behind her down the hall to make sure no soldiers had followed. She entered the room, leaving the door open, since closed doors aroused suspicion.

For the next 20 minutes Raja fixed his gaze on her as she revealed the details of her plan to help John implode the Citadel.

When she finished, Raja gave her the same doleful look as her father did on the tarmac in Srinagar the last time he said good-bye. "If Qadeer catches you, he will make those soldiers in India look like playful schoolboys."

Salena shut her eyes at the bitter memory. She was sure Raja had not intended to pain her, only remind her—strong actions had strong consequences. "This plan will work. It is backed by the Americans."

"They are using you."

"You are wrong. The US does not wish to see Pakistan and India laid to waste, or Kashmir go up in flames."

"Perhaps you are right about India and Pakistan. Both are strategically important to the US. But America cares nothing for Kashmir, or the suffering of the Kashmiri people."

"Kashmir is paradise on earth, and I swear, someday it will be free. Helping the American martyr kill Ali Khan will bring that day closer."

"Do not delude yourself, Salena. Nothing in their plan includes freedom for Kashmir."

"When Khan is dead, I can return home and resume my father's struggle."

"What makes you think the Border Security Force will allow—"

"Excuse me, Dr. Raja. Have you seen … oh, there you are."

Dr. Uddin, an obstetrician who had joined the staff last month, stood at the door holding a patient file.

"I apologize for interrupting, but I have an important question for Dr. Zamal."

"No trouble, she is right here."

Dr. Uddin turned to Salena. "I did not expect you in the hospital so early. Nurse Vander heard from Nurse Laldin you were in the Pediatric Unit. I hope you don't mind."

"Not at all. What do you need?"

"Last night I ran an MRI on Nusrat Afzal. The lungs of her fetus are six weeks premature. I would like your permission to prescribe a steroid, perhaps Dexamethasone."

"Give her Betamethasone instead. Fewer injections will be required."

"The pharmacy ran out. It is on back order."

"Then I must examine the MRI myself. I will be up in five minutes."

"Thank you." Dr. Uddin smiled politely and left the room.

Listening to the fading clicks of the doctor's footsteps, Salena searched Raja's eyes for their intent. "You wanted the truth. Now you have it. Assure me you will do nothing to stop me from helping John Covello."

"The Americans have made you a pawn."

Perhaps if Raja spoke with John himself and got to know him better. "He is sacrificing his life to prevent a war that will destroy us all. When you meet him, you will understand he can be trusted."

"Next you will suggest I help him."

"Never would I ask you to put—"

"How may I help you?"

Raja was speaking to someone behind her.

"I was looking for Dr. Zamal."

Salena turned around to find Nurse Vander from the Maternity Unit standing in the doorway. "What now?"

"I am sorry Dr. Zamal, but a man from Federal Express wishes me to sign for an early delivery."

"Of what?"

"Four gurneys. I was not aware you had authorized such a purchase, and refused to accept them."

"Are you sure they are not meant for Emergency Services?"

"The man said they were addressed to you."

"Very well." This was starting out to be a busy day. "Tell him to wait, I will be up shortly."

"Thank you."

Salena paused a few seconds until Nurse Vander was out of hearing range. "Give me your word you will not interfere with Mr. Covello's mission."

"It is fraught with risk, especially for you."

"I want your word."

"I promise only this. I will not intervene so long as I detect no imminent threat to your life."

"If I am forced to marry Khan, my life is over anyway."

Raja handed her both printouts. "I will never forgive myself if you are caught."

Salena noticed at the corners of Raja's eyes fine rivulets of skin streaking back to his temples, revealing his years. She took the diagrams, glanced behind to make sure no one was watching, then embraced him.

He held her briefly and stepped back. "Go, before someone else comes looking for you."

She stuffed the floor plans in her lab coat. "I am forever in your debt."

"Pay that debt by avoiding danger."

Salena left Room 412 and backtracked to the nurses station. She bade Nurse Laldin good day, and was relieved to find no soldiers waiting for her at the elevators. She boarded the next car, pressed the button for the 5th floor, and wondered who in the world, without her approval, had ordered four gurneys for the Maternity Unit.

CHAPTER THIRTY-EIGHT

The alarm clock on the night table went off at 7:30 a.m., an hour before breakfast was scheduled to arrive at John's room in the Citadel. Groping for the off switch, John shut the buzzer and stared at the ceiling, relieved the morning hadn't greeted him with stomach pain. He relished moments like these, rare since May, when his belly was spared the excruciating agony. He felt so good, in fact, he could hardly believe he'd be dead in four months were he not blowing himself up in three days.

His thoughts turned to Lieutenant Hall and Sergeant Banta. They hadn't yet contacted him about where and when they planned to deliver the 80 sticks of gelatin dynamite. John would deal with the problem of reaching out to Hall and Banta later. Now he wanted a closer look at the Citadel's 3rd floor. If the 3rd floor were vacant, as the floor plans indicated, that was where he intended to position the dynamite. First, though, he must find a way to gain access undetected.

After a hot shower and close shave, John slid open the closet doors beside his bed. The pants, shirts, and business suit CRUSO had given him hung neatly from metal hangers on one side. On the other, he noticed two pairs of cotton trousers and long baggy shirts, one set white, the other emerald green, and both pairs came with matching cloth belts.

If he managed to slip away from the Citadel to track down Hall and Banta, dressed like the locals he'd be less likely to stand out. Anyway, the native garb looked downright comfortable. He opted for the plainer white set.

Even if John missed breakfast, he knew he must return to his room by nine o'clock, the time Qadeer was sending a soldier to escort him to the hospital.

He slid on his watch, and in one pocket shoved a pen and pad from the night table, and in the other, his wallet and a handful of rupee coins. After clipping on his guest badge, he headed for the door.

Grasping the doorknob, he stopped short. On the floor at his feet he spotted a small paper bag.

Inside he found his miniature Harley Davidson ElectraGlide. At least General Khan was a man of his word. Too bad he was bent on starting World War III. John ran his fingers over the Hog's tiny blue gas tank, wishing he could hold Maureen, Karen, and Christie one last time.

John stuffed the tiny Hog in his pocket and opened the door. Glancing both ways, he found the corridor clear of armed guards and security cameras.

He recalled seeing on the floor plans a service elevator abutting the Citadel's northeast face. Last night when Qadeer escorted him to his room, John had mentally recorded their route as they crossed from the hospital and wound their way through the Citadel's serpentine halls. If memory served him, a right turn from his room led north to the service elevator.

John heeded his instincts. He walked quietly through the carpeted hall, and stopped about 20 feet short of an intersecting corridor. According to the schematic, a right turn led down a short hall terminating at the service elevator. Stepping forward, he heard from around the bend a crackling radio, followed by a man's response in a foreign tongue.

Salena had said she'd seen guards posted at the service elevators on the 4th and 11th floors. Apparently the same was true on the 9th floor. John turned and walked back toward where he had started.

He remembered the blueprint showed fire stairs along the east and west sides of every floor. From where he was now, he'd find the nearest stairwell along the east wall, at the end of a hall intersecting the main corridor a few rooms beyond his own.

John passed his room, and when he reached the hall leading to the stairwell, turned left. He walked to the end of the corridor and stopped at a metal door labeled 'emergency use only.' He scanned the door for alarms, and turned the handle. The door wouldn't budge.

A perfect fire hazard, John thought. He could probably set the Citadel ablaze and achieve the same result he planned for Wednesday.

The other stairwell, on the west side, offered a last chance to avoid the well-guarded passenger elevators. He returned to the main corridor and continued down the hall, making periodic turns at shallow angles paralleling the building's octagon shape. He approached another intersecting corridor, which if he were right, should dead-end at the entrance to the west stairwell.

When he turned he found himself staring down a hall half as long as the one leading to the east stairs, but instead of terminating at a door, this hall dead-ended at a beige sheetrock wall. Odd that the diagram had shown a stairwell directly ahead of where he now stood.

There must be another way to enter the Citadel's 3rd floor. With the 9th floor service elevator guarded, the east stairwell locked, and the west stairs apparently nonexistent, he had but one choice—brave the guard at the main elevator bank and look for access on a different level.

He'd try on the 4th floor.

For one thing, on the 4th floor he wouldn't stand out as much as on other, more desolate floors like the one he was on now. On the 4th floor, the pedestrian bridge linked the Citadel to the hospital, and from what John had observed, medical staff, maintenance workers, and military personnel crossed frequently in both directions. He also recalled from the schematics seeing an employee cafeteria, five or six storage areas, and various unmarked rooms on the 4th floor. If stopped and questioned, he could say he'd gotten lost looking for the cafeteria. What John liked most about the 4th floor, however, was its location directly above the floor on which he needed to position the dynamite.

Making his way through the halls, John fiddled with his ID tag, making sure it hung conspicuously on his long white pullover. He entered the 9th floor elevator lobby and encountered a single soldier standing behind a high narrow counter.

"Good morning, Mr. Cattano. Up early today."

"I have a meeting at the hospital."

"You are not authorized to leave this floor without a proper escort. Captain Qadeer's orders."

"Does he think I'll get lost?"

"If you wish to go somewhere, I will call a chaperone."

"Look, Dr. Zamal is expecting me in the Maternity Unit to discuss installation of an incremental, integrated hospital information system to improve survival ratios of preterm infants at heightened risk of neuro-developmental abnormalities. When I tell her who delayed me, she won't be happy."

The soldier glared at John and picked up a radio. "Alpha 9 to Alpha 4. Mr. Cattano is coming down. Expect him in 60 seconds."

The radio hissed back words, but not in English.

John boarded the elevator and rode it to the 4th floor. When he stepped out, a soldier behind the counter called him over and scrutinized his badge. "What is your destination?"

"Heaven, I hope."

"What?"

"The hospital. Next door. I'm meeting Dr. Zamal. Before I walk over, I'd like a cup of tea. Isn't there a cafeteria somewhere around here?"

"The cafeteria does not open for 10 minutes."

John put on his best dejected look. "Darn, I really enjoyed the black tea you guys gave me last night." He bowed his head and started walking away.

"You'll find vending machines across from the cafeteria. Go to the end of the hall and turn right."

John flashed the guard an appreciative smile. "Thanks."

The guard waved him over to the counter at which he stood, and pointed to one of three tiny TV screens lined up beneath the shelf. "Those are the cafeteria doors."

John glanced at the other two monitors. One showed a solid door with the same 'emergency use only' sign as the door on the 9th floor. That ruled out the fire stairs. On the third screen he saw a side view of his own face, and that of the soldier standing next to him.

John again thanked the guard and headed down the hall.

At the next intersection he turned right, passed a pair of bathrooms, and came to a small alcove holding two vending machines. He dropped two 50-rupee coins into the slot, and extracted a Styrofoam cup filled with steaming black tea.

Standing in the corridor outside the alcove, he watched as a wall-mounted camera swiveled in his direction. A minute later three men in officer's uniforms came into view from around a corner. They lingered at the cafeteria doors and eyed John curiously. One officer whispered to the others, and both snickered in reply.

John was about to walk over and ask the group how they liked his native garb when a cashier opened the cafeteria doors from inside. At the same time, nine or ten dark-skinned men wearing civilian clothes approached the cafeteria from the opposite direction.

John assumed the guard at the elevators was watching him on the camera. He filed into the cafeteria behind the three officers, stopped just inside the double doors, and as the swarm of civilians pushed their way in, John nudged his way out, hoping the soldier in the lobby didn't notice him leave.

Back in the hall, he ducked out of the camera's line of sight and considered what to do next. With the east stairwell under surveillance and the service elevator guarded, that left as his only option the west stairwell he couldn't locate on the 9th floor.

Drawing on his memory of the schematics, John made his way to the corridor where the floor plans showed the stairwell entrance. He turned left where he was supposed to, and again confronted a hall abbreviated by a solid sheetrock wall—a hall leading to nowhere.

Something was clearly wrong. The corridor should extend another 15 feet, ending at the entrance to the west stairwell. What lay beyond the wall that blocked his path?

Looking up, he saw white foam ceiling tiles suspended on runners. If he could climb into the space above the tiles, he could look down onto the other side. To do that unseen, he would need access to one of the two rooms on either side of this 15-foot hall to nowhere.

There were no doors within the short hall, only beige painted walls. John reentered the main corridor and glanced left and right for the nearest doors.

About six feet to his right he saw a solid door labeled 'storage.' He tried the handle, but it didn't move. Remembering an on old James Bond movie, John pulled out his phony driver's license and wedged the plastic card between the door's face and strike plates. No dice.

He backtracked along the main corridor, and stopped at a door on his left labeled 'authorized personnel only.' He turned the handle, and to his surprise, the door opened easily. He slipped into a dark room, held the door open a crack, and groped for a switch.

He found one, flipped it on, and closed the door behind him.

John found himself in a room that resembled a small movie theater. Five rows of red cushioned theater chairs, each row with 10 connecting seats, faced a wall of glass. The door he had come through opened onto an aisle running along the theater's left-hand wall. An identical aisle ran along the opposite wall, and a narrow aisle running behind the last row of seats connected both sides of the theater. Folding chairs were set up in the wider side aisles, and speakers were mounted at all four corners of the ceiling.

He flipped two more switches and lit up the space behind the glass wall. When he looked through the window, his heart pounded.

On the other side of the glass he saw the same interrogation room in which Qadeer had questioned him. The restraining seat was empty, but the stainless steel table from which Qadeer had fetched his cattle prod held other devices he had not noticed yesterday.

Black drapes were bunched together along both sides of the glass inside the interrogation chamber, and when John realized he was looking at the chamber from some sort of observation room, chills ran up his back.

Pondering what poor wretch had been dragged in there after him, John had to remind himself of his immediate purpose. He looked up and saw more ceiling tiles. On the other side of the wall to his left should be the 15 foot dead-end hall. He walked about 20 feet down the aisle along the theater's left-hand wall and stopped. At this point, on the other side, he should find whatever lay beyond the hall to nowhere.

He propped a folding chair against the wall and stepped onto its seat. Reaching up, he jarred loose a ceiling tile, and saw three feet of dark open space above his head. Good news. The wall wasn't load-bearing and he should have a clear view over.

John hoisted himself, trying not to scuff the painted sheetrock. With his head and chest fully inside the space above the drop ceiling, he looked down over the wall, and confirmed his hunch. He was peering into a narrow, unlit space about six feet wide—as wide as the abbreviated hall outside—and 15 feet long. As he suspected, the short wall to his right inside the dead space was broken by a door. Above the door, the wall ran straight up into the floor above, indicating the wall was load-bearing. John was willing to bet the door below opened into the west stairwell.

Why General Khan would conceal an emergency stairway John couldn't guess, but now was his best chance to find out.

CHAPTER THIRTY-NINE

John lowered himself back into the interrogation observation room, stepped off the folding chair, and shut all but one set of lights inside the grim theater. Anticipating at some point he'd need to return, he folded up a second chair, stood on the first chair against the wall, and lifted the second chair over his head and dropped it through the vacant rectangle above. The chair clattered loudly as it slammed against the floor inside the dead space beyond the theater.

Leaving one corner of the ceiling tile ajar to allow in light, John scrambled up and over the wall. When his feet hit the floor inside the dead space, his knees buckled and he rolled sideways.

Unhurt, he got up, dusted himself off, and walked to the door he had seen inside the dark, narrow area. He grabbed the handle, the door swung open, and John stepped into a black void.

Firmly gripping the doorknob, his mind played an unexpected trick.

The foot he placed inside the stairwell failed to touch solid ground. When John looked up and saw a point of sunlight shining down from high above he realized his mind hadn't played a trick at all. He had stepped into a hole.

Instantly he tightened his grip on the knob, looked down, and found himself dangling by his right hand from a door that had opened into a deep shaft, probably as deep as the Citadel itself. All that stopped him from plunging into the dark abyss was his hand clenched to the doorknob and the door's hinges attached to the frame.

His fingers started slipping. With his left hand, he reached up and grabbed the knob on the other side of the door. Two arms now shared his body's weight, but he couldn't hang on forever.

John rocked his legs and feet until the door began inching back toward its frame. Each swing of his lower body brought the door closer, until finally, with one powerful thrust, he lifted his legs and propelled his feet through the open door. He latched his toes to the doorjamb, and using his toes for leverage, pulled on his legs and drew his thighs, hips, and torso back onto solid ground.

He caught his breath, grateful to be alive, and peered out over the floor plate into the darkness. Metal bars attached to the wall on his left caught his attention—a ladder. He scanned the rungs up and down, and saw they ran the full height of the shaft.

He noticed in the middle of the vertical tunnel four taut cables, and immediately, he understood what this place was—an elevator shaft.

When working off blueprints to prepare a building for demolition, John had often encountered situations where the schematics varied from actual construction, but a deviation of this magnitude was rare. He speculated that this shaft housed an elevator for Khan's exclusive use, and ran from the penthouse to the sub-levels, skipping all the floors in between.

John glanced at his watch. He had 15 minutes to finish his inspection and return to his room in time for breakfast.

He grasped the metal rungs inside the shaft and climbed down. At the 3rd floor he came to another door. John pulled open the door, and cautiously stepped off the ladder.

Safely inside the 3rd floor, John looked around and smiled. The entire floor was an empty shell, complete with exposed steel columns and not a soul in sight. Unlit light bulbs dangled from overhead wires, but windows running the perimeter of the building allowed in all the light he would need. Along the wall to his right, he spied two half-used, five-gallon buckets of cement compound, and a painter's ladder folded upright. He'd need the ladder to attach dynamite sticks to the overhead beams.

The only significant breaks in the vast space were a concrete rectangle at the center of the floor, which John speculated was the main elevator shaft, and a small concrete square at the other end, which probably housed the service elevator.

For the next few minutes John examined the horizontal and vertical I-beams to determine how and where to attach the dynamite. He thought about jotting down notes, but since Qadeer or one of his goons could frisk him at any time, he decided not to.

He gave the concrete elevator housings a closer look. All four doors of the passenger elevator were ringed by a low cement wall, but the service elevator was clear of any barrier. That could mean trouble. It wasn't unreasonable to assume Qadeer's soldiers periodically inspected the 3rd floor, and he'd have to keep that in mind when he returned to position the dynamite.

He walked to the windows fronting Constitution Avenue. Even at this hour, children were climbing monkey bars on the playground inside the Diplomatic Enclave. Eighty sticks of judiciously placed dynamite would certainly compromise the Citadel's structure, maybe kill most of its occupants, but from what he'd seen so far, making the structure fall inward using only 160 lbs of standard dynamite would be no easy task.

John checked the time. He was five minutes late for his eight-thirty breakfast.

He reentered the shaft of Khan's secret elevator, climbed one flight up, and stepped into the dead space adjoining the interrogation viewing room. He stood on the chair he'd left there earlier and hoisted himself to the top of the wall. Lifting the ceiling tile he'd left slightly ajar, he poked his head down and froze.

Through the glass partition at the front of the theater he could see into the interrogation room. The room was awash in florescent light and three soldiers stood beside the restraining chair. Their lips moved but made no sound. The speakers inside the observation room must be turned off, but from what John could see, it was apparent the soldiers were readying the chair for use.

He theorized the glass wall was actually a one-way mirror. To test his hypothesis, he extracted three sheets of note paper from the pad in his pocket, crumpled them all, and threw them into the theater. A soldier standing behind the chair looking straight at the glass partition didn't flinch as the paper wads flew across the observation room. Having confirmed his hunch, John was about to reenter the theater when the door off the hall opened and two men in tan khakis walked in.

John quietly placed the ceiling square back on its runners, leaving one corner ajar for light. Since exiting the way he'd entered was no longer an option, he considered what to do next. He could reenter the elevator shaft and climb to a higher floor. With a little luck, he might find alternate access to the Citadel's corridors. But even if he emerged unseen, his inexplicable appearance on another floor was sure to arouse suspicion.

Then he remembered the first door labeled 'storage.' He should be able to enter that room from inside the dead space by climbing over the wall behind him.

John moved the folding chair to the opposite wall and stepped onto its seat. He popped out a ceiling tile, hoisted himself, and balancing his weight on the wall's top edge, lifted a ceiling tile above the adjoining room.

The space on the other side was completely dark but for a thin line of light seeping in from under a door below to John's left. This was indeed some sort of storage room, and the door was probably the same locked door he had encountered earlier.

The near-total darkness made gauging the room's size impossible, however, he did make out directly below a row of metal shelves mounted flush to the wall. John lifted his legs and pivoted his body, praying the shelves held. Relieved they supported his weight, he climbed down, and guided by the sliver of light, groped his way to the door. Along the wall he found two light switches and turned them on.

John had expected to find himself in a room no larger than a closet, but instead, he had entered a spacious, irregularly shaped storage area about 30 feet wide. Two of the room's walls, including the one he'd climbed down, were lined with metal shelves holding office supplies, computer accessories, and paper printouts. The opposite wall, with no shelves, was piled high with metal desks. In another corner he saw several rows of black file cabinets, while the center of the floor was cluttered with assorted chairs and cartons of copy paper stacked six high.

No time to explore, John grasped the doorknob, shut the lights, and breathed a little easier when the doorknob opened from the inside. He released the door lock, figuring reentry to the hidden elevator shaft would be less risky through the storage room than through the interrogation viewing room.

Exactly how he'd secrete 80 sticks of dynamite through the halls of the Citadel without raising an eyebrow was a problem he'd have to solve, but for now he couldn't wait to share his good news.

Approaching the employee cafeteria, it dawned on him if Lieutenant Hall and Sergeant Banta failed to deliver those explosives in the first place, his good news was essentially useless.

CHAPTER FORTY

Steps beyond the vending machine alcove, where earlier he had purchased a cup of black tea, John sniffed a foul, familiar odor and heard the voice of a man he was growing to hate.

"So there you are."

John stopped and turned. "Oh, my shadow."

Dragging on his cigarette, Qadeer marched up to him. "Where have *you* been?"

"Why, can't get enough of me?"

Qadeer exhaled his smoke into John's eyes. "Do not worry, Mr. Cattano, I can have plenty more of you."

John waved off the smoke, realizing an argument with Qadeer wasn't worth the trouble. What he wanted now was to tell Salena about Khan's secret elevator, then contact Lieutenant Hall and Sergeant Banta to find out when they planned to deliver the dynamite. "I couldn't sleep, and I was thirsty, so I came down for a cup of tea."

Qadeer's eyes narrowed. "The guard in the lobby said you went to the cafeteria, but I did not find you there."

John held his abdomen with both hands. "Something in the tea didn't agree with me. I've been sitting in a bathroom stall."

"Americans. You all have weak stomachs, not only for pain, but for food as well."

"Are you here to insult me or take me to the hospital?"

"A bit of both, but first I have good news for you."

John felt like saying, 'let me guess, it's really you who's dying of cancer,' but instead, he asked, "What's that?"

"Last night, General Khan called the director of Lady Reading Hospital. He has arranged for you to meet with the hospital's Board of Trustees to discuss the benefits of your software. You are going to Peshawar."

John sucked in a quick sharp breath. It was one thing to sham a man like Ali Khan whose expertise was waging war. Quite another to fool a panel of experts in hospital and health care administration. "When am I supposed to fit a trip to Peshawar in my schedule?"

"Tomorrow morning."

Over the next few days John couldn't possibly spare time away from the Citadel. "But my plane leaves Wednesday."

"Don't argue, all the arrangements have been made. The general has authorized Dr. Zamal to accompany you. She served at Lady Reading Hospital before coming to Islamabad. The general thought it best if she personally introduced you to their staff."

"I can't squeeze in a trip to Peshawar."

"Declining the general's generosity is not an option." Qadeer's tone turned derisive. "Anyway, I look forward to spending more time with you."

"Don't even say it."

"Yes, the general has chosen me to serve as your escort. He wants only his best to protect the woman he loves."

"Not from me I hope."

"Despite our army's crackdown, the dacoits remain a problem."

"Dacoits?"

"Bandits. They sneak down from the mountains and rob motorists along the highways."

"Great." Maybe if John spoke with Khan directly, he could change the general's mind. "Please let me talk to your boss. I'll thank him profusely, but explain I need to spend every minute of the next three days right here in Islamabad."

"Today the general is traveling to … his schedule is full."

"But I—"

"Stop your fretting and follow me."

Silently brainstorming ways to bow out of Khan's offer to sell Med-Link in Peshawar, John followed Qadeer through the Citadel's corridors to the skywalk entrance. They passed the checkpoint unquestioned, and once in the hospital, rode the elevator to the 5th floor.

John approached the nurses station in Labor and Delivery ahead of Qadeer, and saw Salena arguing with a nurse in front of the counter. Standing off to one side was a man wearing a white turban and a Fed Ex uniform, and beside him, what looked like four new gurneys.

Salena turned to the Fed Ex man, who thrust a packing slip in her face.

"I tell you, I did not order them."

"Sorry, ma'am, but your name is right here."

She glanced in John's direction, grabbed the slip from the man's hands, and scratched her signature. The courier handed her a receipt, thanked her, then turned and walked toward the elevators.

Salena smiled weakly at John, and ignored Qadeer. John had almost forgotten about the printer in the Pediatric Unit, and wondered if Salena had retrieved the blueprints.

Qadeer pointed to the gurneys in front of the nurses station, and addressed Salena. "Who ordered these? Why do you need so many? Why are they in the middle of the floor?"

"Instead of asking so many questions, why don't you help me move them?"

Patting the mattress of the nearest gurney, Qadeer snickered. "Do you mistake me for your servant?"

John shook his head. "Forget it big guy, I'll help her."

"Good idea. Work will toughen you." Strutting past John, Qadeer chuckled and shoved his elbow into John's ribs. John grit his teeth to stop the pain from showing on his face.

Qadeer struck up a conversation with a young blue-veiled nurse behind the counter, while John gripped the safety rails of the nearest gurney. Alongside Salena, who pushed a different gurney, he wheeled the rolling cot toward the elevator lobby. "Did you hear we're going to Peshawar tomorrow?"

"I was informed last night after I returned to my room."

"Aren't you worried we're leaving the Citadel?"

"What difference does it make if you do not have the dynamite?"

"Good point." The muscles in John's arms began to ache. "Damn, these gurneys are heavy."

"Please, do not swear in front of me."

"Damn?"

"An American profanity."

"Damn's no curse, it's part of the English language."

"Maybe for you."

"I use it all the time."

"It shows disrespect."

"All right, all right, I'll be more careful." Caught off guard by Salena's reprimand, John changed the subject. "Did you get the floor plans?"

"I did, but not before someone else."

"Who?"

A doctor approached from the opposite direction. Salena greeted her, and waited until she was out of listening range. "Dr. Raja, the friend I spoke of last night."

"So now he knows everything."

"I had no choice, I had to tell him."

"I hope you know what you're doing."

"He is trustworthy."

"Does Farrell know about him?"

"No, but take my word, Raja will not betray us. He gave me the printouts."

Beyond the elevator lobby, they came to a wide corridor, where John paused. "Mind if we rest a minute?"

"Are you ill?"

"Beside my cancer?"

Salena looked down. "I am sorry. For the moment, I forgot. Fatigue is a common symptom of aggressive cancer."

"Don't sweat it." John hadn't meant to embarrass her. "Who knows, maybe Qadeer is on target—I am a weakling."

"No, you are ill."

On John's right a wall of windows overlooked a nursery. He surveyed a dozen basinets with Plexiglas sides, and counted three newborns, all swaddled in pink. Their wrinkled faces and squinty eyes reminded John of how Karen and Christie looked when they were born. "They're so cute, so innocent."

"Unless Khan is killed, when they become women they are doomed to lives of quiet despair."

"Is that really why you're helping America?"

"That … and freedom. Freedom for me and freedom for Kashmir."

"Then what I'm about to tell you should come as good news." John related his discovery of Ali Khan's hidden elevator, his descent through the elevator shaft, and his confirmation the 3rd floor was a vacant shell, ideally situated for positioning dynamite to destroy, or at least cause major damage to, the Citadel.

"That all sounds perfect, but when will your contacts deliver the dynamite?"

"I don't know. They told me to sit tight."

Standing beside the nursery window, Salena cocked her head and eyed him head-to-toe. "You will have no difficulty assimilating with indigenous men in a shalwar kameez."

"In a what?"

"The shirt and pants you are wearing, what most Pakistanis wear."

"To be honest, it's damn … darn comfortable."

"It fits you well."

They continued pushing the gurneys until they came to a short, wide hall on their left, into which Salena steered her stretcher. John followed, parking his gurney against the wall behind Salena's.

They headed back toward the nurses station, and when they passed the nursery, John again walked over to the window.

Standing beside him, staring at the babies, Salena whispered, "You miss your family."

John's words stuck in his throat, and he swallowed hard to get them out. "They made my life worth living. They're the reason I'm here."

Salena regarded him with big, glistening eyes. Her smooth brown skin and full pink lips assured the beauty of any child she might conceive, and he wondered why she had never married. "Do you think someday you'll want children of your own?"

She turned away, facing the glass when she spoke. "That day will come."

They walked back to the nurses station and found Qadeer still flirting with the nurse behind the counter. He saw John coming and smirked. "Do you enjoy working like a mule?"

"You tell me—you're the perfect ass."

"Are you calling me stupid?"

"Of course not. I would never insult stupid people like that?"

Salena pulled her veil across her face, biting back a grin.

"Remove the other gurneys, before I remove your tongue."

John and Salena grabbed the last two gurneys and rolled them away. When they passed the elevators, Salena said, "You should not goad him."

"He deserved it."

"I warned you once. Provoke him too far, and he will kill you."

"I'm gonna die anyway."

"Yes, when you complete your job."

"All I know is this—Qadeer had better be inside the Citadel, right beside Khan, when I bring it down."

"He and all who have brought ruin to Pakistan will be assembled for Glorious Dawn. Already I have seen many of Khan's generals and political puppets arriving at the Citadel for Wednesday's meeting. They gloat at the world, as did Osama bin Laden when he attacked your country."

The very mention of the terrorist's name aroused anger in John. "I have no interest in killing innocent people, and from the Citadel's 3rd floor, that playground across the street looks awfully close."

John and Salena reached the dead-end hall where they had brought the first pair of gurneys. "No doubt the task is difficult, but Allah will guide your hand."

They parked the last two gurneys against the wall. "If only Allah could get me the dynamite."

"Have faith. God is great, he will help us."

John rubbed his shoulders, sore from pushing the heavy stretchers. Their weight didn't seem to phase Salena, who pulled the Fed Ex slip from her lab coat. "When I find out who ordered these gurneys, I shall have a long talk with them." She scanned the air bill. "Planned Resources … an American company. I don't recall ever purchasing from them … and look at that. They're from New Jersey."

In stunned comprehension, John whispered, "Oh my God."

"What is wrong?"

"Where in New Jersey?"

Salena read from the paper. "Long Branch."

"Let me look at that." She handed John the air bill. "425 Westwood Avenue." His back and arms tingled. "The address of my company, Planned Demolition."

"You don't think …"

"I sure do." John examined the last gurney lined up against the wall. He found a zipper along the front side of the mattress and tugged it open. Beneath the zipper he encountered white plastic sheathing. He poked his finger through and tore open a foot long section. "Son-of-a-b … I mean, holy cow. They did it."

CHAPTER FORTY-ONE

L ooking inside the mattresses topping the other three gurneys, John estimated each contained 20 eight-inch sticks of gelatin dynamite, an identical number of electric blasting caps, two coils of insulated hook-up wire, and 10 rolls of duct tape. Inside one mattress, he also discovered two kitchen timers, each equipped with a pressure arm, microswitch, and two wires. As promised, Lieutenant Hall had delivered enough supplies to inflict heavy damage on the Citadel, but unless John found a way to transport these materials across the skywalk and down to the Citadel's vacant 3rd floor unnoticed, the Lieutenant's ingenuity would have been for naught.

Earlier that morning Qadeer let slip Khan was out of town for the day. The general's absence could give John an ideal opportunity to move this cache past the guards on the Citadel side of the skywalk. He hadn't yet thought of what excuse he'd give for wheeling four empty gurneys into the Citadel, but he'd come up with something. Right now, he must deal with a bigger obstacle, an obstacle with a penchant for inflicting pain and blowing smoke in his face.

Standing beside the gurneys, Salena looked over her shoulder. "Qadeer will not let us out of his sight."

John zippered up the mattress on the last gurney. "What I need is a distraction, something big enough to get that worm off my back and keep the soldiers in the Citadel busy."

A nurse in a green veil cuddling one of the pink-swaddled infants paused and peeked down the dead-end hall occupied by John, Salena, and the four gurneys.

While John stayed put, Salena walked up to the nurse and addressed her in a foreign language. John had no idea what Salena said, but the nurse smiled, and nesting the baby in her arms, disappeared.

Salena hurried back to John. "We cannot linger in the hall. Let us go to my office."

"What about the gurneys?"

"I told Nurse Rasheed I was mistaken—I did in fact purchase new gurneys, but these were not the model I ordered. I directed her to forbid anyone from using them. They must be returned to the supplier with no scratches."

"You sure weave a good tale."

"A talent that has kept me alive."

"Good thing I'm a fast learner."

To avoid Qadeer, Salena led John to her office through a back corridor that by-passed the nurses station. When he entered, the first thing he noticed were computer cables lying loose on the floor beneath her desk, with no monitor, CPU, or keyboard in sight. John reached down and picked up the coupler end of a printer cable. "Is this why you couldn't get in touch with Major Farrell?"

"Qadeer has become increasingly suspicious of me. He confiscated my computer, and his technicians are taking it apart."

"What will he find?"

"When I agreed to help Major Farrell, she e-mailed me encrypted files enabling me to chat with her. She explained the communications software was embedded in four obscure Microsoft Excel files, and unless the program was activated by a series of codes and passwords, the encrypted files were impossible to decode."

"Nothing's impossible."

"I agree, Qadeer's technicians will eventually find the encrypted files, but I am praying not until after Wednesday."

John couldn't help but feel a little sad, because for him "after Wednesday" didn't exist. "Yeah, I guess Wednesday can't come soon enough."

"And why is that?" The voice was not Salena's.

John turned and groaned.

Captain Qadeer, cigarette dangling from his fingers, filled the doorway. "I must stick to you more closely."

"Dr. Zamal was just giving me a peek at her patient files."

"Do you forget the need for an escort?"

"Now that *you're* here—problem solved."

Qadeer puffed hard on his cigarette, breathing a bright orange glow into its ashen head. "My presence is required at the Citadel. You must come with me now."

"But I'm analyzing the hospital's in-patient data recordation systems."

Qadeer took another long drag and flicked the half-finished cigarette into the waste basket beside Salena's desk. "Do it later, when I can spare a guard."

Salena glanced down at the trash basket, then shot John a stern, tight-lipped look, as if signaling him to keep quiet. "The captain is right, we can finish our work later."

"But we don't have—"

"Please, Mr. Cattano," she said, almost angrily, "you must abide by the customs of our culture."

John nodded his consent, though he was baffled by Salena's sudden obedience to a man she utterly despised.

Qadeer motioned for John to leave. Walking toward the elevators, tailed closely by Qadeer, John glanced over his shoulder to see if Salena was watching. What he saw startled him.

Her office door was closed and she was nowhere in sight.

Qadeer steered John into an open passenger car and they took the elevator one floor down. On the 4th floor, Qadeer directed John through a series of turns in the hospital halls. When John asked where they were going, Qadeer muttered something about making him wait in a visitors lounge in the Pediatric Surgery Unit.

After what seemed like a mile-long hike, they passed through a set of swinging doors and entered a long, deserted hall. Qadeer instructed him to stop at the third door on the right.

John obeyed, and turned to face Qadeer. "How long before a guard comes to get me?"

Qadeer adjusted his turban, and smirked. "As long as it takes."

Resigned to the delay, John turned the knob to enter the lounge when a shrill, ear-splitting shriek shattered the silence of the deserted hall. The jarring sound was steady at first, then a few seconds later, intermittent.

Qadeer stepped back and glared up at a red box mounted inches below the ceiling on the wall behind John. Along with an ear-piercing noise, the box emitted a flashing white light.

The radio on Qadeer's belt crackled and a frantic voice blared through the speaker. John couldn't understand what the man was saying, but the captain, now holding the radio to his ear, was obviously displeased by what he heard.

After a short exchange, Qadeer belted his radio and scowled.

John made a genuine effort to sound polite. "What's wrong?"

"A fire on the 5th floor. Smoke is filling the halls."

"That doesn't sound good."

Qadeer's eyes thinned, and he stepped toward John. "Never again let me catch you alone with Dr. Zamal."

John considered telling the captain to mind his own business, but thought better of it. "I'll be more careful."

Qadeer spun and marched briskly down the hall and out the double doors.

During the next three days John knew he must exercise discretion. As much as he hated Qadeer, the joy of prodding him wasn't worth squandering his family's future, or Salena's life.

John had no reason to hang around a hospital lounge for a guard who might never show. After making sure Qadeer was nowhere in sight, he walked through the swinging doors. As the panels closed behind him, he remembered the dynamite inside the gurneys. A fire could detonate the charges and innocent people, mostly women and children, could be killed.

John bolted down the hall, searching for the nearest stairway.

CHAPTER FORTY-TWO

Relieved that for the next six hours, at least, she needn't worry about keeping the peace between her boss and India's special envoy, Farrell stretched her legs out under the conference table. Fifteen minutes earlier, Ajay Agarwal announced he needed a rest and had left AMOC-CRUSO for the Depew House at the Indian Embassy, leaving the conference room quieter than at any time since the special envoy had arrived.

At 1450 hours Farrell had asked Stacy to call Dr. Chandler and request he e-mail all available medical reports and test results on John Covello. By 1630 hours, the doctor had faxed copies of John's CT scan, GI series, and PTC results, all confirming John's Stage IV pancreatic cancer. The only documents Chandler hadn't sent were John's ERCP and angiography, and his handwritten notes and charts. After those items were received, John Covello's medical file would be complete.

Chandler had not answered repeated calls to his home or office since 1930 hours, so Farrell had requested the FBI send an agent to the doctor's home in Marlboro, New Jersey to find out why he hadn't forwarded the remainder of John's file.

Though annoyed by Chandler's procrastination, at the moment Farrell had more pressing concerns. Lieutenant Hall had informed her 80 sticks of gelatin dynamite had been delivered to the Maternity Unit at Pakistan National Hospital, but he couldn't confirm Dr. Zamal, who had signed for the gurneys, knew the mattresses were stuffed with explosives. Farrell had tried disguising the airbill enough to avoid scrutiny by Khan's security, yet not so much that Dr. Zamal would dismiss the delivery as an unwanted nuisance.

Farrell now had no choice but to wait for John or Dr. Zamal to contact her.

She pulled out the CT scan Dr. Chandler had faxed earlier. "Based on the medicals we've seen so far, John would've been lucky to see Thanksgiving."

Colonel Daley, sitting across the table, opened his eyes and yawned. "Look at it this way—we gave him a chance to make his life count for something."

Maybe she was exhausted, or just plain cynical, but Daley's comment struck a raw nerve. "That something wouldn't be your promotion?"

"I don't like what you're implying, major."

"I don't like what *you're* implying, sir. His life counted for something long before CRUSO snatched him from his wife and kids."

"Be honest—he was a drain on his family."

"Not the way Maureen's been grieving, not the way his youngest still thinks he's coming home. No way they saw him as a drain. In fact, if the decision had been Maureen's, I believe she would've chosen four months with John over all the money in the world."

"That's a bold conclusion."

"Not according to John's preliminary 3-C's. From all accounts, their marriage was rock solid. True, John's troubles put a strain on the relationship, but she was sticking by him all the way."

"I'm not looking to pick a fight, major. Maybe you're right. My point was that by dying in the Citadel's rubble next Wednesday, John achieves more for his country—more for his family—than dying of cancer in four months."

"That's not how it sounded."

"Sorry, I'm tired. We're both tired." Daley thumbed through a stack of reports on the table. "Speaking of 3-C's, any word on Chandler's?"

"Stacy checked with Special Agent Clarkson around seven. They'll deliver a report, 90 percent complete, tomorrow morning at eight."

"Is Stacy still here?"

"For the duration."

"Did she say if he found anything interesting?"

"As a matter of fact, Clarkson mentioned that last November Dr. Chandler took out two hefty equity lines—one on his trophy house in New Jersey, the other on his condo in Aspen."

"What's so interesting about that?"

"He's two months late on both."

"How much did—"

The conference room door swung open, and in ran Stacy holding a single sheet of light blue paper. She rushed to Daley's chair and handed him the Priority 1 notice. "Sorry, sir. This just came in."

Farrell stood. "What's wrong?"

As Daley read silently, Stacy answered, "The FBI didn't find Dr. Chandler at home, so they searched his office. He wasn't there, either. They were about to call local law enforcement when they scanned a police radio transmission that a Ford Taurus had driven off the road into the Manasquan River. The description of the vehicle matched the model leased by Dr. Chandler. Turned out the car was his."

"So where's Dr. Chandler?"

Handing the notice back to Stacy, Daley turned to Farrell. "In the car. Dead."

"Heart attack?"

"Not with a .45 caliber entrance wound through the base of his neck."

Farrell stared at her boss in astonishment. "Who'd want Chandler dead?"

Daley looked up at Stacy, his gray eyes blazing. "Call Agent Clarkson immediately. Tell him to rush Chandler's 3-C's Report. I want it complete, in my hands, ASAP."

Her emotions wavering between curiosity and concern, Farrell more than ever wished CRUSO had been given a few more days to come up with a qualified candidate for Mission 003.

CHAPTER FORTY-THREE

Sprinting through the hospital's 4th floor corridor, John searched for a stairwell door. He careened around the next corner and nearly collided with two oncoming nurses. The veiled pair glanced at him and moved on. Covering his ears to muffle the shrill shrieks of the alarm boxes, John kept going.

Qadeer had said the fire was on the 5th floor. John remembered the babies in the nursery, and he worried about Salena, too. He must reach the gurneys before the fire ignited the dynamite inside their mattresses.

Beyond the passenger elevator lobby, he spotted a door marked 'stairs.' As soon as he entered, he whiffed the scent of smoke. Nurses, doctors, and patients with taut lips and watery eyes streamed down-stairs along the rail, while John leapt the risers two at a time.

At the 5th floor landing, John opened the door and found the haze grayer and the scent stronger than in the stairwell, but neither the smoke nor smell overwhelmed him. He saw well enough to make out a nurse trotting toward him, head bowed, cuddling a baby, and stepped out of the way at the last second to avoid a head-on collision.

He came to a T in the corridor. A left led to the nursery and the hall where he and Salena had parked the gurneys. A right would take him to Salena's office. The smoke appeared thickest to the right, so that was the direction he headed.

John passed a nurse pushing a wheelchair, and in it, a mother who kept shouting, "Get my baby, get my baby." Covering his nose, he fought his way through dense, gray billows, past the nurses station, and down the hall toward Salena's office.

Through the haze he discerned an approaching figure, a shadow at first, and as it got closer, a clearly defined outline of a veiled woman wearing a lab coat, and she was by no means in a hurry.

"Salena?"

The woman spoke calmly. "Yes, it is me."

John rushed up to her, and when they met, restrained his impulse to pull her close and shield her nose from the smoke. "Are you all right?"

She nodded.

He gently clasped her arm and led her down the corridor, back to-ward the nurses station. As they approached the end of the hall, four soldiers bolted around the corner and raced past them without a glance.

Beyond the nurses station they came to the passenger elevator lobby, and when they reached the stairwell door, Salena pulled her arm away from his. "The gurneys. They are needed to move patients out of the Cardiac Care Unit."

"What are you talking about? Those gurneys are rolling bombs, and this hospital's on fire."

"The fire is contained to one room."

"How do you—" All at once her meaning became clear, and he couldn't believe she had done it. "Which room, or should I guess?"

The smoke had caused Salena's eyes to water, but the gray mist swirling about her flawless face only accentuated their resolve. "You said you needed a distraction."

"I didn't mean to set the whole damn … darn hospital on fire."

"The whole hospital is not on fire. Only my office."

"You really set fire to your office?"

"Not me. Captain Qadeer."

"He couldn't have. You were right there when we left."

"You did not see what happened after he dropped his cigarette into my trash basket, how it burned a hospital menu I discarded this morning."

"No one's gonna believe a single piece of paper set fire to your whole office."

She regarded him with what he perceived as a bashful smile. "Friday night the captain left his newspaper on my desk. It accidentally fell into the basket. So did two of my patient files."

He was mistaken. The smile was devilish.

"I tried to extinguish the fire, I really did, but in my panic I knocked the basket over. After that, well, the carpet caught fire, then more papers. At that point all I could do was pull the alarm—exactly how we were taught. Really quite a mess."

John shook his head and smirked. "OK smart-ass. What's the plan?"

"We will use the gurneys to move patients from the Cardiac Unit, which is also on the 5th floor, down to the 4th floor. From there, we will transport them across the footbridge into the Citadel. The employee cafeteria and surrounding halls of the Citadel are designated patient holding areas during emergency evacuations of the hospital."

John smiled. "And after we drop off the patients, on our way back for more, I happen to get lost in the Citadel and find my way to the storage room I stumbled across this morning."

"You are indeed a fast learner."

"But don't the elevators automatically lock down? How do we get the gurneys to the 4th floor?"

"So long as the service elevator is not in danger of catching fire, it continues to operate for removing patients."

He was impressed with her spunk, but the plan was risky. "Don't you think it'll look suspicious, you and me wheeling patients side-by-side?"

"Not at all. You are a friendly American showing how helpful your people can be during a time of crisis."

"I'm not sure this is a good idea."

Salena frowned. "Maybe Qadeer is right, American men are soft."

"Hold on. What about Patty Krause? She was American, and she blew herself up rather than let Khan's soldiers get their hands on the hi-tech explosives."

"Yes, that took great courage, but she was a woman."

No doubt this pretty lady had a will of steel. "Whether in three days or three months, for me the ending's the same. You have your whole life ahead of you. Don't throw it away."

Salena stared into the smoky haze, and when she spoke, her voice was a whisper. "Dying for a noble cause is never a life thrown away."

He had his doubts, but wasn't about to argue. "All right, let's do it."

Salena led John through the Nursery to the dead-end hall where they had wheeled the gurneys before the fire. When they turned the corner, a nurse was backing one out.

Salena barked, "You may not use that."

The startled nurse spun. "I am sorry Dr. Zamal. I was moving it to the Cardiac Unit."

"That is why we are here. Go downstairs to Pediatrics. Nurse Rasheed needs help with the children."

The white-veiled nurse bowed curtly and hurried off.

John and Salena grabbed a gurney each. As they worked their way through a maze of halls leading to the Cardiac Care Unit, the smoke thinned out and John found himself breathing more easily.

When they reached the Cardiac Unit's nurses station, Salena spoke to a doctor who held a phone to his ear. While talking into the mouthpiece, the doctor nodded at Salena and pointed down a long corridor. Salena waved at John to follow. They entered a room with four beds, two occupied by elderly women. Following Salena's instructions, John helped Salena transfer the women onto the gurneys.

They wheeled the elderly women to the service elevator, where the guard let them board the next car. The elevator attendant let them off at the 4th floor, where John followed Salena across the enclosed skywalk.

On the Citadel side, they encountered a throng of doctors, nurses, and patients crowding the soldiers at the security checkpoint. Nowhere did John see Captain Qadeer. The guards shouted at the mob, ignoring John and Salena, who rolled their gurneys into the Citadel.

In the employee cafeteria, janitors were pushing tables and chairs to the sides, while nurses unfolded emergency cots in the center. A bearded doctor helped John and Salena lower the two elderly women from the gurneys onto padded cots.

Their cargo unloaded, John and Salena rolled the gurneys into the hall, and instead of turning right toward the skywalk, they veered left.

When they came to the storage room door, John twisted the knob and found it unlocked, just as he'd left it. After making sure the corridor was empty, he pulled his gurney into the room, turned on the light, and waved in Salena.

Both gurneys delivered unseen, John shut the door and locked it from the inside. He showed Salena where he had climbed over the wall and through the ceiling.

"How will you get the dynamite to the 3rd floor?"

"I haven't figured that out."

John heard footsteps in the hall. He pressed his finger to his lips, but whoever it was walked quickly past.

Salena tugged on John's wrist. "We must hurry before someone takes the other gurneys."

John shut the lights and they left. The crowd mobbing the soldiers at the skywalk entrance had grown. Taking advantage of the confusion, John and Salena entered the glass-enclosed passage without being stopped. Once back in the hospital, they climbed the stairs to the 5th floor and repeated the process with the second two gurneys.

Before leaving the storage room, Salena's bold, brown eyes lingered on John. She touched his shoulder. "The fire will occupy Qadeer for several hours. Use that time well."

"I'll work as fast as I can."

"Remember, Allah is at your side."

"I'll take help from wherever I can get it."

Salena left, and John locked the door. He extracted from the mattresses the dynamite, blasting caps, wires, timers, and duct tape, and set them on the floor at the base of the metal shelf. From inside one mattress, John dug out a detailed instruction pamphlet, and chuckled. Maybe CRUSO feared his two-year break had dulled his skills.

He yanked the sheets off the gurneys and fashioned a basket around an empty cardboard box. He tied a single sheet to the top of the basket, and twisted the white linen into a rope for lowering the basket to the floor inside the dead space. Examining the tools of his trade, he calculated he'd need five trips to move all the supplies over the wall.

He filled the box and slung the basket over his shoulder, then tied the makeshift rope around his waist. Though the box was heavy, he climbed the shelves with no trouble, and once on top, popped off the nearest ceiling tile. The fluorescent fixtures in the storage room threw off enough light to see inside the dead space. John carefully lifted the basket over his head, leaned over the wall, and slowly lowered it to the floor.

He pulled his legs inside the three-foot high space above the drop ceiling, turned himself around, and lowered himself onto the folding chair inside the dead space. After removing the supplies from the box, he pulled himself to the top of the wall and descended the metal shelves inside the storage room. He again filled the box, and made the same trip three more times without a hitch.

He was halfway up the shelves with his fifth and final load when a click-click-click from behind froze him in his tracks.

The doorknob.

John climbed back down and set the basket on the floor. He tiptoed to the door and shut off the lights, plunging the room into darkness.

The knob turned twice more. Both times, the lock held. Good thing, because anyone who entered and turned on the lights would see in plain view the four eviscerated gurneys and the last box of dynamite.

John heard nothing for several seconds, but the shadows of two feet blocking the sliver of light beneath the door disclosed the presence of someone outside. John's heart raced as he heard the jangling of keys, their insertion into a lock, and a full turn of the doorknob.

As the door opened, and light entered, John scrambled behind the boxes of copy paper stacked in the room's center. The door shut, transforming the room into a black void. He heard a hand scraping against the switch plate.

John had no time to think. He sprang from behind the boxes and lunged at the figure in the dark, slamming the intruder full force. John tackled what felt like a man, and the man fell easily. John straddled him and unleashed a flurry of punches.

The fallen man lifted his arms to protect his face. "No, please, stop."

John kept whaling, aiming for the man's face and neck.

"Don't hurt me, please don't hurt me."

The man sounded like he was about to cry.

"John … John Covello, please don't hurt me."

How did this man know his name? "Stay where you are." John got up, turned on the light, and found himself looking at an older gentleman whose head was covered with a green turban, and whose lip was smeared with fresh blood. "And who, may I ask, are you?"

CHAPTER FORTY-FOUR

Major Farrell placed the handset on the receiver, and related to Colonel Daley what FBI Special Agent Steve Clarkson had just told her. "Twenty minutes ago two Monmouth County detectives picked up a 26-year-old white male of Russian descent. The suspect isn't saying much, but they've identified him as a low-level enforcer for the Chalikoff crime family operating out of Brooklyn."

Daley rolled his chair away from the conference table, clasped his hands across his chest, and rocked. "The Russian Mafia doesn't kill a man unless he owes lots of money and the prospect of repayment looks dim."

"It's too early to draw any conclusions, but Clarkson's office dug around and discovered Chandler owed a total of $250,000 to the Sands and Borgata hotels in Atlantic City. We didn't pick those up on the prelims because neither one's been reduced to judgment."

"So we can't be faulted."

Farrell shook her head, irritated by the colonel's attempt to dodge responsibility. "The fact is, if we had run a complete 3-C's on Dr. Chandler, we would've picked up not only those debts, but the fact that he's missed two payments on his equity line, and that last Monday his S-600 Mercedes Benz was repossessed by a leasing company."

"Sounds like he lived above his means."

"Clarkson said they also found evidence he'd fallen behind on his office rent. At first light this morning, they'll confirm it with his landlord."

Daley said nothing.

Farrell leaned forward. "Colonel, what implication does this have for our mission?"

Daley stopped rocking and took a deep breath. "My feeling? CRUSO's better off with Chandler dead."

"Why?"

"A man as desperate as Chandler might have tried something stupid, like extort money from the government in exchange for his silence."

"About CRUSO's existence?"

"Yes. The Russian mob may have saved us the nasty business of silencing Chandler ourselves."

"I don't buy it. The FBI's totaled everything Chandler owes, and his referral fee would've easily covered all his debts, legitimate or otherwise."

"I know that, and so do you, and maybe in the seconds before he died, Chandler spilled his guts about CRUSO, and swore he'd have the money in a day or two."

Farrell could well imagine a man about to die saying anything to save himself. "I suppose if I were a 26-year-old professional assassin who's heard more sob stories than Jerry Springer, I wouldn't have believed him either."

"Of course not." Daley pulled his chair forward and thumbed through a manila folder on the conference table. "On the down side, now that Chandler's dead, it'll be up to the FBI to piece together John's medical records."

"An hour ago Agent Clarkson woke up a judge in Freehold. The FBI is searching Dr. Chandler's office this very minute."

"How long before we receive a full 3-C's on the late doctor?"

"Clarkson assures me he'll wrap up the report by mid-morning. In light of what's happened, though, we don't need his character profile to conclude he's a bad apple."

Daley closed the folder. "I honestly believe Chandler's affiliation with a shady lender bears no relevance to our mission. The doctor provided us with a reasonably qualified candidate, and to boot, saved Uncle Sam $2,000,000."

According to CRUSO's referral fee policy, if a referral agent died prior to receipt of payment, the government was required to pay the fee to the referral agent's surviving spouse, or if no surviving spouse, next-of-kin—unless the referral agent left no surviving spouse or next-of-kin, in which event, the government was obligated to pay no referral fee at all. Chandler had left no heirs, so with his demise CRUSO's duty to pay had been negated.

Farrell studied Daley's face, hoping her boss's conclusion was correct—Chandler's sleazy dealings had no relevance to John's completion of CRUSO Mission 003. During the next three days, she and Daley would have enough on their plate. What they didn't need were any more surprises coming out of Dr. Chandler's belated background check.

CHAPTER FORTY-FIVE

Kneeling beside the turbaned head of a man wearing dented wire glasses, whose nostrils leaked blood, John confirmed at least some of his punches had reached their target. "How do you know my name?"

"Dr. Zamal."

"Are you her friend who pulled the floor plans from the printer?"

"Yes, yes. Dr. Raja."

John's stomach pulsed painfully as he realized he'd pummeled this man for no good reason. He spotted a carton of paper towels on one of the metal shelves, ripped open a package, and exhumed a handful. "Hold these firmly against the bridge of your nose."

Raja pressed the paper towels to his face, and when he spoke, sounded like a foghorn. "You didn't have to punch me so hard."

"I'm sorry, but I haven't met many kind and friendly people in this country. I couldn't take a chance."

"You Americans, always with your stereotypes. Most Pakistanis are actually a lot like me—courteous and considerate."

"Yeah, like the butchers who murdered Daniel Pearl, and those sickos who burned 50 Christian missionaries alive in their own church."

"Don't you dare compare me to those soulless murderers."

The blood trickling from Raja's nose stopped, and John helped him to his feet. "How did you get a key?"

"From Dr. Zamal, who asked Khan's soldiers at the footbridge. She told them she needed access to the storage room to get paper and pencils for the children moved to the cafeteria."

John checked his watch. Nearly 30 minutes had passed since Salena had left him. "What's going on out there?"

"The fire has been extinguished, but everyone is still running around like crazy. The soldiers are trying to clear the smoke. Dr. Zamal has created quite a mess for Qadeer."

"So you know what she did?"

Raja wrapped a clean paper towel around those stained red from his blood, and stuffed the wad into his lab coat. "Dr. Zamal has decided you will succeed, with or without my cooperation. She is convinced your chances are better if someone helps you. Forgive my lack of enthusiasm, but this plan is dangerous, and in my opinion, doomed."

"Why bother at all?"

"I shall tell you up front, my sole concern is for Dr. Zamal's safety. If you are caught, Qadeer will know someone helped you from the inside. If you are found out today, it will be me, not her, who is seen helping you."

John glanced at the last box of dynamite at the base of the metal shelves. "Truth is, my job will go a whole lot smoother with an extra pair of hands."

"Then I offer them."

Raja's turban hid the color of his hair, but judging from his beard and creased skin, John put him well into his 50's, possibly early 60's. He wondered if Raja had a father-daughter thing for Salena, or maybe something more. "OK, I'll take your help." He pointed to the gurneys. "Roll those into the hall. If someone comes in for office supplies and finds four empty gurneys, that'll look pretty suspicious."

Raja dug deep into the pocket of his white trousers and pulled out a penlight. "Dr. Zamal said you might need this."

John tested the three-inch long flashlight. For a tiny object, it threw off an intense beam. "Where we're going, this will come in handy."

Raja moved the gurneys into the corridor, while John scaled the metal shelf carrying the last box of explosives. Dangling the basket he had jury-rigged from the sheets, he lowered the dynamite into the dead space and came back into the storage room. With John's help, Raja climbed the metal shelf, turned around in the space above the ceiling tiles, and lowered himself to the folding chair.

John shut the lights in the storage room, turned on the penlight, and followed Raja into the dead space. Their faces lit only by the narrow beam, John explained his plan.

Using the ladder mounted to the wall inside the shaft of Khan's secret elevator, they would descend to the vacant 3rd floor, where John would position 80 sticks of dynamite. He'd use Raja's help to carry the dynamite down, and to tape the sticks and wires to the I-beams.

John bundled the explosives and supplies into two sheets, packing one heavier than the other. Lugging the heavier bundle, John led Raja inside the elevator shaft.

As Raja stepped off the ladder onto the 3rd floor, John reached out, gripped the doctor's arm, and pulled him safely from the elevator shaft. They untied the sheets and walked to the windows facing Constitution Avenue. Standing two steps back from the glass, John looked down at the playground across the street.

At half past eleven, the monkey bars crawled with children, some fair, some dark, some veiled, some not, all laughing, tussling, and soaking in the warmth of Pakistan's summer sun. John sucked in a deep breath, and spoke as much to himself as to Raja. "Not a grain of rubble touches those kids. If I can't destroy the Citadel without risking their lives, I'm outta here."

"For an American, you have a strong conscience."

John glared at Raja, restraining his impulse to pound the doctor—this time on purpose. "Go to hell. I'm tired of you people calling Americans heartless and self-centered." Maybe he was tired, or maybe he had simply heard one too many foreigners bash America, but he could no longer contain his anger. "Even after the attacks in New York and Washington, you people still had a hard-on for America. When we dumped that maniac in Baghdad, what did you people do? Sulked—like Hussein was some kind of fallen hero. You know what your problem is? You're jealous. All of you. You're jealous of our freedom and our wealth. We have it, and you don't, so threatening either one brings you joy. That we pulled together and rebuilt so quickly after 9-11 just riled you more. That we took over Iraq in less than a month rubbed it in your face. Maybe if you people weren't a bunch of religious bigots, you might reap a little freedom and prosperity of your own."

Raja removed his glasses and fiddled with their delicate silver frames in an apparent effort to straighten the metal earpiece John had dented. He huffed loudly on the lenses and wiped the glass with the hem of his lab coat. "Let us start working. The task ahead is difficult."

John wasn't about to let Raja squirm away so easily. "So you agree with me."

"Another problem with Americans. They do not listen, they only talk. They know everything, and the rest of the world knows nothing."

"All right, smart ass. I'm listening."

Raja stared John squarely in the eye. "Yes, our government is founded on religious principles, Islamic principles, and I am proud of that. Yours … yours bans God from every public institution—even the most important—the very schools in which your children spend half their lives. Learning about God and morality in school is not bad. Your society worries so much about separation of church and state, but you have gone to the extreme. Any discussion of God's teachings violates your laws. The thought of banning the word of Allah from our schools is abhorrent. The five pillars of Islam are fundamental to building morality and character in our children, the same children who will one day become our leaders. Your courts have banned the Ten Commandments from your schools. What did it get you? Children who kill, children who steal, children who treat their parents like rubbish."

"You can't tell me Pakistan doesn't have kids who steal and talk back."

"Yes, and when they do, they are severely reprimanded. They learn their lesson and go on. In your country, a father who smacks his son for cursing him can go to jail."

"Violence begets violence. Hitting kids doesn't solve the problem."

Raja shook his head. "As I said before. You know everything, the rest of us are ignorant."

"That's not what I meant. I mean we can have different opinions, and still get along."

"Today we do not have time to discuss our differences, much less solve them." Raja pressed his glasses to the bridge of his nose. "But thank you for listening."

John would have liked to learn if they shared any common ground. Too bad in three days he'd be dead. "OK, then let's get to work."

For the next two hours John taped gelatin dynamite to the exposed I-beams. To reach the overhead beams, he borrowed the painter's ladder he had discovered during his solo trip to the 3rd floor. He attached the bulk of the explosives to I-beams nearest the floor's center, concentrating around the passenger elevator shaft.

John made a conscious effort to hide the dynamite sticks and connecting wires as he attached them. Though the 3rd floor contained nothing but steel girders and columns, he was reasonably sure guards would inspect this level at least once before the start of Glorious Dawn.

John had worked with gelatin dynamite as a secondary explosive on several prior demolitions. The tightly wrapped brown tubes, also called nitrogelatin, were packed with a jellylike mass of nitroglycerin, but also contained sodium nitrate, meal, collodion cotton, and sodium carbonate. The gelatin's water-resistant properties made it a favorite among drillers for shattering natural and man-made obstacles encountered underwater or in water-saturated soil.

Nitrogelatin for this job, however, was not what John had in mind. The force of a blast generated by gelatin dynamite did not focus in a particular direction, but discharged in all directions at once. A directed explosion, like the kind generated by a linear shaped charge, was almost always necessary for severing horizontal steel beams from their vertical support members.

John also worried about the sufficiency of the nitrogelatin's explosive power. The sticks weren't marked, but Lieutenant Hall had said each could generate an explosive force of 15,000 feet per second, cream puff strength compared to the RDX-7S Patty Krause was to have delivered to Lieutenant Hall. According to Farrell, the prototype RDX-7S charges generated an explosive force of up to 125,000 feet per second, and would have made imploding Khan's Citadel a foregone conclusion.

Gelatin dynamite also posed the problem of weeping, the separation of liquid nitroglycerin from the absorbent materials packed into each stick to keep the explosive gelatinized. Because settling occurred with gelatin dynamite stored for long periods, stored boxes were turned at regular intervals to reverse the settling flow. John had heard stories of old nitrogelatin sticks exuding their nitroglycerin and seeping through the paper wrapping, making them unreliable, and in some cases, dangerous to handle. John had no idea where Lieutenant Hall had obtained the dynamite he and Raja were using, but dark blotches on some sticks clearly indicated they weren't new.

Holding a dynamite stick in one hand, John stood on the painter's ladder under a horizontal I-beam running perpendicular to the central elevator shaft.

Raja ripped off a two-foot length of duct tape and handed it to John. "That leaves 12."

John had known he was running low on dynamite, but thought he had at least 18 more sticks. "Are you sure?"

"I am sorry, you have already used 68."

No way would 80 sticks be enough to guarantee an implosion. Even with the additional 50 sticks of ammonia dynamite Lieutenant Hall had said he'd try digging up by tomorrow, John would fall short. He estimated at least 120 additional sticks—200 total—were needed to inflict major damage to the structure, let alone cause the building to implode.

John wiped his brow. "I don't have enough to cut the beams. It won't work."

"You cannot give up."

"I need more dynamite."

"Allah will provide."

"While he's at it, maybe he could get me 50 aluminum-sheathed, linear shaped charges with HMX explosive core loads."

"You must have more faith."

"I must have more—"

From somewhere outside the Citadel, a man's voice cried out over a loudspeaker. In an Arabic tongue, his tone rose and fell as if singing a song.

"What the hell is that?"

"The muezzin. He cries out the Adhan."

"Excuse me?"

"The Call to Prayer." Raja walked to the windows facing east. "Come, let me show you."

John stepped off the ladder and followed Raja.

"See, over there." Raja pointed down Constitution Avenue, about five blocks away, to a four-story building topped with a white onion dome. The building's brick exterior, decorated with a brightly colored ceramic tile motif, was magnificent to behold. Men, hundreds of them, most wearing shalwar kameez, streamed through a two-story ogee arch that opened to the sidewalk. "Look at the minaret."

Along one side of the structure rose a long, narrow column capped by a pointed dome. The dome covered an arched pulpit, and inside the pulpit at the top of the tower stood a solitary man chanting into a microphone.

"What's he saying?"

"He declares the first Pillar of my faith. In the name of Allah, the Almighty, the Merciful … there is no God but Allah, and Mohammad is his messenger."

"So in the middle of the afternoon everyone drops what they're doing and prays?"

"Not only in the afternoon. Five times each day."

"Isn't that a pain in the neck?"

Raja rolled his eyes. "How often do you pray?"

Even before the Chicago accident, when John gave up church completely, attending mass on a regular basis meant once a month. "I guess whenever I feel the need."

"You are lucky God is forgiving." Raja turned and walked to the wall of windows facing west.

"Hey, where you going? We're not finished."

Raja picked up one of the sheets in which John had wrapped the dynamite, set it carefully on the bare cement in front of the glass, knelt, and bowed his head. "This is my time to pray."

John couldn't believe anyone but a terrorist could be so pious, yet Raja didn't spew hate. He didn't even sound angry—just devoted to God.

In three days, John's death was a certainty, and not once in the last two years had he turned to his Maker for guidance. Between now and Wednesday, he'd probably be too busy to make his peace with God, and for some odd reason, now seemed as good a time as any.

He walked up to Raja, whose forehead was pressed to the floor. Standing at Raja's side, John gazed out the window at the rugged mountains looming over the city. "Mind if I join you?"

The doctor looked up and smiled. "Not at all, my friend."

For 15 minutes, John knelt and prayed. He remembered Maureen and how much he loved her, and he remembered Karen and Christie. He begged God's mercy for killing Billy Dwyer, and he begged God's forgiveness for the many men he would kill come Wednesday.

They finished praying and went back to work. Standing on the ladder, John pulled a strip of duct tape off Raja's fingertips. "What about Muslim women? Don't they get to pray?"

"Indeed they do, but inside their homes."

"Don't they rate?"

"The Qur'an distinguishes their place in society."

"Yeah, the men make the rules, and the women obey."

"No, I said their role is different, not inferior."

"I wonder if Salena ... Dr. Zamal would agree."

"General Khan has made Dr. Zamal his prisoner. His breed of Islam does not adhere to the word of the Prophet. Dr. Zamal is justified in seeking freedom from Ali Khan."

John wasn't sure Raja would bite, but he decided to try anyway. "You and Dr. Zamal seem pretty tight."

"She is a good person, a kind and generous person."

"How long you know her?"

"We met four years ago, at Lady Reading Hospital in Peshawar."

"I'm giving a lecture there tomorrow."

"Dr. Zamal told me. Prepare well. If you falter, you may expose your ruse."

"In a pinch, I can toss the bull as good as anyone." John got back to the subject. "So how'd you end up here with Dr. Zamal?"

"Last summer I received an invitation from General Khan. He asked me to leave my post at Lady Reading Hospital, and offered me the position of Assistant Chief of Pediatric Medicine at Pakistan National Hospital."

"He must've admired your skill."

Raja tore off a two-foot length of duct tape. "More likely, knowing I was Dr. Zamal's friend in Peshawar, he wanted to keep me where he could watch me."

John thought about how quickly General Khan had invited him to lodge at the Citadel. Maybe the general's hospitality was driven by something other than a desire to woo contacts in the West. "Do you think that's the real reason he's been so nice to me?"

"I am certain."

"I should've known it wasn't my grace and charm."

"Ali Khan despises any man to whom Dr. Zamal exhibits fondness, which means you should be especially careful."

John wasn't sure why, but the thought Salena might like him pleased and frightened him at the same time. "From what I've heard, she's had a rough life."

"You cannot begin to know what horrors she has seen."

"Gotta give her credit, though. She's managed to keep all her aces." John taped the last stick of nitrogelatin to the I-beam above him, looked down, and found Raja eyeing him quizzically. "What I mean is this: She knows what she wants, she knows how to get it, and let's face it— we wouldn't be here right now if she didn't go out and do it."

Raja stared at the floor. "I am sorry to say, you are right."

"Is it really so bad if she goes after what she wants?"

John detected sorrow in Raja's tone. "Too often, to get what she wants, Dr. Zamal puts her life in jeopardy."

John wrapped the timers, leftover wire, and unused duct tape in a sheet, and tucked the white bundle in an overhead I-beam, out of view of the service elevator. His next task—break the bad news to Salena. Not enough dynamite to fell the Citadel, hardly enough to cause major damage.

The two men climbed into the hidden elevator shaft and scaled the rungs to the dead space on the floor above. John peeked over the wall into the storage room, making sure no one had entered, then descended the metal shelves, turned on the lights, and went back to help Raja up and over.

Appearing together in the halls of the Citadel after a five hour absence might arouse suspicion, so they agreed to stagger their departures. Raja would leave first.

The doctor pushed his glasses firmly on his nose. "If Captain Qadeer should discover your identity, please do not implicate Dr. Zamal, even under torture."

John remembered Qadeer had stolen his cyanide caplets. "I won't, you have my word."

"Is your word your honor?"

John's answer instantly came to mind, but he paused several seconds, making sure he truly meant what he was about to say. "Yes, you have my word, and my word is my honor."

"Good." Raja shook John's hand. "Until we meet again, Mr. Covello."

"Call me John."

Raja smiled and left the storage room.

Realizing he still had the penlight Raja had given him, John hid it on a shelf behind some printouts. He checked his watch periodically, and waited several more minutes.

He had no idea how to inform Lieutenant Hall he needed at least 120 sticks of ammonia dynamite, but the thought occurred to him he might call CRUSO directly. Why not phone Ted Dunne, his boss at Advanced Medical Systems, and give him a progress report on his business trip?

Chapter Forty-Six

Turning a corner on the 4th floor, John found himself in a corridor leading to the employee cafeteria. Gurneys and wheelchairs, most unoccupied, were lined up along the walls. A veiled nurse exiting the cafeteria guided an elderly man by his arm. Another nurse pushing a woman on a gurney followed the first pair out. John deduced the fire had been extinguished, and the hospital's staff was returning patients to their rooms.

John grabbed an empty gurney and wheeled it into the cafeteria. A nurse standing beside a cot near the condiment bar motioned him over. After they lifted a pregnant woman onto the gurney, the nurse instructed John to deliver the patient to Room 512.

John got in line behind the convoy of gurneys and wheelchairs clogging the security checkpoint at the skywalk entrance. The guards at the counter, busy placating an irate female patient, didn't notice John as he entered the glass-enclosed tube behind the caravan of wheelchairs.

The soldier working the hospital's service elevator took him to the 5th floor, where John wheeled the pregnant woman to the Labor and Delivery Unit. As he approached the U-shaped nurses station, he heard Salena shouting.

"Wait until General Khan returns. You will be ironing sheets in the laundry room."

Captain Qadeer waved his finger in Salena's face. "Do you know what I think?"

"What you think is irrelevant."

"You set that fire on purpose."

Salena's dark brown eyes grew wide with indignation. "What an absurd accusation."

Qadeer must have noticed John pulling up with the gurney. He turned, glowering. "Didn't I tell you to wait downstairs until I sent for an escort?"

John rolled the gurney against the wall and smiled at Salena, whose soot-smudged cheeks hardly diminished her beauty. "This very pregnant lady belongs in Room 512."

Salena's face lit up when she answered. "Thank you, Mr. Cattano. Thank you very much."

"I asked you a question."

John strolled to Qadeer, who faced Salena in front of the nurses station. "I wasn't gonna stand there while the place was on fire, so I found a quiet corner of the Citadel to prepare for my presentation."

The captain grinned scornfully. "Yes, tomorrow I shall be your constant companion."

Salena glared at Qadeer. "Not after I inform General Khan of your reckless behavior."

John admired Salena's cunning and courage, but pushing Qadeer too far would only make matters worse. "Calm down, Dr. Zamal. The fire's out. Everything's gonna be fine."

"Everything is not fine. I have lost an entire day's work."

Wary of the vicious glint forming in the captain's eyes, John stepped between them. "Captain, I just came from the 4th floor. There's a huge commotion on the Citadel side. The guards look like they need help."

"What kind of commotion?"

"Some lady's outta control. She's going off on your men."

Qadeer's eyes burned like lasers into Salena's forehead. Only after she looked away did Qadeer turn and stomp toward the elevators.

When the captain was out of sight, John spun to confront Salena. "Are you out of your mind, pushing him like that?"

"Look who's talking."

"He means business."

"So do I."

Not much kept this girl down, and he would've yelled at her for jeopardizing his mission, but that steadfast attitude and those alluring brown eyes checked his frustration.

A young orderly walked up to the nurses station and rolled away the pregnant woman John had transferred from the Citadel. After the young man and the gurney disappeared down a hall, John looked around to make sure no one was standing nearby. "Thanks for sending Raja."

"You said you needed all the help you could get."

"We wired the dynamite, but it's not enough. If I detonate what's there, it'll do serious damage to the floor above—maybe knock out a cross beam or two, but it's not gonna take down the building. I have to contact Major Farrell for more explosives."

"Call the number I called yesterday. I spoke with a man named Mr. Ted Dunne."

"Yeah, Mr. Dunne is really Colonel Daley, Major Farrell's superior officer."

"I'd suggest using my phone, but …"

"It's burnt to a crisp."

"Dr. Nayyar is visiting her family in Karachi. We can use her office."

John followed Salena to the fire stairs, and down to the 4th floor. In the hall, they passed a parade of wheelchairs and gurneys returning children to their rooms. When they approached the storage room where Salena had taken him last night, John asked, "Are the kids in the Freedom Ward OK?"

"My children were the first patients I brought back to the hospital."

"How did Kalila do?"

Salena stopped and looked at him, her eyes beaming approval. "You remembered her name."

"After what Qadeer made that kid go through, how could I forget?"

"Do you know Qadeer once raped a little girl, and killed her? He tried paying off her parents, and when they refused, the miserable Satan killed them too."

"Glad to know Khan's chosen the few, the brave, and the demented to lead his government."

"After Ali Khan dies, I am taking Kalila with me to Srinagar. I am the only person she trusts."

John's eyes lingered on Salena a bit too long. She covered her nose and mouth with her blue silk veil and continued down the hall. John followed her into an office where she flipped on the lights and pointed John to a phone. "Remember, all calls are monitored."

John dialed the hospital's switchboard, requested a line to America, and a minute later, the operator came back to say he could place his call. Reading from a phony AMS business card, John punched in the number.

On the third ring, a young woman answered. "Good morning, this is AMS. How may I direct your call?"

"This is John Cattano calling from Pakistan. I'd like to speak with Mr. Dunne."

"Very good Mr. Cattano, please hold."

After a short wait, a man's voice came on the line. "Mr. Cattano, how are you doing?"

John immediately recognized the voice, and resisted the urge to advise Colonel Daley to scratch his ass. "Just fine, and you?"

"Dr. Zamal called yesterday. She said you've already begun analyzing the hospital's existing software systems—even gone as far as identifying beneficial applications of Med-Link for the hospital's medical staff and administrative end-users."

John glanced at Salena. "Despite … or should I say thanks to … a hot little distraction, I made considerable progress this morning. All things considered, I believe Dr. Zamal is quite pleased with what she sees. I've also had the pleasure of meeting General Khan."

"So I've heard."

"The general has been supportive of my effort to upgrade his hospital's software, but there's just one glitch."

"I'm here to help."

"I ran out of marketing brochures. After distributing the 80 in my possession, I'm still short 120 pieces. If I don't get more, no way will I make a lasting impression on my audience."

"I understand."

"Can you get them to me?"

"We're running short. In the next day or so I can probably send 50, but more than that and I'll have to bring the proofs to the printer. The brochures wouldn't be ready until Wednesday, after you fly home."

Yeah, John thought, home to the arms of God. "Can't you rush them? It'd be a shame if I lost the sale because you didn't send me enough."

"We'll do our best."

"There's something else you should know."

"What's that?"

"General Khan has asked me to pitch Med-Link at Lady Reading Hospital in Peshawar."

"You're going to Peshawar?"

"Bright and early Monday morning."

"Are you sure that's wise?"

"The general insists. He's already scheduled a meeting for me with one of the hospital's bigwigs."

"Will that leave you enough time to satisfy your sales objectives in Islamabad?"

"Time's not a problem."

"Call me as soon as you return."

"Will do."

"While I have you on the line, John, one other thing." Daley's tone oozed reproach. "Dr. Zamal tells me you've had difficulty resisting the urge to speak your mind. Your candor has resulted in certain cultural misunderstandings. Is that true?"

"Absolutely."

"Do you think you might restrain that urge?"

"It's tough, but I'll try."

"Your sales quota is on the line."

"I appreciate your concern, Ted, but if you have a problem with how I work, maybe you ought to fire me."

Dead silence on the other end.

"Ted, are you there?"

"Yes John."

"Please, get me those extra brochures so I can finish my job."

"I'm all over it."

They said their good-byes and hung up.

Salena regarded John with eager curiosity. "What did he say?"

"He can't get me more than—"

"Excuse me."

Startled by a voice from behind, John spun to find Raja standing in the doorway.

Salena hastily tucked loose wisps of brown hair beneath her veil. "Raja, what are you doing here?"

His expression grim, Raja entered Dr. Nayyar's office. He nodded to John and addressed Salena. "I need to see you." His voice drifted into a subdued whisper. "It's about your mother."

Salena gulped, and the corners of her eyes misted.

"When I returned to my office, I found an e-mail from Dr. Qureshi. Your mother has taken a grave turn. Her blood pressure has fallen to 80 over 45."

Salena bit her lower lip and bowed her head. She choked out her words. "Is she still in a coma?"

"She has awoken twice, but only for a few moments. Dr. Qureshi gives her a few days, perhaps a week, before her heart gives out." Raja paused, and sighed. "Both times when she was conscious she called out your name."

The tears trembling on Salena's eyelids flowed freely down her cheek.

John checked his impulse to hold her. Instead, he said softly, "I'm sorry."

Salena lifted her head and spoke through tear-soaked lips. "I must go to her." She began marching toward the door.

Raja thrust out his arm, blocking her path. "We have been through this before—you cannot go to Srinagar. The journey is dangerous, and those you leave behind will suffer Khan's wrath."

"My mother is dying."

"Your plan to assassinate Khan is insane, yet I helped. In return, I ask only that you wait until after Wednesday."

"My mother may die by Wednesday."

"You must stay strong."

"She is all I have left in the world."

Raja gently clasped Salena's shoulders. "Do not forget Naji."

Salena wiped the tears from her cheeks, and firmed her voice. "All the more reason I must destroy Ali Khan and return to Srinagar." She freed herself from Raja's grip, stepped back, and turned to John. "Those additional explosives you require. Must they be dynamite?"

Her question caught him by surprise. "I suppose not. Any charge with a directed force would do."

"What about plastic explosives?"

"Sure, depending on the type, they'd work better than dynamite."

"What about Semtex or C4?"

John's jaw dropped. She had rattled off the names of two powerful plastic explosives containing Cyclonite and PETN as their primary respective components. "How do you know about Semtex and C4?"

"A close friend to my father. For 20 years he has fought for Kashmir's liberation."

Raja glanced anxiously at the door, then turned to Salena. "You cannot mean Omar Shah?"

"That is exactly who I mean."

"Omar Shah is a murdering terrorist."

"He is a freedom fighter."

"Wait a second," John said, "what's your father's friend got to do with Semtex and C4?"

Salena spoke with an intensity John had not heard from her before. "My father was a journalist, not a fighter. He abhorred India's occupation of his homeland, but respected human life and refused to kill Indian soldiers. He fought all his battles on the editorial pages of the *Kashmir Monitor*. He and his boyhood friend, Omar Shah, would argue for hours. Omar pleaded with my father to abandon the press and take up arms. In the end, Omar was right. For expressing his views in print, my father was murdered by India's secret police."

"I'm sorry about your dad, but I still don't get the connection to Semtex and C4?"

"I know where to get both."

John ran his fingers along his jaw. "Let me guess. Srinagar."

Salena nodded. "Omar supplies weapons to insurgents in the Vale. He has access to many different explosives."

"How long would it take him to deliver 10 blocks of C4 to Islamabad?"

"I am afraid we must go to him."

Raja nearly shouted, "Have you taken leave of your senses?"

John asked Raja, "Is the trip dangerous?"

"Not only dangerous, but foolhardy. The terrain between here and Srinagar is rugged, and the mountains crawl with Khan's soldiers and sympathizers. Only a lunatic would travel to Srinagar, especially now, with India and Pakistan on the brink of war."

John turned to Salena. "What makes you think your father's friend would give you his explosives, anyway?"

"My father advocated an independent Kashmir, not one controlled by India—or Pakistan. Omar holds the same view. He perceives Khan to be as much a threat to Kashmir's freedom as India. If I contact him, and tell him why I need the explosives, he will gladly give them to me."

John stepped back from Dr. Nayyar's desk. He hadn't bargained on a treacherous quest to Pakistan's frontier to seek out more explosives. The idea had been for CRUSO to deliver the explosives to him. His agreement with CRUSO required he set off an explosion in the Citadel. Even if Khan lived, Maureen got $2,000,000, but if John ended up dead on some desolate mountainside teeming with terrorists, Maureen would receive only half what she needed to rid herself of his debt. His family was better off if he stayed put and worked with whatever materials CRUSO managed to deliver.

John shook his head. "I'm sorry, Salena, we can't go to Srinagar. It's too chancy. We'll wait until my contacts come up with more dynamite."

Raja exhaled an audible sigh. "Thank you for appreciating the risks."

Shielding her face with her veil, Salena lowered her head and turned away from them both. John sensed her desperation, and wished he could help, but Maureen and his children came first. Though Khan alone bore the blame for denying Salena the right to visit her mother, John couldn't suppress a twinge of guilt as an image of his own mother came to mind.

CHAPTER FORTY-SEVEN

Ajay Agarwal had awoken three hours early from his six-hour nap, and was nestled comfortably in his favorite chair in AMOC-CRUSO's largest conference room. Standing beside his own chair, Colonel Daley looked down at Agarwal across the table, and summed up the gist of his conversation with John Covello. "Lieutenant Hall and Sergeant Banta are reaching out to our Pakistani agent in Rawalpindi. They're almost certain they can take delivery of 100 lbs—50 sticks—of ammonia dynamite by tomorrow at 900 hours, Pakistan time. They'll try getting more through another agent in Murree, but they're not real hopeful."

Farrell, two chairs away from Agarwal, had begun tiring of the special envoy's doom and gloom. He rarely had anything constructive to say, and now was no different.

"I am thinking you are not even sure Mr. Covello has planted the first shipment of dynamite."

Farrell guessed Daley had reached the brink of exhaustion, because he made no effort to hide his contempt. "And I'm thinking you don't know what the hell you're talking about. It's obvious he positioned the gelatin dynamite."

"How are you knowing this?"

"I am knowing this because 45 minutes after our Pakistani agent made the delivery, Lieutenant Hall observed a disturbance at Pakistan National Hospital. I'm knowing this because after the lieutenant investigated the cause of the disturbance, he discovered the fire originated in Dr. Zamal's office. And I'm knowing this because I just got off the phone with John Covello, and he told me a hot little distraction helped him make considerable progress."

"Why you did not ask him directly?"

Daley's lips twisted into a derisive smirk. "You'd expect me to ask him straight out, on a call monitored by a dozen ISI surveillance experts, whether he planted and wired 80 sticks of gelatin dynamite in Khan's Citadel. That wouldn't give too much away, would it?"

"You gave him no code word, yes?"

"Yes, I mean no, we didn't give him a code word, but his message was clear—the first shipment of dynamite is set to detonate. Our objective now is getting him more."

"Why are you not delivering the remaining RDX charges?"

Daley sat down, and gestured to Farrell. "You tell him."

Farrell had investigated the possibility of smuggling the last 22 prototype RDX-7S charges to John in Islamabad. If flown via ST-131 transport from McGuire Air Force Base, the charges could reach the *USS Ronald Regan* as early as Monday at 0100 hours. The problem wasn't time, the problem was moving the classified explosives into Islamabad once they were snuck into Pakistan. "During the past 24 hours, Khan's security forces have tripled the number of checkpoints on all major roads in and out of Islamabad. If transporting the RDX-7S was risky before, it's near impossible now."

Daley had created an inch-high mound of shredded scrap paper, and had begun adding more. Tearing a blank sheet of paper in half, he looked across at Farrell. "How much longer before we get the full 3-C's Report on Dr. Chandler?"

"Last I checked, Special Agent Clarkson was targeting 1030 hours."

"Did he have anything new to add?"

"More of the same. Bad debts, nasty creditors. Turns out not only was Chandler in trouble with the mob, he planned to leave the country. Clarkson's team found a one-way ticket to San Paolo taped to the back of his blotter. He apparently planned to take our money and run."

"Why run? He would've had more than enough money to pay off his creditors."

"That I'm not sure of. Maybe he owed more than we know."

"Sounds like Chandler was in a bigger hole than John."

Agarwal must have been feeling left out. Folding his hands on the conference table, he leaned forward, and looked across at Daley. "When Mr. Covello was calling, you told him about Dr. Chandler's untimely death, no?"

Daley shook his head. "John has enough to worry about."

Farrell recalled something else Agent Clarkson had mentioned during their conversation. "The FBI's on-call physician took a good look at John's ERCP and angiography—the two tests Chandler never faxed to us yesterday. Based on his interpretation of the results, John's cancer is far more advanced than Chandler led us to believe. In fact, he speculates John wouldn't have lived another month or two."

Clinging to a half-torn sheet of paper, Daley's hands froze in mid-air. "Chandler said he had three-to-four."

"He may have lied about that, too."

"Why?"

"Maybe he assumed if we knew John's cancer was that far advanced, we would've passed him over as a candidate."

"And he'd lose his referral fee."

Something still wasn't sitting right with Farrell. "I guess that's the most logical explanation." She recalled both prior meetings with John. "But for someone with only two months to live, he still has a whole lot of energy."

"When John's original test results arrive, take them upstairs to Timmy."

Daley was referring to Dr. Timothy Sheehan, CRUSO's Executive Medical Officer. "I was planning on doing just that."

"Let's focus on getting John more dynamite." Daley's bleary eyes fixed on Agarwal. "Maybe your idea isn't so bad. I'll suggest to President Lloyd we transport the remaining RDX-7S charges to the Seventh Fleet. Who knows? Maybe before Wednesday we'll figure a way to sneak them into the Citadel."

With Khan's security forces on such high alert, Farrell had her doubts, but one could never tell. Sometimes opportunity knocked when it was least expected.

Chapter Forty-Eight

After a quiet dinner alone in her suite at the Citadel, Salena had returned to the hospital, not to check on her patients, but to attend to matters far more important.

Her freedom was so close she could taste it, and while John Covello was a courageous man, and more importantly, a kind man who sometimes made her smile, he did not take chances. Who could fault him? He had no concept of the Neelum Valley, Muzaffarabad, and the Jagran Nala. He was unfamiliar with the treacherous roads and mountain passes leading to Srinagar. She, on the other hand, knew them well, and would not give up her last hope for freedom because John lacked a few kilograms of plastic explosive.

Glancing behind her, making sure the receptionist at the pharmacy's drop-off desk did not see her, she slipped on a single latex glove and keyed in the five-digit code to enter the pharmacy's storage room. Once inside, she quietly shut the door.

Wasting no time, Salena unlocked a wall-mounted cabinet on her left and pulled down a blue jar from the top shelf. She transferred four teaspoons of clear liquid into a three-inch plastic vial, then placed the jar back on the shelf. From the same cabinet, she extracted a second bottle and scooped out enough crystalline powder to fill another three-inch tube. She put away the second jar and tucked both vials, tightly capped, inside her pocket.

She regretted Qadeer would not feel the effect of these potent chemicals, but took solace in knowing she had demeaned the captain in the eyes of Khan, then added insult to his injury by blaming the fire for her need to extend her workday well into the evening. So incensed was General Khan by Qadeer's negligence, he had ordered Qadeer to keep away from her while she caught up on her patient rounds and paperwork at the hospital. Khan's only demand was that she return to the Citadel by eleven o'clock.

Salena left the pharmacy through the back door and entered the stairwell from the service corridor. Exiting on the 5th floor, she walked toward the Maternity Unit.

Putting all the pieces in place required she finish one more task, a task which involved substantial risk, since an e-mail transmission over a non-secure line was vulnerable to interception. But she had no choice. The computer in her office was gone, and she must use another.

Salena greeted Nurse Jawaid, who sat behind the counter in Labor and Delivery filling in patient charts. They chatted about the fire Qadeer had started, and the havoc it had wrought on the ward. They reviewed the file of every patient on the floor to determine whether any had missed a scheduled dose of medication.

As was her plan, Salena discovered Nusrat Afzal had not taken her afternoon capsule of Terbutaline. She asked Nurse Jawaid to go immediately to the Pharmacy, order two dosages of the labor-inhibiting drug—one for tonight, another for tomorrow morning—and wait there until the capsules were ready.

The instant Nurse Jawaid boarded the elevator, Salena turned to the monitor on the counter, and typed in a 10-digit code she had stored in her memory long ago. With a little luck, in 60 seconds, she'd get a response, and soon thereafter, an answer to her prayers.

Only 30 seconds passed before the recipient answered with an inquiry of his own:

Salena, how may I help you?

Salena couldn't hold back a satisfied grin. Everything was falling into place with quite less trouble than she had anticipated.

CHAPTER FORTY-NINE

I n his room on the Citadel's 9th floor, John slept soundly until two in the morning, when his stomach pains returned with a vengeance. He tossed and turned until 5:15 a.m., gave up on sleep, and switched on the lamp beside his bed. Trying hard not to think about the 160 lbs of dynamite he and Raja had positioned in the same building only six floors below, John lay on his bed and skimmed the Med-Link marketing brochure.

Yesterday, after dismissing Salena's crazy notion of trekking to Srinagar to procure plastic explosives from a man named Omar, John had returned to his room in the Citadel to prepare for his sales pitch in Peshawar. At nine o'clock, shortly before undressing for bed, he had received a call from one of Qadeer's grunts informing him to be ready to leave the following morning at seven. A Lieutenant Hassan would pick him up.

When John asked why not Qadeer himself, the grouchy soldier snarled something about a change of plans requiring the captain's presence in the Citadel. John suspected the good captain had received a scolding from his boss over the fire he'd caused in the hospital.

Bored of reading the Med-Link brochure, John got out of bed, showered and shaved, and put on the white shirt, paisley tie, and blue pinstripe suit hanging in his closet. Never comfortable in a businessman's costume, John slipped into his Nike sneakers, and threw the black dress shoes CRUSO had given him into a plastic bag.

At precisely 7:00 a.m., a mustached soldier wearing a red beret knocked on his door. The thin-lipped man introduced himself as Lieutenant Hassan, and without a word walked John to the elevator and rode with him to the lobby. The Citadel's magnificent lobby, with its polished basalt walls, and ceiling adorned with tile mosaics and crystalline chandeliers, buzzed with activity.

A tall, turbaned man in a crisp military uniform, surrounded by an entourage of enlisted soldiers, had entered the lobby and was speaking with Captain Qadeer. John assumed the officer was one of many who had begun flocking to Islamabad for Khan's big bash on Wednesday.

Qadeer must have spotted John from the corner of his eye. While conversing with the impeccably dressed officer, Qadeer turned and gave John a hard look that said "drop dead." John smirked, but avoided the captain's gaze, figuring Qadeer might use a game of eye-chicken as an excuse to hassle him. Anyway, what John saw next was considerably more pleasing to behold.

All alone under the canopy at the curb leading up to the Citadel's front entrance stood Dr. Salena Zamal. She had shed her bland lab coat to expose a long, loose azure dress with a matching blue veil. Slung over her shoulder was a brown leather bag in which John guessed she had packed documents for his presentation.

Under cover of the canopy, John and Lieutenant Hassan walked toward her. The searing sun had already baked the morning air, and while the canopy's shade offered scant relief, John longed for clothing more comfortable than a tie and business suit.

Salena did not acknowledge the pair, at least not right away. Instead, she stared down the driveway toward the street.

John and Hassan were less than 10 feet away when she finally turned.

Her expression was stone serious. "Good morning, Mr. Cattano."

"Good morning, Dr. Zamal." John paused, waiting for Hassan to greet Salena next, but the lieutenant ignored her.

John continued, "Lovely weather we're having this morning. Wonderful day for a sales pitch."

Salena looked away, but not before John caught sight of her full pink lips pinching back a grin.

From a service road looping around the Citadel, a shiny black Mercedes Benz turned into the main driveway. When the gleaming sedan eased up to the curb, John was startled when the driver emerged from the passenger side. He then remembered in this part of the world they put steering wheels on the wrong side of the dashboard.

Like Lieutenant Hassan, the driver wore tan khakis, and belted around his waist, a semi-automatic pistol. He was clean-shaven, and wore no turban, an uncommon sight from what John had observed in Khan's Pakistan.

The driver flashed John a friendly grin. "I am Subedar Mazhar. It is my pleasure to assist you."

"Nice meeting you, too."

Mazhar offered to take John's AMS brochure, but John politely refused.

Lieutenant Hassan guided John to what would have been, in New Jersey, the front driver's side. Before getting in, John shed his jacket and shoved the garment into the plastic bag along with his dress shoes.

Sinking into the car's smooth plush seat, John whiffed the scent of new leather. Though he dreaded the journey's destination, at least he was going in luxury.

Salena opened the rear, right door and sat behind Mazhar. Hassan got in last, and sat behind John.

They pulled away from the curb and turned right through the high, wrought-iron gate onto Constitution Avenue.

Almost immediately, Salena lowered her window. Mazhar looked up at his rear-view mirror. "The air conditioner will cool you."

"I prefer fresh air. I hope that is not a problem."

"But an open window will make us hot."

Salena shot a caustic glance at Hassan. "Do you object if I leave the window open?"

The lieutenant said nothing, and Mazhar dropped the issue.

Inside the city, John recognized the same roads his taxi driver had taken on Saturday morning from Islamabad National Airport to the Rawal Regency Inn. Not until they passed the cricket stadium, where Khan had slaughtered thousands in the name of Allah, did John dare speak. He turned and looked at Hassan in the back seat. "Been to any games lately?"

Hassan ignored him.

"Guess you don't like what they play."

John noticed an automatic rifle poised upright against the rear seat between Salena and Hassan. He hoped the weapon wouldn't be needed to fight off the dacoits Qadeer had warned him about.

John gave up on Hassan and looked at the driver sitting next to him. "And you, Subedar? Been to any games?"

Someone in the back giggled. John turned to face Salena. "What's so funny?"

She pulled her veil over her mouth. "Subedar is not his name."

"Isn't that what the lieutenant called him?"

The man at the wheel smiled and said, "Subedar is my rank. Very much like the rank of warrant officer in the American army."

"Sorry."

"To answer your question, no, I have seen no game since they stopped playing cricket."

"Think they'll ever play again?"

The subedar glanced in the rear-view mirror, John supposed, to guage the reaction of his superior officer. "I hear talk, that is all. I enjoyed the cricket games. Those were happy times." In the back seat, Hassan cleared his throat, and Mazhar quickly added, "But I am honored to make any sacrifice necessary to achieve the noble goals of our supreme leader for a greater Pakistan."

They drove south through Rawalpindi on a two-lane road until they came to a ramped intersection, the first John had seen in Pakistan. Mazhar turned off onto the M1 Motorway, a six-lane expressway, each set of lanes separated by a wide grassy median.

John noticed a billboard along the highway written in English and Arabic: 'Islamabad the Beautiful.' The sign depicted a white dove grasping an olive branch perched serenely on the shoulder of a smiling turbaned man. John wondered if Khan might change the billboard before unleashing his nuclear bombs on India—maybe to a skull and crossbones etched on a gravestone.

He turned his attention to the exotic land passing before him. Both sides of the expressway were aflame with terraced gardens—brilliant bursts of red, yellow, and white. Beyond the resplendent array of color, John saw gently rolling carpets of green, and far to the north, majestic gray peaks crowning the horizon.

This fascinating country offered amazing delights for the eye. What a shame everyone here hated Americans. If in two days he weren't meeting his Maker, he might have returned with Maureen someday, after Khan was history, and share with her Pakistan's natural wonders.

A sign ahead read 'Hasan Abdal,' followed shortly by another, 'Taxila' and 'Wah Mughal Gardens.' John asked Mazhar, "Where are we?"

"Thirty-five kilometers northwest of Rawalpindi. Taxila and the Wah Mughal Gardens are world famous."

John hadn't heard of either. "What's in Taxila?"

"Archaeological sites dating back to the 5th century BC. Taxila was a famous center of Gandhara art and architecture. It flourished for a thousand years until the Huns invaded from the north."

A thousand years! John could hardly imagine what the United States, not yet 300 years old, would look like in 700 more. No wonder the people of Pakistan resented America, a prosperous nation having achieved that status in so short a time.

He glanced in the back seat at Salena, who was staring out her open window. The warm air buffeting her face rippled her veil along the sides of her head, and John remembered this was the first time in months she had been away from the Citadel.

Salena regarded John with lips severely pinched and eyes wider than usual. He got the impression she was trying to send him a message. She pulled her travel bag off her shoulder. Resting the bag on her lap, she reached inside and dug out a silver thermos and three paper cups.

The summer sun beating down on the car's black metal shell had transformed its interior into a furnace. Beads of sweat covered Lieutenant Hassan's forehead, and he'd begun looking wilted in his full military dress. John hoped the thermos held something cool and refreshing. "What've you got there?"

Salena jiggled the thermos, rattling ice cubes inside. "Iced tea. Would anyone like a cup?"

"Sounds great," John said.

"I will have some too," Mazhar quickly added.

Salena looked over at Hassan and waited for his answer.

"Very well," he said.

Salena poured iced tea into the top cup and handed it to Hassan, who swallowed its contents in a single gulp. The second cup she lifted over the front seat to Mazhar, who wolfed down the dark green liquid so fast he began coughing.

She placed the third cup, empty, back in her bag.

"What about me?" John asked.

"I mixed this tea from tap water. It will not agree with your stomach."

Retching at the podium before a roomful of doctors certainly wouldn't help his presentation, yet falling ill at the last minute might give him a credible excuse to avoid the talk in the first place. He was about to insist Salena pour him a cup when Hassan slumped forward into John's headrest.

John turned his head. "What's wrong?"

Gripping the steering wheel, Mazhar also looked back. "Lieutenant?"

John boosted himself to his knees, knelt backward in his seat, reached down to lift Hassan's head. "Stop the car!" He glanced at Salena, who stared calmly out the window.

John heard the car's motor revving faster and looked back at Mazhar.

The subedar was hunched over the dashboard, and his hands had dropped from the wheel.

"What the hell."

Before John could react, the car wavered from its lane. He lunged for the steering wheel and looked out the windshield. Dead ahead, about 500 feet, the highway crossed a river.

The subedar sat up, muttered something unintelligible, and collapsed unconscious against the driver's side door. John again pounced for the wheel, but before he could firm his grip, the car veered left, off the highway.

Bumping and bouncing down an embankment, the car's undercarriage scraped against sharp rocks, while its front grill plowed through prickly brush. The river John had seen from the highway was coming up fast.

Instinct took control. John yanked on his door handle and the door flew open. With the riverbank less than 100 feet away, John dove out.

Rolling and tumbling downhill, he clawed at the dirt, the rocks, and the grass. Unable to slow his forward momentum, he rolled over a smooth boulder, and for an instant lost sight of the river. His heart sank when he saw why.

A massive tree trunk lay directly in his path. Helpless to control his direction, he grabbed at the dirt and came up empty. He tried again, and for half a second held a clump of brush. He had slowed his roll—but too little too late.

Even as he balled his body to protect his head, his skull slammed into the tree's rock-hard bark and all at once, the sunlight vanished.

PART III

"If knowledge is power, then ignorance is weakness—and I'm no weakling, not anymore."

—John Covello, Demolitions Contractor

CHAPTER FIFTY

Eyes closed, vaguely aware he was flat on his back, John rubbed his head where it hurt and felt a lump the size of a quarter. He pressed two fingers against the bruise and winced. Warm liquid dripped down his cheek. He wiped his face with the back of his hand, opened his eyes, and saw his knuckles painted red with blood.

Using his other hand to shield the sun from his eyes, he discerned in the harsh light a human figure bent over him. Salena.

She gripped a pistol in one hand, and his suit jacket in the other. He noticed her chin was smeared with blood from a cut on her lower lip. She looked somehow different, younger, than before, and he realized she wore no veil. Her dark brown hair, darker than her eyes, flowed freely off her cheeks, cascading so low its soft ends nearly touched his nose. He smelled flowers, jasmine was his guess, and realized he was sniffing the scent of her hair.

As she examined his arms, face, and head, she spoke in a clinical monotone. "Abrasions on the right hand, minor contusions on the scalp, two-inch laceration on the forehead. Good." Salena reached down and dabbed the blue sleeve of his jacket against his forehead. When she pulled the jacket away, the sleeve had stained purple from his own blood. "We must leave quickly," she said.

"What the hell's going on?"

"I shall tell you when you stand."

"How about a little help? I'm pretty banged up."

Holding out her hand, Salena smiled incredulously. "Trust me, you are not banged up."

Back on his feet, John felt woozy. He spotted the black Mercedes parked on the rocky bank of a river, its right wheels only three feet from the water. "What happened? Where's Lieutenant Hassan and Subedar Mazhar?" Then he recalled the two soldiers had passed out. "What did you put in their tea? What were you thinking? What are you—"

"I shall explain."

"You sure will."

"Hassan and Mazhar are sleeping."

"Bullshit. You drugged them."

"Yes. They ingested a solution of chloral hydrate and pure alcohol mixed with water. They will not move very much for the next six to eight hours."

A sudden pain tore through John's gut, and he doubled over.

Salena dropped John's jacket on the dirt. Still gripping the pistol, she cradled his shoulder with her free arm. "Take slow, deep breaths."

John fell to one knee, did as she instructed, and gradually the pain subsided. He fought to keep calm. "OK, Salena. What are we doing here, and why are we doing it? You must have a very good reason, because from the looks of things, there's no turning back."

"Are you feeling better?"

John slowly rose. "Cut the crap and start talking."

"No reason to be nasty."

"Nasty? Me, nasty? I'm not the one who nearly got us killed."

"You said you needed more explosives."

"That's why I plan to hook up with Lieutenant Hall when we get back to the Citadel. He's getting me more dynamite."

"You yourself said plastic explosives work better than dynamite."

John remembered their conversation yesterday with Raja. "Don't say it. Don't even think it. This isn't some loony plan you've cooked up to get C4 from your father's friend in Srinagar?"

Tears welled in Salena's eyes.

John wasn't sure if he should hit her or hold her. "You know something—you're crazier than Ali Khan."

"Omar Shah will help us."

Bowing her head, Salena spewed out her sentences, as if she knew the second she paused he'd cut her off. "All the arrangements have been made. I contacted Omar last night. We will drive northeast to Azad Kashmir, and make a quick stop in Muzaffarabad. Omar's cousin lives there. He will give us the supplies we need to cross the mountains. Once we enter the Vale, two of Omar's friends will guide us south to Srinagar. Omar lives on a houseboat on Dal Lake. That is where he keeps his explosives. We only need go there and get them."

Shaking his head, John pointed at the embankment. "The only place we're going is up that hill to wave down the next passing car."

"That is not possible now."

Having poisoned two of Khan's soldiers, she was probably right. "When we're a no-show in Peshawar, Khan's gonna send out every troop at his disposal to track down his precious Salena."

Salena reacted in a way John didn't expect. She screamed. "Don't you dare call me his precious Salena. I am not his precious Salena. I will never be his precious Salena."

John's impulse was to yell back, but living with three women for more than a decade had taught him that would just set her off again. He rubbed his chin and spoke with as much calm as he could muster. "Salena, you know what I mean. He'll be searching for us."

The mild approach worked—her tone softened. "Trust me, I have thought this through. We will hide Hassan and Mazhar in the trunk of the car and leave them with Omar's cousin in Muzaffarabad."

"You heard Raja. The trip is too dangerous."

"Omar has already arranged for our passage to the Vale. He said he will do anything to stop Ali Khan from dropping more nuclear bombs on Kashmir."

"What exactly did you tell him?"

"The truth."

John suspected her answer before he asked. "The truth about me?"

"Yes."

"You're a piece of work, you really are. My mission's supposed to be a secret. How much does he know?"

"He knows you suffer from terminal cancer, and you were sent by the US on a suicide mission to assassinate Ali Khan and his ministers and generals. I told him the explosives you intended to use never arrived, that you obtained dynamite from a different source, but when you put the sticks in place you realized there wasn't enough."

"He must've asked why an American would take on a suicide mission. After all, I'm not like one of those al-Qaeda fruitcakes who beg for death in the name of Allah."

"I told Omar you volunteered for this mission because you are a rare American actually moved by the suffering of Pakistanis under the tyrannical regime of General Khan. You deplore that he has unleashed his sadistic henchmen on his own people under the pretense of defending Islam. Your empathy for the oppressed citizens of Pakistan, and your fear of the fate certain to befall Kashmir if Khan is not stopped, motivated you to accept this mission. In fact, your desire to save Kashmir from the clutches of Ali Khan is why I married you."

"What!"

Once more, Salena's eyes welled with tears. "I had no choice."

"Please don't cry, I'm just having a really tough time understanding, that's all."

"In Pakistan a man and woman cannot travel alone unless they are married. Omar would shoot us both if he knew we were not wed. I told him we were married in a civil ceremony. He did not ask many questions. I believe he thinks our marriage is one of convenience. He did express regret you are Christian, but forgave me because your mission is just, and also because Wednesday our marriage will be dissolved with your death."

"Gee, I'm glad Omar's so full of hope for our future."

"He likes you already. Rather than succumb slowly to your illness, you have chosen to die a quick and noble death—the mark of a true Pathan warrior who, like Omar, is willing to fight and die for his beliefs. Your mission to stop Ali Khan in his tracks before he rains more misery on the people of Pakistan and Kashmir gave you the perfect opportunity to fulfill your dream."

"Sounds more like your dream."

"I had no choice but to weave such a tale, not if Omar is to help us procure the C4."

John glanced at the Mercedes parked on the rocky river bank, and for the first time noticed the unconscious bodies of Hassan and Mazhar lying on the rocks behind the car. Salena must have moved the two men herself. "So last night, when I was worried sick about my presentation in Peshawar, you knew all along we'd never get there."

"I had no chance to discuss my plan with you, and even if I did, you would have said no."

"Let's pretend I've lost my mind and I take this crazy trip to Srinagar. If and when we get back to Islamabad with the explosives, won't Qadeer wonder why his soldiers aren't with us?"

"You mock me inferring I would be so ignorant."

"Oh forgive me, sweet Salena, but my family's future's at stake."

"Calm down." Salena tossed her head back and finger-brushed her hair off her eyes. "Dacoits ambushed our car on the road and kidnapped us. Such attacks occur in the frontier all the time."

"Why would anyone believe we were ambushed?"

"Qadeer's men will investigate our disappearance and discover this riverbank is where we were assaulted. We shall leave behind your empty wallet, and those of the lieutenant and subedar. You shall also leave your bloody jacket, and me, my empty travel bag and scarf. The ground here is mostly stones and brush, so it will not be easy for Qadeer's investigators to determine how many bandits attacked us. At twelve o'clock noon, Omar Shah will call the Citadel and identify himself as a spokesman for the Jammu & Kashmir People's League, the counter-revolutionary group who kidnapped us. He will demand a ransom for our release."

"You think Qadeer's gonna buy that?"

"Qadeer is always suspicious, that is his way. Khan, he harbors doubts about my loyalty, but as usual, his lust for me will erase them."

"If by some miracle we reach Srinagar alive, how do we get back to the Citadel in time for Glorious Dawn?"

"Omar knows many people in the Vale, militants and army officers alike. He will use his contacts to secure our return to Islamabad by Wednesday morning."

"No good. I need to get into Khan's Citadel by tomorrow night."

"He will arrange our return for whenever we require."

Wishing he could feel more confident, John waved his thumb toward the two soldiers behind the car. "What about them? Why aren't they with us?"

"Tonight, while the poor lieutenant and subedar fight the dacoits to the death, we elude our captors and hike over the Margalla Hills back to Islamabad. The truth. Omar's cousin will detain them in Muzaffarabad until Khan is dead."

John had no shortage of reasons why they shouldn't go. Khan's soldiers might intercept them on the road to Srinagar. They could get caught in the crossfire, if not between the Pakistan and Indian armies, then between warring terrorist factions. Even if they reached Srinagar unscathed, they only had one day to return to Islamabad, convince Qadeer they'd been kidnapped, and after that, John still had to plant the explosives on the Citadel's 3rd floor.

He shook his head. "I think we'll go back to the Citadel right now. We'll tell Ali Khan the lieutenant and subedar passed out from the heat. It actually works for the best. Their sudden illness forced us to turn around, and I had to bow out of my presentation. All we have to do is—"

"No."

"I didn't finish."

"The answer is no."

"No? That's it? Not even 'let's discuss the options' or 'look at all the angles.' Just no."

"Yes."

John surveyed the scene around him. First, the black Mercedes where Hassan and Mazhar lay still on their backs, then up the rocky embankment where he could make out the guard rail, but no part of the cars or trucks that occasionally whizzed past, and finally, Salena, who for all her strength and resolve was utterly dependent on what he did next.

"Seems awfully coincidental—you coming up with this plan *after* Raja told you about your mother taking a turn for the worse."

Salena stared at the ground, her lower lip quivering.

"Look at me Salena." When she did, he saw the tears getting closer. "Promise me this isn't some elaborate trick to leave Islamabad and stay with your mom. Promise me when we get to Srinagar, you're not gonna skip out on me?"

The brimming tears disappeared, and under the sizzling sun, he could swear he saw fire in those large umber eyes. "Yes, I long to see my mother, and yes, I long to return to Srinagar, but no, I will not abandon you."

"Why should I believe you?"

"If I do not return to Islamabad, too many people will suffer at the hands of Ali Khan."

John couldn't figure this woman out. Like Maureen, she stood fiercely by her convictions and those she loved, yet unlike his wife, Salena could lie and scheme without thinking twice to get what she wanted. Maybe that was how women living under the thumbs of their men had learned to survive. "OK, since you know it all, if I'm dressed in a white shirt and tie, how do I blend with all the other chauvinist husbands of Pakistan."

Salena reached into the brown leather bag at her feet, pulled out a pale green shalwar kameez, and handed it to him.

"You think of everything, don't you?"

"I try."

"I hope you brought a map, too, because I have no idea where the hell we are."

"Please watch your language."

"Sorry."

"And do not worry, I know exactly where we are."

CHAPTER FIFTY-ONE

John changed into the shalwar kameez, while behind the Mercedes Salena tied the hands and feet of Lieutenant Hassan and Subedar Mazhar. Thanks to the chloral hydrate, the two officers would remain unconscious for at least six hours.

John and Salena lifted the lieutenant first, then the heavier subedar, into the trunk of the car. Worried the men might suffocate inside a locked metal compartment under a scorching sun, John climbed into the car's rear seat and gouged four small holes through the leather upholstery into the trunk using a Swiss army knife Salena found in the lieutenant's pocket.

Having previously relieved the lieutenant of his semi-automatic pistol, Salena un-holstered the subedar's sidearm and threw it into the river. She scattered John's dress shoes and bloodied suit-jacket, her empty travel bag and an extra scarf she'd brought along, and the wallets of all three men, emptied of rupees, amongst the rocks and tall weeds along the riverbank.

Standing at the edge of the river with her back to the water, Salena surveyed the rocks and brush leading up the embankment to the edge of the highway. John guessed she was assessing their attempt to make the area look like a crime scene. She must have liked what she saw, because she smiled at him and nodded.

Salena opened the car's rear door, pulled out the rifle John had seen earlier resting against the back seat, and without any warning, tossed it to him.

Having never handled a rifle, John was surprised by its weight. "What's this for?"

"We will be driving through dangerous territory."

John held the rifle away from him like a week-old diaper. "I wouldn't know how to shoot this thing if you paid me."

Salena walked closer and stood at his side. "You are never too old to learn." Salena took the gun from John and gripped it firmly by its butt and muzzle. "This is a Heckler and Koch Gewehr 3—G3 for short. It is manufactured in Germany, and as you can see, it is not an aesthetically pleasing weapon."

"Gee, is it better to get shot by a pretty gun?"

"The G3 has a roller-delayed blowback action." She yanked on something behind the trigger that made the rifle appear longer. "This model is equipped with a retractable stock. On all models the move-ment of the rollers is controlled by the firing pin, which presses the rollers back into contact with the receiver sides."

"You don't say."

"Each magazine holds 20 rounds, unlike an AK-47, which holds 30. The G3 fires at a rate of 550 rounds per minute, with a muzzle velocity of 810 meters per second and an effective range of 500 meters."

"I'll bet you've never baked cookies."

Salena didn't answer, and instead, popped out the clip, inspected the magazine, and shoved the metal cartridge back in place.

"I won't even ask about knitting."

She lifted the rifle's stock to her shoulder and aimed its barrel at a distant tree. "When you fire, do not jerk on the trigger. The touch of your finger must be smooth and gentle."

"Unless my wife's been lying all these years, that part should be easy."

Salena frowned. "Very well. I shoot, you drive. Anyway, better if a man is seen at the wheel. In this country, it is the men who drive."

"Is that why you don't have many car accidents in Pakistan?"

"Actually Pakistan has the highest accident rate in the world."

"Maybe you should drive."

"Do not forget what you told me." Salena tossed him the keys. "You are a fast learner."

"No problem." John walked to the car's left front door.

"Excuse me." She pointed to the steering wheel on the dashboard's right side.

"Oh yeah, I almost forgot. Everything around here is backwards."

"Backwards? You are the one who cannot shoot a rifle."

John slid behind the wheel, started the engine, and slowly drove up the embankment. At the top of the hill, John paused and looked at the nearly empty twin ribbons of highway. "What do I do now?"

"Press the gas pedal, silly."

"I deserved that."

On the westbound lanes of the M1 Motorway, with tall mountains ever present to the distant north, they drove 10 minutes until they came to the next interchange. Salena pointed to a sign for Hazro and in-structed him to turn off the highway. At the bottom of the ramp, John paused at a square red sign, and at Salena's direction, turned right.

Unlike the smooth wide asphalt of the M1 Motorway, the two-lane road they drove on now was narrow and pocked with bone-rattling cra-ters. John was forced to keep his speed under 65 kilometers per hour. "Khan should take better care of his roads."

"President Razzak maintained them diligently, but when Khan took over, he funneled all the country's resources into the military."

"Doesn't an army need good highways to move men and equipment?"

"Tanks do not require perfect roads."

They drove past a cement factory, a power plant, and several decrepit industrial buildings John couldn't identify, but mostly they drove past trees broken by an occasional field of amber grass. John glanced at Salena, who stared straight ahead. He wondered why such a beautiful woman had never found love. Or maybe she had.

Yesterday, after Raja informed Salena her mother's condition had worsened, she said her mother was all she had left in the world. When Raja reminded her about someone named Naji, she replied Naji was all the more reason she must go to Srinagar. John wondered if Naji was a friend, or lover, waiting patiently for her in Kashmir.

For now, Salena's love life could wait, as another, more pressing concern nagged at him. Staring out her window, Salena appeared enraptured by the passing trees and meadows. Knowing she'd been confined to the Citadel since March, John was reluctant to disturb her. "At some point I should contact Major Farrell and Colonel Daley, and let them know what we're doing."

Salena turned her head and saw him looking at her. "Keep your eyes on the road."

To those he liked, John told the truth. "That's hard to do with a gorgeous gal sitting next to you."

For several seconds their eyes met and his pulse raced. He sensed he had embarrassed, yet flattered her. "So when can I call Major Farrell?"

She jerked her veil over her head, and stared out the windshield.

"I'm sorry. I didn't mean to offend you."

"I am not offended, not at all. We are approaching Haripur and I must cover my hair."

"Now I know why Muslim men keep their women hidden."

"Why is that?"

"If they're all as pretty as you, Pakistan would have even more car accidents."

She looked down, unable to hide a coy smile. "It is not a problem to contact Major Farrell. Omar's cousin has a satellite dish on his farm. But Khan's spies monitor the airwaves, so you cannot make the call yourself. After we leave Muzaffarabad, Omar's cousin will call Major Farrell for you. We will tell him what to say."

John chuckled. "You're amazing ... truly amazing."

They drove through a lush green valley into a bustling market town

Salena referred to as Haripur. She said they had reached the southwest corner of the Hazara District in the North-West Frontier Province. A narrow street bisecting the village was packed with people and animals. John saw donkeys, horses, even camels—and all sorts of vehicles— cars, trucks, motorcycles, and tractors—some brassy and new, others so old, they were held together with duct tape and wire. Most of all, John was impressed by the buses. Packed to their roofs with men, women, and babies, their exteriors were painted with geometric designs in a dazzling array of color.

Impressed by her knowledge of the region, John inquired about the large mountains he saw looming east, north, and west of town. From a distance, they appeared significantly higher than the Margalla Hills bordering Islamabad. She informed him to their west lay the Black Mountains, which separated the Hazara and Swat Districts, and to the north and east, an outlying ridge of the Himalayan Mountains.

"You mean like Mount Everest?"

Salena regarded him with a bemused smile. "The Himalayas are spread out over seven countries. What you see from here are the baby sisters of Mount Everest."

"If those are the babies, I can only image their big brothers."

Twenty-six kilometers beyond Haripur they passed through a small village called Havelian, where John read a sign informing him they were now on the Karakoram Highway. Salena explained that the Karakoram Highway, built years earlier in cooperation with China, snaked 1,300 kilometers north through some of the most dramatic mountain scenery in the world, and terminated in the westernmost province of China. To reach Muzzafarabad, she said, they must drive 80 kilometers—about 50 miles—on the Karakoram Highway, where they would turn off near the village of Mansehra.

Twenty minutes out of Havelian, on a gradually inclining road, they approached a town considerably larger than Haripur, also a bubbling blend of humanity, vehicles, and four-legged beasts. Salena told him they had reached Abbottabad, a cantonment town.

"What's a cantonment?"

"A military base."

"Think we'll run into any of Khan's security people?"

"Not if we keep a low profile."

John surveyed the cars ahead of and behind them, as well as those parked on both sides of the street. "Then I guess it doesn't bother you we're driving the only dent-free, late-model, black Mercedes Benz in sight."

The traffic and people jamming the road slowed their progress through the bustling town. They inched through what John deduced was Abbottabad's shopping district—a dusty bazaar packed with noisy stands, colorful tents, and donkey-pulled carts crammed with cloth rolls, cookware, and every trinket imaginable. At one stand, he even saw a merchant hawking familiar pink boxes stacked 20-high—Barbie dolls—the kind Karen and Christie played with for hours on end when little things still made them happy.

Crawling along the narrow road, they finally reached the outskirts of town, where the street was lined with trees. They passed pastel-colored bungalows, lush green gardens, an old Protestant church, and two Christian cemeteries crammed with weathered gravestones, the names of the deceased long worn away after the last British soldiers had departed.

The two lane road leading out of Abbottabad continued its gradual ascent, and with the windows open, John felt a marked drop in temperature. Sniffing the strong scent of evergreen and admiring the incredible alpine vistas, he listened as Salena described their next destination, Mansehra.

She explained that before the division of Kashmir, Mansehra evolved as an important center of trade on the ancient route to Srinagar, and that now the town served as a vital link between the Hazara District to the west and Azad Kashmir to the east. Before America's war with the Taliban, Mansehra housed a large population of Afghan refugees, and when the west installed a new government in Kabul, only about half returned to their homeland.

After a few moments of comfortable silence, Salena posed a question he hadn't given much thought to. "Are you afraid to die?"

John watched the road ahead, pondering his answer, making sure his reply was as honest as his heart would allow. "Not so much afraid to die as I am sad to leave those I love."

"You would have preferred to spend your last days at home with your family."

"Absolutely."

"Then you understand my own sadness—forbidden to see my mother in her final days."

John wasn't about to stop Salena from visiting her mother—not if they reached Srinagar alive. "I don't see why we can't drop in on your mom—being we're going there anyway."

Salena's eyes lit up. "I promise, I will not stay long. I only wish to tell her how much I love her."

"I understand perfectly."

After a moment, Salena's expression turned serious, and he noticed her looking at him. "Have you ever lost someone you loved?"

"My dad. He died from lung cancer four years ago."

"Was he a good man?"

"He was a great father, but like everyone, he had his issues." Worried he might insult Salena, John hesitated before speaking again. "His biggest flaw was his prejudice. My dad thought America was way too lenient about letting in foreigners, especially after 9-11."

If he had offended Salena, it didn't show in her voice. "Do you mean emigrants from the Middle East, South Asia, and other regions where Islam is dominant?"

John hadn't lied to Salena yet, and he wasn't about to. "Yeah. The attack on the Twin Towers really set him off. If my dad had his way, after 9-11 we would've sent every Muslim in America packing for their native countries."

This time it was Salena who hesitated. "Do you ever view your mission as a way to exact revenge for America?"

"Khan's politics don't interest me. I signed on for the money—not for me, of course—but for my wife and kids. That Khan is a Muslim terrorist like the ones who murdered innocent Americans didn't hurt."

"Muslim radicals have ruined countless other lives as well—mostly the lives of Muslim women."

"I thought we got rid of those jerks when we routed the Taliban."

"The war in Afghanistan did not eliminate the extremists. Many escaped into Pakistan, and over the years worked their way into legitimate positions of power in Pakistan's armed forces. Ali Khan is a perfect example. While he rose in the ranks of Pakistan's army, he played a game of compromise, but when he became the country's undisputed dictator, he imposed strict laws on women based on his misguided interpretation of the Qur'an."

John recalled his first meeting with Ali Khan. "I agree—wearing a veil should be a woman's choice—but being forced to cover your head can't be all bad. Khan himself told me Islam views a woman as precious, and making women wear veils protects them from the vulgarity of men."

"You have fallen into a dangerous trap, the same trap as many of my sisters. If the suppression of women ended with demanding they cover themselves with the burqa, perhaps their plight would not be so terrible. But the burqa is where it starts. Have you ever heard of the Zina laws?"

"Can't say I have."

"In 1979, Pakistan's President Zia ul Haq passed the Zina Ordinance. For the first time in Pakistan's history, zina—fornication—became a crime against the state, and along with fornication, punishable by death. This terrible law blurs the distinction between adultery, fornication, and rape. It defines zina as sexual intercourse with a person you are not married to, and rape as intercourse without one's consent. Thus if a woman is raped and cannot prove her lack of consent to the intercourse, the sex act becomes a crime, and the woman becomes the criminal."

"That doesn't make sense."

"Not long ago, I heard the story of a 16-year-old maid named Safia. She was raped by her employer's son and became pregnant. Safia's father had the man arrested for rape, but in Pakistan's courts, the testimony of a man is given more weight than that of a woman, and the pig was not convicted. But poor Safia's pregnancy was evidence of adultery, and Khan's puppets in the courthouse not only sentenced her to death, but fined her family 100,000 rupees."

John smirked. "Why the fine? To cover the cost of a new maid?"

Salena glared at him, and spat her words like bullets. "How dare you joke about such a thing. You have daughters of your own. How would you feel if one of them was raped, then executed by the very people who are supposed to protect them."

John hadn't intended to offend her, only lift her spirits. "You're right, I apologize. That was a stupid thing to say. I'll never make a joke about something so serious again. I'm truly sorry."

Salena turned away, and looked out her window. Not until 10 minutes later, when they approached an intersection marked with a sign pointing to Mansehra, did she again speak. "Make the next right."

John obliged, and within five minutes, found himself driving through a cluster of wood shacks and bland one and two-story concrete buildings enveloped by mountains. Along the narrow road he saw a signpost that read 'Kaghan Road.' "Are you sure we're headed in the right direction?"

"Do you question me because I am a woman?"

John hit the brakes so hard a motorcycle tailing them almost rammed their fender. "Let's settle this, here and now. I made a mistake. I said something totally insensitive. I was trying to make you happy in a really dumb way. You're a good person, Salena. I like you a lot. In some ways you remind me of my wife. Sometimes I get carried away with the jokes, especially now, with so much on my mind. But don't crucify me. I really want us to get along." His tone softened as the stark realization dawned on him. "After all, you're the last woman I'm gonna talk to before I die."

Salena's stern countenance slowly yielded to a restrained smile and she extended her hand. "Apology accepted."

Unsure why he should feel so grateful for Salena's absolution, John said, "Thanks for the second chance."

CHAPTER FIFTY-TWO

The landscape to this point had impressed John, but the natural wonders he beheld during their drive from Mensehra to Muzaffarabad overwhelmed his senses. Towering evergreens blanketed rolling hills, yellow tulips carpeted vast fields, dazzling violets exposed their passion along the banks of swift-moving streams, and blinding white peaks capped distant mountains.

For the next 30 minutes, the two lane road wound gradually uphill until it crossed a trestle bridge over the Kunhar River, then snaked down into the hamlet of Garhi Habibullah Khan. On the opposite bank, in the village center, they came to an intersection. A left turn, according to Salena, led north into the Kaghan Valley, but that was not the direction they were headed.

She added, "If you think the drive to Mensehra was pretty, you should see the Kaghan Valley."

Reluctant to dim Salena's enthusiasm, John spoke his mind anyway. "Too bad I won't live long enough to come back and visit."

The glow in her smile flickered, and she turned facing the dashboard. "You have nothing to worry about."

"I've got plenty to worry about."

"I don't mean on earth."

"Then where?"

"In heaven."

"What makes you think that's where I'm headed?"

"Allah teaches us a person possesses not only a body, but a spirit. The spirit is a seed that grows, like the mortal body grows. To grow your body healthy, you eat good food. To grow your spirit, you do good deeds. The fate of a person's spirit after she dies is determined by her actions during physical life."

"Then I'm in trouble, because my deeds have ruined people's lives."

"What you are doing now—ridding the world of a heartless tyrant—there are few greater deeds."

John recalled the letter he received from Billy Dwyer's father shortly after the Chicago accident. He accused John of being "blinded by his thirst for money to the point he was willing to shed the blood of an innocent child." Not once in the six weeks after John read that letter did he step foot inside his office. He had children of his own, and would never have consciously sacrificed safety to cut costs.

He turned to Salena. "I killed a little boy."

Salena's eyes opened wide, and she stared at him.

"Two years ago."

John explained how he had spread himself too thin as his demolition company expanded, how at the last minute he had warned Chicago's mayor to call off the Demarest implosion because the subcontractor had used Riogel instead of linear-shaped charges, and how after Billy Dwyer's death, he had dug himself into a hole so deep, he never found a way to climb out and start over.

Salena listened silently, and when John was finished, she drew a deep breath. She stared at him for a moment, and finally asked, "Have you ever begged God for His forgiveness?"

"A hundred times a day."

Salena smiled. "He who has transgressed against himself, despair not. Allah forgives the sins of those who seek His forgiveness, for truly, Allah is most merciful."

In another time and place, John would have thought the woman crazy, but considering he was 7,000 miles from home, and in less than 48 hours he'd be dead, he took comfort knowing Salena's God sounded a lot like his own.

The road's topography changed, winding downhill at a leisurely pace through hills, pines, and meadows until it descended into a narrow valley bisected along its length by a swift-moving indigo river. As they entered the valley, John observed bland concrete buildings spread out along both banks, and still others clustered in the hills surrounding the river. Salena told him they had reached Muzaffarabad, the administrative capital of Azad Kashmir, and the home of Omar Shah's cousin. From here on, she cautioned, they must keep their eyes and ears wide open.

When they reached the center of town and turned left on Neelum Road, John understood the reason for Salena's warning. Jeeps, troop transports, armored personnel carriers, and mobile missile launchers crowded the roads. A city of green tents populated by hundreds of soldiers wearing dark green fatigues had overrun a sprawling lawn along the Neelum River. Salena explained that Muzaffarabad was one of five key launching points for Ali Khan's offensive against India, and that for the remainder of their journey through the Neelum Valley they could expect to encounter military convoys.

She pointed to a one-story brick building on the right. "Look, the office of the JKLF."

The building had air conditioners protruding from its windows, and was in better structural condition than most John had noticed in Muzaffarabad. "What's the JKLF?"

"The Jammu & Kashmir Liberation Front."

"Wonderful. I'm in a town where terrorists get to plot their next attack in the cool comfort of their offices. I'll bet they even have conference rooms, afternoon tea, and weekly focus groups."

"They are not terrorists."

"Do they kill people?"

"Only those who abuse freedom-loving Kashmiris."

"Then they're terrorists."

"And the patriots who ambushed the British in Lexington. Were they also terrorists?"

"That was different."

"Why is it always different for America? Don't my people deserve freedom too?"

Now wasn't a good time to start an argument with Salena, not in the middle of a war zone surrounded by a city filled with militants. Rather than answer, he kept quiet.

Passing fewer buildings and more farms along the road, John deduced they were leaving Muzaffarabad. He was about to remind Salena this was where they were supposed to drop off the unconscious soldiers in the trunk, when Salena pointed to a grassy field on the left. "We are here!"

John stopped the car and, peering through the windshield, scanned the meadow along the left. A football field away, he saw a wood frame house painted white. A barn stood apart from the house, and behind the barn was a concrete block garage with three bays, one of which was open. To the left of the garage, on a cement base, stood a satellite dish aimed straight at the sky.

Salena instructed John to turn left down a dirt driveway leading to the farmstead, then back the car into the open bay.

Driving past the house, John saw no one. After backing the Mercedes into the garage, a man wearing a dark blue turban—about John's height, but 20 years older—approached the vehicle on Salena's side.

Salena got out and conversed with the man in a language John didn't know. She handed her keys to the man, who gave them to one of two dark-haired boys roughly the same ages as Karen and Christie. The boys opened the trunk and, in two trips, carried the limp, but breathing bodies of Subedar Mazhar and Lieutenant Hassan into a room behind the garage.

John walked around the hood to join Salena and the older gentleman, who she introduced as Ghazi Shah, Omar's second cousin. When

Salena introduced John as her husband, Ghazi embraced John, then stepped back and scoured him with dark brown eyes. "Omar has told me of your mission. Your cause is just."

"Depends who you ask."

"Fighting for freedom is always just."

John didn't have the heart to tell Ghazi freedom for Kashmir had nothing to do with his mission. Instead, he smiled graciously, and accepted a canteen and backpack handed to him by one of the boys. In return, John gave Ghazi the rifle Salena had taken from Hassan.

Ghazi's sun-worn face broke into a smile when he tossed John a single sleeping bag. "The mountain air can make your skin freeze, even in July. Make sure you keep warm tonight."

Knowing he'd relinquish the sleeping bag to Salena, but not sure how he'd protect himself from frostbite, John shot Ghazi a thumbs up.

Salena handed John the lieutenant's pistol and five fully loaded magazines, which he stuffed into the backpack. Loading the gear into car, John remembered he must ask Ghazi to do something important. He pulled an AMS business card from his shalwar pocket. "Does your farm have a telephone?"

Ghazi took the card. "My satellite allows me to call anywhere in the world, but my best reception is in the middle of the night."

"That's fine." John told Ghazi exactly what he must tell Ted Dunne, and added, "Your conversation may be monitored, so be careful what you say."

"I am always careful what I say." From his own pocket, Ghazi dug out a map. Judging from the concentric black swirls overlaid with red pencil, John deduced it was topographical. Ghazi unfolded the map on the hood of the Mercedes. With John and Salena looking over his shoulders, he pointed to a spot circled in red. "After you leave your car in the forest, here, hike east. Under cover of night, you will climb the mountains. By two o'clock you will reach the safe cave."

John stepped back. "Safe cave?"

"Yes, a cave under a waterfall known only to mujahideen—a place where we hide from Indian soldiers. You can steal four hours of sleep there. At daybreak, you will hike to Kuligam, where you will be met by Abu Kundi and Hani Taj."

"Who are they?"

"My brothers in the struggle for freedom. They will guide you to Srinagar, and deliver you to Omar Shah."

"Are these guys expecting us?"

"Yes, but you must reach Kuligam by nine o'clock. At nine-fifteen, they will assume you were killed or captured, and leave the village. Kuligam is a three-hour hike from the cave, so be sure to start out by six o'clock."

Ghazi folded the map and gave it to Salena, who thanked him for his help. After saying their good-byes, John and Salena drove down the dirt driveway to the main road, turned left, and continued in the direction they'd been headed before stopping at Ghazi's farm.

Settled behind the wheel, John looked over at Salena, who was carefully studying the map. "Is something wrong?"

Salena shook her head dismissively.

"Come on, Salena. What's the problem?"

"No problem at all."

"Don't BS me. Something's on your mind."

Salena hesitated before speaking. "Within the next few hours, Khan's soldiers will be on high alert for a late-model black Mercedes Benz—this Mercedes Benz. We must hide the car in the woods. Ghazi circled a spot on the map between Dowarian and Sharda."

"Isn't that good."

"Not exactly."

"What's wrong?"

"I prefer not to say."

"Why?"

"You might get nervous."

"Don't be ridiculous. Tell me what's wrong."

She looked down at the map, and said softly, "The place he circled is filled with Pakistani soldiers. I know this from listening to Khan and his generals."

"We'll deal with it. Just don't treat me like a wimp."

"But your cancer."

"I'm still a man." John rubbed his hand over his mid-section. "Except for the pain in here, I feel good enough to do anything."

Salena's alluring brown eyes stared at him, as if peering inside his soul. "You are right, my deceptions, no matter how well-intended, dishonor your courage."

"Then I trust you're hiding nothing else from me."

Salena opened her mouth, as if about to speak, then looked away.

"What now?"

"It does not concern you."

"Tell me."

"It has nothing to do with your mission, and will not affect you in any way."

"Just say it."

"You will think less of me as a woman."

John felt suddenly awkward, as if he'd probed somewhere he shouldn't. "You can talk about it if you like. I'm a pretty good listener."

Salena's voice was soft and sad. "I can speak of it to no one."

John wasn't sure if he should press the issue. He sensed she wanted to share something important, and might actually open up if he pushed. Women were like that sometimes, insisting you not pry into their lives, then resenting you when you didn't; and if you persevered and they bared their souls, that meant you really cared. John thought for a moment, and decided when the time was right, he would persevere.

CHAPTER FIFTY-THREE

Azam Qadeer grinned as he gazed out his 4th floor office overlooking Constitution Avenue. The few women who dared venture onto Islamabad's sidewalks all wore burqas, a great improvement from the days when the whores inhabiting Pakistan's capital wore mere dupattas—some only scarves—in public places.

In two years Ali Khan had done much to strengthen Pakistan's moral fiber. The weak leaders before him, most recently Labib Razzak, had abandoned their faith and transformed Pakistan into a puppet of the West. Khan had achieved what no other ruler of Pakistan could. In every city, in every village, he had humbled every woman—every woman but one.

Salena Zamal was Khan's greatest weakness, and Qadeer could not understand why. She was attractive, no doubt, but not the sort of moral Muslim woman Khan should take as his wife. Khan deserved a woman who understood that obedience to Islam meant obedience to her husband. So blinded by Zamal's beauty was Khan, he allowed her to wear a mere head scarf even as his Ministry of Moral Obedience had sentenced hundreds of women to death for doing as much.

But Qadeer sensed Zamal's games of duplicity were about to catch up with her. Her disappearance, along with that of John Cattano, Lieutenant Hassan, and Subedar Mazhar, was no random kidnapping. Though Qadeer's investigators had not yet proven his suspicions, they were working around the clock to collect and analyze the evidence.

While Qadeer suspected the kidnapping was staged, he was not sure why she had chosen now to leave Ali Khan. She could have walked out anytime, slipping past the guards at Pakistan National Hospital. Until today, she had been held captive by fear—fear Khan would expel the spawn of Pakistan's traitors she sheltered in the hospital, and fear Khan would execute her cowardly friend, Dr. Raja. No, Zamal had staged the ambush for another reason.

His problem, as usual, was convincing Khan she was up to no good, and he was about to get another chance. Khan had summoned him to the Citadel's penthouse to find out what steps had been taken to locate and kill the dacoits who had abducted his beloved Salena.

Qadeer left his office, walked to the 4th floor lobby, and boarded the first elevator. Anticipating Khan would have many questions, he recounted in his mind the events that had transpired since mid-morning.

At 10:15 a.m., the director of Lady Reading Hospital had called him with the news neither Dr. Zamal nor Mr. Cattano had arrived for their Med-Link presentation scheduled for 9:30 a.m. Qadeer immediately ordered three army helicopters and four overland reconnaissance parties to trace Subedar Mazhar's route to Peshawar.

At 12:00 noon, the Karachi office of the *Daily Jang* reported a phone call from a man identifying himself as a spokesman for the Jammu & Kashmir People's League, a counter-revolutionary group opposed to Khan's dream of incorporating Jammu & Kashmir into Pakistan. The man claimed to hold Dr. Zamal, as well as an American businessman and an unspecified number of Khan's officers. He demanded immediate cessation of Pakistan's military activity in Azad Kashmir, and 100 million rupees.

Thirty minutes later, a ground reconnaissance patrol discovered the site of an apparent ambush along the M1 Motorway. Tire impressions matching those of the SL-Class Mercedes Benz sedans comprising Khan's civilian fleet indicated the automobile driven by Subedar Mazhar had been forced off the road onto the east bank of the Harro River 10 kilometers west of Hasan Abdal. All material evidence recovered at the scene was immediately delivered to the Citadel. The items found included three empty wallets, Zamal's scarf and travel bag, John Cattano's shoes, and his suit jacket stained with blood. An elaborate ruse, indeed.

Qadeer sought to sway Khan to the same conclusion, but must proceed cautiously. The general's pride still smarted over the fire yesterday morning at Pakistan National Hospital. Qadeer had tried reasoning with his commander. How could one cigarette tossed in a waste basket have caused so much damage in so little time? Khan refused to listen, and instead, had berated him in front of Lieutenant Siddique.

If Qadeer did nothing else, he would restore Khan's sight where it came to Zamal. He got off on the 12th floor and found Khan standing on his balcony under the afternoon sun finishing a glass of ice water.

Khan put down the empty glass and hugged Qadeer in the Pathan way. "Any word of Dr. Zamal?"

"Nothing more than I knew an hour ago."

"I shall not rest until her captors are found and she is returned unharmed."

"I have doubled the number of investigators assigned to her case."

"Have you called Mr. Cattano's employer?"

"I recommend we wait until the call received by the *Daily Jang* is authenticated."

"Who else beside the Kashmir People's League could be responsible for their disappearance?"

"We are examining all possibilities."

"When the call came into the *Jang*, no one else knew they were gone."

"May I speak as a friend."

Khan nodded.

"Is there a chance she made herself disappear?"

"I knew the thought would occur to you."

"As it has to you."

"Dr. Zamal has not fully accepted her future with me, that much I know. But she has made progress, especially these last few days. As the reality of Glorious Dawn draws near, she is gaining an appreciation of the prestige and power that shall accompany her position as my wife."

"What leads you to believe she has accepted her fate?"

"On Friday night, she prepared my favorite meal, jhinga karhai and chapli kabob—with her own hands."

Qadeer wished he could have tested the scraps for ground glass and poison. "Cooking a meal does not mean she has succumbed to your will."

Khan eyed him skeptically. "Now may I speak to you as a friend?"

"Always."

"You shall remain my most trusted advisor, even after I marry Dr. Zamal. Yes, in time I shall seek her counsel, but she can never replace you. Tell me Azam, is that why you fear her?"

A ridiculous notion Azam Qadeer would fear any woman. His only ambition was protecting his friend. "Please, habib, you must consider the possibility Dr. Zamal has staged her abduction."

"I shall think nothing of the sort. She is accepting her role, perhaps even relishing the chance to serve me. And do not forget those little vagabonds who take refuge in my hospital. She would never jeopardize their safety."

"Her desire to flee the Citadel may be stronger than you know."

"Do you believe she would risk the life of that old oaf, Dr. Raja? She knows if she leaves I will have him killed." Khan swept his free hand, palm down, in a dismissive gesture. "No, my friend. Dr. Zamal is in trouble, and it is you who bears the responsibility for her safe return."

"But—"

"I shall hear no more. Find her and bring her back to me. Find the American, too. I wish no further embarrassment."

Qadeer stared at the balcony's concrete floor. "I never intended to embarrass you. I shall do as you wish." Khan's mind was closed. The only way he would convince his commander of Zamal's deceit was to furnish him with irrefutable proof.

Khan took another sip from his glass. "The 7th and 8th Armored Brigades under Lieutenant General Mattu have crossed the Rajasthan Canal at Pugal and broken through to within five kilometers of Bikaner. General Hanif's 4th Division has already crossed the Rann of Kutch and taken Patan and Morvi."

"Gupta's defenses have proven soft."

"The ground assault is proceeding better than planned. The timing is perfect. I am thinking of moving the launch date from Sunday to Thursday. Behari will never expect me to strike so soon."

"In this campaign, surprise means everything."

"On Wednesday, I shall guage the reaction of my generals. They must assure me their divisions will penetrate swiftly into their assigned sectors. Only then will I move up the date." Khan placed his hand on Qadeer's shoulder. "You have been my right arm since the moment we met. In the coming days, I shall need you more than ever. Do not be distracted from the greater cause."

"In what way distracted?"

"Your constant suspicion of Dr. Zamal. She is held against her will, and even now thinks of me. I tell you something else, I am glad this has happened. The terror she feels in the hands of the dacoits shall drive her firmly into my arms upon her return."

No, Ali Khan was not ready for the truth, and Qadeer knew that day might never come, even when presented with hard evidence of his beloved's guilt. Embracing his commander-in-chief, Qadeer knew only one way to assure his mentor's safety. Make Zamal disappear forever—after he found her.

CHAPTER FIFTY-FOUR

The two-lane road ensconced in tall conifers meandered northeast through the Neelum Valley, more or less following the bank of the Neelum River. In some stretches, the road consisted of asphalt, in others, crushed stone. The road was devoid of traffic except for a few banged-up Toyotas, Hondas, and donkey-pulled carts John passed along the way. Only once in the hour and a half since leaving Muzaffarabad did they encounter a military convoy. The mile-long column of jeeps, trucks, and mobile artillery launchers approached from the opposite direction, and none of the grim-faced soldiers staring through the windshields or peeking through the canvas flaps gave John or Salena a second look.

Frequent breaks in the forested road opened to breathtaking views of lush green farms bathed in bright sunlight, extending in wide swaths across the valley on both sides of the river. The owners who cultivated these tidy rows of rice and maize were nowhere to be seen, leaving John to wonder whether humans actually tilled these fields.

Thickets of wild strawberry grew along the road, as did apricot seedlings and walnut trees. Around every bend, sparkling springs bubbled from red-speckled granite boulders protruding from the rich black soil. Twice the river and road switched sides, and in each instance the crossing was a flimsy, wood plank bridge.

In a few spots, dirt paths ran perpendicular off the main road to rope bridges spanning the turbulent river. The flimsy boards dangled perilously close to the roaring current, and despite John's skepticism, Salena insisted the bridges, built by hand, could bear the weight of the trucks and tractors that plied them to reach the cottages and barns scattered on the opposite bank.

They drove into a cluster of ramshackle wood buildings and crumbling stone structures. Salena informed him they had reached the town of Athmuqam, the sub-divisional headquarters for the southern half of the Neelum Valley. "At this point," she said, "only 32 kilometers before we abandon the car and start our hike."

The roofs and walls of most buildings in this settlement had collapsed, or teetered on the brink. Only a handful of elderly men and women dressed in ragged shalwar kameez picked their way through the ruins. John drove slowly to avoid the splintered lumber, shattered bricks, and dazed humanity littering the street. "This place looks like a bomb hit."

Salena stared out her window. "Many bombs have hit, not once, but often."

"I don't see any children."

"If their families were lucky, or blessed with money, they moved to a safer place. If not, they were probably killed by artillery shells."

On a hill up ahead, in a fenced-in compound, the charred and gutted remains of four cement buildings, two and three stories high, stood apart from the rest of the town. "What's that?"

"You would never know it, but Athmuqam once served as a major center of commerce in the Neelum Valley. The town had a bazaar, a post office, banks, a hospital, and a telephone exchange. It even had a college. You are looking at what is left of the tahsil headquarters, where the hospital and college once stood."

Out his window on the right, John noticed a cemetery. Freshly turned dirt in too many places belied the freshly dug graves of dozens of dead. "What happened here?"

Salena pressed the ball of her index finger against the windshield, pointing up and to the right. "Somewhere in those mountains is the Line of Control."

"When I met Major Farrell she mentioned something about the Line of Control. She said it was the cease-fire line between India and Pakistan."

"The Line of Control divides that part of Kashmir governed by Pakistan, and that part controlled by India, and you bear witness that neither side has ceased firing."

"Isn't the Line of Control where Ali Khan started his war against India?"

"He launched his offensives south and east of here, at Kotli, Poonch, and Mirpur."

"What about that city he nuked?"

"Baramulla is 60 kilometers away, on the other side of those mountains."

John's eyes opened wide. "Not that it matters to *me*, but aren't you afraid you'll catch a dose of radiation."

"The mountains separating the Neelum Valley from the Vale of Kashmir are 4,000 meters high. They will shield us from the radiation."

"Not after we climb over them."

"The trail on Ghazi's map crosses the Panji Range east of Sharda, far from Baramulla."

"If that's good enough for you, fine. But don't blame me if we start glowing."

"I am not afraid. I would rather die fighting for my freedom than endure a lifetime of servitude."

John's stomach turned at the sight of an enormous carcass on the shoulder, a dead cow, its bulging brown eyes glued open, and its moist pink belly and cream colored intestines exposed to the elements. Thousands of buzzing flies swarmed over and in the animal, feasting off its spongy entrails. John closed his window. "Who did all this?"

"The Indian Army."

"I thought we were on Pakistan's side of the Line of Control."

"The mountains on your right are teeming with soldiers from both armies. Over the years, India has tormented the Neelum Valley with indiscriminate shelling. In Nagdar, a mortar killed 10 children sitting at their desks in a grade school. Twenty others were mutilated. India has sent commandos into Azad Kashmir to conduct nighttime raids. In Lanjot, they crossed the Line of Control in the middle of the night and massacred 14 people. Six of their victims were women, and five, children. Three men, all sick or elderly, had their heads hacked off."

"Why would they invade the Neelum Valley and go after women and children?"

"India believes Azad Kashmir, with Pakistan's support, harbors many of the jihad warriors who carry out the armed struggle to free the Vale of Kashmir."

"I hate to be your reality check, but is India right?"

Salena turned and stared ahead, stone-faced. "Some militants take refuge in Azad Kashmir, but their cause is righteous."

"No, Salena, both sides are wrong. Cold-blooded killing is never a means to justify an end."

"India has murdered thousands of innocent Kashmiri citizens. Those who fight for Kashmir's independence also fight to stop India's genocide of my people."

"I'm sorry, I disagree. Violence begets violence, and it has to stop somewhere."

"It will stop. When my people are free."

Leaving Athmuqam, John observed sitting on a small boulder a few feet off the road a boy of eight or nine wearing a mop of jet black hair and ragged, dirt-caked clothes. As the car drew nearer, the child smiled and extended his open palm. Driving past, John caught a glimpse of two ragged stumps where the boy's legs had been, and fought back his urge to scream.

They drove through two more war-battered villages, Neelum and Dowarian. Most of the road beyond Dowarian was pocked with holes.

In a few places, John swerved around craters the size of basketballs, and twice, drove on the grass to avoid gaping cavities as wide as the pavement. Narrowly missing a wooden fence post that had fallen across the road, John asked, "Did the shelling cause all this?"

"Yes."

John felt a little sad that a place of such incredible beauty was the site of so much pain. He hoped his death, along with Khan's, would liberate Salena, but he doubted Khan's demise would bring freedom to Kahsmir. "Do you really believe Kashmir will become independent?"

"It is Kashmir's destiny."

"From what I understand, India and Pakistan don't see it that way."

"Kashmiriyat will survive, and Pakistan and India will leave us alone."

"Kashmiriyat?"

"Before partition, Jammu & Kashmir was a land where diverse religions lived in harmony—Muslims, Hindus, Sikhs, and Buddhists. They co-existed in peace, guided by the tenets of Sufi Islam."

"What's Sufi Islam?"

"Sufism is a brand of Islam that stresses gentleness and the treatment of all human beings with equality and dignity. That was Kashmir."

"Sounds like utopia."

"In many ways, it was. For 700 years, the invisible bond of trust, solidarity, and friendliness allowed very different cultures to share a rich variety of music, art, education, literature. Now, Kashmiriyat is all but forgotten."

"What happened?"

"Armed rebellion, the massacre of innocents, occupation by India's army, and the intrusion of Muslim fundamentalists from Pakistan, Afghanistan, and the Middle East. All these events have combined to dampen the spirit of Kashmiriyat. Yet in my heart I do not believe Kashmiriyat has been destroyed, only suppressed, and one day it shall be restored."

"Doesn't sound like an easy job."

"Kashmir must rid itself of India's soldiers, and also the Muslim extremists."

"Isn't Omar Shah a Muslim extremist?"

"He is extreme, not in the practice of his religion, but in his zeal for seeing Kashmir free. The fundamentalists who infiltrate Kashmir from other Muslim countries are the ones mostly responsible for bringing misery to Kashmir."

"I thought that's why India sent troops to the Kashmir Valley. To keep the peace."

John glanced at Salena, and was taken aback by her furrowed brow and stern demeanor. "If keeping the peace was all they did, fine. But India's soldiers have never made the distinction between the peace-loving Muslims of Kashmir desperate to live normal lives, and the militants who commit murder and mayhem. In their quest to bring peace to Kashmir, India's soldiers have tortured and murdered hundreds of innocent Kashmiri Muslims. Now, almost every Muslim in Kashmir despises India for the pain it has brought to my homeland."

"How come I never heard about those atrocities?"

Her tone seethed. "Until your country's wars against al-Qaeda, Iraq, and Syria, Americans lived like moles with their heads in the ground. My people have endured tyranny for decades, and no one in your country cares."

John got the feeling he'd opened the wrong door. He turned and faced forward, keeping an eye on the road ahead as it curved into a thick stand of fir trees.

"Look at me when I am talking to you."

"I'm driving."

"What I tell you now is important."

"You want me to crash?"

"Then listen, and listen carefully."

No woman had spoken to him like that since Maureen blasted him for crawling into his shell after the Chicago accident. Now, like then, he did what was strategically best—kept his trap shut.

"When I lived in Srinagar, before I moved to Peshawar—" Salena stopped, glanced down at the map, then leaned forward and peered out the window. "Slow down! We are nearing the trail where we must turn off."

Tapping the brakes, John saw no opening in the dense forests of pine trees lining both sides of the road. "Are you sure the map is right?"

She pointed across his line of sight. "Over there."

John slowed to a crawl and spotted a narrow path leading into the forest. "I never had a doubt." About 200 yards to their right, a densely treed mountain rose sharply off the valley floor. He looked up at the rear-view mirror to make sure no one was following, then turned the Mercedes onto the trail.

Listening to the sound of low-hanging branches scratching the roof of the car, John discerned above the treetops ahead the nearly vertical side of a mountain. "How much longer?"

"Another 100 meters."

John steered around the next bend through the wall of evergreens, glanced in the mirror, and caught sight of two figures sprinting across the trail, then disappear into the forest. "I don't think we're alone."

"What do you mean?"

John was about to tell her, when a yellow fireball exploded 30 feet in front of the car. The windshield shattered and John reflexively took his hands off the wheel and covered his eyes. A second explosion lit up the woods a few yards to his right. "What the hell's going on?"

"Artillery shells!"

"Who's shooting?"

"I do not know."

While the car was still moving, Salena reached down, grabbed the backpack, and jumped out. Not bothering to brake, John snatched the sleeping bag in the back seat, yanked on his door handle, and leapt from the Mercedes. He rolled three or four times, stopped, and kept his belly pressed to the ground.

What he heard next was more frightening than mortar shells—the shouts of men.

John rose to his knees, scanned the woods across the path, and spotted Salena lying on her side. She wasn't moving, and her eyes were closed. Ignoring the sound of automatic gunfire echoing off the trees, John got up, ran to her, and gently rolled her onto her back.

He lifted her wrist, looking for a pulse, and heard another explosion behind him. He turned and saw the hood of the Mercedes engulfed in flames. The shell hadn't scored a direct hit, but had come close enough to broil anyone inside.

John felt a pulse—she was alive. "Salena, say something." He brushed her hair off her face, and stroked her cheek with his fingers. She was stunning, even in sleep.

Her eyes opened with a start. "The soldiers!"

"Yeah, they're everywhere." John helped her to her feet and hastily slipped on the backpack. Salena gripped the sleeping bag by its tie cords and hung the canteen on her shoulder.

Holding hands, they ran deeper into the woods, leaping over fallen branches and massive rocks bulging from the soil. Somewhere in the forest, closer than before, John heard a deep voice barking orders in an unfamiliar language.

Squeezing John's hand, Salena gasped out her words. "Urdu, they are speaking Urdu."

"What does that mean?"

"They are Pakistani. They think we are with India's Special Frontier Force."

They burst into bright sunlight—a wide, flat clearing in the middle of the forest. Directly ahead lay more pine trees, followed by a slope that rose gradually at first, then steeper and higher until it touched the puffy white clouds above.

They had run halfway across the meadow when John heard from behind a man's angry holler. Salena stopped short, releasing his hand. Inertia carried John a few steps beyond, and by the time he halted his forward momentum, he was 10 feet ahead of Salena.

John heard more shouts, and though he had no idea what the men were saying, John raised his hands and looked over his shoulder. At the edge of the clearing where he and Salena had emerged stood five soldiers in green fatigues pointing semi-automatic rifles in their direction.

Keeping his hands high, John slowly stepped backward until he stood side-by-side with Salena. Making no sudden moves, he whispered, "What do they want?"

Salena dropped to her knees, keeping her back to the soldiers. "They are telling us to lie face down."

"They gonna search us?"

Salena's voice quaked. "They ... they intend to kill us."

"What about the Geneva Convention?"

"The only law in Azad Kashmir is the law of survival."

John lowered his arms and spun.

The five men lifted their rifles in unison, taking aim at him through their sights.

Salena shouted, "Don't!"

John was about to beg for their lives, when a blinding flash of yellow light lit up the ground behind the soldiers. A simultaneous explosion forced John to slap his hands over his ears. The ground shook violently, and John instinctively bent his knees to keep from toppling over.

Salena fell forward onto her hands and knees. She looked up at him, and her lips moved, but John couldn't hear, because another deafening boom muted her words and made the ground shake harder than before.

After the shockwave passed, John helped Salena to her feet. He looked to where the five men had stood, and what he saw made him sick. Beneath a cluster of pines at the edge of the clearing lay such an assortment of arms, legs, and parts of torsos, it was impossible to know how many human beings had once existed.

Before he could speak, John heard directly above a low rumble that swelled instantly into a loud shriek. As John craned his neck at the billowing clouds, a gray shadow with wings screamed over the treetops, moving so fast, John wasn't sure from which direction it had come, or where it had gone. Salena pointed toward the treetops. "MIG-29. India's Western Air Command."

John heard gunfire deep in the forest. "I thought all the fighting was in India."

"Technically, Azad Kashmir belongs to neither India nor Pakistan. Since they are at war, this area is up for the taking by either side."

"All things considered, I'd rather be in Peshawar selling Med-Link."

Salena pulled out Ghazi's map, and for a half minute, studied the black circles and red writing. When she was done, she carefully folded the map, tucked it under her dress, and turned to John. "We should leave this place as soon as possible."

John shot her a wry look. "You think?"

They sprinted to the end of the clearing, reentered the forest, and ran toward the base of the mountain. Salena took the lead, found an unmarked trail, and waved for John to follow. For the next half hour, they jogged the uphill path, until the sound of screaming jets and staccato gunfire gave way to chirping birds and babbling streams.

Chapter Fifty-Five

M ajor Farrell glanced at the line of digital clocks on the wall behind Colonel Daley. The time in Pakistan was 6:35 p.m., and John still hadn't called to confirm his return to Islamabad. Worse yet, CRUSO's two attempts to locate John had proven futile.

An hour earlier, Farrell, posing as Ted Dunne's executive assistant, phoned Lady Reading Hospital to inquire whether Mr. Cattano had met with the hospital's administrators over dinner to discuss Med-Link's capabilities. She was eventually transferred to the evening shift administrator, a polite gentleman who knew absolutely nothing.

The administrator told Farrell a salesman from an American software company, accompanied by Dr. Zamal, had been scheduled to give a presentation at 9:30 a.m. The pair never arrived. When Farrell asked if anyone had phoned Islamabad to find out why, the administrator replied, "I doubt it. Tardiness and broken appointments are no surprise when dealing with Islamabad." Farrell thanked the nice, but useless gentleman, and hung up.

While that conversation hadn't shed any new light on John's location, it was the next call, placed by Colonel Daley posing as Ted Dunne, that elevated Farrell's concern from worry to panic.

Daley had phoned the security office at Khan's Citadel to ask hard questions about Mr. Cattano's whereabouts. Passed to five different lackeys who hadn't a clue, he told the fifth he needed answers or he'd be forced to contact the US embassy. Daley's threat must have ruffled some feathers. A sixth man, clearly agitated, came on the line and said, "I give no shit who you call. We do not know where he is, and we are trying to find him too." The man hung up without giving Daley a chance to reply.

That was 10 minutes earlier, before Farrell and Daley had begun a losing battle convincing India's special envoy that John Covello was alive and well somewhere in Pakistan.

Ripping a sheet of paper in half, Daley said, "If he'd been caught, Ali Khan would've paraded him around on Al-Jazeera for all the world to see."

Agarwal waved him off. "Not if Khan is torturing him first, prying information about your agency before killing him."

The thought that John may have been captured and was undergoing interrogation by Khan's thugs tied Farrell's stomach in knots. CRUSO's first operation against Russian crime boss Yegor Kotenov had been carried out by a former Marine. Caught setting the charges, the terminally ill man didn't hesitate to bite the cyanide caplet. John was different, and might not act quickly enough to end his life. He had no prior military training, and was unprepared to respond to the intense physical and psychological pressures certain to be inflicted at the hands of an expert.

Farrell had to remain optimistic. "Our support operatives inside Islamabad have spent the last three hours attempting to secure information on John's status. So far nothing they've learned indicates his identity has been compromised."

"But nothing indicates it hasn't."

Daley tore both halves of the paper down the middle. "The jerk who just hung up on me sounded damn sincere about finding John. I'd bet my life Khan's people have no idea where he is."

"Then where did your Mr. Covello go? On a tour of the Pakistan countryside?"

"You're an irritating SOB, Agarwal. Anyone ever tell you that?"

"What is this meaning, SOB?"

Farrell threw her hands in the air. "Please gentlemen, bickering does not solve the problem."

The intercom's red light started blinking. Farrell pressed the speaker button. "Yes Stacy?"

After four consecutive days and nights punctuated by three naps in the officers lounge, Stacy's voice still sounded strong. "Dr. Sheehan needs to see you."

At least something had gone right. FBI Agent Steve Clarkson had driven down from New Jersey in the middle of the night, and at 4:30 a.m., had hand-delivered full 3-C's reports on John Covello and Dr. Chandler, along with John's complete medical profile. When Dr. Timothy Sheehan, CRUSO's chief medical officer, arrived for work that morning, he set aside all other obligations to review and sign off on John's medicals.

"Please tell him I'll see him as soon as I'm free."

"I'm sorry, major, but Dr. Sheehan insists on ..."

Across the table, Daley shouted something at Agarwal. Farrell held up her hand as if to stop traffic. "I'm sorry, Stacy. What was that?"

"Dr. Sheehan must see you immediately."

"OK, I'm on my way." She released the intercom button and announced, "Tim Sheehan needs me up in the lab. Can I trust you two alone?"

Daley shrugged his shoulders, scowling.

Agarwal stared at her, baffled.

"I'll return as soon as I can. Meanwhile, please keep your conversation to a minimum."

CHAPTER FIFTY-SIX

No sooner had they reached the mountain's summit, than Salena beckoned John to follow her down a winding trail leading to the bottom. John struggled to counter his own weight as he trotted down the steep slope in the Himalayan foothills, narrowly avoiding nose-to-bark contact with one tree trunk after another. This was the last challenge John thought he'd be facing four days earlier when he'd grappled with whether to call Dr. Chandler's government contact.

His little-bit-of-heaven by the Jersey Shore, marred by persistent bill collectors, was a lifetime away. Maureen, Karen, and Christie, though certain to be first in his mind when he drew his last breath, had also become a memory.

Salena's agile movements as she descended the serpentine path put his own clumsy effort to shame. He decided if forced to choose anyone beside his three women in Brielle with whom to share his last day on earth, he'd have picked Salena Zamal.

Though her flawless dark features and lissome frame made her easy to be near, they weren't the only reasons he'd have chosen her. Against insurmountable odds she pursued a cause she would lay down her life for. How could he not admire her? While he withdrew from work and family after Billy Dwyer's death, she doggedly pursued freedom for herself and her homeland. Next to this woman, he felt small and ashamed.

Salena waited for him on a narrow stone shelf jutting out from the heavily treed hillside. Preoccupied with fighting to stay upright while dodging football-size pine cones dangling from overhead branches, John hadn't paid much attention to the terrain beyond the forest. He caught up with Salena, and stood beside her on the slim rock outcropping.

Having climbed halfway down the mountain, their view to the south and east was shielded by a hill across a wooded glen below. To the west the sun lay hidden behind the mountain they had just descended, casting the pines blanketing the dell into gloomy shadow.

Rarely during their downhill trek had John and Salena spoken. Until now, Salena had maintained a brisk pace, and she was prudent to do so, since they must cover 20 kilometers in seven hours if they were to set up camp in a cave where, according to Omar's cousin, they could sleep the night without fear of attack from Indian soldiers.

Salena sipped water from a round canteen slung on her shoulder. After handing the canteen to John, she removed her blue veil, and freed her chestnut hair. "I hope you do not mind. The dupatta makes my face sweat."

John admired her luxuriant mane. "Yes, in fact, I do mind—forcing me to gaze upon the face and hair of such a beautiful woman. How revolting."

Salena drew a sharp breath, and yanked her veil back over her head.

"I'm only kidding. Of course I don't mind."

"Are you certain?"

"You've been stuck in Khan's Citadel way too long."

She again removed her dupatta, and stuffed it in the backpack. "Omar will like you."

"Why, because I'm a Christian and I'll be dead in two days?"

"No, because like a true Pathan warrior you are willing to sacrifice your own life to save the lives of many."

John was certain he'd accepted CRUSO's offer for one reason—to save his family from financial ruin. Now, on a rock ledge in the lower Himalayas, soldiers of warring nations lurking all around, and this magnificent lady standing beside him, he wasn't at all sure his only motivation was saving his family. "Yeah, maybe some good will come of this."

Salena stared at the darkening treetops in the valley below. "Yes, perhaps the liberation of Kashmir."

"Don't bet on it."

"I yearn for the peaceful coexistence of all religions in the Vale." Her eyes brimmed with tenderness and passion. "I swear, I will live to see that day. I only wish I could see it with you."

Flustered by her honesty, John studied Salena's expression, attempting to unravel its intent. He had never felt so alone, yet at the same time, so at peace with his surroundings.

They resumed their trek down the mountain, and at the bottom, crossed the wooded glen. By the time they started up the next hill, the sky overhead had turned dark purple. John looked back and saw the setting sun had left an orange glow along the top of the ridge they'd left behind. He removed two flashlights from his backpack and handed one to Salena.

Two or three times in his early 20's, John had camped overnight with friends along the Delaware River, but he'd never hiked an unmarked trail. He wondered if CRUSO might bend its rules and pay Maureen his full $2,000,000 failure compensation if before returning to the Citadel he fell to his death off the side of a mountain.

The sky was now black, and a gibbous moon accompanied by a million stars cast eerie shadows between the prickly limbs of the pine trees all around them. During their uphill climb, the temperature must have dropped 30 degrees.

At around 9:30 p.m., John began hearing sporadic machine gun fire and bursting mortars in the distance. Every five minutes or so, an artillery shell exploded loud enough so that John guessed it had struck within a mile of their position, but under the stars and conifer canopy it was impossible to see any smoke and know exactly where the shell had landed. Salena's assurance such artillery exchanges across the Line of Control were common did little to allay his fear.

Salena pulled two wool blankets from John's backpack, and wrapped one around her shoulders and the other around John's. When John saw she was still shivering, he insisted she take his blanket, but with equal insistence, she refused. "A chill will make you susceptible to illness. If you catch cold, you will lose more strength than the cancer has already sapped."

"I'm not a damn sissy."

"Please, your language."

At the hill's summit, they could hardly see through the darkened forest. The canopy of branches all but blocked the moonlight, yet they refrained from using flashlights to fix their location, fearing their beams might draw the fire of soldiers on patrol in the surrounding woods.

The bombs and guns continued their intermittent clatter, and sounded closer than before. They hiked downhill for another half hour, descending into a narrow valley split in half by a stream. Crossing the water on a path of smooth rocks, the narrow trail led to another uphill climb on the opposite bank.

John was about to suggest they try an alternate route, away from the battle, when a fiery white explosion lit up the pine trees in the woods to their right, and shook the ground like thunder.

Instinctively, they started running uphill. John tripped over a thick root snaking the ground and dropped his flashlight. The chrome tube popped open and all three batteries scattered downhill.

He abandoned the flashlight, scrambled to his feet, and ran toward Salena, who had stopped, turned, and was looking back. John caught up, wheezing. "Don't worry … I'm good … lost my flashlight."

"Stay close and move fast."

Each uphill step grew steeper until John was forced to lean forward and claw at the ground to avoid falling backward. Salena struggled even harder, holding her flashlight in one hand and digging at the dirt with the other.

John panted, "Your flashlight ... give it to me."

Salena glanced back. "You do not know where you are going?"

"Sure I do. Up the hill and away from the bombs."

Salena handed him the flashlight and John scuttled ahead. Every few seconds, he glimpsed over his shoulder to make sure she was keeping pace.

Scratching at the ground with one hand, he shone his beam uphill through the trees. As the incline leveled off, John heard Salena call out from behind. "Wait, I am stuck."

John stopped short, and on his hands and knees, slid backward, braking with his toes at Salena's side. He shone the flashlight over Salena and saw the hem of her dress had caught on a branch. The canteen had rolled away, but she still held onto the sleeping bag. He scrambled behind her, untangled the dress, and reached for her hand. Salena pulled with more strength than he expected. Standing precariously on the slope, he lost his footing and fell face down, squarely on top of her.

Their noses barely an inch apart, and their faces illuminated by the flashlight wedged between them, John wasn't sure how to extract himself from this awkward position. For a few seconds, he didn't move. He didn't want to. Her eyes remained riveted to his, and he wondered, could it be?

This wasn't the time to find out. He whispered, "We'd better get going."

She didn't say a word, but watched his every move as he pushed off the ground and stood. He reached down, braced his legs, and lifted her to her feet.

After the initial explosion had triggered their frantic ascent, no more shells had been fired. They continued their climb, but without the same urgency. In fact, John had shed his anxiety completely, and he wasn't sure if it was because the shelling had stopped, or because his fingers were woven with Salena's.

The ground leveled off, and they walked side-by-side with little exertion. Aiming his flashlight low to keep the trail in sight, John was speculating how Salena might react if he tried kissing her, when he heard a loud snap in the darkness ahead.

Salena let go of John's hand, dropped the sleeping bag, and clutched John's arm.

"You hear it too?"

"Yes."

"An animal?"

"I am not sure, but whatever made the sound lies directly in our path."

"It's probably nothing." John shone his flashlight on each tree in the forest ahead. It was dead center between the third and fourth trees where the beam caught the helmeted heads of two soldiers sitting in a jeep, staring straight at them.

John grabbed Salena, and with his back to the jeep, shielded her body and waited for the soldiers to shoot or shout. Salena wrapped her arms around his waist, and he felt her body quake. He pressed his lips to her ear. "Don't be afraid."

Nothing happened. No shooting, no shouting, nothing. John drew a long, deep breath into Salena's hair. Her scent evoked a feeling he hadn't known for months. She smelled wild, almost feral, and John hesitated to let go.

He did, finally, and slowly turned, keeping Salena shielded. He pointed the flashlight at the jeep's grill, then at the two soldiers sitting in the front seat. A flapping flag mounted to the antenna explained the sound. Training the light on the soldiers' faces, he understood why he hadn't been shot.

The soldiers sat rigid, their startled eyes locked in their sockets focused straight ahead. John got up, then helped Salena, and together they walked toward the jeep. Halfway there, Salena gasped. "Land mines!"

John froze and pointed the flashlight down. Shining the beam across the ground, he saw every few feet in all directions places where the soil had been dug out and filled in. In some spots—including one John had stepped over—dry pine needles had been piled over the disturbed earth.

Salena clutched John's arm. "PMN anti-personnel mines."

"Is that good or bad?"

"PMN mines contain large amounts of explosive and are difficult to neutralize."

John shone the light on the jeep's shattered headlights and crumpled windshield. Both soldiers' chests were splattered with blood. "I don't plan on neutralizing anything. I just want outta here."

"When I was little, my father warned me if I ever wandered into a minefield, keep still and wait for help."

"Maybe if we wait long enough, Khan himself will come and rescue us."

"He also taught me how to retrace my footsteps."

"I'm listening."

"First, inspect the ground around your feet for signs of exposed mines and tripwires."

"I see plenty of those."

"As you start walking back, turn your body in the direction of your rear foot."

"I don't get it."

"If your right foot was behind your left foot when you stopped, turn around by turning right."

"What if you're with someone else?"

"My father didn't say."

"Maybe you weren't listening." John aimed the flashlight straight down and scrutinized the ground around their feet. Seeing no mines beneath their legs, John carefully stepped around Salena and took the lead. He shone the flashlight on the ground in the direction they'd come from, and estimated the edge of the mined area lay 20 yards away near a low cluster of arborvitae shrubs. "What next?"

"Place your foot completely within your print. Don't tiptoe or you may lose your balance."

"Makes sense to me." John directed the beam in a straight line from their feet to the low-growing shrubs. "I've got bad news."

"What?"

"The ground got hard. We left no footprints."

"He did not say what to do in such circumstances."

"We'll wing it." Clasping Salena's hand, John took every step with care and deliberation, constantly focusing the beam on the ground. After 10 minutes they came to within a few feet of the arborvitaes, where John turned to Salena. "I hope Omar's cousin uses EverReady batteries."

"Is that important?"

"Never mind, we're almost there."

The last six feet appeared clear of mines, but John and Salena took their time anyway. When they reached the shrubs, Salena wrapped her arms around John and said, "Thank you."

John stroked her hair and allowed his fingers to caress the rim of her ear. "I'm glad you're safe."

He was sure Salena would have let him kiss her, and though grateful for the comfort of her arms, he wasn't sure kissing her was fair—to her, to Maureen, and to himself. Salena must have read his hesitation. She took a deep breath, and stepped back. "We have a problem."

At that moment, John's only problem was the hardening in his pants. "What else is new?"

"The mines make the trail ahead too dangerous."

"Do you know another way?"

Under the beam of the flashlight, Salena studied the map, and under the starry sky, John studied Salena. The moon's creamy light blurred the lines of her face, transforming her into a milky-skinned princess. Breathing in the aroma of jasmine mingling with her body's natural oils, he understood why she had driven Khan mad. She *had* to know the power she held over men. When she glimpsed him out of the corner of her eye, he fought the impulse to pull her close and press his lips to hers.

Salena folded the map and stuck it inside the sleeping bag. "We must go back to the stream we crossed before and hike two kilometers north. Three large rocks in the water mark the start of another trail. From there we hike five kilometers southeast until we come to a waterfall. Behind the waterfall we will find Ghazi's cave."

"Do you think we'll get caught in any more mine fields?"

"I promised you the truth. There is a chance, not only of encountering more mines, but Indian commandos."

John realized his chances of reaching Srinagar were as good as getting killed by a soldier's bullet. "If anything happens to me, promise you'll go on alone to Srinagar. You won't go back to Islamabad."

She shook her head.

"Please, Salena, Khan wouldn't dare hurt those kids in the Freedom Ward, or your doctor friend."

"All will bear the brunt of his rage."

"Qadeer is analyzing your computer. Eventually he'll figure out what you've been up to."

"I will not abandon my children, or Dr. Raja."

John knew he wouldn't change her mind, but cared enough to persist. "Your father's friend in Srinagar can protect you."

"If I do not return, and Khan discovers I was plotting with the Americans, he will never rest until he finds me. And when he does, he will send Qadeer to slaughter all who helped me, and then he will allow Qadeer to do with me as he pleases."

"As long as I'm alive, I'll never let that son-of-a-bitch harm you."

She moved her mouth close to his ear, and whispered, "Get us through these mountains, and I will make sure no one harms *you*."

CHAPTER FIFTY-SEVEN

Captain Timothy Sheehan was a Navy man who President Lloyd had appointed as CRUSO's Executive Medical Officer on the advice of the Secretary of Defense.

That Sheehan held all the right credentials and knew all the right people gave Farrell all the more reason to massage her temples and shake her head. She had learned to smell trouble a mile away, and standing in Sheehan's office, regarding this fair-skinned man whose face bore the pallor of too much desk-work, the stench was unbearable.

Sheehan lifted a manila folder from off the top of a waist-high cabinet between them. "Ordinarily, our lab is given a month to verify a candidate's diagnosis, but as you know, time constraints imposed on this mission severely limited our staff's ability to corroborate Dr. Chandler's tests."

"Rest assured, doctor, you'll get blamed for nothing."

Sheehan took a deep breath that sounded a lot like relief. "Diagnosis of pancreatic cancer is often tricky, and involves a multi-pronged approach. Physical examination, routine X-rays of the gastro-intestinal tract, and blood tests don't often reveal exocrine or endocrine cancer. More invasive techniques are required once pancreatic cancer is suspected. For example, a barium swallow."

"That's when you drink barium sulfate and your insides light up."

"Specifically, the upper digestive tract is made visible on X-ray film. Mr. Covello underwent this test, along with an ultrasound, which helps distinguish cancer from pancreatitis. But an ultrasound isn't foolproof. Sometimes it fails to detect an existing tumor. Sometimes it suggests a tumor where none is present. That's why Dr. Chandler ordered additional tests."

"I read his preliminary report. He also obtained a CT scan, an ERCP, and a PTC."

"The CT is more accurate than ultrasonography, and while it's useful for locating cancers that alter the shape of the pancreas, the CT can easily overlook early or small tumors. The more conclusive tests include the ERCP and PTC, which is why we spent so much time, at least initially, examining those. The only test Dr. Chandler didn't perform was an actual biopsy. He didn't need to since the other procedures conclusively disclosed the tumor's presence. It took us awhile to verify Mr. Covello's results because we initially devoted our resources to evaluating the more advanced diagnostic procedures. We didn't spend much time—at least at first—scrutinizing the results of the basic tests—his abdominal cavity X-ray and routine blood analysis. You understand, major, those don't go to the root of diagnosing pancreatic cancer."

"So what's wrong with prioritizing your work?"

Sheehan stared at her a long time, and finally said, "Sometimes you miss the obvious."

Feeling herself draw shorter, faster breaths, Farrell made a conscious effort to slow her breathing. "Go on."

"The anomaly was first brought to my attention by Joan Shapiro, my senior radiologist. She examined Mr. Covello's CT scan and found his appendix at the bottom of the caecum in the lower right side of his abdominal cavity."

"Isn't that where it's supposed to be?"

Sheehan pulled a CT film from the manila folder and clipped it to a fluorescent illuminator mounted on the wall above the cabinet. He pointed to a cross section showing a two-inch long, white nub protruding from a larger white mass Farrell surmised was John's large intestine.

"There it is, plain as day."

"Fine, what's the big deal?"

CRUSO's chief doctor extracted a four-page stapled report from the file. "This is John's medical history dating back to birth. Collaborating with New Jersey law enforcement authorities, our team procured the information under the pretense it was required in connection with identifying John's body following his boating accident."

"Standard procedure. I don't understand where there's an issue."

Sheehan folded back the first page and pointed to the top line of the second. "At six and one-half years of age John Covello suffered an acute inflammation of his appendix requiring an emergency appendectomy." Sheehan wiped his brow. "I'm sorry to inform you, major, but your mission operative has no appendix."

Farrell gripped the edge of the cabinet, and reread the top line of the second page to verify she'd heard Sheehan correctly. "Do you understand what you're saying?"

"When Joan pointed out the inconsistency, we immediately began looking for others. Within two hours we found one—this time in his blood work."

Distracted by the enormity of what Sheehan was implying, Farrell struggled to concentrate on his every word.

"We ran DNA tests and came up with two scientifically irrefutable conclusions. First, the individual from whom the blood was drawn has the same type as John, O-negative."

"Isn't that rare?"

"Only seven percent of the population. So we thought our fears might prove unfounded. But another test—a DNA screen performed half a dozen times by three different technicians—confirmed our hypothesis: The blood was drawn from an individual who absolutely could not be John Covello."

"Why's that?"

"Because the blood was taken from an individual with two X chromosomes."

"How could that be?"

"It can't, not if it were drawn from a man."

A zillion questions whirled in Farrell's mind, and she didn't know where to start. She decided with the obvious. "If the blood didn't come from John, whose is it?"

"We contacted Special Agent Clarkson and requested another search of Dr. Chandler's office, this time to pull the files of all his patients diagnosed with cancer." Sheehan opened a second folder on the cabinet, and extracted another set of documents. "Clara Hansen has been Dr. Chandler's patient for seven months. She's a 61-year-old woman who lives in Sea Girt, New Jersey. She suffers from Stage IVB pancreatic cancer."

Farrell grit her teeth for no other reason than to make sure she still felt something. Her head started spinning and she heard herself breathing hard.

"An inspection conducted by Clarkson's staff, confirmed by our own people, indicates Mrs. Hansen's file was tampered with. For one thing, standard tests normally found in the file of a pancreatic cancer patient—CT scan, ERCP, and PTC—were missing. More importantly, we discovered several tests in Mrs. Hansen's file bearing Mr. Covello's name."

"The bastard switched the files."

"At least the results, and he was pretty damn good. Using an ordinary word processing program, and an expensive color printer, he replaced the headers on Mrs. Hansen's printed test results with the headers from Mr. Covello's test results. Looks like Dr. Chandler hadn't finished finagling the files, and probably planned to cover his tracks more carefully, but I understand a hitman's bullet put a premature end to any such intentions."

"What about John's pain? He's complained of severe stomach pain for months."

"With good reason." He lifted another page from John's folder and placed it on the cabinet in front of Farrell. "We found Mr. Covello's upper GI series and endoscopy results inside Mrs. Hansen's file. It's easy to understand why the poor man's hurting. He suffers from a severe duodenal ulcer."

"A simple ulcer?"

"Actually, it's not so simple. His duodenum wall is nearly perforated. If he doesn't receive appropriate treatment within six weeks, bacteria entering his abdominal cavity will cause peritonitis requiring emergency hospitalization and surgery. I suggest he begin a regimen of H-2 blockers and antibiotics—along with medication to protect the mucosal lining—and he should begin as soon as possible."

Farrell scrutinized Sheehan's face as if he were an alien from a distant galaxy. "Doctor, you don't understand. John Covello is in Pakistan, God knows where, determined to implode General Khan's command and control center in 48 hours, and when that building comes tumbling down, he plans to die inside with everyone else."

Sheehan's cheeks flushed, and he looked down. "Oh yeah, that's right."

Farrell's worst fears about CRUSO's objectives and methods had been realized. They were the same fears President Lloyd had expressed when he'd chosen her to serve as Daley's assistant. On the day he summoned her to the Oval Office, they'd held a frank discussion about the ethics of sending a man or woman on a suicide mission, even a man or woman already marked for death.

They both understood the rise of terrorism justified extreme measures. After all, terrorist organizations didn't think twice about sending human beings to blow themselves up for a cause. Still, something didn't sit right with the president, or her, about paying a dying man's family lots of money to die a little sooner—even for the sake of national security. Despite his misgivings, President Lloyd had come to realize in a world plagued by ruthless terrorists and rogue heads of state, circumstances might arise where a suicide mission offered the logical solution. That was why he tolerated CRUSO, and why he'd asked her to serve in the agency as his watchdog. To make sure power wasn't abused and careless mistakes weren't made. To make sure the large sums involved didn't cloud judgments. On all counts she had failed.

Farrell never cried easily, but for the first time in as long as she could remember, tears were about to come. She swallowed back her anger and guilt, and asked Dr. Sheehan one last time, perhaps wishing their conversation had been a bad dream. "Are you absolutely sure the test results were switched?"

"I have no doubt whatsoever."

What she must do next was almost unthinkable. Inform Colonel Daley and President Lloyd they had sent a basically well man on a suicide mission, and that CRUSO must now focus on extracting him from Pakistan. But how could they pull John out of Pakistan when no one knew where to find him?

An even more disturbing thought occurred to Farrell. What if the colonel proposed they do nothing—let John complete his mission and keep the president in the dark? Farrell dismissed the notion as absurd. Anxious though Daley was for the mission's success, he wouldn't dare suggest something so monstrous simply to improve his chances for brigadier general.

CHAPTER FIFTY-EIGHT

From what the moon and stars allowed John to see, the waterfall was no more than 15 feet wide along the top, and plummeted 20 feet straight down before crashing into a wide pool cluttered with boulders. According to Salena, behind this waterfall they would find a cave where Kashmiri freedom fighters on the lam hid from Indian army patrols.

John squeezed sideways through a foot-wide gap between the sheet of falling water and a jagged stone wall. Salena followed closely, shining her flashlight through the gap. John shut his eyes against the cold spray, and stepped cautiously to avoid slipping on the wet rock floor.

They entered a shallow cavern roomy enough to sleep 20. In the beam of the flashlight John noticed a ring of small stones filled with ashes, and a pile of dried pine branches a few feet beyond. John could easily imagine a band of terrorists holed up here overnight, choosing their next victims and plan of attack. Osama bin Laden could very well have taken refuge in a place like this after he fled Afghanistan.

Helping John out of his backpack, Salena asked him if he wouldn't mind lighting a fire while she set up the sleeping bag.

Despite the twin advantages of stick matches and dried wood, John failed miserably in three attempts. Salena must have noticed him fumbling over the circle of stones. She walked over, knelt beside him, and stared down at the two dozen charred matchsticks on the floor beneath his hands. He sensed she was trying not to make him feel like an idiot when she said, "Perhaps you should look in the backpack to see if Ghazi packed us dinner."

John frowned at his failure. "I'm sorry. I'm just not good at campfires."

She studied his face, first his eyes, then his mouth, and back to his eyes. "You are good at what is important."

"Like what."

"You are an expert in demolitions, you have a good sense of humor, and you know how to protect a woman."

John smirked. "Yeah, like you really need my protection."

"We help each other. That is what makes us a team."

A chill ran up John's spine as he remembered Maureen had spoken those same words the day he left her for the last time. Afraid to die alone in a strange land, he longed to hold Maureen, feel the warmth of her breasts against his chest and the comfort of her arms around his back. But the life he had lived before CRUSO was gone.

John got up, crossed the stone floor, and knelt in front of the backpack. Rummaging through the bag, he wondered if Salena expected him to stand guard through the night while she caught a few hours sleep.

He pulled from the backpack three round flatbreads wrapped in old newspaper, and two chunks of smoked lamb bundled in leaves. Neither looked particularly appetizing, but he really wasn't hungry anyway.

Salena quickly kindled the dry branches into glowing flames that filled the cave with yellow light. She rose and walked toward him, and as she approached, they exchanged smiles.

She knelt beside him, and their eyes met. "So what is there to eat?"

"Filet mignon and a bottle of French Merlot."

The flickering light revealed a subtle smile on Salena's lips. "I am not hungry either."

He pretended to ignore her steady gaze. "We've had a long day, and tomorrow promises to be just as long. You should get some sleep." John nodded toward the fire. "I guess I'll park myself over there." As he reached for a folded blanket at the foot of the sleeping bag, Salena grabbed his hand.

"No."

He froze.

"You will not sleep by the fire."

He stared at her long, lithe fingers enveloping his, and sighed. "OK, I'll go outside and keep a look out."

"That is not necessary. No one will find us here."

"Then what am I supposed to do?"

She firmed her grip on his hand. "Do not forget, you are my husband."

John's heart pitter-pattered like a kid who'd gotten a date with his high school crush. "Are you sure?"

"I have never been more sure."

Salena un-zipped the sleeping bag, and John pulled off his sneakers. His feet, free after a grueling day, throbbed with relief. Salena slid in first, turned her back to him, and moved to one side. John took off his watch, and slipped in beside her. When Salena zippered up the bag, John wasn't sure where to put his hands. He didn't wait long before Salena offered an answer.

"Hold me. Our joined bodies will keep us warm."

"Like a furnace."

Salena removed her veil, and in the cozy space, squirmed around to face him.

His pulse pounded as he drank up the sight of her large brown eyes reflecting the dancing flames, her long chestnut hair rippling along her face, and her smooth dark cheek nearly touching his. The sweet scent of jasmine overwhelmed him, and he closed his eyes and rubbed his temples, unable—unwilling—to deny the magnetism between them.

"Are you all right?"

"Too good," he replied, and when he opened his eyes, he found her staring at him with an intensity he could no longer escape.

Her voice fell to a whisper. "I must share a secret with you, then you must decide."

"I thought you had no more—" Then he remembered she had begun telling him something before they abandoned the car. "Nothing you can say will make me change my mind."

She riveted her eyes to his, parted her lips, and ran the tip of her finger along his cheek. "After my residency in America, I returned to Srinagar to live with my mother. She had taken ill with pneumonia, and the women's hospital was in dire need of physicians. I was home only three months when my life changed forever."

He felt her shudder in his arms.

"One October night five men from the Border Security Force came to my mother's house. They broke down the door and accused me of giving medical aid to Muslim terrorists. In front of my mother, they dragged me outside and gagged me. My mother was sure I was about to meet the same fate as my father. To this day, her screams live in my nightmares.

"They drove me to a police station, where for six hours they interrogated me about my political beliefs. At first I answered honestly, but after countless kicks and slaps, and four cigarettes extinguished on my skin, I told them lies, whatever they wanted to hear. I told them Kashmir should always remain part of India.

"Just when I thought they would release me, they dragged me to another room. They shouted at me and called me terrible names. They said I was a whore. They grabbed my hair and threw me on a metal table. My back was cold, and I remember cracks in the ceiling shaped like a rose. One man pulled my arms over my head while the others ripped off my dupatta. They made fun of my veil and said whores did not need veils. Then they tore off my nightgown."

John clenched his teeth, wishing a slow, painful death for those who had hurt her. He found himself caressing her cheeks, wiping tears from her eyes.

"They raped me for I don't know how long, taking turns, until they made me bleed. After they were done I was convinced they would shoot me. Instead, they drove me home and left me naked on the street, wishing they had."

John kissed a teardrop off the corner of her mouth.

"I treated my own injuries, and in two months, my body healed, but not my heart. To forget what happened, I lived for my work, but the soldiers and police were everywhere, even in the surgical suites. Whenever they looked at me, it brought back the pain. Finally, I left my beloved Srinagar. I left my mother, I left ..." Salena closed her eyes, buried her face against his throat, and began to sob.

As her body shuddered, John snuggled closer and stroked her hair. "I'm sorry Salena. If I could go back in time, I'd kill those assholes before they hurt you."

He thought of his daughters, and their vulnerability. He longed to be at their sides every waking minute so no man could ever harm them.

The sobs subsided, and Salena fell quiet. John wrapped his arm around her waist, and kissed away the last of her tears.

"Only my mother, my dear friend Raja, and now you, know of my shame."

"You have nothing to be ashamed of. Nothing."

"But I do."

"You did nothing wrong."

"In this land, if a woman is raped, she is deemed to have provoked the act. Fanatics have twisted the words of Allah, turning the victim into the criminal, forcing countless Muslim women to carry a lie to their graves. A woman who admits to her rape is forever marked. She will never find a happy life with a good Muslim man."

John now understood why this intelligent and attractive woman had not married. What had happened to her also explained Naji. At the time of her rape, Salena had been in love with him. Maybe she had told Naji the truth, and he had spurned her, or maybe, fearing his rejection, she had left Srinagar without divulging her secret.

Knowing how alone she must have felt these last five years, he longed to reassure her. "If a woman is caring, compassionate, and intelligent, that's all that matters. Her rape should make no difference to a man, and if it did, the man would be a lowlife who didn't deserve her anyway."

She bit her lower lip. "What would you have done?"

"Stuck by you all the way."

For a long moment, her eyes scoured his, and when she spoke, her voice was a whisper. "I tried to hate him, but I could not."

"Hate who?"

Salena shook her head. "I cannot say."

John wouldn't force the issue. He had learned this woman bared her soul in increments, and tonight she had shared a secret so personal, so tragic, he wasn't sure he had a right to know more.

She sniffled and wiped her nose. John finger-stroked her hair, eliciting a soft moan, and tenderly kissed her forehead.

Salena slid her hand under his shirt, then down his arm. "Forgive me for burdening you with my past."

"Nothing about you burdens me."

Her fingernails gently raked his chest. "Tell me John Covello. What secrets lie within you?"

He had already told her about Billy Dwyer's death, but not how the tragic incident had almost cost him his family.

Salena's eyes glimmered with understanding. "The good in you, John. That is what they will remember. Only a good man feels such deep sorrow after what was truly an accident."

"Maureen thought I'd stopped loving her."

"You are wrong. She knew you cared, even after the accident."

"How could she? I closed my heart."

"Women have a special gift. They can always see within a man's heart."

John clasped Salena's hand and drew it close to his chest. "What lies within mine?"

She answered with a seductive gaze that left him powerless to resist.

Slowly he moved his fingers downward, skimming the soft lines of her back, her waist, and her thigh. Instinctively, her body arched toward him, and in one forward motion, she was snugly in his arms. Her lips parted, and their tongues locked and writhed, and after a brief taste of paradise, she pulled away and gazed at him with a desperate, urgent yearning.

Her rapid breaths felt warm and moist against his face, and his lurching heart could no longer ignore the fire in her eyes and the stiffening in his groin. He pulled her firmly to him, and in response, she thrust her eager tongue into his mouth. What happened next was a blur, as all rational thought fled him, replaced by blind desire for the corporal warmth that would soon be denied him forever.

CHAPTER FIFTY-NINE

Farrell wasn't surprised by Daley's silence, figuring he simply needed more time to absorb the incredible truth about John Covello. Ajay Agarwal's reaction, on the other hand, startled her.

Leaning forward in his self-appointed chair at the long conference table, Agarwal's brown eyes bulged, and he shook his fist at her. "He is one man, no? One man comparing to the lives of 20 million Indians and 10 million Pakistanis. It is beyond my comprehension you are having any doubt whatsoever."

Farrell turned in her chair, and facing Agarwal, planted one elbow on the polished tabletop. She carefully considered her response. After all, a single sentence from Agarwal to Behari could trigger a chain of events igniting a nuclear catastrophe in South Asia.

"John accepted CRUSO's offer on the pretense he would have died within four months from pancreatic cancer. Failure to disclose the truth to President Lloyd not only violates our legal duty to our commander-in-chief, but breaches every ethical and moral principal on which CRUSO was founded. Simply put, CRUSO does not send healthy men and women on suicide missions."

"And why should this be? The Tamil Tigers in Sri Lanka, Hamas in the Middle East, and the PKK in Kurdistan—for decades all are using the suicide mission to great effect." Agarwal's tone shifted from shrill to defiant. "Do not be forgetting the words of your own secretary of defense after al-Qaeda attacked your country. 'The terrorists operate in the shadows and must be dealt with in the shadows.' Is that not the very reason for CRUSO existing? To deal with terrorists and their sponsor states on their own terms?"

"If you're comparing tactics and procedures, yes, CRUSO does employ the suicide mission as a weapon against terrorist organizations and hostile governments, but unlike Hezbollah, Hamas, and other militant groups, we don't knowingly send healthy citizens to their deaths."

Agarwal's face broke into a smug grin that at once frightened and infuriated Farrell. She looked across the table at Daley to glean his reaction, but he was busy tearing sheets of scrap paper, and appeared not to notice.

The special envoy's eyes bored through Farrell. "You yourself make my case for allowing Mr. Covello to complete his mission."

"How's that?"

"When you recruited Mr. Covello, you did so under the belief he was terminally ill, no?"

Farrell nodded warily.

"When he boarded the jet to Bahrain, you were believing he would be dead in a few months, is that not true?"

"Your point, Mr. Agarwal."

"You just told me your agency does not knowingly send healthy citizens to their deaths, and CRUSO did not send a healthy man on this mission knowingly."

Farrell shot out of her chair. "That's ridiculous. We were tricked into believing John was terminally ill. If we hadn't been forced to select a candidate under such rigid time constraints, we would've discovered Chandler's crime and revoked John's eligibility before the mission ever got underway."

Agarwal cocked his head and looked up at her with a sympathetic smile. "Please, major, I am asking only that you weigh your decision carefully. Measure the life of one man against the lives of millions."

"Whether ten or ten million lives are at stake, CRUSO does not force men and women to kill themselves."

"Did not John Covello make his decision of his own free will?"

Farrell aimed her index finger at Agarwal. "Now you make *my* case, sir. People base decisions on available information. If a person bases a decision on a lie, he has not made the decision of his own free will. He may believe the decision was his own, but in truth, the information was manipulated to achieve the desired result. John accepted CRUSO's offer on the information his premature death was inevitable. That information was false. I can well imagine him making a different decision had he known he was suffering from a readily treatable ulcer, not inoperable cancer."

"You cannot deny at the time he accepted your offer, the information was true."

Farrell rolled her eyes. "You don't get it, do you?"

"No, I think you are not understanding me. In two days Khan and his generals will be finalizing plans to unleash the full fury of Pakistan's nuclear arsenal on my nation. We intend to stop Khan with or without America's help. If that means deploying our own nuclear warheads to preempt his aggression, so be it. If Khan manages a counterattack and we lose millions of citizens, that is a dear sacrifice we must endure for the greater good of the republic. But Major, you have an operative on the ground, and yes, I am admitting at first I was skeptical. I was not believing Mr. Covello would enter the Citadel." Agarwal grimaced, as if it pained him to concede John's success. "He did. I was not believing your agents could smuggle 80 sticks of dynamite into Pakistan National Hospital. They did. I was not believing Mr. Covello could plant that dynamite. And he did. Think of the countless lives spared on both sides of the Line of Control if your operative returns to Islamabad, takes delivery of the ammonia dynamite, and finishes the job he was sent there to do."

Farrell dropped into the leather chair and sighed. There was no convincing the special envoy. Fortunately, the decision to intercept John and bring him home was not Agarwal's to make. She turned and looked across the table at Daley, and Agarwal did the same.

With the edge of his hand, Daley shoveled the torn paper scattered on the table into a perfectly circular inch-high mound. He admired his handiwork from two angles, first shifting his head to the right of the pile, then to the left. Satisfied with his effort, he looked up smiling.

Slowly, almost imperceptibly, the curl on Daley's lips faded, and for a full minute he nodded pensively. Finally, he said, "You know, Mr. Agarwal, I can almost buy your argument about sacrificing the life of one for the lives of millions. Allowing events to unfold as planned might work out quite conveniently. John believes he has terminal cancer, so in his mind, he has nothing to lose. What's more, his wife and children already think he's dead." Daley stroked his chin and stared thoughtfully at his scrap paper heap. "However, I have a few problems with not informing the president. First of all, too many people know the truth about John's illness—Captain Sheehan, his medical staff, and for that matter, Agent Clarkson and his team at the FBI. More importantly, even if no one but the three of us in this room knew the truth, I'm not about to commit treason. That's exactly what I'd be doing if I failed to inform my commander-in-chief of a material change of facts. Don't get me wrong, your suggestion is tempting. Nobody wants a nuclear war that might be avoided but for one man's death. But unless I'm willing to risk 20 years in Leavenworth, that's not my call."

Then the colonel did something Farrell had never seen him do. He scraped the hundreds of bits of paper into his hand, tilted his head up at the ceiling, and wearing a sickly smile, tossed them high in the air. Farrell watched her boss's tired, gray eyes follow the shower of confetti fluttering to the table. As the last of the scrap paper hit the fine wood surface, she got the feeling Daley had just witnessed his only chance for brigadier general crash and burn.

CHAPTER SIXTY

Azam Qadeer enjoyed his time alone in the Truth Revelation Center, as General Khan cleverly called the Citadel's interrogation room. Of the hundreds of rooms in the Citadel, here was where he felt most alive, for here he held the specter of life and death over Khan's enemies. Here grown men wept before him, begging for mercy. Here the fiercest Afridi tribesmen inevitably succumbed to his exquisite skill in the art of inflicting pain. And here he most often satisfied his lust for broken women.

Qadeer recalled a particularly delightful occasion when he questioned a Kalesh girl from Chitral whose only crime had been her father's allegiance to Labib Razzak's minister of agriculture. The faster her body writhed under the pain of nail-studded clamps squeezing her tender parts, the deeper he penetrated her, and the louder the cheers of those who encouraged him to an all-too-quick release.

During the last few months he had not been given the chance to practice his special talents on the devious sex, but he remained hopeful his drought was about to end. What better prize than Salena Zamal. But first he must prove her betrayal.

Qadeer's analysts had worked two days studying files offloaded from Zamal's PC, looking for any sort of telltale code embedded in her operating system and applications programs. So far they'd found nothing, but his experts had merely scratched the surface.

Qadeer extracted his box of Red Lamps from his pants and fished out the last cigarette. He crumpled the box and tossed it in a pail under the stainless steel table he longed to share with Khan's whore.

He pondered his other riddle, Mr. Cattano. The arrogant American carried himself convincingly as a software consultant, but Qadeer distrusted him nearly as much as he did Zamal. Before their supposed abduction, Zamal and Cattano had spent much time together walking the 4th and 5th floor halls of Pakistan National Hospital. He had personally observed the pair during their Saturday night stroll to the nurses station in the Pediatric Unit. Something about those two he couldn't put his finger on, a bond stronger than that of salesman and customer. How conveniently they had been kidnapped only two days before Glorious Dawn.

No, Zamal and Cattano were definitely scheming. But why had Advanced Medical Systems called four times in the past five hours looking for Mr. Cattano? Qadeer himself had taken the last call from a

Ted Dunne, the company's owner, and had detected in his voice genuine concern for his employee's safety. The pompous American even threatened to contact the US ambassador unless he received more specific information regarding Mr. Cattano's location. Qadeer also knew Mr. Dunne had telephoned Lady Reading Hospital. If John Cattano were anything more than a sharp-tongued salesman, why would those who pulled his strings openly seek information on his whereabouts.

Then there was Lieutenant Siddique's report of two American men snooping around the hospital's main entrance that very evening. When stopped and questioned, they claimed to work for their country's embassy. Their paperwork seemed in order, at least to the untrained eye of the soldiers posted at the door, and they were allowed to leave.

Qadeer mulled whether he should bother Khan with such vague hints of sedition, or wait until he received concrete evidence against Zamal—proof she had staged her own abduction, and proof she was somehow linked to Cattano.

Gazing upon the stainless steel table, he sucked a long drag from his cigarette. As he exhaled, the door behind him opened.

"Captain."

Qadeer turned as Lieutenant Siddique entered the interrogation chamber and dipped his head in respect.

"I apologize for disturbing you, but I bring important news."

Qadeer nodded.

"Lance Corporal Shafi called from Salkhata. At 1305 hours his men encountered an SFF squad 30 kilometers northeast of Athmuqum. Sweeping the area of enemy soldiers, his men discovered a car hidden in the forest off the main road—the Mercedes Benz Subedar Mazhar was driving to Peshawar."

Why would Zamal have gone to the Neelum Valley? Perhaps her plot was nothing more sinister than an escape to Kashmir. But why involve Mr. Cattano? "Have you made a positive ID."

"The license plates match, but the car was damaged by artillery fire."

Qadeer's chest tightened, fearing the answer to his next question would dash all hope of having his way with pretty Salena. "Were any bodies recovered?"

"No, sir. Shafi's troops scoured the area. The only dead are 10 of our own, and seven Rashtriya Rifles."

"Did Shafi move the vehicle?"

"Not yet. He is awaiting your instructions."

"Good, I will go to Athmuqum at first light." Only after Qadeer had personally inspected the car would he inform General Khan of his conclusions. Intuitively, though, he knew that what he was about to find would vindicate him in the eyes of Khan. Then, after he tracked Zamal down and dragged her to the Truth Revelation Center, he would tie her to the stainless steel table and do with her what he had dreamed of for many, many months.

CHAPTER SIXTY-ONE

Daley had phoned the president half an hour earlier with the shocking news. When informed John Covello stood as good a chance as any man to live a long and healthy life, the president said little. Instead, he summoned them to the Situation Room for an emergency meeting.

Farrell, Daley, and Ajay Agarwal rose from their soft leather chairs, and just as they walked out the door, the intercom inside started buzzing. Farrell hustled back to the phone, and pressed the speaker button. "Yes Stacy."

"Good, I wasn't sure I'd catch you. I have a telephone call for Ted Dunne."

"From Islamabad?"

"No, Muzaffarabad. It's a gentleman who says he's delivering a message from your man in Pakistan."

Farrell glanced at Daley and Agarwal, and realized their mouths had all dropped at the same time. "Put the call through."

Daley added, "On speaker."

"Very well, sir."

Seconds later a deep, accented voice echoed off the room's walnut paneled walls. "Hello? Hello? Mr. Dunne?"

Daley replied cautiously, "This is Ted Dunne. Who is this?"

"Hello?"

"Ted Dunne here. Who am I speaking with?"

"Cousin to Omar Shah, but my name is not important. Your man in Pakistan has a message for you."

"Is he OK?"

"Allah will keep him safe."

"What does *that* mean?"

"Please, our connection is poor. Let me tell you his message. He says ... I could not wait for your delivery. I have found my own supplier. I am picking up the materials myself, but to get them I must travel to Srinagar."

Farrell turned to Agarwal, whose brown eyes bulged from their sockets.

"How is he getting there? When's he leaving? Who's the supplier?"

"Never mind. He is on his way."

"To Srinagar?"

"Yes, my map will guide him over the mountains from Sharda. When they reach the Vale, my friends will show them the road to the city."

"He's headed for the Kashmir Valley?"

"Do not worry, he is with his wife, and she knows the Vale as well as anyone."

Daley grabbed his forehead. "Wife? What wife?"

"He is a brave man. He will stop at nothing to fulfill his destiny."

"Wife? Destiny?" The line went dead, but Daley didn't notice. "What destiny? How can I reach him?"

Farrell said meekly, "Sir, the connection is lost."

"Get that man back on the line!"

Stacy answered through the intercom. "I'll try, sir."

Daley shook his head. "Son-of-a-bitch. He's found someone to supply him more explosives. Someone in the Kashmir Valley."

Farrell nodded in agreement. "And I'd venture a guess his wife is Dr. Zamal."

"That explains their disappearance."

"But what do you suppose he meant about destiny?"

"Beats me, but at least we can tell the president we know where John's headed."

Farrell noticed Agarwal's lips puckered in a frown.

Colonel Daley snapped, "What's wrong with *you*?"

"If Mr. Covello reaches Kashmir, he is on India's soil. How are you being so confident the prime minister will cooperate with your agency to find him."

"Are you suggesting the prime minister would ignore President Lloyd's request to undertake a search and rescue effort to extract John, even if he knew full well John is no longer authorized to complete his mission?"

Folding his arms across his chest, Agarwal's expression turned from sullen to smug. "That is exactly what I am suggesting."

Daley glared back. "With or without your prime minister's permission, once we get the green light, we're finding John Covello and bringing him home."

Agarwal grinned. "We shall be seeing."

Stacy's voice came over the intercom with the answer Farrell had expected. She hadn't been able to reconnect with the caller from Muzaffarabad.

"OK, let's go," Daley said, glowering at Agarwal. "I can't wait to see what Behari says after the president gets through with him."

Last to leave the conference room, Farrell turned off the lights, not nearly as sure Prime Minister Behari would heed the president's request to help find John in the Kashmir Valley, especially when doing so precluded any chance of assassinating Khan and stopping a nuclear war.

CHAPTER SIXTY-TWO

The prime minister's dark cheeks dominated the 60-inch flat-panel monitor mounted to the Situation Room wall. Sitting before a camera in a subterranean command center in the Aravali Hills near New Delhi, Behari gazed at the lens in such a way that his piercing eyes followed you around no matter where in the room you moved. The effect reminded Farrell of a haunting picture of Jesus her mama kept taped to the refrigerator door in her childhood home. Wherever she walked, His eyes followed.

Behari awaited the president's response, and Farrell, sitting beside Daley, waited too. If Edward J. Lloyd were the same principled leader whose political aspirations she had supported over the years, he'd already made up his mind, and she and Daley were there only to lend moral support.

The president looked directly at the giant monitor. "Your argument is cogent, sir, but surely you understand I cannot allow Mr. Covello to complete his objective under false pretenses. His candidacy for any suicide mission would have been a nullity had we known the truth prior to commencement of the operation."

A muscle flicked at the corner of Behari's mouth. "I hope you appreciate the irony."

"How so, Mr. Prime Minister?"

"Following the attack on Baramulla, you urged me to postpone a retaliatory strike—give Mr. Covello an opportunity to infiltrate the Citadel and topple Khan's government. I was skeptical. When I learned he had not only gained access, but positioned 160 lbs of dynamite, I was encouraged. I began to believe he might succeed, and I could soon close India's silos. Now, after winning my confidence, you ask my help finding Mr. Covello solely to guarantee his failure."

"I'm sorry, sir, but that is precisely what I'm asking."

Behari's eyes seethed as he glared at the president. "Now millions will die."

"Not if Secretary Parker's diplomatic efforts in Beijing succeed. The secretary's latest report indicates he's made incremental progress toward convincing Premier Jintao to exert his influence on General Khan."

"I am afraid slow but steady will not win this race. In New Delhi, Tuesday is less than four hours old, Glorious Dawn but a day away. I assure you, by Wednesday afternoon General Khan will know my nation's resolve to meet force with force."

"I implore you, give diplomacy a chance. If China withdraws its support of Pakistan, Khan will have no choice but to cease his aggression against your country."

Behari shook his head. "Premier Jintao will gladly play both sides until Pakistan and India obliterate each other. Nothing would please the premier more than a vulnerable India, allowing him to seize all of Ladakh and any other territory in northern India he desires for China."

Farrell considered Behari's statement, and concluded he might have a point. After partition, China's favors rained heavily on Pakistan. Not only had China shunned India, the world's largest democracy, but in 1962 had gone to war with its southern neighbor along their common border in the Himalayas. China inflicted a crushing defeat on India, and in the process annexed 13,000 square miles in the Aksai Chin region of Jammu & Kashmir. China also claimed 35,000 square miles in India's northeastern state of Arunachal Pradesh, and regarded India's Sikkim state as disputed.

As the curtain rose on the 21st Century, relations between the two titans of Asia thawed, partially because China had begun to appreciate India's potential as a lucrative trading partner. More importantly, Pakistan's position on Kashmir evoked considerable angst amongst the Chinese leadership.

Beijing had expressed increasing concern about the copycat effect Kashmir's independence movement could have on the 10 million Muslims inhabiting China's oil-rich Xinjiang region. Acting on these fears, China had recently conducted several joint military exercises with the Indian Army, demonstrating to Pakistan that Beijing could make nice to leaders on both sides of the Line of Control. Premier Jintao had also made clear to Ali Khan, and before him, Labib Razzak, that while a negotiated settlement of the Kashmir dispute was essential, Beijing would not support any form of independence for Kashmir likely to fuel the secessionist yearnings of Xinjiang's restive Muslims.

Thus while China maintained friendly relations with Islamabad, it kept a diligent eye on the growing influence of Muslim radicals in its own western provinces. China's recent overtures to New Delhi served to counter-balance the rise of Islamic extremism in South Asia, a realization apparently not lost on President Lloyd.

The president stepped closer to the screen. "I am confident Premier Jintao does not wish India brought to its knees. A victorious Khan bent on spreading Islamic fundamentalism will only further destabilize Xinjiang."

"China will do what is best for China. Perhaps Premier Jintao and General Khan have already negotiated a secret treaty—Jintao will allow Khan to annex India's northwest provinces if Khan checks the influence of his mullahs in Xinjiang."

In Farrell's view, Behari had hit the nail on the head. She knew for a fact the president hadn't disclosed to India's prime minister the disturbing images picked up two hours earlier by the DIA's Anstat-4 satellite. Twenty Chinese fighter jets and 15 Chinese transports had linked up with the 15 Pakistani PUMA's and eight Pakistani T-80UD's already in place at Skardu.

Behari continued, "If I authorize a pre-emptive strike against Islamabad, Lahore, Peshawar, Quetta, and Karachi, and all verifiable missile platforms in Pakistan, I assure India of no less than a stalemate."

The president rubbed his eyes and sighed. "Then God help us all, because the political and economic shockwaves of such a calamity will extend far beyond the subcontinent."

The prime minister stared at the president with lethal calm. "Then I urge you to reconsider your request, and allow Mr. Covello to complete his mission."

President Lloyd turned and looked at Farrell. His eyes lingered on her, as if he were hoping she'd jump up and say it was all a terrible mistake—Chandler had not deceived CRUSO, and John could proceed with his work.

Meeting the president's gaze, Farrell shook her head gloomily.

He turned and faced Behari. "I'm afraid John's mission is over. He should never have been sent in the first place."

Sanjay Behari concluded the conference by informing the president he must confer with his cabinet before diverting military resources to a search and rescue effort aimed at finding Mr. Covello. He promised to inform the president of his cabinet's decision by 1700 hours, DST. Before the screen went black, President Lloyd reminded the prime minister John's consent had been obtained through fraud.

The White House meeting was adjourned and all rose. The CIA Director, National Security Advisor, and India's special envoy left the room immediately. As Farrell followed Daley out, she noticed the president waving at her to stop while he chatted with Secretary of Defense Anne McClellan.

Farrell told Daley she'd catch up with him in the Ellipse parking garage. Her boss replied with a curt nod, and disappeared down the hall.

Standing beside the oval conference table, waiting for the president to finish up with Anne, Farrell studied the presidential seal on the wood paneled wall. There were times she still couldn't believe she'd been allowed to enter the inner circle of the most powerful man on earth. Other times, like now, she wished she hadn't.

On her way out, Anne flashed Farrell a bleak smile. The door closed, and she and the president were alone. He sat at the table's head, and motioned for her to sit beside him.

"I haven't seen your brother since last September, not since we hacked our way through 18 at Tam O'Shanter."

Farrell's brother played golf with the president and Secretary Parker once a year on Long Island. "I haven't seen George since Easter."

The president nodded. "It's been a busy year."

"What do you need, sir?"

"Your job description calls for you to put yourself in harm's way, but understand, what I'm about to ask is a request, not an order."

"I'll do whatever I must."

"Life on the subcontinent may get pretty dicey during the next 24 hours. Not a place most would choose to go."

"Do you want me there?"

"Yes, as my personal liaison to oversee John's rescue effort— assuming the prime minister agrees to help."

Farrell had never considered the possibility of seeing John alive again. How would she greet a dead man brought back from the grave? She'd worry about that later. What mattered most now was finding him before he got himself killed. "When do I leave?"

"The ST-131 is idling on the runway at Andrews."

"I'll inform Colonel Daley."

"Don't bother. Anne's speaking with him now. She'll accompany you to Andrews and share our latest intelligence on Kashmir. She'll also give you a dossier on the prime minister."

"Thank you, sir."

The president regarded her thoughtfully. "Do me a favor Denise. Come back alive, preferably with John Covello."

"I will, sir. Count on it."

CHAPTER SIXTY-THREE

Awakened to the sound of rushing water, John kept his eyes closed and breathed the erotic scent of Salena's hair tickling his nose. A biting chill stung his face, but the down sleeping bag, and Salena's smoldering skin, warmed his legs and torso. He became aware of his arm wrapped around her waist and his hand cupped over her breast, and figured this wasn't a bad way to start his last full day on earth.

His legs entwined with Salena's, John rubbed his feet against hers and moved closer. Salena shimmied backward, leaving no space between them. She squeezed his hand around her breast, released her grip, and brushed his hand gently over her stout nipple. He took the hint and massaged one breast, then the other, until he elicited a grateful moan. Instinctively, his member stiffened and wedged tightly against her backside.

If he didn't stop now, he'd lose control, so he moved his hand down to her belly. She must have misread his intent and gently steered his hand over her pubic hair to the moist tissue between her thighs. No way would he insult this fine woman, so he obliged her. With each rotation of his finger, Salena's moans grew louder and longer until her instinctive thanks echoed off the cavern walls.

John glanced at the thundering wall of water behind which they'd slept, and noticed faint light on the other side. He pulled his hand away and reached for his watch.

"What are you doing?" she whispered.

"Just checking the … damn!"

"Is something wrong?"

"It's six-thirty. We have to be in Kuligam by nine."

The seductive smile on her face melted into a look of profound disappointment. "We can stay here a little longer, and hike to Kuligam a little faster."

John kissed the tip of her nose. "I'll make it up to you."

She lifted her chin and their lips met. "You had better."

Unable to resist her Pathan beauty, he moved his mouth over hers, devouring its pink warmth, then probed deeply with his tongue until he was forced to stop for air.

John hungered for more, but they had to go. If they didn't reach Kuligam by 9:15, they'd lose their guides through the Vale. He pulled up his shalwar trousers, wiggled out of their fluffy cocoon, and put on his Nikes.

John stood for a moment staring at the back side of the waterfall, now dimly lit by the soft glow of dawn. Captivated by its sparkling beauty, he walked slowly toward the cascading torrent, and as he stretched out his hand to touch the water, he heard Salena shout from behind. "Watch out!"

He spun his head and saw Salena, fully dressed, crouched to the floor. "What's wrong?"

"On the other side—something moved."

John saw nothing beyond the translucent curtain of water.

"There!" Salena pointed to the slim opening where the edge of the falls met the cavern's rock wall.

John detected a moving shadow. He turned to Salena, who was slinking toward the backpack, he guessed, to retrieve the pistol inside.

A deep voice boomed off the rock walls. "Do not move!"

John wheeled to find a bearded man wearing a white turban pointing a rifle at him. Before John could react, a second man, wearing neither beard nor turban, but carrying a rifle, stepped from behind the opposite end of the waterfall. The clean-shaven man marched toward Salena, and ordered her to lie on the floor.

Salena did not move, and as the man reached her, he dropped his rifle and grabbed at her arms. Refusing to be held, she punched at the man's chest in a futile struggle to stay free.

John ran toward Salena, but before he got close, a pair of arms encircled his chest and started pulling him backward.

John gripped the arms, and imbued with unknown strength, bent forward and flipped his attacker over his back. A brown-bearded face and two startled eyes ogled up at him from the stone floor. John pounced on the man, and grabbed a black revolver tucked in his leather belt. Straddling the man's belly, he pointed the muzzle at his forehead, cocked the trigger, and screamed at Salena's assailant, "Stop or I'll kill him!"

John had never fired a gun, and didn't know what to expect if he did, but if the man clutching Salena so much as bruised her, he was prepared to find out.

Salena's attacker backed away. "Don't shoot! Don't shoot!"

John glared down at the man between his legs. "Who are you? What do you want?"

"My name is Abu Kundi."

"Bullshit! Abu Kundi is waiting for us in Kuligam."

The bearded man did something odd. He grinned broadly. "Then it *is* you."

"Who?"

"Dr. Zamal's new husband."

"If you know who we are, why the guns?"

"Five factions of the separatist movement use this cave as a hiding place. Each is the sworn enemy of the other. Only a fool would enter here with his weapon down."

Salena nodded her approval, and John stepped back.

Abu Kundi slowly rose, and flattened down the sleeves of his white kameez. After introducing his black-haired companion as Hani Taj, he explained what had happened. Late last night a BSF platoon had conducted a cordon and search operation in Kuligam looking for freedom fighters. They drove off with 11 boys and posted guards on all roads in and out of the village. "I knew if you tried to enter you would stumble into a snake's den. Hani and I slipped out in the middle of the night to intercept you."

John handed Abu Kundi back his pistol. "You obviously knew where to find us."

"Ghazi told me which trails he mapped for you. Consider yourselves lucky to be alive. This area is saturated with soldiers from both armies." Abu Kundi smiled through his dense beard. "But I know these mountains like I know my mosque. I will get you safely to Srinagar."

John picked up the backpack, and left behind the sleeping bag. He had no intention of camping out tonight. If all went according to plan, when they reached Srinagar, Omar Shah would give them plastic explosives and arrange for their return to Pakistan. By nightfall they'd be safely in the Citadel, having escaped the dacoits who'd abducted them on the road to Peshawar.

Trailing Abu Kundi and Hani Taj, John and Salena passed through the gap between water and rock on the west side of the falls. Pausing to admire the dawn's early light, John prayed for a memorable last day on earth, and though he had no way of knowing it now, his prayers were about to be answered in a way he could never have dreamed.

CHAPTER SIXTY-FOUR

On a mountain slope in the lower Himalayas bordering the northern edge of the Kashmir Valley, Abu Kundi stood beside a low mound of sawed-off pine branches hidden behind a fir tree a few yards off the trail. Clutching a fistful of the green-needled branches, he pointed to the mound and called out, "Two more martyrs for freedom."

John followed Salena and Hani Taj into the trees, and saw beneath the pile of evergreen branches the bodies of two clean-shaven, brown-faced young men. Neither had seen his 18th birthday, and each had been shot twice, once in the forehead, once in the chest. These children hadn't been dead long, as the reddish-black fluid coagulating around each bullet's entry point glistened under the sun's warming light.

John spun, folded at the waist, and retched. Salena clasped his shoulders. "They sacrificed their lives fighting for what they believed in."

Wiping bile from his lip, he heard Abu Kundi say, "For every mujahideen who dies, four line up to take his place."

Maybe he was sick and tired of hearing about Kashmir's martyrs, or maybe he knew zealous Muslim boys like these were instilled with hatred from the time they were babies—or maybe he understood these wasted lives were cut from the same cloth as those who'd murdered 3,000 innocents in New York, Washington, and Pennsylvania, and who'd butchered thousands of civilians in Iraq and Syria. Whatever it was, something inside him snapped.

He turned and screamed at Abu Kundi. "Bullshit! These boys aren't martyrs. They're kids, plain and simple. People like you poison their hearts with hate and fear and nonsense about virgins and glory. They didn't deserve to die any more than their victims. You people think life is something to throw away like garbage. I'd give anything to hang onto a few more years, yet you people kill each other like it's nothing. And don't give me that crap about justice and freedom. Yeah, the Indian soldiers who rape and murder Kashmiri civilians are no better, but that doesn't justify wasting the lives of children to fight your wars."

Abu Kundi's eyes narrowed and pierced John with simmering fury. "You will never understand. You did not die for the freedom you so cherish in America. No doubt the young patriots who battled the British were labeled militants and terrorists by England's king. You are a liar if you tell me the boys who died in the American Revolution wasted their lives like garbage. So why are we, who fight for our independence, labeled murderers by those who already enjoy the sweet nectar of freedom."

"Great speech, Kundi, but the American patriots fought soldiers, not civilians. George Washington didn't go around blowing up busloads of holiday shoppers, or office buildings filled with hard-working mothers. He didn't bomb discos filled with teenage girls guilty of enjoying their youth. It's your tactics, Kundi. They suck."

Abu Kundi's nostrils flared, and his beard quivered. "To set the record straight, I do not go around blowing up mothers and girls. I belong to the Kashmir Guard. We fight only Indian soldiers and their puppet regime in Srinagar. We never bomb civilian targets, and for your information, whenever we destroy a police station, we call a newspaper first to warn of the attack."

"Oh great, just what the world needs—kinder, gentler terrorists."

Salena nudged herself between the two men and turned to John. "Try to understand. There are two sides to the story. Abu Kundi is right. My people have suffered for decades under what he and I, and a million others, believe with all our hearts to be foreign occupation of a sovereign nation."

John wasn't looking to start a fight with Salena, but before facing God's judgment he needed to understand how basically decent people could kill innocent human beings as casually as putting on pants. "Help me out, here. Explain why I shouldn't feel lucky to be leaving an insane world seething with hatred."

Facing John, Salena slipped her hands into his, and spoke more out of hurt than rage. "Ali Khan and Sanjay Behari each have their own view of Kashmir's destiny. Khan believes Kashmir's Muslim majority justifies accession to Pakistan. By waging war on India, he intends to fulfill that destiny. Behari believes the Instrument of Accession signed by Hari Singh in 1947 closed the issue forever and made Kashmir an integral part of India. After partition, the countries battled for a middle ground that stopped at the Line of Control. To this day, both believe they are the rightful owners of all of Kashmir.

"Squeezed into the vise between India on one side, Pakistan the other, are ordinary Kashmiris like me who ask only to be left alone, but neither India nor Pakistan recognize our right to self-determination. Neither understands to achieve peace Kashmiris must choose for themselves to join Pakistan, stay with India, or remain free."

"Your people's thirst for freedom doesn't justify killing civilians."

"Death to innocent Kashmiris comes from all sides, even those who claim to fight for Kashmir's independence."

"And that makes sense *how*?"

"It does not. Over the past two decades dozens of militant groups have come and gone in Kashmir, each touting different agendas and methods. Some groups support accession to Pakistan, like the Hizbul Mujahideen and Lashkar-I-Toiba. Others, like the Jammu & Kashmir Liberation Front and The People's League, insist on nothing less than complete sovereignty. Still others have very specific and limited objectives, like Tehrik-ul-Mujahideen, which exists to protect a small community of Sunni Muslims known as the Asidih. There is even a group comprised solely of women who seek to establish an Islamic state in Kashmir and force women to wear burqas and stay locked inside their homes.

"Many of these groups are filled with radical elements from outside Kashmir—places like Pakistan, Yemen, Iran, Saudi Arabia, and other countries that know nothing of my people's heritage. None of these foreign terrorists understand the desire of Kashmiris—whether Muslim or Hindu, Buddist or Christian—to live together in peace. Sadly, the extremists leave behind death and destruction, and eagerly kill anyone who does not adhere to their beliefs."

Gripping Salena's hands, John nodded toward the dead boys covered in branches. "Then Kundi just assumes Indian soldiers killed those two. They could've as easily been shot by their own Muslim brothers. Is that what you're telling me?"

Abu Kundi, who was listening intently, said, "You are right. I cannot know for certain who pulled the trigger, but Indian soldiers are nevertheless responsible."

"How's that?"

"If India's occupation force withdrew from the Vale, the militants would no longer have a reason to fight."

"Wrong, Kundi. If the Indian Army packed up and left tomorrow, with all those hothead terrorists running around, each espousing their own brand of bullshit, I'd bet you'd see a lot more death and destruction in Kashmir than you see now."

Salena squeezed John's hands. "What Abu Kundi means is this: the first step toward peace requires India to recognize the right of Kashmir to exist as a sovereign nation. That much should be clear to you."

"Yeah, clear as mud."

John's thoughts turned to Karen and Christie. He wished he could have lived long enough to remind them how lucky they were to have been born into a free and tolerant society, a country whose highest priority was the protection of human and civil rights. Until he had come to this war-torn land, even he had taken those rights for granted.

CHAPTER SIXTY-FIVE

The descent from 9,000 feet at the northern cusp of the Kashmir Valley offered John his most breathtaking view yet of Salena's homeland. John, Salena, and their two guides passed emerald green rice paddies cut from the hills in tiers, and crossed over sparkling, snow-fed streams where John watched trout leap clear to their tails. The further they descended toward the valley floor, the more John observed nature's bounty blessing this fertile land. Tangled strawberry vines, cherry trees, apricot, and apple trees—all grew in wild abundance as if a spell had been cast upon the hills by an ancient god who instilled life in the soil, the water, and the very rocks beneath their feet.

They hiked for long stretches beneath fir, pine, and silver birch trees that opened suddenly into vast, sprawling fields resplendent with yellow, white, and purple flowers; then just as quickly, returned to the cool, dark shelter of evergreens reaching majestically toward a brilliant blue sky. At every step, John inhaled nature's fragrance—wild spruce, sweet jasmine, and always the bracing scent of fresh pine from off the mountains.

Abu Kundi and Hani Taj opened a 50 yard lead in the dense woodland, leaving John and Salena alone to enjoy the beauty of their surroundings. John fought the urge to reach out and hold Salena's hand. He longed for another chance to share their hearts and bodies as they had last night, and hoped she felt the same.

At a section of the trail winding downhill through the forest, John heard the sound of a flute. The long, soft notes played a simple, haunting melody that made John think of white-frocked angels floating near the gates of heaven.

Salena explained, "A bored shepherd blowing into his giraw. We must be nearing Kuligam."

When John was a boy, his mother read stories to him of shepherds playing flutes as they tended their flocks. Listening to a real shepherd play a real flute in the shadow of the Himalayan Mountains was as close to living a fable as he could imagine. "The music is pretty … but not as pretty as you."

Salena smiled shyly. "Every summer, when I was a little girl, my father took us to a guest house on Wular Lake. If we had time, I would show you."

"If we had time, I'd go."

After another hour of downhill hiking, the forest floor leveled off. When they crossed a sparkling brook, John noticed Abu Kundi and Hani Taj waiting for them up ahead. Beyond where the two men stood, sunlight shone through the trees, and when John reached them, he saw they had come to another clearing at the edge of the forest. Across a seemingly endless meadow of yellow flowers he saw a dilapidated wood house that looked more like a chicken coop than someone's home. To the left of the shanty, about 100 feet away, was a barn twice as large as the house, and behind the barn and the house stood rows and rows of green stalks six to eight feet tall.

Abu Kundi pointed to a wall of pine trees beyond the stalks. "Across this farm is the jeep trail that will lead us to Ganderbal. The trail is narrow. It bypasses Bandipur and allows us to avoid the roads."

Salena voiced John's concern. "It will take too long to reach Srinagar on foot."

Abu Kundi grinned. "I have no intention of walking 65 kilometers."

"Have you arranged for a jeep?"

"In a way."

John wasn't pleased with Abu Kundi's insinuation. "Do you have a jeep or not?"

"My own jeep is in Kuligam, 12 kilometers west of here, but security forces have sealed the town. Even if we snuck in, we could not leave."

"Where's the jeep you have in mind?"

Abu Kundi nodded toward the barn. "I hope in there."

"I don't like the idea of stealing."

"Who is stealing? I will offer to pay."

John scanned the field of yellow flowers, the maize stalks beyond, and the area around the house and barn, and saw not a soul. "What if nobody's home?"

"We will borrow."

John wasn't thrilled with taking anything from anyone, especially a destitute farmer, but they needed to reach Srinagar quickly. He and Salena followed Abu Kundi and Hani Taj to the shanty's front door. Close up, the house appeared in worse condition than it had from the forest. John was convinced if he huffed and puffed, he could topple this house of rotting boards held together with rusted nails.

Abu Kundi knocked twice, no one answered, and he knocked again. He waited another minute and unhitched the clasp. Holding his rifle at his hip, aiming it forward, he opened the door. Hani Taj drew his rifle too and followed Abu Kundi inside. John felt Salena rummage through the pack on his back, and when he turned to look, she was holding a pistol.

The door opened into a single room that served as the home's kitchen, dining room, and den. The room was sparsely furnished, its inhabitants obviously poor. Some would have called the rickety hand-made table and chairs rustic. John called it pathetic.

Salena bolted the front door and locked them in. Abu Kundi opened two doors into bedrooms at the rear of the common area, and reported both empty. He guessed the home's occupants were either out running errands or had been taken into custody by the Border Security Force. Hani Taj opened cabinets searching for food, while Abu Kundi rummaged through drawers looking for supplies they could use on their journey.

In the short, narrow hall separating the two bedrooms, John noticed a rectangular door in the wood plank floor. The door's hasp was unlocked. He reached down, pulled up the door, and found himself star-ing down the barrel of a rifle. Clutching the rifle was a bearded man wearing a blue kameez and black vest. Beside the man stood a boy about Christie's age, also holding a rifle. Huddled in the cellar's dark recesses, barely visible, cowered a young girl in a black veil.

In retrospect, John could have slammed down the door and run, but at the time, he was too scared to move. He said weakly, "Oh guys, I think the three bears are home."

John's companions turned and gasped.

As the man in the cellar climbed up the stairs, he shoved open the trap door and sent it flying back on its hinges, crashing to the floor. "Drop your guns. All of you."

A sharp pain bored through John's belly. He took two backward steps and looked at Salena, who set her pistol on the kitchen table. When Abu Kundi and Hani Taj hesitated, the man holding the rifle fired a single shot.

John was turned toward Salena, and he didn't see the man pull the trigger, but heard the bullet whiz past his ear.

Abu Kundi shouted, "OK, we will do as you ask." He lay his rifle on the floor, and Hani Taj did the same.

"We are freedom fighters," Kundi said. "We have come to buy your food and rent your jeep."

The man whose home they had invaded looked around at the open cabinets and drawers. "You are a liar. You have come to steal."

Abu Kundi held out his palms. "We have taken nothing. We are on a mission to liberate the Valley."

The man sneered and cocked his rifle. "I know who you are. You claim to fight for Kashmir's freedom, but in truth, you bring only death." He nodded over his shoulder at the boy and girl at the bottom of the cellar steps. "You are the same beasts who killed their mother because she did not wear a veil. You rob and murder anyone who does not think like you. It makes no difference if we are Indian soldiers or simple Kashmiris who wish to live in peace."

"But peace is what we want for you, too."

John got the impression that wasn't what the farmer wanted to hear.

His words seethed. "You all think you know what is best for us—break away from India, join with Pakistan, start a new country. Yet what do you bring? Misery and death."

"Allah be my witness, our mission is different. We are here to stop Ali Khan from destroying the Vale."

"Your only business here is to butcher my lambs to feed your faces, steal my son to fill his mind with hate, and rape my daughter to satisfy your lust." The man lifted his rifle and squinted down the barrel at Abu Kundi. "Those things you may do, but I swear, I will kill two of you before you kill me. Which two will it be?"

From outside the cabin, John heard the sound of squealing brakes. Hani Taj, standing nearest to a window, leaned back and peeked out. "BSF."

Salena's body stiffened and Abu Kundi's eyes opened wide. Bending down to pick up his rifle, Abu Kundi said, "Shoot us if you will, but we must be on our way." Aiming his gun at the floor, he added, "If you are smart, you and your children will join us."

Hani Taj picked up his rifle too, and along with Abu Kundi, dashed past the father, around the open floor hatch, and through a bedroom door. Salena stood motionless in the kitchen while the man pointed his rifle at John.

John heard car doors slamming shut. He wanted to tell this father lots of things, but only had time for one. "I'd never hurt you or your family. Life is too great a gift."

Someone banged hard on the door, and an angry voice shouted, "Let us in."

Salena carefully reached for her pistol on the table. "We must go now. If you come with us, we will protect you."

"I have survived armies and militants for 20 years. I do not need your protection."

Salena tucked the pistol under her dress. "You are making a mistake." She ran past the farmer, stopped at the bedroom door, and motioned for John to follow.

The soldiers outside pounded on the door. John knew the flimsy lock wouldn't hold. Staring down at the man's daughter, a girl younger than Christie, he said to the father, "Come with us. That lady knows what she's talking about."

The man shook his head.

Praying the farmer wouldn't shoot, John walked past him, around the cellar door, and into the bedroom.

The tiny bedroom's only window was a glassless square cut crudely out of a wood plank wall. From nails above the window hung a black cloth to keep out the elements. Salena pulled back the cloth and jumped out.

John ran to the window to see where everyone had gone.

Abu Kundi and Hani Taj were crouched outside the first row of maize stalks 50 yards behind the house. They pointed their rifles in his direction, John guessed, to cover him and Salena, who had already run halfway to the freedom fighters.

John's mind must have been playing tricks. He couldn't stop thinking about the father and his young children who'd lost their mother. John threw his legs over the sill and jumped to the ground. Instead of running toward the stalks, he hugged the outer wall and inched toward the corner of the shanty.

Peering around the warped boards to the front of the house, he saw two jeeps parked one behind the other. In the cargo area of the second jeep he saw a machine gun mounted on a tripod. John turned his head toward the front door, and watched mesmerized as the burliest of the soldiers kicked harder and harder until the door's brittle boards shattered to pieces.

John's heart pounded as the horrible sounds blurred together. Shouts in English, answered in a foreign tongue, high-pitched shrieks and desperate screams, and finally, a single, ear-splitting gunshot.

He looked at his hands and saw them trembling. He glanced back at Salena, who waved frantically from the edge of the maize field. More screams and pathetic sobs. John wiped his face and looked down at his hand, stunned to see his palm wet from his own tears. Most things he did by choice and some he did out of necessity. What John did now he did by instinct.

Running back to the bedroom window, he pulled open the black curtain and climbed in. He crawled to the side of a straw-stuffed mattress and glimpsed over the bed. The bedroom door to the living area was open, and what John saw inside made him sick. The two children were huddled on the floor over the lifeless body of their father. Tears streamed down the boy's cheeks, and the girl wailed, "Poppi, poppi."

The burly soldier grabbed the boy's arm and pulled him to his feet. "Where are you hiding them?"

John noticed a pistol handle protruding from under a frayed pillow at the bed's headboard. He reached over and wrapped his hand around the warm metal grip.

The soldier slapped the boy hard across the face, "Tell me now or you will join your father in hell." The wailing girl hugged her father's bleeding torso tighter.

Gun in hand, John stood. Avoiding the door's line of sight, he walked silently around the bed, and as he approached the door, he heard floorboards creaking toward him. He slid behind the door just as it opened into the bedroom.

A man in green fatigues, about John's height, walked into the room. In a single fluid motion, John grabbed the soldier around his neck and shoved the pistol into his temple. Drawing on all his strength, he pushed the man forward into the living area.

The soldier who had struck the boy let go of the child's arm.

John said coolly, "Lose the guns or this man dies."

Three of the soldiers immediately placed their rifles on the floor, but the hands of the man beside the boy inched toward his holster. John screamed, "Drop it, or I swear I'll kill this son-of-a-bitch."

The soldier's eyes opened wide. "An American. If there is one thing I hate more than a stinking terrorist from Pakistan, it is a stinking terrorist from America."

John's voice cracked. "Why … why did you have to kill him?"

The soldier in John's grip must have detected weakness. He spun, broke free, and dropped to the floor.

John screamed, "Stay down or I'll shoot."

The soldier who'd slapped the boy smiled and said, "I don't think you can do it."

"I will. I swear, I'll kill him."

"Go ahead. I dare you."

John pointed the gun at the young soldier curled up on his side. He had a dark face and a mustache, and was no older than 25. He was someone's son, brother, or husband, maybe even father, and John couldn't do it. He couldn't pull the trigger.

The gloating soldier who had dared John yanked his pistol from his holster and aimed it at John's head. "You foolish American, now it is your turn."

An explosion shattered John's eardrums and he waited to fall. Instead, the soldier about to shoot dropped his pistol, gaped down at his own chest, and pressed his hands over a gushing fountain of blood that splattered the boy's face. The soldier teetered backward, then toppled forward onto the legs of the dead father.

John heard a woman shout from behind. "Get down stupid!"

John dropped to the floor and heard a barrage of gunshots. On his hands and knees he scrambled into the bedroom and saw Salena firing her pistol from behind the door. Hani Taj was firing crouched behind the bed. John heard more shots from the other bedroom and guessed Abu Kundi had entered from a different window.

Hani Taj yelled, "Get out, both of you. We will hold off these swine."

John glanced back and saw the teenage boy grab hold of his sister and scramble into the cellar. He prayed for their safety, and wondered what would become of those poor children left with no family.

Protected by a spray of bullets from Hani Taj's rifle, Salena jumped out the window. John leapt out after Salena, grabbed her hand, and they ran toward the stalks. A bullet whizzed past John's head and they both turned. The jeep with the machine gun mounted on back was racing toward them.

Salena shouted, "We will never make it to the maize field."

Realizing they were easy targets, John looked around and saw only one place to run. "The barn!"

"Too far."

"It's our only chance."

With 100 feet of grass in between, the barn looked hopelessly out of reach. Even as he estimated how long it would take to get there, a hail of bullets chewed up the turf around their feet.

John squeezed Salena's hand. "Let's go."

CHAPTER SIXTY-SIX

Pulling Salena by the hand, John ran zigzag across the meadow, toward the barn. The jeep bore down on them hugging the line of stalks to their right, cutting them off from the maize field. John glanced back at the jeep and saw two soldiers, one at the wheel, the other standing in the rear, firing the pedestal-mounted machine gun.

The staccato bursts abruptly ceased, and John looked toward the shanty. Abu Kundi was shooting at the jeep from the bedroom window. The jeep's driver veered toward the house, while his gunner sprayed a torrent of bullets in Abu Kundi's direction.

Their pursuers momentarily distracted, John and Salena reached the barn's double doors. The handles yielded at John's first tug and they slipped inside.

He shut the doors, found the hasp, and slid the lock into place. Windows high in the rafters sent shafts of sunlight streaming to the barn's dirt floor, and the stench of manure made breathing difficult. John looked around and spotted a cluster of hay bales stacked waist-high. He grabbed Salena's hand and they scurried for cover.

Leaning back against the hay, catching his breath, John gasped his words. "I'm sorry ... I shouldn't have ... shouldn't have gone back in."

Salena's eyes showed no trace of anger. "Perhaps the soldiers did not see us come in here."

John smirked. "Yeah, sure, and maybe I'm not dying."

She snuggled against his side and laced her fingers through his. "What you did back there ... I remember the night the police came for me ... you did not even know that family." She squeezed his arm tighter. "I am so proud of you John Covello."

"If I hadn't gone back, we'd be safe in the cornfield."

Salena stared straight ahead, her eyes revealing a hint of sorrow. "That night, if someone had risked their life for me ..."

"If I were there, I would've stopped them—or died trying."

"I know."

"Then back in the house, why'd you call me stupid?"

A playful smile brightened her face. "Because next time someone points a gun at you and dares you to shoot first, do it."

John chuckled, then turned his head toward the barn doors. The shooting outside had stopped. "Maybe you're right, the soldiers didn't see us. Maybe Abu Kundi—"

A man's voice, amplified by a bullhorn, filled the barn. "If you surrender peacefully, we will shoot only one of you."

John sighed. "Or maybe they know exactly where we are."

Salena pulled her pistol from under her dress.

"How many rounds you have left?"

"Three clips of 15, not counting six in here."

The soldier's voice, cruel and derisive, sounded again, "Whoever chooses to die, come out now. I am losing patience."

John felt a shiver run through Salena's body. He encircled his arm around her shoulders and drew her close. "Maybe we can shoot our way out."

"They have bigger guns and more bullets."

"You've got better aim."

"By now they may have called for reinforcements."

"Then we'll slip out the back."

"They will see us. We cannot outrun a jeep in an open field."

John took his arm away and pivoted to his knees. Whiffing the fetid air, he looked over the hay bales at the opposite wall. "There, in that stable, it's a horse."

Salena turned and knelt beside him. "Do you know how to ride?"

John scanned the barn's interior, first one wall, a dark corner, then another wall, and finally, his eyes froze on an object propped against an elm-staved barrel overflowing with animal feed. "I sure do, but not a horse."

John stood and reached for Salena's hand. "Come on."

They sprinted across the barn, where leaning against the barrel was the sweetest sight John had seen since he'd met Salena—a shiny chrome engine, an electric blue fuel tank, a padded double seat, two tires filled with air, and most importantly, a key in the ignition. It wasn't a Harley, but for what John had in mind, a Harley wouldn't do.

He yanked the key from the ignition and popped open the gas cap. "Where exactly does that trail behind the cornfield lead?"

"If I remember correctly, southeast around Wular Lake to Ganderbal. If we can reach Ganderbal, we will have only 20 kilometers to Srinagar."

John peered into the tank, checking the fuel level. "It'll have to do." He pushed the cap in place. "How far from here to—"

The tone of the soldier outside turned angry. "I am growing impatient. Do not make me come in and get you."

"How far from here to Ganderbal?"

"About 25 kilometers."

He mumbled, "Thirty miles to Srinagar ... quarter tank ... it'll be close."

Salena ran her hand over the black vinyl seat. "I do not understand. You want me to ride with you on the back of this machine—all the way to Srinagar?"

"I'd have Scotty beam us there, but he's chasing Tribbles in Sector 5."

Salena gave him a look of utter bafflement.

"Of course you'll ride with me. Unless you prefer we stay and serve tea to our guests."

Outside, the jeep's engine raced. Salena pulled up the hem of her dress and started lifting her leg over the seat.

"Hold on, let me figure this thing out." The word Enfield was imprinted in gold letters on the electric blue tank. He remembered an advertisement for the Royal Enfield Bullet he'd read in a biker magazine. He recalled the motorcycle was actually built somewhere in India.

John grasped the handgrips and swung his foot over the seat. Feeling the controls, he saw several differences between the Enfield and any bike he'd ever ridden. For one, when he pressed his right foot on the brake pedal, he found the gear lever instead, and surmised the pedals were reversed. He was more concerned he couldn't locate the start button, until he remembered the bike only came with a kick-start.

He shoved the key in the ignition, made sure the clutch was in neutral, and slid the stop switch to the run position. He found the choke lever, pushed down, and with his left hand pulling on the decompressor lever, slammed his heel onto the kick start.

Nothing, not even a rumble.

He tried again. Same result.

Scanning the controls, he saw no other buttons to push.

The soldier on the bullhorn sounded closer. "If you don't come out now, excuse us for barging in."

John glanced at Salena. She had turned and was pointing her pistol at the barn doors. Without looking back, she asked, "What is the trouble?"

"I'm doing something wrong. Give me a minute."

Gears outside started grinding, as if the jeep was moving in reverse.

"You do not have 15 seconds."

The jeep squealed to a stop, and its engine gave three loud revs in fast succession.

Salena turned her head. "Is there petrol in the tank?"

"I already checked. There's plenty of ... shit ... I mean dammit, that's it!" He bent down, peered under the gas tank, and saw the fuel-cock in the off position. "It'd help if I let some gas in the carburetor."

He snapped the lever into the on position, pulled up on the decompressor handle, and gave the footstart a long, smooth kick. The engine rumbled to life. "Let's go!"

Salena jumped on and hugged John tight.

The jeep's grill splintered the barn doors like matchsticks. John kicked the clutch into gear and twisted the throttle full open. By the time the soldiers caught sight of them, John had sped out the shattered doors, crossed the meadow, and was plowing through the maize field toward the forest on the other side.

Stalks whipped past on both sides, stinging John's face, but it felt like heaven to ride again—even if the locals were out to kill him. On level ground, he tried kicking the Enfield into 5th gear, and was disappointed when his foot met firm resistance. He wouldn't win any races with this bike.

Just as his eyes, nose, and mouth adjusted to their stalk-whipping, John burst out the other side. A narrow dirt strip separated the last row of maize stalks from the pine trees ahead. He braked, shifted into neutral, and turned to Salena.

"Any idea where the trail begins?"

Salena studied the forest line, then pointed right. "I think at those birch trees."

John rode to where Salena had pointed and sure enough, found a trail that disappeared into the dense forest. Before going in, he stopped the bike and looked back. From this vantage, the farmhouse appeared miniscule. He heard occasional gunfire, but the shots sounded far away.

Bowing his head, he mourned the murdered father, and imagined those poor children with no parents huddled in the corner of their basement. He thought about going back, but just then, the jeep and its two occupants burst through the stalks and peeled straight at them.

The bullets started flying and John started swearing.

He had hoped to salvage a quiet moment with Salena. Now he'd be lucky to salvage their lives.

CHAPTER SIXTY-SEVEN

The road between Dowarian and Sharda had been swept clear of Rashtriya Rifles, leaving Captain Qadeer free to strut in a lazy circle around the seared Mercedes. For a reason he couldn't quite fathom, he found the smell of burnt paint invigorating.

The Citadel's finest crime scene investigator, Jameel Sawad, had accompanied Qadeer on his trip to the Neelum Valley. Despite the vehicle's close encounter with an artillery shell, Jameel had lifted an abundance of fingerprints. This very moment, in the mobile lab parked on the main road, he was comparing prints dusted from the steering wheel, dashboard, and door handles with those on file for Dr. Zamal, Lieutenant Hassan, Subedar Mazhar, and most recently, John Cattano.

Qadeer stopped beside the rear passenger door, and peered through the window at the leather interior. His penis could not help but stand erect. The rear seat of a Mercedes was where he had bedded the child he had plucked from the streets of Rawalpindi during the hectic days of the revolution. Those were frantic times, ridding Pakistan of Labib Razzak's spineless leadership. Devotion to duty left little time to release pent up carnal needs, and the petite brown-eyed girl with long black hair wandering the streets outside the Odeon Cinema looked so much older than 10.

While she pleased his senses, had he known her age, he might not have taken her as he did, tearing her and watching her bleed to death beneath him. Five hot showers did little to relieve the sickening sense he had failed to cleanse his flesh of her bodily fluids. The girl's father and mother had not believed him when he explained their daughter had been attacked by a gang of Razzak's henchmen. Too bad they put up such a fuss, for even as the sobbing parents begged for their lives, they professed to believe in Khan's goal of a greater Pakistan.

Qadeer heard someone approach from behind. He smoothed down his crotch and turned.

Lieutenant Siddique bowed and sneezed, wiping mucous on his khaki pants.

"Are you allergic to pine trees?"

"No, I have a cold."

"Feel better soon, for these next two days will test your stamina."

"Yes, sir."

"Has Jameel completed his analysis?"

Siddique nodded.

"And?"

"A positive match on all four occupants."

"Where were the prints found?"

"All over, but what is most unusual—Mr. Cattano's prints overlay those of Subedar Mazhar on the steering wheel and on the front driver's side door handle. Dr. Zamal's prints covered the front passenger door handle. Not where Jameel had expected."

Qadeer mulled Siddique's implication. If the four had been accosted by dacoits, why was Cattano at the steering wheel with Zamal at his side? He licked his lips. "And the prints of the kidnappers?"

"That is what Jameel found strangest of all. There were none."

CHAPTER SIXTY-EIGHT

Salena's arms tightened around John's waist. He gunned the throttle, and took off into the woods with a jeep and two irate Border Security officers in hot pursuit. The trail wound four kilometers over mild dips and swells through a thick forest of birch and pine trees. Up ahead John could see a steep incline he knew he'd have trouble climbing, especially riding with a passenger.

Since he wasn't about to leave Salena to the wolves, he drew on memory to coax the bike uphill. He'd spent his 13th summer at his aunt's bungalow in the Pocono Mountains, where from dawn to dusk he rode his cousin's motocross bike in the hills outside Stroudsburg.

Coming up fast on the trail's sharp rise, he downshifted to third gear and gunned the engine to the red line. As he hit the incline, he downshifted to second. The engine stayed in the powerband, and the bike shot up the slope.

Near the top of the hill, the engine strained. John dug his heels into the foot pegs, downshifted again, and prayed for a few more rpm's. He rocked the bike back and forth, willing the motorcycle up the last 10 feet, and though the rocking did nothing, he inched his way to the top.

Clearing the crest, John saw the trail ahead take a slight dip, then level off. As he gained speed on flat ground, he noticed bark chips snapping off the trees on his left. Glancing over his shoulder, he saw the soldiers less than 30 yards behind, and realized the flying bark was being shot off by the jeep's machine gun.

On this level stretch through the forest, John managed to gain yardage. The Enfield's screaming single-cylinder drowned out the sound of gunfire, but he saw pebbles kicking at the bike's wheels, and deduced he was still in the shooter's range. Looking for a curve in the trail, he saw one ahead that veered down, to the right, into a deep valley.

Erosion ruts carved into the downhill bend bounced the bike like a basketball. He recalled a technique he'd learned during his Pocono summer, and shouted back to Salena, "Lean on the foot pegs."

Following his own advice, John bent his knees and lifted his butt, so that only his legs, not his body, absorbed the rough terrain. Salena must have understood. He felt her body rise slightly off the seat, and she shouted, "Much better."

The bark chips and pebbles stopped flying and John looked back. The jeep was nowhere in sight. Not counting on the chance the soldiers had stalled or gotten stuck in a rut, John turned on the juice.

For the next 10 minutes the bike jumped, bounced and slid beneath him, as he dodged ruts, roots, and an occasional small mammal. He came up suddenly on a fork in the trail and hit the brakes. Keeping one eye on the road behind them, John shouted over the idling engine. "Which way?"

Salena took a full minute studying the trees and diverging trails, and finally said, "We are coming to a river, so it depends."

"On what?"

"Would you prefer to cross the slow way, and hope the raft is working, or the quick way, and cross a suspension bridge."

John's eyes popped open. "When you say suspension bridge, I assume you don't mean like the Golden Gate."

"Not quite as sturdy."

"How reliable is the raft?"

"According to what my father once told me, it operates from May through August every day except Fridays, Saturdays, and Wednesdays, and only from eleven in the morning until two in the afternoon, except on Muslim, Hindu, and Buddhist holidays, and even then, only if the temperature is higher than 36 degrees Celsius."

"I'll take my chances with the bridge."

"Good idea. Go half a kilometer, and keep the bike steady when you cross the planks."

"Planks?"

"Never mind. You will see when we get there."

Revving the engine, John turned right onto the rising trail. As they approached the crest, John noticed the shrubs and trees thin out, which made him nervous, since less vegetation meant less cover.

The road leveled off, and as Salena had predicted, he found himself stopped on a barren hilltop staring down at a ravine about 100 feet wide by 100 feet deep spanned by a wood plank bridge with more than a few planks missing. The bridge reminded John of an Indiana Jones movie he had once seen on late-night TV. Like in the movie, the bridge didn't look sturdy enough to hold the weight of a pea, let alone him, Salena, and the Enfield.

He wiped the sweat from his hands onto his shirt, and turned to Salena. "Are you sure this is safer than the raft?"

"Look down there." Salena pointed to the nearest bank of a dark blue river below. A few yards offshore broken logs and smashed lumber protruded from the water.

"I see your point." The raft had likely been hit by a mortar, either from the militants or the Army—a distinction in John's mind becoming blurrier by the minute.

As he approached the bridge, John fed gas to the engine, slowly at first, then a bit more when the front wheel touched the first board. The three-foot planks were barely wide enough to fit the bike, but the bridge's width was John's least concern. It was the rocking beneath the wheels that put John's heart on afterburners.

He felt Salena turn around on her seat. Too nervous to look back, he shouted, "What's going on?"

She yelled, "Do not worry about me. Get us across."

He heard a single gunshot directly behind him and nearly jumped off his seat. "What the hell are you doing?"

"Your language, please."

Training his eyes on the next few planks, he swallowed hard, and said between clenched teeth, "What, may I ask, are you doing?"

"Giving us insurance."

John's curiosity won out. He turned his head to see Salena pointing her pistol at the planks they'd crossed. She fired another shot, and John watched a board fall away from the ropes and drop into the river. He realized she was making it impossible for the soldiers to follow on foot, but a scary thought crossed his mind. "Will that make the bridge collapse?"

Taking careful aim at the next board, Salena squeezed off another round, severing the plank from the rope. "That depends how long you take to cross."

John revved the throttle, counter-balancing his weight against the bridge's sway. Even in first gear, doing two miles an hour, they made steady progress.

With only 30 feet to go before reaching firm ground, he heard Salena shout, "They're back."

John turned and saw the jeep stopped at the bridge's entrance. The soldier in the rear had abandoned the machine gun, moved to the front seat, and was aiming a rifle over the windshield.

Hastily gunning the motor, John caused the Enfield to slip on the rickety, rocking planks. He slowed, glanced back, and saw the soldier on the passenger side stand up and take aim. Salena fired one shot in the jeep's direction, and the startled soldier ducked behind the dashboard.

John gradually opened the throttle. Just as the bike started moving, he felt a massive jolt followed by an undulating shock wave. "Shit!"

He turned his head and watched the jeep back up, stop, and drive dead center into the right-hand support beam. Another powerful jolt forced the bike sideways. If not for the rope handrail, they would've fallen into the river. The son-of-a-bitch was trying to take out the bridge.

Salena gripped John's waist with one hand and fired her pistol with the other, managing to squeeze off four rounds. She pulled the trigger again, and nothing came out.

"That's my last clip." She tossed the pistol into the river and wrapped both hands around John's chest.

John steadied the motorcycle and watched the jeep back up as the soldiers prepared for a third run at the right-hand log anchoring the bridge. The first two jolts had slackened the span, causing the wood planks to lean sharply right along the bridge's entire length. With only 15 feet to the precipice ahead, John fought harder than ever to keep the bike balanced. He stabilized the Enfield with his feet, and half-rode, half-walked the bike the last few yards.

John glanced back and saw the jeep ram the log at full speed. This time the timber jutting from the ground snapped, and the jeep kept going—clear over the bluff. John watched in horror as the car and its occupants plunged into the river.

With only one support beam in place, the handrail and few planks still attached to the rope began twisting around like a corkscrew starting on the side where they'd entered the bridge.

Salena screamed, "Go, go, go!"

John didn't think. He yanked the throttle open and prayed. The rear wheel dropped out from under him at the same second the front wheel touched dirt. Just enough forward momentum kept the bike from falling backward into the river.

Both wheels planted on the opposite ledge, he braked, turned off the ignition, and looked behind. A few wood planks dangled from a single rope, and in the river far below, the jeep sank quickly. Even though they'd tried to kill him, John was relieved to see the driver and gunner swimming toward shore.

His eyes met Salena's, and he realized she was staring at him, mouth agape.

"Who taught you to ride like that?"

"My daddy."

"He taught you well."

John smiled. She was right. From riding a dirt bike to imploding a 50-story office building, his father had always encouraged him to do his best. "I think he would've been proud."

The sound of voices came from the ravine, and he and Salena looked down. The first soldier out of the river was shouting into a waterproof radio.

Salena gripped John's arm. "He will call in our position."

"It'll take their friends time to get here." He scanned the bike's control cluster and saw the gas gauge hovering over 'E.' He unscrewed the cap and looked in the tank. "We're using gas faster than I'd expected."

"Do we have enough to reach Ganderbal?"

"How far?"

"About 15 kilometers."

John made a quick calculation. "Every motorcycle has a reserve supply, but nine miles … that's cutting it close."

"What time is it?"

He glanced at his watch. "Quarter to one."

Salena cast her eyes to the ground. "By now we should have reached Srinagar." She rested her head on his shoulder, and said sadly, "I should never have taken you on this journey. Perhaps we should return to Sharda, and ask Ghazi to drive us to Islamabad."

Through her windblown hair, John stroked Salena's earlobe. "That's not like you to give up."

She pressed her head against his open palm, obviously enjoying his caress. "I do not care how many friends Omar Shah has, by the time we reach Srinagar, it will be too late for him to arrange our return to Pakistan."

John mulled her words and guessed she was probably right, but these last four days, in the midst of wanton murder, maimed children, and the brutality of war, he found something he thought he'd lost forever—his desire to live. Driven to despair by Billy Dwyer's death, he had run from everything important. He smiled to himself at the irony of having revived his love of life the day before he planned to die.

No way would he concede defeat in his final hours. He kissed Salena's cheek. "We're going to Srinagar and getting the C-4, and not only that, I'm taking you to see your mom. And after that, we're going back to Islamabad to finish what we started. That's a promise."

Her brown eyes sparkled an emotion John had difficulty reading, somewhere between joy and admiration. He felt his cheeks burn, and turned away. Starting the bike in a single kick, he grabbed the handgrips and eased the bike forward on the trail to Ganderbal.

CHAPTER SIXTY-NINE

Shifting his weight in synchrony with each rise and dip in the trail, John savored his ride through the wooded foothills of the Kashmir Valley. Salena hugged his chest more tightly than she had to, but he enjoyed the sensual comfort of her strong arms and supple body.

Before the Chicago accident, at least once every summer he and Maureen made a day of riding his ElectraGlide through the secluded back roads of northwest New Jersey. They'd find a shady spot along the Delaware River, wrap themselves in a blanket, and make love all afternoon under the tall oaks. He should never have allowed his guilt and self-pity to destroy their intimacy.

On a gradual rise in the trail, Salena tapped his shoulder.

John eased up on the throttle, and called back, "Is something wrong?"

"Over the next hill you will come to a marker. When you see it, stop."

"What's there?"

"I will show you."

John downshifted and proceeded slowly. Twenty yards past the top of the hill he spotted a small wood sign nailed to a tree trunk with the word 'Lookout' painted in white letters. Near the base of the tree he noticed a footpath that wound through the forest and disappeared through a thicket of tall mulberry shrubs.

John shut off the Enfield, and Salena dismounted. He propped the bike on its kickstand, unscrewed the fuel cap, and saw no gasoline inside. Salena didn't ask, and he didn't offer. Instead, John checked his watch, and said, "I thought we were in a hurry."

"This will only take a minute. It was papa's favorite place." She started down the footpath, and with a quick wave, beckoned him to follow.

John walked behind her, watching her subtle curves sway beneath her long blue dress. He loved Maureen, but yearned for Salena. Maybe he was wrong caring so much for a woman he hardly knew, but Salena had given him something he could never again share with Maureen.

They hiked in silence through the thicket of mulberries, and when they emerged on the other side, John stopped in his tracks and stared out in awe. They had walked onto a wide precipice overlooking an expansive valley. Straight to the horizon everything was green, but for an occasional white smudge marking the location of a town or village.

They walked to the cliff's edge and stood at the abyss. Salena pointed down at the nearest collection of buildings. John could make out cars and trucks plying the roads in and out of town.

"That is Ganderbal to the south, where the trail ends." She turned and pointed west.

In the distance John observed a swath of blue, and beyond the blue, massive, snow-capped mountains.

"Wular Lake," she said. "Kashmir's largest."

John stepped carefully along the cliff's edge, and Salena followed. He stopped when he noticed a vast gray stain on the southeast horizon. "What place is that?"

Salena eyes glimmered. "Our destination."

"Srinagar."

She threw her arms around his neck, and stared into his eyes. "You are the bravest man I have ever met." Their lips touched and he responded, gently at first, then with the craving of a man driven by desire. When their tongues finally parted, he caressed her full, pink lips with his finger. "I've learned a lot from you."

"And I from you."

"Yeah, sure. Twenty years from now you won't even remember my name."

She pushed his hand away. "On the contrary, you have ruined me. Any man I meet must compete with the memory of you, and I cannot imagine anyone coming close."

John stroked her hair, and with the tip of his tongue probed her neck, her ear, and the rim of her lips, then bathed his tongue in the soft, wet heat of her beckoning mouth. He closed his eyes and held her kiss, and when he stopped, he noticed a patch of wildflowers growing nearby. "Close your eyes and don't move."

"Where are you going?"

"Shhhh."

Salena smiled and shut her eyes.

John picked a handful of flowers from a plant whose white petals emitted a sweet, seductive fragrance. He bunched the stems and held them out to Salena. "Open."

Salena's eyes grew wide. She held the flowers as gently as a newborn puppy, pressed them close to her face, and started to cry.

"I'm sorry, I thought you'd like them."

She sobbed through her words. "I do ... I love them ... you do not understand."

He'd heard that complaint from every women he'd known. "I get it. When a girl likes flowers, she cries, and when she hates them, she laughs."

"They're my favorite … my favorite in the whole world."

"Now I understand completely. What kind are they?"

"Jasmine."

"You act like no man's ever given you flowers."

A tear ran down her cheek and paused at the corner of her mouth. "No man has—no man I cared about."

John's neck tingled.

"Before Major Farrell sent me the message you were coming, I had thought about killing myself."

"Why?"

"Death was a better choice than life."

"Swear to me, after I'm gone, you'll never think about hurting yourself."

Her fingers brushed his neck. "When you came, you brought hope, not only for me, but for all Kashmiris. When Khan is dead, I will live free."

"And if he survives?"

Salena bowed her head.

"Swear no matter what happens, you won't give up."

"For what reason would I live?"

"People need you. The children at the hospital, Dr. Raja, your patients. You take your life, and they lose everything." He forced a smile. "Besides, I can't go to my grave thinking this world might lose someone as special as you."

She wiped her cheeks and gazed into his eyes. "I love you, John."

At that moment he felt the same about her, but was too scared to admit it. He gathered her into his arms, held her snugly, and kissed her once more. Finally, reluctantly, he pulled away and said, "We'd better get going."

Her eyes refused to break their hold. "I will remember this day forever."

Hands entwined, they spent one last moment admiring the Vale's beauty, then turned toward the path leading into the woods.

They hadn't walked two steps when three men burst through the mulberry bushes wielding automatic rifles, shouting, "Hands in the air, hands in the air. Hands in the air, or die!"

CHAPTER SEVENTY

With their backs to the cliff and hands held high, John and Salena stood side-by-side facing their assailants. All three wore brown shalwar kameez, dark beards, and white turbans, and all clutched rifles similar to the German G3 Salena had borrowed from their Pakistan Army escorts on the road to Peshawar.

Avoiding the icy stare of the tallest man, who stepped forward and approached them, John whispered to Salena, "Who are *these* guys?"

Salena answered without turning her head. "I cannot be certain. Definitely not army regulars."

The tall man's granite face seemed to have forgotten how to smile. He walked behind John, patted down his shirt, and barked, "What are you doing here?"

John saw no reason to lie, sort of. "Spending a few moments alone with my bride. Who are you?"

Towering a full head taller than John, the man planted himself, legs apart, in front of John's face. "We are Allah's tools. Liberating Kashmir is our jihad."

Freedom fighters. That couldn't be all bad. John addressed Salena from the corner of his mouth. "Tell them who you know."

Salena shot him an incredulous look.

"Go ahead, tell them about Omar."

The tall man stepped to his left, and facing Salena, undressed her with his eyes. "Tell me, pretty one, who is Omar?"

Clutching high above her head the flowers John had picked, she answered hesitantly, "Omar Shah … of Srinagar."

The man flashed an evil grin, revealing brown stumps for teeth. "Omar Shah? I do not know him."

"He is a freedom fighter … like you."

"Like me? Not at all. We are Lashkar-e-Jabbar."

John heard Salena stifle a gasp, and assumed that wasn't good. Salena had explained different terrorist groups touted different causes. Their only common denominator was the means by which they achieved their ends. Hoping to divert the man's attention from Salena, John said, "Hey, aren't you both fighting the same enemy?"

The stumped-tooth ruffian shuffled sideways to face John. "You are American, are you not?"

"Yes."

"Married to a Muslim?"

"Yes."

"Have you converted to Islam?"

"No."

"Do not say you are Christian."

"Then I won't."

The man thrust his chin forward. "Do you know my brother was killed by an American bomb dropped on Kabul?"

John clenched his teeth to curb his tongue, but failed. "Do you know a young father from my hometown was blown up by a car bomb in Fallujah?"

The bearded man smiled. "That pleases me."

John checked his impulse to smash his fist into this jerk's face. "Please, let us leave and go about our business."

"Why did you marry a Muslim, not a Christian?"

John looked at Salena, and for a few seconds, their eyes met. "Love doesn't know the difference."

The man's visage transformed into a glowering mask of rage. "You have made this woman a whore." He screamed at Salena, "Where is your burqa?"

"I do not practice purdah."

"You are no better than the American scum you married."

Salena lowered her arms, and when she spoke, her words seethed. "He is a braver man than you will ever be."

John knew her opinion wouldn't sit well with this Osama wannabe. Again attempting to deflect attention, he said, "I have lots of rupees. Let us be on our way, and they're all yours."

"I will gladly take your rupees. After I take your life."

John lowered his arms and held Salena's hand. "I've had enough of your crap. Shoot us if you must, but we're outta here."

Pulling Salena by the hand, John stepped around the head honcho and his followers, and walked toward the mulberry shrubs leading into the forest.

A single shot rang out, and immediately, sharp pain pierced his left shoulder.

John's mind went numb as he realized he'd been hit. Instinctively, he slapped his hand on his upper arm. Everything sounded far away—the shouts of the terrorists, Salena's screams, and the barked commands. Two pairs of hands grabbed his elbows, dragged him to the edge of the cliff, and flung him to the ground.

On his back, clutching his shoulder, he stared at his injured arm. Unable to dam the river of red oozing between his knuckles, John strained his neck to look behind, and saw only blue sky.

The bearded leader walked to John's side, pointed his rifle at John's chest, and grinned. "Before you die, you will see what happens to whores who defy the word of Allah."

He heard Salena shriek, "Let me go, let me go."

Fighting the pain, John lifted his head and saw one of the men kneeling between Salena's legs. He pulled off her underwear, while the other man pinned her arms.

John cried out, "Don't hurt her."

When Salena kicked the kneeling man, his partner slapped her hard across the face.

John rolled on his side, and got up on his hands and knees. The terrorist standing nearby slammed his rifle against John's skull, dropping him instantly.

Dazed and in pain, John noticed something roll past his head. He craned his neck and watched the jasmine bouquet he'd picked for Salena tumble across the ground and break apart until all the white petals scattered in the sky over the cliff behind him.

Salena's screams were too much to bear. His only thought was saving her. He again rolled on his side, then stretched his bloodied hand toward the leader's ankle. The giant thug jumped out of reach and laughed derisively, pointing toward the center of the precipice. "You are missing the show."

John looked back and saw one of the men gag Salena with her own panties. John boosted himself to his hands and knees and lunged at the leader, who hopped out of range, laughing even louder.

John heard the metallic click of a cocking gun. "Say good-bye to your little slut."

At that instant a tremendous gust of wind blew John down, away from the ledge, and rolled him onto his side. He heard a thunderous roar and loud rhythmic thumping, followed by ear-piercing, staccato bursts.

Guns. Big guns.

Shielding his face against the fierce wind, John looked up and couldn't believe his eyes. A big black helicopter hovered over the precipice, shooting not at him, but at the militant leader standing a few feet away. John rolled on his side, and kept rolling until he bumped into something hard. When he realized it was Salena, he looked around, and saw her attackers were gone.

John knelt at her side and shouted over the cacophony of rotors and turbines. "Get up, Salena, get up."

Sobbing softly, Salena grabbed her panties, and then his hand. On her feet, she turned toward the chopper hovering over the cliff. "Indian Army."

The leader of the terrorists lay on the ground a few feet from the ledge. His skull had been blown apart, and soupy brain matter stained his dark kameez. The other two thugs stood at opposite sides of the precipice, shooting at the helicopter. As John ran toward the line of mulberry shrubs, the man on his right grabbed his chest and collapsed forward.

Holding Salena's hand, John spotted a path and together they scrambled through the thicket. Running through the forest at top speed, he ignored the throbbing pain in his upper arm. The gunfire behind them ceased, and he heard a change in the drone of the chopper's engine, as if the helicopter were moving.

They found the Enfield where John had left it. When he grabbed the handlebars, he cried out in pain and nearly dropped the bike.

Before now, Salena hadn't realized he'd been shot. Gripping his arm, she said, "Let me have a look."

He winced and let her inspect his injury, awed by her instant transition from helpless victim to studious clinician.

"Looks like a penetrating wound."

"Obviously it penetrated."

"I mean there is no exit wound, the bullet is still inside you." She tore a blue strip off her cotton dress, and under John's kameez, wrapped his arm and shoulder. "You're lucky. No bone injury, only soft tissue damage." She yanked on both ends of the strip, and tied a tight knot.

"Make it looser."

"Tight stops the bleeding."

His arm bandaged, John found he could grasp the bike with less pain. He straddled the seat and kicked the engine to life. Salena jumped on and hugged his waist. To conserve gas, John opened the throttle slowly.

Every bump and rut in the trail sent daggers through John's arm, but self-preservation took control, and he fought to keep the bike upright and moving. His eyes shifted from the road ahead to the gas guage. The red needle now fluttered below the 'E.' He glanced up and saw no sign of the helicopter above the treetops.

Five minutes after they'd resumed their journey, the engine sputtered.

John eased up on the throttle, and as the bike moved, he reached under the gas tank and turned the fuel cock to reserve. Most reserves held a half gallon, enough to get to the next service station. Figuring he wouldn't find any gas pumps on this trail, he hoped whatever fuel was left would be enough to take them to Ganderbal.

Around the next bend through the forest, John saw a steep rise, but instead of winding uphill, the trail disappeared into a tunnel. The entrance came up fast, and they plunged into darkness. Just as quickly, they came out the other side and were met by a furious wind that nearly toppled the bike.

John looked up. The helicopter.

Salena tapped John's right shoulder and pointed to the sky.

He nodded, and shouted, "I see it." He kept riding, and the chopper followed. At any second he expected a rain of bullets, but the big bird's side-mounted machine guns stayed silent.

The Himalayan air again played tricks on his mind. Over the din of whirling blades and roaring rpm's, he thought he heard a voice call out "stop hello," then "crazy John," but he knew that couldn't be.

The trail began a gradual, winding descent through the forest. Taking advantage of the slope, John rode in neutral, so gravity, not gas, spun the wheels.

He saw a break in the trees ahead, and realized why the Indian soldiers hadn't fired—they were waiting for a clear shot. Out in the open they were goners, but he had no choice.

The forest ended abruptly, and the trail continued straight on a downhill slope through a vast meadow of lavender. At the base of the purple hill—about a mile away—the dirt road disappeared between a cluster of one and two-story buildings.

Salena shouted in his ear, "Ganderbal."

She firmed her grip on his waist, and then it happened. The engine sputtered and died.

"We're out of gas!"

The hill's sharp angle kept the wheels spinning at 50 kph. Descending toward the village they passed a horse-drawn cart and a bevy of women shrouded in burqas. A powerful gust from the overhead rotors blew one woman's basket away, and in his handlebar mirror John saw a green billowy figure shaking her fist at the sky.

They reached the buildings at the bottom of the hill, where the road leveled off. During their two minute descent into Ganderbal, the soldiers in the helicopter could have picked them off as easily as hens in a chicken coop, yet they hadn't even tried. Surely they knew the man and woman on the motorcycle were the same pair who'd fled the farm near Kuligam.

Maybe the Indians wanted him alive, but from what he'd learned, life here was cheap. Why go through the trouble of capturing them when killing them was so much easier? He didn't know the answer, but he did know this—he wasn't stopping to find out.

CHAPTER SEVENTY-ONE

Riding on inertia made steering the Enfield a chore, and the throbbing pain in John's arm didn't help. He sounded the horn, and at the last second, an old man in a black robe dangling a cage with two live chickens leaped out of the way.

As they rolled further into Ganderbal, the town's dirt streets grew more congested. The army helicopter on their tails kicked up a whirlwind of soil, sand, and pebbles, forcing women in bright blue veils to scuttle for cover in dingy shops along both sides of the street. Men in ankle-length pullovers hawking wares off horse-drawn carts paused and looked up in disbelief at the low-flying helicopter. More than once, John screamed at ogling women and children who had stopped in the middle of the road and craned their necks to the sky. So far, no one on the street seemed to know it was him and Salena the chopper was after.

As the Enfield's forward momentum slowed to a crawl, the street emptied into a large town square lined on all sides by an eclectic array of two and three-story buildings. The middle of the square was jammed with carts, tents, and covered stands, whose owners sold everything from blankets and pottery to live hens and linens.

Entering the market, John steered the bike down the first row of peddler's stalls. Three stands in, the bike rolled to a stop, and he and Salena jumped off. The chopper's twirling rotors spawned a whirlwind of sand and dust, wreaking havoc on unsecured stalls and tents. Merchants frantically covered their wares and panicked shoppers scurried in all directions.

A green tarp flew over John's head, and one of two white-turbaned men chasing the airborne canvas bumped John's arm, making him see stars. Salena gently stroked his shoulder to ease the pain.

Above the din of the screaming turbines, John shouted to Salena, "What now?"

Before Salena could answer, John heard a voice in the sky and looked up. A soldier standing in the chopper's bay door was yelling into a bullhorn. At least he wasn't nuts—the voice he'd heard on the trail had come from the helicopter. Straining to listen over the screaming engine and the shouting mob, he couldn't understand what the soldier was saying. He caught bits and pieces, and thought he heard the words "Hello Joe."

By now, the fierce wind whipping the outdoor market had dislodged every tent in the row where John and Salena stood. Scarves, hats, shawls, even wicker baskets, pelted their faces, and the dust and sand limited visibility to a few yards.

Salena grabbed John's hand. "I know what to do." Shielding her face with her veil against flying debris, she led John down the aisle in the direction from which they'd entered. At the end of the aisle, in front of a cloth shop, she picked up a roll of white cotton that had blown off a display table. She groped her way through the swirling dust along the store's outer wall, and when she reached the corner, slipped into a narrow gap between the cloth shop and the next building.

They had entered an alley about four feet wide between two buildings fronting the square. Salena moved a few yards into the narrow space, until the wind no longer buffeted their backs. From inside the alley, John had a limited view of the square, but he deduced from the rising whine of the overhead engine the helicopter was on the move.

Salena pulled down her veil. "I have been to Ganderbal twice. We are in the old city, five or six blocks from the bus depot. If I am not mistaken, a bus leaves for Srinagar every hour."

"How long's the ride?"

"Express, about 45 minutes."

John checked his watch. "Srinagar by two-thirty, Omar Shah by three. Not much room for error, but it sounds like a plan. Let's go."

"Wait, first let me change your dressing." John lifted his kameez and she unwound the bandage from his arm and shoulder. Wiping off dried blood from the entry wound, she scrutinized the hole left by the bullet. "No bone was damaged, so after the round is removed, you should make a full recovery." Realizing her mistake, she clapped her hand over her mouth.

He could have said something sarcastic, but instead, gently swept away stray wisps of hair off her cheek. "When I'm with you, I forget too."

She pressed her head to his chest and wrapped her arms around his middle. "If only tomorrow never had to come."

"Let's make the best of the time we have."

She pulled away and gazed at him with an unmistakable yearning. He thirsted for her touch, but quenching his desire would have to wait for a quieter moment.

Salena tore off a yard-long strip of the white cotton she'd taken from the cloth shop. "To conceal the blood, I must again wrap the bandage tightly. It may hurt."

"Better I'm in agony than arousing anyone's suspicion."

She flashed him a demure smile and firmly bandaged his arm in fresh white cotton. When she was done, she handed John his shirt, stained dark red at the shoulder. "Before we reach the bus station, I must buy you a new kameez."

Favoring his injured arm, John squirmed into his shirt, then followed Salena deeper into the alley until they emerged behind the cloth shop onto a narrow, crowded street. Somewhere behind him, John heard the helicopter flying over the city.

After a 15 minute walk past squalid shops and food stands along Ganderbal's dusty streets, including a quick stop to buy him a new shirt, they stopped on the sidewalk of a wide road across from a one-story whitewashed building. A large green sign hung over the building's entrance: 'Sudhari Depot.'

They crossed the street, entered the lobby, and went to the ticket window with the shortest line. Salena informed him he'd be the one buying the tickets. She explained when Muslim couples traveled together, the man made all the arrangements, including the purchase of bus and train fare.

When John's turn came, he stepped to the window and requested two tickets for the one-thirty bus to Srinagar.

From behind the grating the agent looked up at him through bulky, black glasses. "Will you be wanting express or local?"

"Express."

"How many pass you buy you?"

"Huh?"

"You knowing how many pass you buy you, no?"

Salena stepped close to John and said, "Two please."

The man glared at John. "Four hundred fifty rupees."

John fumbled through his pants, pulled out some notes, and handed the man what he hoped were enough to cover the cost of the tickets.

The ticket agent frowned. "Why you don't having Indian rupees?"

John growled back, "Why you don't speaking normal English?" John's big toe exploded with pain where Salena rammed it with the heel of her sturdy shoe. She plastered a phony smile on her face. "Would you be so kind as to accept Pakistani rupees?"

"If you be giving me 800 rupees only."

"Very well." She turned to John wearing an exaggerated smile and said through gritted teeth, "Please give the nice man another 350 rupees."

"Anything you say, hon." John passed more notes under the metal bars and grabbed the tickets.

They walked to the bus and John boarded first. Every seat was filled, except in the last row, where an empty bench seat stretched window-to-window. He led Salena down the aisle, and as they sat, the driver closed the doors and pulled away.

From under her veil, Salena regarded him. "You are beginning to convince even me we are married."

John reached for Salena's hand, but she gently brushed it away. "We are riding on a bus in Kashmir, not New Jersey. No public affection is allowed."

"That stinks."

"Yes, but when in Rome—"

"Yeah, I know," John said, staring into Salena's glimmering eyes.

Salena snuggled closer to John's arm and rested her head on his right shoulder. "Does your wound hurt?"

"Only when it's touched."

"When we visit my mother at Lal Ded Hospital, I will have one of my friends remove the bullet and give you enough anesthetic to last you through tomorrow."

Exhausted, John pushed his head back in the seat and enjoyed the chance to relax rather than shoot or get shot at in the foothills of the Himalayas. Through the window he saw a military convoy sharing the road with the bus, and on the shoulder, a long line of civilians, mostly women and children, and hollow-eyed elderly, traipsing away from town. In the midst of dealing with his own survival, he had almost forgotten he was in a land preparing for war.

Salena must have been exhausted too. Her head leaned heavily on his shoulder, and her breathing quickly fell into a soft, steady pattern. He thought about Maureen, and how much he missed her, but he thought about Salena too. Had he met her first, he could easily imagine having asked her to marry him.

Succumbing to fatigue, John drifted to sleep, but not before he had a strange dream filled with loud, urgent voices—amplified voices from somewhere in the sky that called out his name.

CHAPTER SEVENTY-TWO

John's eyes opened with a start when he realized the bus wasn't moving.

Sitting in the rear seat, his view of the road ahead was blocked by the heads of the passengers in front of him. So as not to disturb Salena, who slept soundly with her head on his shoulder, he shifted his eyes right and left to figure out what had happened.

Along both sides of the road, which had widened from a narrow concrete strip into three lanes of asphalt in both directions, he observed dilapidated shops and row houses. He carefully lifted his arm to check the time, and when he saw they'd slept nearly an hour, he assumed they were approaching Srinagar.

Their bus was stopped in the middle lane, and though every window was open, the heat was stifling. John craned his neck for a better view, and discovered the reason for the holdup.

Three lanes of traffic were merging into two, and all vehicles were being searched a pair at a time. The checkpoint resembled a toll booth, and of six portals, only the two right-hand lanes were in use.

Stopped at the front of the lines were a red compact car and a commuter bus identical to the one they were sitting in. A grim-faced soldier swept a long-handled mirror under the car's chassis, and aboard the bus John noticed a soldier taking his time walking up and down the aisle.

Salena began to stir. John nudged her awake and whispered, "We've got trouble."

Salena's eyes opened wide. She looked around, made a quick assessment, and said, "Keep up the act. We are an ordinary married couple visiting my mother in Srinagar."

They were neither married nor ordinary, but under the circumstances her suggestion made sense. Anyway, the girl was smart, beautiful, and could turn any man's head, so until he died, he might as well pretend she was his.

The next six cars were cleared to pass, then came their turn.

As the bus inched forward, Salena advised John to sit still and avoid eye contact with any soldiers who came aboard. Looking into their eyes would be interpreted as a challenge to their authority.

A solitary soldier in green fatigues clutching a machine gun climbed onto the bus. After a few words to the driver, he marched slowly down the center aisle, scrutinizing every rider.

No one spoke, and no one moved. Halfway down the aisle the soldier paused and stared at an elderly gentleman gazing out the window.

"Open the bag old man."

The gray bearded man appeared surprised he was the object of the soldier's order. He lifted a brown bag from his seat, and held it toward the soldier over the lap of a boy sitting next to him.

"I said open it."

John thought the old man said "a blanket for my granddaughter," but from the back of the bus, he couldn't be sure. In any event, the soldier must not have liked what he'd heard. He lifted his rifle and pointed it at the man's head.

"Please, please, it is only a blanket." He was on the verge of tears.

The soldier glared at the boy sitting next to him. "Do you know this man?"

The child's voice quivered. "He is my ... my poppi."

From where John sat, he couldn't judge the boy's age, but he sounded about nine or 10.

"Empty the bag ... slowly."

The boy took the bag from his grandfather and pulled out a folded blanket, then reached inside and grabbed something else.

"I said slowly."

The boy held up what looked like a doll—a baby girl dressed in a white gown.

"Why was that toy hidden under the blanket?"

The old man answered, "It is a surprise for my granddaughter."

The soldier lowered his rifle and snatched the doll from the boy's hands. "What are you hiding inside?"

"Nothing, I swear. It is a toy for Leena. She is sick. I thought a doll would make her smile. Nothing is hid—"

"Shut up, old man." The soldier tucked the doll's legs under his armpit, gripped its head, and with a single twist, wrenched the baby's head from its body. He peered into the torso and grunted.

The boy shouted, "Why? Why did you do that? My sister is sick, it was a gift."

The soldier dropped the doll's head on the floor, and stomped her face with his heel, crushing her eyes, nose, and mouth into the back of her skull. He glowered at the boy. "Shut up, or you will come with me."

The grandfather wrapped his arm around the boy's shoulder and pulled him close. "Hush Saalih, we can buy Leena another doll."

"But you saved two months to buy *that* one. She—"

The old man cupped his hand over the boy's mouth. "Hush now."

The soldier smirked. "You'd better listen to your grandfather."

John recalled only three times he'd chosen violence as a solution. Two were in grammar school, and the third, when he once slugged a guy who'd flirted with Maureen when they were engaged. Ordinarily, he wouldn't have clocked a man for admiring Maureen, but the jerk had pinched her backside right in front of his face.

Though he abhorred violence, he understood why the people of Kashmir, beaten down by the military and the militants, harbored resentment toward both. If he wasn't sure he'd be shot, John would've knocked the shit out of this scumbag who found courage pointing guns at old men and young boys.

The soldier continued down the aisle toward the back of the bus. As the pitiless goon inspected another man's package, John whispered to Salena, "Pretend you're sleeping. I'll do the same." John sagged in his seat, closed his eyes, and turned his face into Salena's veil.

The sound of clumping boots came closer and stopped, came closer and stopped, came closer and stopped at John's feet. Except for the sound of John's own breathing, the bus was silent.

A sharp object poked his left shoulder, and he bit down hard to keep from hollering. Pretending to stir from sleep, he turned his head slightly, then resumed deep, rhythmic breathing.

After what felt like forever, the footsteps resumed, but this time they were moving away. Only when John was sure the soldier had gotten off the bus did he open his eyes.

The bus driver closed the doors, and proceeded through the six-lane plaza.

John took a deep breath, relieved they'd escaped so easily.

Rubbing his shoulder, he turned to look out the back window. At that instant, a jeep carrying two soldiers zipped past the back of the bus and skidded to a stop in front of the checkpoint. Holding what looked like a photograph, one of the men leaped out and ran to the soldier who'd inspected their bus.

The bus had traveled about 50 yards when the soldier who'd stomped the doll started yelling and pointing at John, who was looking out the back window. Two other soldiers started blowing whistles and sprinted after the bus. Through the bus's open windows, the driver must have heard the shrill sounds, because the bus slowed to a crawl. The two soldiers, joined by four more, were catching up and shouting at the top of their lungs.

Only after he understood their words did John jump out of his seat, grab Salena's hand, and run up the aisle.

"The American, the American. Stop the bus, you have the American."

Halfway up the aisle, Salena tugged on John's hand.

"What's wrong?"

Her eyes were desperate and wild. "Do not let them take me. Kill me first."

John gripped her hand tighter. "No one's gonna take you—or me, cause we're outta here."

"How? We are trapped."

"Only if we stay put." John towed Salena the rest of the way, running past frightened passengers recoiling in their seats. By the time John reached the driver, the bus had stopped in the center lane with its pneumatic doors wide open. Six Indian soldiers were less than 20 yards behind.

John's decision was instant. He leaned over the farebox and scowled at the driver, a pencil thin man whose dark brown skin contrasted sharply with his bright white uniform. Grabbing the driver by his crisp white collar, John lifted him off his seat and turned him around.

"You can no take my bus."

John flashed the driver a broad, facetious grin. "Have a nice day," and heaved the hapless man down the front steps, and out the open door. John squeezed around the farebox and wedged himself into the driver's seat.

Sprawled on the asphalt, the driver sat up and pointed his finger at John. "You can no take my bus." He scrambled to his feet and ran at the door.

Salena stepped forward of the white line, and when the driver gripped the door handle to lift himself, she swung her foot forward with full force, and rammed the flat of her shoe squarely onto his face. The man staggered backward covering his nose with both hands.

John skimmed the instrument panel and pressed a red button labeled 'front door.' The doors hissed closed and John looked up. "Which way to Srinagar?"

CHAPTER SEVENTY-THREE

Standing at John's shoulder, Salena's voice rang loud and clear. "Straight ahead."

Having never driven anything longer than a cargo van, John scanned the steering column for a transmission lever, came up empty, and scoured the control panel. The panel contained an LCD showing an outline of the bus with built-in indicator lights warning the driver what doors were open and what signals were on.

Startled by hands pounding on glass, John looked left and saw two unhappy soldiers standing outside the bus's double-leafed doors. The more wild-eyed of the pair pointed at John and shouted, "He is the one!"

Focusing his attention on the instrumentation, John spotted a column of buttons along the side labeled 1, 2, 3, and D, R, and N. Praying he'd found the gear selector, John pressed the brake pedal, hit number one, and shifted his foot to what he hoped was the accelerator.

The banging on the doors stopped, and John realized the bus was moving.

When the digital speedometer reached 30, John pressed the "2" button, and the bus lurched. Salena grabbed a metal pole at the last second to keep from slamming into the windshield.

John apologized, and said, "I'm better at riding a bike than a bus." In the side-view mirror, he saw the backs of six soldiers running toward two jeeps parked at the checkpoint.

Looking ahead, John noticed more buildings on both sides of the highway. Every structure was made of wood or concrete, and all were in dire need of face-lifting, though occasionally John spotted a well manicured garden tucked between the shabby homes and apartments.

John was curious why Salena longed to return to a dying city. Maybe she believed if the fighting stopped, Srinagar would again see its glory days. He glanced up over his shoulder. "How are the passengers doing?"

Clutching a pole for support, Salena looked back. "They are very quiet."

"More like scared shitless."

Salena frowned at the floor.

"I mean highly anxious."

The speedometer read 60, but it didn't feel like 60, until John remembered he was reading kilometers, not miles per hour.

They came to an expansive lake on the left. Along its far shore rose a ridge of high, jagged mountains. Facing the lake were more buildings, all connected, with signs written in Arabic, and a surprising number in English. They passed a Hotel Greenway, Joe's Electronics, and Trade Asia, leaving John to wonder if there was anywhere left in the world that hadn't been commercialized.

Three lanes narrowed to two. The intersecting streets on the right, blocked by concrete posts, teemed with pedestrians. Ladies in silk veils and colorful dresses, and men with shiny black hair in loose shirts crowded the shops and sidewalks.

Salena pointed at the lake. "That is Dal Lake, where we will find Omar Shah."

"Didn't you say he lives on a houseboat?"

"Yes, it is called *The Hemingway*."

Dividing his attention between Dal Lake on his left and the mounting traffic ahead, he noticed hundreds of wooden boats of all sizes docked bow-first along the shoreline. "How are we supposed to find—"

A horn blared. John checked his rear-view mirror, and saw the flickering headlights of a jeep. "Damn, they're on us."

A second jeep pulled out of a side street on the right, and John heard gunfire. The soldiers must be crazy, shooting at a busload of civilians. When he didn't hear shattering glass, he realized they were aiming for the tires. He tugged the steering wheel hard, and swerved from one lane to the other.

Directly ahead a traffic light glowed red. Two compact cars were stopped in the left lane, and in the right, a single three-wheeled vehicle that looked like a scooter with a covered seat attached to the back. John slowed the bus as he approached the intersection, and when he pulled to within 20 feet of the scooter's fender, the signal turned green.

The tiny vehicle, holding a driver and two passengers, didn't move. John slammed the hub of the steering wheel, sounding the bus's horn. The driver of the mini-taxi looked back in wide-eyed terror, gunned his scooter, and careened onto the sidewalk.

After crossing the intersection, John checked the side-view mirror. The lead jeep was squeezing along the bus's right side, and the right lanes were heavy with oncoming traffic. If John sideswiped the jeep, he'd send it careening into a head-on collision. He had no desire to kill anyone, but if he let the jeep pass, he'd be surrounded and forced to stop.

John steered the bus on a gradual angle to the right, slowly muscling the jeep into the oncoming lanes. He heard screeching brakes, glanced back, and saw the jeep stopped dead center on the double yellow lines.

When he turned and looked forward, his heart sank. Three blocks ahead a line of short concrete pillars blocked both lanes of traffic. They were coming to the end of the highway and the start of a stone bridge, now a pedestrian mall, filled with food vendors, craft stands, and shoppers. "Which way?"

"This is center city. Every street is crowded."

The soldiers in the jeeps stopped shooting, and started honking. In his side-view mirror, John noticed a soldier holding up his hand. Maybe Kashmir's occupiers weren't all that ruthless. In the last hour they'd had three chances to kill him, and each time, they'd spared his life.

John wasn't about to stop and ask why, and with the bridge less than a block away, he had to do something now.

Salena pointed over his shoulder. "Over there! Chinar Bagh."

Ahead on the right, John saw a break in the storefronts filled by lush green grass and tree-lined walks.

"We will try for Munawar."

The names meant nothing to John, but Salena had grown up in this city. He waited for a gap in the traffic, leaned on the horn, and crossed the two oncoming lanes.

A flock of ladies in black burqas walking on the sidewalk scattered in different directions as the bus jumped the curb, crossed the sidewalk, and drove onto the lawn of a large park. Pounding the horn, John steered the bus onto a wide concrete walk lined with graceful trees.

"Chinar Bagh is one of my favorite spots in Srinagar," Salena said, nodding to the elegant green trees along the promenade. "Those are chinars. In autumn they take my breath away."

John glanced in the mirror, confirming the two jeeps were still on his tail. "I know some really pissed off soldiers who wouldn't mind taking your breath away." When he turned his attention forward, he saw directly ahead a dozen small children huddled around three adults. John hit the horn and didn't let up, but the children and chaperones in the middle of the walk stood frozen in fear.

John tugged the wheel hard left, swerved onto the grass, and immediately encountered another obstacle—a family of five lounging on a blanket. He again blasted the horn, and the startled parents and children leapt to their feet and ran. The bus rolled over a hibachi, two lawn chairs, and what looked to John like a pot of yellow rice.

Salena pointed to a large structure with a pointy top. "Go that way."

"What is it?"

"A mosque that backs up to a canal."

Approaching the far end of Chinar Bagh, John's gut twisted. Along the park's perimeter a line of some 30 soldiers bent on one knee pointed their rifles at the bus's windshield. Hoping the Indian Army was still feeling charitable, John aimed the bus toward the mosque behind the kneeling troops, and pressed hard on the gas.

When the bus came to within 20 yards of the soldiers, the formation broke rank and let John pass.

The bus leapt the curb, and as they neared the mosque, John eased off the accelerator. "Where to now?"

"That way!"

Salena pointed down a narrow street lined with dilapidated three-story shops and walkups. Little wider than an alley, the cobblestone street swarmed with pedestrians.

"Way too crowded."

"Do you trust me?"

"Of course, dear."

"Go slow and avoid the people."

"You mean no bonus points for hitting old ladies?"

She glared down at him. "That is not funny."

"Sorry." Driving 10 kph through a sea of humanity, he leaned on the horn, drawing angry stares from shoppers in no hurry to get out of his way. Glimpsing in the side-view mirror, John saw the two jeeps had been joined by two more along with an armored personnel carrier. All five vehicles drove single file behind the bus. "Don't you think it's a little odd they aren't shooting?"

"They do not wish to harm the passengers."

John inched past a merchant hawking watermelon off a cart, swiping the man's butt with the bus's right side. When the blue-turbaned peddler banged his fist on the fender, John waved in the mirror and smiled.

Salena grabbed John's left shoulder, and he yelped in pain.

She flinched. "Sorry, I forgot." Stroking his shoulder with one hand, she pointed over the throng with the other. "There is where we get off."

Fifty yards ahead, in the direction she pointed, the street of connecting storefronts bent sharply right. All John saw at the street's elbow was a series of display windows with colorful signs in Arabic mounted over each door. "You're not taking us shopping, are you?"

"No, but if my memory is correct, we are going on a cruise."

John swung his right thumb over his shoulder. "I hope our friends in the jeeps won't be joining us."

"They won't if we move quickly."

Squeezing through the horde at a snail's pace, the 50 yards felt like 500, but eventually they reached the turn in the alley. John looked around the bend and nearly wet his pants. Not only were there more shops, apartments, and people, but more soldiers—at least 50—and a tank blocking the end of the street with its turret trained at the bus.

"Unless that boat of yours drops out of the sky, this ride's over."

Salena pointed to a tiny dress shop straight ahead. "Press the horn and drive into that store."

"What?"

"You heard me. Drive through the window."

"Then what?"

"Follow me."

"Yeah, OK, I trust you … I must be out of my freakin' mind." John leaned on the horn and pressed the gas. Closing his eyes, he lowered his head, and the next sounds he heard were shattering glass, splintering wood, and shrieking passengers. The bus came to a dead stop, and after the clamor subsided, he heard only silence.

John turned, looked down the center aisle through the bus's rear window, and saw he'd driven the bus completely into the shop.

Surveying the shop's dim interior, he saw dresses, shawls, and clothes racks filling the long, narrow space. He realized the bus had wedged itself between the store's walls, and there was no space on either side for a man to fit through. That must have been Salena's plan—block the soldiers and buy them time.

He glanced around looking for her.

"Down here."

She stood in front of the bus with her hands on her hips, having jumped through the bus's shattered windshield.

"Hurry. The soldiers will soon be upon us."

John stood and wiggled from behind the steering wheel. Before joining Salena, he turned and regarded the stunned passengers, all of whom sat perfectly still staring at him bug-eyed. Genuinely sorry for any inconvenience he'd caused them, he announced, "Thank you for your patience, and please accept my apology for taking you out of your way."

He walked down the aisle toward the back of the bus, and stopped beside the gray bearded man and his grandson who'd been harassed by the soldier at the checkpoint. Digging into his pocket, he extracted the wad of money Colonel Daley had given him, and said to the boy, "I hope your sister feels better soon." He peeled off 5,000 rupees and tucked the notes in the boy's hand. "Go buy her another doll."

John spun, ran up the aisle, and climbed out the window. He sprinted toward Salena, who was waiting for him at the back of the store.

She led him through a rickety six-panel door into bright sunlight. The rear yards of the connected, three-story buildings consisted of narrow concrete patios backing up to crumbling stone steps leading down to a brown-water canal. Plying the wide canal were some 40 or 50 canoe-like boats with curtain-shrouded canopies rising from their centers. Piloted by a single oarsman, some boats transported produce, others flowers, and still others held nothing but their captains.

Salena scanned the waterway in both directions, then leapt down the steps two at a time toward one of the covered boats moored at the bottom of the stairs three buildings down. At the base of the steps behind the adjoining yard, she stopped and looked back. "What are you waiting for?"

Unsure what to expect from this woman next, John followed her down the stone steps to a narrow concrete walk abutting the water's edge. By the time he caught up with Salena, she was already haggling with the boat's captain.

"... no, we are not in trouble."

"I know trouble when I see trouble. You two in trouble."

"Please, how much to Dal Lake?"

"I come from there now."

The canoe's owner was a soft-spoken, older gentleman with a gold turban piled neatly on his head. John noticed the pointed ends of his boat held woven willow baskets crammed with dazzling displays of roses and tulips. At the boat's center stood a rectangular canopy about five feet high, five feet wide, and six feet long, with beige curtains hanging from all four sides.

Salena turned to John. "Give me your money."

Glancing back at the dress shop door, John pulled the bundle of rupees from his pocket.

In full view of the boat's pilot, she flicked her thumb through the bankroll. "I shall pay you well."

"My flowers. They will die if I do not get them to market in time."

"Will 50,000 Pakistani rupees compensate you for your risk?"

The man's jaw dropped and John was convinced he was about to salivate. After 20 seconds of silence, Salena played a game of her own. "Very well, I will take my business elsewhere." She spun and grabbed John's arm.

"No, please. Hop in. Enjoy the ride."

Salena counted out 50,000 rupees and handed them to the driver. She stripped off five more notes and stuffed them in the man's hand. "A little extra to row fast and keep quiet."

The man helped John and Salena aboard, cast off his lines, and rowed toward the middle of the waterway where dozens of identical canoes shuttled up and down the canal.

Walking toward the covered canopy, Salena asked the oarsman, "Do you know *The Hemingway?*"

The man smiled. "The boat of Omar Shah."

"Take us to him." Salena disappeared through the canopy's curtain. Following her in, John beheld a cushioned bench seat upholstered in red velour and stacked high with black velour pillows. Lowering her veil, Salena sat squarely in the middle, leaving John little room on either side.

"Am I supposed to stand?"

She shook her head. "It has been a long time since I have ridden in a shikara, and never alone with a man."

He understood, and sat close to her. Caressing her cheek with his fingers, studying her perfect brown eyes, he heard from somewhere outside the thunder of pounding boots and the shouts of angry men.

CHAPTER SEVENTY-FOUR

John reluctantly pulled away from Salena and peeked through the canopy's curtain. He observed Indian soldiers combing the backyard patios of the decaying shops and apartments along the canal. The shikara wallah, as Salena referred to the covered canoe's driver, had earned his generous fare by quickly blending in with dozens of similar boats crowding the bustling waterway.

Though they'd shaken their pursuers, John knew more difficult obstacles lay ahead.

The first was time. They had less than 24 hours to get the explosives from Omar Shah and return to the Citadel before the start of Glorious Dawn. The second was Azam Qadeer. Assuming Omar could arrange for their fast transport to Islamabad, they must convince Qadeer they'd been kidnapped by dacoits and had managed an escape.

John stepped away from the curtain and walked to Salena, who sat on the red velour seat. Despite the time constraints, he was ready to indulge her wish to visit her dying mother. While completing CRUSO's mission was now largely out of his control, pleasing Salena was not.

He sat beside her and listened enamored as she described Srinagar's former beauty and lost innocence, before the violence had torn the city apart. He could see in her eyes she loved this place, and despite what the soldiers had done to her in Srinagar five years earlier, she longed to return. She spoke of the future, and how she planned to live out her days in the house of her childhood after the Indians and militants were driven from her homeland.

With every fiber of his heart, John yearned to fulfill Salena's dream, but even if he pulled off a miracle and assassinated Khan, he knew Kashmir would never be free. Too many interests vied for control here— New Delhi, Islamabad, and the militant groups—each with their own vision of Kashmir's fate. John kept quiet and listened. He refused to steal this woman's fantasy, and even if he tried, the fire in her eyes when she spoke of Kashmiri independence burned too bright for logic to douse.

Salena stood, and before John could stop her, she threw open the curtain behind the bench seat.

"What are you doing? The soldiers will—"

They had entered a vast lake as blue as the azure sky, ringed by mountains whose rugged slopes climbed to jagged peaks touching the bottoms of billowing white clouds. Standing beside Salena, John scoured the lakeshore, discerning houses and houseboats, lush green gardens, and far in the distance, a tremendous domed mosque with a pink minaret gleaming under the brilliant sun.

Salena wove her fingers through his, and with a seductive radiance in her smile, she whispered, "Is not Dal Lake lovely?"

Awed as much by his companion as by the splendors around them, John said softly, "The only thing lovelier is you."

He looked across the water in the direction from which they'd come, and noticed close to shore, on Srinagar's outskirts, a solitary hill rising from the valley floor. The hill's summit wore a crown of russet brick walls, and when he pointed out the structure to Salena, she said he had spotted Fort Hari Parbat on Sharika Hill. Her eyes glimmered as she described the history of the 16th Century fort constructed during the reign of Akbar.

Captivated by her enthusiasm and charmed by her voice, John listened intently as she spoke of Dal Lake and her childhood memories. She described the lake's floating gardens, where water farmers cultivated plants and vegetables. She spoke of its famous lotus flowers, and pointed north where she said lotus plants grew in abundance. Straining his eyes, John made out a thin line of floating green, and wished they had more time to explore the lake's wonders.

All around them, shikaras topped with gaily colored canopies sliced the lake's mirrored surface. Standing beside John, Salena snuggled against his arm. "I remember the last time I rode a shikara on Dal Lake. Poppa did something the elders would have frowned upon—he held my mother and kissed her in front of me. He did not believe it wrong for married couples to share affection in front of their children."

"Your dad sounds like a wise man."

"When I was a girl, I dreamed of riding alone in a shikara with someone special." She regarded him with beckoning eyes. "Someone I loved."

John remembered Naji. Two days earlier she had told Raja that Naji was all the more reason she must return to Srinagar. John wondered if Naji was someone with whom she had dreamed of taking that shikara ride.

Salena closed the curtain and tugged on John's hand, pulling him to the bench seat. He kissed her tenderly at first, and then with a passion matched only by her own. If they wound up stranded in Srinagar, he wouldn't care, so long as they were together.

After too short a time in her arms, he heard the boatman call out, "We are here."

Reluctantly John broke their embrace and parted the curtain. The driver paddled toward the back of a wooden houseboat moored near two others along a desolate stretch of the lakeshore. A covered veranda ran the width of the boat's stern, and hanging from the porch rail was a sign painted in white script: 'The Hemingway.'

Along the wood railing stood a giant of a man with crow black eyes and a sun-toughened face wearing an apple green turban. A fleshy stub protruded from the right side of his head where there had once been an ear.

"Salena."

"Omar Shah."

The oarsman lashed the shikara to the houseboat, and Salena climbed through a gate in the rail. She reached into her dress, turned to the driver, and handed him a fistful of rupees. "Please wait for us, we will not be long. I trust this amount will cover the cost of your flowers for the day."

The grinning shikara wullah stared at the notes. "It will cover their cost for a month."

John climbed aboard the houseboat and stood on the porch beside Salena.

Salena tipped her head in respect at Omar, who studied her face. "You share your father's nose—and his determination."

"Thank you."

A hint of sorrow entered the big man's eyes. "His determination is what killed him."

"I am mindful of my deeds."

"You must remain so." Omar moved away from Salena, and stood facing John.

John didn't consider himself short, but toe-to-toe with this guy, he felt like a runt.

Omar gripped John's right hand and squeezed. Sensing a challenge to his testosterone, John did all he could not to wince.

"You must be very special for Salena to marry out of her faith."

"I couldn't help it. I was born Catholic."

"We can't all be as lucky as the children of Mohammed."

John didn't think the children of Jesus had it so bad, but under the circumstances, he held his tongue.

Omar Shah freed John's hand and led them through a door covered with a white cotton scrim shading a full-length window. They entered a parlor, where John was amazed to find delicately carved walnut paneled walls and varnished hardwood chairs. The chairs were upholstered in red velvet, and might well have furnished Queen Victoria's palace. Elegant sconce lamps dressed up the walls, and a fully stocked, ceiling-high mahogany library stood behind a 19th Century secretary in mint condition. The pine secretary was flanked by two end tables covered with white silk doilies. One table held a polished silver tea service that resembled something Maureen once bought for her mother at Bloomingdale's.

"How soon can we return to Pakistan?" Salena asked.

The burly man stared down at the hand-embroidered red and gold carpet gracing the parlor floor. "I called Ghazi last night, but you had already left. The news is bad. Very bad."

"What news?"

"Travel to Pakistan is impossible. You cannot go back."

Salena shook her head in disbelief. "Travel to Pakistan has always been difficult, but never impossible."

Omar Shah walked to the table beside the bookshelves, and from the silver service, poured three cups of steaming tea. "Something big is about to happen. Every route from the city is blocked by Border Security Forces or regular army units. Not an oxcart leaves Srinagar without a search, and all boats on the Jhelum River beyond Safa Kadal are turned back."

When he brought the tray over, Salena lifted one of the silver cups. "What if we escape the city through Shirazi Bagh and travel north past Shalimar Bagh to Telbal."

"Heading north and west will take too long, not if you must reach Pakistan by nightfall."

John thanked Omar for the tea and drew a long sip, paused, then wolfed down the rest.

Omar must have noticed him enjoying the sweet beverage. "That is my finest kahva. I shall pour you more."

John set his empty cup on the tray. "Thanks, it's the best I've had."

Handing John his refill, Omar addressed Salena. "I'm afraid I have more news—sad news. A Hindu friend with reliable contacts in the Jammu & Kashmir Rifles informed me Hani Taj was killed in the gunfight outside Kuligam."

Salena closed her eyes and bowed her head.

"Do not mourn his loss. He died a martyr."

She said softly, "He was so young."

"Ease your sorrow, for Abu Kundi escaped to the mountains, but not before killing two BSF goons. His only regret—not joining Hani Taj as a martyr in paradise."

John had seen too much wanton death in the last 24 hours to check his tongue. "Bullshit! Hani Taj didn't deserve to die, and neither did the soldiers who Abu Kundi murdered."

Salena and Omar turned to him with the same startled look.

"That's right, if Hani Taj and others like him didn't consume themselves with hate, maybe they'd find a peaceful way to bring freedom to Kashmir."

Omar slammed his cup on the table. "You are in no position to speak. You know little of my people's struggle."

John recalled the young girl in the farmhouse wailing over the slain body of her father. "I know your people's struggle destroys families."

"Jihad requires sacrifice."

"Including the lives of innocent civilians?"

"All Kashmiris—regardless of age or gender—must be ready to die for the cause."

This was one subject they'd never agree on. "Look, I'm not here to argue. Just give us the explosives, and we'll find our own way back to Islamabad."

"I tell you, travel to Pakistan is dangerous."

"That's what I heard about travel to Srinagar."

"Then you do not know."

"About what?"

"The Rifles have orders to capture the American who escaped the shootout near Kuligam. They want him alive."

"Why?"

"My friend isn't sure, but the order comes directly from the commander of the Jammu & Kashmir Rifles."

"Maybe they're curious why an American was fighting on the side of Kashmiri militants."

"Perhaps, but if you do attempt the journey, do not let them capture you. They will beat the truth from you."

"I'd sooner kill myself than let them take me alive."

Omar regarded John pensively, rubbing his ear stub. He glanced at Salena, then back at John. "If that is your word, I will give you all the explosives you can carry."

"I never break a promise."

"Do you favor C-4 or Semtex?"

"Both are stable, but I'm more familiar with C-4."

"Are you sure? My Semtex comes from Romania. No plastic tags, and it is reformulated to avoid sniffer detection."

John hadn't considered that at some point he might pass through a bomb detection system. After the war on terrorism had shifted into high-gear, gas chromatography explosive detection systems had popped up everywhere, but he didn't recall seeing sniffer devices at the entrances to Pakistan National Hospital or Khan's Citadel. "I'll take my chances with the C-4."

"How much do you need?"

A quarter pound of C-4 rolled into an eight-inch long cigar could slice a steel I-beam as effectively as a blow torch. A pound of C-4 carefully positioned at a building's four corners could bring it down. Taking into account the Citadel's octagon shape and 12 stories, John mentally reviewed numbers he'd crunched during his hike over the lower Himalayas. "Ten pounds should do the trick."

"That's all?"

"The lighter we travel, the better."

For a full minute, Omar Shah stared down at his silver cup. John and Salena exchanged tight-lipped glances, until finally Omar turned to John and announced, "My friend with connections in the Indian Army—he may be able to smuggle you across the border at Bhatea."

Salena's eyes lit up. "That is wonderful."

"Do not yet celebrate. I offer my C-4 as a donation to the jihad, but my friend's services do not come free."

Salena pulled out the bankroll of rupees. "How much will it take?"

Omar's gaze fixed on the bulky wad. "Pakistan rupees? 200,000."

Her mouth dropped. "You must be mistaken."

"My friend is taking a great risk."

"That is nearly all we have left."

"I am not even sure 200,000 will do it."

"Very well."

"Mind you, I get no commission."

Surveying the opulence around him, John somehow doubted that. He asked Omar, "How long before you can contact your friend?"

"Give me an hour."

"Good, we'll have time to visit Salena's mother."

Omar slapped the heel of his hand against his forehead. "Allah forgive me, I nearly forgot." He regarded Salena with dark, doleful eyes. "I have more news, bad news—this from a friend at Lal Ded Hospital. Last night your mother's blood oxygen dropped to critical levels. If she has not already expired, her time is at hand."

By now John could read Salena, and he knew she was about to cry. Good manners or not, he turned to the second love of his life, and ignoring his pain, comforted Salena with the full strength of his arms.

Her soft curves locked in his embrace, she whispered, "We must go to her immediately."

CHAPTER SEVENTY-FIVE

John climbed from the patio of Omar Shah's houseboat onto the shikara's deck, reached up for Salena's hand, and helped her aboard. Standing at the rail of his floating home, Omar bid them farewell, and promised to greet them with a platter of rista meat balls and seekh kababs upon their return to *The Hemingway*.

The sharp pains tormenting John's stomach over the past few weeks had bothered him little since he'd awoken. He'd eaten neither breakfast nor lunch, and was looking forward to a home-cooked meal before the return trip to Islamabad.

As the shikara wullah cast off the lines, Salena called out to Omar they'd be back in two hours. When Omar asked why so long, she said she had someone else to see after they visited her mother. She didn't mention who, but John had a feeling it might be Naji, the other man in her life, and though he had no right to feel jealous, he found himself resenting this guy before he even met him.

The boatman paddled into the lake's deeper waters, then pointed his boat toward Srinagar's main canal. Salena instructed the boat's pilot to deliver them to the foot of Amira Kadal. She explained to John that Amira Kadal was one of nine bridges spanning the Jhelum River in center city, and was within walking distance of Lal Ded Hospital.

From the middle of Dal Lake, John admired the tall mountains sheltering the valley from the east. Cumulous clouds skirted the scraggily ridge, but refused to venture beyond, leaving the sky above the lake crystal blue.

Closer to the city along the shoreline John saw hundreds of wooden houseboats, some ornately carved, others plain, but elegant. Many were given whimsical names to beckon travelers, names like *Singsong*, *Magic Sammy*, and *Playful Child*. What a wonderful place Kashmir must have been to visit. If the threat of terror ever ended for good, John could well imagine this enchanting land again becoming a magnet for tourists.

As the buildings of Srinagar loomed larger, Salena instructed the oarsman to tell her when Amira Kadal was in sight. She led John under the shikara's canopy and closed the curtain. "We must be careful. Border Security Forces are posted on every bridge."

John agreed they were safer under the canopy, then asked her a question that had bothered him since they'd left *The Hemingway*. "What if Omar's connection falls through?"

Salena sat on the velour bench seat. "Omar is resourceful. He will help us."

"What if he can't?"

She tapped the cushion, inviting him to sit beside her. "You know I must return to Islamabad, if not tomorrow, then as quickly as Omar can arrange for a guide. The lives of Raja and my children in the Freedom Ward are at stake."

John sat and stared into her eyes. "You're an amazing woman."

During a long silence, Salena's eyes roamed his face, and when finally she spoke, he detected a tremor in her voice. "If Omar cannot deliver us to Pakistan in time for Glorious Dawn, when I leave Srinagar, you will not accompany me."

"What's that supposed to mean?"

"Going back to the Citadel may be dangerous. If Qadeer's technicians have discovered the code hidden in my computer, Qadeer will know I was plotting with your government. You need not share my risk. If we cannot leave Srinagar today, I will go alone. I will tell Khan you were murdered by the dacoits along with Lieutenant Hassan and Subedar Mazhar. Meanwhile, you can escape to the east, perhaps to Kargil or Ladakh, before Khan launches his missiles."

John smiled. She truly did not understand the power she held over him. "Yeah, like I'm ever gonna let you make the trip alone."

"And why not?"

Caressing her cheek, he coaxed her mouth to his. "Because you and me, we're a team, and we're gonna stay a team til the end." Their lips met and their tongues danced with a fervor that made him dizzy, yet in the midst of their passion, he remained troubled, and forced himself to pull away. He held her hands and looked her straight in the eye. "I need to know something, and I want the truth."

"I would never dishonor you with a lie."

"Do you still love this Naji fella?"

Her eyes opened wide and she smiled, then the crescent of her lips grew into a broad grin, until finally she burst out laughing. "Yes … yes, I still love Naji."

John dropped her hands and slid to the end of the bench seat. "Then why … I mean, how could you …"

Salena kept laughing, and laughed until tears welled in her eyes.

Pain jabbed at John's belly. "What's so funny?"

"You are."

"I get it. You think it's a big joke I'm just another pathetic jerk who fell in love with you."

"No."

"Then what?"

"Because, silly ..." She thrust her chest forward, leaning so close he thought she was about to kiss him, "Naji is a little boy." And then she did.

John pulled away, confused. "What do you mean 'a little boy'?"

She smiled playfully. "You know ... what you were before you grew into a man."

"Very funny. How do you know this kid?"

"He was abandoned by his mother when he was a baby, and now lives in an orphanage near Lal Ded Hospital. He is very special to me."

John realized he must have sounded like a fool making an issue over a little kid. "Oh, yeah, no problem. We'll visit whoever you want."

Salena peeked through the curtain, and her expression hardened. "We do not have much time, and I must prepare you for what you will see when we visit my mother."

"I've been around sick people before."

"No, I mean the condition of the hospital. The war for independence has exacted a terrible price on Kashmir's hospitals. The Indian government has cut off money to buy medicines, vaccines, and basic supplies. Do not expect a facility like Saint Barnabas in New Jersey. What you see will horrify you."

"Dirty sheets? No big deal."

"You do not understand. When I worked at Lal Ded Hospital, there was an epidemic of viral meningitis, and the government refused to give us medicine. Two hundred women and children died. Cancer patients are rarely treated and almost all suffer painful deaths. X-ray machines, blood testing equipment, incubators, sterilization devices— all sit broken. Even the sickest patients are crammed five to a room."

"What's the government's problem?"

"They believe Kashmir's hospitals aid the freedom fighters."

"Are they right?"

"As doctors, we take an oath to treat all people, no matter who they are, or where they come from."

"At least they don't stop you from practicing medicine."

"There you are wrong. More than once Border Security Forces have turned back ambulances transporting critical patients—after the soldiers drag the drivers from their vehicles and beat them senseless. Doctors, too, are not immune from abuse. Many of my colleagues were harassed, some arrested, for treating young men the BSF claimed were militants. Once, in the middle of performing a Cesarean section, the police raided the hospital and forced me to leave the operating room at gunpoint. Five hours later, after interrogating all of us like common bandits, they allowed me to return. The poor woman had already bled to death and her infant girl had drowned in her mother's amniotic fluid. So prepare yourself for much worse than dirty sheets."

"I had no idea."

"If you succeed in killing Khan, I intend to use the money your government gives me to repair the broken equipment, buy the medicines, and make Lal Ded Hospital the finest women's hospital in all of Kashmir."

"Like I said, you're an amazing woman." John remembered another question he'd been meaning to ask. "Does Lal Ded mean 'the dead'?"

Salena's lips formed a bittersweet smile. "Lal Ded was a 14th Century mystic and poetess. She married at an early age and was neglected, nearly starved, by her mother-in-law. She ran away to learn yoga and meditation, and under the influence of Muslim scholars, traveled the Vale preaching a gospel of brotherhood, unity, and tolerance. Her poetry speaks to Hindus and Muslims alike about social equality and the oneness of God. She is the embodiment of Kashmiriyat."

How ironic last Friday he couldn't give a damn who was president in his own country. Now, surrounded by people for whom freedom was only a dream, and immersed in a culture he hardly knew existed, he found himself wishing he could pound the crap out of extremists on both sides of the Line of Control for stealing Kashmiriyat from Salena and others who longed to bring tolerance back to this beautiful land.

Before John could ask her more about Lal Ded, he heard the shikara wullah speak quietly through the curtain. "We have reached Zero Bridge."

John got up, snuck a peek, and saw they had left the lake and entered a tributary flowing through the heart of Srinagar. A stone bridge ahead teemed with soldiers marching in both directions. He turned and looked at Salena. "We'll never reach the hospital without being noticed, especially if they're looking for an American."

Salena rose and glimpsed through the curtain. "I have an idea."

"An invisibility cloak?"

"You are not far off." In a hushed tone, she summoned the shikara's pilot, who poked his gold-turbaned head between the curtains. She informed him they'd had a change of plans. Rather than drop them off below Amira Kadal, he was to leave them halfway between Amira Kadal and the bridge preceding Badshah Kadal.

The captain nodded, and disappeared. Salena told John more about the life and poetry of Lal Ded, and how Muslims and Hindus had found common ground in her teachings. John listened quietly, riveted by her enthusiasm.

Within a short time the shikara wullah again thrust his head through the curtain to inform them they had reached their destination. Salena instructed the driver to pull up to stone stairs leading to the back of a dilapidated three-story building. At the top of the steps, John noticed an alley running between that building and a brick structure next door, possibly a factory.

When Salena rose abruptly, John did the same.

She held up her hand. "Wait here."

"Where are you going?"

"Give me five minutes." She vanished through the curtains.

John heard Salena cross the boat's bow, say something to the shikara's captain, and the next thing he knew, she was gone. He peeked outside and caught sight of her blue veil as she disappeared between the two buildings at the top of the steps.

Under the shikara's canopy, a wave of loneliness washed over John. He heard few sounds—no honking horns, no hustle and bustle—as if all Srinagar's inhabitants tiptoed silently through the streets to avoid drawing attention to themselves.

Solitude forced him to grapple with mixed emotions. On one hand, he hoped Omar Shah came through with a quick ride to Islamabad, giving him a chance to complete his mission. Yet, he liked the idea of living out his last few months in Kashmir, but only with Salena at his side. If he could convince her to change her mind, maybe they could flee the Vale together, and find a place in the mountains where the nuclear fallout wouldn't touch them.

Startled by a noise at his back, John spun to find Salena clutching two bundles of cloth, one light blue, the other, dark green.

"I told you I would not be long." She handed him the green bundle. "Put this on."

"What is it?"

"A burqa."

"You're kidding."

"I swore I would die before wearing one of these." She unfurled the orthodox Muslim garb, threw it over her head, and her lovely eyes disappeared behind a thick netting with tiny face holes to see and breathe through.

"You seriously expect me to wear this."

She replied as if she were speaking through a cotton wad. "If I must wear it, so do you. Besides, I spent top rupee to buy the largest size I could find."

For a moment, John stared at the green bundle in his hands, then reluctantly, pulled the cloth over his head.

Holding his hand, Salena guided him out from under the canopy.

Through pin size peep holes stifling his airflow he saw Salena hand the oarsman another fistful of rupees. "This is for your kindness," she said, and handed him more. "This is for your silence."

"Thank you."

"Return to this spot in 90 minutes."

"I shall be waiting."

Stumbling up the stone stairs, John tripped twice. Both times Salena caught him. After a third fall, he asked, "How do women function in these things?"

"I know a few men I would love to see wear this for a day or two."

An image of Azam Qadeer trapped beneath a burqa popped into his mind, and he chuckled out loud.

Along every street, down every alley, armed soldiers moved amongst the shoppers and merchants. On every corner, John saw soldiers crouched behind fortified bunkers pointing rifles over the tops of sandbag walls. On one block, they passed two gutted apartment buildings, side-by-side, with only their facades and a common wall left standing. The ruins reminded John of photos he'd seen of bombed out Berlin at the end of World War II.

Walking beside Salena in his cloth cocoon, John's self-awareness faded as he noticed others traipsing the streets of Srinagar shrouded head-to-toe. About six blocks from the canal, Salena paused on the sidewalk across from a bleak, four-story concrete building extending an entire city block.

Salena leaned close and whispered, "We are here."

John kept his voice low. "Are you ready?"

"If my mother is alive, she may not know I have come."

"Every parent knows when their child is near."

"I am not sure this is a good idea."

Surprised this brave woman had suddenly grown cold feet, John gently grasped her burqa and found her elbow. "Let's do it."

Two soldiers standing outside the hospital's double doors kept watchful eyes on everyone strolling the sidewalk. Three burqa-clad women approached the entrance and entered unquestioned. Bending his knees to appear shorter, John nudged Salena, and they crossed the street. John held his breath when they reached the doors, and exhaled slowly after they entered without evoking a glance.

John's peripheral vision was nonexistent, but from what little he saw through the cloth mesh, he knew this place had seen better days.

The formerly white walls of the sparsely furnished lobby bore grimy black stains. In one spot, John noticed a chest-high blotch with long red drip marks streaking to the floor, and he wondered if someone had been shot there. On another wall hung a black-and-white print of a beautiful young woman whose long dark hair and luminous round eyes resembled Salena's. John had a hunch she was the Kashmiri poetess for whom the hospital had been named.

A pair of elevators lay straight ahead, and blocking their path, a husky soldier in battle fatigues standing beside a walk-through metal detector.

Salena moved in front of John and stopped at the portal.

The dark-skinned soldier gave her a harsh look. "What is your business?"

"I am visiting a patient."

The soldier grabbed Salena's arm through her burqa. "You idiot. Who? Who are you visiting."

John's impulse was to knock this jerk on his ass and bind him in one of their cloth shrouds.

Salena answered calmly, "My mother."

The soldier's thick hand clenched Salena tighter. "Who is your mother?"

"Hafeeza. Hafeeza Zamal."

The soldier released her, and the edge disappeared from his voice. "Wait here, I will call upstairs for authorization."

The soldier crossed the lobby and picked up a phone beneath the picture of the dark-haired lady.

John whispered, "You don't know how much I wanna grab that jerk and kick the shit out of him."

"You mean pummel him, and I would too, but violence accomplishes nothing."

"It'd make me feel a whole lot better."

"Forget it. When you live here, you expect their abuse."

"I'd never get used to that kind of crap."

"I did not say get used to it. I said expect it."

When the burly soldier returned, he pointed down a corridor beyond the elevators, and spoke to Salena in a tone that struck John as oddly polite. "Walk to the second set of stairs. Go one flight up and turn left. Your mother is in Room 204—third door on the right."

Just as he thought they'd get past this goon with no more hassles, John walked through the metal detector and an ear-splitting alarm echoed off the lobby walls. Immediately he remembered the toy Harley.

John was prepared to shed his burqa and bolt for the front door, when the soldier did something highly unusual. He waved them on without a word.

They entered the hall where the soldier had pointed, and when John was sure they were out of earshot, he said to Salena, "That was easy. Way too easy."

Passing the first set of stairs on the right, John sensed the eyes of the soldier in the lobby boring through his back, though he dared not turn to confirm his suspicion. Nearly every door off the hall was closed, and those left open revealed darkened rooms, as if the hospital had been abandoned. Even the three women in burqas who had entered the hospital a moment before had disappeared. He whispered, "Do you get the feeling we're being watched?"

"The Indian Army watches everyone."

"Isn't it a little strange the soldier in the lobby didn't frisk me?" They came to a set of doors wedged open by dirty towels forced under their bottoms. John peeked around the doorjamb and saw the second set of stairs. "I'll go first. If this is a trap, run like hell."

Lifting his foot to climb the steps, he tripped on the hem of his burqa. "Damn."

Salena helped him up, and he continued climbing. He paused on the first landing, where he could see the closed double doors on the second floor. "Something's definitely wrong. That soldier was sweet as pie after he called upstairs."

"What should we do?"

"Maybe turn around, and—"

Footsteps from above echoed through the stairwell. He couldn't tell how many people were coming, but definitely more than one. He poked his head between the staircases, looked up, and saw two women descending from the third floor, both wearing long white dresses and white veils. One had a stethoscope dangling from her neck, the other held a black doctor's bag. John got an idea.

"How many rupees do you have left?"

"Barely enough to pay Omar's friend."

"If this is a set-up, and we get caught, it won't matter if we're short a few rupees."

"What are you thinking?"

"I'll tell you as we go. First, lose that tent you're wearing, or we'll lose our chance."

CHAPTER SEVENTY-SIX

Crouched next to Salena on the fourth floor landing, John peeked over the railing.

"Hurry! Hurry!" The urgent cry came from the stairs below. "They are escaping to the river!"

The clamor of boots in hot pursuit bounced off the walls as a dozen soldiers poured into the stairwell from the second floor corridor. Descending the steps two at a time, the soldiers disappeared through the open doors on the first floor.

John was right, the Indians had known they were coming, but how? He'd work on that later. Now they must go to Salena's mother before the soldiers discovered his ruse.

After removing his burqa, John had politely stopped the two women he'd seen coming down the stairs. Both were nurses who jumped at the chance to earn 25,000 rupees each. They need only don the burqas John and Salena had worn into the hospital, exit the building through a side door, and walk past the main entrance toward the Jhelum River. Salena warned the two women the soldiers might chase them, and if that happened, they should run toward the river.

After the last echo of sprinting boots faded, John rose and led Salena down two flights of stairs. Along the way, he cautioned, "We don't have much time."

From inside the stairwell on the second floor landing, he peeked into the hall through a window in the double doors. Seeing no one, he cracked the doors open and looked both ways.

Still nobody in sight—only an empty gurney with bloodstained sheets parked along the wall. Taking Salena by the hand, he opened the door and turned left down the corridor.

The soldier in the lobby had said Salena's mother was in Room 204. When they came to the third door on the right, sure enough, '204' was stenciled above the doorframe. The door was open, the lights were out, and the blinds were drawn, but in the darkness John detected a human form lying under a blanket on a bed next to the window.

Salena released his hand and ran into the room. He followed, locked the door, and turned around to find Salena kneeling beside the bed.

John crept up behind her, and as his eyes adjusted to the dim light, he looked over her shoulder. Lying on a flimsy mattress with her eyes closed was an elderly woman with long gray hair. She was connected to wires and an IV drip, and a pair of slim tubes fed oxygen through her nose, but at least she was breathing. Her dark, wrinkled face bore an uncanny resemblance to Salena's, so strikingly similar, John swore he was looking at an age progression of the younger woman kneeling at her side. Looking past the ruts and lines crisscrossing Hafeeza's face, John knew she had once been beautiful, maybe as pretty as Salena.

Salena whispered something to her mother, but the frail woman did not respond. John had worked miracles to get them this far, but he could offer no magic to help Salena's mom.

Feeling a little awkward, John surveyed the room. He was sickened by its stench and filth. He noticed three other metal frame beds, all topped with scrawny mattresses stripped bare. The empty beds surprised him, since Salena had described the hospital as overcrowded. Then he noticed a military radio standing upright on the floor next to one of the beds. That eliminated any doubt the soldiers had set a trap.

He walked to the blinds, peeped through the slats, and found himself staring down onto the street in front of the hospital. If the soldiers returned before he and Salena left the room, John figured he could barricade the door with a bed frame, and buy them time to jump out the window. But even if they hit the sidewalk in one piece, they still must contend with the 50 soldiers who, from what John could see through the window, had begun chasing his well-paid decoys.

John glanced at Salena, who caressed her own cheek with the limp palm of her mother's hand. He wished he could give Salena all the time she needed, but the opportunity for escape was limited. When the soldiers discovered they'd been duped, they'd return to the hospital in a flash.

He bowed his head and walked to Salena's side. Through muffled sobs, Salena murmured into her mother's ear. Hafeeza lay perfectly still and said nothing.

John placed his hand on Salena's shoulder, and when he did, she rocked back and forth on her knees, weeping openly.

"If only I'd gotten you to Srinagar sooner."

She looked up at him, tears dripping down her cheeks. "It is not your fault."

Unsure if he believed what he was about to say, he said it anyway. "I know your mother can hear you. She just can't answer."

Salena's lower lip quivered. "If only that were true." She turned again to face her mother.

John heard shouts in the street, and seconds later, squealing tires.

He ran to the window, peeked out, and his stomach knotted. Two blocks away, in the middle of the street, a dozen soldiers surrounded the nurses with pistols drawn. Stripped of their burqas, the two women pointed up at the hospital window, directly at John.

He hurried back to the bed, ready to hoist Salena to her feet, when Hafeeza's head turned on the flimsy pillow. She faced her daughter and opened her eyes. "Salena."

"Umma."

John's jaw dropped. Hafeeza's eyes were a duplicate of her daughters. He strained to listen as they spoke.

"Salena ... you heard my prayers."

"Yes, umma, I am here."

"You found your way ..." Her feeble voice cracked, and she started to wheeze.

"Please, umma, do not speak." Salena leaned closer. "Not a day has gone by I have not thought of you. I wanted so much to see you again."

"And Naji?"

"I have come to see him, too."

"Please take Naji home. You belong together."

"Soon, umma, I promise. Very soon."

"I love you, Salena, and do not fear. Where I am going, I can watch over you both."

"You will always be in my heart, umma."

Hafeeza tightened her grip on Salena's hand, turned her head, and her huge brown eyes stared straight at the ceiling. An audible gush emitted from her mouth and her eyes froze open. Salena threw her arms around her mother and sobbed quietly.

John made a fast sign-of-the-cross, reached down, and gently shut Hafeeza's eyes. "I'm sorry, Salena, but the soldiers are here."

Salena tucked her mother's flaccid wrist under the covers, and tore herself away with a choking cry. "Good bye, umma."

Looking down at Hafeeza, John said, "She must have been a fine woman to raise a daughter like you."

Salena kissed John's cheek, dampening his face with her tears, and whispered, "Thank you. I am ready to go."

John opened the door and saw the hall empty. "We can't go out the way we came. Do you remember another exit?"

"The out-patient annex, but the annex fronts a busy street."

"What about a side door?"

"There is a service entrance in the basement, but we must cross the main lobby to reach it."

John heard the sound of barked orders and storming boots some-where to his left. "Anywhere else? Anywhere at all?"

For several seconds Salena stared straight ahead, then her eyes lit up. "The mosque on the first floor. Beyond the mosque is a garden. Through the garden is a gate to an alley. Along the alley are doors to shops and walkup flats. We can find a place to hide there."

"Show me the way."

Salena moved past John, and started running. John sprinted after her, following her around a series of sharp bends in the hall. She took him down a narrow set of stairs connecting the first and second floors. At the foot of the stairs, Salena stopped short in front of an archway opening into a dark room with a high ceiling. She lifted one foot and turned to John. "Remove your shoes."

"Thanks, but this is no time for a foot massage."

"We are entering the mosque."

John glared. "Salena. Reason with me here. We've got a hundred soldiers hot on our tail who'd like nothing better than to skewer us alive, and you want me to take off my shoes."

"It is disrespectful to enter a mosque with shoes on."

If she weren't so damn sincere—and beautiful—he might have ig-nored her. Instead he reached down and pulled off his Nikes. "Can we flee in desperation now?"

"Yes." She ran through the arched doorway.

John followed, holding tight to his sneakers. The carpeted prayer hall was large, dim, and devoid of people and furniture. He noticed be-neath his feet a red carpet cleverly patterned with repeating rows of large rectangles—built-in prayer mats for worshippers. In a narrow ves-tibule on the opposite side of the prayer hall, Salena stopped and slipped into her shoes.

Shoveling his feet into his own sneakers, John said, "Too bad I've gotta die. I would've liked to learn more about Islam."

"Are you unhappy as a Christian?"

"No, I like my religion, but back in America I had lots of friends who were Jewish and Protestant—I even knew a Buddhist. We each viewed God a little differently, but that didn't stop us from being friends. Look at you and Raja, the first Muslims I ever got to know, and you're two of the nicest people I ever met." He stroked her cheek with one finger. "If knowledge is power, then ignorance is weakness—and I'm no weakling, not anymore."

Salena bit her lip, cupped her hand against his ear, and whispered, "I love you John Covello."

His heart skipped about ten thousand beats. "I hope what I'm about to do isn't disrespectful." He closed his eyes and kissed her, and would've kept kissing her if he didn't hear the shouts of men getting closer. He pulled away. "Let's move."

Salena opened the door and they stepped into a large sunlit garden hemmed in on three sides by the hospital's four-story walls. Covered walkways bordered by brick flowerboxes ran the full length of the walls, and round stucco planters overflowing with yellow roses and pink tulips filled the courtyard. A circular fountain with a clay statue of Lal Ded on a pedestal occupied the middle.

About 25 feet beyond the statue, John saw their ticket out—an iron gate, wide open.

They ran halfway through the garden on a crushed stone path when John heard a click. It sounded like a cocking gun and came from behind the flowerbox on his left. All at once, 20 soldiers on both verandas popped up with big, black rifles pointed at their chests. Another 20 jumped from behind the round planters.

A voice bellowed, "Freeze, or die."

John stopped in his tracks. Salena wrapped her arms around him and screamed, "Make them shoot me."

It took John a full ten seconds to register the chase was over. No miracle escapes, no lucky breaks, but what a run it was. Even as the two rows of guns targeted his chest, he embraced Salena.

She was right. No matter what happened, they were dead, so why not end it here and now. No interrogations, no torture, no rape. End it in the arms of a woman he loved. "Look at me Salena."

Her eyes were wide and filled with fear. "Don't let them take me alive."

He kissed her forehead. "I won't, but first let me thank you. Thank you for opening my heart and my mind." Holding Salena, he faced left and squinted at the line of soldiers aiming their rifles from the porch.

A graying man with a pudgy face wearing a uniform cluttered by ribbons stepped from behind a planter on John's right. "Drop your weapons."

John locked eyes with the Indian officer. "I'm carrying a gun, and one of us is about to die." He whispered into Salena's ear. "I love you," then reached under his shirt and waited for the hail of bullets to rip into his body.

Instead of guns, he heard a woman shout, "John Covello, don't do it!"

His hand froze in his shirt. He knew that voice.

She called out again. "Show me your hands, slowly."

The voice came from the statue. As he extracted his hand from his kameez, an attractive woman with dark brown hair cut in a pixie stepped out from behind the fountain. She was African-American, and wore a green military jumpsuit with stars and stripes stitched on the shoulders.

A cold shiver ran up his arms, across his shoulders, and down his spine.

Major Denise Farrell.

PART IV

"The world has changed. Beating an enemy who carries no flag requires flexible thinking."

—Major Denise Farrell, Deputy Director, CRUSO

John held out both hands so Major Farrell and the 50-plus soldiers surrounding him and Salena could plainly see he held no gun. "Is that you Major Farrell?"

"Yes John."

"What are *you* doing here?"

Farrell stood beside the fountain, and from what John could see, she wasn't armed. The graying Indian Army officer who had ordered him to drop his gun stepped alongside her.

Farrell clasped her hands at her waist, as if praying. "Please John, hand over your weapons." She turned to Salena, who clung to John's right arm. "You too, Dr. Zamal."

A minute ago John would have let Salena hold onto him forever, but for some reason, he felt oddly shy in front of Farrell. Still unsure his eyes weren't playing tricks, he barely heard himself say, "We don't have any."

The Indian officer took one step forward, coming to within a yard of John. "Then you won't mind if my men search you." He nodded to five soldiers standing nearby. Two lowered their rifles and strode toward John and Salena.

The first soldier to reach them grasped Salena's shoulder, and started pulling. She firmed her grip on John's arm, and shrieked, "Don't touch me!"

The second soldier came up on John's left and gripped his wounded arm. Razor pain shot through his bicep. He yanked his right arm free of Salena's hold and slammed his fist into the soldier's nostrils. The stunned soldier staggered backward, holding his face.

What little control John had, he lost. He pivoted and grabbed the ears of the soldier pulling on Salena, and throttled the young man's head. The soldier let go of Salena, and started punching at John.

Salena screamed, "Stop! He is sick!"

When the soldier kept punching, she unleashed a fierce kick to the man's groin. He grabbed his crotch, doubled over, and fell to his knees, moaning.

Three other soldiers rushed forward. Before John could see if Salena had been hurt, another set of fingers tugged on his shoulders. John balled his hand, cocked his fist, and wheeled. He stopped his arm mid-swing when he saw the target was Major Farrell.

"John! Please. Calm down." Farrell scowled at the Indian officer. "Make your men stop."

The graying soldier licked his lips, clearly unhappy to give the order. He spat out his words. "Stand down!"

The three soldiers who had joined the fracas backed away.

Farrell said to John, "Is it OK if I search Dr. Zamal myself?"

John was breathing hard and fast, and had trouble getting his words out. He looked at Salena, who nodded her assent, and John, in turn, nodded to Farrell.

With 40 muzzles aimed at their chests from under the covered verandas, John allowed the Indian officer to pat him down while Farrell frisked Salena.

Farrell was done first, and said, "She's clean."

The Indian officer said, "So is he."

Farrell addressed John. "Please allow me to introduce General Naresh Prasad. He commands India's elite regiment, the Jammu & Kashmir Rifles."

General Prasad extended his hand.

John shunned the gesture and puckered his lips with disdain. "Are you the same savages who rape Kashmiri girls and butcher innocent schoolboys?"

Farrell huffed angrily. "Things haven't changed, have they John?"

"A lot has changed."

"Not your mouth."

"I call it like I see it."

"Maybe you haven't seen everything."

"You can't imagine what I've seen."

Prasad retracted his hand. "Never mind, major." He threw Salena a hard look. "I might feel the same if I had heard only one side."

"I've heard enough to know too many good people die in this valley." John reached for Salena's hand and gently pulled her to his side. "I swear, general, if you harm one hair on this girl's head, I'll come back from my grave and haunt you as long as you live."

Farrell eyed John quizzically, glanced at Salena, then looked back at John. "I see you two have become well acquainted."

"You could say that."

Farrell approached Salena and shook her hand. "I regret our second meeting could not have occurred under more pleasant circumstances."

"As do I."

John remembered Farrell had met Salena in February at a convention in New York City. He also remembered Farrell hadn't answered his question. "So why'd you come?"

"General Prasad has put a hospital room at our disposal. Once we're inside, I'll explain." Farrell took two steps toward the nearest veranda. "This way please."

John clasped Salena's hand, and started following.

Farrell turned. "Only you, John."

Salena latched herself to John's arm.

"If she doesn't go, I don't go."

"What I have to say is private."

"I have nothing to hide from Salena, and after what she's done for America, neither should you."

Farrell studied him, as if struggling to understand his motive. "If you insist."

"I insist."

"Very well. Come along Dr. Zamal."

Farrell led them past the round concrete planters to an inside corner of the courtyard. They climbed two steps into the shade of a covered veranda, walked past the backs of the soldiers, who had lowered their rifles, and stopped at a wooden door facing the garden.

John followed Farrell into a rectangular room about the size of Maureen's walk-in closet. Two wood chairs and a round table filled half the space. The major offered Salena one chair, John the other, and both politely refused.

Farrell shut the door and turned to John. "May I speak honestly?"

"As opposed to bullshitting?" He winked at Salena. "I mean lying."

The major wasn't smiling. "You're not funny, John. I can't believe you would've let those soldiers kill you. You have no idea what I've gone through to keep you alive."

John moved closer to Salena, this time fighting off his impulse to hold her hand. "We've done a pretty good job keeping ourselves alive."

"No, John, you're not in a body bag because of me. Those Indian soldiers in the helicopter near Wular Lake could've as easily shot you as chased you through the forest. Same when you hijacked that bus in Srinagar. And when you pulled your little stunt here in the hospital, masquerading two locals as yourselves, if I hadn't insisted otherwise, you'd be dead."

That confirmed what Omar Shah had told them on the houseboat. The soldiers who'd been chasing them were trying to capture, not kill them. But why? "I'll bet you're worried we won't get back to Pakistan in time for Glorious Dawn, and now you're here to give us a lift. How'd you know where to find us?"

"India's Intelligence Bureau learned Dr. Zamal's mother was a patient at Lal Ded Hospital. They knew if Dr. Zamal were going to Srinagar, she'd attempt a visit, and when she did, you'd probably go with her."

"Not bad. I sure hope you brought what's left of the RDX-7S, because—"

"Please, if you'd let me—"

"Speaking of which, I gotta tell you. Patty Krause was one brave lady sacrificing her life to keep your precious secret."

"Her bravery was exemplary, but—"

"Now you're here to deliver what she couldn't. Don't worry, major, I'll finish what I started. Just give me those charges, and get me back to Islamabad."

"That's not why I'm—"

"If you're thinking I've changed my mind, don't. In fact, more than ever—"

Farrell screamed at the top of her lungs, "Dammit John! Will you shut your trap and let me finish?"

John raised his eyebrows, startled by the major's outburst. "Sorry." The disturbing notion occurred to him that CRUSO had aborted his mission. "What's the problem?"

Farrell took a deep breath and exhaled slowly, her brown, oval eyes holding him in their grip. "The problem is you should never have been chosen as a mission candidate."

"Why? I'm damn good at what I do."

"I agree."

"I screwed up once, and for two years I've paid the price. But you should've seen me in the Citadel. Once I got going, it was like old times. Sure, the conditions weren't optimal, but give me that hi-powered RDX, and tomorrow I'll guarantee you one hell of an implosion."

"You are pretty amazing, which makes pulling you off this mission the hardest decision of my career."

He had to finish his work, if not for Maureen and his daughters, then for Salena and her dream of a free Kashmir. "I can do this, I know I can."

Farrell shook her head. "You don't understand. You shouldn't be here because you don't have pancreatic cancer. Cancer's not going to kill you—not in the foreseeable future."

He probably hadn't heard right. "What kind of cancer *do* I have?"

"You don't. You're not dying at all."

John's legs started to wobble. He grabbed the back of the nearest chair. "The pains, what about the stomach pains?"

"Duodenal ulcer. Severe case, according to CRUSO's staff physician."

"But Dr. Chandler. He showed me the results, the X-ray. You're mistaken. It's pancreatic cancer. I saw it."

"Turns out Dr. Chandler was a desperate man in serious financial trouble. He switched your test results with those of another patient who tested positive for pancreatic cancer. He did it for CRUSO's referral fee. Now he's dead, presumably murdered by those he owed."

This couldn't be happening. "He set me up?"

"Exactly."

"You didn't find out until after I was gone?"

"Unfortunately, no."

"I only have an ulcer?"

"A bleeding ulcer, and it should be treated immediately. You're at risk for peritonitis. In fact, we'll start you on H-2 blockers as soon as I fly you out of India."

John's arms and legs went numb. He stumbled onto the chair, lowered his head, and stared at the wooden tabletop. Too many questions swirled in his head. What about Khan's Citadel? What about stopping nuclear war? And Maureen. Did she know he was alive? What would become of Salena?

Salena! John's head shot up and his eyes darted around the room. They found Salena standing in a dim corner, gazing at the floor.

He was supposed to spend his last day on earth with this incredible woman. Together, they would prevent a calamity like the world had never seen. John took a deep breath, rose, and walked to Salena, stopping less than a foot away.

She kept her eyes down.

In such a small room, Farrell would hear even if he spoke softly, but he whispered anyway. "Please, Salena. Don't ignore me."

"What is there to say? I am happy for you."

He knew she wasn't, not really. "You don't have to go back to Khan."

Salena lifted her chin and challenged him with those large, shimmering eyes. "Have you done nothing but ignore me? If I do not return, many will suffer."

John stood before this woman admiring her as never before. She possessed the compassion to take in homeless children in the face of Khan's disapproval, the devotion to cross mile-high mountains to visit a dying mother, and the sensitivity to make him feel like a man when his manhood was all but lost. At the same time she had courage, tenacity, and strength. In all those ways, she reminded him of Maureen. Yet she had something more—the experience of having grown up in a land ravaged by war, rape, and death, of having lived most of her life in fear, if not of an occupying army, then of barbaric religious extremists.

Beyond the loss of Maureen's $10,000,000 had he done CRUSO's bidding, John appreciated the dire consequences of his mission's premature end. The obvious result was a nuclear holocaust in which millions would perish. But just as important, at least to John, if Salena survived the war she would be forced to marry Khan and live the rest of her days as his slave. And his friend, Raja, if the bombs didn't kill him, would likely end up dead at the hands of Qadeer.

Going home was the easy choice. Uncle Sam might even pay him for his troubles—give him enough to clear his debt, and throw in a little extra to keep him quiet.

John turned and looked straight into Farrell's eyes. "Have you lined up another demo man?"

"On such short notice? Impossible."

"So that's it. I take my ball and go home. End of game." John scratched his head above his ear. "Doesn't anyone care?"

"Yes, about 25 million Indian civilians fleeing their homes this very minute, along with the leaders of every civilized society on earth. Yes, John, I'd say a whole lot of people care."

"Where's the rest of the RDX-7S charges?"

Farrell's eyes narrowed, and she cocked her head. "On an aircraft carrier in the Arabian Sea. Why?"

John glanced at Salena, who was now watching him closely. He turned again to Farrell. "Does Maureen know I'm coming home?"

"We thought it best to wait until we were sure you'd be captured alive."

"Don't tell her. Not yet."

"I don't understand."

"I'm not going home—not today."

Farrell's eyes grew large. She stepped around the table and walked toward him. "What are you saying?"

"You already know."

"But why?"

"Major, I don't have a death wish. In fact, now that I'm healthy, putting my life on the line comes with a few more strings attached."

Farrell stopped short and regarded him with a wry smile. She was surprised, but apparently not shocked. "OK, John, assuming we get authorization to proceed, what are your terms?"

CHAPTER SEVENTY-EIGHT

Before John laid out his conditions for returning to Islamabad, he was curious why anyone might object to his finishing off General Khan. "Whose authorization do you need?"

Farrell's smile disappeared. "For starters, President Lloyd."

"Why? What's changed? Khan's still meeting with his generals tomorrow."

"Yes, but frankly, John, CRUSO never contemplated a scenario where one of its candidates finished an operation and returned home breathing. That's not the way—"

Farrell was interrupted by three hard knocks on the door, and before she could answer, the door swung open. Filling the threshold shadowed by the cloister was General Prasad.

Farrell said politely, "We haven't finished."

Prasad eyed John warily, then glanced at Salena, who stood in the far corner. "I am checking to make sure your operative did not perform another vanishing act."

"That's the problem," Farrell said. "He's not going anywhere."

John stepped toward the door. "Come in, general. Your government has a lot more riding on what I'm about to say than mine."

The general's eyes narrowed to puzzled slits.

"I suppose he's right," Farrell said, "you might as well join us. I have a feeling you'll find this quite interesting."

The general closed the door and stood beside the table. "What, exactly, will I find interesting?"

"It appears I flew halfway around the world to take John home, and now he wants to stay."

"Stay? But why?"

"For a reason I expect we're about to hear, John wants to complete his mission."

Prasad grinned. "I hear your government pays handsome sums to the families of its suicide operatives. Perhaps Mr. Covello wishes to spend his fortune while he is alive to enjoy it."

Farrell stared at the floor for a moment, weighing the general's statement, then looked at John. "If you're staying for the money, no need to risk your life. President Lloyd has agreed to a compensatory settlement of $5,000,000. Return to the States with me, swear your silence about CRUSO, and the money is yours."

"You don't get it, neither one of you. It's not only about money."

Farrell moved around the table and stood beside Prasad. "What else *is* it about?"

"If Khan lives, India and Pakistan go to war, right?"

Farrell nodded.

"But this time we know for a fact the nukes are gonna fly. Whether they go off here or in Times Square, atom bombs don't bode well for my kids' futures." He glanced at Salena, who was watching him intensely, then turned to Farrell and Prasad. "On my way to Srinagar, I saw horrors I'm gonna have nightmares about the rest of my life. In Salena's homeland, people are hurting—squeezed by India, squeezed by religious lunatics, and now squeezed by Khan. The plight of Kashmir has to end. It has to end here. It has to end now."

Prasad snickered. "Learned diplomats with lifetimes of experience have tried solving the Kashmir problem. Wars have been fought and men have died over the region. What makes you think a neophyte like you can make any difference?"

"Because, general, at this moment, a neophyte like me is the only person alive who can stop Khan from bombing your country back to the Stone Age."

"What exactly do you hope to accomplish?"

"I'll make sure your country isn't leveled, and I'll keep America from getting sucked into a war nobody wins." John walked to Salena's side, and this time he didn't care who saw. He held her hand. "But most of all, I'll keep my promise to this incredible woman who taught me more about freedom in four days than I've learned in 40 years."

Farrell drew a deep breath. "I know what I'm hearing, and I can't believe it. You can walk out of here with $5,000,000, be back in New Jersey before dark, but you're willing to return to Islamabad and implode Khan's Citadel."

Prasad's lips arced into a broad grin. "I believe that is exactly what John is saying."

John's words bit like vinegar. "To you, general, it's Mr. Covello."

Prasad's smile disappeared.

"You'd better get serious, because I'm not finished. I'll raze the Citadel and bury Khan's war dogs, but I have a few conditions, and only one of them is money."

Farrell said, "We're listening."

"First, I get to live—which means you give me remote detonators for the dynamite I've already planted. Same for the RDX-7S charges.

Second, my fee doubles. Uncle Sam put me through hell these past four days, and twenty million ought to smooth things out nicely. For sure it'll make me forget all about CRUSO."

"Anything else?"

John lifted Salena's hand, woven in his. "Her share also doubles—to five million. If it weren't for this lady, I'd never have gotten inside the Citadel to begin with. And unlike me, she has noble plans for the money. I figure the more she gets, the more good she can do."

"I'll pass your wish list along to the president, but your conditions seem reasonable to me."

"Oh, no. You're not getting off that easy. I'm just warming up."

"What else?"

"From America, nothing." John turned to Salena, whose eyes met his. "This one's for you, kid." He scrutinized General Prasad. "Get ready to make an important decision."

"I'm listening."

"The way I see it, if Ali Khan is alive tomorrow night, nuclear war is a done deal. Khan launches his missiles, you launch yours, and whoever isn't dead in the first five seconds will probably wish they were."

"That about sums it up."

"I heard all about the total destruction one teensy weensy atom bomb did to six square kilometers of Baramulla. Imagine what a dozen carefully targeted, bigger bombs would do to cities like Delhi, Calcutta, and Bombay."

Prasad's dark brown eyes glinted off the single light bulb dangling from the center of the room's ceiling. "The results would not be pleasant."

"So I take it you'd rather not lose seven cities and 20 million people in a storm of fire and brimstone."

"I'm sure the prime minister would not mind adding more money to what your government is already paying."

"Damn you, I said it's about more than money." John looked into Salena's eyes. "This woman believes my mission will somehow bring freedom to Kashmir. And you know what, general? I hope seven cities and 20 million Indian citizens are worth giving my lady a shot at making her dream come true."

Prasad stared at John, stone-faced. "What do you want from my government?"

"Only this: India withdraws every last soldier from Jammu & Kashmir, including its lovely Border Security Force, and since nobody wants terrorists filling the void, a multi-national peacekeeping force goes in and roots out as many militants as possible. After that, separate elections are held in the Kashmir Valley, Jammu, and …" John whispered to Salena, "What's that other part of Kashmir you told me about?"

"Ladakh," she said softly.

"Yeah, that place, too. The elections in each district will be fair and impartial, and monitored by UN observers. Since India's had a hard-on for Pakistan since both countries were created, it's probably a pipe dream to think India would allow Kashmir to become part of Pakistan. So the Kashmiri people get two choices—stay with India or become independent. From what Salena tells me, Jammu would probably vote to stay with India. So would Ladakh." John gripped Salena's hand tighter, afraid if he didn't she might let go. "But I have a feeling the Valley would choose independence. I could be totally wrong, maybe it'd stay with India. The point is the Kashmiri people were never given the chance to decide—a chance they should've had back in 1947."

Prasad stood silently, looking as inclined to laugh out loud as suggest John go to hell. Finally, he said in an even tone, "What about Pakistan-occupied Kashmir?"

Farrell interjected, "I think the general means Azad Kashmir."

"No," Prasad snapped, "I mean the puppet regime in Muzaffarabad whose strings are pulled by Islamabad."

John scratched his head. "Ladies and gentlemen, we don't have time to argue semantics. The general's right. What's good for the goose is good for the gander. The former president of Pakistan … the one Ali Khan kicked out …"

Salena whispered the name in his ear.

"Yeah, Labib Razzak. Before Khan gave him the boot, I understand he and the prime minister were holding talks over Kashmir's future. But that's where it stopped. Talks and more talks. Years and years of bullshit. So here's the deal. If I pull this off, and Razzak gets a second shot at playing Pakistan's president, the people of Azad Kashmir and all the other areas of Kashmir under Pakistan's control get the same choice as the people in the part of Kashmir occupied by India. Vote to join Pakistan, or become free states. But first, the Pakistan Army leaves and the UN troops go in to hunt and kill as many terrorists as they can find. Maybe Azad Kashmir decides to stay with Pakistan, maybe it doesn't, but at least the people get a choice. If they do choose freedom, who knows, maybe Azad Kashmir and the Kashmir Valley become one again."

Farrell chuckled, then quickly covered her mouth. "I'm sorry. I'm just amazed."

"At what?"

"You've gotten quite an education."

John released Salena's hand. Mesmerized by her beauty, inside and out, he reached out to stroke her hair. She pulled back, which was probably what he deserved, but he couldn't stop looking at her. "I had the best teacher in the world."

Farrell coughed to get his attention.

John reluctantly turned away and looked at the major.

"Do you truly believe you can finish this mission?"

John uttered his words with the force of steel. "Get me to the Citadel in time, and I'll give you a pile of rubble—with Khan and his cronies at the bottom."

CHAPTER SEVENTY-NINE

General Prasad stood beside Major Farrell, shaking his head, eying John skeptically. "For good reason my men believe you are insane."

Before the Chicago accident, John's friends had referred to him as unique and interesting, but never crazy. "Who says I'm nuts?"

"The soldiers of my regiment who chased you across the Vale. But their reasons are not mine. If you believe Prime Minister Behari will even consider your demand for a plebiscite allowing Kashmiris to choose independence, you are truly demented."

Farrell stepped away from Prasad, frowning. "Don't be so quick to dismiss the idea." She walked halfway around the circular table, putting equal distance between John and Salena on her right, and General Prasad to her left. "Hanging in the balance are the lives of 30 million people, maybe more, depending on prevailing winds. Not counting the millions killed instantly by the blast, DIA models suggest as many as 25 million people in India and Pakistan will suffer radiation doses of 600 rem or more, with another 10 million exposed to levels between 100 and 600 rem. And that model assumes half the nuclear warheads of both countries are destroyed before they ever leave the ground."

John had anticipated resistance from Prasad, but Major Farrell's support came as a welcome surprise. He let her continue, remembering how much he had trusted her when they'd met at Lakehurst Naval Station.

"Put the situation in perspective, general. True, India's 120 nuclear warheads far outnumber the 75 we estimate Khan has the ability to launch from missile and fighter jet platforms. True, the destructive capacity of India's arsenal is twice that of Pakistan's, and yes, India may ultimately prove the superior nuclear power. But tell me general, are the deaths of 30 million human beings—most of them Indian citizens—worth keeping a territory whose people don't want you there in the first place?"

"You are forgetting the Shimla Pact. India and Pakistan are bound to resolve their differences by peaceful means through bilateral negotiations. No outside intervention is necessary. If Mr. Covello achieves his objective, and Labib Razzak is restored to power, the two nations may continue their peaceful discourse over Kashmir's future."

"Cut the crap, general. You and I both know the Shimla Agreement is a diplomatic dinosaur. According to its own terms, both countries agreed to promote a friendly and harmonious relationship and establish a durable peace so each could devote its resources to the task of advancing the welfare of its people. The sad reality, at least for the people of Kashmir, has been war, begetting terrorism, begetting military repression, begetting more terrorism. Kashmir's wheel of destruction will spin forever unless the cycle is broken now. John recognizes that truth, and frankly, I admire him for making a plebiscite one of his conditions."

Prasad stood silently for a moment, gazing at the table. He rubbed his eyes, and sighed. "Policy decisions are not mine to make. I am only a soldier."

Farrell nodded. "As am I, and as soldiers we know the insanity of war."

"I will contact the prime minister to discuss what has transpired." The general added, almost as an afterthought, "I will recommend he give careful consideration to Mr. Covello's offer."

"I will call President Lloyd and suggest the same."

Prasad lumbered to the door, and pausing with one hand on the doorknob, glanced back at Farrell. "You know, the prime minister will view Mr. Covello's conditions as blackmail."

Farrell locked eyes with the general. "Suggest to the prime minister he view John's offer not as a threat, but as an opportunity. If he allows free elections to finally resolve the Kashmir dilemma, history will regard him as a great statesman. If he refuses to budge, and 30 million perish in a nuclear war, I wonder how history will perceive him then."

General Prasad left the room shaking his head.

After the door clicked shut, and the three were alone again, Farrell asked John, "If we get you back to Islamabad, how will you finish the job?"

"My plan is to integrate the dynamite I previously wired with the RDX-7S charges. I could also use 16 delay connectors—semiconductor bridges if they're available—and for the dynamite and RDX systems, a composite wireless electronic detonator, minimum range 200 feet, and a time chart for the detonators."

"None of that should be a problem."

"As for the bullet in my arm ..."

"What?"

"I forgot to mention, when we were in the mountains, a few stray terrorists roughed us up. One of them shot me. I think he had a problem with my attitude."

"You don't say."

John waved his finger at Farrell. "It's not what you think. I didn't mouth off. We were just trying to protect ourselves."

"I'll ask the general to have one of his medics examine you."

"I'm fine." John smiled at Salena, who didn't smile back. "I had my personal physician with me."

"Won't the injury interfere with your mobility?"

"As a matter of fact, a bullet hole backs up the story I plan on feeding Khan. Salena and I were ambushed by bandits on the road to Peshawar. If Omar did what Salena asked—"

"Whoa. You're not referring to the same Omar whose cousin called CRUSO and said you two were married?"

John winked at Salena, hoping to elicit a smile. Instead, she wiped her hair from her face and turned away. "That's a story for another day. But if Omar did what he was supposed to, Khan's security people got a call from our kidnappers demanding a hefty ransom for the return of Dr. Zamal, John Cattano, and two Pakistani Army officers. If you deliver me to the outskirts of Islamabad tonight, I'll call the Citadel to say I escaped from the kidnappers and hiked east through the Margalla Hills. Khan will be so worried about searching for Salena, he won't have time to—"

"Wait just a minute." The voice was Salena's, and her bold eyes pierced him. "Khan will have no reason to search for me because I am going with you."

"Forget it. Qadeer already suspects you're up to something. He'll hound you the second you walk into the Citadel."

"There is no choice. We must return together."

"I know, you're worried about Raja and the kids in the Freedom Ward. But tomorrow night, after Khan and his stooges are history, you can return to Islamabad free of fear."

"You are not thinking. Qadeer is as suspicious of you as he is of me. When you return to the Citadel, he will keep you under constant surveillance. You will have no opportunity to sneak back to the 3rd floor. If I go with you, I can distract Qadeer."

"I've seen that mutant look at you, and I don't trust him."

Farrell said softly, "I think the doctor makes a good point. She can deflect his attention while you position the charges."

Salena's eyes implored him. "You know you need me."

Reluctantly, very reluctantly, John had to admit Salena was right. He'd like nothing more than to keep her far from the Citadel, but in truth, he couldn't have planted the dynamite in the first place had she not kept Qadeer off his tail.

John cupped Salena's chin with his hand. She swallowed hard and their eyes met. "You can come. But promise me you won't let that sick son-of-a-bitch anywhere near you."

Her eyes got watery and she nodded.

"I swear, if he hurts you, I'll shove a stick of dynamite so far up his ass he'll vomit nitroglycerin, and then I'll blow his sorry butt straight to hell."

A tear slipped down Salena's cheek. "Please do not … do not say hell." She pulled away and dropped her eyelashes quickly, as if to hide her heart.

Longing to keep her in his life forever, and saddened by the distance she was putting between them, he remembered something Salena said she must do when they came to Srinagar. He addressed Farrell. "I have another request. Nothing earth-shattering, but it's mighty important to this lady here."

Farrell's voice was soft, and her tone subdued. "What is it, John?"

"While you and Prasad call your bosses, Salena and I have someone to visit."

"May I ask who?"

"A little boy. He's in an orphanage not far from here, and this time, I don't want helicopters, tanks, or jeeps chasing us. In fact, an armed escort would be nice."

"I can make that happen. Who's the boy?"

"I don't know, and it doesn't matter. If he's important to Salena, he's important to me."

CHAPTER EIGHTY

During the three minute ride in an open jeep to the orphanage near Hazuri Bagh, Salena sat against the door, as far from John as possible, and stared out her window as if she were a million miles away. Before leaving Lal Ded Hospital, she told him their destination was a home for orphans, many of whom suffered physical deformities. She also said the orphanage was funded by private donations and was managed by a Kashmiri-based foundation called HELP—Human Effort for Love and Peace—and that was the last she had spoken to him.

The jeep, driven by an officer of the Jammu & Kashmir Rifles, pulled up to a two-story, brick building at the end of a long block lined with rundown shops peddling wares from copper pots to wicker cricket sticks. From the outside, the orphanage appeared in dire need of help. Half the façade's bricks had fallen away, exposing large mortar cavities, and the glass was gone from two large picture windows where someone had taped clear plastic to keep out the elements.

Salena climbed from the jeep and stood next to the vehicle with her back to John.

John stared at her veiled head, and didn't budge from his seat.

She turned around. "What are you waiting for?"

John was anxious, but he wasn't sure why. He wasn't surprised Salena had insisted on visiting a homeless boy. Everything he'd learned about this beautiful Kashmiri woman told him she was warm, kind, and caring, especially when it came to kids. The knot in his gut came from somewhere else. "You ever gonna be nice to me again?"

Her perplexed expression looked pretty convincing. "Whatever do you mean?"

John slid across the jeep's rear seat, folded his arms across the top of the door, and looked up at her. "Save the bullshit for someone else. From the second you found out I wasn't dying, you've treated me like a complete stranger, not like a man who cares the world for you."

The phony confusion vanished from her face. "Do not make me sick. You know the truth, and the truth is killing me. How foolish I feel looking at you, talking to you, just being with you, but my heart gives me no choice. I only pray Allah will someday heal my pain."

"I'm sorry, Salena, but it's not like I expected this."

Tears brimmed in her large, brown eyes. "Do you know what hurts more than anything?"

John shook his head, reluctant to answer.

"Your heart is not torn apart like mine."

No matter what he said to convince her she was wrong, he'd come off sounding like a selfish oaf, but he had to try. "You can't imagine how much I care for you—how meeting you, loving you, has changed my life forever."

He detected a slight thaw in her eyes. "We can discuss this until the Day of Resurrection and nothing will change. I am going inside." She spun and marched toward the building.

John jumped from the jeep and ran to catch up with her, more confused than ever how to reconcile his feelings for Salena and Maureen.

They entered the building through a windowless door. Standing beside Salena in a narrow foyer, John's senses were immediately assaulted by the stench of urine and the wailing of babies. A frail, gray-haired man who walked with a stoop appeared from a door on the right. He had a wrinkled face, the color of cocoa, and his dark brown eyes had seen more than a little pain. John was surprised when Salena greeted the elderly man with a hug and a smile. "Hello Rukan."

His voice was a contradiction—rough like gravel, but soft as a whisper. "Salena, what a pleasant surprise."

"I have business in Srinagar and can only stay a short time, but I shall return in two days, perhaps permanently."

"That will bring great joy to Naji."

"And to me as well." She introduced John as a good friend.

John shook a frail hand that packed a firm grip.

Rukan turned to Salena. "Can you spare a few minutes with the children?"

"Of course." She grabbed a yellow smock hanging from a wooden peg, and handed it to John. "Put this on."

The yellow fabric was so thin in spots, John could've poked his finger through. "What do I need this for?"

"Have I yet given you bad advice?"

He pulled the smock over his head, and knotted two frayed strings at his waist. While Rukan stood in the foyer talking to the Indian officer who'd driven them to the orphanage, John followed Salena into a room at the end of a narrow hall.

In a rectangular space little larger than a budget motel room, John beheld five rows of rickety cribs, many with legs held on by duct tape. Babies with twisted bodies and open sores lay in the cribs, while on the floor, small children played with lumber scraps and cardboard boxes that passed for toys. Every little body was clothed in tattered hand-me-downs, and every tiny foot was coated with dirt.

John turned, ready to bolt, when something pulled on his shalwar cuff. He looked down at a baby boy grasping his leg, bawling at the top of his lungs. A little girl with no hair hobbled over and wrapped herself around John's other leg. He picked up the boy, who rested his head on John's shoulder and became suddenly quiet.

Fighting his impulse to run, John forced himself to look into the gaunt faces of the discarded young, and when he did so, struggled to hold down his bile—a boy with one leg and no arms, a two year old girl with no eyes, and too many with purple scabs marring their malnourished limbs.

Salena started walking between the first two rows of cribs.

John gently pried the little girl from his leg and followed. Nearly every little head was shaved, and when John asked why, Salena told him shaving their heads was necessary to stop the spread of lice and other blood-sucking parasites. Many babies obviously hadn't had a diaper change in days, and several wallowed in their own excrement.

Toddlers healthy enough to stand wobbled toward Salena with their arms extended. Salena paused at every crib, lifted every tiny occupant, and held each child a full minute before setting him or her down, then moving onto the next. It dawned on John these kids craved the touch of a warm body. John lowered the boy in his arms, and followed Salena's lead, picking up as many babies as he could. He rocked some, held others, and each time he lifted a crying child, the crying stopped at once.

He helped Salena change the diaper of every infant in the room, and all the while, he thought of Karen and Christie, healthy and safe in Brielle.

John followed Salena to a row of bassinettes lined up against the wall. In the hooded cradles lay babies tinier than any of the others. One boy who Salena said was seven months old, but looked like a preemie, lay still with his eyes squeezed shut and mouth wide open. John clenched his fists and bit back tears when he realized he was looking at a baby so weak his cry made no sound.

Salena touched the baby's forehead. "He is burning with fever."

John noticed the boy's arms and legs were covered with insect bites. "Why don't they give him antibiotics?"

Salnea frowned. "You did not listen. Hospitals, orphanages, all are low on medicine. The best he can hope for is an ice bath."

John remembered what Salena had told him on the shikara less than two hours earlier, and felt foolish for having asked.

She walked to a corner of the room where a ring of dirty pillows lay scattered on the floor. Salena sat on one pillow, and instantly, three toddlers scrambled toward her. A little girl with stumps for legs dragged herself along the floor and clawed her way into Salena's lap, pushing herself between two tiny babies Salena cradled in her arms.

John looked around the room. Some children cried inconsolably, others rocked in eerie silence, and a few banged their heads against the bars of their cribs. All begged for attention, and never, ever before— not even on the morning of the Chicago implosion—did John feel more utterly helpless than he did at that moment.

Salena chatted awhile with the legless girl, then rose and said fare- well. Leading John to a door near the bassinets, Salena stepped into an unlit corridor. Walking single file through the hall, they passed two open doors. A room on the left served as a storage closet, but John saw nothing on its three rows of shelves but a single sack of rice. Peeking into an open door on the right, John observed grimy tiles and inhaled the pungent odor of stale urine.

At the end of the hall they came to a windowless room three times the size of the nursery. Low, round tables, each with two or three chairs tucked under, took up most of the space. On the scratched tabletops lay worn textbooks, and remnants of pencils and crayons. Children slightly older than those in the nursery sat in half the chairs, though some of the bigger children held toddlers on their laps, helping them draw on sun- yellowed scrap paper.

Salena explained they had entered the classroom. Trained teachers were in short supply, so the handful of older children who could read and write often taught the younger boys and girls.

A veiled girl of 11 or 12 who'd been reading alone on the floor looked up and called out, "Miss Salena, Miss Salena." Instantly, John found himself engulfed in a sea of young people.

Salena hugged the children one at a time, and as John watched, a little boy about seven or eight grabbed his hand. "Who are you?"

After Salena introduced him as "Mr. John from America," the children peppered him with questions about life in the United States. What kind of car did he drive? Did he play baseball? Who was his favorite movie star? Did he live in a mansion or a sky- scraper?

A teenage boy with jet black hair standing on the fringe of the circle asked John, "Does anybody in America care about Kashmir?"

John rubbed his chin, not sure what to say. Thankfully, Salena answered for him. "For too many years America has forgotten the people of Kashmir, but that is about to change. Mr. John has come to give Kashmiris a chance for freedom."

She failed to mention his success hinged on pulling off an almost impossible feat, but caught up in Salena's enthusiasm, John added, "I'll do everything in my power to restore peace to your beautiful land ..." He smiled at Salena, "... and to your beautiful people. The terrorists and the soldiers had their chance, and failed. The children of Kashmir have suffered long enough. You all deserve a better life, and we intend to make that happen."

A cheer went up from the children, and John's heart raced as he read hope in their eyes. How could he let them down? Almost any risk was worth keeping the promise he'd made to Salena, and now, to these innocent victims of violence.

After a few more minutes chatting with the boys and girls, Salena broke away from the crowd, walked to another door, and motioned for John to follow.

John said good-bye to the children, and met Salena at the door. "These kids need new books, new pencils and pens, maybe a couple of blackboards." He glanced at a young girl cradling the bristle-end of a broomstick. On the tattered straw end she had drawn a smiley face in black marker, and it occurred to John she was holding the broom like a doll. "And they definitely need new toys."

"Since the war for freedom began, the number of Kashmiri orphans has tripled. Every Indian rupee spent in Kashmir goes to fighting insurgents—none to the children."

Trailing Salena down a short hall, John said, "General Prasad doesn't know it yet, but he's about to make a generous donation."

John followed Salena into the next room. Here he saw only five children, all boys, and each seemed to live in his own world. A teenager sat cross-legged on the vinyl tile floor holding a workbook on his lap. Its cover was torn off, and the book looked to John like a math primer. The young man stared down at the first page, his dark eyes as wide as quarters and his body perfectly still, as if gazing long enough at the words and numbers might actually give them meaning.

This space was brighter than the other rooms John had seen so far, lit up by the sun's rays beaming through small windows set high in the opposite wall. On a large oval rug in the far corner sat a scrawny boy of five or six wearing navy blue shorts and a white T-shirt. He gazed at an old TV whose color image had long ago faded. On the washed out tube a jolly gray dinosaur began singing a happy alphabet song, and the boy, whose right leg was missing, clapped along.

Salena asked John to wait at the room's entrance.

She walked to the one-legged boy and knelt on the rug behind him. The boy turned, and recognition flashed in his enormous brown eyes. "Miss Salena." He threw his arms around her neck.

Salena sat beside the boy and held him tightly. "I missed you so much, Naji."

The boy gripped Salena as if he would never let her go. "I missed you too."

John didn't intend to stare, but the force of their chemistry was too strong to resist.

Salena pulled away. "I love you."

Naji replied, "I love you too."

John was struck by the similarities—the shapes of their eyes, the lines of their cheeks—and all at once, he knew. He should have known all along. No wonder visiting Naji had been so important, and suddenly John felt stupid and humbled.

He wondered if the resemblance was as obvious to everyone else as it was to him. Salena didn't seem to care. These last five years, how much pain had she endured, forced by war, terror, and shame to live apart from her son? Standing alone, watching them play, John was vaguely aware of tears dripping down his face.

Salena waved John over, and he could see she'd been crying, too.

Not at all sure he could handle this, he dabbed his face with the sleeve of his kameez and went over to where they sat.

Salena touched Naji's shoulder. "I'd like you to meet Mr. John."

Naji's face turned stone serious, and he thrust out his hand like a little man.

John reached down and grasped it. "Pleased to meet you, Naji."

Naji's eyes lit up. "You are American."

"Yes I am."

"Someday I will visit America."

"When you come, I will show you New York City."

Naji turned toward Salena with yearning eyes. "Can we go there soon?"

Salena's fingers swept her son's brown hair along the sides of his head. "Soon. I promise. Very soon."

Wondering how many promises had been made to this boy and never kept, John was sure of one thing—his wouldn't be one of them. "Do you know the Statue of Liberty?"

"The big lady who stands for freedom."

"Would you like to visit her?"

Naji's eyes grew wide with wonder, and he nodded.

"When you come to America, we will go on a boat ride, and I will take you up to her crown where you can see all of New York."

Naji pulled hard on John's hand. He got the message and sat on the rug beside mother and son, and for half an hour the three talked and played and laughed.

At one point, Naji pulled five marbles from his pocket and held them out to John in his cupped hand. He proudly explained in meticulous detail how he had acquired each of his prized possessions, pointing to one in particular—clear and smooth with a dark blue center—which he'd won from a boy twice his age.

When John promised to send Naji a pail full of marbles, the boy's eager eyes grew bigger still, as if he couldn't imagine owning so many marbles at once.

John glanced at Salena and noticed her staring at him. Just as their eyes locked, a harsh voice from behind broke the magic. "Mr. Covello, Dr. Zamal. Time to leave."

John snapped his head toward the door. Their Indian driver stood in the threshold.

"A decision has been made. General Prasad has instructed me to take both of you to the Badami Bagh cantonment where you will be informed of the outcome."

Naji buried his head in Salena's chest, and hugged her fiercely.

Salena stroked her son's head. "Please do not be afraid. I will be back for you soon."

CHAPTER EIGHTY-ONE

Taxiing on a runway at Badami Bagh cantonment in Srinagar, Major Farrell explained to John they were flying in a Reprocured C-2A Greyhound, a 57 foot long twin turboprop designed to provide logistics support to aircraft carriers. Serving as the US Navy's carrier-on-board delivery workhorse, the C-2A could accommodate cargo, passengers, or both. This particular plane had been outfitted to provide airlift for diplomats and dignitaries, and when John asked Farrell which category he fell in, she bluntly told him neither.

The passenger cabin was configured to seat 28 people in seven rows of four with a narrow aisle dividing the paired seats. John sat in a front row seat, across the aisle from Farrell. Each well-padded chair was upholstered in indigo blue, and felt slightly more comfortable than standard accommodations in commercial coach. In the last row, in a double seat on the opposite side from John, Salena sat alone staring out a porthole.

Shortly after takeoff, Farrell began explaining what was expected of him over the next 24 hours, and for that matter, the rest of his life.

Leaning over the armrest, maintaining steady eye contact, Farrell said, "I suppose no one ever guessed you'd go through with this."

John studied Farrell's face for any telltale shift in expression or avoidance of eye contact that might belie a trick or a trap. "I wouldn't have, not if they hadn't agreed to my terms."

"For President Lloyd, the decision was easy. Twenty-five million, including payment to Dr. Zamal, doesn't come close to the billions in foreign aide we'll be dishing out in South Asia if Khan starts a nuclear war between Pakistan and India."

"Maybe I should've asked for more."

"Don't push it, but in truth your compensation request was the least of the president's worries. He was sure Behari wouldn't agree to replace India's troops in Kashmir with a UN task force. I suppose in the final analysis, the prime minister decided pulling out of a territory where his country's presence is hated beats losing seven cities and 20 million people."

"Either that, or Behari expects me to fail. That way, he gets to bomb Pakistan with a clear conscience, knowing he did everything conceivable to cooperate with America before resorting to nuclear war."

"You're being cynical. No one expects you to fail. In fact, before we left, I called Colonel Daley, and set-up is proceeding on schedule."

As the C-2A Greyhound leveled off to a cruising altitude of 20,000 feet, Farrell described the groundwork being laid for the completion of John's mission. The CIA had already placed an anonymous call to Khan's Citadel. Claiming to represent John's abductors, the man who called vowed to execute the two Pakistani Army officers still in captivity as retaliation for the daring escape of the American businessman and Pakistani doctor. If the CIA had done its job, the call would be traceable to an isolated valley in the Margalla Hills within a three hour hike of Islamabad.

As Farrell spelled out the details of the military operation about to drop him and Salena back in the lion's den, some of the technical terms she used, like surge capability and 60-gunner, went over John's head, but he didn't stop her for an explanation—the gist of how events were supposed to unfold was perfectly clear.

Last Saturday, after Patty Krause had blown herself up, CRUSO had begun devising a new plan to deliver the remaining RDX-7S charges to John. On Sunday morning, the army's last 21 prototypes had been transported to the *USS Ronald Reagan*, an aircraft carrier positioned 200 miles south of Karachi in the Arabian Sea. That was where John, Salena, and Farrell were headed now. Farrell estimated their arrival time at 5:45 p.m.

After a 30 minute stopover on the *Ronald Reagan* to pick up the RDX-7S charges and refuel the C-2A Greyhound, it was off to a US Army airfield in Afghanistan 12 miles east of Jalalabad. To get there on schedule, they'd have to fly over Iranian Baluchistan. In the event Teheran's generals objected to the unauthorized use of their airspace, a dozen F-14 Tomcats and 10 F/A-18 Hornets were tagging along for the ride.

From Jalalabad it was the job of the Nightstalkers—the 160th US Army Division Special Operations Aviation Regiment—to ferry John and Salena across Pakistan's North-West Frontier Province to a drop-off point in the Margalla Hills 10 miles north of Islamabad. To occupy the Pakistan Air Force with something other than the four AH-64 Blackhawk helicopters flying toward the Margalla Hills, at the same moment John and Salena lifted off from Jalalabad in the west, the Indian Air Force would launch air strikes against multiple targets along Pakistan's eastern border. The primary objective of India's attack was not to inflict damage and casualties, but to draw Khan's air defenses away from Pakistan's western front. After the Nightstalkers confirmed safe delivery of their package—Farrell's obtuse reference to him and Salena—the Indian Air Force would break off the fight, and withdraw to their bases.

The Margalla Hills were further east than the Nightstalker crews would have preferred to fly, but dropping John and Salena close to Islamabad was imperative. Leave them too far west, and it might take Khan's security men two or three hours to find and retrieve them. Since the operation's success depended on John returning to the Citadel by nine o'clock tonight, two or three hours was too much to waste.

Lieutenant Hall and Sergeant Banta, who'd already received their instructions, would drive into the Margalla Hills to meet John and Salena at their drop-off point. For reasons Farrell promised to explain, John must hand over the RDX-7S charges to Lieutenant Hall. Hall and Banta would then drive him and Salena to Daman-e-Koh, a popular tourist spot overlooking Islamabad. There, at Kashmirwala's Restaurant, John would make two phone calls.

The first was to Ambassador Stephen Kline at the US Embassy, who would be expecting John's call. After informing the ambassador of his escape, John was to phone Khan's Citadel for the same reason, and to request a ride back to the Citadel. While Khan's security men were driving out to Daman-e-Koh, Ambassador Kline would lodge a formal protest with the Pakistan government for having failed to provide adequate protection to an invited guest of Dr. Zamal. The ambassador would also demand John receive an immediate, comprehensive medical evaluation. Hopefully, all the fuss raised by the US ambassador would remove any suspicion of a feigned abduction in the mind of Khan's security chief, Azam Qadeer.

Nevertheless, John and Salena would likely be searched upon their return to the Citadel. That was why John must turn over the 22 RDX-7S charges to Lieutenant Hall after landing in the Margalla Hills. It was Lieutenant Hall's job to deliver the explosives back to John after he regained entry into the Citadel.

To make that job easier, at 9:45 p.m. Ambassador Kline would visit Pakistan National Hospital to see for himself how John was recovering from the bullet wound he sustained during his escape. Posing as embassy aides, Lieutenant Hall and Sergeant Banta would accompany the ambassador. Sometime during their visit, the two CRUSO operatives would transfer possession of 22 RDX-7S charges back to John.

Farrell said, "I'm not sure how Hall and Banta plan to package the RDX, but count on something interesting."

John recalled the gurneys stuffed with explosives. "I'm sure you're right."

"The package will be smaller this time. The RDX charges, the 50 feet of detonation cord, and the wireless detonator can all fit in a cereal box."

"Don't forget the delay detonators and time chart."

"Those too. Once our operatives hand over the materials, it's up to you to plant the explosives and bring down Khan's Citadel without killing anyone in the Diplomatic Enclave."

"Or in the hospital next door."

"Of course."

"Don't expect me to set off a firecracker if there's a chance it'll take out the hospital."

"It's your call, but whatever happens, it's essential you detonate on time. Our agents monitoring traffic in and out of the Citadel confirm all but 11 of Khan's guests—and we expect about 70—have arrived for Glorious Dawn. We anticipate the rest will show up tonight or early tomorrow. Since we have no idea how long the actual meeting will run, you're instructions are to detonate between one and 1:10 p.m."

"Consider it done."

Farrell studied John's face, and when she spoke again, her tone was softer. "Have you given any thought to where you'll be when you set off the charges?"

"Probably in the hospital, while I'm getting my bandage changed, or maybe outside across the street. I'll figure it out."

"Be careful."

"I'll be a lot more careful than I was in Chicago."

"Any questions?"

"Yeah, after I implode the Citadel, how do I get the hell out of Pakistan?"

"Lieutenant Hall will call us on his cell phone the instant the building falls. As soon as we get word, Pakistan's former president and nine of his cabinet members, now on the ground in Kabul, will be flown to Islamabad. Hall will then pull up to the curb outside Pakistan National Hospital and pick you up."

"Salena's going too."

"If that's what she wants." They both turned their heads and looked down the aisle at Salena, who still peered out the window. Farrell continued, "You'll be flown back to the *Ronald Reagan*, where you'll leave immediately for the US. If anyone in Pakistan asks what happened to Mr. Cattano, Ted Dunne will say his consultant fled the city when he heard a counter-coup was in progress."

"Mr. Cattano's a smart man."

"After a quick stopover at McGuire Air Force Base, we'll chopper you out to the Atlantic Ocean 10 miles southeast from where your Boston Whaler sank. Within 20 minutes, a New Jersey State Police boat will spot you clinging to your Whaler's wreckage. Having survived five days in stormy seas, you're sure to make the local news. Be careful what you say." Farrell looked at her watch. "Taking into account the time difference, at this hour tomorrow you'll be safe at home, and a whole lot richer."

The thought of going home gave John the shivers. He couldn't wait to hug his wife and daughters, but living life as if he'd never met Salena was unthinkable. Even now John wasn't sure if he survived his mission and the time came to say good-bye he'd have the strength to leave Salena. He spoke softly, hoping Salena wouldn't hear. "What happens to Dr. Zamal?"

Farrell answered matter-of-factly, "I suppose that's up to her."

"Will you fly her back to Srinagar?"

"Wherever she asks." Farrell paused, searching John's eyes for an answer. Finally, she said, "I don't mean to pry, but technically, it's official business. What happened between you two out there?"

What could he say when words were useless? The horrors he'd witnessed, the emotions he felt, how his life had changed forever—no one would understand. "Let's put it this way. Imagine before I met Salena I was blind. She helped me see. How do you not care for someone who restores your sight."

Farrell stared at him, nodding, but John knew she was being polite. He turned and watched Salena gazing out the window, then excused himself and walked to the back of the plane.

Salena didn't see him standing in the aisle next to the empty seat beside her, or at least that's what she pretended. John cleared his throat.

Her head spun and their eyes met.

His impulse was to take her in his arms, squeeze her, and never let go. Instead, he glanced at the porthole she'd been looking through. "What's so fascinating out there?"

She sat upright and faced straight ahead. Her long, flowing hair shielded her eyes. "I was looking at the Vale, but now it is gone."

So many times during their journey across the mountains she had reassured him. Now it was his turn. "With a little luck, by tomorrow afternoon Khan will be dead and your homeland on the fast track to freedom. You and Naji can finally live together in peace."

She whispered, "Why have I waited all my life for this chance, yet now I feel so empty?"

John knew exactly what she meant, and was about to tell her so, when Farrell called out from the front row. "Excuse me, John." She was holding a cell phone, waving him up. "I have an important call for you."

CHAPTER EIGHTY-TWO

John took the cell phone from Major Farrell and recognized the voice of President Lloyd.

"Please accept my apology on behalf of the United States government for having placed you in this unfortunate circumstance."

"What, with all the stress of a failed business and faltering marriage, I was ready for a long getaway weekend."

"We should have foreseen the possibility a referral agent might take advantage of the time pressure CRUSO was under to identify a qualified candidate."

"Isn't that ironic? Chandler's dead and gets no money, and I'm alive and get to enjoy it. Wasn't it supposed to work the other way around?"

"The people of America are grateful you have agreed to complete your objective."

"Excuse me, Mr. President, but that's horseshit. The people of America have no clue what I've been through, nor what I'm about to do, and if I understand the terms of our agreement, they'll never know."

"I'm speaking figuratively, John."

"Then why don't you just say 'thanks for saving my ass, Mr. Covello, because if Ali Khan lives to start World War III, there's a good chance I'm a one-term president.'"

"I understand your need to express anger, and anticipated you might release pent-up frustration, nevertheless, it is essential you comprehend the extraordinary consequences of your mission. Nuclear war, even if contained to the subcontinent, will adversely impact every nation on earth."

"Then I'd better pay very close attention to what I'm doing."

"I'm also calling to inform you of a change in your compensation. Implode the Citadel with Ali Khan and his generals inside, and your total payment will be increased from $20,000,000 to $30,000,000."

"Gee, is that tax-free?"

"According to my understanding of the re-assimilation plan, your payment will take the form of a tort claim settlement, all of which will be allocated toward reimbursement for personal injury and emotional distress resulting in physical illness. In that event, yes, your compensation is fully exempt from federal income taxes."

"Great, but I gotta tell you, Mr. President. If India reneges on its promise to let the Kashmiri people vote for independence, you can keep your tax-free dollars and throw me in jail, because I'll go to every newspaper who'll listen and spill everything I know about CRUSO and Dr. Chandler and Patty Krause and all the others who do your dirty work." John noticed Salena get up and walk toward him. "I never break a promise, Mr. President, and I promised a young lady who's worth a hell of a lot more than $30,000,000 that Kashmir gets a shot at freedom. If that doesn't happen, there's no deal, not for fifty million."

"I have Prime Minister Behari's word that upon Labib Razzak's re-installation as Pakistan's president, and verification the Pakistan Army has left Azad Kahsmir—the part of Kashmir where—"

"I know, go on."

"…India will commence withdrawal of its Border Security Force and regular army regiments from the Kashmir Valley, Jammu, and Ladakh. A multi-national peacekeeping force will replace the Pakistan and Indian armies to maintain security until UN-sponsored elections are conducted, possibly as early as September."

"Make that happen, and I'm off the map."

"When this mission is over, Mr. Covello, you'll be walking around with highly classified material in that swollen head of yours, and that's where it has to stay. If you succeed, you're a hero, but the fact remains, you'll never get the recognition you deserve."

"I don't give a rat's ass about recognition. I just want Behari to keep his word."

"He will Mr. Covello, and again, thank you."

"You're welcome."

John handed Farrell the cell phone and met Salena's gaze.

"I overheard what you said to your president."

"Was that who I was talking to?"

For the first time since leaving Srinagar, Salena smiled.

John asked Farrell, "What else do I need to know?"

"I've covered it all."

"I'll fill Salena in."

John led Salena to the same two seats in the last row where Salena had come from. He maneuvered into the window seat, and Salena sat beside him.

John explained everything Farrell had told him about the military operation to deliver them to the Margalla Hills. Salena had heard of Kashmirwala's Restaurant, but had never been there. Listening to John, her glimmering eyes gradually grew heavy, and at one point she yawned and apologized.

John was exhausted too, and after he finished Farrell's instructions, he asked her if she needed a nap. She nodded, and John slid toward her, but was stopped by the armrest separating their seats. Recalling the warmth of her body in the back of the bus during their ride to Srinagar, John gripped the armrest. Before he could flip it away, Salena placed her hand on his and shook her head.

"You sure?"

She nodded, but it was a sad nod just the same.

John shut his eyes, and in the midst of deep slumber, was roused by a vivid nightmare. In his dream, John detonated the charges he'd planted in the Citadel, and panicked when he saw concrete walls and steel columns crumbling all around him. When he realized it was only a dream, he looked out the porthole and saw what had actually woken him was the C-2A Greyhound bouncing to a stop on the deck of the *USS Ronald Reagan*.

John's abbreviated sleep left him feeling more sluggish than when he'd closed his eyes. He descended the turboprop's stairs, and lagged behind Farrell and Salena across the carrier's massive flight deck. Back home he'd seen a History Channel program featuring enormous aircraft carriers, but never thought he'd step foot on one. He had intended to take his daughters to the Sea-Air-Space Museum in Manhattan when both reached their teens, but that would've meant doing so in the last two years, and during the last two years, he hadn't done much of anything.

After he returned to Brielle, that was all going to change. When Salena and Naji visited America, he'd take them to see Lady Liberty. After that, they'd hop a cab to Pier 86 for a tour of the *Intrepid*. Naji would gape at its size alone.

In front of a portal on the carrier's deck they were met by an officer holding a black briefcase. Farrell introduced the officer as Lieutenant Commander Raymond Garcia. Following Farrell, Salena, and Garcia down a narrow corridor inside the ship, John wondered how he would explain Salena to Maureen. Even if he cooked up some half-baked story—like she was a long-lost college friend, purely platonic—Maureen would know the truth the instant she saw him look at her.

They climbed two sets of narrow stairs and entered a small, sparsely furnished room with a large window overlooking the carrier's deck. John glimpsed out and witnessed a buzz of activity. He noticed sailors wearing different colored jerseys and asked Garcia what the colors meant.

The lieutenant commander pointed to a man and woman wearing purple jumpsuits shoving a hose under the C-2A Greyhound. He explained each color defined a sailor's function, making the job of identifying who did what a whole lot easier. For example, the "grapes" gassing up the C-2A specialized in aviation fuels. The men and women in blue jerseys worked as plane handlers, elevator operators, tractor drivers, or messengers. Anyone wearing a red jersey might be an ordnance disposal or crash and salvage expert.

John was about to ask what the green jerseys did when a blue-eyed woman with short, blonde hair donned in nurse's whites strolled into the room and handed John a white tablet and a cup of water.

Holding the pill, John stared at her.

"Is something wrong?"

It had been days since he'd seen a woman with blonde hair and blue eyes. "Nothing, I'm sorry. What are you giving me?"

"A 40 milligram dose of Omeprazole. Reduces the amount of acid produced by the stomach. It'll lessen the frequency and intensity of your stomach pain."

Farrell interjected, "For obvious reasons, we're giving you a single dose, but when you return tomorrow, you'll get another."

John smirked. "Why waste perfectly good medicine on someone who could end up dead."

"You know what I mean. First thing … well maybe not the first thing … when you get back home, make an appointment with your doctor to treat that ulcer."

"Can you recommend someone good? My doctor died unexpectedly."

Farrell shook her head. "I can't take much more of you John."

The nurse fished into her pocket and handed John two clear caplets filled with light blue powder.

"What are those?"

Farrell answered, "I asked General Prasad if when he frisked you he found the cyanide caplets I'd given you in Washington."

"Khan's lackey took them."

"What did he do with them?"

"Hopefully, swallowed a few."

"That wouldn't be good, John, not now."

"He probably tossed them."

"I hope so. These are your replacements."

"You're being way too generous."

"Sorry, but it's an integral part of the deal."

"Should I be surprised?"

The blue-eyed nurse left the room and Farrell turned to Lieutenant Commander Garcia, who handed Farrell the black briefcase he'd carried into the room. Farrell set the briefcase on a small waist-high shelf, and snapped open the latches.

John spied inside a red container the size and shape of a cigar box, and instantly knew what it held. He'd seen the same box in a conference room at Andrews Air Force Base four days earlier.

Farrell opened the lid and carefully removed a six-inch long, bow-shaped tube. "These charges are identical to the ones Sergeant Banta showed you in Washington. How about a quick refresher?"

John reached for the RDX-7S charge, and Farrell passed it to him gingerly.

Gripping the thin, three-ounce tube, John scrutinized the tiny buttons and digital display built into one side. He recalled Banta's lesson on the function and capability of these unique linear shaped charges. They came with a force velocity regulator allowing the user to adjust each charge's explosive force from 2,000 feet per second to 125,000 feet per second, three times stronger than any charge John had used in his commercial demolitions business. Thanks to a precision blast containment system, the direction of each charge's explosive force could be aimed to within an accuracy of one foot. A programmable timer enabled a user to stagger each charge's detonation in .0005 second increments.

John remembered another unique characteristic of these classified prototypes—their independent charging and ignition systems. Linear shaped charges required a shock to trigger their explosive capabilities, usually generated by a blasting cap wired to an external source of electric current. The RDX-7S explosives featured a self-contained charging system that could ignite the blasting cap after an interval set by the user on the charge's built-in timer. For all practical purposes, each charge could be detonated independently, and in theory, used like a hand grenade. Though John wasn't planning on tossing these babies around, the fact he wouldn't have to wire the charges together made the job of positioning them incredibly easy.

John handed the metal tube to Farrell. "No refresher necessary—piece of cake."

Farrell placed the charge back in the container. "These are the army's last RDX-7S prototypes for at least six weeks. If it isn't necessary to use them all, don't."

"I'll keep that in mind."

Farrell snapped the box shut and flipped it over. John observed in the box's underside a recessed square, and at the bottom of the square, a black button and a silver toggle switch.

"This is something I hadn't expected to show you."

John had a hunch what it was, and took a shot. "If I'm caught with the box, hit the toggle, press the button, and no more explosives, and no more John."

"You learn fast."

Now that he wasn't dying of cancer, John wondered what he'd really do if Qadeer caught him.

Salena turned away from the window overlooking the flight deck, and walked over to them. "John will have no need to destroy the explosives. I will do everything in my power to distract Khan until Glorious Dawn convenes."

There was a knock on the door, and Garcia answered. A clean-shaven sailor standing in the doorway saluted his commanding officer. The two spoke for less than a minute.

The sailor left and Garcia walked over. "Satellite surveillance has confirmed CIA ground intelligence. During the last three hours 10 mobile launchers have been moved to within three miles of the Indian border from Kel, south to Sukkur. All seven Indian cities identified by the NSA and DIA as targets of Glorious Dawn are now within striking distance. President Lloyd has placed the Seventh and Third Fleets at DEFCON 2."

Farrell took a deep breath and turned to John. "Time's a wasting. Let's roll."

CHAPTER EIGHTY-THREE

From a clearing atop a plateau in the Margalla Hills, John and Salena waved good-bye to the four Blackhawk helicopters flying toward the setting sun on the western horizon. They turned away only when the drumbeat of rotors faded behind the jagged peaks of the Second Ridge. India's ploy must have worked. Skimming the trees across the plains and valleys of northwest Pakistan, the Nightstalkers confronted no aircraft during their 70-minute flight to the jeep trail on a hill five miles north of Daman-e-Koh.

Jostled by the ride from Jalalabad, John's left arm pulsed in pain. He listened to the rhythmic chirps of the evening insects and the occasional caw of an unseen bird. Alone with Salena for the first time since riding in a shikara on Dal Lake, he felt suddenly awkward. They had spoken little since leaving the *USS Ronald Reagan*, though twice on the helicopter he'd caught her looking at him, and now with one last chance to bare his soul, he wasn't sure how to begin.

Salena had turned away, and was standing at the edge of a sharp drop-off staring down into a valley darkened by the shadows of the hills. The dying sun was slowly yielding to what could be John's final night on earth. If he had something to say, he'd better say it now, before Lieutenant Hall and Sergeant Banta came to pick them up for the ride to Daman-e-Koh.

He placed his hand on Salena's shoulder. Without looking back, she jerked away.

John blamed only himself, having fallen too hard and too fast, though he'd never have done so had he thought he might live. But now it was too late, for both their hearts had made the leap. "Eventually you'll have to talk to me."

Salena's lustrous hair swirled as she spun her head and glared at him. "Fine, you want to talk? We will talk. What time is it? How is the weather? Maybe I can tell you what species of flora and fauna thrive in the Margalla Hills? Did you know jackals and leopards make their home here? What about the story of how the Margalla Hills became a nature preserve? What would you like to talk about?"

John bit back his frustration. "Damn you, Salena. You know what I—"

They must have heard the same distant rumble at the same time. In unison, they crouched. John gripped the handle of the briefcase holding the RDX-7S charges and moved in front of Salena.

He was sure the sound was an approaching engine—the only question was whose. Spotting a willowy shrub to his right, John whispered for Salena to follow. Walking low to the ground, they crossed the clearing and ducked behind the shrub's dense leaves.

The clunk and rattle of shifting gears grew closer until yards in front of the leafy bush brakes squealed and a motor stopped. A door clicked opened and a voice called out.

John stood holding the briefcase. "Over here."

Lieutenant Hall and Sergeant Banta sprinted from an unmarked jeep, and the four shook hands all around. John introduced Salena as Dr. Zamal and noticed she had veiled her head. "You guys are prompt," he said.

Hall took the black briefcase from John and looked up. "It's getting dark and our schedule is tight. Let's move."

"Don't you wanna hear about my trip?"

Banta smirked. "Rumor has it you survived a few close scrapes in the wilds of Kashmir."

"Let's just say I'm ready for a long stretch of deserted beach and a half-gallon jug of frozen margaritas."

John and Salena squeezed in the rear seat of the capped jeep, while Banta drove, and Hall rode shotgun. The prospect of a clear, moonlit night did little to eliminate the need for high-beams as they negotiated a series of hairpin turns through the dense nighttime forest.

During the bumpy 12 minute ride to the outskirts of Daman-eh-Koh, Hall reiterated Major Farrell's instructions. In two hours, Ambassador Kline would visit Pakistan National Hospital, and Hall and Banta, posing as Kline's aides, would return the RDX-7S charges to John.

"So what's it gonna be?" John asked, "A box of chocolates, a new bathrobe?"

Hall and Banta exchanged glances. "The sergeant and I have a difference of opinion as to what looks least suspicious, but don't worry, by 10 o'clock tonight you'll have those charges."

The winding trail straightened out, and they ascended another hill. By now, the sky had turned dark purple, and was filled with twinkling stars. When they reached the summit, Banta steered slowly into a sharp turn and stopped short.

Directly ahead and far below John beheld a vast expanse of sparkling lights arranged in an orderly grid—Islamabad glowing like a shimmering jewel.

Hall turned to John from the front seat. "This is your stop."

From their vantage high above the city, Pakistan's capital resembled an enchanted fairyland. "It's beautiful."

"Snap a few photos next time you're in town." Hall pointed out the open window on his left. "It's a three minute walk to Daman-eh-Koh. At this hour, Kashmirwala's Restaurant should be easy to spot. It's the only building with lights on. You'll find two telephone booths in the lobby."

Salena climbed out and John followed. Standing at the jeep's window, he shook the lieutenant's hand. "Thanks for the lift."

"Good luck, and don't forget—you're Mr. Cattano, and you survived a grueling ordeal in a hostile land and barely escaped with your life."

"But that's what really happened."

Hall suppressed a smile. "If you detonate the charges from inside the hospital, exit immediately through the main doors. We'll be parked on Constitution Avenue in a blue BMW bearing the seal of the US Embassy. If you run into trouble, we'll shoot whoever gets in your way."

"Wouldn't it suck if I got that far and ended up dead?"

"If you get that far, you have my personal guarantee you're going home alive."

"Then I'll count on that Beamer ride."

Hall's expression turned serious. "One more thing. I want you to know, if you had chosen to go home, the sergeant and I would've been stuck in Islamabad when the nukes went off. We owe you."

From the beginning John understood these two men had put their lives in his hands. "I won't let you down."

The CRUSO agents sped off, leaving John and Salena in a thick cloud of dust. John didn't mind the additional dirt on his already filthy shalwar kameez. A grimy appearance added truth to their tale.

John wiped his eyes and turned to Salena. She was gone.

After five frantic seconds of scouring the darkness, he spotted the back of her veil. She had taken a 20 pace lead, and was fast putting distance between them.

He ran to catch up. "Where's the fire?"

"You heard Lieutenant Hall. We have three minutes to get to Kashmirwala's Restaurant."

Between the branches of the trees ahead, John discerned flickering lights. "Look, we're almost there. You can spare half a minute."

"You do not know for certain that is the restaurant."

John planted himself in front of Salena, and grabbed her arms more roughly than he'd intended. "I don't care if we stand here all night, we're gonna talk this out."

She tried pulling away, but John gripped tighter.

"I said we're talking."

Her eyes turned to slivers. "If I refuse, what will you do, hit me?"

"Ordinarily, no, but if that's what it takes."

With a jerk of her shoulders, she freed herself. "We have no time for this game." She stomped off, leaving John alone in the dark feeling like an idiot. Women could be tough at times, and often logic didn't work. He'd try for the heart.

He ran to catch up, speaking as he walked beside her. "I love you, Salena, and that's a fact. Outside the orphanage, you said my heart's not torn apart. You couldn't be more wrong. I'm so screwed up, I don't know what to feel. I don't have cancer, and should be dancing in the streets. But it's sick—it's almost like I wish I were dying again. At least when I was dying, you loved me back."

Salena stopped short, but refused to look at him. "If you want the truth, John, I do wish you were dying. At least then no other woman could have you. But now, after tomorrow ..." Her misting eyes met his. "... I must live the rest of my days knowing you are out there, some-where, but not with me."

"Why can't we have a relationship? Maybe not the way we did here, but like good friends who've shared rough times."

She turned, faced him squarely, and slapped him hard across the face.

John gasped. "What was that for?"

"I gave you every part of me, yet so easily you would think of me as your friend. You are a liar. Your love extends only as long as your linga."

"That's not fair."

She stormed off and disappeared around a bend in the trail. So much for an appeal to the heart.

John saw no point in running to catch up. Instead, he strolled down the path in the direction she'd gone. Coming around the bend, he saw on the left a one-story building with double wooden doors, and colored lights strung along the eaves. A sign on the lawn lit up by a pink flood-light read 'Kashmirwala's Retreat: On Top of the World.'

Salena stood outside the doors. At least she had waited for him.

Ambling up the concrete walk, John noticed along one side of the building a crushed slate parking lot where he counted a dozen cars, and beyond that, a breathtaking vista of the city's glittering lights. John guessed this eatery was popular with young couples—or in an Islamic republic—young married couples.

When Salena looked up and saw John approach, she stepped inside.

John opened the wood doors and found himself standing in a dimly lit foyer with walls papered in sea-green felt. The only person around was Salena, who stared down at the light blue carpet beside one of two telephone booths Lieutenant Hall had said they'd find in the lobby.

Ignoring Salena, John entered the nearest booth and made his calls, first to the US Embassy, whose receptionist played her shock and surprise with Golden Globe excellence. The ambassador's performance was even better. After thanking God for his safe return, Ambassador Kline assured John he'd call Ted Dunne at Advanced Medical Systems, then file a formal complaint with Pakistan's Minister of Domestic Security.

John made his second call with greater trepidation. Listening for the slightest hint of suspicion in the voices of the low-ranking grunts who bounced his call from one underling to another, John was eventually put through to the Citadel's evening security chief. Avoiding the details of their ambush and captivity, John explained he and Salena had escaped their abductors somewhere west of Islamabad, and though he'd been shot in the arm, they had hiked across the Margalla Hills to Daman-e-Koh. John read the officer's surprise as genuine, and after a long wait on hold, was told three jeeps were coming to pick them up. He and Salena were to wait inside the restaurant until the soldiers arrived in 10 minutes.

Disregarding the officer's instructions, John hung up the phone and walked outside, not bothering to see if Salena followed. Under a bright gibbous moon, he sauntered across the parking lot, stood at the edge of its crushed slate surface, and stared down from the mountain at the gleaming lights of Islamabad.

He listened to the summer bugs screeching in the night and the occasional crackling of gunfire from the city, and after four or five minutes, he heard slow-moving footsteps crunching the ground behind him. He turned and saw Salena approach with her head bowed.

She stopped directly in front of him and looked up. John's heart dropped when he saw her cheeks sopping wet and her eyelids puffy.

"Forgive me for striking you. I am ashamed of myself." Her moist lips quivered and she looked away. "I do not understand how we can share anything less than everything we have already given. I cannot love and forget, I can only love and never forget. This is how I was raised, and I must remind myself, this is not the way of the Americans."

John couldn't stop himself. He wrapped his arms around Salena's waist, drew her close, and was grateful to God for the feel of her hands pressing his back, pulling him to her. "I swear, had I met you in a different time, I'd be yours and yours alone. Maybe you're right. It's not possible to share anything less than what we had in Kashmir. But damn, Salena, I can't imagine life without you."

Through soft sobs and streaming tears, Salena struggled for words. "As I cannot imagine life without you … but if I live with any chance of seeing you again … my heart will never be free."

Staring into the depths of her soul, John lowered her veil and stroked her hair. "No matter what happens tomorrow, never forget me. If I live or die, I'll always love you." He kissed her forehead, and whispered. "I don't know how to stop loving you."

Pulsing red light lit up the trees all around them, and the sounds of the night were shattered by the whine of fast-approaching vehicles.

Salena whispered into his ear. "You will have to learn, John. We will both have to learn."

They backed away from each other as the trio of jeeps pulled into the parking lot. A knot twisted through John's gut knowing he might never hold this woman again.

CHAPTER EIGHTY-FOUR

Leaning against the observation room wall in the Truth Revelation Center, Azam Qadeer smelled a rat—two rats, in fact—and both were scurrying to the lair.

From the moment his senior security officer informed him John Cattano had called from Daman-e-Koh with a tale of how he and Dr. Zamal had escaped their abductors and trekked 20 kilometers over the First and Second Ridge of the Margalla Hills, the captain suspected the two were up to no good. If Cattano had indeed been shot in the arm, a claim he could easily verify, most likely it was Lieutenant Hassan or Subedar Mazhar who had fired the bullet.

Qadeer also doubted the authenticity of the call he had received at 4:08 p.m., allegedly from Cattano's kidnappers. The Citadel's surveillance experts had traced the wireless signal to Martyr's Valley east of Haripur, and when Qadeer ordered three Alouette attack helicopters to investigate, nothing or no one was found. The nameless caller also claimed Hassan and Mazhar, both alive and healthy, had been taken to Azad Kashmir.

The physical evidence gathered thus far failed to corroborate the claims of the kidnappers, and now, of John Cattano. How had the American's fingerprints gotten on the steering wheel of the Mercedes Benz found in the Neelum Valley—far from Haripur and the Margalla Hills? Why were no fingerprints of his alleged abductors found anywhere in or out of the car? More importantly, Cattano and Zamal could not have acted alone. A third party had to have placed the call from Martyr's Valley.

Qadeer had even considered the possibility the US government was conspiring against Ali Khan, and that John Cattano, foul-mouthed buffoon though he was, had been sent to do America's bidding. If that were true, why the ranting phone call from Ambassador Kline 10 minutes earlier challenging the adequacy of the Citadel's security?

Answers had proven elusive, but Qadeer was confident he would get some soon—when he questioned Dr. Zamal.

The door to the observation room opened, and in walked a regal figure wearing a long, white robe. "I though I might find you here."

Qadeer saluted General Khan, who walked down the aisle and embraced the captain. Glancing at the glass wall dividing the viewing seats from the deserted chamber, Khan said, "I dislike this place. Implementing Allah's will should not require the use of such harsh tools of persuasion."

Qadeer thought better of reminding Khan the success of his coup was due in large part to the effectiveness of such tools. "Perhaps some-day they will not be necessary."

"May it come to pass." Khan turned away from the glass partition. "How much longer before Dr. Zamal and Mr. Cattano arrive?"

Qadeer glanced at the clock on the theater's rear wall. "Five minutes."

"I have a job for you, and then I wish you to join me in celebrating the return of my beloved."

Qadeer had his own plans for Khan's beloved. "After the medical staff has examined Dr. Zamal, may I have your permission to meet with her?"

Khan eyed him skeptically. "Poor Azam, you have gathered not one crumb of evidence against Dr. Zamal. For three days your computer experts have dissected her computer, and found nothing."

"This afternoon Sergeant Maqbool informed me his lab has de-tected irregularities—lines of encrypted code embedded in her Excel program files. He is deciphering their meaning and may have answers as early as tonight. I merely wish to ask the doctor a few questions that will make his job easier."

"I have warned you before, you swim in treacherous waters when you doubt the allegiance of my betrothed. I will not allow her to be questioned, not unless you have proof. Until then, I wish you to share my joy?"

So long as the bitch breathed, he would feel no joy. "As you command."

Khan clasped Qadeer's shoulder. "Is there anything else?"

Qadeer was reluctant to press, but in light of the fingerprint evidence, he had no choice. "I wonder about Mr. Cattano. How is it he left his finger-prints all over the car's steering wheel, and the dacoits not one thumbprint?"

Khan's eyes narrowed. "Your distrust of Dr. Zamal sufficiently tries me. Surely you do not allude Mr. Cattano is her accomplice?"

"During the time he was here, they seemed to have gotten along well." The instant Qadeer uttered the words, he knew he had over-stepped his bounds.

Khan removed his hand from Qadeer's shoulder, and inhaled a long, deliberate breath. "Do you mean to imply she is attracted to Mr. Cattano?"

"No, I mean they have spent much time together ... in the hospital wards."

"Did your men not accompany them?"

"At all times."

"Then dare not question her fidelity."

"Do I have your permission to interview Mr. Cattano?"

Khan's eyes bored through him. "I am told he took a bullet to his arm. He may have saved Dr. Zamal's life. Yet you would interrogate this man like a criminal when he may be the only reason she lives."

"What if he were not shot escaping thieves or counterrevolutionaries? What if he was shot in a struggle with Lieutenant Hassan and Subedar Mazhar?"

Khan chuckled. "Your imagination runs away from you."

"Please forgive me for speaking my mind, but it is you who denies reality."

"I shall hear no more. I am happy beyond reason Salena is coming home, and if Mr. Cattano was instrumental in her escape, I demand you treat him as her savior."

For the sake of protecting his charge, he had no choice but to push the issue. "I wonder, my general, even if I offer you proof, will you remain blind to the truth?"

Khan pressed his lips into a derisive grin. "Say you are right. For what purpose do Dr. Zamal and Mr. Cattano conspire? To murder me? Though Dr. Zamal is a reluctant bride—which shall change the day I annex Kashmir to Pakistan—do you seriously believe she would try killing me knowing the attempt guarantees her execution?"

"What if her plan included a means of escape?"

"Salena ... Dr. Zamal is not capable of such deceit."

"But—"

"Enough!" Khan held up his palm. "Speak no more of your suspicions until you offer incontrovertible evidence." The general turned and walked up the aisle. He stopped at the door and looked back. "You have so fouled my mood, I nearly forgot why I came."

"Please forgive me."

"Behari shall require two full days to evacuate India's cities. To insure our warheads inflict maximum casualties I am rescheduling Glorious Dawn for 0700 hours tomorrow. If all goes well, I shall issue the launch order tomorrow at dusk. That means I cannot wait for Generals Masood, Rehman, and Saboor to arrive at midday. You must call them immediately and convey my order they are to fly to Islamabad tonight. I need everyone present, no exceptions, when we convene tomorrow morning."

"Yes, my general."

"After you make the calls, meet me in the hospital to celebrate Dr. Zamal's return."

"It will be my privilege."

Khan nodded and disappeared into the halls of the Citadel.

Qadeer stood alone for a moment, mulling what to do about Khan's delusion Salena might one day return his love. As he started up the aisle, Lieutenant Siddique walked through the door and saluted.

"What is it?" Qadeer asked.

"The jeeps have arrived."

"Was Mr. Cattano shot?"

"A single round to the arm."

"What is Dr. Zamal's condition?"

"Both appear ragged, but—" Siddique let loose a ferocious sneeze. "…but otherwise they are healthy."

"Did you carry out my instructions?"

"Yes, they were driven to the hospital in separate jeeps, and escorted to different floors."

"Good." Qadeer noticed large beads of sweat glistening on Siddique's forehead, and his skin looked paler than usual. "Have you taken medicine for your cold?"

"Sir, I have not had time."

"You look feverish." Qadeer remembered the pills he had swiped from the ill-mannered Mr. Cattano. "In my office, on the corner of my desk, you will find an aspirin bottle. Take two capsules and a short nap. I need you healthy this evening to assist me with a very special interrogation."

"Thank you, sir."

Siddique saluted and walked out, leaving Qadeer to ponder how he might obtain quick and conclusive proof of Dr. Zamal's guilt—and Mr. Cattano's complicity.

CHAPTER EIGHTY-FIVE

John was less surprised by the fact he and Salena were driven back to Islamabad in separate jeeps than he was by the speed with which the soldiers waiting at Pakistan National Hospital whisked Salena away without allowing them so much as an exchange of glances.

John was escorted to a wheelchair at the curb, then rolled into the hospital through the Emergency Room doors on the main level. He was taken to a 2nd floor examination room, where a male doctor who John didn't recognize gave him a cursory check-up. After the doctor left, a male nurse came in, removed the white cloth Salena had wrapped around his arm, and tossed it in a covered chrome basket. As the nurse dressed his wound with sterile gauze, John restrained an odd impulse to jump off the table and retrieve Salena's bandage to take back home and hide in his sock drawer for the rest of his life.

Sitting on the examination table, John waited alone less than a minute before a soldier in tan khakis entered the room to say General Khan extended his deepest appreciation for John's heroism in returning Dr. Zamal safely to the Citadel. The general regretted he could not thank John personally, but he fully intended to do so after verifying Dr. Zamal had not been harmed.

The soldier spun and left the examination room, leaving John by himself to stare at the antiseptic white walls and glossy white cabinets and drawers. He thought about what Salena had said outside Kashmirwala's Restaurant, and she was right. If he lived, and they kept in touch, the moment he got her alone, he'd hold her close, not as a friend, but as a lover.

This woman had snatched his heart and turned it inside out. In two amazing days, she had profoundly altered his perspective on so much that had never before mattered. Not until their journey to Kashmir had he so cherished his freedom and the value of human life. More importantly, she had made him understand the absolute necessity of moving forward even when your past still haunted your present.

As John grappled with all the reasons he shouldn't stay and live out his days in seclusion with Salena, a nurse entered the room. The short gentleman with a round chocolate face informed him a hospital room had been readied on the 3rd floor where he could recuperate as long as he wished. If he preferred, however, he could return to his suite on the Citadel's 6th floor. Remembering CRUSO's plan included an imminent visit by Ambassador Kline, John opted for the hospital room.

The nurse wheeled John to the 3rd floor, and settled him in. Folded at the foot of the room's only bed, John found a clean pair of silk pajamas, and hanging in the closet, a freshly pressed shalwar kameez. Keeping in mind the work to come, John bypassed the pajamas for the comfortable South Asian garb, while the nurse fetched purple flowers for a ceramic vase on the windowsill. John climbed on the bed, lay on the top sheet, and pulled the beige cotton spread up to his chest.

As the nurse turned to leave, John couldn't help but ask, "How is Salena?"

The pudgy-faced man regarded him sternly. "Dr. Zamal is well."

John had closed his eyes for less than a minute when a middle-aged woman shrouded in a green dress and matching veil marched into the room and announced to John he had visitors. He thanked the nurse, and asked her to show them in.

A tree of a man in a charcoal suit ducked under the doorframe and walked to John's bed, hand extended. "Good evening, I'm Ambassador Kline," and as if he already didn't know, added, "You must be Mr. Cattano."

John felt like saying, 'no, I'm Elvis Presley, and this is where I've been hiding since 1977,' but he remembered Farrell's warning the room might be bugged. "Yes, thank you greatly for your concern over my ordeal."

Two men in navy blue jackets, white shirts, and bland business ties walked in behind the ambassador. John recognized the shorter, olive-skinned man, Sergeant Banta, but saw no sign of Lieutenant Hall.

He noticed none of the men bore gifts.

The ambassador introduced his companions as Martin Wolfe and Joseph Cruz, and the four made small talk, patently avoiding the specifics of John's bold escape, and for that matter, any description of his captors. Maybe these guys did know what they were doing. John realized if he invented too many details and someone was listening, they'd have a mountain of lies under which to bury Salena.

As Ambassador Kline chitchatted, Sergeant Banta removed a pen and paper from inside his jacket, set it on the table beside the bed, and started scribbling. When he was finished, Banta held the note in front of John's face while Ambassador Kline rambled on about the Mets' latest victory over the Braves. Reading the note, John's mouth went dry:

2 calls/1 e-mail to Khan's
generals intercepted @ 2100.
Glorious Dawn now @ 0700,
not 1300, tomorrow. Can do?
Nod yes or no.

John had planned on meeting Salena first thing in the morning, hoping she might create another diversion to help him reenter the Citadel's vacant 3rd floor. If Khan convened his meeting at seven o'clock, six hours earlier than John had expected, he might have to find his own way to sneak in and plant the explosives.

Unsure whether to proceed, John remembered an axiom he once held dear, and had all but forgotten after Billy Dwyer's death. Salena's courage had reminded him. Damn the odds and screw defeat, if it's important enough, never give up.

John nodded three times, and Banta promptly balled up the paper and popped it in his mouth. The sergeant walked to the door, stopped at the threshold, and signaled with his eyes to someone in the corridor. Sure enough, in walked Lieutenant Hall, dressed more like a Mafia don than a special ops army officer. He carried under his arm a stuffed, pink Porky Pig.

Hall sauntered to the bed and spoke in a southern drawl that sounded strange coming from the Hall he'd known before. "Howdy, I'm Bob Davis, staff aide to Ambassador Kline. Glad to make your acquaintance." He handed John the plush toy. "Had some trouble gettin' this here pig inside. Forgot Muslims shun pork. Guards downstairs wanted nothing to do with poor Porky—wouldn't even touch him."

Certain Hall knew damn well Muslims hated pork, John turned the doll over several times, scrutinizing its pink material.

"Don't go squeezing that little guy too hard."

"Shucks. I was hoping I could snuggle up with him under the covers."

"You feel the urge to squeeze anything, try his nose."

John gripped the pig's nose.

"Not now."

"I see."

John rested Porky on his pillow, and for the next several minutes, the five men spoke fervently about nothing. Before leaving, Ambassador Kline encouraged John to sleep, and promised he'd make a follow-up call to Ted Dunne at AMS when he returned to the embassy. Though the ambassador assured John he'd visit again tomorrow, if John had his way, he'd never see the diplomat again, except maybe on TV.

Sergeant Banta, the last to reach the door, gave John a parting wink.

So that was it. He had the incentive, he had the courage, and he had the pig. All he needed now was a miracle.

S alena stood beside the hospital bed in the examination room, shut her eyes, and imagined the hands clasping hers belonged to John Covello. Only until tomorrow must she pretend. After that, she would never again be forced to veil her head, or her heart.

She inhaled slowly and deeply, and looked into the face of Ghalib Ali Khan.

He neither smiled nor frowned. "I am comforted with the knowledge of your safe return. Now you must rest."

"I am not sure why, but I cannot sleep. Perhaps I am beyond fatigue, or perhaps the thought of having sipped from the cup of death keeps me awake."

"I too have not slept. Glorious Dawn has occupied much of my time, but during your absence, my mind was unable to focus fully on the great days ahead for Pakistan. Allah has returned you to me, for He knows without you I am half a man." Khan's grip tightened around her hands, and they began to hurt. "I missed you, my flower."

Forcing herself to stare into the eyes of the man who had stolen her freedom, Salena said nothing.

"Did you miss me as well?"

"More than you can imagine."

"I struggled to find meaning from your ordeal, and hoped your brush with death might renew your appreciation of my love."

"It has, kind master."

"I am grateful those evil men did not have you long. Eventually they would have defiled you and relegated you to a life of shame." Khan released her hands. "Praise Allah for Mr. Cattano's bravery. His timely escape kept you pure."

"How is Mr. Cattano? Has his wound been disinfected?"

"I am told his wound had been cleansed before he arrived—I presume by you."

"I did what I could."

Khan spoke through clenched teeth. "The touch of his arm, how did it feel?"

"All I did was bandage it."

"Mr. Cattano is handsome, is he not?"

Salena shuddered under his penetrating gaze. "He is not a man I would choose."

Khan nodded slowly, studiously. "Your abductors? What cause did they espouse?"

Salena recalled the story Omar Shah was to have given the *Daily Jang*. "Independence for Kashmir."

"I fail to comprehend why the People's League abducted you, when it is your betrothed who seeks Kashmir's liberation?"

"To my abductors, annexation to Pakistan does not mean freedom, but replacing one master for another."

"Fools. Don't they see Pakistan shall serve the needs of Kashmir's Muslims better than their Hindu jailers?"

"These self-proclaimed liberators of Kashmir fear the Islamic extremists more than the Hindu moderates."

Khan's eyes blazed. "I will kill them all! Muslims who defy my will, and Hindus wherever I find them."

Realizing she had pushed Khan too far, and knowing in less than a day his corrupt views of Islam no longer mattered, she said, "I did not intend to upset you, only answer your questions."

Khan walked to the room's window, where heavy white drapes prevented any view of the nighttime sky. He looked back at Salena. "Questions indeed. Captain Qadeer has many he wishes to ask you."

Tomorrow she must create a distraction for John, but a lengthy interrogation at the hands of Qadeer was not what she had in mind. "Can his questions wait for another day?"

"I have ordered the captain to hunt down your captors and bring them to swift justice. He is understandably anxious to learn what he can of their location and numbers. He asked to interview you tonight, but I insisted tonight was too soon." Khan came closer. "We shall see about tomorrow. This evening, you shall rest."

"I was hoping to check on my patients before retiring to the Citadel."

Khan snickered in a way that made her stomach turn. "Which patients—the wives of my generals, or the gutter rats you hide in my hospital?"

"To be honest, both. I have seen neither my patients, nor the orphans, since Sunday. I am long overdue analyzing Reema's blood sugar counts, and I should really check on Shatha. When I last saw her, she was unusually despondent. And of course, Nusrat always requires tending. She must think I abandoned her, so if I—"

"Stop! You have made your point." Khan gripped her forearms, smiling. "Actually, I am glad to see you eager to resume your duties, even to visit your beggar children. Your insolence makes me feel as if you never left."

"In truth, I lost two days of work."

"Very well, go for one hour. After that, return to the Citadel. Three guards shall accompany you—both to assure your safety, and guarantee your obedience." Khan must have thought himself funny. He laughed, digging his fingers deeper into her soft flesh.

"Thank you, kind master."

"Tomorrow, though, you must answer the captain's questions."

"As you wish."

"He has vowed diligence in resolving the answer to his puzzle."

"What puzzle is that?"

Khan released her arm, and scrutinized her face. "Perhaps I shall ask you now, my flower. How many men abducted you?"

Salena knew to keep her answers short and vague. "It is difficult to say. Much of the time I was blindfolded. Perhaps four or five, maybe more."

"Who drove the Mercedes?"

"Our kidnappers, of course."

"Then Qadeer is right, it *is* rather odd."

Salena sensed she had given a wrong answer, but wasn't sure why. "Everything happened so quickly. I was frightened. I cannot remember the exact timing and sequence of events."

"But the kidnappers drove."

"I told you, they covered my eyes. Much of the time I could not see."

"Is it possible they put you in the front seat without your knowing?"

"I suppose. Why?"

"My soldiers discovered the Mercedes deep in the Neelum Valley. Mr. Cattano's fingerprints were found on the steering wheel; yours all over the dashboard and front passenger door handle."

Salena did everything humanly possible to stop from gasping. "When I was blindfolded, I … I did hear someone order Mr. Covel … Cattano to drive."

Khan smiled down at her. His voice was smooth like a velvet rasp. "Do not worry my love. All the answers shall come." He kissed her forehead. "For now, wait here for your three protectors, and when they come, tend to your patients. After that, sleep well, for tomorrow brings a glorious dawn and a new beginning for Pakistan."

CHAPTER EIGHTY-SEVEN

Knowing the plush Porky Pig brushing his ear held enough explosives to topple most man-made structures wasn't enough to keep John from shutting his eyes and battling sleep. After all he'd endured since last Thursday, he understood why exhaustion was catching up, but if he held onto his wits one more night, he could spend the rest of his life recharging his batteries.

Lying on the hospital bed, John mulled how he might gain access to the Citadel's 3rd floor before seven o'clock tomorrow morning. The nurse had offered him the option of recuperating in his room in the Citadel. If he accepted, and went back, he might talk his way past the guards on the 6th floor, ride the main elevators down to the 4th floor, and return to the storage room abutting the dead space. From there he would enter the shaft housing Khan's secret elevator.

If the guards asked why he was leaving his room, he'd say to fulfill his sudden urge for the black tea dispensed by the vending machines across from the employee cafeteria. But still, the plan had holes. The explosives, delay detonators, and wire would not fit into his pockets, and explaining why he was taking along his stuffed Porky Pig would be tough. Moreover, since he needed three or four hours to set the RDX-7S charges, synchronize their timers, position the delay detonators, and double-check the connections of the gelatin dynamite already in place, the guards were sure to become suspicious of his lengthy absence. Even if he could explain his plush companion, and come up with a logical reason for a three-hour tea break, he had no way of getting into the storage room, which by now must be locked.

John heard footsteps approach his bed. He opened his eyes to find staring down at him a silver-bearded gentleman wearing an emerald green turban and a pair of dented wire glasses.

"Raja."

The doctor's tone was not nearly as friendly as the last time they'd spoken—after the fire on Sunday, when they'd tried to convince Salena a trip to Srinagar was out of the question.

"Are you insane?"

John had no clue what Raja knew. "What do you mean?"

"Don't forget, Mr. Cattano, Mr. Covello, or whatever you call yourself, Dr. Qureshi is one of my oldest and dearest colleagues."

John pressed his finger to his lips, signaling Raja to shut up.

"I will not silence myself. How could you put Salena's life in danger?"

If the room were bugged, Raja had given him away. "Doctor, I have no idea what you're talking about."

"You know perfectly well I am referring to the Assistant Director of Lal Ded Hospital in Srinagar, the same hospital where Salena's mother passed away this afternoon, the same hospital where you and Salena were almost killed at the hands of Indian soldiers. How dare you put her life in jeopardy? You are a clever liar. You had me believing you cared about Salena's safety. You are nothing but a lying—"

"Hold on."

"…American scoundrel whose only gratification you seek is your own."

"Are you finished?"

"Qureshi also said …"

Apparently not.

"…an American army officer was present, and she knew your identity. After you met with an Indian general, you and Salena were driven to an orphanage, I presume, to visit Naji."

"Are you going to let me talk?"

"You think me a fool, but I knew Salena would steal your heart."

Expecting a battalion of Qadeer's goons to barge in at any second, John sat up, jumped off the bed, and glared at Raja. "Let me talk."

Raja took a hesitant step backward.

If someone had been listening, they were dead anyway, so he might as well speak his mind. "Yes, we did go to Srinagar, yes, we did see Omar Shah, and yes, we were almost killed—several times, in fact—but my first inkling I was taking a wild ride to Kashmir came when I woke up lying on my back along a riverbank in the middle of nowhere with Dr. Zamal standing over me teaching me to shoot a German machine gun."

"She planned the journey without you?"

"Yes, and it's amazing we survived, but thanks to you, if this room's bugged, we're all gonna die."

Realizing his mistake, Raja snapped his head both ways, and said meekly, "I am sorry."

John and Raja stood facing one another, waiting for Khan's soldiers to storm in and drag them away. Instead, the chubby-faced nurse who had wheeled John from the Emergency Room walked in and asked, "Is there a problem?"

John looked at him innocently. "Should there be?"

"I heard loud voices."

"We're happy to see each other."

"Patients are sleeping."

"I'll keep it down."

The nurse left, and John and Raja stood another two minutes without saying a word. Finally John whispered, "I think we're all right."

"I am truly sorry. I lost my composure."

Speaking softly, watching the door behind Raja, John related everything that had happened since yesterday morning when he and Salena had left the Citadel. He skipped certain parts, like last night's sleeping arrangements in the cave, and how he and Salena had spent their time under the shikara's canopy on Dal Lake. He did tell Raja about the US ambassador's visit, but said nothing of where the RDX-7S charges were concealed, or even that they had been delivered.

When he heard John wasn't dying from pancreatic cancer, Raja was stunned. "Why did you return?"

"Who else is gonna stop Khan from obliterating South Asia?"

"This is not your war. You could have gone home to your family."

"I made a promise to Salena, and I never break a promise."

Raja smirked. "A valiant American who keeps his word. I can think of nothing more obnoxious."

John ignored the dig. "I was counting on her to help get me into the Citadel's 3rd floor."

"Impossible. Three armed soldiers are following her everywhere. Qadeer already suspects Salena of no good. If you so much as look at her, you put her life at risk."

John mulled the possibility of slipping past the Citadel's guards without Salena's help. As he weighed his options, an idea occurred to him that wasn't completely nuts. He glanced at the pink pig beside his pillow, then looked at Raja. "If Salena can't help me, you must."

"What can I do?"

"Help me finish what we started."

"I will not go into the Citadel. I am staying in the hospital—all night, if necessary—to make sure Salena is not harmed."

"I'm not asking you to go to the 3rd floor."

"Then where?"

"Just across the skywalk, into the Citadel."

"When you get there, do you have a plan?"

John did, but one obstacle remained. "You don't happen to have that storage room key Salena gave you?"

"In all the commotion Sunday, I never had a chance to return it."

Raja dug into his lab coat, pulled out a ring of keys, and removed a gold-plated key. "It's right here."

John grabbed the sides of Raja's head, and kissed his forehead. "You're one clever man."

"It was an oversight."

"I don't care, you're still clever." John took the key, faced the bed, and picked up the pig. Scrutinizing the seam where Porky's nose was sewn to his face, he saw the stitching had been tampered with. The original seam had been replaced with half-inch wide stitches, which at the right time, would make pulling off his nose a cinch.

John poked his finger between two stitches under the animal's nose, widened the gap between the threads, then pushed the key into the stuffing. He placed Porky on the night table and turned to Raja. "That was easy."

Raja cringed. "Bad enough someone brings the likeness of an animal into Khan's hospital, but of all animals, that most detested by Muslims."

"Exactly why they chose Porky. He's part of the plan to get the explosives into the Citadel, the plan you're gonna help me with."

Raja sounded less than enthusiastic. "What time should I return tomorrow?"

"Tomorrow's too late. Khan moved up his meeting to first thing in the morning." John glanced at his watch. "If I'm gonna blow the Citadel in nine hours, I've gotta get in tonight."

Raja tugged the short hairs of his trim beard. "When do you propose we go?"

"No time like the present."

Chapter Eighty-Eight

John lifted Porky Pig from the night table and presented him to Raja. "I will not touch that vile animal. 'Forbidden to you are dead meat, blood, and the flesh of swine.' The Qur'an strictly forbids the consumption of pork."

"I'm not asking you to eat the damn thing. Just hold it."

Raja pinned the bloated waist of the stuffed animal between the fingertips of both hands and held it straight out. "This wretched toy is rather heavy."

"Made in America. Built solid."

"I do not understand how it helps you get the explosives into the Citadel?"

Having pegged Raja as the nervous type, John thought twice about telling him he already held the most powerful demolition charges on earth. "Trust me, Raja, my government is proficient in the techniques of clandestine transport."

"Will they attempt the same trick as with the dynamite?"

"Maybe." John pulled a white plastic bag from the night table drawer and crammed his dirty shalwar kameez and underwear inside. He tied his Nikes and waved his arm in a sweeping motion toward the door. "After you."

Raja started walking, and just before reaching the threshold, stopped and turned. "I wager the explosives are taped to your body."

"Stop guessing. I'll tell you after we cross the skywalk."

"If anyone asks, why am I with you?"

"You'll see."

Raja entered the corridor, and John limped out after him, favoring his left leg. "Wait for me, doc."

Raja looked back. "When did you injure your foot?"

John hobbled to catch up and whispered, "Now you know why you're with me." He grasped Raja's free arm and the two continued through the hospital's desolate halls. At the nurses station, two soldiers in tan fatigues watched them approach.

When they reached the soldiers, the taller of the two grimaced at the stuffed animal under Raja's left arm and asked John where he was going. The male nurse who had wheeled John to his room, and who now sat behind the counter, looked up. "Good evening Mr. Cattano, Dr. Raja." The nurse addressed the soldiers. "Mr. Cattano has General Khan's authorization to return to his room in the Command and Control Center."

The soldier nodded. "I'll radio ahead."

The nurse said to John, "Please return to this station tomorrow morning at eight-thirty for a follow-up blood test and urinalysis. Before that, eat no solid foods for eight hours."

"Can I do the tests earlier?"

The nurse glanced down at his desktop calendar. "What time is convenient?"

"Seven-fifteen. After that, I have an appointment elsewhere."

"Seven-fifteen will be fine. Ask for Nurse Aasim."

"Will do."

The soldiers let them pass, and arm-in-arm John and Raja slowly made their way to the main elevator bank. Raja pressed the "up" button and they boarded the first car to arrive. Alone in the elevator, Raja pressed '4' and yanked his arm from John's grip. "I'll bet they put them in a flower pot in your room."

"Put what?"

"The explosives."

"Be cool, Raja."

"Why can't you tell me?"

"I have more important things to tell you."

"Such as?"

"You said Qadeer's guard dogs are watching Salena."

"They have not let her out of their sight."

"You have to get to her and tell her Khan moved Glorious Dawn to seven o'clock tomorrow morning. Make sure she's nowhere near the Citadel when it blows. Of course, same goes for you. In fact, I'd feel better if you two were together when I detonate the explosives."

"What should we do after the Citadel is destroyed?"

The elevator stopped, and they got out on the 4th floor. Clutching Raja's arm, limping beside him, John turned down the hall leading to the skywalk. He kept his voice low. "The instant you hear the explosion, escort Salena to the hospital's main lobby. That's where we'll meet. A car will be waiting outside to pick up me and Salena. The minute my government confirms Khan and his cronies are dead, they'll fly President Razzak to Islamabad. The hours between the implosion and Razzak's return could get pretty hairy, so it's a good idea if you tag along."

"Are you sure you want me?"

"Don't be silly." John wondered if he'd have time alone with Salena before CRUSO flew him back to America. "Please come for Salena's sake. After I leave, I'd prefer if she had a good friend with her."

They reached the small lobby on the hospital side of the skywalk. John said to Raja as much as to himself, "Are you ready?"

"For what?"

"To prevent World War III."

"How do they say in your country? Let us do it."

Raja walked, and John limped across the skywalk. At the checkpoint on the Citadel side they found two guards waiting for them.

What John did in the next few seconds would either get him shot, or safely to the 3rd floor. He recognized one of the two soldiers at the counter. As John hobbled toward the checkpoint, the soldier said, "Good evening, Mr. Cattano. How are you feeling?"

"A bit tired."

The other soldier stepped from behind the counter holding a black wand, some sort of metal detector. John was well aware the wire and detonators inside the stuffed animal would set off the alarm.

"Please step forward," the guard instructed.

John handed his watch and bag of dirty clothes to the soldier, who passed the wand along John's left side, head-to-toe, and repeated the process on his right. The soldier then hand-patted John's shirt and pants and circled the wand around the plastic bag.

The soldier nodded, and John shuffled to the opposite side of the counter. He turned and noticed Raja biting his lower lip. After the torments Qadeer and his goons had put him through, the doctor had good reason to be nervous.

The soldier holding the wand scowled at Raja. "What is that unholy creature in your arm?"

Raja swallowed hard. "It's ... it's not ... I don't—"

"I'm sorry," John said. "It's the gift Ambassador Kline gave me when he stopped by the hospital. I apologize for his insensitivity."

The guard slammed the wand on the counter, grabbed Porky Pig from under Raja's arm, and thrust him into John's hands like a lit firecracker. "You cannot take this upstairs. Get rid of it."

"Gladly, but where?"

The first guard pointed down a hall off the small lobby. "Go that way and around the corner. You will find a garbage pail next to the vending machines."

"Across from the cafeteria?"

"Yes."

"I've been there. Any chance the cafeteria's open?"

"The Citadel is housing a great many guests tonight. To accommodate them, the cafeteria will remain open until midnight."

"Our kidnappers barely fed us, and I'm dying for some sweet black tea. Do you think I might stop in and grab a cup?"

"After you discard the pig."

"Of course."

The second guard pressed the point. "Do not pass this way again with that filthy animal."

"I won't. You have my word."

The guard picked up the wand and passed it along Raja's left and right sides, then frisked the doctor the same as he had John.

After a pair of nods from the soldiers, John and Raja walked slowly down the hall and around the corner toward the employee cafeteria. John carried the pig, and Raja held John's clothes.

Raja asked, "How did they miss the charges taped to your body?"

"Because they're not there."

"Please, I would like to tell Salena you have the explosives."

"Then tell her."

Raja stopped short. "You are being entirely too mysterious. I will say nothing to Salena unless you tell me where the charges are hidden."

John released Raja's arm, took a step back, and smiled. "My friend, you carried them into the Citadel yourself."

Raja looked at John puzzled, then slowly lowered his gaze to the plush Porky Pig tucked under John's arm. Behind his wire rims, Raja's eyes grew large. "You mean ..."

"Sorry, but I figured if they saw *you* holding the pig they'd make you get rid of it a lot faster than if *I* held it."

"You are right, better I did not know."

John took the plastic bag from Raja. "Go find Salena. Tell her I never break a promise. Her nightmare is about to end."

Raja embraced John. "May Allah light your way."

CHAPTER EIGHTY-NINE

In the vending machine alcove across the hall from the employee cafeteria, out of view of the cameras trained on the cafeteria doors, John removed his dirty clothes from the plastic bag and shoved them into a covered garbage pail beside a candy dispenser. He carefully extracted the storage room key from Porky's nose and slipped the pig into the empty bag. Holding the plastic bag, John walked into the cafeteria, avoided eye contact with the suits and uniforms seated at roughly half the tables, and purchased a cup of sweet black tea to go.

Carrying the Styrofoam cup and the plastic bag, he left the cafeteria, found his way to the storage room door, and let himself in. After flipping on the lights, he walked to the metal shelves against the wall he was about to climb, bent down, and stuck his hand behind a stack of computer printouts. He found Raja's penlight where he'd left it Sunday, snapped it on, and shut off the storage room lights.

Clenching the penlight between his teeth, he gripped the bag with Porky inside and scaled the shelving unit. After sliding away a ceiling tile above the top shelf, he lowered his legs into the dark dead space between the storage room and the interrogation room viewing area. His feet found the folding chair he'd left against the wall, and he stepped down.

Inside the dead space he opened the door to the shaft housing Khan's secret elevator. Hearing no cables move, he stepped onto the metal rungs attached to the wall, descended, and when he reached the floor below, slowly pulled open the door.

The bulbs dangling from the girders were unlit, but the vacant 3rd floor was not entirely dark. The lights of Islamabad shone in from the windows, casting eerie thin shadows from vertical I-beams onto the cement floor. John had no choice but to work without lights. Turning them on would attract the attention of the soldiers patrolling the Citadel on the ground, as well as those stationed on the hospital roof next door. He wasn't too concerned, though. Between the penlight and the city lights, he'd have no trouble seeing what was essential to complete his task.

John walked to the middle of the deserted floor, pulled Porky from the plastic bag, and with a firm tug, tore off the pig's nose. The seams along the belly gave way, and out spilled everything he needed to assure Ali Khan met his death under tons of debris.

John counted 21 RDX-7S linear-shaped charges with built-in delay elements, and 10 delay connectors to fix the interval between the firing signal and base detonation for the gelatin dynamite. Tucked in Porky's hindquarters he found a time chart for the delay connectors, and in the pig's rump, a single remote detonator with a handwritten note rubber-banded around its black casing.

The note, signed by Lieutenant Hall, apologized for delivering only 10 delay connectors when John had requested 16, and explained why only one remote detonator had been supplied. The detonator's radio frequency had been calibrated to send simultaneous firing signals to the delay elements in the RDX-7S charges and the electronic lead lines attached to the gelatin dynamite John had already positioned. That meant he need not worry about simultaneously pressing four buttons—two on each detonator to charge and fire the blasting caps. The hand-held detonator resembled a TV remote with a single dial and two buttons, and slipped easily into his shalwar pocket.

John set to work attaching the high-powered RDX prototype charges to the vertical beams he deduced would cause the Citadel to fall in on itself, not outward against the hospital, or across the street on the Diplomatic Enclave.

Demolishing a building was a lot like felling a tree. To topple a tree south, a lumberjack cut the trunk on its south side. To fell a skyscraper south, a demolitions contractor detonated charges on the building's south side first. An implosion—the collapse of a building within its own footprint—required a different approach. Thinking of a high-rise as four separate columns of equal size, the contractor positioned the explosives so that when detonated, each column fell in the direction of the building's core, not outward to any side.

Denied the advantages of 3D computer modeling or actual test-blasting, John judged where to position the linear charges based solely on experience and instinct. For a 12-story building, cutting the vertical support columns on the 3rd floor would effectively collapse the building, and timing the detonations so that the columns at the center blew out first, followed milliseconds later by columns along the perimeter, would collapse the building inward.

If this were a commercial job, he'd also position charges on the Citadel's 8th and 9th floors. Blowing columns on a structure's upper floors facilitated clean-up by pulverizing the building's materials into fragments. For this project, though, John didn't give a damn about what sort of mess he left behind—so long as no harm came to innocents.

After working 20 minutes, John concluded he'd need only 18 of the 21 RDX-7S charges to slice the primary support beams bearing the weight of the Citadel's upper floors. For any demolition task, too many explosives was worse than just enough, and for this job, 18 charges were all he needed. John couldn't wait to see Farrell's expression when he handed her back three of her top-secret charges unscathed.

John positioned the 18 pencil-thin tubes without breaking a sweat, and when he was done, had plenty of time to relocate 36 of the 50 gelatin dynamite sticks he'd positioned on Sunday, taping two sticks to each column loaded with an RDX-7S charge. He attached the dynamite to the sides of the columns facing away from the building's core and set their delay switches to ignite 5 milliseconds after the RDX-7S charges severed the I-beams. The dynamite would in essence push the vertical support beam toward the center of the building after the RDX-7S charge cut the beam in half.

Relocating the dynamite actually took more time than placing the RDX-7S charges, and after setting the delay elements for the dynamite, John shone the penlight on his watch and saw the entire job had taken less than two hours. As midnight approached, he considered how to return to his room in the Citadel without calling undue attention to himself. Mulling his choices, it occurred to him he need not return at all.

He would set his watch alarm for 6:30 a.m., and exit the Citadel first thing in the morning. Spending the night on the vacant 3rd floor instead of his 6th floor suite minimized the chance he'd bump into Captain Qadeer over the next few hours, or even worse, that he'd be found by Qadeer if the captain came looking for him. The more he thought about staying put and avoiding a confrontation with the captain, the more he liked the idea. The biggest problem with staying was inventing a story for the guards at the sky bridge in the morning.

By sunrise a different pair of soldiers would be on duty. He'd tell them he couldn't sleep and had gone to the 4th floor in the middle of the night—while the previous guards were posted—to buy tea from the vending machines. Why he'd taken nine hours to buy a cup of tea might be hard to explain, but John supposed he could concoct a tale of grueling constipation, then falling asleep in a bathroom stall. Worst case, he could run across the sky bridge holding the detonator, and when the soldiers chased him, literally blow the floor out from under their feet.

John found the sheet Raja had used as a prayer mat on Sunday, and moved it against the wall of the main elevator shaft in the center of the floor. He sat in the darkness with his back against the cool cement knowing he'd done a good job. This implosion would be clean, not perfect, but he was confident the steel columns would collapse to the building's core.

After setting his watch chime for 6:30 a.m., John patted his pockets, making sure they held the detonator and three leftover RDX charges. He closed his eyes and saw Billy Dwyer's face, and knew then and there if God let him live past tomorrow, what happened in Chicago was behind him forever.

CHAPTER NINETY

Flanked and tailed by Khan's three soldiers in the corridor leading to the Labor and Delivery Unit, Salena whiffed the faint scent of smoke left over from the fire she had started on Sunday. These particular soldiers had accompanied her before, though never at the same time, and were familiar with the rules. When they came to the automatic doors separating the visitors area from the rooms of the female patients, the soldiers abruptly stopped. Salena informed her guards she'd be on the ward longer than usual, as she hadn't seen her patients in three days.

Khan had commanded she return to the Citadel in one hour, but Salena hoped to stretch one into three, possibly more. She had no desire to ever again step foot in the Citadel, and would spend the entire night in the hospital if she could find a way to elude her escorts. She also feared running into Qadeer, who had found incriminating fingerprints inside the abandoned Mercedes. He was certain to put the evidence together eventually, so the longer she managed to avoid him, the more likely she would never again see him alive.

Only one of the soldiers stood outside the ward, guarding the automatic doors. The other two sauntered into a visitors lounge off the hall and plopped onto a blue vinyl sofa in front of a TV. Salena entered the Labor and Delivery Unit, and went directly to the nurses station where she had moved her patient files after the fire.

Sitting behind the counter, Nurse Jawaid asked Salena how she was holding up. Preferring to avoid small talk, Salena replied she had never felt better, and was anxious to return to her duties. She picked up five manila folders at one end of the U-shaped counter and set off to visit her most difficult patient first.

Fortunately, she found Nusrat asleep. Salena stood a full minute at the foot of the woman's bed pretending to check her chart, then visited the rooms of four other women she prayed John would soon make widows. Some, like Nusrat, whose haughty self-importance endured only because her husband belonged to Khan's inner circle, were about to get what they deserved. Others, like Shatha, beaten into suicidal depression by her husband, were about to receive an answer to their prayers.

She completed her rounds on the 5th floor and returned to the nurses station, leaving behind her patient files for what she hoped was the last time. Instead of joining her escorts outside, she headed back toward Nusrat's room, passed Nusrat's door and the doors of all her patients, and at the end of the deserted hall, entered a stairwell and walked one flight down.

Her destination was the Freedom Ward, and her route took her through the Pediatric Unit. As she approached Room 412, the empty patient room Raja chose to escape the scrutiny of Qadeer's listening devices, she was surprised to see a light on at 10:30 p.m. She tiptoed to the door, peeked in, and saw Raja sitting behind a small table, staring down at his files.

Without making a sound, Salena walked in. When Raja looked up, he shot out of his chair and met her halfway. "You are supposed to be upstairs checking on your patients."

"How do you know that?" she asked, not surprised he had been watching over her.

"Never mind. Where are the soldiers?"

"Glued to a TV in the visitors lounge. I came downstairs to check on the children."

Raja leaned closer. "The halls are not safe with Qadeer about."

"Is he on the floor?"

"I have not seen him all day, but you never know when or where that human waste will appear." Raja looked past Salena's shoulder, then placed his hand on her arm. "Please accept my condolences on your mother's death."

"I am not sad. She is in paradise." Salena hesitated, but had to ask. "Have you heard anything of John?"

Raja frowned. "An hour ago I helped him enter the Citadel."

"Is he there now?"

"When I saw him last, he was headed for the storage room on the 4th floor carrying an ungodly stuffed toy filled with explosives."

"Ambassador Kline. But why is he placing the charges so soon?"

"That is why I am here. I suspected you might visit the Freedom Ward, and I have an important message from John."

Salena's heart fluttered. "What did he say?"

"Ali Khan has moved Glorious Dawn to seven o'clock tomorrow morning."

"How can that be? The meeting is scheduled for one."

"Khan is apparently launching his attack on India sooner than anyone expected."

"Then it is fortunate John and I returned from Kashmir when we did."

"About your journey to Kashmir ..." Raja folded his arms across his chest. "John told me all about it. Your drive through the Neelum Valley, your hike over the Himalayas, your bus ride to Srinagar. If I weren't privy to your passion for the Vale, your trek might have surprised me."

"Please understand."

"I understand only because you have returned alive."

"Did he reveal the most important reason I must live?"

"If he succeeds, Sanjay Behari has agreed to allow a referendum for Kashmiri independence. You can finally go home to Srinagar."

"And to Naji."

"Yes, and Naji, too."

"Did John tell you he is not dying, that he returned to Islamabad of his own accord?"

Raja looked down at the carpet. "He did. He also told me he came back because he made you a promise."

"He said that?"

Raja nodded.

"John is a good man."

"I must ask you a difficult question." The proud doctor lifted his eyes. "Do you love John?"

Salena had no idea what John had told Raja about their time in the Himalayas and on Dal Lake, but she hoped the American had respected her honor. "I did have fond thoughts of him, but circumstances have changed, and I have driven those thoughts from my head."

"And from your heart?"

"I tell you, my feelings for John are not that way. Not anymore." She looked down.

"I do not believe you, Salena, for the pain you feel now I suffer every day—loving you and knowing you will never love me in return."

Avoiding Raja's gaze, she confessed, "It is true, I cannot erase him from my mind, but like you, I have no choice. He is married and will soon go home."

"Does he know the depth of your emotions?"

She could not help but recall John's seductive touch. "Yes, and I am certain he feels the same."

"What will you do Salena?"

"I do not know … but I do know this. I am deeply sorry I hurt you."

Raja forced a smile. "Why? You did not make me fall in love with you. I did that."

Salena heard footsteps in the hall and turned to see a nurse walk past the door. "I must go."

"Be careful, and whatever you do, leave the Citadel by 6:30 a.m. John wants us both in the lobby downstairs when the charges go off."

"A car from the US Embassy will be waiting outside."

"Of course, you already know." Raja gently took hold of her hands. "I am truly happy for you. Before long, you shall satisfy your two strongest desires. Freedom for Kashmir, and freedom for yourself."

But not all her desires, she thought.

Salena said good-bye and left the room. Walking briskly but silently through the late-night halls of the Pediatric Unit, she prayed her love for John might one day wane. If such a day came, she might visit John in America, perhaps even meet his family. She would take along her son, and if fortune smiled upon her, a husband too. Newfound love offered the swiftest relief for a broken heart, though she could not imagine, not yet, craving any man as she craved John Covello.

She left the Pediatric Unit and stopped at the metal door to the storage room housing her orphans. Before going inside, Salena spied a circular clock on the wall. It was nearly 11:00 p.m., and the soldiers upstairs would soon grow anxious. She must make her visit brief, return to the 4th floor, and fabricate a cogent reason why she needed more time with the sleeping wives of Khan's officers.

Salena entered the dimly lit Freedom Ward, and heard the rhythmic breathing of little ones whose respite from despair lasted only as long as the night. She lowered her dupatta and walked to the last cot on the left. Not unexpectedly, she found Kalila lying atop her skimpy blanket, eyes open.

Kalila popped up and embraced Salena.

"More nightmares?"

"They said you left the hospital."

Salena had already decided if the Americans freed her from Khan's grip, she would take Kalila home with her to Srinagar. Though Major Farrell had no way of knowing, tomorrow's flight from Islamabad required one more seat. "I had important work to do."

"I thought you ran away."

Salena sat on the cot beside Kalila, and swept long strands of black hair away from her cheeks. "Nothing or no one could make me leave you. In fact, I bring important news. Do you wish to hear?"

Kalila's hair bobbed with her nod.

"There is a good chance tomorrow you will have a new home."

"You found a mummy and poppi for me?"

"Would only a mummy do?"

"If she loves me."

"Of course she loves you."

"Who is it?"

Salena planted a gentle kiss on Kalila's forehead. "Me."

Kalila's eyes lit up, and her mouth opened, as if she were about to scream. Salena pressed her finger to the girl's lips and looked around at the other children.

Kalila whispered, "I am sorry … I am so … so very happy."

"Me too."

"But where will we live?"

"Where I grew up. In Kashmir."

"This must be a dream."

"It is not, but please sleep, for tomorrow you will need all your energy." Salena hugged Kalila, then kissed her lips.

The child lay on her side and Salena pulled the thin blanket to her neck.

"Will you sleep with me?"

"The monsters again?"

"Yes, but when you are my mummy, they will go away."

Salena longed to tell her monsters did not exist, but in a world where children watched parents butchered at the hands of barbarians, monsters of the human kind were all too real. Salena lay on her side, snuggled to Kalila's back, and wrapped her arm around the girl's waist. "I love you."

Kalila whispered, "I love you, too."

Lying beside her new daughter, Salena fell into a deep, dreamless slumber and would likely have slept through the night had she not been awakened by the muffled shouts of men—angry men—stomping through the halls outside. She rose, and at the nearest nightlight, checked her watch. She'd slept over an hour.

This was not the first time Salena had forced her escorts to search for her, but never before had they screamed her name with such fury.

"Who are those men?"

Salena turned to find Kalila sitting up, rubbing her eyes. She went to the girl and knelt beside her. "When I find out, I will scold them for waking my children. Go back to sleep."

Kalila shook her head.

"Please try," Salena whispered. "Tomorrow is a big day."

Kalila sat up and wrapped her arms around Salena. "I am scared."

"I will return, if not tonight, tomorrow morning. Be patient a little longer. Can you do that for me?"

"I will try, but please do not forget me."

"Never, Kalila. Never."

Salena strode to the solid metal door, and yanked it open. In the hall she spotted the backs of five burly soldiers in green combat fatigues lugging rifles and radios through the Pediatric Unit's double doors.

After closing the door behind her, Salena called out, "What is this fuss about?"

All five men spun at once. The red-turbaned soldier leading the group, now at the rear, stepped through the four men blocking him.

Instinctively, Salena clenched her teeth and balled her fists.

Azam Qadeer.

"There you are, bitch."

Stunned silent, Salena froze. Qadeer's eyes narrowed until their white's disappeared, leaving thin black slivers scrutinizing her like a vulture eager to devour its prey. He marched up to her, lifted his large calloused hand, and struck her hard across the face. "Where is your veil?"

Salena staggered backward against the storage room door, more dazed than hurt. Rubbing her cheek, her mind raced, trying to make sense of the senseless. "Why are you here? Why did you hit me?"

Qadeer barked at his men, "Take her."

"What have I done?"

Two sets of burly hands grabbed her wrists and yanked them hard behind her back. She heard the click of handcuffs and no longer had use of her hands. *John had been caught.*

The soldiers dragged and pushed her down the hall toward the elevators. She could not see Qadeer, but smelled his foul tobacco somewhere behind her.

She heard a shriek. A child's shriek. She strained to look over her shoulder, and saw Kalila running toward her.

The girl darted around Qadeer's groping hands, and entwined her frail arms around Salena's waist. "Don't hurt her, don't hurt her."

Adrenaline took over and Salena writhed free of the soldiers.

Kalila's grip tightened. "Please don't hurt Miss Salena."

Salena screamed, "Go back, Kalila. Go back."

A lascivious grin curled Qadeer's lips, and his eyes widened in a way that made Salena sick. Khan's twisted enforcer pulled a billy club from his belt and whacked the child hard across the back.

Kalila shrieked but still held tight.

Salena screamed, "You demented ass!"

Qadeer again lifted the club, but before he could smash the child's back, Salena lurched in the path of its downward arc.

Her thigh took the full brunt of solid wood, her legs buckled, and she stumbled to her knees.

Somewhere close by Salena heard the screams of women begging Qadeer to stop. Two veiled nurses kneeling beside her struggled to pull Kalila away.

For an instant, Salena locked eyes with Kalila. "Please go back. If you do, I promise you a new home, a good home."

Through Kalila's tears, Salena saw terror she had once known herself, and at that moment wished nothing more than to slash off Qadeer's testicles and shove them down his throat.

The nurses managed to pull Kalila off, but the child would not go willingly. The two women dragged the girl backward down the hall toward the Freedom Ward, and even as she disappeared through the metal door, Kalila reached out for Salena.

Two soldiers grabbed Salena's arms, jerked her off the floor, and shoved her in front of Qadeer.

Salena stared at the captain, refusing to flinch. "You fool, when I inform General Khan of your despicable acts, he shall slit your throat."

Qadeer smirked, then smiled, and finally, he laughed, and only when tears came to his eyes did the hideous peals subside. "You are the fool, for it is Ali Khan who has sent me."

CHAPTER NINETY-ONE

John's eyes shot open as his brain registered sound—intermittent beeping from his watch. He had forgotten he'd fallen asleep against a wall on the Citadel's vacant 3rd floor. When he looked around and saw vertical I-beams, steel girders, and bright sunlight gleaming through tinted windows, for a blessed instant he thought he had dozed off while preparing to implode a condemned building for Planned Demolitions, Inc.

When the sober truth hit, John wondered if he'd live to see another dawn.

He massaged his left upper arm, throbbing with pain. Steadying himself against the concrete wall, John rose, rubbed his legs, and lumbered to the windows overlooking Constitution Avenue. He admired the green slopes of the Margalla Hills, hoping there might come a time he could return to Pakistan with Maureen and his daughters to tour this magnificent country unafraid of getting kidnapped, killed, or both. One thing he did know—the globe in his den would never look quite the same.

John turned his attention to the walled compound across the street. Half a dozen children were already playing on the school's jungle gym. He watched a small boy in a blue T-shirt push an even smaller girl on a swing, and though he could not hear their voices through the glass, their eyes and mouths belied laughter. He swallowed hard. If he had done any less than his best work last night, those children could end up dead.

He also considered the lives of the poor souls caught in the Citadel at the moment of detonation who didn't deserve to die—janitors, cooks, and servants earning a living in the wrong place at the wrong time. Maybe Colonel Daley had been right. Collateral damage was a necessary consequence of achieving the greater good, and John couldn't think of a good much greater than preventing a calamitous war in which tens of millions would perish.

John watched a young mom walk her son into the school across the street, and recalled his last image of Maureen. She stood at their kitchen window as he steered his Boston Whaler into the Manasquan River. He had waved to her, but she didn't wave back. In fact, she had been crying. God, how he missed her, and for the first time since he'd slept with Salena in the cave, he yearned to hold Maureen and look into those strong blue eyes and caress her soft, golden hair. He loved Salena, but he didn't belong with her. He belonged home, and home was Maureen, Karen, and Christie.

As he thought about his family, reality sank in. If he survived the next 45 minutes, he'd get paid $30,000,000, first to satisfy his debts, then to spend wantonly on his wife and daughters. He'd even have money to squander on himself. No disrespect to the Royal Enfield that had saved his life, but nothing came close to the big, deep ride of a Harley Davidson ElectraGlide.

John would miss Salena, but after today they'd both get a chance to wipe the slate clean, maybe not completely, but enough to erase most of the suffering they'd endured during the last few years.

He patted his shalwar pockets and confirmed he hadn't dropped the detonator and the three unused RDX-7S charges. After checking the time, 6:40 a.m., he walked to the shaft housing Khan's secret elevator, which in 21 minutes would exist no more.

He planned to climb inside the shaft of Khan's elevator to the 3rd floor. From the dead space between the storage room and interrogation room theater, he would shimmy over the wall into the storage room, enter the Citadel's 4th floor corridors, and stroll past the employee cafeteria to the sky bridge. He'd tell the guards he was headed to the hospital for his blood and urine tests, and hopefully, they'd let him pass.

From prior crossings into the hospital, John knew the guards wouldn't frisk him leaving the Citadel. He was more concerned Qadeer's men had discovered he hadn't gone back to his room last night, and would detain him for questioning. John had already decided if the soldiers got nasty, he'd make a dash for the hospital and activate the detonator on the fly. The Citadel would fall in about eight seconds, so he'd wait until reaching the skywalk's halfway point before pressing the 'fire' button.

On the other hand, if he passed the guards with no problem, once in the hospital, he'd find a relaxing spot with a good view, hit the 'charge' and 'fire' buttons, and stand back. As the Citadel collapsed like a house of cards, he'd watch the results of his work with more pride than guilt, satisfied he had rid the world of yet another threat to international peace, and in the process, freed a woman he loved from a life of misery.

John glanced at his watch. Kick-ass time.

He entered the elevator shaft, climbed the ladder one floor up, and entered the dead space between the storage room and the theater where warped minds enjoyed the spectacle of human misery. With no light to guide him but Raja's penlight, he stepped onto the chair and nudged aside a ceiling tile directly above. Ignoring steady pain in his injured arm, he hoisted himself to the top of the wall and saw the lights still out in the storage room. He was about to swing his leg over, when behind him, on the other side of the wall, he heard men talking.

The interrogation room was occupied.

John couldn't make out what they were saying, but he heard three distinct voices. One of them laughed. In John's book, anyone who found joy in the agony of others deserved to die, and if he had his way, in about 12 minutes, every man there would meet that fate.

He swung his leg up and over the wall. Bracing his arm for leverage, preparing to swing his other leg over, John heard a long, shrill wail, a scream borne of abject terror, amplified by speakers inside the gallery.

Then he heard sobs, followed by a woman's voice.

"By the mercy of Allah, please stop."

John's belly collapsed under a torrent of nausea. He knew the voice behind the sobs.

CHAPTER NINETY-TWO

John's response was automatic—he wasn't leaving the Citadel without Salena. He lowered himself back into the dead space and carried the chair to the opposite wall. Standing on the seat, he quietly lifted the nearest ceiling tile and peeked inside the interrogation room.

Through the glass barrier he saw Salena tied to the same chair he had occupied when Qadeer had interrogated him on Saturday. Her wrists were cuffed to a hasp behind the chair's back, and her ankles were bound by sturdy rope to its metal legs. Another rope, looped around her neck and tied to the handcuffs, prevented her from moving her head forward.

Salena's blue dupatta lay on the floor beside the chair. Her long hair partially curtained her face, but not enough to shield her tear-stained cheeks and her left eye—purple, puffy, and half-closed. The front collar of her dress had been torn, rendering her cleavage bare.

Qadeer stood beside Salena clutching a cigarette in one hand and his cattle prod in the other. His tone was eerily calm, as if no further decision need be made regarding Salena's fate. "Where is he?"

Salena whimpered, and when she spoke, the speakers amplified her desperation. "I do not know. Why would I know?"

Qadeer placed his hands on the arms of the interrogation chair and leaned into her face. Salena turned her head, averting his gaze. Qadeer grabbed her chin and forced her to look at him. "That bastard poisoned my most loyal soldier. Tell me where he is now, or I will enjoy this pleasure all day long."

"I swear, I do not know."

Qadeer released her chin, stood erect, and nodded to one of two soldiers standing to the side. The soldier walked up behind the chair, gripped Salena's arms, and squeezed them together at the elbows. The strain on her shoulder blades forced her chest forward, gagging her at the same time.

Qadeer lifted the cattle prod and pressed its glistening U-shaped tip between her breasts. "This is for Siddique."

Even with restraints, Salena's body jolted forward and she shrieked hideously.

The asshole must have given one of his subordinates the cyanide. John regretted only that it hadn't been Qadeer himself who'd swallowed the capsules.

For several seconds, Qadeer held the prod to Salena's tender parts. When he pulled the tip away, her head dangled forward. The rope around her neck kept her torso upright, and her chest heaved, as her screams turned to sobs.

Think, you idiot, think. Looking down into the viewing room from the gap in the ceiling, John counted three soldiers. Two sat in the front row on the opposite side of the theater. The third stood in the aisle and was facing forward next to the chairs where the other two sat. The pair in the chairs, engrossed by Qadeer's cruelties, leaned forward in their seats.

He could jump into the room, sprint between the first and second rows, and grab one of the soldier's guns. He'd shoot the three men in the theater first, and by the time Qadeer, on the blind side of the one-way mirror, realized something was wrong, he'd nail the shithead and his two flunkies through the glass.

The problem was time. He needed 10 seconds to leap into the theater, and run the 15 or so steps to the other side of the room. Before he got anywhere near them, he'd be shot dead.

No matter what, he wasn't leaving Salena, and since he had little chance of surprising the soldiers, he had but one choice. He'd run at them while holding the detonator's 'charge' button, and as his last living act, press the 'fire' button, and topple the Citadel.

Leaning on the top edge of the wall, legs dangling in the dead space, John reached into his left pocket. Remembering he had placed the detonator in his right pocket, he was about to extract his hand when his fingertips touched three tubular objects.

Of course, the charges! The three spare RDX charges.

Each explosive contained independent charging and ignition systems. Their timers could be set to ignite the blasting cap after whatever interval the user programmed. Why not set the blast intensity to its lowest level, the timer for 15 seconds, and lob a charge across the gallery?

John lowered himself into the dark cavity between the storage room and the viewing room, and pulled a single charge from his pocket. Clenching Raja's penlight in his teeth, focusing its beam on his hands, he set the force regulator to 2,000 feet per second, and the ignition timer to 15 seconds. He'd wait until climbing back on the wall before activating the countdown.

Through the speakers in the viewing room John heard Qadeer's voice. "You bitch. I will make you beg for death."

John shut the flashlight and stuffed it in his pocket, held the RDX-7S charge in his teeth, and pulled himself to the top of the wall. He saw Qadeer drop his cigarette, grab Salena's hair, and scream into her battered face.

"Where is Cattano!"

Perched on his stomach along the wall's top edge, John removed the charge from his mouth and depressed a round switch recessed in the top of the tiny cylinder. The digital display started ticking down from 15.0000.

Gripping Salena's hair, Qadeer slammed the back of her head against the chair and lifted the electric prod.

13 … 12 … 11 …

He inserted the prong down Salena's dress and pressed the metal against her breasts.

9 … 8 … 7 …

Khan's enforcer screamed, "You whore, where is he!"

John couldn't wait, not another second. He hoisted his feet to the top of the wall, crouched low, and dropped through the square opening in the ceiling.

Bending his knees to cushion the impact, John hurled the charge across the theater to where the soldiers were bunched. The charge struck the wall behind the standing soldier, and bounced in the aisle behind him. The standing soldier turned toward John, their eyes met, and he yanked a pistol from his holster.

The last thing John saw before diving to the floor was the soldier's gun pointed at his head. John squeezed his eyes shut and shielded his head with his arms.

A deafening explosion shook the room, and searing heat tinged John's hair, and when the noise and heat subsided, John leapt to his feet. The three soldiers—what was left of them—lay sprawled on the floor. A blood-soaked arm on a legless torso quivered, and John realized the man was alive.

The blast left a jagged, gaping hole in the one-way mirror. So as not to be seen by Qadeer and the two soldiers in the interrogation room, John dropped to his hands and knees, and crawled up the side aisle toward the rear of the viewing room. When he reached the aisle behind the last row of seats in the five-row theater, he crawled toward the middle seat.

Peeking between the backs of two seats midway in the last row, John observed the soldiers in the interrogation room approach the shattered partition. Qadeer followed the pair, while 15 feet behind him Salena sat in the metal chair with her head dangling.

He'd have to use another charge. He removed a second cylinder from his left pocket, set the explosive force to 2,000, and the ignition timer to 10 seconds. He waited for Qadeer and his lackeys to walk closer to the glass, away from Salena.

When they came to within a foot of the shattered partition, John activated the timer and tossed the tube over five rows of seats to the front row of the theater. Glimpsing between the seats, John saw one soldier standing at the breach in the glass bend down and pick up the charge. The brown-turbaned man studied the narrow cylinder close to his face. His eyes opened wide, John ducked low, and an ear-splitting, glass-busting boom consumed the viewing room.

The dust settled and John stood. Surveying the damage, he saw the explosion had blown out all but a few shards of glass jutting from each side of the partition, leaving nothing but a badly damaged, foot-high wall rising from the floor. Just inside the viewing room, a charred head, eyes stuck open, lay on the floor gazing at the ceiling. Another soldier's burnt, half-naked corpse had blown 10 feet inside the interrogation room. If John's adrenaline weren't pumping like a piston, he'd have vomited at the site of the broken men scattered on the floor.

John sprinted down the last row of seats to the far side of the theater. When he reached the aisle, he walked slowly toward the front row where he'd blasted the first group of soldiers.

As John stepped over the legless man, an arm reached out and grabbed his ankle. John kicked his leg free, picked up a rifle within the dying man's reach, and saw it was similar to the German rifle Salena had taken from Lieutenant Hassan on the road to Peshawar. Grinding glass fragments beneath his sneakers, John stepped through the shattered partition and spotted Qadeer, face-up, on the floor in front of Salena.

Qadeer's bright red turban had unraveled around his skull, exposing thick black hair matching the color of his wide-open eyes and the soot now covering his face. John approached Qadeer cautiously, uncertain if he were alive. Only when John reached the captain's feet did he get an answer.

Legs straight out, the dazed Qadeer sat up and groaned. Blood trickled from his nose and dripped from a dozen cuts in his skull where John spotted embedded glass fragments.

John moved to the captain's left side and glared at the monster who'd made so many suffer. "Normally, Azam, I never hit a man who's down, but in your case, I'll make an exception." John lifted the rifle, and smashed the stock squarely against Qadeer's temple.

The captain's head snapped forward, and his body went still.

Confident Qadeer was a threat no more, John reached down and yanked a pocket knife and key ring off the captain's belt. He walked behind the metal chair and sliced the ropes holding Salena's neck, then removed the cuffs binding her wrists, and the ropes around her feet.

He stood, and came around the chair to face Salena. Kneeling in front of her, he cupped his hand under her bruised chin and gently lifted her head. Up close the devastation wrought by Qadeer's fist on her tender flesh made John yearn for another whack at the vicious scumbag.

Her un-purpled right eye opened, and her voice was barely audible. "John."

"Come on, Salena, we gotta go." John picked up the rifle and slung it over his back. He slid his free arm under Salena's shoulder and lifted her to her feet.

Salena leaned against John as he guided her over what remained of the glass partition. Inside the viewing room, he walked her up the aisle along the opposite wall from where the first soldiers had fallen. Nearing the exit at the rear of the theater, John heard shouts in the hall. He locked the door handle and came to a quick conclusion.

They'd have to climb down to the vacant 3rd floor through the hidden elevator shaft. Though the passenger elevators didn't stop at the 3rd floor, the service elevator did. He'd ride the elevator one floor up, and pray every guard in the Citadel had been ordered to the interrogation room. Once back on the 4th floor, even if forced to fight his way to the skywalk, he had one rifle and one RDX charge, and that should be enough.

He thought about using his last charge to blast his way into the dead space, but he might need it to take out the guards at the skywalk checkpoint. John brushed Salena's hair away from her cheek, restraining his anguish as he looked at her. "I know a way out, Salena, but we have to climb a wall. Do you think you can do it?"

Salena slowly lifted her arm off John's shoulder and nodded.

Holding Salena's hand, he backtracked down the aisle and stopped under the hole in the ceiling through which he'd entered. He found a folding chair, placed it against the wall, and helped Salena up. "There's another chair on the other side. Lower yourself slowly, and don't be scared. It's dark in there."

Her will to live must have been strong. With a powerful boost from John, she lifted herself to the top of the wall, scrambled through the ceiling, and when she spoke, her voice was a rock. "I am in. Hand me the rifle."

John stepped on the chair's seat and lowered the rifle by its sling into the dead space until Salena took up its weight. As John pulled himself up, he heard a burst of gunfire beneath his feet. His last glimpse of the interrogation room theater was the door busting open and green uniforms pouring in.

Inside the dead space, John took the rifle from Salena and guided her to the door leading to the shaft housing Khan's secret elevator. As he held the knob and inched the door open, a wall of air sent him staggering backward.

The elevator had gone past—Glorious Dawn was about to convene.

John entered the shaft first and helped Salena onto the metal rungs along the wall. He heard shouts from somewhere above, then an explosion. The concussion nearly knocked him off the ladder. Barely clinging to the rungs himself, he reached up and slammed his hand against Salena's back to stop her from falling.

John guessed the soldiers had blasted their way into the dead space.

He continued his descent, with Salena following, until he reached the 3rd floor. He stepped through the door, glanced around, and saw nothing but steel girders and I-beams. Helping Salena inside, John heard more shouts, this time from the elevator shaft.

Qadeer's soldiers were right behind.

John wove his fingers through Salena's. "It's time to blow this joint."

He couldn't believe this brave woman actually managed a smile.

As the rifle on his shoulder slapped his back, John raced with Salena across the open concrete floor. He stopped short at the service elevator, and pushed the 'up' button.

A motor whirred to life. John glanced across the floor at the door from which they'd emerged, and saw a green uniform climbing through.

John aimed his rifle and pulled the trigger. Nothing happened.

Salena grabbed the gun and snapped a lever. "You forgot to turn off the safety."

He smiled, remembering all the reasons he'd fallen in love with her. "Thanks."

Two feet from John's ear, a bullet ricocheted off the cement wall housing the service elevator. John squeezed the trigger and fired back. The soldier disappeared into the shaft, presumably dead or about to die.

John heard the elevator stop behind him, spun, and pointed his rifle at the parting doors. The car was empty.

Another burst of gunfire erupted from the door across the floor, and as he followed Salena into the open car, John heard someone shout. "Go back, go back! The service elevator!"

Though he intended to get off at the floor above, John pressed every button from '4' through '12,' hoping to confuse their pursuers, at least for a few seconds, as to where they'd actually stopped.

As the elevator cab decelerated, John wrapped his arm around Salena's shoulder. "You ready to finish what we started?"

Her one good eye sparkled. "I have been ready for a very long time."

Planting himself in front of Salena, John trained his gun straight ahead as the doors split apart. Breathing fast and shallow, he braced for a firefight.

Fluorescent light poured into the elevator, nothing more—not a soul in sight.

John remembered the service elevator was on the Citadel's east side. They'd have to turn left off the elevator and run a quarter way around the octagon to reach the skywalk lobby.

Holding his finger to the gun's trigger, John led the way as Salena kept glancing back. Surprised no one blocked their path, John was amazed when he came around the last bend.

Not a single guard stood anywhere near the counter at the skywalk entrance. All Khan's security men must have been diverted to the disturbance on the 3rd floor.

John grabbed Salena's hand and they bolted toward the abandoned checkpoint. Twenty feet from their destination John heard an ugly and familiar voice scream from behind.

"You will never escape!"

Qadeer was alive.

Gunfire snapped at their heels and tore a line of holes in the sheetrock wall to their left. John stumbled and Salena bumped him from behind. Still clutching her hand, he shouted, "Don't stop."

John recovered his balance and kept running. He found himself half-pulling Salena, who must have exhausted her strength. They reached the high counter at the sky bridge entrance and ducked behind for cover.

"Stay down," John said, as he slowly rose from a crouched position and pointed the rifle over the counter. He pulled the trigger and let loose a barrage of bullets.

After 10 seconds of silence, John glanced at Salena, sitting against the wall behind the counter. Her head was bowed and her tangled brown hair covered her face. The skywalk entrance was six feet away, and all they needed do was cross.

John reached for Salena's hand. "Come on, we're almost there."

Salena slowly lifted her head, and emitted a soft moan. Something was wrong—terribly wrong.

Kneeling beside her, he brushed her hair from her eyes and stifled a gasp. A crimson stream flowed from the corner of her mouth.

Slipping his hand between the wall and her back, John gently nudged her shoulders forward. A bright red circle stained the wall midway down her spine, and her own blood had turned her blue dress dark purple where Qadeer's bullet left a gaping wound close to her heart.

"Salena, can you hear me?"

She nodded and whispered, "I am sorry, John."

Tears coursed from the corners of her eyes, but John was afraid to wipe them, fearing any touch to her bruised skin would cause her more pain.

John knew to apply pressure to bleeding wounds, but the bullet's damage was deep in her chest. Though he had no idea how to treat such an injury, a hospital lay 20 feet away. He had to get her there, and fast.

John buried his lips in her hair. "Hold on tight, I'm gonna carry you."

She squinted at him through her tears. "Go, before they kill you. Give me …" Fluids gurgling in her lungs forced her to stop speaking. She coughed, spat up blood, and whispered, "Give me the rifle. I can stop them."

John's chest tightened. He stroked stray wisps of hair away from her forehead. "You and me, Salena, we help each other. That's what makes us a team."

He slid his arms under her knees and around her shoulders, and as he braced himself to lift her, machine gun fire splintered the countertop above them. The first volley, followed instantly by a second, shattered a glass frame on the wall above Salena's head. Instinctively, John crouched forward, shielding Salena from the falling shards.

John pivoted, aimed his gun over the counter, and pulled the trigger. His gut plunged when he heard only a click.

"Please John, go … go now."

Their location no longer a secret, John had one more chance. He pulled the last RDX-7S charge from his shalwar and set its force to maximum blast. He set the timer to five seconds, pressed the igniter switch, and tossed the tube down the hall. Using his back as a shield, he protected Salena and waited for what seemed an eternity as a continuous barrage of gunfire chewed up the checkpoint counter and the wall behind them.

A tremendous explosion rocked the floor, knocking John to his side.

There was no time to think. If Khan and his generals, secure in the Citadel's sub-basement, didn't know something was wrong before, they sure did now.

Ignoring the pain in his wounded arm, the thick smoke in his lungs, and the tears burning in his eyes, John cradled Salena, scooped her off the floor, and carried her across the sky bridge.

CHAPTER NINETY-THREE

H olding Salena in his arms, John entered a small lounge on the hospital side of the skywalk, and found it deserted. He screamed for a doctor and nobody answered. He screamed again, and saw veiled heads poke out from doors along the corridor. None stepped forward.

John lowered Salena onto a vinyl sofa in front of a window facing the Citadel. Kneeling beside her, he knew Salena's injury was severe, but in a hospital she might be saved.

She took quiet, shallow breaths. "Do it John … do it before Qadeer finds us."

John detected no pain in her eyes, and every muscle in her face was relaxed. "Don't worry, Qadeer is—"

"Dead?"

John whirled on his knees and came face-to-face with the barrel of a black, semi-automatic pistol. Clutching the pistol was Azam Qadeer, bloodied and bruised, but standing.

"Move away from your dying whore and I will finish her off."

John had rarely known hatred, but the anger engorging him now squeezed every drop of compassion from his soul and replaced it with blind desire to destroy this man. Qadeer was going to shoot him anyway, so why not go out with a fight. "You sorry asshole, I'm not moving anywhere." John extended his leg and swept it against Qadeer's left ankle.

At the last second, Qadeer limped backward, avoiding the arc of John's foot. He sneered down at John. "You fool, I see you have run out of tricks."

Propped by his arms, sliding on his butt, John moved a few inches closer. Again he swept his leg over the gray carpet trying to hook Qadeer's ankle.

Qadeer hopped backward, barely lifting his foot away before John made contact.

As the captain's derisive laugh echoed off the walls, John shimmied closer. Uncertain how long Qadeer would toy with him before pulling the trigger, John made a third attempt to trip Khan's stooge, but again, Qadeer hobbled backward.

A siren went off, and John knew instantly the high-pitched wail came from the Citadel. If he didn't detonate the charges now, Khan and his war-mongers would escape.

Qadeer glanced toward the skywalk entrance, then looked down at John. "I grow weary of this silly game." He extended his arm straight out, and aimed the muzzle at John's skull.

John thrust out his leg one more time, and swept it full force toward Qadeer's ankle.

The captain jumped backward and his body froze. His eyes grew as big as doorknobs, and the pistol dropped from his hand, hitting the carpet with a thud.

Qadeer tilted forward, slowly at first, then faster and faster, until John realized if he didn't move now the beast would fall directly on top of him. He pivoted sideways as Qadeer's body whooshed past and slammed the floor, face-down.

Lying on his belly, looking at Qadeer, John was confused. A syringe protruded from Qadeer's back, and his arms and legs convulsed. The monster's vapid eyes trained on John, then slowly slid into his head until all that remained were the whites.

John heard a man's voice. "That's right, you animal, take your time dying."

He looked up at a distinguished gentleman wearing a bright green turban whose eyes gleamed behind silver-wired spectacles.

John jumped to his feet and grabbed Raja's arm. "Please help ... she's been shot."

They ran to the sofa where Salena lay.

"Raja," she whispered.

Wincing at the sight of her purpled eye and her cheeks laced with contusions, Raja gently rolled her to her side and inspected the bloody hole in her back.

John knelt beside the sofa, close to Salena's face. "Hang on, Salena, please."

She struggled for air. "John ... my children ... tell Kalila I am sorry."

John tried to sound like nothing was wrong. "Sorry for what?"

"Do not waste ... waste what time I have ... I promised Kalila a family ... Tell her I am sorry."

John caressed her cascading hair. "Of course."

"... and please do not leave Naji without a home."

Raja lowered Salena onto her back, and when John read the doctor's face for an answer, tears that broke into muffled sobs told him all he needed to know. He dug deep in his pocket, pulled out the remote detonator, and pressed the 'charge' button.

"I will find your son a good home. I promise."

She looked up at the ceiling, and smiled weakly. "How did you know?"

John lifted Salena's arm, balled her fingers into a fist, and placed her hand on her bosom. "A boy that handsome could've come from only one beautiful lady."

She turned and looked at him. "Do it ... do it now."

John tasted the salt of his own tears dripping between his lips. Ashamed he couldn't be as brave for her as she had for him, he gazed into her eyes and heard himself say, "I love you."

"Do it."

With his finger on the 'charge' button, he wrapped Salena's hand around the detonator. "You deserve the honor." He guided her index finger to the 'fire' button. "Now."

Salena pushed the button and stared straight up.

John turned away and looked through the window at the Citadel's south wall. For five seconds he heard nothing but Raja's soft weeping and Salena's strained breathing.

Then it happened—a chain reaction of muffled explosions in rapid succession and a giant ashen cloud ballooning upward from the 20 foot alley between the hospital and Khan's Citadel. The floor beneath them began to tremble, and the window facing the Citadel cracked. John gripped Salena's hand tighter, and leaned forward to protect her face from the hurtling steel and cement he was sure would breach the glass.

*   *   *

General Khan was the last to react, as if everyone but him had heard the siren wailing in the subterranean amphitheater. His mullahs and generals were leaping the aisle stairs three at a time, running for the exits. Even as two bodyguards lifted him off his feet and carried him back from the podium, Khan could not understand the reason for the commotion.

This was his Citadel, after all. None of his enemies would dare attack his command and control center, and risk destroying the hospital and school so near to his sanctuary. Even precision guided missiles posed too great a danger to the women and children nearby. Who would be so brazen?

Then, for a flicker of an instant, when he looked up and saw hurtling toward him a brown steel buttress, did the stark reality of what was about to occur reach his conscious mind. In that frozen frame of time, he could not deny his fate. As he had been forced to accept his beloved's betrayal, he must now accept the fact of his imminent mortality.

*   *   *

The floor stopped shaking and the window overlooking the Citadel—cracked in three places—held firm in its frame. Billows of smoke rising from the alley shrouded any view of what lay beyond, but kneeling beside Salena, John knew if debris hadn't crashed into the hospital by now, it wouldn't at all.

Mesmerized by the swirling kaleidoscope of dust, ash, and soot, John barely heard Salena whisper, "What happened?"

John slipped his arm under Salena's neck and shoulders, and carefully lifted her head. "See for yourself."

The whirling eddies of smoke began to thin and shafts of sunlight filtered through. Behind the settling dust, Khan's Citadel had been reduced to a mound of rubble as high as the sky bridge, now snapped in two. Staring at the mountain of twisted steel and broken cement, John said, "You did good, Salena. You did real good."

When Salena did not reply, John turned and saw she hadn't heard his praise. Her eyes had closed, and her lungs had ceased their desperate struggle. He prayed she knew from somewhere beyond that what she had done was right and just, and because of her, India, Pakistan, and her beloved Kashmir, had been spared a nuclear holocaust.

Placing her head on the sofa and kissing her still warm lips, John knew cities and countries were not all she had saved. "Thank you, Salena."

He bowed his head and clenched his teeth, fighting back more tears. They came anyway and he wept without shame, comforted by the truth Salena had at last found freedom.

Raja's hand touched his shoulder.

John rose and the two men embraced, consoling each other their loss. Finally, Raja pulled back and said, "It is time for you to go home."

CHAPTER NINETY-FOUR

Alone in the ST-131's second-to-last row, John gazed out the portal and searched for the horizon. Half-blinded by the sun, he couldn't distinguish the turquoise sky from the teal sea, so he turned away and closed his eyes.

Four hours had passed since he'd imploded the Citadel, been flown to Kabul, and boarded the supersonic jet for McGuire Air Force Base in New Jersey. In eight hours he'd be home, a place only yesterday he thought he'd never see again.

The RDX-7S had done its job. It wasn't his cleanest implosion, but considering he hadn't the benefit of proper preparation, he'd done damn well. Plummeting debris had cracked or shattered every window along the hospital's north side, but not a man, woman, or child inside was hurt. Better yet, across Constitution Avenue, inside the Diplomatic Enclave, the school and playground were unscathed.

Far different was the story less than 200 feet away, where every human caught inside the Citadel had perished, or so was the preliminary finding of rescue workers, real and disguised, who'd rushed to the scene. American intelligence put enough confidence in those early reports to sneak Labib Razzak back into Islamabad within two hours of the Citadel's collapse.

Though the terrible lessons of the Chicago disaster would remain with John forever, and though he never need work another day in his life, he pondered the challenge of rebuilding Planned Demolitions, Inc. He had imploded a building under the worst conditions imaginable, and hadn't harmed anyone he didn't intend to—no Billy Dwyers left behind to haunt his waking hours.

He missed the awe in Christie's eyes when she pressed the 'fire' button and stood transfixed by the synchronized destruction of outdated edifices her father's hand had wrought. For no other reason than that, he'd try again.

Footsteps approached, and by the time John chose to open his eyes, Major Farrell slipped into the seat beside him.

John had meant to tell Farrell something since yesterday. "Guess I'm the first CRUSO candidate to take the 'un' out of unrecoverable."

Despite what must have been the most harrowing week of her career, Denise Farrell was wide-eyed and perky. She managed a smile. "That you are, John."

John leaned close to her ear. "Please tell me once we're off the Jersey coast, you're not gonna dump me out and let me drown—make some hapless fisherman stumble across my floating body. It'd be perfect."

"Perfect for what?"

"Guaranteeing I don't shoot my mouth off to the media."

Farrell's smile got bigger.

"Don't laugh. That way, the Treasury gets to keep its thirty million."

"I think you watch too many *X-Files* reruns."

"Seriously, everyone at home already thinks I'm dead."

"You sure you don't work for the CIA?"

"See, I was right."

Farrell's smile disappeared and she stared at him long enough to make him nervous. Finally, she said, "Yes, the scenario has been discussed."

"I'm sure Colonel Daley led the debate."

"Understand something John. Real government is not a homogeneous parade of automatons all marching to the same drummer. The world has changed. Beating an enemy who carries no flag requires flexible thinking. Not just a diversity of cultures and races, but a diversity of ideas to come up with the best possible solution to any given conflict or problem. Too many of us on the inside, good soldiers nevertheless, don't let our patriotism get in the way of distinguishing right from wrong."

"So you're not gonna leave me in the ocean to die?"

"No, but on the other hand, Big Brother will be watching you the rest of your life. The second we have an inkling you opened your mouth to anyone, bank accounts, brokerage accounts, IRA's, 401-K's, all mysteriously disappear. The IRS will hound you, Maureen, and I'm sorry to say, your girls, too, when they grow up. And no matter how hard your children try, no matter how good their grades, they'll find they can't buy their way into beauty school. And that's just the beginning. No financial institution in America will grant you, your wife, or your children a loan. On top of that, you'll—"

"OK, OK, I get the picture."

Farrell's smile returned. "In other words, stick to your end of the bargain—a lifetime of silence—and we'll stick to ours."

"I hope that includes a vote for Kashmir's independence."

"Secretary Parker has already left Beijing for New Delhi to negotiate the logistics."

"Fair enough."

John wondered if Raja, too, would stick to his word. The gentle doctor swore he'd never divulge John Cattano's true identity. He told

John even if he tried, no one in their right mind would believe one man had destroyed the Citadel.

John intended to stay in touch with his new friend, even if Uncle Sam cringed. In the moments before John boarded the ST-131, Raja vowed to help John stand by the last promise he'd made to Salena.

Then John recalled something he'd said to Farrell yesterday before flying back to Islamabad. "Sorry I used up all those high-tech charges."

"If they saved your life, they were well spent."

Already memories were fading, and he wasn't about to let that happen. "I wish they'd saved Salena's too."

Sitting erect on the edge of her seat, Farrell folded her hands on her lap, tilted her head, and studied his face. "You fell in love with her, didn't you?"

He swallowed hard at the question, but denying those feelings wasn't possible. Not yet. "Yeah."

"What about Maureen?"

"I'd never have let myself love Salena if I thought for a second I'd be going home."

"Will those feelings affect your marriage?"

John sat back in his padded chair and pushed his skull against the soft headrest. "I'll work it out."

Farrell stared down at the cabin's low-pile carpet, and for the first time since Friday, avoided looking at him when she spoke. "I'm truly sorry. What we did was a terrible mistake. The worst kind."

John grinned broadly, which Farrell must have thought strange. "Everyone makes mistakes."

Farrell rose. "Try and get some sleep. I'll wake you when we're within 20 minutes of Jersey."

Though he'd asked her for reassurance five times in the last four hours, John wouldn't rest until he heard it again. "I know it wasn't part of our bargain, but can you make it happen?"

"Are you sure it's what you want?"

"Right now, it's the only thing I'm sure of."

"I'll see what I can do."

CHAPTER NINETY-FIVE

The ST-131 rolled to a stop at the end of a runway that seemed to go on forever. John was hustled down the stairs into a waiting jeep and driven along with Major Farrell to a small, concrete building on the outskirts of McGuire Air Force Base.

John stepped from the jeep and looked around. Though July had 10 days left, a mid-August haze filtered in just enough sun to lay down shadows. The building they had come to stood alone at the edge of a flat forest of low-growing pines and sand-stunted brush typical of southern New Jersey. John had hiked often with Maureen and his girls through the state's coastal forests, but never before had the Pine Barrens smelled so sweet.

John noticed a green army truck parked alongside the building. He called to Farrell over the jeep's roof, "Don't tell me. Colonel Daley's waiting for us inside."

She shook her head, grinning, and led John to the front door of the bland building in the middle of nowhere.

Its interior was just as dull. John counted three closed doors off a short hall—to the left, right, and straight ahead. Farrell led John to the room on the left, where inside, John was surprised to find a beige carpet, a burgundy leather couch, and two rocking recliners.

"We use this place for mission debriefings. Not just CRUSO, but the CIA, the FBI, and six other agencies you're better off not knowing exist."

The recliners looked awfully inviting. Still, something about lounging, even for a minute, in this desolate haven so soon after a near-death experience didn't sit right with John. "Maybe it works for you CIA types, but if I'd managed to survive a grueling, overseas mission that nearly got me killed ..." John paused, rubbing his chin. "... I'd be anxious to get home."

"Soon enough." Farrell waved John to the nearest recliner.

"Now I know. You've got that army shrink in the back room."

"Lieutenant Hawley? No. My instincts told me you'd pass on the psychological debriefing."

"Very good, Major Farrell."

Farrell glanced at a mahogany grandfather clock beside the sofa. "The helicopter arrives in half an hour. Before then, I need to explain some details we didn't work out on the jet. And you need to get properly dressed."

John looked down at his legs and chest. "You're right. I'd have a tough time explaining where I picked up a shalwar kameez floating around the Atlantic Ocean."

"We saved your clothes from last Friday."

"Do I have to give up my Nikes?"

"You can afford a new pair."

It still hadn't sunk in he was about to become a multi-millionaire. "I suppose you're right."

"We've tattered your shirt and pants a bit, scored them with burn marks, and sprayed them with gasoline."

"You guys are scary."

Farrell nodded at the recliner. "Sure you don't want to sit?"

John eyed the pliant leather. "If I do, you'll have to pry me out with a crowbar."

"Very well." Farrell sat on the edge of the sofa's armrest. "The torn bow of your Boston Whaler has already been delivered to the drop-off coordinates. I'll fly out with you. Once we arrive, you'll be lowered in a Heli-Basket. Last week's storm has moved into the North Atlantic. Seas are in the one-to-two foot range, and the ocean temp is around 72. When I leave, hold onto the wreckage, and after you've had a good salt-water soaking, you'll be picked up by the New Jersey State Police."

"Why not Coast Guard?"

"Too many people already know about CRUSO. Some years back a lieutenant with the New Jersey State Marine Police assisted the federal government with a covert bust in Ocean County. Since then, he's worked on a number of clandestine federal operations where the Garden State's involved. His name is Larry Bateman, Lieutenant Bateman, and he's already been briefed."

"You have every base covered."

"We hope. Lieutenant Bateman can also fudge your post-rescue paperwork. Close any holes in your story of five harrowing days at sea."

"Like what?"

"Like the fact your bullet wound goes down as a shrapnel injury from an exploding engine."

"Good point."

"Fortunately, you've lost a few pounds, a fact consistent with your ordeal. How you survived five days without fresh water also works. Your Whaler's bow, the largest piece left, contains a built-in storage well. You drank the rainwater that collected inside." Farrell stood and eyed John head-to-toe. "You look exhausted."

"Imagine how I feel."

"Actually, that's good. Someone lost in stormy seas for as long as you should look worn and haggard."

Farrell directed John to the building's back room, where he found a young soldier in tan fatigues holding the blue jeans and polo shirt he'd dressed in last Friday. As Farrell promised, they'd been charred and ripped to look like they'd survived an explosion. John changed into his costume, making sure he didn't forget Christie's toy Harley, then met Farrell in front of the concrete building at the edge of the forest.

Standing shoulder-to-shoulder, they stared across the concrete tarmac at a line of trees a mile away. She said without turning, "No amount of money will compensate you for what you endured over there, and you'll never get the credit you deserve. Just know some of us deeply appreciate your sacrifice. Whether you did it for your family, for Dr. Zamal, or for your country doesn't matter. You saved a lot of lives."

"I should've saved one more."

"If your request is granted, you will."

The drone of approaching rotors sounded from somewhere overhead. John's gut knotted. "Showtime."

Pausing only long enough to land and take them aboard, the dark green helicopter lifted off and flew east over a landscape once familiar to John, but which now looked somehow different. Crossing the Garden State Parkway, they flew parallel to Route 37 and quickly approached the Atlantic Ocean.

Through the haze, John discerned the giant Ferris wheel on the Seaside Heights boardwalk. Last Thursday Karen had asked if she could go there with friends and spend a few dollars of her summer earnings. Maureen reminded her money was tight and told her no. John couldn't suppress a smile knowing he could buy the whole damn boardwalk now if he wanted to.

As they hovered over the drop-off point, John saw 60 feet straight down the front third of his Montauk's baby blue hull floating in calm seas. An unmarked vessel, which John assumed had delivered his Whaler's remains, was headed south.

In the chopper's cargo hold, two sailors in red jumpsuits readied the Heli-Basket. Holding a radio, Farrell quietly observed the final preparations of CRUSO's elaborate hoax. Only when one of the sailors motioned John over did she walk up to him.

Her eyes were bloodshot, and if John didn't know better, he'd swear she'd been crying. Or maybe exhaustion had caught up with her, too.

The whining turbines forced her to speak loudly. "As soon as they lower you, I'll put in a call to the Marine Police as a private pilot who's spotted a man clinging to wreckage. I'll give the coordinates, and your ride should arrive in 15 minutes."

"Will I ever see you again?"

"If you do, John, that's not a good sign."

"You swear you're not gonna shoot me when I'm in the basket."

Farrell frowned, and did something John would not have expected. She wrapped her hands around his shoulders and squeezed him tight.

He hugged her back, and when she pulled away, John saw he'd been right. Her cheeks were moist and she rubbed her eyes.

"Get out of here. Enjoy the rest of your life, and enjoy your family. You have lots of explaining to do to Maureen—and I'm not just talking about your adventure at sea."

"She'll be good with it, I know she will. It's the red tape that worries me."

"I'll do everything in my power to cut through it."

The cargo door slid open, and John descended in the Heli-Basket. The cool salt-water dunking woke John fast, and before his body acclimated to the ocean's temperature, the basket was gone, and then the helicopter. Grasping the rubber rail attached to the top edge of his ruined Whaler, John followed the helicopter until it became a silent dot and winked out over the western horizon.

John waited, but not for long. As he bobbed clinging to the front third of his Whaler, he spotted a boat coming straight at him, and for the first time his heart raced at the prospect of seeing Maureen and his girls.

When the white fiberglass vessel pulled closer John recognized the blue and gold markings of the New Jersey State Police. A hand attached to a muscular arm reached down from the boat's deck and lifted John from the water.

On his feet, John stood face-to-face with a handsome gentleman slightly taller than he, and a few years older. Wrinkles fanned from the corners of hardened, brown eyes. Clearly, this man had seen more than most. "I'm Lieutenant Lawrence Bateman. You, I presume, are John Covello."

"You know perfectly well who I am."

Bateman winced, and looked behind him.

Two young troopers ran from the boat's cabin holding a stretcher, and John realized he'd stepped out of role. "I mean, yes sir, I am. Thanks for coming. I never thought anyone would find me."

"Amazing you held on for five days under such trying conditions."

"For the most part, the waves were rough, but every now and then the seas calmed just enough to give me hope."

"Your wife's been notified. She was all kinds of happy."

"And my daughters?"

"Overjoyed." Bateman's eyes narrowed, and he looked slightly perplexed. "But I have to tell you, your younger daughter wasn't a bit surprised."

"That's Christie for you. She made me take along my good-luck charm."

Bateman nodded. "Apparently, it worked."

CHAPTER NINETY-SIX

Half paying attention to Colonel Daley, who walked beside her, Denise Farrell admired the flowers blooming from the potted pomegranate trees lining the walks of the Pentagon's inner courtyard. She loved gazing upon their bright orange petals in the spring, and sipping the tangy-sweet nectar of their fruit come autumn. She'd even nurtured one in her sunroom at home, but for some reason, no matter how hard she tried, the government-grown pomegranates always flowered brighter and tasted sweeter than her own.

Daley must have sensed her wandering mind. "Do you think he'll do it?"

"I'm sorry, colonel, it's been a long week. Will who do what?"

"Will John keep his mouth shut?"

Farrell had never met anyone quite like John Covello, but then again, her job constantly introduced her to unusual people. And maybe John wasn't all that unique. Any citizen thrust into a similar situation might have performed as well. After all, this was America, and Americans of every color and creed had displayed great courage in the face of the terrible trials foisted upon them at the start of the 21st Century.

Whatever his reasons, John had given 10 times more than she, Daley, or President Lloyd had a right to expect. If John, too, understood the significance of what he'd done, and the importance of CRUSO's role in the world, despite his ordeal, he'd remain silent.

"He'll honor his word, if we keep ours."

"The way things are shaking out, we may pull it off exactly the way he asked. With Razzak back in office, Pakistan's silent majority is literally dancing in the streets. Behari not only jumped on the peace train, but took over as engineer, and eleven militant groups in Kashmir have agreed to a cease fire. The only jittery player is Premier Jintao, worried Kashmir's plebiscite sets a bad example for separatists in Xinjiang."

"I've discussed the issue with President Lloyd. He hopes his public and private assurances the Kashmir vote is unique will satisfy the premier."

Colonel Daley paused and looked up at the brilliant morning sky. "What about that other matter John asked you to handle?"

"The paperwork's moving faster than I expected."

"Pays to know people in high places."

"Speaking of which, please accept my congratulations. I'm looking forward to the ceremony next month."

The colonel smiled. "Yes, brigadier general does have a certain ring to it." His smile vanished, and he gave Farrell a long, pensive look. "Have you considered my recommendation to the president?"

From the beginning she'd harbored strong doubts about CRUSO, as did President Lloyd who'd appointed her. In spite of her concerns, Daley had recommended she take his place when he retired next June. "I'm not sure I'm up for the job."

"What's that supposed to mean?"

"I let Chandler slip through."

"This mission was an exception—put together under the threat of imminent nuclear war. We had three days to prepare."

"I should've done a better background check."

"You're not listening. We had no time."

"I sent a healthy man on a job meant for someone dying."

Daley shook his head. "The system isn't perfect. It's made up of people and machines, and neither is flawless. We did our absolute best under impossible circumstances."

"We put that man through hell."

Daley sighed. "Did you ever think maybe we did him a favor?"

She hadn't looked at it that way before, but the colonel could be right. John had gotten much more than money from his difficult journey. She only hoped he had found his way home again. And while selecting John for CRUSO Mission 003 had been a terrible mistake, he turned out to be the best mistake she'd ever made.

EPILOGUE

Lying unopened on the kitchen table, the hefty Sunday editions of the *Asbury Park Press* and *Newark Star-Ledger* smelled of fresh newsprint. Appreciative his girls had saved him the walk to the mailbox, John eyed the headline splashed across the top of the *Newark Star Ledger*: "World Lauds Behari As Peace Comes To Kashmir." He chuckled, but not out loud.

After reading the article's first three paragraphs, John deduced the rest had nothing more to say than a story he'd read off the Internet last night before heading up to bed. He opened the front page. Every story inside directly or indirectly addressed events in India and Pakistan.

Relieved the media had finally relegated his saga of personal courage and survival at sea to the graveyard of extinct news, John put down the paper, poured himself some coffee, and walked into his den overlooking the Manasquan River.

Maureen had left their bed an hour before him, and was nowhere in sight. Through the den window, he spotted Karen checking out the controls of his new Sugar Sand offshore jetboat moored to the backyard bulkhead. No sign of Maureen there, either.

Last night they'd run low on milk. Maybe she'd driven over to Shop Rite to pick up a gallon, and if she were reading his mind, a pound of bacon and a box of Funny Bones too.

John looked down at the globe perched on its chrome stand. Two months had passed, and still his eyes couldn't help but fixate on those green and mauve countries, side-by-side, with the larger of the two, India, a light purple mass extending nearly as far north as green-colored Pakistan. The cartographers would soon be hard at work again, replacing India's purple head with a new color nestled between Pakistan, India, and China.

Setting his coffee mug on an end table, John plopped in the club chair against the window and clicked on the TV. He flipped through the channels and found no respite from world events. Not particularly interested in watching Barry Stokes land redfish in the flats of southern Louisiana, he resigned himself to CNN, but everything Brian Walters reported he already knew.

The July 21 counter-coup in Islamabad staged by elements loyal to President Razzak had been eclipsed on September 2 by an event of profound historic significance. Ten weeks after General Ali Khan detonated a nuclear bomb over Baramulla, India's Prime Minister Behari and Pakistan's President Razzak announced a joint initiative aimed at stabilizing relations once and for all. India and Pakistan agreed to withdraw their respective forces from the occupied territories of Jammu & Kashmir and the Northern Areas. A 75,000 strong multi-national UN task force spearheaded by Russia, Ukraine, and United Korea—supported by troops of France, Italy, and Australia—had already entered the region to prevent a bloodbath between Muslims and Hindus similar to that which had followed partition.

The US, bogged down managing yet another fragile peace in the Middle East, offered logistic, but not military support. President Lloyd, however, wholeheartedly endorsed the initiative, and praised Sanjay Behari as South Asia's greatest peacemaker since Mahatma Ghandi.

After showing a video clip of UN tanks rolling into Srinagar, CNN's Brian Walters commented on how quickly the peace deal between India and Pakistan had been arranged. A series of intense secret meetings between Razzak and Behari had led to the mutually acceptable solution, but neither would elaborate on what had prompted the negotiations. Speculation had surfaced the agreement was brokered behind the scenes by the UK, Russia, and China. While these three nations welcomed the move toward permanent peace on the subcontinent, none claimed credit for facilitating the accord.

President Lloyd's face filled the high-definition tube with an interview excerpt John hadn't seen before. The president commented, "Sometimes nations simply grow weary of war, and no outside catalyst need trigger a lasting peace."

John spat out a mouthful of home-brewed coffee and gasped for breath.

Walters came back to discuss how last Wednesday and Thursday, under watchful UN eyes, separate plebiscites were conducted in Jammu, Ladakh, Azad Kashmir, Hunza, Gilgit, Skardu, and the Kashmir Valley. Each region was given a choice between independence, and depending on its geographic proximity to India and Pakistan, full incorporation into one country or the other. Early results indicated the people of Jammu and Ladakh had voted to join India, while those of Hunza, Gilgit, and Skardu had opted for accession to Pakistan. In Azad Kashmir and the Kashmir Valley, the overwhelming majority had voted for freedom.

No surprises there, but John was mildly amused when Walters reported no group had yet claimed responsibility for the explosion that destroyed General Khan's command and control center in downtown Islamabad, killing him and nearly every member of his inner circle, and setting the stage for Razzak's return. China pointed the finger at special forces from India backed by the US, but Prime Minister Behari and President Lloyd scoffed at the accusation, stating the nature of the explosion, actually an implosion, indicated the destruction of the Citadel could only have occurred from within. The very idea Indian commandos had penetrated the Citadel and positioned explosives in the manner required to produce such an implosion was preposterous.

John had enough. He turned off the TV, walked into the kitchen, and poured another mug of coffee. Stirring in the last drop of milk, he heard the front door open.

He set his mug on the counter and called out, "Maureen?"

She answered from the living room. "We're home." Maureen waltzed into the kitchen holding a plastic bag in one hand and a white-capped prescription bottle in the other. "You forgot to renew your Misoprostol."

John kissed her cheek as she whizzed past carrying a grocery bag to the counter.

"And don't forget your appointment with Dr. Jeffers tomorrow. I'm tempted to rat you out."

Last night John and Maureen had taken the kids to the Point Pleasant boardwalk. "I stopped after two funnel cakes when I could've done three."

"Even one is bad for you."

"Is that what Jeffers said?"

"Everyone knows greasy foods don't help an ulcer." She opened the refrigerator, wedged the milk between a carton of orange juice and a bottled water, then shoved the bacon in the meat drawer. John kept quiet when she crumpled the plastic bag without extracting a single Funny Bone. She turned and looked at him. "It's amazing your stomach didn't keep you up all night."

Maureen had decided to let her hair grow a few inches longer, and he'd begun noticing the difference. He hadn't asked her to, but he wondered if it had something to do with his sideways glance on the boardwalk last month at a mom around her age with long brown hair. In truth, he'd love her if she were bald, but he appreciated her decision to indulge his fantasies.

He walked up to his wife, wrapped his arms around her waist, and squeezed her. "Thanks for caring, kid."

"Don't mention it."

The top two buttons of her blouse were open, and he was awfully tempted, but with children around, fondling her now wasn't a good idea. "Where's—"

The sound of skipping feet caught John's attention. He pulled away from Maureen and turned to find a young girl with dark brown eyes and long black hair prancing into the kitchen. The eight pounds she'd gained in four weeks had shown up mostly in her face and arms, and her dark skin appeared smoother and healthier.

She looked up at John. "When can we ride on the boat?"

Though she'd spent her first six years landlocked in Rawalpindi and Islamabad, Kalila loved swimming in the Atlantic Ocean and cruising the waters of Barnegat Bay.

John knelt before her. "Can you wait until after lunch?"

Kalila nodded. "Where will we go today?"

Their pediatrician had assured them the bruise on her back would eventually heal. Children were indeed resilient, she'd said, but it wasn't the physical scars that worried John most. "Is there any place special you'd like to go?"

"The island, the one where we made a picnic on the sand."

"Tice's Shoal. Great idea."

"Thanks Mr. J—Poppi." Every now and then she still slipped. "Is Christie awake?"

Maureen answered, "I think she's out on the deck. She said something about teaching you to play slapjack."

Kalila hugged John, and gazed at him with those eyes that marveled at every new sight. "Can I steer the boat?"

John rustled the hair on top of her head. "Sure, just steer clear of the whales."

She bolted out the back door shouting to Christie to wait before dealing the cards.

John rose and walked to his wife. "Isn't it great how she's taken to us?"

"You'd never know the suffering she's seen."

After John was rescued off the Atlantic coast, he'd kept his secret from Maureen—for all of about two hours. Maureen was no dummy. If John hadn't told her the truth about his overseas mission for the US government, she'd have eventually put the pieces together—SeaStar's lightning speed settlement, his sudden urge to adopt an orphan from Pakistan, and the frequent e-mails from a man named Dr. Raja.

They decided Karen and Christie should never be burdened with the real reason their father had left home for five days, and whenever their daughters, Kalila included, started asking questions, Maureen did her best to help John change the subject. After all, he and his wife helped each other, and that's what made them a team.

John slid his hand around his wife's midriff, and pulled her to him. "Up for another day at Tice's Shoal?"

"So long as you don't sneak any fried chicken."

"I promise, I'll be a good boy today."

She kissed his neck, then whispered in his ear, "I hope not tonight."

"You have my word."

Her blue eyes smiled. "Why don't you go outside and play with the kids? I have to run upstairs for a minute."

"Don't be long."

"I won't." She disappeared into the living room.

John had shared everything with Maureen—well, almost everything—about his trip to Islamabad and his dangerous trek with Dr. Zamal to the Kashmir Valley. When he described the pain and poverty of the countless orphans General Khan had left in his wake, Maureen was fully supportive of his decision to adopt Kalila.

So far his wife had voiced no regrets. If anything, it was he who'd forgotten how much time young children consume. During the last three weeks, he'd ridden his new Harley only once. Between a family refreshed and a business reborn, he rarely had time for himself.

The most difficult question for John in the days after coming home was how to fulfill his last promise to Salena. He had considered adopting Naji along with Kalila, but knew in his heart Salena would not have chosen an American life for her son. She had died so Naji might grow and flourish in a free Kashmir.

It was Raja who'd suggested the answer. Two weeks after the Citadel was destroyed Raja accepted a post as the new director of Lal Ded Hospital. Since he was moving to Srinagar anyway, why not adopt Naji as his son? John could think of no better role model for Naji than the brave and kindly man who had cared so much for Salena.

Gazing at the floor, John tried not to think too much about the Kashmiri woman who had changed his life. True, time had a way of healing all wounds, but some scars left their mark forever. He considered checking his e-mail before heading outside to join his daughters, but he doubted Denise Farrell had sent him another message.

The day after Labor Day, he had opened his Outlook Express to find an e-mail with no subject line that could have come from only one person. Apparently, CRUSO wasn't sure what to do with Salena's $5,000,000, and Major Farrell—now Lieutenant Colonel Farrell—wondered whether he'd like that money for himself to defray the cost of raising a larger family.

John replied $30,000,000, tax free, was quite enough, and instructed Farrell to use half of Salena's share to fund a trust for Naji naming Dr. Raja as trustee. Million dollar donations were to go to Lal Ded Hospital and the orphanage he and Salena had visited in Srinagar.

As for the balance, he asked Farrell to check on two dozen homeless children living in a large storage closet on the 4th floor of Pakistan National Hospital. Salena's last half million was to pay for private rooms for each child, along with all the toys they desired.

He hadn't heard from Farrell since, though last Monday he did receive an e-mail from Raja, who described how easily Naji had taken to his prosthetic leg. Raja also thanked John for his generous donation to Lal Ded Hospital, and assured him the money would be spent on supplies and equipment, and also to fund restoration projects. John reminded Raja restoration of the hospital was Salena's dream, and it was Salena who should be thanked, perhaps by building a memorial to her in the hospital's garden next to the statue of Lal Ded. Raja thought the idea splendid, and promised to keep John posted on the progress of improvements.

John heard Maureen come downstairs, and when she walked into the kitchen looking awfully sexy in that white sundress of hers—the one hugging her curves in all the right places—his instinct was to march her right back up to their bedroom. But alas, the children.

His thoughts must have been clear. "You can hold off until tonight."

"If I have to watch you looking like that all day, tonight's gonna end too soon."

She smirked. "Why are you still here? I thought you'd be out back."

"I was thinking how lucky I am."

"I think we're both pretty lucky."

John backed Maureen against the refrigerator and caressed her neck with kisses. "You're the best."

Maureen moaned appreciatively, then pulled away and led John through the back door onto the deck.

Warm sunshine and a gentle breeze made the day ideal for cruising Barnegat Bay. Karen, still fiddling with the Sugar Sand's controls, waved when she saw them come out, and Christie and Kalila, sitting in resin chairs around a patio table, played a lively game of slapjack.

John and Maureen walked to the deck's railing, and side-by-side stared out over the glimmering waters of the Manasquan River.

Without turning, Maureen asked, "Do you think I'll ever get to see Kashmir?"

John was already planning for the day he and Maureen could visit Raja and Naji in Srinagar. "Definitely, after the political situation settles down."

"Where would we stay?"

John's first thought was of a fine wooden houseboat moored along the shores of Dal Lake owned by a man with one ear. Perhaps Omar Shah, deprived of a living peddling guns and bombs, might open *The*

Hemingway to tourists. "I happen to know someone with a really nice houseboat where I'm sure we'd be welcome. And I hear he makes a mean dish of rista meat balls and seekh kababs."

Maureen studied his face, as if laboring to read his expression.

"What?"

"Nothing, I guess. It's just that you learned so much about Kashmir in such a short time."

Mesmerized by the sun-sparkled tips of the river's waves, John gently clasped the hand of his beloved and whispered, "That I did, kid. That I did."